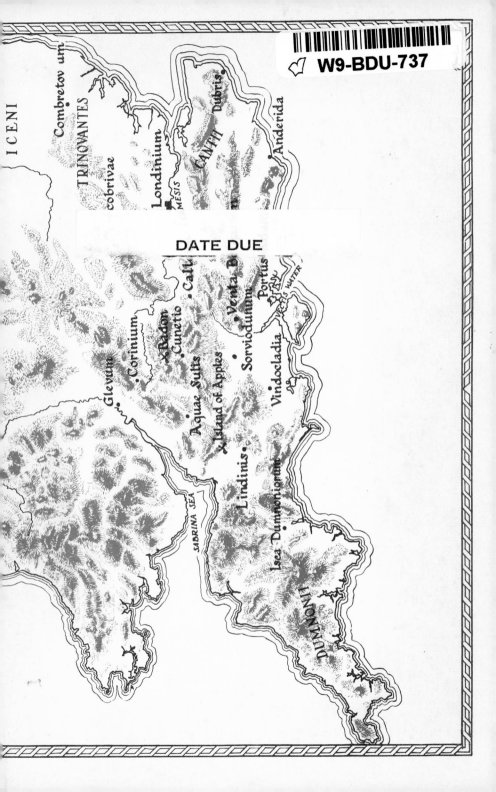

W9-BDU-737

DATE DUE

ICENI

Combretov um

TRINOVANTES

cobrivae

Londinium

CANTII

Dubris

Anderida

MESIS

Call

Venta B.

Corinium

xBadon
Cunetio

Aquae Sulis

Portus

Glevum

Sorviodunum

Island of Apples

Vindocladia

Lindinis

Isca Dumnoniorum

DUMNONII

SABRINA SEA

SWORD AT SUNSET

By Rosemary Sutcliff

Rosemary Sutcliff

Sword at Sunset

COWARD-McCANN, Inc. New York

CARL A. RUDISILL LIBRARY
LENOIR RHYNE COLLEGE

Copyright © 1963 by Rosemary Sutcliff

All rights reserved. This book, or parts thereof, may not be repro-
duced in any form without permission in writing from the Publisher.

HIC JACET ARTHURUS REX QUONDAM REXQUE FUTURUS is from Francis
Brett Young's *The Island,* published by William Heinemann Ltd.
Reprinted by permission.

.823.914
Su8s

45600

Sept. '63

Library of Congress Catalog
Card Number: 63–10159
MANUFACTURED IN THE UNITED STATES OF AMERICA

HIC JACET ARTHURUS
REX QUONDAM REXQUE FUTURUS

Arthur is gone . . . Tristram in Careol
Sleeps, with a broken sword—And Yseult sleeps
Beside him, where the westering waters roll
Over drowned Lyonesse to the outer deeps.

Lancelot is fallen . . . The ardent helms that shone
So knightly and the splintered lances rust
In the anonymous mould of Avalon:
Gawain and Gareth and Galahad—all are dust!

Where do the vanes and towers of Camelot
And tall Tintagel crumble? Where do those tragic
Lovers and their bright-eyed ladies rot?
We cannot tell—for lost is Merlin's magic.

And Guinevere—call her not back again
Lest she betray the loveliness Time lent
A name that blends the rapture and the pain
Linked in the lonely nightingale's lament,

Nor pry too deeply, lest you should discover
The bower of Astolat a smoky hut
Of mud and wattle—find the knightliest lover
A braggart, and his Lily Maid a slut;

And all that coloured tale a tapestry
Woven by poets. As the spider's skeins
Are spun of its own substance, so have they
Embroidered empty legend—What remains?

This: That when Rome fell, like a writhen oak
That age had sapped and cankered at the root,
Resistant, from her topmost bough there broke
The miracle of one unwithering shoot

Which was the spirit of Britain—that certain men
Uncouth, untutored, of our island brood
Loved freedom better than their lives; and when
The tempest crashed around them, rose and stood

And charged into the storm's black heart, with sword
Lifted, or lance in rest, and rode there, helmed
With a strange majesty that the heathen horde
Remembered after all were overwhelmed;

And made of them a legend, to their chief,
Arthur, Ambrosius—no man knows his name—
Granting a gallantry beyond belief,
And to his knights imperishable fame.

They were so few . . . We know not in what manner
Or where or when they fell—whether they went
Riding into the dark under Christ's banner
Or died beneath the blood-red dragon of Gwent.

But this we know: That, when the Saxon rout
Swept over them, the sun no longer shone
On Britain, and the last lights flickered out;
And men in darkness murmured: Arthur is gone . . .

FRANCIS BRETT YOUNG

AUTHOR'S NOTE

JUST as the saga of Charlemagne and his paladins is the Matter of France, so for fourteen hundred years or so, the Arthurian Legend has been the Matter of Britain. A tradition at first, then a hero-tale gathering to itself fresh detail and fresh glories and the rainbow colors of romance as it went along, until with Sir Thomas Malory it came to its fullest flowering.

But of late years historians and anthropologists have come more and more to the belief that the Matter of Britain is indeed "matter and not moonshine." That behind all the numinous mist of pagan, early Christian and medieval splendors that have gathered about it, there stands the solitary figure of one great man. No knight in shining armor, no Round Table, no many-towered Camelot; but a Romano-British war leader, to whom, when the Barbarian darkness came flooding in, the last guttering lights of civilization seemed worth fighting for.

Sword at Sunset is an attempt to re-create from fragments of known facts, from likelihoods and deductions and guesswork pure and simple, the kind of man this war leader may have been, and the story of his long struggle.

Certain features I have retained from the traditional Arthurian fabric, because they have the atmosphere of truth. I have kept the original framework, or rather two interwrought frameworks: the Sin which carries with it its own retribution; the Brotherhood broken by the love between the leader's woman and his closest friend. These have the inevitability and pitiless purity of outline

[vii]

that one finds in classical tragedy, and that belong to the ancient and innermost places of man. I have kept the theme, which seems to me to be implicit in the story, of the Sacred King, the Leader whose divine right, ultimately, is to die for the life of the people.

Bedwyr, Cei and Gwalchmai are the earliest of all Arthur's companions to be noted by name, and so I have retained them, giving the friend-and-lover's part to Bedwyr, who is there both at the beginning and at the end, instead of to Lancelot, who is a later French importation. Arthur's hound and his white horse I have kept also, both for their ritual significance and because the Arthur —or rather Artos—I found myself coming to know so well, was the kind of man who would have set great store by his dogs and his horses. When the Roman fort of Trimontium was excavated, the bones of a "perfectly formed dwarf girl" were found lying in a pit under those of nine horses. An unexplained find, to which, in Artos's capture of the fortress and in the incident of "The People of the Hills," I have attempted an explanation. So it goes on . . . Almost every part of the story, even to the unlikely linkup between Medraut and that mysterious Saxon with a British name, Cerdic the half-legendary founder of Wessex, has some kind of basis outside the author's imagination.

Having, as it were, stated my case, I should like to express my most warmly grateful thanks to the people who have, in one way or another, contributed to the writing of *Sword at Sunset*—among them the Oxford University Press, for allowing me to use certain characters which have already appeared in *The Lantern-Bearer*. Among them also the authors of many books from Gildas in the sixth century to Geoffrey Ashe in 1960; the oddly assorted experts who returned detailed and patient answers to my letters of inquiry about horse breeding; the Canadian friend who sent me the poem *Hic Jacet Arthurus Rex Quondam Rexque Futurus* and the Intelligence Corps Sergeant and his young woman who found its origin for me after both I and the aforesaid Canadian friend had dismally failed to do so; the Major of the 1st East Anglian Regiment, who sacrificed three sunny afternoons of his leave from Staff College to help me plan Artos's campaign in Scotland, and to work out for me in three colors on a staff map the crowning victory of Badon.

Contents

CONTENTS

GLOSSARY

Abus River—Humber
Anderida—Pevensey
Aquae Sulis—Bath
Bodotria Estuary—Firth of Forth
Burdigala—Bordeaux
Calleva—Silchester
*Castra Cunetium—Castledykes
Cluta—Clyde
Combretovium—Baylam House
  (Suffolk)
Corinium—Cirencester
Corstopitum—Corbridge
Cunetio—Mildenhall
Deva—Chester
Dubris—Dover
Durocobrivae—Dunstable
Eburacum—York
Garumna—Garonne
Gaul—France
Glevum—Gloucester
Isca Dumnoniorum—Exeter

Island of Apples—Glastonbury
Lindinis—Ilchester
Lindum—Lincoln
Londinium—London
Luguvallium—Carlisle
Metaris Estuary—The Wash
Môn—Anglesey
Narbo Martius—Narbonne
Portus Adurni—Portchester
Sabrina Sea—Bristol Channel
Segedunum—Wallsend
Segontium—Caernarvon
Sorviodunum—Old Sarum
Tamesis—Thames
Tolosa—Toulouse
Trimontium—Newstead
Vectis Water—The Solent
Venta Belgarum—Winchester
Vindocladia—Badbury
Viroconium—Wroxeter
Yr Widdfa—Snowdon

*Latin name of author's own invention

[xi]

CHAPTER ONE

The Sword

NOW that the moon is near to full, the branch of an apple tree casts its nighttime shadow in through the high window across the wall beside my bed. This place is full of apple trees, and half of them are no more than crabs in the daylight; but the shadow on my wall, that blurs and shivers when the night wind passes and then grows clear again, is the shadow of that Branch the harpers sing of, the chiming of whose nine silver apples can make clear the way into the Land of the Living.

When the moon rises higher, the shadow is lost. The white radiance trickles down the wall and makes pools on the coverlet, and then at last it reaches my sword lying beside me—they laid it there because they said I was restless when it was not ready to my hand—and a spurt, a pinpoint, of blazing violet light wakes far, far down in the dark heart of Maximus's great amethyst set into the pommel. Then the moonlight passes, and the narrow cell is cobweb gray, and the star in the heart of the amethyst sleeps again; sleeps . . . I reach out in the grayness and touch the familiar grip that has grown warm to my hand in so many fights; and the feeling of life is in it, and the feeling of death. . . .

I cannot sleep, these nights, for the fire of the wound in my groin and belly. The Brothers would give me a draught stronger than the fire, if I let them; but I have no wish for the sleep of poppy juice and mandrake that leaves a dark taste in the mind afterward. I am content to wait for another sleep. And meanwhile there is so much to think of, so much to remember. . . .

Remember—remember across forty years, the first time that ever I held that blink of violet light in my hand, answering not to the cold whiteness of the moon, but to the soft yellow radiance of the candles in Ambrosius's study, on the night that he gave me my sword and my freedom.

I was sitting on the foot of my sleeping couch, busy with the twice-daily pumice stone. On campaign I generally grew my beard and clipped it short, but in winter quarters I always tried to keep a smooth chin in the Roman manner. Sometimes that meant the butchery of goose grease and razor, and left me scraped and raw and thanking many gods that at least I was not, like Ambrosius or old Aquila my friend and mentor in all that had to do with cavalry, a black-bearded man. But there was still pumice stone to be got when one was lucky, for it took more than the Franks and the Sea Wolves to quite close the trade routes and pen the merchant kind within their own frontiers. One of the merchant kind had come into Venta Belgarum only a few days since, with pumice stone and dried raisins and a few amphorae of thin Burdigala wine slung in pairs on the backs of his pack ponies; and I had managed to buy an amphora, and a piece of pumice almost the size of my fist, enough to last me through the winter and maybe next winter also.

When the bargaining was over, we had drunk a cup of the wine together and talked, or rather he had talked while I listened. I have always found pleasure in hearing men tell of their travels. Sometimes the talk of travelers is for listening to by firelight, and best savored with much salt; but this man's talk was of a daylight kind and needed little salt, if any. He talked of the joys of a certain house in the street of sandalmakers at Rimini, of the horrors of sea-sickness and the flavor of milk-fed snails, of passing encounters and mishaps of the road that brimmed with laughter as a cup with wine, of the scent and color of the roses of Paestum that used to serve the Roman flower markets (he was something of a poet in his way). He told of the distances from such a place to such another place, and the best inns still to be found on the road. He talked—and for me this had more interest than all the rest—of the Goths of Southern Gaul and the big dark-colored horses that they bred, and the great summer horse fair at Narbo Martius. I had heard before of the horses of Septimania, but never from one who had seen them with his own eyes and had the chance to make his own judgment of their mettle. So I asked many questions, and laid by his answers, together with certain other things that had long been in my heart, to think over, afterward.

I had thought of those things a good deal, in the past few days, and now it came upon me as I sat there rubbing my chin with the pumice stone and already half stripped for sleep, that the time had come to be done with the thinking.

Why that night I do not know; it was not a good time to choose; Ambrosius had been in council all day, it was late, and he might even have gone to his bed by now, but I knew suddenly that I must go to him that night. I leaned sideways to peer into the burnished curve of my war cap hanging at the head of the couch, which was the only mirror I had, feeling my cheeks and chin for any stubble still to be rubbed away, and my face looked back at me, distorted by the curve of the metal, but clear enough in the light of the dribbling candles, big-boned as a Jute's, and brown-skinned under hair the color of a hayfield when it pales at harvesttime. I suppose that I must have had all that from my mother, for assuredly there was nothing there of dark narrow-boned Ambrosius; nor, consequently, of Utha his brother and my father, who men had told me was like him. Nobody had ever told me what my mother was like; maybe no one had noticed, save for Utha who had begotten me on her under a hawthorn bush, in sheer lightness of heart after a good day's hunting. Maybe even he had not noticed much.

The pumice stone had done its work, and I set it aside, and getting to my feet, caught up the heavy cloak that lay across the couch and flung it around me over my light undertunic. I called to my armor-bearer whom I could still hear moving in the next room, that I should want him no more that night, and went out into the colonnade with my favorite hound Cabal padding at heel. The old Governor's Palace had sunk into quiet, much as a war camp does about midnight when even the horses cease to fidget in their picket lines. Only here and there the china saffron square of a window showed where someone was still wakeful on watch. The few colonnade lanterns that had not yet been put out swung to and fro in the thin cold wind, sending bursts of light and shadow along the pavements. The snow had driven in over the dwarf wall of the colonnade, but it would not lie long; already the damp chill of thaw was in the air. The cold licked about my bare shins and smarted on my newly pumiced chin; but faint warmth met me on the threshold of Ambrosius's quarters, as the guards lowered their spears to let me pass into the anteroom. In the inner chamber there was applewood burning above the charcoal in the brazier, and the aromatic sweetness of it filled the room. Ambrosius the High King sat in his big cross-legged chair beside the brazier, and Kuno his armor-bearer stood in the far shadows by the door that opened into his sleeping cell beyond. And as I halted an instant on the threshold, it was as though I saw my kinsman with the clear-seeing eye of a stranger: a dark fine-boned man with a still and very purposeful face; a man who, in any multitude, would wear solitude almost as tangibly as he wore the purple mantle flung about his shoulders. I had been aware always of that solitude in him, but never so sharply as in that moment, and I was thankful that I should never be High King. Not for me that unbearable peak above the snow line. Yet now I think that it had little to do with the High Kingship but was in the man himself, for I had known it in him always, and he had been crowned only three days.

He was still fully dressed, though he sat forward, his arms across his knees, as he did when he was tired. The slender gold fillet that bound his dark brows gave back a blink of light to the brazier, and the straight folds of the cloak that glowed imperial purple in the daylight was ringstraked with black and the color of wine. He looked up as I entered, and his shuttered face flashed open as it did for few men save myself and Aquila. "Artos! So you too do not feel like sleeping."

I shook my head. "Na; and so I hoped that I should find you awake."

Cabal padded in past me, as one very much at home in that place, and cast himself down beside the brazier with a contented sigh.

Ambrosius looked at me for a moment, and then bade his armor-bearer bring some wine and leave us. But when the stripling had finally gone, I did not at once begin on the matter that had brought me, only stood warming my hands at the brazier and wondering how to make the beginning. I heard the whisper of sleet against the high window and the thin whining of the draft along the floor. Somewhere a shutter banged in the wind; steps passed along the colonnade and died into the distance. I was acutely aware of the small firelit room, and the darkness of the winter night pressing in upon its fragile shell.

A gust of wind swooped out of the night, driving a sharp spatter of sleet against the window, the aromatic smoke billowed from the brazier, and an apple log fell with a tinselly rustle into the red cavern of the charcoal. Ambrosius said, "Well, my great Bear Cub?" and I knew that he had been watching me all the time.

"Well?" I said.

"What is the thing that you come to say to me?"

I stooped, and took up a lichened log from the basket beside the brazier, and set it carefully on the fire. "Once," I said, "when I was a cub indeed, I remember hearing you cry out for one great victory to sound like a trumpet blast through Britain, that the Saxon legend might be broken in men's minds, and the tribes and the people might hear it and gather to your standard, not in ones and twos and scattered war bands, but in whole princedoms. . . . You gained that victory at Guoloph in the autumn. For a while at least, the Saxons are broken here in the South; Hengest is fled; and the princes of Dumnonia and the Cymri who have held back for thirty years got drunk three nights since at your Crowning Feast. It is maybe the turning of the tide—*this* tide. But still it is only a beginning, isn't it?"

"Only a beginning," Ambrosius said, "and even that, only in the South."

"And now?"

He had pulled off the great arm ring he wore above his left elbow; an arm ring of red gold wrought in the likeness of a dragon, and sat turning and turning it between his fingers, watching the firelight run and play in the interlocking coils. "Now to make strong our gains, to build up the Old Kingdom here in the South into a strength that can stand like a rock in the face of all that the seas can hurl against it."

I turned full to face him. "That is for you to do, to make your fortress here behind the old frontier, from the Thames's valley to the Sabrina Sea, and hold it against the Barbarians. . . ." I was fumbling for the words I wanted, trying desperately to find the right ones, thinking the thing out as I went along. "Something that may be to the rest of Britain not only a rallying place, but as the heart is to a man and the eagle used to be to a legion. But for me, there is another way that I must go."

He ceased playing with the arm ring and raised his eyes to mine. They were strange eyes for so dark a man; gray like winter rain, yet with a flame behind them. But he never spoke. And so after a while, I had to stumble on unaided. "Ambrosius, the time comes that you must give me my wooden foil and set me free."

"I thought that might be it," he said, after a long silence.

"You thought? How?"

His face, normally so still and shut, again flashed open into its rare smile. "You show too clearly in your eyes what goes on behind them, my friend. You should learn to put up your shield a little."

But as we looked at each other, there was no shield for either of us. I said, "You are the High King, and here in the South it may be indeed that you can rebuild the kingdom and restore something of the heritage; but everywhere the Barbarians press in; the Scots from Hibernia harry the western coasts and make their settlements in the very shadow of Yr Widdfa of the Snows; the Picts with their javelins come leaping over the Wall; northward and eastward the war boats of the Sea Wolves come creeping in along the estuaries, near and nearer to the heart of the land."

"How if I made you Dux Britanniorum?" Ambrosius said.

"I should still be your man, under your orders. Do you not see? —Britain is broken back into as many kingdoms as before the Eagles came; if I hold to any one king, even you, the rest of Britain will go down. Ambrosius, I shall always be your man in the sense in which a son going out into the world remains son to his father. Always I will play my part with you as best I may in any wider plan, and if you should be so sore pressed at any day that without me you cannot hold back the tide, then I will come, no matter what the cost. But short of that, I must be my own man, free to go where the need is sorest as I see it. . . . If I were to take a Roman title, it would be the one borne by the commander of our mobile cavalry forces in the last days of Rome—not Dux, but *Comes* Britanniorum."

"So, the Count of Britain. Three calvary wings and complete freedom," Ambrosius said.

"I could do it with less; three hundred men, if they were a brotherhood."

"And with three hundred men you believe that you can save Britain?" He was not mocking me, he never mocked at any man; he was simply asking a question.

But I did not answer at once, for I had to be sure. Once the answer was made, I knew that there could be no unmaking it again. "With three hundred men properly mounted, I believe that I can thrust back the Barbarians at least for a while," I said at last. "As for saving Britain—I have seen the wild geese flighting this autumn, and who can turn them back? It is more than a hundred years that we have been struggling to stem this Saxon flighting, more than thirty since the last Roman troops left Britain. How much longer, do you think, before the darkness closes over us?" It was a thing that I would not have said to any man save Ambrosius.

And he answered me as I do not think he would have answered any other man. "God knows. If your work and mine be well wrought, maybe another hundred years."

The shutter banged again, and somewhere in the distance I heard a smothered burst of laughter. I said, "Then why don't we yield now, and make an end? There would be fewer cities burned and fewer men slain in that way. Why do we go on fighting? Why not merely lie down and let it come? They say it is easier to drown if you don't struggle."

"For an idea," Ambrosius said, beginning again to play with the dragon arm ring; but his eyes were smiling in the firelight, and I think that mine smiled back at him. "Just for an idea, for an ideal, for a dream."

I said, "A dream may be the best thing to die for."

Neither of us spoke again for a while after that. Then Ambrosius said, "Pull up that stool. It seems that neither of us has much thought of sleep, and assuredly there are matters that we must speak of." And I knew that a part of my life had shut behind me, and ahead lay a new way of things.

I pulled up a stool with crossed antelope legs—it was stronger than it looked—and sat down. And still we were silent. Again it was Ambrosius who broke the silence, saying thoughtfully, "Three hundred men and horses, together with spare mounts. What of baggage?"

"As little as may be. We cannot be tied down to a string of lumbering wagons, we must be free-flying as a skein of wildfowl. A few fast mule carts for the field forge and heavy gear, two to three score pack beasts with their drivers—those must be fighting men too, when need arises, and serve as grooms and cooks in camp. The younger among us to act as armor-bearers for their seniors. And for the rest, we must carry our own gear as far as may be, and live on the country."

"That may not make you beloved of the country on which you live."

"If men would keep the roofs on their barns, they must pay with some of the grain in them," I said. It was the first of many times that I was to say much the same thing.

He looked at me with one eyebrow faintly raised. "You have the whole thing at your fingers' ends."

"I have thought about it through many nights."

"So. Three hundred mounted fighting men with spare horses, mule carts, pack beasts—geldings I take it?—with their grooms and drivers. Have you thought where they are to come from?" He leaned forward. "I make no doubt that you could raise the whole number and more, many more, from among the ranks of the war host; you have whistled all the best of the young men to follow you, as it is; and I should be left with Aquila and a few veterans who held to me for old time's sake." He tossed the glinting arm ring from right hand to left, and back again. "Only I cannot raise and man my fortress with a few grandsires. I will spare you a hundred fighting men of your own choosing, from among the trained troops, and a draft of twenty horses every other year from among the Arfon horse runs for so long as you need them. The rest, both mounts and men, you must find for yourself."

"It's a beginning," I said. "The problem of horses troubles me more than the men."

"Why so?"

"Our native horse breeds have dwindled in size since the Legions ceased to import mounts for their cavalry."

"They acquitted themselves none so ill at Guoloph last autumn —you of all men should know that," Ambrosius said, and began to hum very softly, part of the triumph song that old Traherne our harper had made for me on the night after that battle. *"Then came Artorius, Artos the Bear, thundering with his squadrons from the hill; then the world shook and the sods flew like startled swallows*

[8]

*from beneath his horses' hooves . . . like leaves before a wind,
like waves before a galley's prow the war hosts of Hengest curled
back and scattered. . . ."*

"It is in my mind that Traherne had been drinking to our victory and the Gods of the Harp spoke to him in a blaze of heather beer," I said. "But as for the horses: they are fine little brutes, our native hill breeds; swift and valiant, and surefooted as mountain sheep—and not much larger. Save for Arian there's scarce a horse in all our runs that is up to my weight with even the lightest armor."

"Armor?" he said quickly. We had always ridden light, in leather tunics much like the old Auxiliary uniform, with our horses undefended.

"Yes, armor. Chain-mail shirts for the men—they would have to come as and when we could take them in battle, there are no British armorers that have that particular skill. Boiled leather would serve for the horses' breast guards and cheekpieces. It was so that the Goths broke our Legions at Adrianople close on two hundred years ago; but the Legions never fully learned the lesson."

"A student of world history."

I laughed. "Was I not schooled by your old Vipsanius, whose mind was generally a few hundred years and a few thousand miles away? But he talked sense now and then. It is the weight that does it, the difference between a bare fist and one wearing the cestus."

"Only you need the bigger horses."

"Only I need the bigger horses," I agreed.

"What is the answer?"

"The only answer that I can think of is to buy a couple of stallions—the Goths of Septimania breed such horses—of the big forest strain, sixteen or seventeen hands high, and a few mares, and breed from them and the best of our native mares."

"And as to price? You'll not get such beasts for the price of a pack pony."

"They cost, on the average as I gather, the stallions each as much as six oxen; the mares rather more. I can raise perhaps the price of two stallions and seven or eight mares from my own lands that you passed on to me from my father—without selling off the land, that is: I'll not betray my own folk by selling them like cattle to a new lord."

[9]

Ambrosius was staring into the red heart of the brazier, his black brows drawn together in thought. Then he said, "Too long. It will take too long. With twice as many you might have enough of your big brutes grown and broken to mount at least your best men in three or four years; within ten you might well be able to mount your whole force."

"I know," I said, and we looked at each other through the faint smoke drift and the tawny upward glow of the brazier that threw into relief the old brand of Mithras between Ambrosius's brows that scarcely showed by daylight.

"You spoke of yourself a while since, as of a son going out into the world," he said at last. "So be it, you are all the son I ever had or ever shall have, and the Lord of Light forbid that I should send you out with an empty hand. We are none of us rich in these days, and one cannot build a fortress for nothing, or you should have more. I will give you the price of another ten beasts." And then before I could thank him, he rose with the controlled swiftness that was part of him, and turned away, saying, "More light, Bear Cub, the candles are at your elbow."

And while I lit a twig at the brazier and kindled the thick honey-wax candles on the writing table, he crossed to the big chest against the far wall, and stooped and flung back the lid. The candle flames sank, and then sprang up into the shape of laurel leaves, gold fringed with the perfect blue of the sky's zenith at the heart, and the room that had been lost in shadows sprang to life, the bull's-head frescoes on the walls, the scroll ends of Ambrosius's treasured library making a dim black-and-gold lozenge pattern in their shelves; and the storm and darkness of the night seemed to crouch back a little.

Ambrosius had taken something long and narrow from the chest and was turning back the folds of oiled linen that had been bound about it. "A while since also," he said, "you spoke of my giving you your wooden foil. Let this serve instead— Give me your own in exchange for it." And he turned and put into my hands a sword. It was a long cavalry spatha exactly like the one that I had carried since I became a man; and not knowing quite what to do, I drew it from its black wolfskin sheath, and let the light run like water on the blade. It was a fine weapon, perfectly balanced so that as I cut the air with it, it came up again into my hand almost of its own accord; but so did my own blade. Then I made a discovery. "Ambrosius, it is your sword!"

I suppose he saw my bewilderment, for sitting down again in his chair by the fire, he half smiled. "Yes, it is my sword. But not all my sword. Look at the pommel."

The hilt was of bronze finely inlaid with silver along the shoulders, the grip bound with silver wires, and as I reversed it, holding it point down, I saw that set into the pommel was a great square amethyst. It was so dark in color as to be almost of the imperial purple, and as I moved it, suddenly the light of the candles gathered in it, and far down through the lucid depth, a spark of violet radiance blazed for an instant like a small fierce jet of flame. And above it, clear on the pale surface sheen of the gem, I saw an imperial eagle, intaglio cut, grasping in its claws a double M; and spelled out around the edge, turning the sword to catch the light on the letters, the single word IMPERATOR.

"Do you remember that?" Ambrosius asked.

"Yes, you showed it to me once; it is Maximus's seal." It had been kept always at Dynas Pharaon in the home hall of the Lords of Arfon, and so had escaped the rising that swept so much away. "But it was not in any sword then."

"No, I had it set for you, and the sword seemed the most fit setting."

I remember that I stood for a long time looking at the great seal, waking and losing the star in the heart of the amethyst, oddly moved by the link across the years with my great-grandsire, the proud Spanish general who had married a princess of Arfon and so founded our line before his own legionaries had proclaimed him Emperor and he had marched out to his Gaulish campaigns and his death at Aquileia. After his execution, one of his officers had got his seal back to Arfon, to the princess his wife; and now it seemed to me that I was holding the whole history of our line in the dark depth of the gem that was so nearly the color of an emperor's mantle. A stormy and a bitter history, but a proud one; of Maximus himself; of Constantine, the son he had left, sweeping down from the Arfon glens, out of the very snows of Yr Widdfa, to drive back the Saxon hordes, dying at last of a murderer's javelin in the throat, here at Venta in his own hall. Ambrosius had told me that story often enough; he had been only nine years old, and

Utha two years older, for they were the sons of their father's old age; but he had told me once that he still dreamed of the firebrands and the shouting, and being carried off across somebody's saddle-bow with a cloak flung over his head. It had been days before he knew that he and Utha, snatched away by a faithful few of their father's household warriors, were all that was left of the Royal House of Britain; months before he knew that Vortigern of Powys, Vortigern the Red Fox, their marriage-kinsman, had usurped the chief power in the land. Vortigern's story was in the seal, too; Vortigern the dreamer of magnificent twilight dreams, to whom all that had to do however distantly with Rome was a worse thing than the menace of the Saxon hordes; who had brought in Saxon war bands to hold down the Picts for him, and found too late that he had called the Wolves in over his threshold. And there in the seal, too, was I, who now held it. . . . My mother died when I was born, and either because he felt himself guilty of her death, or because I was, after all, a son, Utha took me into his household and put me to nurse with the wife of his chief hunter; and after Utha's death on a boar's tusk, Ambrosius took me in his stead. I was four summers old then, and thrust among the hounds for the place next to his knee, and when I got it, was content. I was, as he had said, the only son he ever knew, and assuredly he was all the father I had ever needed. Through the years of waiting and making ready that were the years of my own growing up, through the years of long-drawn warfare that followed, quickening at last to our autumn's victory, I had ridden with Ambrosius since I was fifteen and first judged man enough to carry my sword. Therefore it had not been easy to tell him tonight that henceforth I must ride alone. But I think that he had known it already.

Again the star blazed up in the royal depth of the amethyst, and I thought of another thing, and looked up. "Ambrosius—you cannot give me this. The sword, yes, I take that gladly in exchange for mine; but the seal is another matter. It is of the Royal House, even as you say."

"Well? And are you not of the Royal House? Not your father's son?"

"My mother's also," I said.

"Who, then, should I give it to?"

"You have not so many gray hairs that you need take much

thought of that as yet. When the time comes—Cador of Dumnonia, I suppose." I saw in my mind's eye the dark reckless face of the Prince of the Dumnonia, close to Ambrosius's at the coronation feast. Thin and fiery like the fierce spirit that our people make from grain. A warrior, yes; but a High King . . . ?

"He has less of the royal blood in him than you, and that on the mother's side."

"He is not a bastard," I said. And the word sounded harshly in my own ears.

There was another silence; Cabal whimpered in his sleep, chasing dream hares, and the sleet spattered more sharply at the window. Then Ambrosius said, "Bear Cub, has that left a scar?"

"No, for you took care that it should not. But because of it, you must not give me this seal of the Royal House."

He took up again the heavy gold bracelet that he had laid aside when he rose to fetch the sword. "You mistake. I could not give you this that can be worn by right only by the princes of the House. The other was Maximus's private seal and nothing more. In its way it is more potent than the arm ring, but it is mine to give—to my houndboy if I choose, and I choose that it should follow, shall we say, the dexter line of the royal blood. . . . I have known for a long while that a night such as this must come, and I have known as long, that when it came you must take my sword with you, Bear Cub, because I love you; and Maximus's seal because you are its true lord."

"The light burns like a star in the heart of it," I said. "Maybe I can make it shine a small way further, into the dark. . . . I think we're both a little drunk, Ambrosius."

But I do not think that we had touched the wine.

CHAPTER TWO

Left-Hand World

MORE than two months later I was squatting beside another fire—of crackling furze and heather roots that blazed on the open turf before a herdsman's bothy. It seemed to me bright as only a hill fire could be, just as the clear luminous darkness that pressed behind it could only be the darkness of the hills.

Behind me in Venta I had gathered my hundred men, and now, with a handful of those who were closest to me, I had come up into the Arfon herding grounds to see for myself what Ambrosius's promised drafts might be likely to yield in the next few years, and choose out the best brood mares for my great stallions from among my own horse kind.

Spring had come to the valleys of Arfon though the white mane of winter snows still lay far down the north side of Yr Widdfa; and the night was full of the voices of running water, and from the heather slopes behind the bothies, the curlews were calling as they would call almost all night long. But under the voices of the high hills, my ears seemed still to throb with the soft thunder of unshod hooves. All day they had been rounding up the horse herds, bringing them in to this deep valley of Nant Ffrancon that in time of danger could give sheltered grazing to all the horses and cattle of Arfon. The made horses had been brought up in small bands, sometimes even singly, to show their paces; and I had stood here in the loop of the stream where the herdsmen had their bothies and their branding pens, to see them brought in; and afterward the leggy two-year-olds whose breaking had been begun that winter, the wild-eyed colts with matted manes and tails, and burrs in their

[14]

woolly winter coats; awkward and scary, the short hill turf flying in sods from under their stampeding hooves; the mares brought up more quietly, nervous and willful, with bellies beginning to drop as foaling time drew near; the herdsmen on their little swift beasts handling them as a dog handles sheep. It had been a good sound, a good sight. All my life the sight of a made stallion or a mare with her foal running at heel has been to me a thing to shake the heart with delight.

Now the sweating business of the day was over and, herdsmen and Companions, we had gathered together around the blaze, huddling our cloaks about us against the cold that prowled with the darkness at our backs even while our faces scorched. We had eaten broiled mountain mutton and great hunks of rye bread and mare's-milk cheese and wild honey; our bellies were full and our work done, and as we sat talking, most of us, I think, still about the horses, content folded us around like a homespun blanket.

But for me, the blanket was somewhat threadbare, and a little cold wind blew through. It was good, unbelievably good, to be in the mountains again; but I had come to them as a man comes to the house he has longed for—and found that among my own hills and my own people, something in me had become a stranger.

Beside me, huddled in a wolfskin mantle, sat old Hunno, lord of my own horses, who had known me all my life. We had withdrawn from the general talk around the fire, but we too were speaking of horse matters, at least horses came into it.

"So the mountain horse runs will not be good enough for you, after these lowland years," the old man was grumbling into the beard that clothed his face as gray lichen clothes a twisted thorn branch.

I had a strong desire to shake him until the yellow fangs rattled in his head, since it seemed that I could reach him in no other way. "There is no question of that. Have I not told you three times already? The mountain pastures are good, but they are too remote for the training herd. How long, think you, it would take to bring a draft of horses down from here even to the beginning of the lowlands? Seven days at the least; seven days that we could maybe ill afford; and if our need came at a time of storms when the rivers are in spate, we might not be able to get them out at all. The horse runs of the Deva Promontory are good also, and from Deva the roads run clear across to Eburacum or south even to Venta, for quick movement."

"And so you will speak with Kinmarcus of Deva?"

"I have already spoken with him—before he rode north again from Ambrosius's crowning, and he will yield me the grazing leave. There has always been a strong link, remember, between Deva and the Lords of Arfon."

He snorted like an aged ram. "And doubtless you will be picking out men of the Deva runs to herd these great new horses for you? Men that only know how to ride on a flat level and have never roped a wild stallion among the rocks on a slope like a falcon's stoop."

"You know the answer to that well enough, you sour old devil," I said; and then as he remained stubbornly silent, "Well? Will you come?"

He lowered at me under the fringe of his shaggy sheepskin hat. "If I come to be your horse master in the lowland runs, who's to take the reins here and handle these great new breaking runs that you plan?"

"Amgerit, your son," I said. "You know that he will take them anyway, when you grow too old."

"It is in my heart that I begin to grow old already—too old to be dragging up my roots from the mountains that saw me born."

"If you say so," I said. "It is for you to choose." And I left him to it. I thought that in the end he would come; but I could not do as I would once have done, taking him by the shoulders and shaking him, laughing and threatening until I had his promise, because of the strangeness that had come between me and my own world; and I knew that he was as much aware of the strangeness, the barrier, as I was.

Young Flavian, Aquila's son and my armor-bearer, was deep in argument with one of the herdsmen. I saw the white scar on the boy's temple, heritage of a riding fall in his childhood, when the night wind lifted his dark forelock, and the bright eagerness of his eyes as he drove home some point with a finger into the palm of his hand; and the brown wind-burned face of the herdsman, as vehemently denying the point, whatever it was. I saw Owain and Fulvius who had been boys with me and knew these hills as well as I did, as one passed the beer jar to the other, and wondered

[16]

whether they also felt the strangeness of their homecoming. I saw Bericus tossing a greasy knucklebone from hand to hand and watching the fall of it idly as a man playing right hand against left watches the fall of the dice. I saw the farsighted hard-bitten faces of the herdsmen, most of them as well known to me almost as the faces of my Companions. I felt the harshness of Cabal's mane under my fingers, and the softness of his pricked ears; I listened to the calling of the curlews in the dark, trying to lay hold of familiar things again for a defense against the desolation that had come upon me out of nowhere and for no clear reason.

Presently somebody called for a tune, and a boy among the herdsmen, with a smooth olive face and warts on his hands, brought out an elder pipe and began to play, softly as a wandering wind at first, then jauntily as a water wagtail, passing with little runs and trills from tune to tune, while the men about the fire joined in from time to time, or were silent to listen. Some of his tunes were those of working lilts and old songs that we all knew; others, I think, he had made himself from something that he heard in his own head. A small merry piping, but it seemed to me that it spoke to me with a tongue that I had known before I was born, and that Yr Widdfa crest itself stooped nearer to listen. And when the boy finished and shook the spittle from the end of his pipe and thrust it again into his belt, it was as though for a few moments we all went on listening to its echoes.

Then someone moved to throw more furze branches on the blaze, and the silence broke; and most of us had some praise for the piper, so that he flushed like a girl and stared at his feet. And when the talk had turned to other things, I said to old Hunno beside me, "It is a long time since I have heard the music of my left-hand people among my own hills."

"Your left-hand people?" said Hunno.

"My left-hand people . . . Half of me is Roman, Hunno. I think that is so strong in your mind tonight that you have wakened it in mine. My right-hand people are those who built squared forts and drove the great roads straight from city to city through whatever lay between; men who deal in law and order and can argue a question in cold blood—a daylight people. The left side is the dark side, the women's side, the side nearest to the heart."

"A sore thing, you'll be telling me, to belong to two worlds."

[17]

"At the worst, it might be to be torn between the tree and the stallion. At the least, it is to be always a little in exile."

He nodded under his shaggy hat. "Sa sa." And then, grudgingly, "It is in my mind that I will come down into the Deva runs when you are wanting me."

The next day I spent for myself. I had done what I came to do, and tomorrow I must take the road down from the mountains; the long road south through Britain and across the Narrow Sea and south again all the length of Gaul to the horse markets of Septimania; and once I set foot on that road, God knew when I might walk my own hills again. In the cool first light of morning, with a crust of rye bread in the breast of my tunic, and Cabal, eager for the day, loping ahead, I left the rest of my little band to their own devices, and took to the hills, as I had done when I was a boy, before ever Ambrosius led his war hosts down to drive out the Saxon hordes and retake his father's capital; in the days when Arfon was still my world, and the world still whole and undivided.

At the head of the valley, the stream came down in steep white water, and the alders gave place to rowan and bird cherry. The day was strengthening; the hillside still in shadow, but the light suddenly thrilling like birdsong. I struck away from the stream and began to make my way up the open hillside, Cabal leaping on ahead as though the feathers of his heels were wings. Below me, when I turned to look back, the great valley of Nant Ffrancon fell away, green under the gray and blue and russet of the mountains. I could make out the loop of the stream with its rusty smoke of spring-flushed alders, and the huddled bothies where we had slept, and all down the valley the darkling speckle of the horse herds at graze. Then I turned my back on the valley and climbed on, up into the solitude of the high hills, into a world that was very old and very empty, where sound was the crying of the green plover and the siffling of the little wind through the dun grass, and movement was the cloud shadows racing from hill to hill.

I walked for a long time, keeping to the high ground, with the white crest of Yr Widdfa rearing always above the shoulders of the mountains northward; and long past noon, came to the crest of a mountain ridge, where an outcrop of starling-colored rocks, stripped by storms on the seaward side, made a rampart against

[18]

the wind, so that landward of it there was shelter and a thin warmth. It was a good halting place, and I settled there to my hunk of bread. Cabal lay down beside me with a sigh, and watched me eat. A small mountain flower, a star of petals royally purple as the amethyst in my sword hilt, sprang from a cushion of hairy leaves in a cleft of the rocks within reach of my hand, and before me I had the whole mile-wide sweep of the hillside to myself, save for the carcass of a sheep picked bare by black-backed gulls. I finished the dark nutty bread, tossing the last piece to the expectant Cabal, and did not at once push on, but sat with my arms around my updrawn knees, letting the high solitude soak into me. I have always dreaded to be lonely, but it was the loneliness of being set apart that I dreaded in those days, not the mere fact of being alone. . . . It was warm, surprisingly warm, here in the sun and out of the wind, and it was as though sleep came creeping up through the grasses; little by little I slipped into an easier position, my head on Cabal's flank; and sleep gathered us both in the same instant.

I woke to hear Cabal's troubled whining, and felt a changed air on my face; and opened my eyes and came to my elbow in the same instant, staring about me. Where the mile-wide sweep of hillside had dropped away to rise again to the crests across the valley was nothing but soft wreathing whiteness, a few paces of tawny hill grass, blurring into the drift. The mist had come rolling up from the sea while I slept, as such mists do come, without warning, and swiftly as a horse may gallop. Even as I looked, it thickened, smoking across the crest of the rocks above me in swathes of drifting moisture that tasted salt on the lips.

I cursed, but cursing was no good; and considered what next, for I was not familiar with this particular stretch of the Arfon mountains. I could wait where I was for the mist to clear, but I knew these sudden uncanny hill mists; it might be three days before that happened. Or I could find a stream and follow it down. One was never far from running water, among the high hills. The danger of that was that the stream might lead me over a rock fall or into a bog, instead of safely off the hills; but to a hillman born and bred as I was, that danger was small so long as I kept my wits about me.

Cabal was already up, stretching first his front and then his hind legs, and stood watching me expectantly, his tail swinging behind him as I got up and stretched in my turn. I stood for a few moments to get my bearings. Then I whistled him after me and set off downhill into the mist. I moved slowly, steering by the fall of the land and pausing now and then to listen, until at last I caught the purl of quick-running water seemingly still very far below me; and three steps farther on, all but stumbled head foremost into a stream coming down in green spate from the melting snows. It would lead me in the wrong direction for Nant Ffrancon, but that could not be helped; the rest would know, when the mist came down, that I was safe enough among my own glens, and wait for me until I could make my way back to them.

Presently, as I followed the water down, the steep fall of the valley leveled somewhat, and the ground underfoot changed from moor grass to a dense aromatic carpet of bog myrtle interlaced with heather; and I began to feel for the firmness of every step. Then it dropped again, and the stream plunged after it in a long slide of black water smooth as polished glass under the overarching tangle of hawthorn trees, and rough pasture came up to meet me among the hillside outcrops of black rock, and almost in the same instant I snuffed the faint blue whisper of woodsmoke.

I whistled Cabal in closer and, with a hand on his bronze-studded collar, checked to listen, then went on again. Below me I heard the lowing of cattle, and through the mist a huddle of squat buildings loomed into view. There was a soft flurry of hoofbeats and horned shapes shouldering up through the smoking wetness; a knot of cattle being driven in for folding. I had not realized it was as late as that. One of the little rough-coated milch cows broke away from the rest and headed into the mist, her eyes wild and her heavy udder swinging. I stepped into her path, waving my free arm and making the noises that came to me from my boyhood and I had not used since; and she wheeled away, lowing, her head down, and cantered back toward the opening in the turf wall. Cabal would have bounded after her but for my hand on his collar. A sullen-looking boy in a wolfskin came panting up at the heels of this herd, with a great walleyed bitch running low at his knee, and as the last of the cattle pelted through, we came together in the gateway.

He looked at me, slantwise a little, under down-drawn brows, while the dogs—seeing that the other was a bitch, I had released

Cabal—walked around each other in inquiring circles. "She is forever wandering away. My thanks, stranger." The boy's gaze moved over me appraisingly, and fastened upon the heavy gold Medusa-head brooch that clasped my tunic at the shoulder, then returned to my face. Clearly he wanted to know what a man with a brooch like that was doing alone in the mountains, but a kind of sullen courtesy forbade his asking.

I said, "I was caught way up the glen yonder by the magic mist —I am from Nant Ffrancon over the mountains. Will you give me shelter for the night?"

"The shelter is not mine to give; you must ask the woman."

But I had turned in beside him, after the cattle. We were within the gate gap now, and a man who by his face was the boy's father had appeared to help him close the entrance with its dry thornbush for the night. He too stared at me slantwise under his brows, while the cattle milled around us. They seemed a very silent couple.

I was in a farmsteading like many another below the mountains; a huddle of low-browed bothies of turfs and gray stone, roofed with a dark rough thatch of heather; store sheds, byres and houseplace, all huddled within the turf walls that gave nighttime shelter from the wolves and the dark. But I had never been in this steading before, this steading with the white wetness of the mountain mist smoking out of its hunched shoulders. And for a moment I had the unpleasant fancy that it lay at the very heart of the mist as a spider lies at the heart of its web; and that when the mist lifted, there would be only bare hillside where the steading had been.

But even as the thought brushed across my mind, I knew suddenly that I was being watched—watched, that is, by someone other than the man and the boy. I turned quickly, and saw a woman standing in the houseplace doorway. A tall woman clad in a tunic of rough saffron wool worked about the neck and sleeves with crimson, which gave her the look of a flame. A heavy mass of dark hair was loosely knotted about her head, and her eyes looked coolly back into mine out of a face which bore what I took at that first sight to be the burned-out remains of great beauty. Yet she could not, I thought, be more than a few years older than myself, twenty-seven or eight, maybe. She stood with one hand on the leather door apron which still quivered where it had just fallen back into place behind her; yet there was a stillness about her, as though she had been standing there a very long time, maybe a lifetime or so—waiting.

This, clearly, was the woman of whom I must ask my night's shelter. But she spoke first, low-voiced and with less courtesy than her herdboy. "Who are you, and what do you come seeking here?"

"For the one, men call me Artos the Bear," I said. "For the other, a night's shelter if you will give it to me. I am from Nant Ffrancon over the mountains, and the mist came upon me unawares."

I had the odd impression, as I spoke, that something had flashed open behind her eyes; but before I could tell what lay beyond, it was as though she veiled them again, deliberately, so that I should not look in. She stood as still as before, save that her gaze moved over me, from my head to my rawhide shoes. Then she smiled, and drew aside the door apron. "So—we have heard that Artos the Bear was running among the horse herds of Nant Ffrancon. It grows cold since the mist came down; let you come in to the hearth fire, and be welcome."

"Good fortune on the house, and on the woman of the house." I had to duck low to pass in through the doorway, but once inside, with the thick peat reek stinging in my throat and eyes, the house-place was roomy enough to be half lost in shadows beyond the reach of the firelight.

"Wait," the woman said, moving past me. "I will make more light." She disappeared into the farther gloom, and I heard her moving there, softly, as though on furred paws. Then she was back, and stooping to kindle a dry twig at the central hearth. The twig blossomed into flame at the tip, and from the flame-flower she kindled the waxen candle she had brought with her from the shadows. The young candle flame sank and turned blue as she shielded it with her hollowed hand, then sprang erect, and the shadows crowded back under the deep thatch as she reached up and set it on the edge of the half loft in the crown of the roof.

I saw a spacious living hut, the usual standing loom beside the door with a piece of striped cloth on it, piled sheepskins on the bed place against the farther wall, a carved and roughly painted chest. The woman drew forward a stool spread with a dappled deerskin to the flagged space beside the hearth. "Let my lord be seated; there will be food by and by."

I murmured something by way of thanks, and sat down, Cabal watchful at my feet; and sitting there with my elbows comfortably on my knees, I fell to watching her as, seemingly brushing off all consciousness of me, she returned to the cooking of the evening meal. Watching her so, as she knelt in the fire glow, turning from the herb-scented stew in its copper cauldron to the barley cakes browning on the hearthstone, I was puzzled. Her tunic was of rough homespun, scarcely finer, though certainly brighter in color, than that which any peasant woman might have worn, and the hands with which she turned the barley cakes were rough-skinned, the hands of a peasant woman in texture though not in shape; and yet I could not see her as woman to the man outside. Also, the more I looked at her face in the firelight, the more my mind was teased with a half-memory like a fugitive scent that always eluded me, just as I thought I had it. Yet I was sure that I had never seen her before. I should never have forgotten that ruined beauty once I had seen it. Maybe she was like someone? But if so, who? I had an uneasy feeling that in some way it mattered deeply that I should remember, that a great deal depended on it. . . . But the more I tried to lay hold of it, the further the nagging memory slipped away.

At last I turned from it to the puzzle that could be more easily solved. "The man I saw outside . . ." I began, and left the end of the sentence trailing, for I was feeling my way.

She looked up at me, her eyes bright and faintly mocking, as though she knew what was in my mind. "Is my servant. So is the boy, and so is Uncle Bronz, whom you will see in a while. I am the only woman here, and so I cook for my servants—and for my guest."

"And for the lord of the steading?"

"There is no lord of the steading." She sat back on her heels and stared into my face; the hot barley cake must have scorched her fingers, but she seemed not to feel it, as though her whole awareness were in her eyes. "We are such barbarians, here in the mountains where Rome's feet seldom trampled, that a woman may possess both herself and her own property, if she be strong enough to hold them."

She spoke as one half scornfully explaining the ways of her country to strangers, and I felt the blood rise in my forehead at her tone. "I have not forgotten the customs of my own people."

"Your own people?" She replaced the barley cake on the hearthstone, laughing a little. "Have you not? You have been long enough in the lowlands. They say that at Venta there are streets of houses all in straight rows, and in the houses are tall rooms with painted walls, and Ambrosius the High King wears a cloak of the imperial purple."

I laughed also, pulling at Cabal's twitching ears. This woman was not like any that I had known before. "Do not hold the straightness of the Venta streets against me. Do not deny me a place in my mother's world because I have a place in my father's."

CHAPTER THREE

The Birds of Rhiannon

PRESENTLY the three men and the walleyed bitch came to their supper, shouldering in like oxen out of the wet, with a silver bloom of mist drops hanging in their hair and the homespun and wolfskin of their garments, and took their places about the fire, squatting on their haunches in the spread fern. I had the only stool in the place, and they looked at me sidelong and upward, knowing me for who I was, and more silent even than I judged was usual with them because I was there.

The woman gathered the hot barley cakes into a basket, and unhooked the bronze stewpot and set it beside the hearth, and fetched hard white cow's-milk cheese and a jar of thin heather beer. Then she poured her own share of the stew into a bowl, took a barley cake, and withdrew to the women's side of the hearth, leaving the rest of us to fend for ourselves on the men's side.

It was the most silent meal that I have ever eaten. The men were tired, and wary in my presence like animals with a stranger's smell among them; and on the far side of the fire, the woman kept her own dark counsels, though more than once when I glanced toward her, I knew that the instant before she had been watching me.

When we had thrown the bones to the dogs, and wiped the last drops of soup from the bottom of the crock with lumps of barley bannock, when the last lump of cheese was eaten and the beer jar drained, the farm men rose, and shouldered out once more into the night, bound, I supposed, for their own sleeping places somewhere among the byres. Thinking that maybe I should go too, I drew one leg under me to rise. But the woman had risen already, and was looking at me through the peat smoke. It seemed as though

her eyes were waiting for mine; and when I met them, she shook
her head, smiling a little. "Those are my servants, and when they
have eaten they go to their own places; but you are my guest;
therefore stay a while. See, I will bring you better drink than you
had at supper."

And as I watched her, she seemed to melt rather than draw back
into the shadows under the half loft. She was an extraordinarily
silent creature in all her movements, silken-footed as a mountain
cat; and I guessed that she could be as fierce as one also. In a
while she returned, bearing between her hands a great cup of polished birchwood darkened almost to black by age and use, and
ornamented around the rim with beaten silver; and I rose as she
came toward me, and bent my head to drink from the cup as she
raised it, my hand resting lightly over hers in the gesture which
custom demanded. It was more heather beer, but stronger and
sweeter than that which I had drunk at supper; and there was an
aromatic tang under the sweetness that I did not recognize. Maybe
it was no more than the flavor of the wild garlic in the cheese
lingering still in my mouth. Over the tilting rim of the cup I saw her
looking at me with an odd intensity, but as I caught her gaze, I
had once again that impression that she had drawn a veil behind
her eyes so that I could not look in. . . .

I drained the cup, and released it again into her hands. "I thank
you. The drink was good," I said, my voice sounding strangely
thickened in my own ears, and sat down once more on the skin-
spread stool, stretching my legs to the fire.

The woman stood looking down at me; I felt her looking; and
then she laughed, and tossed to Cabal some dark sweetmeat that
she had been holding in the hollow of her hand. "There, for a dog
that is better than heather beer," and as Cabal (greed was his
failing always) snapped it up, she sank to her knees beside me and
letting the empty cup roll unheeded into the folds of her skirt, began to mend the fire. She settled on more peat, and heather snarls
and birch bark to make a blaze, and as the dry stuff caught and
the flames licked out along the strands of it, the light strengthened
and leapt up and reached to finger the very houseplace walls. A
strange mood of awareness was coming over me, so that it was as
though I had one less skin than usual. I was aware as though they
had been part of my own body, my own soul, of the houseplace
brimming with light as the great cup had brimmed with heather

beer, and with the same wild sweet half-forgotten, half-remembered tang of magic; I was aware of the dark thatch like sheltering wings, and beyond the golden circle the night and the mountains and the salt mist crowding in: the very texture of the pale night moth's fur as it fluttered about the candle flame, and the last year's sweetness of the sprig of dry bell heather in the fern by my foot.

There was another scent, too, that I had not noticed before, a sharp aromatic sweetness lacing the mingled homespun smells of thatch and cooking, wet wolfskins and peat smoke. It came, I realized, from the woman's hair. I had not seen her take the pins from it, but it fell now all about her, a dark silken fall like the slide of water under the hawthorn trees, and she was playing with it idly, flinging it this way and that, combing it with her fingers, so that the disturbing sweetness came and went like breath, whispering to me in the firelight. . . .

"Tell me where I may find a place to sleep among your byres, and I will be going now," I said, more loudly than was needful.

She looked up at me, holding aside the dark masses of her hair and smiling in the shadow of it. "Ah, not yet. You have been so long in coming."

"So long in coming?" Something in me that stood aside from the rest knew even then that it was a strange thing for her to say; but the firelight and mist and the scent of her hair were in my head, and all things a little unreal, brushed with a dark moth-wing bloom of enchantment.

"I knew that you would come, one day."

I frowned, and shook my head in a last attempt to clear it. "Are you a witch, then, to know the thing that has not yet come to happen?" And even as I spoke, another thought sprang to my mind. "A witch, or—"

Again she seemed to read my thinking; and she laughed up into my face. "A witch, or—? Are you afraid to wake in the morning on the bare mountainside, and find three lifetimes gone by? Ah, but whatever happens tomorrow, surely tonight is sweet?" With the speed and liquid grace of a cat, she slip-turned from her kneeling position, and next instant was lying across my thighs, her strange ravaged face turned up to mine and her dark hair flowing over us both. "Are you afraid to hear the music of the Silver Branch? Are you afraid to hear the singing of Rhiannon's birds that makes men forget?"

I had not noticed the color of her eyes before. They were deeply blue, and veined like the petals of the blue cranesbill flower, the lids faintly stained with purple like the beginning of corruption. "I think that you would not need the birds of Rhiannon to make men forget," I said thickly, and bent toward her. She gave a low shuddering cry and reared up to meet me; she tore the bronze pin from the neck of her tunic so that it fell loose, and caught my hand and herself guided it down into the warm dark under the saffron cloth, to find the heavy softness of one breast.

The skin of her hands was hard, and her throat brown where it rose above her tunic, but the skin of her breast was silken, full and unblemished; and I could feel the whiteness of it. I dug in my fingers, and the delight under my hand set up a shivering echo like a small flame in my loins. I was not like Ambrosius; I had had my first girl when I was sixteen, and others since; not more perhaps, or less, than most of my kind. I do not think I ever harmed any of them, and for me, the taking had been sweet while it lasted and not much mattered afterward. But the thing in me that stood aside knew that this would be different, promising fiercer joys than ever I had known before, and that afterward, for all the rest of my life, the scars would last.

I struggled to resist—drugged, enchanted, whatever I was, I strove to fight her; and I am not weak-willed. She must have felt the struggle in me. Her arms were around my neck, and she laughed, softly and crooningly. "Na na, there is no need that you should be afraid. I will tell you my name in exchange for yours; if I were one of *Them*, I could not do that, for it would give you power over me."

"I do not think I want to know it." I dragged the words out.

"But you must; it is too late now. . . . I am called Ygerna," and she began to sing, very softly, almost under her breath. It might have been a spell—maybe it was, in its way—but it only sounded like a singing rhyme that I had known all my life; a small caressing song that the women sing to their children, playing with their toes at sleeping time. Her voice was sweet and soft as wild honey; a dark voice:

"Three birds perched on an apple spray,
And the blossom was not more white than they.
And they sang to the souls who passed that way.

[28]

A King in a cloak of white and red
And a Queen with goldwork round her head
And a woman with loaves of barley bread . . ."

The song and the voice were calling to me, calling to the part of me that had its roots in my mother's world, offering the perfect and complete homecoming that I had failed to find. The Dark Side, I had called it, the women's side, the side nearest to the heart. It was calling to me now, arms wide and welcoming, through the woman lying across my knee, finally claiming me, so that the things I had cared about before the mist came down were forgotten; so that I rose when she did and stumbled after her to the piled sheepskins against the wall.

When I awoke, I was lying still fully clothed on the bed place, and the leather apron had been freed from its pegs and drawn back from the doorway; and in the gray light of dawn that watered the shadows, I saw the woman sitting beside me, once again with her stillness upon her, as though she had been waiting maybe a lifetime or so for me to waken.

I smiled at her, not desiring her any more, but satisfied, and remembering the fierce joy of her body answering mine in the darkness. She looked back at me with no answering smile, her eyes no longer blue but merely dark in the leaden light, the discolored lids more deeply stained than ever. I came to my elbow, aware, without full looking, of Cabal lying still asleep beside the hearth, the fire burned out to frilled white ash, and the cup with its silver rim lying where it had fallen among the fern. And in the woman, too, it seemed that the fires were burned out and cold, deadly and dreadfully cold. A chill fell on me as I looked at her, and the thought came back to me of waking on a bare mountainside. . . .

"I have waited a long time for you to wake," she said without moving.

I glanced at the light that was still colorless as moonstone beyond the doorway. "It is still early."

"Maybe I did not sleep as sound as you." And then, "If I bear you a son, what would you have me call him?"

I stared at her, and she smiled now, a small bitter twisting of the lips. "Did you not think of that? You who were chance-begotten under a hawthorn bush?"

[29]

"No," I said slowly. "No, I did not think. Tell me what you would have me do. Anything that I can give you—"

"I do not ask for payment; none save that I may show you this." She had been holding something hidden between her two hands; and now she opened them and held out what they contained. And I saw that it was a massive arm ring of red gold, twisted and coiled into the likeness of the Red Dragon of Britain. I had seen the mate of it on Ambrosius's arm every day of my life. "On a morning such as this one, Utha, your father and mine, gave this ring to my mother before he rode on his way."

It was a long moment before I understood the full meaning of her words. And then I felt sick. I drew my legs under me and got up, pressing back from her, while she sat watching me under her dark cloak of hair. "I do not believe you," I managed at last. But I knew that I did believe her; the look in her face told me that if she had never told the truth in her whole life, she was telling it now; and I knew at last, now that it was too late, that the likeness that had so puzzled me was to Ambrosius. And she had known; all the while she had known. I heard someone groan and scarcely knew that it was me. My mouth felt stiff and dry, so that I could scarcely form the words that were in my throat. "Why—what made you do it?"

She sat playing with the dragon arm ring between her hands, turning and turning it, just as Ambrosius had done, that night in Venta. "There could be two good reasons. One is love, and the other, hate."

"I never harmed you."

"No? For the wrong, then, that Utha, Prince of Britain, did to my mother before you were born. Your mother died at your coming—oh, I know—and because you were a son, bastard or no, your father took and reared you at his hearth, and so you see the thing with your father's eyes. But I was only a daughter; I was not taken from my mother, and she lived long enough to teach me to hate, where once she had loved."

I wanted to look away, not to stare into her face any more, but I could not turn my eyes from her. She had given me her body in a kind of flaming and devouring ecstasy, last night; and it was an ecstasy of hate, as potent as ever that of love could have been. I smelled hate all about me, tangible as the smell of fear in a confined space. And then, as though at last the veil were torn aside, I saw what was behind her eyes. I saw a woman and a child, a woman and a girl, beside the peat fire in this place, the one teaching and the other absorbing that caressing, soul-destroying lesson of hate. All at once I saw that what I had taken for the ruins of beauty in Ygerna's face was the promise of beauty that had been cankered before ever it could come to flowering, and for one instant pity mingled with the horror that was rising like vomit in my throat. But the two figures in the peat smoke were changing, the girl becoming the mother, and in her place a boy, with his face, his whole soul, turned to hers, drinking in the same lesson. Dear God! What had I let loose? What had my father let loose before me, into the world?

"If it is a boy," said Ygerna, and her gaze went beyond me, as though she too were seeing past and future, "I shall call him—Medraut. I had a little white rat with rose-red eyes called Medraut, when I was a child. And when he is a man, I will send him to you. May you have much joy of your son when that day comes, my lord."

Without knowing it, my hand had been fumbling with the hilt of my sword which had lain beside me—strange that she had not disarmed me while I slept. My fingers tightened on it, and it was half out of the wolfskin sheath. A little hammer was beating in my head. "I should like—very much—to kill you!" I whispered.

She swept up from the floor, dragging back the torn breast of her gown. "Why do you not then? See, here is the place. I will not cry out. You can be well away from the steading before my servants find what is left." All at once there was a wailing note in her voice. "It might be the best way for both of us. Now—kill me now!"

But my hand dropped away from the sword hilt. "No," I said. "No."

"Why not?"

I groaned. "Because I am a fool." I blundered past her, thrusting her aside so that she stumbled to her knees, and sprang for the door as though all the fiends of darkness were behind me. Cabal, who had roused and come to crouch against my legs, snarling and shaking his head in a way that I remembered afterward, leapt past me into the milky daylight. The steading was already astir. I heard the milch cows lowing, and the thornbush

[31]

had been pulled aside from the gate gap. I plunged out through it, and behind me heard the woman laughing, a wild, wailing laughter that followed me long after I had ceased to hear it with the hearing of my body.

The mist was thinning fast, growing ragged and fitful, sometimes smoking around me as thick as ever, at others lifting to show half a hillside of sodden bilberry and last year's heather. At the foot of the valley my feet found a track that crossed the stream and headed in the direction I needed, and I turned along it, splashing thigh-deep through the ford. Presently the distance cleared, and Yr Widdfa frowned down on me from the north, with mist still scarfing its lower glens. I knew where I was now, and turned aside into the steep hazel woods that flanked the lesser heights.

Once I stopped to vomit; but I had not eaten that morning, and though I seemed to be retching my heart up, nothing came but a little sour slime. I spat it into the heather, and went on. Cabal ate grass in an urgent and indiscriminate way very different from his usual careful choosing, and was sick also, throwing up all that was in him with the ease of a dog. It would have been the drugged sweetmeat she gave him last night. I have wondered, in after years, why she did not poison him and be done with it, especially since she must have seen that I loved the dog. But I suppose her hatred was so focused on me that she had none to spare. Maybe she even feared to lessen its power by dissipating it.

A long while after noon, I struck the hill track from Dynas Pharaon, and came dropping over the last hill shoulder into the head of Nant Ffrancon. Among the first birch and rowan trees I checked, and stood looking down. The valley lay outstretched below me, sheltered under the dark hills. I saw the greenness of it freckled with the grazing horse herds, smoke rising from the clustered bothies in the alder-fringed loop of the stream. It was all as it had been yesterday, when I turned here to look back; and the sight steadied me with its message that whatever happened to a man or a thousand men, life went on. Something in me deep down below the light of reason had been dreading to find the valley blasted and sickness already rife among the horse herds. But that was foolishness; I was not the High King that my doing should bring evil on the land. The doom was for myself alone, and I knew already that it was sure. However unknowingly, I had sinned the

Ancient Sin, the Great Sin from which there is no escaping. I had sown a seed, and I knew that the tree which sprang from it would bear the death apple. The taste of vomit was in my very soul, and a shadow lay between me and the sun.

Cabal, who had been waiting beside me with the patience of his kind until I should be ready to go on again, suddenly pricked his ears and looked away down the track. A moment he stood alert, his muzzle raised into the little wind that came up from Nant Ffrancon; then he flung up his head and gave a single bell-deep bay. From below among the birch woods was a boy's voice calling, long-drawn and joyful. "Artos! My Lord Arto-os!"

I cupped my hands about my mouth and called back. "Aiee! I am here!" and with Cabal leaping ahead of me, I went on downhill.

Below me two figures came into view where the track rounded the shoulder of the birch-clad outcrop, and stood looking up; and I saw that they were Hunno and young Flavian. The old horse master flung up an arm in greeting, and Flavian, outstripping him, came springing eager as a young hound up the track to meet me. "Sa sa! It is good to see you safe! We thought that you might be somewhere on this track." He was shouting as he came within word range. "Did you find shelter for the night? Did you—" He reached me and I suppose saw my face, and his voice stammered and fell away. We looked at each other in silence while old Hunno climbed toward us; and then he said, "Sir—what is it? Are you hurt?"

I shook my head. "No, I—I am well enough. I have dreamed evil dreams in the night, that is all."

CHAPTER FOUR

The Horses of a Dream

I CAME down from Arfon, having settled with Hunno all things as to the new grazing grounds, and gathered the few fourteen and fifteen hand mares that I could find among my own horses. Having gathered also the best part of a score of tribesmen to swell the number of the Companions—fiery youngsters with small idea of obeying orders, but maybe I and the men they would be serving with could hammer that lesson into them; and they were as brave as boars and rode like the Wild Hunt itself.

We descended upon Venta to find that Ambrosius had ridden westward to inspect the Aquae Sulis end of the old frontier defenses, and I snatched with a sense of reprievement the delay in coming face to face with him again. There were plenty of other men that I must face and drink with as though the world was still as it had been when I rode for Arfon earlier in the spring. It was hard to believe that it was still the same spring, but I had had time by now to raise a shield of sorts, and I made a good enough showing. I think that Aquila, my father in arms and horse management, guessed that something was amiss, but he was a man with the ancient scar of a Saxon thrall ring on his neck, and too deep and painful reserves of his own, ever to poke into another man's hidden places. At all events, he asked no questions save about the horses, and I was grateful. But indeed I had small leisure for brooding, in the few days that I remained in Venta. There were arrangements to be made for the horses, my score of tribesmen to be divided among the squadrons of the Companions, under the captains best able to handle them. Arrangements also for the Companions themselves in my absence; the question of the Septimanians' purchase gold to be dealt with. Ambrosius had already given me his promised share in weighed gold armorings—coinage meant nothing, nowadays—but what I had been able to scrape together from my own lands and even my personal gear took many forms from iron and copper currency rings to a silver brittle bit set with coral, and a fine red and white bullskin and a pair of matched wolfhounds. And the better part of one day I spent with Ephraim the Jew in the Street of the Golden Grasshopper, changing all these things, save for the hounds, into weighed gold, and haggling like a market crone over the price. Even at the end, I remember, he tried to leave his thumb in the scales, but when I pricked it up with the point of my dagger, he smiled the soft smile of his people, and held both hands up to show me that the measure was fair, and we parted without malice.

The hounds were bought by Aquila. I do not think that he could afford them, for he had nothing but his pay from the war chest, and a wife to keep on it, even now that Flavian had become my affair. Save for his horses the only thing of value that he possessed was the flamed emerald signet ring engraved with its dolphin badge, which had come to him from his father and would one day go to his son; and there was generally a patch somewhere about him. But I would have done the same for him in a like need.

All the multitude of nameless preparations to be made for a long journey were made at last and with nineteen of the Company, I set out from Venta. So many would eat badly into our gold, but I did not see how we were to do with less, especially if we were to get the stallions overland to Armorica and so avoid the long sea voyage. The gold we carried sewn into the wadding of the thick riding pads, and wore above our elbows only an arm ring each for immediate use.

Three days later we rode into this place, this place among the reedbeds and the western marshes, which the Celts among us call the Island of Apples; and found Ambrosius's big black stallion Hesperus tethered with a few other horses among the trees of the monks' orchard—for there were holy men here then, even as there are now, and as they claim there had been almost since the time of Christ. We tethered our horses with Ambrosius's, under the apple trees where the grass grew sweet and tall for grazing, and followed the young brown-clad Brother who had taken us in charge, up to the long hall beside the wattle church, which formed as it were the center of the cluster of small thatched cells, like the queen cell in a humblebee's nest. The place was thick with the smoky light of the fat-lamps hanging from the rafters, and the Brothers were already gathering to the evening meal of bread and kale broth, for it was a fast day, and Ambrosius and his handful of Companions sat with the Abbot at the head of the rough plank table. I had been dreading the meeting, fearing, I think, not so much what he might see in my face as what I might see in his; fearing in some confused and nightmare way that because I had seen the likeness to him in Ygerna, I must see the likeness to Ygerna in him. Indeed if it were not for shame, I would not have taken this road at all, but held westward by the lower way and so shirked the meeting. . . .

I did not look at him fully as I walked up the timber hall, and knelt with bowed head before him, according to the custom. He made the gesture to me to rise, and I got slowly to my feet, and looked at last into his face.

Ygerna was not there. There was a surface likeness of form and color, the dark skin and the slender bones beneath it, and the way the brows were set. It was that that had tugged at my memory with its unavailing warning. But the man whose face flashed open to smile at me out of the strange rain-gray eyes was Ambrosius as he had always been. The breath broke in my throat with relief and I bent forward to receive his kinsman's embrace.

When the simple meal was over, we left the Brothers to their souls and our own men to playing knucklebones about the fire, and went out, the two of us, with Cabal stalking as usual at my heel, to sit on the low turf wall that held the orchard from the marsh; and talked together as we had had no chance to since the night that Ambrosius gave me my sword.

The moon was up and the mist rising over the marshes and the withy beds like the rising tide of a ghost sea; the higher ground stood clear of it, islands above high-water mark, rising to the steep thrust of the hill crowned with its sacred thorns; but at the lower levels of the orchard a lantern tossing its way along the horse lines had a faint golden smoke about it. The first pale petals were drifting from the apple trees, with no wind to flurry them abroad. Behind us we heard the quiet voices of the camp and the holy place. The marsh was silent until somewhere far out in the mist a bittern boomed, and was silent again. It was a very peaceful place. It still is.

After a while, carefully keeping to the obvious, Ambrosius said, "So we meet on your road to Septimania."

I nodded. "Yes."

"You still feel that you must needs go yourself on this journey? You do not feel that the sorer need of you is here?"

I was dandling my sword between my knees, looking out into the mist that crept nearer across the marsh. "God knows I have thought the thing over through enough of nights. God knows how bitterly I grudge a whole summer's campaigning; but I cannot trust another man to pick my war-horses for me; too much depends on them."

"Not even Aquila?"

"Aquila?" I said reflectively. "Yes, I'd trust old Aquila; but I cannot find it in my mind to think that you would lend me Aquila."

"No," Ambrosius said. "I would not—I could not lend you Aquila; not both of you in one year." He turned toward me abruptly. "What of your men, Bear Cub, while you're away?"

"I lend them back to you. Hunt my pack for me, Ambrosius, till I come again."

For a while we talked over the mares I had chosen for my breeding herd, and the plans that I had made with Hunno, and the money I had raised off my own estates; of the defenses that Ambrosius had been riding here in the West, and a score of other things, until at last we fell silent again, a long silence while the mist and the moon rose together, until presently Ambrosius said, "It was good, to get back to the mountains?"

"It was good, yes." But I suppose something in my voice rang false, for he turned his head and sat looking at me fixedly. And in the stillness, somewhere among the reedbeds the bittern boomed again, and again was silent.

"But something I think was not so good. What was it?"

"Nothing."

"Nothing?"

I felt my hands tighten on my sword hilt until the pommel with its great square-edged amethyst cut into my palm, and forced a laugh. "More times than once, you have told me that I show all things too clearly in my face. But this time you ride your own fancy. There is nothing there to show."

"Nothing?" he said again.

And I turned deliberately to face him in the full white moonlight. "Do I seem changed in some way?"

"No," he said slowly, consideringly. "More as though you found us—our world—changed; or were afraid to find it so. When you came into the holy men's hall this evening, you held yourself as long as might be, from looking into my face. And when you looked at last, it was as though you feared to see the face of a stranger—even an enemy. It is—" His voice dropped even lower, and all the while he had been speaking scarcely above his breath. "You make me think of a man such as the harpers sing of, who has passed a night in the Hollow Hills."

I was silent a long time, and I think I nearly told him all the story. But in the end I could not; I could not though my soul had depended upon it. I said, "Maybe I have passed my night in the Hollow Hills."

And even as I spoke, up beyond the apple trees the bell of the wattle church began to ring, calling the Brothers to evening prayer; a bronze sound, a brown sound in the moonlight, falling among the apple trees. Ambrosius went on looking at me for a moment, but I knew that he would press the thing no further; and I remained for the same moment, playing with the hilt of the great sword across my knees, and letting the quiet of the moment soak into me before I must rouse myself to go forward again. "If I were indeed newcome from the Hollow Hills, at least this must be the place of all others, with the bell calling my soul back to the Christian's God. . . . It is a good place—peace rises in it as the mist over the reedbeds. It would be a good place to come back to in the end."

"In the end?"

"When the last battle is fought and the last song sung, and the sword sheathed for the last time," I said. "Maybe one day when I am past fighting the Saxon kind, I shall give my sword to whoever comes after me, and come back here as an old dog creeps home to die. Shave my forehead and bare my feet, and strive to make my soul in whatever time is left to me."

"That is the oldest dream in the world," Ambrosius said, getting to his feet. "To lay down the sword and the Purple and take up the begging bowl. I don't see you with bare feet and a shaven forehead, Artos my friend."

But even as he spoke, it seemed to me that the great purple amethyst in my sword pommel tilted a fraction under my finger, as though it were not quite secure in its bed. I bent quickly to examine it and Ambrosius checked in the act of turning away. "Something amiss?"

"I thought Maximus's seal felt loose in its setting. Seems secure enough now, though; probably I imagined it. . . . I'll get the next goldsmith I can find, to take a look at it, all the same."

But the bell was ringing louder, and the sound of singing stole down through the apple trees, and if we were to pay the Brothers the small courtesy of joining them at prayer, we must move. I got up, stirring the unwilling Cabal with my foot. "Up, lazy one!" and with the hound's cold muzzle thrusting into my hand, walked with Ambrosius up through the orchard. I thought no more about the loosened amethyst, until a later day reminded me. . . .

Well before spring had given place to summer, I and my small band were in Dumnonia, and lodged with Cador the Prince, while we waited for a ship. I had thought to find him in the old frontier town of Isca Dumnoniorum, or at his summer capital on the Tamara River; but it seemed that Cador had as little liking for cities as have the Saxons, and so those few waiting days were spent up on the skirts of the high moors where he had his Dun with his warriors and his women and his wealth of cattle gathered about him, like any wild Hibernian chieftain.

On the last evening, we came back from hunting with a couple of the proud red deer that roam those hills slung across the backs of the ponies. It had been a good day's hunting, and for a while, just for a while, I seemed to have outdistanced certain pursuing hounds of my own. We came up to the Dun, with our shadows running far ahead of us through the brown of last year's heather and the fragile green of the spring-sown barley; and the pleasant tiredness that comes of a day's hunting was in all our limbs. Cabal ran at my horse's forefoot apart from the rest of the pack. He was the greatest of them all though Cador had fine hounds, too. We clattered through the broad gateway of the Dun, and among the

byres and stables of the forecourt, where the tall weapon stone
stood for the warriors to sharpen their blades in time of battle, we
handed over the ponies and the kill to the men who came for them,
and went on together, toward the inner court.

A knot of women sat before the doorway of the long timber
hall, in the thin shade of the ancient half-sacred whitethorn tree
that grew there. "Sa sa! The fine weather has brought the women
out like midges in the sunlight," Cador said, as we came in sight
of them. The sight was a good one to see. The dappling sunspots
quivered on the blue and russet and saffron of their tunics, as the
small lazy breeze stirred the whitethorn branches and brought
down the first thin drifts of fading petals; and they were talking
softly, like a huddle of colored birds, some of them spinning, one
girl combing out wet hair to dry in the sun; while Esylt, Cador's
wife, sat in their midst, restringing a broken necklace of amber
beads, with something small and mewing like a kitten in the soft
folds of a fallow doeskin at her feet.

I knew that Cador had a son, born since Ambrosius's crowning,
and named Constantine for my grandsire, but I had not seen him
before, though I had heard him yelling like a hungry lamb in the
women's quarters. Cador had been ashamed to show any interest
in the thing before other men, but now that he could do so without
seeming eager, I think he was pleased to show it off to the stranger
within his gates. At all events, his step quickened as we came into
the inner court.

Esylt looked up with a melon-shaped bead of amber between
her fingers, her eyes narrowed against the watering sunlight. "You
are come home early, my lord. Was the hunting not good?"

"Good enough to show the Bear that there are other hunting
runs than those of his own mountains," Cador said. "We killed
twice." He bent down, his hands on his knees, to peer at the small
squirming thing in the doeskin, then glanced aside at his woman
with a snapping flash of white teeth. "Why then, should I not come
home early from my hunting? Is it that I might find something or
some*one* that I am not meant to find?"

"There are three men hidden in the folds of my skirt, and the
fourth lies there," said Esylt, pointing to the child with the hand
in which she held the thread. "If you would know *his* father, you
have but to look at him."

It sounded like a quarrel, but it was a game, the kind of half-fierce, half-laughing game that boys and hounds play together in mimic war. Also it was born of the fact that Cador knew that there was no one that he was not meant to find, and so could afford the jest. I had never seen a man and a woman make that kind of play together, and it seemed to me good.

"So, but I cannot see it all; it might be a small pink pig. What is it bundled up like that for?"

"Because the sun is westering and the wind grows cold," Esylt said, suddenly laughing. "He is much the same as he was this morning. But see, if you would have it so," and she turned back the folds of deerskin, so that the man-child lay naked in its nest, save for the bead of coral that every babe wears around its neck to keep off the Evil Eye. "There is your pink pig."

Cador grinned at it. "Small and useless," he said, studying to keep the pride from his voice. "When he comes of an age to bear his shield, *that* is the time when it may be worth while to have a son."

And for me, at his words, there was suddenly a shadow over the sky, and the hounds were on my track again.

Cabal, who should have been a bitch for his interest in all young things, thrust forward his muzzle to snuff at the babe, and I stooped quickly to catch his collar and pull him back. He would not have dreamed of harming the thing, but it was in my mind that the mother might be frightened. And as I stooped, Maximus's seal in my sword hilt sprang from its faulty setting, and fell into the nest of deerskin beside the babe and rolled against his far neck, to lie there an instant holding the fires of the sunset in a small fierce flame of imperial purple.

Esylt stooped and caught it up next instant and gave it back to me, and everybody spoke at once, the women exclaiming over the lucky chance that it had not fallen somewhere among the heather, Cador peering into the empty socket of my pommel; while my men and his crowded around to see. And I laughed, and made a jest of the thing, and tossed the gem in the hollow of my hand. It was all over in the time that it takes a gust of wind to sweep up over the shoulder of Yr Widdfa and die into the grass. But an old woman under the May tree whispered something to her neighbor, and they looked from the child to me and back again, as I

[41]

turned to follow Cador into the hall. And I caught the gist that was not meant for my ear. "It is a sign! A sign! Constantine is an emperor's name. . . ."

That was the first time I ever saw Constantine Map Cador face to face. The last was only a few days ago—I am not sure how many, it is hard to keep count of time—when I named him as my successor before the whole war host. That was on the eve of the battle. The Lord God knows how he will bear the leadership, but he is the last of the line of Maximus, and at least he is a warrior. The choice had to fall on him. . . .

"You had best take that down to Urian my swordsmith," Cador said. "Blades are the business of his heart, but he can make shift to bed a jewel as surely as any goldsmith of Venta Belgarum."

And so I went down to the lower Dun, following the directions that he gave me, and found Urian the Smith to reset the great seal for me.

I was still standing propped in the forge doorway, watching the little bullock-shouldered smith—for I would not let the seal out of my sight until it was once more securely in its place—when a step sounded behind me, and I turned to find Fulvius, who had gone down to the coast with a couple of Cador's men to see about our passages, coming from the direction of the stables.

"Well?" I said. "What fortune?"

He grinned, the grin that even when we were boys had always made me think of the little jaunty rough-haired dogs that one puts down rat holes, and wiped the dust and sweat of his ride into streaks across his forehead with the back of one hand. "Well enough. I found a ship sailing for Burdigala in two days' time, and contrived to strike a bargain with the master. She'll be coming back with a cargo of wine, but she's going out in ballast with only a few raw bullhides for cargo, and he was glad enough to hear of some passengers to make the trip more profitable."

"How much?" I demanded.

"An arm ring to every four heads—that's if we don't mind the likelihood of drowning."

"All things must have a first time," I said. "Does she leak like a sieve?"

"She looks sound enough, but nigh as wide as she's long. Na,

I'd say on second thoughts we are more like to die of seasickness than drowning."

That night we sat late after the evening meal, discussing the problem of horse transport. Cador had promised to find me two suitable vessels and have them ready on the far side of the Narrow Sea by the middle of August, which, with luck, would leave us six weeks or so before the autumn gales, for the five or six trips that would be needed to get all the horses across. But the problem was how they should be adapted in such a way that they could be returned to their normal use again afterward. The Roman horse transports had been built with entry parts below the waterline, through which the horses were loaded while the vessels were high and dry, and which were closed and caulked afterward. But what shipmaster would allow his ship to have great wounds cut in her underwater body? And we could not afford to buy ships, nor build them, even if there had been the time to do so. In the end it was decided that part of the decking must be torn up, and the horses drugged and slung into the holds by means of slings and pulleys, the deck planks being replaced after them. It was a desperate measure, and I think we all prayed to God that it would not result in the deaths of either men or horses; horses almost more than men, for they would be harder to replace. But there was no alternative that any of us could see.

The next day, leaving Cabal chained in an empty byre and howling his furious despair behind us, we rode down to the coast. (It was the only time in his life that he was parted from me, and I felt much like a murderer.) And on the morning tide of the day after that, we sailed for Burdigala, packed close into the space left by the stinking bullhides, in a vessel that, as Fulvius had said, was almost round, and wallowed like a sow in litter, into the troughs of the seas, so that one wondered at each weltering plunge whether she could ever shake clear again in time for the next crest. We were very wretched, and presently we lost count of time, so that we had little idea of how many days we had been at sea when at last, having neither foundered nor fallen in with Sea Wolves, we ran into the mouth of a broad Gaulish river. When we came ashore I was surprised to find, never having been to sea before, that the wooden jetty heaved up and down beneath my feet with the long slow swing of the Atlantic swell.

At Burdigala we found a party of merchants gathering for the next stage of the journey, for it seemed that to the horse fairs of Narbo Martius, the merchant kind gathered from all over Gaul and even from the nearer fringes of Hispana beyond the mountains that men call the Pyrenaei; not only horse traders, but those who came to trade among the horse traders, in anything from sweetmeats to swords and painted pottery to ivory Astartes and cheap horoscopes. We joined ourselves to this party, and while we waited for the latecomers, set about buying the nags that we should need for the next stage. We picked small sturdy brutes, with no looks or graces to add to their price, yet such as we might be able to sell again at Narbo Martius without too much trouble. I had thought that the strange tongue might make bargaining difficult, but everyone spoke Latin of a barbarous kind—at least it sounded barbarous in our ears, but maybe ours sounded as barbarous in theirs—and with the aid of a certain amount of counting on our fingers and shouting, we managed well enough. They are a goodly people to look upon, the Goths; tall men, some as tall as I am, and I have met few men of my own height in Britain; fiercely proud, fair-haired but with more of yellow and less of red than our own mountain people have. Strange to think that these loyal vassals of the Eastern Empire were the great-grandsons of the men who, seventy years ago, had sacked Rome and left it a smoking ruin. If they had not done so, perhaps the last Legions would not have been withdrawn from Britain. . . . But there is no profit in such speculating.

The last comers joined the band, and we set out for Tolosa.

All the wide valley of the Garumna seemed, as we made our way eastward along what remained of the old road, to be wine country. I had seen a few vineyards, mostly falling into neglect, clinging to a terraced hillside here and there throughout southern Britain, but never great stretches of vine country such as this. A smaller, darker people than the Goths were at work tying the vines along the roadside, and from time to time we could see the great river that cast its gray sinuous curves across and across the countryside—but myself I have always loved best a mountain stream.

On the fifth evening, our numbers swollen by other, smaller bands that had joined us on the road, we came in sight of Tolosa where the distant mountains began to thrust up into the sky. We spent a day there to rest the horses and mules before the roughest part of the journey and get in supplies for ourselves. Everything for four camps among the mountains, said the fortune-teller, who had taken that road many times before, and liked to bestow advice. And next morning, our numbers increased still further by the men who had joined us in the town, we rode out again with our faces to the hills.

As the road lifted, and the vast vale of the Garumna fell behind us, the tall crests of the Pyrenaei, deeply blue as thunderclouds, marched in a vast rampart across the southern sky. But by the second day I saw that we should not touch the mountains; they rose on either hand, maybe twenty miles away, and between them lay a lesser hill country through which the broad paved road ran, terraced sometimes, or causewayed across a ravine, toward Narbo Martius and the coast. We jogged on at the same slow pace, pausing in what shade we could find during the heat of the day, passing the nights huddled about our fires, for even in summer it could be chill at night, while the beasts stamped in their picket lines at the distant smell of wolf, and the guard sat huddled in their cloaks and longed for morning. We—the Companions and I—slept sword in hand, with the precious riding pads for pillows. We did not distrust our fellow travelers; in such bands it is a law that no man robs his brother, for the sufficient reason that in robber country where there are broken men among the hills, any breach in the traveling band may let in the enemy, and therefore any man caught in such an act is driven from the band to make his own way, which, lacking the protection of their numbers, is likely to be a short one. Nonetheless, there was always the risk of a night attack by the hill robbers themselves, and we were running no risks.

But on the fifth day, without having met any worse trouble than somebody's mule being overbalanced by its load and slithering into a ravine, we reined aside from the road into the shade of a long skein of pine trees where a brown hill stream ran quietly over a paved ford, to make our last noontide halt. And sitting in the shade after we had sparingly watered the horses, and washed the worst of the white dust out of our own eyes and mouths, I looked down over the gently dropping countryside to Narbo Martius and the sea.

This was a different world from the vine country around Tolosa;

the hillside covered with a dense mat of aromatic things—thyme and broom and stone bramble were the only ones I knew—and the quivering air was full of the hot rising scent of them and the darker scent of the pines. The land turned pale and sunburned below us, growing more and more bleached and barren as it went seaward, and the sea was a darker blue than any that I have looked down on from the headlands of Dumnonia, though I have known that the color of a kingfisher's mantle. A little wind shivered up through the woods that followed the valleys, so that the thin scatter of gray-green trees turned to silver—wild olives, somebody said they were, later—and here and there the pale discs of the threshing floors caught the heat-drained sunlight and shone like silver coins. Strange to be in a land where one could be so sure of the weather that one threshed in the open.

But of all the scene before me, the thing that claimed and held my gaze was the pale checkered smudge of a town on the far-distant coast. Narbo Martius; and somewhere among its horse guards and in fields, the stallions and brood mares that I had come to buy; the horses of my dream.

CHAPTER FIVE

Bedwyr

AT sunset, with the dust haze that rose from the hooves of
the pack beasts turned to red-gold clouds in the westering
rays, we clattered under the gate arch into Narbo Martius, and
found the place thrumming like a bee swarm with the crowds
pouring in to the horse fair. It must have been a fine place once,
one could see that even now; the walls of the forum and basilica
still stood up proudly above the huddle of reed thatch and timber,
with the sunset warm on peeling plaster and old honey-colored
stone; and above the heads of the crowds the air was full of the
darting of swallows who had their mud nests under the eaves of
every hut and along every ledge and acanthus-carved cranny of
the half-ruined colonnades. The smell of the evening cooking fires
was the arid reek of burning horse dung, such as the herdsmen
burn in the valleys of Arfon.

The two or three inns which the place still possessed were already
full and spilling over with merchants and their beasts, but the open
spaces within the city walls had been roughly fenced off with hurdles
and rope and dead thornbushes, to serve as camps for the lesser
folk and latecomers, and when the trading band broke up, we
found a place in one of these, where a couple of score of mules and
their drivers were already encamped among their newly unloaded
bales, and an ancient merchant sat under a striped canopy, scratching himself contentedly beneath his earth-colored blanket robes,
while his servants made camp about him. There was of course no
service of any kind, no one in charge of anything, save for an
immensely fat man with green glass earrings in his hairy ears, who
lolled under the awning of a wine booth—it was good wine, though;

[47]

we tried it later—nor was there any food for the men, though we found that fodder for the beasts could be got close by. So while Fulvius and Owain, who were our best foragers, went off to buy cooked food, the rest of us watered and tended the horses and made camp as best we could in the corner of the corral not already occupied with kicking and snarling mules.

When the other two returned, we supped off loaves with little aromatic seeds sprinkled over the crust and cold boiled meat with garlic and green olives whose strange taste I was by this time getting used to; and washed it down with a couple of jars of drink from the wine booth. Then we lay down to sleep save for Bericus and Alun Dryfed, who took the first watch.

For a long while I lay awake also, listening to the nighttime stirrings and tramplings of the camp and the city, and looking up at the familiar stars that had guided and companioned me so often on the hunting trail, every fiber of me quivering with a strange expectancy that concerned something more than the horses that I should buy tomorrow. It had been growing in me all evening, that mood of intense waiting, the certainty that something, someone, was waiting for me in Narbo Martius—or that I was waiting for them. So might a man feel, waiting for the woman he loved. I even wondered if it might be death. But I fell asleep at last, and slept quietly and lightly, as a man sleeps on the hunting trail.

The midsummer horse fair, held on the level ground above the shore, lasted for seven days, and so I should be able to make my choice with care and maybe time for second thoughts, but by evening on the second day I had bought well over half the horses I wanted, by dint of much vehement bargaining—duns for the most part, and dark brown, so dark as to be almost black, with a white flame or star on the forehead—and it was beginning to be harder to find what I sought, or maybe I was becoming harder to please as I grew more used to the big powerful animals that filled the selling grounds.

Yet it was on the third day that, as I pushed my way through the crowd at the far end of the sale ground, with Flavian beside me, I found the best horse that I had seen yet. I suppose he had been brought in late, when the best of the others were gone. He was a full black, black as a rook's wing. There are more bad horses among the black than any other color, but a good black is own brother to Bucephalus. This was a good black, standing a clear sixteen hands at the shoulder, with a good broad head and high crest, power in every line of him, and fire in his heart and loins to beget some of his own kind. But as I stopped to examine him more closely, I saw his eyes. I would have turned away, but the man in charge of him, a bowlegged individual with small twinkling eyes and a lipless gash for a mouth, stayed me with a touch on my arm. "You'll not see a better horse than this in Narbo Martius this year, my lord."

"No," I said. "I should think most likely not."

"My lord would like to look him over?"

I shook my head. "That would be a waste of your time and mine."

"Waste?" He sounded as though I had used a forbidden word, almost awed at my iniquity; and then, his voice turning soft as fur, "Did ever my lord see such shoulders? And he just five years old. . . . One was telling me that my lord sought the best stallion in Septimania—I suppose he was mistaken."

"No," I said, beginning again to turn away. "He was not mistaken. A good sale to you, friend—but not with me for the purchaser."

"Na then, what does my lord find amiss with him?"

"His temper."

"Temper? The temper of a sucking dove, Most Noble."

"Not with those eyes," I said.

"At least let you see his paces." We were on the edge of the open ground where the horses were shown off, and the crowd was packed dense behind me, but I could have pushed my way through easily enough. I do not know why I hesitated; not, I think, for the stallion's sake, magnificent as he was, certainly not for the man's persuading tone. The finger of Fate was on me, I suppose; for the enrichment and the bitter loss that came of that moment's hesitating have been with me all my afterdays.

The horse dealer had summoned someone from the crowd with a jerk of the head; and a man stepped forward in answer. I had seen him before, distantly, among the men who showed off the horses for prospective buyers. I recognized him by the lock of fair hair that sprang from his temple, mingling oddly with the darkness

[49]

of the rest of his head; but until now I had noticed nothing else about him. Yet there was enough to notice, when one came to look. He was a very young man, maybe midway between myself and Flavian for age, but lean and sinuous already as a wolfhound at the end of a hard season's hunting; naked save for a kilt of lamb-skin strapped about his narrow waist, the wool showing at the edges, and something that looked surprisingly like a harp bag was slung from a strap across his bare shoulder. But in the brief moment while he stood looking to the horse dealer for his word, the thing that I chiefly noticed was his face, for it seemed to have been put together somewhat casually from the opposite halves of two com-pletely different faces, so that one side of his mouth was higher than the other, and his dark eyes looked out from under one gravely level brow and one that flared with the reckless jauntiness of a mongrel's flying ear. It was an ugly-beautiful face and it warmed the heart to look at it.

"Hai! Bedwyr, the chieftain would see the Black One's paces, that he may judge of his mettle," said the dealer, and I did not contradict him because, of all foolish reasons, I wanted to see how this young man with the surprising Celtic name handled such a horse.

The horse was of course already bitted and bridled, but not saddled. The boy swept me a swift low bow, and turning, set his hands on the great brute's shoulders, and next instant was astride the glossy back, and catching the reins out of the dealer's hands as the great brute began to dance and snort and sidle, swung him out onto the open trampled turf. Watching him as he put the Black One through his paces, I found myself judging the rider's mettle as well as the horse's, noting how lightly he handled the savage "wolf" bit, while never for one instant losing the control; and the way the Black One himself, who I was very sure would have been a plunging fury with almost any other man on his back, not only answered to his authority but seemed to enter into the thing with him as they wheeled and circled and changed paces, and came sweeping in a cloud of dust around the full circle of the open space; so that when at last they came to a trampling halt before me, I could have sworn that the horse, as well as the man, was laughing. . . .

"See, my lord, and he is not even sweating," said the dealer's voice in my ear; but I had to think of the long road home; above all, of the sea crossing. I longed to take this superb black thunder-storm, but if I did, he would almost certainly cost us a man's life, or another horse's, maybe more, to get him home.

"He is a good horse—with the right rider," I said, aware of the man Bedwyr looking down at me under that flaring eyebrow, with a curious intensity widening his eyes, "but he is not good for my purpose." And I turned on my heel and pushed my way into the crowd again, followed by Flavian in a cloud of mute protest, for he was still young enough to be sure that if one only wanted it badly enough, one could hook Orion out of the sky on the end of a cockle pin.

He looked back once, and sighed. "It's a pity," he said.

I glanced down at him, and because he looked so young and forlorn, found myself calling him by the name that had been his when he stood nose high to an otter hound. "It's a pity, Minnow." And felt that the pity of it included the man as well as the stallion.

But it was to be only a few hours later that I saw the man with the pale forelock again.

Every evening after the first, we had had our own small fire in the corner of the corral, for dried dung cakes cost little, and a sack of them went a surprisingly long way. And that evening we were gathered around it as usual, eating the evening meal, when a step came past the horse lines and a shadow loomed out of the crowded shifting dark, and took substance in the smoky light of the fire. The small licking flames seemed to leap up at his coming, and the pale lock of hair gave him the look of having a white swan's feather caught at his temple; and I saw that he held in his hands a small thickset harp of black bog oak, on the strings of which the firelight played as on running water.

He came in the usual way of wandering harpers, who sit them-selves uninvited at any man's fire, sure of a welcome and a hearing and a meal for the song they sing; and making me the same swift bow that he had made in the horse ring, he folded onto his narrow haunches between Flavian and Bericus, settling his harp onto his knee and into the hollow of his shoulder before most of us were aware of him at all. We had been talking of the horses, cavalry talk, sweet and nutty on the tongue, but at his coming a gradual silence fell, and face after face was turned expectantly to the new-comer; horse talk one could have at any time, not so a harper.

[51]

But having gained our whole attention, Bedwyr seemed in no hurry to begin his song, and remained for a few moments fondling the well-worn instrument, so that watching him I was reminded suddenly of a man making his falcon ready for flight. Then with no beginning, no awakening chord, it was as though he flung the bird free. But it was no falcon, and though it leapt upward in bursts and upward rushes as a lark leaps toward the sun, it was no lark either, but a bird of fire. . . .

Old Traherne was no mean harper, but I knew, even while my own heart leapt out on the winged and rushing notes, that this was harping such as I had not heard in Ambrosius's hall.

Presently it sank and grew little, infinitely little, and sad. I watched a stalk of dry shepherd's purse among the dung cakes catch light and glow for an instant into beauty stranger than ever it had had in life, before it crumbled into a pinch of blackened fibers. And the harp music seemed one with it, lamenting the loss of all beauty, that might fall in a single grass seed. . . . Now it was swelling again, rising to the heights of Oran Môr, the Great Music, and the lament was for lost causes and lost worlds and the death of men and gods; and as it grew, it began to change. Until now it had been sound without the limit of form, but now it was taking on a fugitive pattern, or rather the pattern was growing through the storm-rush of the music, and it was a pattern that I knew. The harper flung up his head and began to sing, his voice strong and true, with an odd brooding quality in it that matched the song. I had expected a song of the Goths and the South, forgetting his unlikely name. Instead, I found that I was listening to a song of my own people, and in the British tongue; an old nameless lament that our women sing at seed time to help the wheat to spring; for a dead hero, a dead savior, a dead god, for brightness laid in the dark and the dust and the long years rolling over. Why it should help the corn in its springing, we have forgotten with our minds, though our bones still remember; but in its way it is a song of death and rebirth. I had known it all my life, as well as I had known Ygerna's small song of the birds on the apple spray; and as I had waited when I was a child for the wheat to spring again, for the rekindled hope of the ending, so I waited now for the promise of the hero's return. *"Out of the mists, back from the land of youth,"* sang the harper, as though to himself. *"Strong with the sound of trumpets under the apple boughs* . . ." I had heard that song so often ended on a crash of triumph as though the lost hero were already returned to his people; this time it ended on one clear note of distant hope that was like one star in a wild sky.

The harp song was silent, and the harper's hand fell from the leaping strings to lie at rest on his knee. For a long moment we were all silent about the fire, and the sounds of the camp washed in upon us without breaking the stillness of our own circle. Then Owain leaned forward to remake the sinking fire, building the brown dung cakes upon each other with the grave and thoughtful deliberation that was very much a part of him, and the spell was broken, so that I was aware of the dark faces of the mule drivers gathered on the fringe of the firelight, and the angry squealing of a mule somewhere beyond; and close beside me the old merchant, standing with his hands in his beard, and the faint aromatic smell that came from his robes as he rocked gently to and fro, his head cocked as though still to listen; and the murmur that came from him too, "Sa sa—so the women used to sing when I was a boy—singing the lament for Adonis, when the crimson anemones are springing from the rocks . . ." which was strange, for he understood no word of the British tongue.

I saw the harper looking at me through the blue smoke drift of the dung fire. But it was Fulvius who spoke first. "I should scarce have thought to hear that song in Septimania, unless it was one of our own pack that gave tongue to it."

Bedwyr the Harper smiled, his crooked mouth touched with mockery. "I am from the settlement that the Emperor Maximus made with his Sixth Legion veterans in Armorica and my father's mother was from Powys. Does that answer your question?" His speaking voice was deep, a singer's voice, and touched with mockery also.

Fulvius nodded, and passed him the wine jar. Flavian set the basket of cold meat and olives before him, and he accepted both without comment, returning the harp gently to the embroidered doeskin bag like a man rehooding his falcon. The mule drivers, seeing that there would be no more singing, at least for a while, had drifted away.

I said, "It explains how you came to have the songs of Britain

[53]

in your harp bag, but scarcely why you should choose one of them for us. Do we wear Britannicus branded on our foreheads?"

"All Narbo Martius knows that the chieftains are from Britain to buy stallions and brood mares," he said, eating bread and olives in alternate bites. And then he said the thing that I knew he had come to say. "Why did you refuse the Black One? He would sire fine sons."

"Does all Narbo Martius know that the stallions are for siring?"

"Is it not clear to see? Every horse that my lord has chosen, the points that he has looked for are those that make for strong breeding, in the stallions as well as the mares. My lord has been buying, not these horses but their sons. . . . Why turn from the Black One?"

"We are from Britain, as you have said yourself. That means a long road north and a sea crossing. If I mistake not, the horse is a killer."

"Your true killer slays for pleasure like a wildcat," Bedwyr said. "This one's heart is angry, that is a different thing. He is what he is because he was mishandled in his colt days."

"You know him, then?"

"I never saw him until today. But brother may know brother . . ."

That was the only time, I think, in twenty years, that I ever heard him speak, however indirectly, of his own colt days, and I would sooner, I think, have asked Aquila how it felt to wear a Saxon thrall ring, than have probed into what he did not choose to tell me.

"I think maybe you are right. Certainly he handled well enough for you," I said, and scarcely noticed at the time, though I remembered it after, how he looked up at that as though a new thought had opened in him, and then returned to the meat in his hand. "But nevertheless, he must find another master than me."

But I wished that it need not be so. The Black One had taken my fancy more than almost any other of the horses that I had seen in Narbo Martius.

The wine jar came my way, and I drank and passed it on to Bericus beside me, and returned to an earlier thing. "And now— since you know so clearly what it is that we do in Narbo Martius, do you make fair return, and tell us what brings you here, so far from your own hunting runs."

On the face of it, it was a foolish question to ask of a strolling harper, but there was something about this man that set him apart from the ordinary wandering minstrel drifting from lord's hall to fairground; a purpose about him that was at odds with any kind of drifting; and I thought it unlikely that a professional harper would have turned his hand to the kind of work that he had been doing that morning.

And suddenly his eyes, meeting mine through the acid smoke, flashed into a mocking awareness of what I was thinking. "I am on my way to Constantinople, in hope of joining the Emperor's bodyguard," he said, and watched me to see what I would make of it.

"I think you hope that I will not believe you," I said, "but oddly enough, I do." I was leaning forward as he was, arms across knees, and we spoke to each other through the dung smoke as though the others around the fire did not exist.

"I wonder why."

"Because for one thing, if for some reason you were lying, you would choose a less wild tale to tell."

"Sa! I will remember that for a future need; if I wish to lie and be believed, always to make the lie great enough. Does the tale seem so very wild, then? They say that nowadays, with the Ostrogoths pressing against the frontiers, the Emperor will give his sword to any good fighting man of any nation that comes his way. And it will be good to see Constantinople, and a splendor that does not lie in ruins; good to have a sword, and a cause to use it in." For one moment his manhood and his mocking reserves fell away from him, and I saw through the smoke a boy looking at me with hopeful eyes.

"It is only the length of the road that makes it seem strange. I have heard that now the old posting services are dead, for a traveler without great store of gold it takes the best part of two years."

"So—but I am well on my way already, and as to the gold, my harp and the odd task such as I had today will see that I do not starve." Bedwyr reached for another olive and sat tossing it idly from hand to hand, and the boy was a man again, and the subject closed. "Doubtless I should travel swifter with a Lucitanian colt between my knees. But I should see less of the road on the way, and since I shall travel it but once, I'd as lief see more of it than a cloud of my own dust."

"Are they so swift then, this Lucitanian breed?"

He looked at me, still tossing the olive from hand to hand. "The mares are served by the west wind, so I have heard, and the foals are as swift as their sire, but live only three years. You should strike a bargain with the west wind, my lord—it might come cheaper in the long run than buying Septimanian stallions."

"I can well believe in this Powys-born grandmother of yours, for you have a true Cymric tongue in your head. . . . But as for me, I need size and strength in my war-horses—the striking power of Camulus's thunderbolts, not the speed of the west wind."

"War-horses?" he said.

"Did you think I wished to breed them for the Hippodrome? Our need is for war-horses, in Britain. Here it has been the Goths, but with us it is still the Saxons, and compared to the Saxon, the Goth is the very flower of gentleness. Gaul has not known the tearing of the Sea Wolf's fangs, and for the most part Gaul has had the sense to lie quietly in the dust while the conquerors ride over. But in Britain we choose another way, and our need is for war-horses."

He sat back on his heels, and looked at me with level eyes. "Who are you, my lord, that speak of Britain as a chieftain speaks of his war band?"

"I was named Artorius on my ninth day, but most men call me Artos the Bear," I said, thinking that the name would mean nothing to him.

"So. We have heard that name—a little—even in Armorica where the Sea Wolves do not run," he said; and then, "Truly my lord should take the Dark One, for they are worthy of each other."

And suddenly we were all laughing, whirled up into choking mirth by his persistence; and Bedwyr laughed with us, over the rim of the wine jar that he had caught up; but it seemed to me that the laughter only brushed his surface as a puff of wind brushes the surface of a dark pool.

That night when we lay down to sleep with our feet to the fire, I could have laughed at my idiot fancy of the night before, for the day was passed and nothing, apart from the newly purchased

horses in the picket lines, had come of it, after all. Yet I thought
about Bedwyr in the time that followed, almost as much as I
did about the black horse, and next day constantly found myself
looking out for them in the sweating and trampling and the dust
clouds of the horse yards. The horse I glimpsed twice, though I did
not go near him again, and guessed that other men besides myself
must have seen the killer in his eyes, that he hung so long in the
market. Bedwyr I did not see at all in the horse yards; but at
evening I passed him among the crowd about one of the cheap wine
booths. He was drunk, to judge by the flush along his cheekbones
and the hectic brightness of his eyes; he had a little dark red rose
stuck behind one ear, and flourished a wine jug at me as I passed,
shouting something about damping the dust on the road to Constantinople.

On the evening of the fourth day, suddenly weary of Narbo
Martius and its uproar that was so much more blurred and raucous
than the uproar of a war camp, I did not at once return to the
city when the selling grounds began to empty, but let the rest of
the band go on without me, and myself strolled down through
the ill-kept olive gardens that rimmed the open ground, and sat
on the stone curb of a well, looking out over the pale levels toward
the sea which was turning to pearl-shell colors as the sun westered.
It was good to be alone for a while, and have quiet enough for
my bruised ears to hear the faint hushing of the little wind that
rose each evening, in the olive trees behind me, and the dark
drip of water from the well, and the soft clonk of goat bells, and
to watch, far off, the fishermen drawing in their nets. This
would be our last night in Narbo Martius, and I knew that when
I got back to the evening fire, every man of the Company would
be there. On other nights, many of them had hurried through
their supper and gone about their own pleasures; the laughter and
rough horseplay in the wineshops, and the women of the city kind
and not expensive. But I could not risk thick heads and maybe a
hunt through Narbo Martius for some fool still dead drunk in a
harlot's bed, when the time came to break camp in the morning.
So I had given the order and made sure that it was understood;
but I knew that I must not bide long in my quiet place below the
olive gardens, taking for myself the freedom for my own pleasure
that I had denied to Fulvius and the Minnow and the rest. I think

that few of them would have grudged it to me if I had, but it was not in the bargain.

Just until the shadow of the low-hanging olive branches reached that crack in the stones of the well curb, I told myself. It had the breadth of a hand to travel yet. . . .

That time I heard no step coming through the long grass under the olive trees, but a shadow, fantastically long in the westering light, fell across the wellhead, and when I looked up, Bedwyr was standing within a spear's length of me, his figure blotted darkly against the sunset. "How does the horse buying go?" he asked, without any other greeting.

"Well enough," I said. "I have chosen all my stallions, all but one of my brood mares. Now we have all things ready for striking camp, and tomorrow I shall take the first reasonable beast that I can strike a bargain for, and with good fortune we should be on the road north by noon."

He came and sat himself on the ground at my feet, leaning his head back against the warm stones of the well curb. "There are yet three days of the fair to run. Why then so great a hurry, my Lord Artos?"

"It is a long road north, and at the end of it a sea crossing. Even with good weather we must needs rest the horses at least one day in four. And at the best, we shall reach the coast with a month to spare before the autumn storms."

He nodded. "You will have transports of some kind?"

"If Cador of Dumnonia has been successful—two trading vessels with the decks torn out for getting the horses into the holds."

"And how many horses do you reckon to get across at each trip?"

"Two to each tub. To try for more would be to strike hands with disaster."

"So. I see wisdom of not lingering among the wine booths of Narbo Martius."

"That relieves my mind," I said gravely, and he laughed, then shifted abruptly to look up at me.

"The Black One is still for sale."

"I have all my stallions."

"Sell one again. Or another stallion instead of the last mare?"

"Certainly you do not lack for cool affrontery."

"You want him, don't you?"

I hesitated, then admitted it fully to myself for the first time. "Yes, I want him, but not enough to pay for him as I am very sure I should have to do, with the life of a man or another horse."

He was silent a moment, and then he said in a curiously level tone, "Then I ask another thing. Take me, my Lord the Bear."

"What as?" I asked, without surprise, for it was as though I had known what was coming.

"As a harper or a horse holder or a fighting man—I have my dagger, and you can give me a sword. Or"—his strange lopsided face flashed into a grin, his one reckless eyebrow flying like a banner—"or as a laughingstock when you feel the need for laughter."

But though I had known, in a way, what was coming, I was not sure of my reply. Usually I can judge a man well enough at first meeting, but this one I knew that I could not judge. He was dark water that I could not look into. His reserves were as deep in their way as Aquila's but whereas Aquila, whose past was bitter, had grown them through the years as the hard protective skin grows over an old wound, this man's were a part of himself, born into the world with him as a man's shadow.

"What of Constantinople and the Emperor's bodyguard?" I said, a little, I think, to gain time.

"What of them?"

"And the splendor that does not lie in ruins, and the bright adventure and the service to take?"

"Could you not give me a service to take? Oh, make no mistake, my Lord Artos, it was the other I wanted. That was why I got drunk yesterday; it was no use though. I am your man if you will take me."

"We have need of every sword hand," I said at last, "and it is a good thing to laugh sometimes—and to have the heart sung out of the breast. But . . ."

"But?" he said.

"But I do not take a hawk without having made trial of him. Nor do I take an untried man into the circle of the Companions."

He was silent for a good while, after that. The sun was behind the mountains now, and the evening sounds of the olive grove were waking, the creatures that they call cicadas creaking in the branches, and the voices of the fisherfolk coming up faintly on the wind. Once he made a small swift movement, and I thought he was going to get up and walk away, but he stilled again. "You choose more delicately than they say the Eastern Emperor does," he said at last.

"Maybe I have more need." I leaned down and touched his shoulder, scarcely meaning to. "When you are captain of the Emperor's bodyguard, you'll look back on this evening and thank whatever god you pray to, that the thing turned out as it did."

"Of course," he said. "When that day comes, I shall thank—whatever god I pray to, that it was not given to me to throw all that away, and go crawling back over those five hundred miles or so that I was already on my way, to die at last in a northern mist with the Sea Wolf's fangs in my throat."

I said nothing, for it seemed to me that there was no other word to say. And then he turned to me again, his eyes full of a cool dancing light that was nearer to battle than to laughter. "If I get the Black One back to Britain for you, without its causing the death of himself or any other horse or any man, will that seem trial enough? Will you take me then, and give me my sword in recompense?"

I was more surprised at that than I had been at his first asking to join us, and for a moment the surprise struck me silent. Then I said, "And what if you fail?"

"If I have not died in the failing, I will give you my life to add to that of the man or the other horse. Is not that a fair bargain, my Lord the Bear?"

Before I knew that my mind was made up, I heard my own voice saying, "We will go now and look into the Black One's mouth and feel him over, for I have not even touched him as yet. And if the horse be all that he seems, then it is a fair bargain, Bedwyr."

And I remember that we spat in our hands and struck palms like men sealing a bargain in the marketplace.

On a wild night of late September, with the first of the autumn gales beating about the thatch, we supped again in Cador's mead hall, I with the great gaunt joyful head of Cabal on my knee; behind us the long road and the choking summer dust cloud rolling up through Gaul, behind us the urgent struggle to get the last of the horses across before the weather broke. And the torchlight and the heather beer seemed the more golden for the triumphant knowledge of fine big-boned Septimania stallions and the brood mares picketed within the ring fence of the Dun.

Bedwyr, with dark smudges beneath his eyes—for the last crossing, with the Black One on board, had been no easy one, and he had not slept, even in his accustomed place at the great brute's side, for two nights before it—had come from his fairly won place among the Companions and sat on the harper's stool beside the hearth and sang for us, or maybe for himself, the triumph song of Arwas the Winged after he slew the Red Boar.

CHAPTER SIX

The Laborer and the Hire

THEY broke at noon, and all the rest of that day and most of the next we had driven them, among the willow-fringed islands and the reedbeds and the wildfowl meres; we had fired their winter camp (they should be well used to the stench of homesteads going up in flames). We had cut off the stragglers and burned their narrow dark war boats in the mouth of the Glein. Now, at evening on the second day, we came up from the river marshes toward the monastery on its island of higher ground, where we had left the baggage beasts.

We were a full band, three hundred cavalry, four hundred counting grooms, drivers, armorers, et cetera—or we had been, two days ago. We were somewhat less this evening, but in a few weeks we should be up to strength again; we always were. There were no captives with us. I have never taken captives, save once or twice when I had need of a hostage.

Cabal trotted as usual at my horse's off forefoot. Bedwyr rode on my sword side, and on the other, Cei who had blown in like a blustering west wind to join us when first we made our headquarters at Lindum, just two years ago. A big, red-gold man with hot-tempered blue eyes, and a liking for cheap glass jewelry that would have become either a Saxon or a whore. Those two had proved themselves in the past summers when, sometimes alone, sometimes with the half-trained warriors of Guidarius, the local ruler, we had attacked the settlements of Octa Hengestson, and driven back his inland thrusts again and again. And the time was to come when I counted Bedwyr the first and Cei the second of my lieutenants.

Bedwyr had unslung his harp from its accustomed place behind his shoulder, and was plucking the strings in triumphant ripples of notes that broke in waves of brightness, managing his horse with his knees the while. He often played and sang us home from battle. "After the sword, the harp," as the saying runs—and always it seemed to help our weariness and our wounds. When the tune was recognizable, Cei lifted up his voice in a deep grumbling buzz that was his nearest approach to singing, and here and there behind us a man took up a snatch of the familiar tune; but for the most part we were too spent to join in.

The sun was sinking as we pulled up out of the rustling reedbeds, and the vast arch of the sky was alight with a sunset that seemed to catch its mood from Bedwyr's harping and break in waves and ripples of flame. Never, even among my own mountains, have I known such sunsets as those of the eastern marshes, winged and shining skies busy as market crowds or streaming like the banners of an army. The standing water among the reedbeds caught fire from the sky, and overhead the wavering lines of wild duck were flighting.

On the lower levels only just clear of the marsh, the monastery's horses were grazing. It was horse country, though most of the beasts, sturdy though they were, were too small for our needs; too small, that is, if we had had any choice in the matter. But it would be seven or eight years yet before we could hope to draw much from the Deva training runs. We had lost upward of a score of horses in the past two days, and they would be harder to replace than the men.

The countryman in charge of the herd (the horse herding and breaking was the only work of the community not done by the Brothers themselves) took one look at us from the hummock of land that was his lookout post, and tossing up his spear ran back toward the monastery building. We heard him shouting, "They are coming! They are back! Holy Brothers, it is the Count of Britain!" And a few moments later the bell of the little church began to throb out its round bronze notes in greeting and rejoicing. "Truly, we are to have a hero's welcome!" said Bedwyr; and he let his hand fall from the harp strings, so that the weary smother of hoof-beats behind us grew suddenly louder.

The fire was fading from the sky as we reached the gateway in the thorn hedge; the huddle of reed-thatched sleeping cabins and farm buildings about the church and wattle dining hall were dark against the fading brightness of the west, and the few wind-stunted apple trees of the monks' orchard were pale and insubstantial clouds of blossom; and suddenly I thought of that other community over toward the sunset in the Island of Apples. The Brothers and the poor folk who had taken refuge with them had come crowding down to their gateway, save for whichever Brother it was who was still ringing the bell. Their hands reached out to us, their anxious faces were full of questioning; they called down blessings on us as we clattered through. They had brought a lantern with them, and by its light I saw the haggard face of a woman with a babe asleep at her shoulder, and that Brother Vericus the ancient Prior was crying.

In the clear space between the ring hedge and the huddled buildings, I dropped from the saddle and pulled off my war cap. The others were dismounting all about me, clattering to a weary standstill, more than one of them swaying with the weakness of a wound. The sharp yellow gleam of the lantern was in my eyes, and people pressing about me, catching at my hands, or my knees, and I was aware of the tall spare figure of the Abbot moving toward me; aware that I was expected to kneel down for his blessing as I had done when we rode out. I wanted to get the wounded under cover, but I knelt down. Cabal lay beside me with a grunt.

"How went the day, my son?" He had a beautiful voice, like the bronze notes of the bell still floating out above us.

"We burned their winter camp," I said. "There is one Saxon settlement the fewer to foul the grass, and this place may rest secure from the Barbarians, at least until the next thrust."

His hands were light as skeleton leaves on my head. "May the Grace of God be upon you. And may your shield, under His, be over all Britain, as it has been over us this day; and may you find His peace when the fighting is over."

But it was not the Grace of God that I wanted at that moment, it was salves and bandage linen and food for my men. I got to my feet again, slowly, for I was so tired that I could scarcely bear my own weight up from the ground. "Holy Father, I thank you for your blessing. I have wounded men with me—where may I send them for tending?"

"Wounded men, alas, we had expected," he said. "All is ready for you in the hall; Brother Lucius, our Infirmarer, will go with you."

The drivers whom we had left behind with the baggage train were already busy with the horses, and some of the village men among them. I saw Arian lead off with my bronze and bullhide buckler clanking softly at the saddletree, then turned to the business of getting the wounded together. Gault, one of my best youngsters, had a long spear wound in the thigh, and slid half fainting into the arms of his friend Levin, who had ridden close beside him all the way; but the rest of us were able to walk, and we went up to the hall together. I had a gash in my sword arm—most of our scathes, as usual with horse soldiers, were in the sword arm, or in the thigh below the guard of the thick leather kilt—and it was still oozing red.

In the hall they had hung extra lanterns from the rafters to see by, and pushed back the trestle table to make a clear space. There were small bundles of gear and possessions stacked within the doorway, easily to be caught up for a hurried flight. With the Sea Wolves so near, the Brothers and their refuging village folk had been prepared for flight when we came, and they had left all things ready in case the worst should happen after all.

Those of us whose hurts were slight stood back against the wall while the more sorely scathed were tended. After the chill of the spring evening it was very warm in the hall, for they had lit a fire, to boil water and heat the searing iron. The smoke hung among the rafters and made drifting yellow wreaths around the lanterns; it grew hot, and there began to be a thick smell of salves and the sweating bodies of men in pain, and once or twice, when the searing iron came into use, the sickening reek of scorched flesh. The first time the iron was used, it was on Gault, and the boy cried out, short and sharp as the scream of a hawk. Afterward he wept, but I think he wept because he had cried out, not for the pain.

Brother Lucian, working with the sleeves of his habit rolled to the shoulder, and the shaven forepart of his head shining sweat-beaded in the lantern light, had two or three helpers, amongst them a young novice, whom I had noticed before. A yellow-haired overplump lad with a good straight pair of eyes, and a way of slightly dragging his left foot. Watching him now, somewhat anxiously at first, for he was so young that I doubted his skill, I saw that he knew what he was doing, and that he cared deeply for the doing of it. Once he glanced up and saw me watching him, but his eyes returned instantly to the work of his hands, without, I think, even being fully aware of mine. I liked the singleness of purpose in him.

When it came to my turn, it so happened that the Infirmarer was still busy upon someone else, and the novice turned to me as I came forward to the table under the lanterns. I was just going to pull off the clotted rag, but he stayed me, with the authority of a man who is about his own trade.

"No, let me. You will set it bleeding again." He took up a knife and cut through the rag, eased away the stiffened folds and looked at the gash.

"It is not much," I said.

"Clench your fist," he ordered, and when I had done so, he nodded. "It is not much. You are fortunate. A nail's breadth farther that way, and it might have severed the thing that bids the thumb answer to your will." He bathed the gash and salved it, drawing the edges together, and lashed it. His hands were less plump than the rest of him, very sure of their work, strong and gentle at the same time, with a gentleness that had nothing soft in it but could be swiftly ruthless if the need arose. Also they were the hands of a fighter. And I thought for the first time that it was a pity that the healing art should lie altogether with the Church; better the old way when the healer had been part of the world, when army surgeons had marched with the Legions. Somehow I could not see these hands as belonging to one shut away into sanctuary, their healing shackled always to the dictates of one religion.

He fastened off the bandage and I thanked him and turned away, and in a little we went out, those of us who were still on our feet, to join the rest of the Companions, who had unhelmed and loosened off their war gear, and were kneeling about the candlelit doorway of the wattle church—there would have been room for less than half of us within—for it was the hour of evening prayer. The Abbot spoke the Thanksgiving prayers. His stately words meant little to me, but I remember that there was a late blackbird singing in the orchard, and the wind came siffling up from the marshes, and I had my own Thanksgiving prayer within me, because there was one less settlement of the Sea Wolves in Britain. Afterward they brought out and held up before us their chief treasure; some bones from Saint Alban's foot, I think it was. The light from the open doorway woke colored fires in the goldwork and enamel of the reliquary, as the Abbot raised it between his hands; and I heard the soft awed gasp of the village folk, who lived, as it were, in the shadow of its sanctity.

Then mercifully there was food at last. We made camp in the orchard, and ate there, for, like the church, the hall would not have held half of us, let alone the huddled refugees of the countryside. The brown-clad Brothers served and ate with us; and the Abbot served me with his own hands.

We had a fire, well clear of the apple trees, and by the flicker of it I saw the young novice watching me, more than once. And late that evening, as I crossed the monastery garth toward the bothy where our sorest wounded had been housed, I met him coming from there, swinging a lantern in his hand and walking with that faint drag of the left foot that I had noticed before. "How is it with Gault and the others?" I asked as we came together, and jerked my chin in the direction of the bothy.

"I think that if they do not take the wound fever, they will do well enough. How is it with that arm, my Lord Artos?"

"Well enough, also. You're a good surgeon."

"It is my hope that I shall be, one day."

I would have gone on, but he lingered as though there was something he wanted urgently to say; and I found myself lingering also. Besides, he had been catching at my interest all evening. "Is that why you entered the religious life?" I asked after a moment.

"There is nowhere that one can learn or follow the healer's craft outside the Church, in these days," he said; and then, speaking as though the words stuck a little in his throat, "That is a good enough reason for my choice of life, but lest it should fail me, I've another." He thrust forward his bare left foot from the thick folds of his habit, and glancing down at the sudden movement, I saw that it was turned inward, wasted and drawn up like the cramped claw of a bird, and the reason for his slight lameness became clear. "I am a younger son. I possess nothing of my own save a certain skill with wound salves and black draughts; I had the normal weapon training that all boys have, but as my father was at pains to make clear to me, I'd not be likely to find a lord overeager to take a fighting man as slow-footed as I am into his hall."

"I wonder if he was right," I said.

"My Lord Artos is kind. I have wondered the same thing—now and then. But I expect he was."

"I am willing to believe, at all events, that you will make a better surgeon than you would have made a soldier," I said. "Why do you make this defense, as though I had accused you of something?"

His eyes were bright and wretched in the lantern light, and he laughed a little drearily. "I don't know . . . I suppose because it is a time for taking the sword, and I would not have you think—" He caught at the words as though to have them unspoken again. "No, that is presumption; it sounds as though I were fool enough to think that you—that you—"

"Might waste my time thinking of you at all," I said, rescuing him from the stammer. "My way is the sword and yours is prayer, and both are good. It should not matter to you what I think of you."

"It will always matter to men, what you think of them," he said; and then on a lighter note, "Nevertheless, it is good to follow the healer's craft."

"It is a craft not without its uses when men take to the sword, Brother . . . What name do they call you by?"

"Gwalchmai."

Gwalchmai, the Hawk of May; it was a piteously ill-fitting name, for he was built more like a partridge than a hawk.

He hitched up the lantern and began to swing it. "It's comic really, isn't it? My Lord Artos, they have made the guest place ready for you—but they will have told you that."

"They told me. But I had liefer sleep with my men in the orchard. God's night to you, Brother Gwalchmai." And we went our separate ways, I to see for myself how Gault and the other three were doing, and he, swinging his lantern in blurred gouts of light before him, on across the garth to the place where the novices slept.

Presently I went back to my Companions, and slept a good sleep under the apple trees, wrapped in my cloak and with my head on Cabal's flank for a pillow. There is no pillow in the world so good as a hound's flank.

Next morning "the bloom began to wear off the bilberries," as they say; and it was Brother Lucian the Infirmarer, in all innocence of heart, who first showed me that it was so. I had been down to the low pastures to look at the monastery's horses—particularly those who were part broken ready for the autumn markets. There were four or five of them big-boned enough to be of some use to us, which might serve to fill up our losses; and I was considering in my mind the price to offer for them. I might be able to get the price out of Guidarius—after all, we were fighting his battles—or failing that, there was something in the war kist, for a few of us had lands of our own; we had sold off the poorer yearlings from the breeding runs, and the Saxon weapons and goldsmiths' work that we took from time to time fetched a good price. It mostly went on horses, but not when I could get them in any other way, for I had always to keep something in reserve against the days when gold might be the only way there was.

My mind was so full of horses that I all but walked through the old man, who had turned aside very kindly on seeing me, to tell me that I need have no fear for the wounded, for they would be well cared for, after we were gone.

I stared at him, scarcely understanding, for the moment, what he meant. "I am very sure of it; but, Brother Lucian, we are not yet saddling up."

"Na na," he said, smiling. "The day is yet very young."

"The day on which we ride out from here has not yet dawned, Brother Lucian," I said bluntly, and saw the startled look in his milky old eyes.

"But surely—surely, my Lord Artos, you will wish to be away back to Lindum now that the work of your swords in this part of the Fens is done?"

They were not trying to drive us out, I realized that; it was simply that it had never occurred to these fools in their enclosed world that men and horses who have been at hard stress for many days together must be rested when the chance offers. "My men need full three days' rest, and so do my horses; today and to-morrow and the day after, we remain within your gates; and on the day after *that,* we ride for Lindum."

"But—but—" He began to bleat like an elderly she-goat.

"But what, Brother Lucian?"

"The stores—the grain—always there is shortage in the spring-time. We had our own poor folk to feed, these past few days—"

"But no longer," I said; for the country folk had for the most part scattered back to their own lives, with their dogs and their cattle, their ducks and their pigs, now that the danger was passed over.

"They ate while they were here," he rallied and pointed out, reasonably enough. I could see the thoughts scurrying among mouths and grain baskets inside his head. "There are close on four hundred of you, with the grooms and drivers; even should you eat sparingly as we do ourselves, which—forgive me, my Lord Artos—is not to be expected of fighting men—even should you eat as sparingly as we do ourselves, you will swallow up more than a month's supplies, and your horses will graze bare the pasture that was for ours and our milch cows."

I broke in on him. "Brother Lucian, will you go now to the Abbot and ask him to receive me."

"The Holy Father is at prayer."

"I can wait while the prayer is done, but no longer. Go now and tell him that the Count of Britain would speak with him."

The Abbot received me within an hour, seated in his cross-legged chair in the hall where last night our wounds had been dressed, the more senior of the Brothers ranged about him. His head might have been that of a king on a golden coin. He rose to greet me, courteously enough, and then seated himself again, his blue-veined hands on the carved arms of the great chair. "Brother Lucian brings me word that you wish to speak with me."

"Yes," I said. "It seems that all is not clear between us as to when I and my Companions leave this place."

He bent his head. "So Brother Lucian tells me."

"And so that the matter may be settled, and trouble neither you nor us with uncertainties hereafter, I come to ask your hospitality for today, tomorrow and the morrow after. The third morning from now, when my men and horses are rested, we leave for Lindum."

"That also, Brother Lucian has told me; and that he made clear to you our position, our shortage of stores after the winter. We are not used to feeding four hundred men and as many beasts over and above our own poor folk that it is our duty to care for."

"There is good pasture hereabouts on the Fen fringes. My horses will not graze it out in three days. Most of us are hunters and we can find our own meat. And as to the grain and stores—" I leaned over him; I had not begun to be angry yet, because I could not believe that he grasped the true situation, and I was trying to make him understand. "Does it not seem to you, Holy Father, that the men who kept the roofs on the barns have earned the right to some of the grain in them? Many of us are wounded, all of us are spent. We must have three days' rest."

"But if the grain is not there?" he said, still kindly. "It *is* not there, my son. If we feed you for the three days that you demand, we shall not have enough left to keep us even in perpetual fast, until the harvest comes again."

"There is still grain to be bought in the Lindum corn market."

"And with what shall we buy this corn? We grow our own food; we are not a rich community."

I was angry now, and I said, "Not so poor, either, that you have nothing to trade. Saint Alban's foot lies in a goodly casket, even the bones themselves would fetch a good price."

He jerked upright as though at the prick of a dagger point, and his face purpled under his eyes, while the watching monks gasped and crossed themselves and cried "Sacrilege!" and swayed like a barley field in a flurry of wind.

"Sacrilege indeed!" the Abbot said in a grating voice. "Sacrilege worthy of the Saxon king, my Lord Artos, Count of Britain!"

"Maybe. But to me, my men are a greater matter than a few gray bones in a golden casket!"

He made no answer; indeed I think he was beyond speech for the moment; and I went on relentlessly. I had meant to ask for the horses at a fair price, ill though we could afford it. But now I had decided otherwise. "Holy Father, do you remember a certain saying of the Christos, that the laborer is worthy of his hire? Two days ago, I and my Companions saved this place from the fire and the Saxon sword, and for that, our hire is three full days' keep, and the four best horses in your pastures."

He found his voice then, and cried out on me for a despoiler of the Church, and that I should leave such ways to the Sea Wolves.

"Listen, Old Father," I said. "It might well have served me better to wait until the Sea Wolves had overrun this place, and

[71]

taken them in the Fens farther westward, farther from their ships.
I might have lost fewer men and fewer horses had I done that.
And why should I do as I have done, and then ride away, asking
for nothing in return?"

He said, "For the love of God."

It was my turn to be silent. And a sudden quiet came over the
hall, so that I heard the drone of the wild bees that nested in the
thatch. I had thought him grasping, without either justice or charity
in his heart, willing to take the lives of a score of my men and
the sweat and blood of the rest of us, and give nothing in return;
but I saw now that it was simply that for him the love of God had
a different meaning to the meaning that it held for me. And my
anger died away. I said, "I also have loved God in my way, but
there are more ways than one. I have never seen the flame on the
altar nor heard the voice in the sanctuary; I love my men who
follow me, and the thing that we are prepared to die for. For me,
that is the way."

His face gentled a little, as though at the passing of his own
anger, and suddenly he looked old and tired. But I did not relent;
neither of us relented. After a few moments, he said coldly and
wearily, "We are not strong enough to persuade you to leave us
until you choose to go; and if we were as many and as strong as
you, God forbid that, remembering your blood shed for us, we
should deny you hospitality when you demand it. Stay then, and
take the four horses for your guerdon. We shall pray for you, and it
may be that our prayers and our hunger before next harvest will
soften your will toward another community at another time such as
this."

He sat back in his chair, signifying with one old thick-veined
hand that the thing was over.

We stayed out our three days, encamped in the monks' orchard
while the horses grazed under escort in the marsh pastures, and
Caradawg, our armorer, set up his field forge and was busy with
his mate, dealing with sprung rivets, beating out the dints in shield
boss and war cap, and replacing the damaged links in mail shirts.
We had a fair number of mail shirts by now, though they were
slow-gathering, since only the great men of the Saxons possessed
such war gear and so it was only when a chief was killed or taken
that we were able to add to our store. (And the winning of a war
shirt had become a matter for eager rivalry among the Com-

panions, in consequence, who wore them as a hunter cuts a notch in his spear.) The rest of us took our turns of horse guard, and sprawled about the fires mending here a broken sandal strap and there the gash in a leather tunic, and ceaselessly trapped and hunted for the pot. But there was no longer friendship between us and the Brothers.

My lads did not take it kindly when I told them what had passed; Cei, I remember, proposed that we should fire the place as a sign of our displeasure, and some of the wilder ones were with him. And when I cursed him and them into a kind of sense, he consoled himself by eating himself almost to bursting point at every meal, in order to make as big a hole in the grain store as might be. The Brothers went about their own life, whether at prayer or at work on the farm, so far as possible as though we were not there, save for Brother Lucian and the boy Gwalchmai, who came and went in their care of the wounded as before. I knew that, even as the old Infirmarer had assured me before the trouble started, I need have no fear for the wounded after we were gone. They were good men, these brown-robed Brothers, though I longed to shake them until their back teeth rattled in their shaven heads. When, on the third morning, I ordered Prosper my trumpeter to sound for breaking camp, and at last the pack beasts were loaded and all things ready, they came out with the Abbot to the place before the gateway, to see the last of us, without anger. The Abbot even gave me the blessing for a departing guest. But it was done for duty's sake, and had no warmth in it.

The horses, fresh after their days of rest, were trampling and tossing their heads. One of the pack mules tried to bite his neighbor's crest and started a squealing fight. I turned to mount Arian, and as I did so, met the gaze of Gwalchmai the novice fixed upon me, where he stood on the outer fringe of the Brothers. I have never seen any face so wide open, so completely without defenses, as Gwalchmai's that moment. The wind from the marsh was ruffling the fair hair on his forehead; he licked his lower lip, and half smiled, and then looked away.

"Gwalchmai," I said, with the purpose scarce formed in my mind.

His gaze whipped back to mine. "My Lord Artos?"

"Can you ride?"

"Yes."

"Come then, we can do with a surgeon."

I would have left him to follow with our wounded when they came back to us, but Gault and the rest would want for nothing in Brother Lucian's care, and I knew that if I did not take the boy now, I should not get him.

"Stop! Are you not content with our four best horses, that you must take from among our Brothers also?" the Abbot cried; and he made a strange gesture, spreading his arms like wings in their wide-falling sleeves, as though to protect the huddled Brotherhood behind him.

"The boy is but a novice, and still free to choose for himself! Choose, Gwalchmai."

He took his gaze slowly from mine, and turned it to the Abbot. "Holy Father, I should make but a poor monk, with my heart elsewhere," he said, and came out from among the Brothers to stand at my stirrup. "I am your man, my Lord Artos, for all that there is in me." And he touched the hilt of my sword as one taking an oath.

The Abbot protested once again, more vehemently than before, then fell silent, while his monks and my own Companions, silent also, stood looking on. But I do not think that either of us heard what the old man cried out.

I said, "So, that is good, for I think there is in you that which we need among the Companions," and turned in the saddle to bid a couple of the drivers to bit and bridle one of the monastery horses and fling a rug across his back.

While they did so, Gwalchmai, as composedly as though his leaving with me had been arranged for many weeks beforehand, set to tightening his rawhide belt and girding up the hampering skirts of his habit.

"Have you nothing that you wish to fetch? No bundle?" I asked.

"Nothing but what I stand up in. It makes for light traveling." He never looked at the Abbot, nor at any of the Brothers again. Someone gave him a leg up, and he settled himself on the riding rug, and gathering up the reins, wheeled his horse among the rest of us. Man after man swung into the saddle, and we clattered and jingled out and down toward the fenland fringes and the old legionary road that runs due north from the Glein crossing toward Lindum.

CHAPTER SEVEN

Frontiers

NOT unnaturally, the Abbot complained of me to the Bishop of Lindum; but the Bishop, though zealous, was a small man, shrill but ineffectual, like a shrewmouse, and not hard to quell. Nevertheless, that was the start of the ill blood between myself and the Church, which has lasted almost ever since. . . .

Six years went by, and all their summers were spent in arms against Octa Hengestson and his son Oisc who was now of an age to lead men. Lindum, with its ill-kept roads radiating from it like the spokes of a wheel, was the perfect base for the campaigning of those years, and there, in the old fortress of the Ninth Legion, made over to us by Prince Guidarius, we set up our winter quarters, from which to strike out southward toward the Glein and the shores of the Metaris Estuary westward along the open sea coast, northward to drive the Sea Wolves back into the Abus River.

Meanwhile, I knew that Ambrosius had made his stronghold against the Dark and was taking his stand there against old and mighty Hengest and against a new enemy, one Aelle, who had landed with his war fleet south of Regnum and made himself a sore menace to the British eastern flank. All that had nothing to do with me now; but nevertheless, I think that I would have abandoned Guidarius for the time being, and left the work half done and doubtless all to do again, and ridden south to Ambrosius if he had sent for me. But he did not send, and so I went on with the work at hand.

They were hard years, and we did not always carry home the victor's laurels but sometimes only our wounds to lick. But by

the seventh autumn, Lindum Territory and the northern part of the
Icenian coast was almost clear, and so unhealthy for the Saxon
kind that for a while their crazy war boats no longer descended
on the coast with every east wind that blew. (We used to call the
east wind "the Saxon Wind" in those days.) And we knew that
when spring opened the country, and the time for the war trail
came again, it would be time to strike north across the Abus
against Eburacum, where Octa and his hordes had made their new
war camp in the old Brigantian country.

That autumn, Cabal died. I had never gone into battle without
him running at my stirrup since he was three parts grown, and all
that last summer he went with me as he had always done. But he
was old, very old, gray-muzzled and scarred by wounds, and in
the end his valiant heart wore out. One evening he lay as usual at
my feet beside the fire in the hall, and suddenly he raised his head
to look up at me, as though he were puzzled by something that
he did not understand. I stooped and began to fondle the soft hollow under his chin, and he gave a small sigh and laid his head in
my hand. I did not realize what was happening, even then; only
his head grew heavier and heavier in my hand, until I knew that
the time had come to lay it down.

I went out then, and stood leaning on the colonnade wall for a
long time in the darkness.

But there was little time, after all, to spare for grieving over a
dead hound that autumn.

Not many evenings later, we were once again in the hall, the
mess hall of the old legionary fortress, where the badges and titles
of the ill-fated Ninth Legion were painted on the peeling plaster
over the door. There were hounds sprawled about the central fire,
hounds belonging to one or other of the Companions. I watched
Fulvius's red bitch suckling her puppies, and thought how perfectly
easily I could come by another hound to fill with his padding and
the rattle of his long nails, the silence that walked at my heels. But
he would not be Cabal. Only fate could send me another Cabal.
. . . Supper was over, and the lads were about their evening's
amusements. Beyond the fire, two of them, stripped to their breeks,
were wrestling, while a knot of others gathered about them to
watch and cheer them on. I could hear their panting breaths and
the laughter and advice of the onlookers. In a corner somewhat

withdrawn from the rest, Gwalchmai leaned over a draughtboard, confronting Flavian, my onetime armor-bearer. They had long since formed a liking for playing draughts together, those two, maybe because they played almost equally badly. We had sweated the fat of Gwalchmai in the past six years, and he no longer bore the least resemblance to a partridge; a lean wiry young man with a quiet face. I had done well, I thought, when I whistled Gwalchmai from his fenland monastery; his father had been wrong, for he had proved himself a formidable fighter on horseback, though on foot his lameness made him slow; but above all he had proved himself the surgeon that I had taken him for. More than one of us owed our lives to him by now. Whatever mistakes I might make in the men I took for my Companions, I had certainly made none there, nor in Bedwyr's case, nor in Cei's. Those three, above all others, had become, as it were, an inner core of the Brotherhood, in the years since we first rode together.

Cei slept with his back against one of the benches, his legs in their black and crimson trews stretched wide to the fire. Presently he would get up, shake himself like a dog, so that his bright glass arm ring and necklaces jingled, and stroll off to the Street of Women at the lower end of the town. When Cei slept in the evening it generally meant that he had plans for a night with more amusing things in it than sleep. Some of us mended harness or cast the dice, talked idly by fits and starts, or simply stared into the fire, waiting for Bedwyr sitting on a white bullskin at my feet to sing again. It was never any use to clamor for song or saga from Bedwyr; when he chose, he would give it of his own free will, harping the bird off the tree, and when he did not choose, nothing on the earth would force him.

A movement in the shadows caught at the tail of my eye, and glancing that way, I saw where on one of the side benches, withdrawn as though into a world of their own, Gault and Levin leaned on each other's shoulders and shared the same ale cup, talking together in low voices and with quiet laughter. It is a thing that happens on campaign, where women are scarce, every commander knows that; but sometimes, as with those two, it becomes a part of life.

Bedwyr saw where I was looking, and said with a breath of laughter, "It is as well, perhaps, that our good Bishop Felicus is not here to see that. The Church would hold up its hands in horror and talk of mortal sin."

"Mortal sin . . . But then the Church and I have seldom seen eye to eye, these six years or so. If it keeps the lads happy and in fighting trim . . ." For it did keep them in fighting trim, each of them striving to be worthy of his friend, each to make the other proud of him; and I have known the love of a yellow-haired girl to make life too sweet and unnerve a man's sword hand, before now.

"Give me a whole squadron of such sinners—so that they be young—and I'll not complain."

"What when they grow old?"

"They will not grow old," I said. "The flame is too bright." And I knew the grief that I suppose all commanders know from time to time, when they look about them at the men who answer to their trumpets; grief for the young men who will never grow old. . . .

A hurried step came along the colonnade, and Owain who was on guard duty appeared in the doorway (we always mounted a light guard whether in camp or winter quarters, especially since Ambrosius had sent me word that Hengest was gathering a war fleet in the Tamesis mouth). "Artos, one of the scouts has come in, and another man with him. They say they must have word with you at once."

"I'll come," I said. "Keep the next song until I get back, Bedwyr," and got up and went out with Owain into the autumn darkness of the colonnade.

The two men were waiting for me in the Sacculum where the Legion had kept its Eagle, its altars and its pay chest. We kept our own pay chest there now, and the muster roll, and the Red Dragon on its painted spear shaft propped in one corner; and it was the place where I usually saw any scouts or messengers that came in. This man I knew of old; he was one of Guidarius's hunters, who knew the northern marshes as a man knows his own bean patch; a little ferret of a man, but completely reliable. The other was a stranger to me, a tall youngster carrying the woad-stained war buckle that proclaimed him for one of the Brigantes, and wearing the gold tore of a chieftain about his throat—like my own mountain people, the folk of the Northern Moors had gone back to their old ways in dress as in most other things, since the

Legions left. I listened to what they had to tell me, and when they were finished, dispatched them to get a meal and a night's rest, for clearly they were too spent for our company that night. Then I went back to the mess hall, and called Cei and Bedwyr out to me.

We went back to the Sacculum, and Cei, still yawning his way out of his interrupted sleep, kicked the door shut behind us. "Well?" he grumbled. "What's the word? I was just going down into the town." Cei generally woke from sleep in a grumbling mood.

"I'll not keep you long," I said. "There'll still be plenty of the night left. And while you're with her you can bid good-bye to Cordaella or Lalage or whoever it is this time."

His eyes opened fully, and his temper sweetened in the moment while I looked at him. "Sa sa! It is like that, is it?"

And Bedwyr, who had come out still carrying his harp, and was leaning against the wall watching us, struck a little spurt of notes that was like an exclamation.

"It is like that. It seems that we have wrought too well, hereabouts, for Earl Hengest's peace of mind. He has come up to the aid of his son—landed on the coast north of the Abus and heading for Eburacum."

"So that was what he was gathering his war boats for," Bedwyr said. And I nodded.

Cei hitched at his sword belt. "And so now we march north to meet them."

"Yes."

Bedwyr said, "It is something late in the year to be riding out on a new campaign."

"I know. It is in my mind that Hengest knows it also, and is banking on the knowledge." I began to walk up and down the small room; four paces from the window to the door, four paces back again—I have always found it easier to think walking. "If we leave him to himself now, with the whole winter to strengthen his position, he will be all the tougher nut to crack open in the spring; and there is always the risk that he may make the first move, and come down on *us*. We have a month of possible campaigning weather left—if we're lucky. We must risk the weather breaking early."

[79]

"Aye well, there'll be girls in Eburacum, I dare say," Cei remarked philosophically.

Bedwyr quirked up that flaring eyebrow, and the laughter flickered in his voice. "Is it *any* girl for you, Brother Cei? *Any* girl in *any* city?"

"Any girl that is warm and willing." The golden man turned to me. "What is the word, Artos?"

"How soon can we march?"

"In three days," they both said together; and Cei added, "That is for the Companions; for Guidarius's men—who can say?"

I was looking at Bedwyr. His fingers were still on the harp strings, but he made no sound. He lifted his eyes to meet mine, gravely considering, under their odd brows. "Who can say?— Guidarius, I suppose. But it is in my heart to wonder if we can count on the Lindum men at all."

I had been wondering that also. We had fought through all those last coast summers together, Guidarius's ragged war host acting as spearmen and mounted archers—their sturdy dependable little horses were well suited to that work, and for scouting, though they had not the weight for a charge; and we knew each other as well as men can who have fought together for more than seven years. It was not them that I doubted, but Guidarius himself. "That's as may be," I said. "Let the others know, and get things moving, Bedwyr. I must go and speak with Guidarius now, but I'll be back in an hour."

"And myself?" said Cei, his thumbs, as they most often were, in his sword belt.

"Go and bid good-bye to Lalage. You can take over double your share of work in the morning, to even the count."

I went out through the main gate of the camp, hearing it already beginning to stir and thrum behind me, and across the street to the old Governor's Palace, close to the Forum. The bitter-smelling mist of early autumn was creeping up from the river marshes, over the lower town, and the lantern that hung in the entrance to Guidarius's forecourt shed a yellow pool of light on to a drift of yellow poplar leaves across the threshold. It was indeed perilously late in the year to be riding out on a new campaign.

I roused the doorkeeper who was sleeping peacefully with his

empty beer jar beside him, and told him that I must speak with
the Prince Guidarius.

Guidarius was in his private apartments, spending a domestic
evening with his wife and daughters. The room seemed, when I
was shown into it after a maddening delay, to be very bright with
candlelight, very hot from the brazier which glowed clear red in
the midst of it, and very full of girls.

Guidarius, reclining on a wolf-headed couch with his wife sitting
dutifully at his feet, was very Roman as to outward seeming, his
pouchy face carefully shaved, the few remaining hairs of his head
trimmed short, his paunchy little body clad in a Roman tunic of
fine white wool, and his wife's gown cross-girdled in the classic
manner, as few women still wore it, even when I was young. I
never saw him without a feeling of surprise that he should have
turned back, after the generations that his fathers had been magistrates and even provincial governors, to the title of Prince, that
had been theirs before the Eagles came. Other men, yes, it had
happened up and down Britain, as our old native states woke out
of the Roman years, but not men who still wore Roman tunics and
swore by Roma Dea and supped, as Guidarius had clearly done
(for the remains were still hanging around his ears), with wreaths
of rosemary and autumn violets on their bald heads.

He looked up when I entered, and nodded affably. "Ah, my
Lord Artorius. I grieve that you were kept waiting, but you know
how it is, we must all ease our shoulders from the cares of state
sometimes; I am never easy to gain access to when I am spending
a quiet hour with my family."

"I know how it is," I agreed. "But my business is urgent. I would
not have broken in on you else."

He stared at me a moment, then made shooing gestures to his
women folk who had already risen uncertainly to their feet; and
they fluttered out, leaving behind them a half-played game of
draughts, a wisp of some soft embroidered stuff with the needle
shining in it; all the pretty clutter that collects where women have
been.

When they had gone, and the heavy curtain had fallen across
the doorway behind them, he swung his feet to the floor and sat
up. "Well? Well well? What is it?"

I walked over to him. "Prince Guidarius, I received word not an hour since, that Earl Hengest is come north to the aid of his kinsmen; he has landed beyond the Abus and is heading for Eburacum."

He looked at me, startled, and then the blood rose into his mottled cheeks. "*You* received? Why was the word not brought in the first place to me?"

"The thing is beyond your frontiers," I told him. "But I am the Count of Britain, and therefore my frontiers are wider than yours."

It was foolish, when I should have been trying to conciliate him, but something about the man had always raised my hackles, since the first day that I entered Lindum, and the years that I had tried to work with him had not altered that. But truly, I think it would have made no difference if I had crawled on my belly at his feet.

He made sounds in his throat, then evidently decided to let it pass; only he said testily, "Well, well, young dogs bark loudest, so they say. Though you be Alexander himself, pull out that stool and sit down. It gives me a crick in the neck to be trying to talk to you while you stand over me like a pine tree."

I did as he bade me, and then went on with what I had it in me to say. "I am come to bring you the word now, and to tell you that I am marching north in three days."

He stared at me in good earnest then, with a frown puckering his forehead. "It is too late in the year to start a new campaign," he said at last, much as Bedwyr had done.

"Almost, but not quite."

He shrugged. "You should know best; you are, as you have pointed out, the Count of Britain. Well, I suppose if you can finish the thing in one good sharp encounter, you may be back here and snug in winter quarters before the bad weather sets in."

"Prince Guidarius, we shall not be coming back, neither before the winter sets in, nor after," I said.

He looked at me with his chin dropped. "Not—coming back?"

"Not coming back."

He seemed suddenly older, and as though there was less bulk inside his skin. I leaned toward him, making myself sound reasonable. "We should have gone in the spring, in any case, that you know; and you will have no more trouble with the Sea Wolves through the winter. How then is it a worse thing that we go now?"

"Next spring is half a year away." He made a small helpless

gesture. "I suppose I hoped that you would change your mind before the time ran out."

I shook my head. "You have two good leaders in Cradock and Geranicus, and I have broken in your men for you. They were brave men when I came, but a brave rabble; now they are trained troops—even disciplined after a fashion—and will rally to you swiftly at need. You should be able to hold off the Barbarians for yourselves now; and the most crying need for me is elsewhere."

Silence hung between us for a long tight-drawn moment, and then he gave his plump shoulders a little jerk, as though to straighten them, and I thought I saw beneath the pouchy lines of his face something of the fighting man he had been in his youth. I should not have to fear for the land between the Abus River and the Metaris after I was gone. "Then it seems that there is no more to be said."

"Something more—I want four hundred of your men to march north with me."

I thought his eyes would start clean from his head. "Roma Dea! Man, man, you have upward of a hundred of my best warriors sucked into the circle of those Companions of yours at this moment! And you must have had as many more through the years! What further would you have?"

"Four hundred, of their own choosing and mine, to go with me as auxiliaries, as spearmen and archers on this campaign. There will be—I have told you before—no more trouble with the Sea Wolves for this year at least; and when the autumn's fighting is over, and Earl Hengest safely out of Eburacum, I will send them back to you."

"Those that are left of them."

"Those that are left of them."

"And meanwhile, no man, not even you, my most war-wise Count of Britain, can say for sure *what* the Sea Wolves will do, for they are as unpredictable as the winds that bring them to our shores; and my fighting strength will not stand the loss of four hundred men."

I cut in on him. "No man, not even you, my most wise Prince of the Coritani, knows more surely than I do what is your fighting strength and what loss it will stand."

The new strength in his face was gathering itself against me now.

"It is enough for us to hold the Sea Wolves from our own pastures; why should I send my young men to fight in the Brigantes' country?"

Suddenly it was I who felt old and tired and helpless. "Because if we stand alone, state and princedom and tribal hunting run each within our own frontiers—state and princedom and hunting run, we shall fall one by one, each within our own frontiers. It is only if we can stand together that we shall drive the Saxons back into the sea."

I do not know how long we argued the thing; but it seemed a very long time. I think once he came near to offering me the whole four hundred, if I would return for another year when the autumn's fighting was over, but by that time we knew each other well—and he thought better of that particular offer before it was spoken.

In the end I did none so badly, for I came away with the grudging promise of two hundred, on my oath on Maximus's great seal that they should indeed come back when the fighting for Eburacum was ended.

The mist had crept up from the lower town, scented with woodsmoke and sodden leaves, and was making a wet yellow smoke about the courtyard lantern as I passed out again into the street. The chill of it was on my own heart. How shall we stand against the Barbarian flood? What hope is there for us even for Ambrosius's hundred years, if we cannot learn to stand together, shield to shield, across our own frontiers?

The two days that followed were filled with the usual turmoil of a war host making ready for the march; rations and gear being issued and packed in the great leather-topped pack panniers, sheaves of arrows and spare weapons issued and checked, horses brought in from autumn pasture and fitted with new leather foot shackles, armor and war gear given a final overhaul to make sure that all was in perfect order; and all day and all night Lindum rang with the deep bell-clink of hammer on armorer's anvil and the neighing of excited horses from the makeshift picket lines. During those two days also, there must have been many partings in and around the old fortress city. By this time upward of a hundred of the Companions were, as Guidarius had said, men from the Coritani, and many of the others had girls in the town. A few (God knows I had always tried to hold them back from that when

I could) had married since we first made our headquarters there.
Partings heavy with promises to come back one day, or send for
the girl . . . Partings taken lightly with a kiss and a bright new
necklace and no promises at all . . . Yet it was not all partings,
for when we marched out at last, the strength of our baggage train
was increased by twoscore or more of hardy girls, riding in the light
carts that carried the mill and the field forge, or walking with a
fine free swing, their skirts kilted to their knees, among the drivers
and the laden pack ponies.

It is not an ill thing for a war host to carry a few women with it,
so that they be hardy and fierce enough to fend for themselves and
not drag on the men; for their cooking has its uses, and their care
can mean the difference between life and death to the wounded.
The trouble, of course, with a few women among many men starts
when several men desire the same girl at the same time, or when
one man wants one especial girl for himself against all comers.
That is when the Brotherhood starts to break. Dear God! *That is
when the Brotherhood starts to break.* I let it be known through
the war host that at the first whispering of trouble over the women
to reach my ears, I should abandon the whole gaggle of them
wherever we might happen to be. Then I let the matter rest.

The young chieftain and the hunter who had brought me word
of Hengest's coming acted as our guides. For the first three days the
hunter led us northwestward, by the road and then by looping
marsh ways that followed the firm ground among the reedbeds and
winding waters and thickets of thorn and sallows, where left to
ourselves we should have been hopelessly lost within an hour, and
where, even as it was, the horses were often fetlock deep in the
dark sour-smelling ooze. One twilight we passed the burned-out
remains of a Saxon settlement that had been our work in the previous year, and something—a wildcat, maybe—screamed at us from
the ruins. After three days we began to pull up out of the marshes,
into softly undulating country and low hills, where the wind over
the dead heather made a sound that was harsh in our ears after the
softer wind-song over the marshes that we had known so long. And
on the fourth evening we struck the road from Lagentus to Eburacum and turned north along it. The hunter was out of his territory
now, and turned back to his own hunting runs, and the young
chieftain entering his own countryside took his place as guide.

Two marches northward the road crossed a river by a broad paved ford, covered by one of the gray derelict guard posts that still stud the countryside. And there we met the Saxon war host under its white horsetail standards.

Whether they had wind of our coming and were advancing to meet us, or whether they had thought to come down behind us in the old Lindum position and take us unawares, I do not know; nor does it matter now. We joined battle at first light of a squally October morning, the rain sweeping across the sodden wrack of last year's bracken. They had the advantage of ground, their left flank on the soft ground by the river, their right guarded by dense thorn scrub. They outnumbered us badly, thanks to Guidarius, and the rain slackened our bowstrings, while of course it had no effect on the hideous little throwing axes with which many of them were armed. On our side we had the advantage of cavalry, which on that narrow front did no more than even the odds. By midday it was over; a small, wicked, bloody business. Neither of us gained the victory, and both were too badly mauled to fight again that year.

Hengest and his war host fell back on Eburacum and we on Deva that men still call the City of Legions. It was an obvious choice for our winter quarters, with wide grazing behind us and the cornlands of Môn none so far away. But it cost us something to get there, and more than one of our wounded died on the road. We got through at last, none too soon, and rode into Deva in a full gale from the west and driving rain that was already turning the dried-out summer moors into oozing mosses; men and horses alike blind weary and on nodding terms with starvation. We were used to living on the country but among the mountains in October the living is not rich for man or beast.

The young chieftain came with us, carrying a wounded shoulder, to see us well into the mountains, but would come no farther. His own village was scarce a day's march eastward, he said, but when we came back in the spring, he would rejoin us. We gave him one of the pack beasts to ride, for he was weak with the wound; and he rode off on his different way from ours, turning once to wave from the skyline before his own hills hid him from view. I have wondered sometimes whether he reached his village. We never saw him again.

CHAPTER EIGHT

Wind from the North

I DID not know Deva well, but there had always been friendly
dealings between Arfon and the City of Legions; and I had
been there once or twice when I was a boy, and again when we
brought up the Septimania horses, and the last time only a few
years since when I had seized the chance in an open winter for a flying visit to Arfon and Deva to see for myself how things went in
the breeding and training runs, instead of sending Bedwyr or Fulvius in the spring, as I had done in other years. So now, as I heard
Arian's heavy hoofbeats crash hollow under the gate arch, I had a
sudden sense of refuge and return to familiar things. And certainly
it seemed that Deva remembered me. The people came running as
we rode wearily up through the weed-grown streets toward the gray
frown of the fortress; only a handful at first, then more and more
as the word spread, until when we clattered in through the un-
guarded Praetorian Gate, half the city was running at our horses'
heels, calling greetings and shouting for news.

In the gale-swept parade ground I dropped from Arian's back,
staggering as my cramped legs all but gave under me, and stood
with a hand on the horse's drooping rain-darkened neck, to look
about me while the rest clattered in and dismounted likewise. I
had thought that the old fortress might be already full of squatters
from the city, but save for a few ragged ghosts that came spilling
out from odd corners even as I watched, the place was as empty
as the Legions had left it. The drift away to the country which was
thinning most big cities nowadays had perhaps come about more
swiftly at Deva, because Kinmarcus, who had no more liking for
towns than had Cador, had gone back to make the capital of his

little border princedom at the Dun of the Alderwoods where his forebears had ruled before the Eagles came. The town was dying in its sleep, as a worn-out old man dies; and meanwhile there was room to spare for everybody, and no need to spill uphill into the deserted fortress.

Bedwyr and Cei were beside me, still holding their weary horses. Gwalchmai was busy among the mule carts as they rolled in with the wounded. "Get some of the barrack rows cleared out and the men under cover," I said. "We shall have to use some of the spare barrack rows and the main granary for the horses—there'll not be stabling for above sixty; this place hasn't been used since before the Legions took to cavalry." I turned on a soldierly-looking old man leaning on a finely carved staff, whom the townsfolk had made way for as for one in authority. "Old Father, do you command here?"

His straight mouth twitched with sudden humor. "In these days I am never sure whether to claim the title of Chieftain or Chief Magistrate; but it is true that I command here, yes."

"Good. Then we need wood for the fires, food for ourselves and fodder for the horses. As you see, they are in no state to be turned out to graze at the present. Can your people manage that?"

"We will manage that."

"Also fresh salves and linen for the wounded—the little man over there with the crooked foot will tell you what he wants, and whatever it is, for God's sake give it to him."

"To the half of my kingdom," said the old man. He glanced about the throng of staring townsfolk, and changing his tone so that it might have been another man who spoke above the booming of the wind, quickly and without fuss called out this one and that and gave them their orders. Then as men and women scattered to do his bidding, he came, leaning on his staff, to stand beside me in the little shelter that the end of a barrack row gave from the driving rain. "It will be some time before the fodder can come, there is not so much fodder in Deva as will feed this number of horses, and we must send out to one or two of the big farms for it; but it will come."

"You are good hosts," I said, tugging at the thongs of my iron war cap and pulling it off.

"Maybe we should be worse hosts to strangers, but are you not

[88]

of the breed of the Lords of Arfon?" (I smiled inwardly at the careful way that it was framed.) "And do not your brood mares graze as it were under our very walls? We count you as a friend—as Artos the Bear, before ever we remember you for Artorius, Count of Britain."

"It is a useful title. It gives me some kind of authority among the princes. But Artos the Bear has a more friendly sound."

Around me the Companions with the grooms and drivers were already hard at work. A starved-looking young priest had appeared from somewhere to help Gwalchmai with the wounded, and the weary horses were being led away. Amlodd, the cheerful freckle-faced lad who had taken Flavian's place as my armorbearer, came to take Arian from me, and I would have turned away about my own work, but the old man stayed me with a brief touch on my arm, his gaze following two of the Companions who stumbled past at that moment, supporting a third into the shelter of the nearest doorway. "You have been fighting and have come sorely out of the battle, and you will have other things to do tonight than tell the story; but remember, when you have the leisure, that we should be glad to know what has befallen—that is a matter which concerns us with the rest of Britain."

I said, "There is not much to tell—a drawn battle, south of Eburacum. But you can sleep tonight without fear of Saxon fire in the thatch. There's no wolf pack on our heels. . . . Meanwhile there's one thing more I need; one of your young men to saddle up and ride to the Dun of the Alderwoods with word for the Prince Kinmarcus that we are in his city and I would come to speak with him as soon as may be."

But I did not ride to the Dun after all, for three days later Kinmarcus himself rode in with a small band of hearth companions.

We had been getting the best-recovered of the horses out to pasture, to ease the strain on the fodder situation, and I returned to the fortress to see him dismounting from a dancing wild-eyed pony mare on the parade ground before what had once been the officers' block, while his men stood by with the carcasses of two red deer slung across the backs of a couple of ponies in their midst.

He roared like a gale of wind when he saw me (a great voice he had for so small a man), and came to fling his arm around my shoulders as far up as he could reach. "Sa sa sa, my Bear Cub! It is sun and moon to my eyes to see you after this long while!"

"And trumpets in my heart to hear you again, Kinmarcus my Lord!"

He boomed with laughter. "The youngster brought me your word, that you were here in Deva and would come to speak with me; but I was for hunting in this direction, and so I but carried the trail a little farther, and here I am—with the fruits of my hunting for a guest-gift."

"A fine gift! We shall feast like heroes tonight!"

He stood with his little legs straddled, and stared about him at my men and his own as they hauled away the carcasses for jointing, his bright masterful gaze disposing of them all in one sweep. "And meantime, while the feast is cooking, is there somewhere in this buzzing hornets' nest where a man can talk with a chance of hearing his own voice without everyone else hearing it too?"

"Come up onto the ramparts. We keep a lookout over each of the gates, but no pacing sentries between. We can talk in peace up there."

But when we had climbed the steps to the southwest corner of the rampart walk, he did not at once begin to talk of whatever it was that had brought him (for I was sure that, friends as we were, this was no mere friendly visit), but leaned beside me on the coping, looking away toward the mountains. The storms of the last few days had rained and blown themselves out; it was a day of broken light and drifting cloud shadow; and Yr Widdfa and his bodyguard of lesser heights stood clear, dark-bloomed with drifting shadows against the tumbled sky. It seemed to me, looking in the same direction, that the light wind that siffled across the ramparts brought with it the smell of the high snows, and the chill heart-catching scent of leaf mold the mossy north sides of trees that was the breath of the woods below Dynas Pharaon where I was bred. And then, as so often happened when I turned toward my own mountains, it seemed that the whisper of peat smoke was on the same wind, and the aromatic sweetness of a woman's hair. I wondered whether I had a son among those blue-shadowed glens and hidden valleys; a son seven years old, and trained in hate since first he sucked in the venom with his mother's milk. . . . No, I did not wonder; I knew. One can feel hate at a distance, as one can feel love. . . . I caught back the scent of the woods below Dynas Pharaon, and clung to it in spirit as a man clings to a talisman in a dark place.

I suppose I shivered, for Kinmarcus beside me laughed and said, "What is it? A gray goose flying over your grave?"

"Only a cloud over the sun."

He glanced at me aside; it was a stupid thing to have said, for there was no cloud over the sun just then; but he did not press the thing further. "And now, let you tell me what has passed this autumn."

So it was to be my turn first. I told him. There was little enough to tell and the story was soon done.

"And so you are come back here to Deva, to lick your wounds, and make your winter quarters."

"Yes," I said.

"And what as to supplies?"

"That was among my chief reasons for choosing Deva; the grazing ground for the horses, the Môn barley for us. I sent Bedwyr my lieutenant with the baggage carts and a small escort off to Arfon this morning, to get what he can. I'd have given them a few days' longer rest, but with winter upon us, I daren't. We can only pray to God, as it is, that they will get the grain through in time—and that the harvest has been good in Môn."

"And meanwhile?"

"Meanwhile, we 'live on the country.' I've paid your folk what I can. I can't pay the fair price for our keep, there's not enough in the war kist, there never is; and *what* there is goes mostly to the horse dealers and the armorers."

"And to Arfon for corn?"

I shook my head. "That counts as tribute from my people. Some will come actually from my own estates. I am of the breed of the Lords of Arfon, as your chieftain here put it. They will let me have the corn. . . . For the rest, there's always the hunting—the stored grain in the granary and the boar in the woods; that is the way the outposts used to live in the old days, isn't it?"

Silence fell between us for a while, and then at last Kinmarcus said, "What thing was it that you would have come to the Dun to speak with me about?"

I turned a little, leaning one-elbowed on the coping, to look at him. "I want men."

He smiled, that swift fierce smile that leapt into his face and out again, leaving it grave. "It is in my heart that you can gather men to you with little help from any princeling, my friend."

"Given a free hand, yes."

"In Lindum, the hand was not free?"

"Free enough, while the men were needed only to clear the Sea Wolves from within their own frontiers. I must have men to follow me out of the Deva hunting runs without let or hindrance from their Prince, and across the mountains to Eburacum in the spring."

"Your hand is free," he said. "Set up your standard, and the young men will come like June bugs to a lantern. Only leave a few to defend our own women and our own hearth places."

"The Scots raiders?"

"The Scots raiders, and others. Maybe the Saxon wind blows across the mountains." He shifted abruptly, before I could ask his meaning, head up into the wind that lifted back his fallow-streaked mane of hair. "What after Eburacum?"

"It is not only Eburacum, though Eburacum is the heart of it. It is the whole eastern end of the Brigantes country. After that we go wherever the sorest need calls us; southeast into the Iceni territory in all likelihood. The Saxons call all that part for their own North-folk and Southfolk, already."

Kinmarcus said abruptly, "And yet I believe that if you are wise, you will take the way north, beyond the Wall, and that without overmuch delay."

I looked at him quietly, aware that this at last was what he had come to say. "What is the reading of that riddle, my Lord Kinmarcus?"

And he returned my look, eye into eye. "I also have a thing to speak of and a tale to tell," he said. "It is so that I did not wait your coming, but hunted toward Deva. If the signs and portents do not lie, by next midsummer the heather will be ablaze through half the lowlands of Caledonia; by harvest, the fire will have leapt the Wall."

"Another riddle to answer the first. What does it mean?"

"There has been unrest in southern Caledonia for a year and more. We have felt it stirring, we who hold the princedoms of the

North. Even so far down from the Wall as this, we have felt it, but the thing was formless, like a little wind on a summer's day that blows all ways at once through the long grass. Now the thing has taken form and we know from whence the wind blows. The Saxons have called in the Painted People to their aid, promising them a share of the fat pickings when Britain goes down; and the Painted People have sent out the Cran Tara, even overseas into Hibernia, summoning the Scots, and made common cause with certain of the British chieftains who think they see the chance to break free of all bonds and stand proud and alone—the fools, hastening to set their necks under the Saxon's heel."

"Earl Hengest's heel?" There was a small shock of cold in me.

"I think not. Possibly Octa has a hand in it, but it is more likely in my mind that the thing lies with the true Saxons of the north coast. Oh aye, with us the one name serves for all, but Hengest is a Jute, remember, and the Sea Wolves have not yet learned to combine." His voice dropped to a brooding note. "If they learn before we do, then that is the end of Britain."

"How do you know all this?" I said, after a pause.

"By a mere trick of chance, or as some might say, by the Grace of God. Not many days since, a currach bound for the Caledonian coast was driven off course by a northwesterly wind and came ashore on ours. The men on board were an embassy of some kind, for they carried no weapons save their dirks, though they were of the warrior kind, and among the wreckage there were green branches such as men carry on an embassy for a sign of peace, and nowhere any sign of the whitened war shields. Only one man came alive out of the wreckage, and he had been broken senseless across the rocks. The men who drew him to land would have finished him then and there, as one finishes a wounded viper, but he cried out something about the Painted People and the Saxon kind. That was enough to make the man with the dagger hold his hand. They carried him up to the fisher huts in the hope that there might be more to be got from him—and sent word to me."

"Torture?" I said. I am not squeamish where the Scots or the Saxons are concerned, but I have never liked the business, needful though it be at times, of roasting a man over a slow fire or slipping a dagger point under his fingernails to come at the thing he has to tell. It is not pity, but merely that I feel too sharply the skin parch and blister, the dagger point shrieking under my own nails.

"In the state he was in, if we had tried torture then, he would have found his escape by dying under our hands; so we let him bide for a few days, in hope that he might regain strength a little, and in the end there was no need. The fever took him. It was a talking fever, and he talked for a day and a night before he died."

"You are sure that his story was not the mere raving of delirium?"

"I have seen many men die in my time; I know the difference between the raving of delirium and a man crying out in fever the secrets on his heart. . . . Besides, when one comes to think of it, the story is a likely one, isn't it?"

"Horribly likely. If it be true, pray God they cannot get the fire blazing before we have had time to deal with Hengest in Eburacum. That must come first—it is in my mind that next year is likely to be something of a race against time."

That night we did indeed feast like heroes, and afterward made merry, though we missed Bedwyr and his harp. And next morning after we had made certain plans and exchanged certain promises between us, Kinmarcus rode off with his companions, the little wild-eyed mare dancing under him like a bean on a bake stone.

The day that followed was a good day; one of those days that do not greatly matter in the pattern of things, but linger, comely-shaped and clear-colored in the memory when the days of splendor and disaster have become confused. I had had no time until then to spare for anything farther afield than the in-pastures where some of our mounts were already out at grass. But that morning, after Kinmarcus was away, I sent for Arian, who was rested by that time, and with Cei and Flavian and young Amlodd, rode out to look at the horse runs.

Winter, which had seemed almost upon us, had drawn back a little, and the day had the softness of early autumn; a light west wind soughing across the gently undulating levels, the sun veiled by a silver haze, and the shriveled brown leaves drifting from the long belts of oak coppice shaped askew by the Atlantic gales, that crested many of the faint lifts of land. Here and there, little dark cattle turned to stare at us with slowly moving jaws as we rode by —fewer than there would have been last month, before the autumn slaughtering—or a knot of ponies would scatter and canter a bow-shot away, then turn to stare also, tossing their rough heads and snorting. Near the villages men were at the late autumn plowing followed by a wheeling and crying cloud of gulls, and the smell of moist freshly turned earth was a thing to shake the heart. A few miles from Deva we came to the huddle of turf bothies among hay and bracken and bean stacks, where the herdsmen lived; and were told by a small man with a squint to make one cross one's fingers and the bowlegs of one born on horseback, that Hunno was out with the herd. So we headed for the long shallow valley of our own training runs.

In Arfon our breeding runs were enclosed for the most part with dry-stone walling, for loose stone is plentiful among the hills; here, too, there was some stone, but it was less easily come by, and in some places, taking advantage of scrub and coppice there already, the dry-stone gave place to hedges of roughly steeped thorn, while at the lower end, which was marshy, the valley was closed by a dike and turf wall.

We met old Hunno on a small rough-coated pony, with a strip-ling whom I did not know riding another behind him, jogging up from the marsh end of the valley. Clearly he had been making his daily round of the boundaries. He looked exactly as he had done when I saw him last, exactly as he had done since I first remem-bered him; the wide lipless mouth, the little bright eyes peering out from the shadow of the enormous sheepskin hat he always wore—I could swear it was the same hat, too. "Heard you was back in Deva." He greeted me as though we had last met maybe a week ago. And then, faintly accusing, "I been expecting you any time these last three days."

"I could not come before," I said. "Too much else to see to. How does it go, Hunno old wolf?"

He gestured with a hand like a knotted furze root. "How does it look?"

But I had no need to follow his pointing finger. I had been look-ing, all the way down from the head of the valley, joying in the sight of young horses grazing by the stream, war-horses in the making, as a miser joys in the gleam of gold trickling through his fingers. "It looks well enough from here," I said. We had never dealt in superlatives together, but we smiled, eye into eye.

"Come and take a look at closer quarters." He jerked his chin toward the water, and we rode on together. Amlodd my young armor-bearer, who was a friendly soul, had dropped behind to join the unknown stripling, and Hunno and Flavian, Cei and I rode ahead in a bunch. Many stallions had sprung from those five Septimanian sires, three-, four-, and even a few five-year-olds; and one look at the big-boned youngsters who scattered at our coming and then turned back in curiosity was enough to tell me that the plan was working out. Not all of them were as tall or as heavy in build as their sires, but all stood at least two hands higher than our native breed.

"All broken?" I asked.

"All rough-broken. A few of the three-year-olds are not finished yet. It's none too easy to get enough men for the task, not what I'd call skilled men, not in these fat Lowlands." Hunno spat with great accuracy into the silky head of a seeding marsh thistle, in token of his opinion of the Lowland horsemen.

"You'll have enough breakers *this* year, at all events."

By the time that we had seen all we wished to see in the training runs, and Hunno had signaled finish to the lads whom he had called up to put the best of the young stallions through their paces, the autumn day was drawing on. And as we went up over the brow of the ridge heading for the one breeding run that we had in the Lowlands, Hunno said, "Best come up to the corral, and we'll drive the rest for you. If you try riding the whole valley, 'twill be dusk before we're half done, and you'll likely miss the best of the colts."

I nodded; we were in Hunno's hands, and this was his kingdom, and on the crest of the ridge, among the wind-shaped thorns that grew there, reined in and sat looking down the gentle slope seaward, toward the breeding run maybe half a bowshot away. The valley before us was better sheltered than the one we had left, with thick low oak woods on the seaward side, a good place for its purpose; and at the upper end of it, among his quietly grazing mares and their foals, I could see the dark masterful shape of the stallion. The long sweep of the valley was only lightly enclosed, for there were few wolves in those parts, and if any of the little native stallions who ran free on the marshes should attempt to break into the mares, the lord of the herd would deal with him; while, with a

stallion contented among his own thirty or forty mares, there was
far less risk of a breakout than among the unmated youngsters in
the training runs.

I wheeled Arian and we set off again for the stone-walled corral
at the head of the valley, passing as we went the furze-roofed
shelters for the mares at foaling time, and coming to the corral gate
we tethered the mounts to a thornbush and Cei and Flavian and I
settled down to wait, while Amlodd went off with the other two to
help drive the horses.

The black stallion had been watching us ever since we came
down to the edge of his domain, not uneasy, but wary on behalf
of his mares; he snorted and tossed his head, his mane flying up
in a dark cloud, and came up at the trot, in a wide unhurried
circle to come between us and them.

"The Black One takes good care of his own," Flavian said.

Old Hunno called out to him softly and unintelligibly as he
trotted by on his shaggy pony, and the great horse ruckled down
his nose in greeting. Bedwyr had been right about that one.

Hunno and his little troop trotted on, dwindling small into the
distance, casting about the lower end of the valley, half out of
sight among the furze and thorn scrub that dipped toward the
marshes. And presently we saw the whole valley moving toward
us. We heard the shouting of the drivers, and a few moments later
the soft smother of unshod horses on the grass. They came up at a
trot, long-drawn-out like a great skein of flighting duck, the herdsmen on their little rough ponies shepherding them on the flanks;
and for a moment I was snatched back to a spring day in Nant
Ffrancon, eight years ago. They were being herded in through the
opening with shouts and cries, the wild-eyed mares with their colts
still running at heel, the yearlings and the rough-coated two-year-
olds who would be for that winter's breaking; awkward, scary,
curious as to the meaning of this thing. And among them still, a
little gray in the muzzle now but still mighty, on guard over his
own, the Black One. I saw Amlodd riding with the herdsmen,
flushed under his freckles and bright-eyed as a girl in love; and
after the hurdles had been set up at the wide entrance, he dropped
from his horse's back and came to me with the bridle looped over
his arm, laughing and breathless. "Oh my Lord Artos—sir—I should
have made a good herdsman if I were not your armor-bearer!"

[97]

"By the time that you are captain of the third squadron," said Flavian, naming his own rank and speaking from experience, "you'll have served often enough as both, I promise you." And he tossed the knot of bright hawthorn berries that he had been playing with, into the hand that the boy flung out to catch it, and turned to the trampling mass of horses.

I went first to the Black One, who in the way of his kind had drawn out from the rest to stand a little to one side, where he could have all things under his eye. He stood with his head alertly up to watch our coming, swishing his tail behind him, but no more uneasy than he had been at first, because of the familiar figure in the old sheepskin hat who walked with me.

"If you had been Bedwyr the Harper," Old Hunno said, "he would have come to you."

"I wonder—does a horse remember so well from year's end to year's end?"

"He doesn't forget the man that won and mastered him," Hunno grunted. "No more than a woman forgets the man that had her virginity—it's the same thing in a way."

I gave him a lick of salt, which he took with aloof deliberation, accepting with it the fact that I was not an enemy; and having made that clear to him, I turned in with Flavian and Cei to see my fill of the mares and their young. We moved in and out among them, pausing to look at this one and that, examining, judging, feeling latent strength and responsiveness in slim haunches and supple neck, while Hunno forced up a head with back-laid ears or slapped aside a woolly rump to make way for us in the press. And afterward, those that seemed to me the finest were brought out to us separately, mare and foal, yearling and two-year-old, colt and filly. In all of them the same thing was apparent, the increase of height, the added weight of bone.

"God is good," said Cei, who was a religious man after his own fashion.

Finally I beckoned Hunno over again. "The chestnut mare over there, with the white foal—bring them out to me."

I had been noticing that mare and foal ever since they were driven up to the corral, or rather, I had been noticing the foal, but had kept him until the last, childishly enough, lest the rest of the day, coming after, should seem a lesser thing.

Hunno cut them out from the herd and brought them to me, and I had a feeling, seeing his grin, that he also had been saving this foal for the last, hoping that I would not call for him before. I set about gaining the dam's confidence first, fondling her neck and making small love talk into her twitching ear (for with the mother's confidence the foal's would come the more easily), before I turned my attention to the young one. He was a rawboned stallion foal, much younger than most of his kind; indeed, I judged him to have been born at summer's end or early autumn, as sometimes happens when a mare comes late into season or remains horsey after her proper time. He was not white as yet, but gray as a signet, yet any who had encountered such a foal before could see that by the third year he would be white as a swan. An uncommon color nowadays; but they used to say that there was Libyan blood in most of the Roman cavalry mounts, and there were many white horses of that breed, and he must have been a throwback in color through his mother to some cavalry horse of the Eagles. One could sense the promise in him already, as he stood beside his mother, uncertain of himself, torn between his desire for the reassurance of the milk that he had almost outgrown, and his curiosity as to these men he had never seen before. The fire of his mother's race was in him, and the power and steadiness of his sire's. He was only a very little afraid of me, especially when he saw that his mother was content to let my hand rest on her neck. Among my own hills, the foals that run wild on the mountain grasslands and are rounded up only twice a year come wild as hawks to the breaker's hand; but those that are born of tamed mothers in the home runs, we are accustomed to handle from the day of their birth, and these "gentled" foals are always the more easily broken when the time comes. So the smoky foal was used to men's hands on him. He was a little shy of me, because my hand was a stranger's, but my palm to lick —there must have been the taste of salt on it still—soon won him over, and he allowed me to gentle the harsh furry tuft where his crest would be, and draw a finger down his nose to the soft muzzle, caressing him, feeling the promise of him, the small half-shy response under my hand. I knew all at once and with complete certainty that here was my war-horse of a future day when staunch old Arian should come to honorable retirement. I always rode a white horse in battle; it is not that I find them better than horses of another color, but that a white horse marks out the leader clearly for his men to follow; it also marks him clearly for the enemy, but that is a thing that there is no help for. Besides, it is not to the Saxons alone that the White Horse is sacred, else why should men, before even the Legions came, have cut a white Dragon Horse half a hillside high in the chalk above the vale that runs to the very heart of the land? It is fitting that a white horse and no other color should lead the war hosts of Britain into battle. . . .

Autumn-foaled and autumn-found—I knew the name that was his as by right; I should call him Signus, for the four stars of Signus the Swan, that comes winging up into the southern sky just at the time of the autumn gales.

I gave it to him now, as a kind of covenant between us. "Signus —Signus, I call you. Remember that, small one, against the day that we go into battle together."

And the foal ducked his head and then tossed it up again. It was no more than my hand on his muzzle, but it looked like agreement. We all laughed, I remember; and the foal, suddenly turning shy, backed a little, and wheeling about on long splayed legs, turned himself to the comfort and reassurance of his mother's milk.

Later, sitting on our hams about the crackling furze fire in the herdsmen's bothy, Old Hunno brought out a jar of fermented mare's milk (it is wonderful what unlikely things can be used to make fire-drink) and the peeled willow wands on which he kept the tallies, both of his own and those which Amgerit his son sent down to him every year from the Arfon breeding runs, that the whole record might be kept as one. There, marked by variously shaped notches on the white wands, was the record of every foal born in the last seven years. Round about ninety to a hundred foals a year, save for the third year, when there had been less than half that number. "That was a bad black year," Hunno said, "a wet spring, a drowned spring, both here and in the hills. And there was more than a score of foals dropped dead, besides them that sickened later; and we lost heavily among the mares too. But this year— Ah now, this year has been a good one; see—" The old brown finger with its ridged and back-curved nail moved up the newest and whitest of the willow wands, touching mark after mark. "A hundred and thirty-two-three-four-five—a hundred and thirty-six, seventy-three of them colts; and we have lost no more than nine. The number of births goes up, look you, because we have added certain of the young mares to the breeding herd."

Besides the occasional losses, there had of course been some horses that did not come up to the needful standard, besides mares who were stallion-shy or consistently bad breeders, and Hunno had sold off these poorer beasts as I had bidden him, to pay for fodder or occasionally for other horses; but save for these sales, we had kept faithfully to the original plan, however sore our need, of not drawing on the herd until it had had time to become well established. But now the time had come when we might safely begin to do so and we looked at each other about the furze fire with brightening eyes. "We have done well to wait so long," I said, "and now, thanks to your good stewardship, Hunno old wolf, we can begin to draw on the herd."

He nodded. "What have you in mind?"

"All the half-bred stallions of four and five years old—the Septimanians are enough to serve as many mares as we possess—possibly some of the three-year-olds, too, come the spring, when they are fully broken. That should give us something over two hundred and fifty."

"What of the surplus mares?"

"Not for us," I said. "Too precious to be risked in war save in the last ditch. Let them go back to free range in the hills; they may do something to improve the stock, and we can call them in again in another year should we need them."

There was a great content in me. We should be able to replace half our present mounts, who were mostly fen horses by that time, good willing brutes but without much fire; and they could go to form a reserve with the rest of the newcomers. (Never wise to put too many raw mounts into the battle line in any one year, however well trained they be.) We had never been able to count on a reserve of spare mounts until now; and God knew how sorely we had sometimes needed them. God, as Cei had said, was good.

When the jar was empty and many things had been talked over, we took our leave, and set out once more for Deva. The mare's milk was the most potent liquor that has ever come my way. I have always had a hard head, but that night the stars were the color of honeysuckle and soft as the stars of midsummer. I think we sang

CARL A. RUDISILL LIBRARY
LENOIR RHYNE COLLEGE

a little, on the road back to the City of Legions. But it was not all the mare's milk.

It was well into the second watch of the night when we got back, but a handful of men who were none of mine were standing under the lantern at the entrance to the old officers' courtyard. They were well-set-up lads, all young and hard, and they had their weapons with them. What they wanted I thought I could guess, even before one of them—it was the youngster who had carried my message to Kinmarcus—stepped forward to my stirrup. "Sir, my Lord Artos, may we have a word with you?"

"I expect so." I dismounted and handed Arian over to my armor-bearer, with an extra pat because I felt all at once the guilt of disloyalty to him. "Take over," I said to Cei, and gesturing the newcomers to follow me, led the way to my quarters. The lantern was lit and there was a small fire burning in an earthenware brazier, and I sat down beside it, holding out my hands chilled from the bridle rein, for the softness of the past day was turning raw, and looked at the young men crowding before me. "Well? What is the thing that you wish to say to me?"

The one who had been my messenger answered for the rest. "Sir, we have brought you our swords, we would join the Company that rides with you."

I looked into their eager and earnest faces. "You are very young, all of you."

"Fion is the youngest of us, and he will be eighteen next month. We are all made men and carry our own weapons, my Lord Artos."

I leaned forward studying them, face after face. What I saw there pleased me, but certainly they were all very young. "Listen," I said. "There are two degrees of following me. I want men for the Company, yes; I always want men for the Company. But I want also—" I hesitated, seeking for the word: "Auxiliaries and irregulars; men to serve with me as light horsemen, as archers and scouts and spearmen, as faithfully as my Companions serve with me as heavy cavalry; men who will follow me out over their own frontiers when the need arises, and hold to me for as long as I need them—knowing always that as soon as I can spare them, in a year, or two, or three, they will be free to return again to their own homes. For the men who ride with me as my Companions, the thing is very different. From them I demand loyalty to myself and to each other, alone and for all time—or at least until the last Saxon looses his hold from the last headland of the British coast. We are a brotherhood, and for us there can be no bond outside, and no release after a few years. By your faces you would seem to be such men as my heart calls to, and gladly I will accept your swords in one degree or the other; but before you decide, in God's name think. You have all your lives to live, and afterward there can be no way back with honor."

They glanced at each other; one, a red-haired youth, licked his lower lip, another fidgeted with the handle of his dirk. "Go home," I said. "Talk it over, put it under your pillow and sleep on it; and come to me again in the morning."

Another man shook his head. "We came this evening to lay our weapons at your feet, and we would not go back to our own hearths again with the thing still unsettled. "Give us leave to speak together in your doorway for a few moments, my Lord Artos."

"Surely, for as many moments as you wish." I drew my dagger and fell to burnishing it with the tail of my cloak, abandoning them and their councils. They drew aside into the doorway, and I heard the low mutter of their voices for a while. Then the pad of their feet came across the floor, and I looked up to see them standing before me again. The boy who had been my messenger stood a little out from the rest, and two more with him. As before, he acted as spokesman for the rest.

"My Lord Artos, we have taken council together and we have decided. These behind me will serve you truly in the second of the ways you offer. They have bonds of their own that cannot be broken; two of them have wives and bairns—but we three, Finnen and Corfil here, and myself, Brys Son of Bradman, we have no bond to hold us, therefore we bind yours upon us gladly. If you will have us for your Companions, then we are yours under the Red Dragon, without thought of sitting at our old hearths again."

And another asked, "Is there an oath to swear? Whatever it is, we will swear it."

"You have sworn oath enough," I said.

And so the first of the gathering that Kinmarcus had foretold was well begun, the gathering that was to continue through all the dark months ahead until, when spring returned, I found myself with a goodly war host at my back.

[103]

CHAPTER NINE

War Horns in the Spring

W E had all but given up hope of Bedwyr's return, when at last he appeared with the grain carts and the escort, looming out of a snowstorm that drove sideways in mealy drifts before a black wind from the northeast. Men and horses alike were near to the point where they drop and do not rise again; but behind him the light baggage carts were piled high with grainskins or covered with roped-down tent cloths. "It is a thing that has its uses, to be a prince in Arfon," he said when we brought him and his fellows into the mess hall. "Even one born under a hawthorn bush," and he staggered down beside the fire and sat there, his head hanging, while the snow thawed on his eyelashes. I think he was not more than half conscious. "They say—the harvest was good in Môn. There will be a few more cartloads in the spring, if the roads are open early enough."

Somebody brought him a cup of heather beer, and he drank it off, and a little color came back into his ashen face. When I left him to oversee the storing of the grain, he had unslung the doeskin harp bag from his shoulders, and taken out his beloved harp, and begun to finger the white-bronze strings, making sure that no harm had come to it from the cold.

That winter we had no time to go out of condition, no time for the dullness of spirit that sometimes comes over a winter camp and must be guarded against as one tries to guard against fever and the flux. We had oats and barley in the granary now, but it had to be ground, and since if we wanted to eat meat we must get it for ourselves, some of us were always on the hunting trail. It was as I had said to Kinmarcus, we lived as the outposts had done in the old days, the corn in the granary and the boar in the woods; only with us it was mostly red deer and sometimes wolf—wolfmeat is none so bad eating, if one is hungry enough. There was much work needed about the camp, too, for the old fortress had been little but a ruin when we rode in.

There were the cavalry horses to be tended also; daily weapon practice lest the eye grow slow and the sword arm stiff; armor and gear to be reviewed, and new men and horses broken in. And on Sundays the priest who had helped Gwalchmai with the wounded on that first night of all came up from the city to preach God's Word on the weed-grown parade ground. Most of us gathered to these services, though I think that among the ranks who stood bareheaded in the cold to listen, and afterward turned man to man with the kiss of peace, there were some who made their own prayers to Mithras or even Nuada of the Silver Hand and the remote and misty gods of their own hills. The kindly little priest would have been saddened if I had told him that, but it has never seemed to me to matter very greatly. I have always been a follower of the Christos, because it has seemed to me that the Christian faith is the strongest and best fitted to carry the light forward into the darkness that lies ahead. But I have prayed to too many different gods in my time, to set any very great store by the names that men cry out to for aid, or the form of prayers they use.

The months wore on and the months wore on, and there came no further news out of the north, by the ways that were closed by snow and mire and storm waters. But though there was no more news, I heard much, that winter, concerning Caledonia, all the same.

From Daglaef the Merchant, I heard it. He came jogging into Deva by the road from the Wall, only the day before Bedwyr and the grain carts returned from Arfon, riding a good horse and followed by a string of four pack mules with their drivers, and two couple of white-breasted Caledonian boarhounds running in leash behind him.

By and by word drifted up to the fortress that one Daglaef the Merchant had returned to his own place for the winter, after a whole summer spent, as he had spent summers before, trading in Caledonia. A great thing it is, to be one of the merchant kind, who can pass safe and welcome where a war host could scarce win through. I made haste to inquire of Lucianus, he who was chieftain or chief magistrate, as to the man's trustworthiness, and Lucianus's report on him being good ("I have never yet got anything cheap from Daglaef, but on the other hand I've never bought a pot from him that cracked the first time spice wine was poured into it, nor a cloak in which the colors ran, nor a hound that turned out to be not the one I paid for"), I sent to Daglaef himself, bidding him to sup with me.

He came, a square-built, sandy-gray man with a small bright eye that seemed always cocked for a bargain, wrapped in a mantle of magnificently dressed badger skins; and when supper was over and we drew to the brazier, began proceedings by trying to sell me a dagger of Eastern workmanship, with the ivory hilt carved into the likeness of a naked woman.

"Na," I said, "I have already a dagger that feels familiar to my hand. It was not for your wares that I called you here."

"For what, then? Assuredly not for the honor of my company, my Lord the Count of Britain?" He grinned at me, slipping back his mantle in the warmth, and began to play with the string of silver and coral beads at his throat, in the way that I came to know later was a habit with him.

"For your knowledge of what lies beyond the Wall."

"That is easily summed up—hills and heather, and northward among the forests of Mannan, a people who speak a dark tongue and can seldom be trusted to keep a bargain."

"And fire smoldering among the heather," I said.

He ceased to finger the bright beads. "So you know of that."

"Something of that—and I would know more. I would know also the shape of the land and the run of the roads beyond the Wall."

"I am a merchant, and frontiers and tongues and peoples are not for me as they are for other men. Are you so sure, then, that I shall tell you the truth?"

"Lucianus says he never had a cloak from you in which the colors ran, nor a hunting dog that turned out to be not the one he paid for."

"So." Daglaef cocked an eyebrow at me with cheerful effrontery. "But I am very sure he told you also that he never had anything cheap from me—let alone free."

I took a gold currency bracelet—I could ill spare it—from my wrist, and tossed it to him. "I am prepared to pay, so that the hunting dog proves to be the one I paid for."

He laughed, tossing the bracelet between his hands, then abruptly stowed it away beneath his mantle, and thrusting aside the strewn fern with his foot, pulled a bit of half-charred stick from the fire. "The land and the roads first, then. . . ."

It was late, when at last we were done with my questions and his answers, and with his badger-skin robe already swathed about him to depart, he tried again to sell me the dagger with the hilt like a naked woman. I bought it as a gift for Cei.

After that, Daglaef the Merchant came on another evening, not to sell, but simply as one man to sit by another's fire and drink a pot of beer and pass an hour or two. He was a great talker, and listening to him on those long winter evenings, as I have always loved to listen to the talk of travelers, I heard tales of strange lands and stranger peoples, of beasts as large as mountains moving and with tails at both ends, of long sea voyages and distant cities; but also, in and out between all these things, much more concerning Caledonia and the Caledonians.

It was February, and I remember that there were snowdrops appearing through the sodden brown of last year's fallen leaves in what remained of the Commandant's garden, when Flavian came looking for me one evening. I had formed a fondness for the place, scarcely larger than a good-sized room, shut within half-ruined walls; it had a quiet of its own, remote from the bustle of the fortress, that made it a good place to come to when I wanted to think. I had been pacing up and down and then sitting on the bench of green-stained marble, thinking of the things that Daglaef the Merchant had told me, and wondering how they were going to fit into any plan of action; and when I turned to go back to my quarters, there he was, just behind me.

I noticed that there were three snowdrops, fully out, stuck into the shoulder strap of his worn leather tunic, which struck me as odd, more like Cei than Flavian. "Sir—" he began. "Sir—" and seemed for the moment unsure how to go further.

"Well," I said, "what is it, Flavian? Not trouble with the squadron?"

He shook his head.

"What, then?"

"Sir, I—I have come to ask leave to take a girl from her father's hearth."

I cursed inwardly. It happened from time to time, and for the Company it was a bad thing. "You mean legally, before witnesses?"

He nodded. "Yes, sir."

I sat down again on the bench. "Minnow, I've never forbidden the Companions to marry, you know that; I have no right, and besides, I am well aware that I should have no Company if I did; but none the less, I don't like it. Let a man take the girl he fancies to bed with him when he wants to laugh and make love, and be warm in the winter nights; there's no harm in that, and afterward he is a free man to kiss and ride away. But the bond that he forges when he takes a wife—that is not good for men who fight the kind of war that *we* fight."

Flavian's face was troubled but perfectly steady in its resolve. "Sir, the bond is forged already; going before witnesses can make no difference. We belong to each other, Teleri and I."

"In every way?"

"In *every* way." His eyes were clear and quiet, and they never wavered.

"Then if it makes so little difference, why marry her?"

"So that if—if there's a child, no one can point a finger at her."

"So the Minnow also has done his begetting under a hawthorn bush." I was silent for a while, crumbling the chill emerald moss from the back of the bench under my fingers. I understood the three snowdrops now. Teleri must have stuck them there with the fingers of love, while they spoke, no doubt, of how he would come to me for my leave to marry her. "Who and what is she, this girl?" I asked, after a while.

Flavian had been standing stiffly before me all the while. "Just a girl—little and brown like a bird that you hold in your hand. Her father is a wool merchant."

"You have little enough to offer. Will he give her to you?"

"Yes, because I am of your Companions, and because there might be the babe."

"If I give you leave to marry her, you know how it must be, don't you? You leave her in her father's house when we march in

the spring; and it may be that one day we shall come back to make
our winter quarters in Deva again, and it may be not; and it may
be that one day you will be able to send for her to some other
place, or again it may be not; but either way you leave her in her
father's house. I'll have no virtuous wives following the camp to
cause trouble, only whores."

"I understand—we both understand that, sir."

I heard myself sigh. "So be it, then. Go and tell her. And Minnow, hand over the squadron to Fercos first. You need not come
back into camp tonight."

"*Yes,* sir." He looked down and then up again. "I don't know
how to thank you, sir, I have not the words—but if I could serve
you more truly than I have done since the days that I was your
armor-bearer, I would." His grave face flashed for a moment into
its rare laughter. "If it would give you the least satisfaction to have
my hide for a riding rug, you have but to say the word."

"I think Teleri might like it better on your back than Arian's,"
I said. "Go now. She will be waiting."

He drew himself up in the old formal legionary salute, and
turned and strode away.

I remained sitting on the weather-stained bench, hearing his
tread fade into the distant sounds of the camp, and I knew that I
would have given everything I possessed in the world, to be as the
Minnow was tonight. Everything save the leadership of three hundred men and the thing that we fought for. But when I came to
think of it, that was all I did possess.

Spring came, and we heard the curlews calling far into the night
as they came in from the salt marshes to nest on the higher ground.
Bedwyr set off once more for Arfon, and once more got back with
the grain carts filled; green flame ran through the woodlands, and
above the marshes the furze was on fire. A wild unrest seized us
all, but as yet there was nothing we could do save wait.

There began to be rumors of black war boats on the coast far
north of the Wall; of Pictish envoys having been seen in this place
and that. One day a hunter with wolfskins for sale came to me
from the North, saying: "My Lord the Bear, last autumn the Cran
Tara went out, and now the Scots and the Painted People and the
Sea Wolves are hosting. I saw a band of the White Shield Warriors

on the track from the west with my own eyes, and they say that Huil Son of Caw stands at the Dun of his forefathers to lead them." Two days later one of my own scouts came in with the same story and showed me a Scottish arm ring with dried blood like rust between the coils to prove it. Kinmarcus had been right, and this year would indeed be a race against time. . . . And still, as yet, there was nothing that we could do but wait, praying that the waiting time would not be long.

That is the disadvantage of cavalry in the North or in mountain country; one cannot march until long after the true start of the campaigning season. One must wait until there is grass enough to feed the horses, and that may be May, even the start of June in a late season; whereas those who go to war for the most part on foot, as the Saxons do, can take the war trail a month earlier. We had no means of knowing whether Hengest and Octa would use that advantage to march on us while we were still bound in winter quarters, or whether they might be waiting for reinforcements, or planned to make their stronghold at Eburacum and hold it against us when we came. It was hard to wait so, for Hengest to take the initiative, and for myself, I have always hated to fight on the defensive, though many of my greatest fights have been defensive ones. But I thought that in the long run, our advantage might equal theirs, simply because if the battle was finally joined close to Deva, we should have short supply lines, whereas theirs would be perilously long—always supposing that the menace from the North did not strike before Hengest did. Everything depended on that.

So we lived through that April in a growing fever with one eye always cocked toward the dark moorland shoulder of Black Bull, a day's march away, where the nearest of our watchers and signal fires waited. And at last it came to May Day Eve. . . .

That evening Cei and I had been out to sup with old Lucianus. Bedwyr was not of our company, for it was a law among us that all three were never out of camp at the same time. We had drunk a good deal, for it was one of those parties of the old imperial pattern one seldom met with now, in which the women withdrew as soon as the meal was over, and the men chose a drinking master and got down to the business of the evening. Our host had brought up in our honor the last of his treasured amphorae of Red

Falernian, and when at last we came up the street and turned in through the fortress gates, the rich fumes of it were still in our heads, making the stars dance widdishins and our feet seem curiously far away. And as neither of us wished to wake next morning with dizzy heads and tongues like old leather, we turned aside from the sleeping quarters as by mutual consent, and climbing the steps to the narrow rampart walk, leaned there side by side, with our hot foreheads to the little thin east wind.

"Ah now, that is better!" said Cei, thrusting back the russet hair from his forehead, and snuffing like a hound. "No air down there in that cursed house."

Fulvius, whose turn it was to take the second watch, had come strolling along the rampart walk to lean his elbows on the coping beside us. He laughed, the quiet laugh of a man on night watch. "Too many vine leaves in your hair?"

Yesterday, with the long strain of waiting which had begun to shorten tempers all around, Cei would have flown into a fury over that, but tonight the wine seemed to have mellowed him, and he answered peacefully enough. "Did you ever see a man with vine leaves in his hair walk up that deathtrap of a rampart stair without a stagger?"

"I've seen you walk the Bath Gardens wall at Lindum without a stagger," I said, "when you were so dripping with vine leaves that most other men would have been lying on their backs in the kennel singing murky love songs to the stars."

"I have a headache," said Cei with dignity. "It was too hot in that cursed place of Lucianus's. Shouldn't have had the brazier glowing like that—May Eve, not midwinter."

"There'll be plenty of folk besides Lucianus keeping good fires tonight," said Fulvius. "You can see fifteen Beltane fires from the ramparts here—I've counted them a score of times since I came up, for want of something better to do."

Almost without thinking, with some idea, I suppose, of finding more than Fulvius, I began idly to do the same. I have always loved to see the fires on the hills at Beltane, making the old magic of returning life. One always burned on the high hill shoulder behind Dynas Pharaon, and many a time when I was a boy I have helped to drive the bellowing cattle through the sinking flames to make them fruitful in the coming year. I leaned my back against the rampart, and looked across the camp toward the western mountains, thinking of those fires; but that way the hills were dark. It must have been more than fifty miles away, even had there been no mountains in between.

Plenty of other fires, though, some near, some very far, like red seeds scattered in the dark bowl of the night. Turning slowly I also counted my fifteen, and could make it no more. And then suddenly, so far off that I could not be sure in the first few moments whether I was seeing it at all, there was another. I looked away, and then back again; it was still there, the faintest spark of ruddy light clinging to the skyline of the mountains away eastward. "Sixteen," I said. "Sixteen, Fulvius—there, on the rim of the mountains."

They both looked where I pointed, and were silent a moment, picking it up. "It is a star rising over the rim of High Wood," said Cei.

Fulvius made a swift gesture of denial. "Na! This isn't the first night I've kept watch up here; there's no star rises at this hour over the crest of High Wood, no star as red as that anywhere, not even the Warrior. It's a fire all right—but it wasn't there when the Beltane fires were lit. It wasn't there fifty heartbeats ago."

A sudden silence caught us all by the throat. I felt my own heartbeat quicken and knew that it was the same with the other two. And then, on the bare crouched shoulder of Black Bull, only fifteen or twenty miles away, in almost direct line between us and the sixteenth fire, there was a sudden blink of light that wavered and sank and spread, and sprang up even while we watched with straining eyes, into a ragged flower of flame.

"The Saxons," I said. And I remember the relief that broke over me like a wave that the long months of waiting were over and Hengest was here while the Northern menace still hung on the edge of breaking. I remember also that the last fumes of the Falernian were gone from my head as though a wind had risen and blown them clear away.

"God be praised that they chose Beltane!" Cei said.

I had been thinking the same thought. It had troubled me a good deal that any fire or smoke signal lit for us must be clear to the Saxons also, warning them all too surely that their advance had been seen and the advantage of surprise lost to them, and so putting them on their guard. But on May Eve, with the whole country aspark with Beltane fires, the signal would carry no meaning for them.

"How long do you reckon we've got?" Cei said.

"Four days, maybe. Enough, but not more than enough." I had turned back to the rampart steps. "Go and rout me out Prosper and his trumpet. I want everybody on the parade ground."

This time it should be we who picked the battleground. The enemy must advance by the old military road, for to trust to the mountain herding paths, or strike across country through the damp-oak scrub and the peat bogs that filled the valleys would be to go leaping on disaster. And knowing this, we had in fact chosen our place some time ago. It was a spot some five or six miles in advance of Deva, where the road from over the mountains, dipping into a marshy valley, forded a little river, then climbed again gently, almost lazily, up the western slope. The soft upward swell of the valley on that side, the Deva side, was crested by a long comb of thorn and tangled oak woods that reached for a mile or more in either direction; and through this narrow belt, as through a hedge, the road ran straight to the west gate of the City of Legions. In the old ordered days the trees had been cut back in the usual way, for a bowshot on either side of the road, but now all manner of quick-growing scrub had come creeping back, hazel, crack willow, black-thorn and bramble, making a tangle that was almost as difficult to break through as the woods on either hand—and as good cover for men.

In this place, on May Day morning, we set about preparing a welcome for Hengest and the Sea Wolves.

We began by felling trees to make a couple of rides through the woodland belt, for the quick bringing up of cavalry, and toward noon on the second day (we had taken our time over this work, not wishing to make a clumsy havoc that would show at a distance) a little dark mountain man of the breed that we sometimes used as scouts came drumming up the road on a shaggy black pony about the size of a big dog, to bring us word of the Saxon war host.

He was brought to me, where I was overseeing the careful screening of one of the ride mouths, and dropping from his pony's back, stumbled and stood swaying, his head bent, his arm across the neck of the wretched little beast that stood with heaving flanks beside him.

"You have ridden hard, my friend," I said. "What news do you bring?"

He tipped back his head slowly, thrusting the matted hair out of his eyes, and looking up at me with narrowed gaze as a man looks up into a tree. "You are he that they call Artos the Bear?"

"I am Artos the Bear."

"So. It is good. Then the Sea Wolves passed at sundown last night, and made their camp among the fringes of Forest Dhu."

"How many? Can you number them at all?"

"I did not see them. They are as the ants that swarm out when a child kicks at an ants' nest; so said the man from beyond Broken Hill. But he carried this—it was given to him by the man before him, and he passed it on to me." The little man took from the breast of his mangy wolfskin mantle a slim billet of wood which reminded me of the peeled willow wands on which Hunno kept his tallies. But this was the tally, not of a horse herd but a Saxon war host; and as he gave it into my hand I read the roughly carved numbers on the shaft: MCDLXX. Close on fifteen hundred men, maybe somewhat more, maybe somewhat less—I knew how difficult it could be to judge numbers when one was not used to it. But still, somewhere around fifteen hundred. The Saxon war host had already trebled its size since last autumn. Had the Picts, despite Kinmarcus's opinion, already leapt over the Wall to join forces with the Sea Wolves of Eburacum? Or had Earl Hengest called up reinforcements from across the North Sea? Well, it made no difference for the moment; it was the numbers that mattered, not where they came from. Against them, allowing for the usual hurts and sickness, I could put something over two hundred and fifty of my own heavy cavalry into the field, and about five hundred tribesmen, more or less trained by now, who had gathered to me as auxiliaries and irregular troops during the winter. If I put the drivers into the fighting line, about a hundred more; and doubtless when the time came there would be a rabble of citizens, valiant and willing, but not much use save in pursuit. The horses would do something, a great deal, to even the desperate odds against us; but not enough. . . .

I handed the man over to my own lads, with orders to feed him

and the exhausted pony, and let them rest in the field camp while
someone else belted back to Deva with their news. Then I sent for
Bedwyr and Cei, and showed them the tally stick. Cei swore at
sight of it, and Bedwyr, with his left eyebrow flying more than
usually like a mongrel's ear, whistled long and liquidly. "It seems
that we shall have hot work when the time comes, my brothers."

"Something too hot for my liking," I said. "Therefore I think,
since I've no mind to gamble against loaded dice when there's any
other way, that we must do something to ease the odds a trifle."

"And that something?"

"Bear traps," I said.

"Strange. I always thought that bear traps were dug for the bear,
not by him."

"Not in the case of this particular bear."

So we set the tribesmen to digging; midway between the stream
and the woodshore a long string of trenches and potholes with
gaps between for the passage of cavalry, cutting straight across the
road and reaching for somewhat over half a bowshot on either
hand. The road crossed the stream on a broad paved ford, at a
spot where the bank was fairly firm, but save for that one spot the
water ran wide and shallow, in a chain of pools between marshy
sallow-fringed banks where a man could become bogged down by
a single unlucky step. Therefore we judged that the Saxons would
not be able to fan out until they were well clear of the valley bottom
and the half bowshot was enough. We cut the trenches about three
feet deep and three to four feet wide, and set a few short stakes,
their ends sharpened and hardened by fire, along their floors for
good measure. And then, just as one does with a bear trap, covered all over with a light latticework of branches, scattering above
it the sodden tawny wreck of last year's bracken still clothing the
hillside at that point. The place where the trench crossed the road
might have been a difficulty, but as the valley was soft, the road
just there was a corduroy of logs carried on a brushwood bed, and
it was a simple matter, after we had cut the trench across, to lay
the logs back over a flimsy hurdlework just strong enough to carry
them but no more. One or two of the logs had rotted through and
had to be replaced, but that might have been done simply in an
attempt to keep the road in some kind of repair; and when the
thing was finished, the hillside looked just as it had looked before.

The spare earth we carried back into the trees, in every trug and basket that Deva could provide.

The thing was finished, and with maybe a day to spare.

That night we camped behind the belt of woods, as we had done ever since the work started, and I called Bedwyr to me. "Beer all around, I think, Bedwyr. The men are all tired; they have worked like heroes and tomorrow they must fight like heroes. But for God's sake see that they don't drink too much. I can't afford to find myself with a camp full of walking corpses in the morning." I went to look for Cei myself, and when I found him in the horse lines, took him aside and issued a private ultimatum. "Cei, I've given the order for beer all around. Don't swill too much of it."

His indignation was, as usual, ludicrous. "Have you ever known me drunk?"

"I've never known you *show* drunk; but nevertheless, it makes you reckless afterward."

He looked at me, half laughing, half indignant still, then flung an arm clashing with blue glass and copper wire bracelets across my shoulder. "I'll not lose you Britain, for the sake of a horn of sour beer."

CHAPTER TEN

Battle Before Deva

LATE that night another of the little dark hillmen rode in on another shaggy pony, to bring us the latest word of Hengest's advance. He was clear of the mountains and into the fringing lowland hills, and his forward scouts were making camp on the wooded flanks of Black Bull. By noon tomorrow, the waiting should be over.

But there was always the chance that the enemy might try a night march, and so there was no lingering next morning. A meal of bannock and hard yellow cheese was doled out to the men at first light, and before the sun was well clear of the woods that crested the opposite ridge, we had taken up our fighting positions; the foot soldiers among the dense low scrub that flanked the road, the mounted archers and the Cymric longbows in the shadows of the trees on either side of them. On the far left, I knew that Bedwyr was waiting with his cavalry wing, as here on the right I held the other. Behind us, among the trees, Fulvius was with the reserves, and away among the woods across the valley, drawn well back from the Saxon's line of advance, Cei—stone-cold sober, for he had kept his promise to me with regard to the heather beer— was lying up with another squadron of fifty or so mounted tribesmen, ready to take the Sea Wolves in the rear, or cut off their line of retreat when the time came.

Hengest, it seemed, had not made a night march, and the day crawled slowly on with no sign of his coming. It was a soft day of veiled sunlight, with a silver bloom on the distant hills, and the milky scent of the hawthorn blossom along the woodshore came and went like breath on the little wandering aimless wind that

[117]

seemed at times to lie down and go to sleep in the young bracken. A day when one could not quite believe in the red evening on which the sun must go down. The slow hours wore away; nothing stirred among the wayside scrub save from time to time that small fitful wind silvering the hazel bushes; only in the half shadow under the trees, now and then the jink of a bridle bit or the low voice of a man soothing a restless horse told where the cavalry waited—waited. . . .

I put up my hand to feel that the knot of hawthorn was still in the forehead band of my helmet—it had become a custom with us of the Company always to ride into battle with something of the kind about us, both for identification and as a kind of grace note, a mark of pride. A gadfly bit my old Arian, and he tossed up his head, snorting and trying to flick his tail which was knotted up for battle in the usual way, that no enemy might grab him by it to hamstring him. Somewhere among the far woods the first cuckoo of the year called repeatedly, the sound soft and bloomed with distance. Beyond the scrub, the shining midge clouds danced in the sunshine.

Noon was long past, the shadows of the opposite hillside had gathered themselves up small under the trees, and our own shadows were beginning to flow cool down toward the stream, when there was a kind of dark quiver along the skyline of the opposite ridge, where the Eburacum road lifted over it. I had been staring that way so long that for a moment I could not be sure that it was anything more than the skyline crawling under my tired eyes. I blinked, trying for clear sight, and the flicker came again, more strongly this time, more unmistakably.

The waiting of that interminable day was over.

A few moments more, and it was as though the dark lip of a wave lifted over the crest of the ridge, clung there an instant and then spilled over. And so we saw again the Saxon war host.

They were spreading down into the valley, a swarm of ants, as the scout had said, their center on the road, their wings spread out, thick rather than far, over the firmer ground on either side. The level rays of the westering sun struck jinks of light out of their darkness, the broad fire-flake of a spearhead, the round boss of a shield, the comb of a helmet; and among them the streaming white horsetail standards caught the light and seemed to shine of themselves, harshly bright as the sun-touched wings of a wheeling gull against a thunder sky.

The scout had not been far astray in his estimate; there must be around fifteen hundred of the enemy. It seemed to me that I could feel already the faint trembling of the ground under their advancing feet. I was in the saddle by that time, and I said to Prosper my trumpeter, sitting his horse beside me with the silver-bound aurochs hunting horn we had always used to sing us into battle, "Sound me the 'Mount and Make Ready.'"

He set the silver mouthpiece to his lips, and the familiar notes rang out, not loudly but with a haunting echo under the trees, and instantly there was a stir to the right and left and behind me, as man after man swung into the saddle.

"Now the 'Advance.'"

One cannot use too many different cavalry calls; it is confusing to the men and horses who must obey them, but I had passed to each of the chiefs and my squadron captains, that the first time the Advance sounded that day, it meant simply that the Companions and the spears and javelin men, but not the archers, who were to remain under cover just within the fringe of the scrub, were to move out from the woodshore into the open so that they could be seen by the enemy, and there halt.

While the soft echoes still hung under the branches, there came a brushing and a cracking of twigs, and a surge forward through the undergrowth, the beat of hooves on last year's fallen leaves, and the jingle of bit and harness, and our battle line moved out into the open and drew rein on the clear ground before the woodshore. I bent forward for the dappled bullhide buckler with its boss of gilded bronze that hung from my saddlebow, and swinging it high to my bridle shoulder, gathered up the reins again, sensing rather than hearing the movement echoed all around me. We had begun of late years, as we got larger and heavier horses, to practice the new Byzantine style of warfare. It was far more effective than the old hacking sword charge, but it still seemed strange to me to ride into battle with the slim ashen spear shaft balanced in my hand instead of the familiar sword grip.

The Saxons had seen us; their dark mass checked an instant in its advance, then they set up a great shout, and the quiet valley and the cuckoo's calling were engulfed in the hollow booming of the Saxon war horns that seemed to burst to and fro from wooded crest to wooded crest. And the dark battle mass came rolling on again at an increased pace. That was what I had wanted; for that I had given the order to advance into the open; for it needed no mere orderly oncoming, but the hot-blood hurly of a charge to bring the bear traps into their full use.

"Play me a tune," I said to Prosper. "Just a tune that sounds like mockery."

He grinned, and again putting the mouthpiece to his lips, answered the strident bellowing of the war horns with a lazy rendering of the hunting call that sics the hounds on when the quarry comes in sight. Probably they did not know what it meant, but the mere sound of it was an insult; and across the valley we heard the yell that they set up, and the war horns bellowing again. They were sweeping down toward the ford, the white horsetails lifting and flowing out on the wind of their going, and my old Arian flung up his head and neighed his own defiance to the war horns.

I had wondered how the new crossbred horses would stand up to their initiation. All that winter we had been training them on, breaking them to crowds and hostile shouting and the boom of war horns, teaching them to charge unbroken against men with blunted spears, to stand undismayed against the rush of yelling warriors, to run straight on a target, to use their own ironshod forefeet as weapons; for to get the most worth out of a war-horse, he as well as the man on his back must be a fighter. They had learned well and willingly in the main, with the proud eagerness to understand and do what is wanted that most of the horse kind show, once the first struggle of breaking is over. But would they remember their training now? Now, when the spears were not blunt and they caught the smell of blood?

The Saxons had almost reached the stream; a close-knit mass, shield to shield, shoulder to comrade's shoulder, and as they came, quickening into a loping wolf run, we heard the deadly sound of the Saxon war cry that begins as a murmur like the murmur of distant surf, and swells and swells at last into an appalling roar that seems to shake the very hills. They had taken to the water now, their center crossing by the ford, those on either side splashing as best they could through the shifting shallows, and as they came I saw in their forefront, under the white horse standards, Hengest

himself, in the brave midst of his house carls. An old gray-gold
giant, with the golden arm ring of an earl coiled about his sword
arm, and the low sunlight clashing like cymbals on the bronze-
bound ox horns of his helmet; and at his side a lesser man of half
his age but with something of the same brutish splendor, who
could be no one else than Octa his son.

Of necessity the Saxons had lost their close formation through
the shallows; men were being pushed too far out, so that the battle
line became ragged; the stream was all a yeasty thresh and the
spray sheeted up about them, bright in the level sunlight. They
were across now, closing the ragged shield mass, roaring uphill at
the full charge, though their battlefront was taking on the shape of
a bent bow as the struggling flanks were slowed by the soft ground.

Old Arian began to dance under me, snorting, and I quieted him
with a hand on his neck; he was always impatient for the charge
before the trumpets sounded. Other horses were catching the fret
from him; men, too; suddenly I felt as though I were holding
straining hounds in leash, waiting for the moment to slip them
against the quarry.

I had not long to hold them. The van of the dark onsweeping
mass was halfway up the gentle slope. Another spear's length. The
terrible rhythmic battle shouting broke into a ragged outcry, as
between one step and the next, the innocent bracken-clad hillside
opened to engulf the foremost surge of the great man-wave. The
first rank plunged from view almost before they could yell their dis-
may; those behind could not stop, thrust on by those behind again,
and pitched down on top of their comrades. One of the horsetail
standards lurched and went down, and in a bare heartbeat of time
all was wild confusion, twisting and struggling bodies and the furious and anguished cries of men.

But with the trenches caved in all along their length, the Saxons
could see what lay before them, and the surge forward began
again. Some of the men had chance-struck the gaps of solid ground
between, and were hardly checked at all, some jumped the trenches
or swarmed across over the very bodies of their comrades, while
those in the trenches who had escaped the sharpened stakes began
to scramble out. The war horns were bellowing like wounded bulls.
Nevertheless, the bear traps had done their work, and the impetus
of the charge was broken.

I was aware suddenly, as though they were a part of myself, of the archers hidden among the hazel scrub, each with an arrow notched to his drawn bowstring. The timing was perfect, the struggling chaos along the trenches had barely begun to sink, when the dark flight of arrows that I had been waiting for leapt from among the bushes and thrummed like a cloud of hornets into its midst. Men were down in good earnest now, and I felt how the hidden bowmen stooped forward each one for another shaft from the ground before him or the loose battle quiver hanging at his saddle-bow. . . .

Far along our own line I heard the shout of command, and our spearmen, yelping their own short sharp battle cry, were running forward down the hill. The few Saxon archers on the flank, unable to see where our bowmen loosed from under cover, turned their own short deadly arrows against the spears—and the moment had come to slip the hounds.

"Sound me the charge."

The man beside me set the great horn to his lips, and winded the one long blast that set the echoes flying like startled birds all up and down the valley. From away to the left, almost in the same instant, Bedwyr's trumpeter took up the note; a great shout rose from our men, and both cavalry wings broke forward, the spears that had been resting upright swinging down as one to the horizontal. I crouched low into the saddle, feet braced into my stirrups against the coming shock, feeling through every fiber of my being the balance of the leveled spear against palm and fingers, hearing the flying thunder of the squadron's hooves behind me.

We took them on both flanks, and at the full gallop.

They had no chance to form the shield wall; for the first moments of impact it was not battle as I counted battle, but sheer red butchery. But whatever evil may be cried against the Sea Wolves, no man ever yet called their courage in question. Somehow they closed and steadied their ranks; they fought like heroes; their archers stood like rocks though their numbers grew steadily fewer under dark hail of the long British war shafts, and loosed their own arrows without pause into our ranks. The house carls of the center held us with spear and seax long after the light throwing axes were spent; their naked and stained berserkers flung themselves upon our very spearpoints to dirk our horses from underneath. After-

ward, I was glad that the thing had after all been a battle and not
a massacre. At the time I saw all things through a crimson haze,
and felt very little.

The sun was gone, and the dusk was creeping up the valley like
the slow inflowing of the tide, when they broke at last and turned
to fly. They streamed away, a tattered shadow of the host that had
stormed across the stream in the late sunlight, seemingly so short
a time ago; and as we swept after them, down to the ford, the
single high note of a horn sounded once more, and Cei and his
wild riders swept down upon them out of the far woods.

In the swiftly fading light, the main number got away, all the
same; and leaving Cei to harry them into the hills, the rest of us,
who had borne the chief heat of the fighting, drew off and turned
back toward the long wooded ridge below which the struggle had
taken place, and the work that still waited for us there.

Some of the archers, with the pack train drivers and the women,
were already moving among the fallen figures, looking at each to
see if it were friend or foe, dead or wounded. Our own dead were
being carried aside for burial, the Saxons left for the ravens and
the wolves if any chanced not yet to have drawn off into their
summer fortresses; they would make the Eburacum road un-
savory for a while, but we had other things to do than bury Saxons.
The Saxon wounded were being cleanly knifed; I doubt if they
gave as clean an end to our own men in like case, but I have always
set my face against mutilation, at least of living men, and the few
women who had tried it in the early days had found their mistake.

I abandoned the scene, and when Amlodd had taken Arian
from me (the old war-horse was still sidling and snorting, and
there was blood and brains on his ironshod forehooves) went to
see how it was with our own wounded. A swarm of good folk from
Deva were helping to get the more sorely hurt into carts and farm
sledges. We could not care for them in the camp, and at first light
tomorrow we must be away after the Saxons, to follow up the
day's victory, so it was better for them to be got back to Deva,
even if a few of them died of the jolting on the road. There would
be folk in plenty to care for them; even a surgeon, good though
generally drunk.

A great fire had been lit in the midst of our last night's camp on
the Deva side of the woods; and the carts and sledges were drawn

up on the farthest fringes of the firelight; and Gwalchmai, with a filthy rag twisted around his own left forearm, was limping serenely among the wounded, looking to each as he was brought in through the trees, with the priest and a few of the women to help him. His face was gray and still, with the gentleness and complete withdrawal from all other matters that came to him only when he was plying his craft. I wanted to speak to him, ask him how badly we had suffered; I wanted to speak to some of the men themselves; but that must wait. I never forced questions on Gwalchmai when that look was on his face. I think I had always the feeling that to thrust myself between him and the thing he was doing would be in some way an intrusion.

So I left him and his wounded, and went back to the great fire where the standard had been set up and the food was already being given out and Bedwyr was waiting for me.

"Who is seeing about burying our dead?" I asked.

"Alun Dryfed is in charge just now. I've given orders for the work to be done in relays, for the grave must needs be dug deep, here in the wilderness."

"Save for the amount needed to make good the road, we can use the earth from the trenches to raise a good-sized mound over them for safety."

He nodded, looking into the fire under that one level and mocking eyebrow. "You'll want Brother Simon to patter a few prayers over them before we cover them in?"

I never learned what god Bedwyr worshipped, if any; it certainly was not the Christos. Maybe it was the thing between hand and harp string. . . . "Seeing that we have a priest among us we might as well make use of him," I said. "But there's time enough for the prayers when he has done helping Gwalchmai with the wounded. The living first, the dead after."

"All things in their proper order. Well, there are a good few more of the Saxon kind to feed the wolves than there are for the Christian prayers and the grave mound."

"Yes," I said. "So far as I can judge as yet, our losses have been surprisingly light compared with theirs."

He cocked that flaring eyebrow at me. "Surprisingly? When one thinks of those bear pits?"

I was silent for a moment, and then I said, "It was not the kind of fighting that I would choose. I thought at the first after the Companions came in that it was going to be a massacre. I am glad it flowered into a battle after all."

"You're a strange man, my Lord Artos the Bear. There are times when I think that you come near to loving the Saxon kind."

"Only when I am actually at his throat and he at mine. Not be-fore—and not after."

Two of my own squadron came out from the black gloom of the trees, dragging a body between them. A body that, judging by the way they handled it, was Saxon and none of ours. They flung it down in the full red glare of the firelight, rolling it over onto its back with a silent triumph that shouted more loudly than any voice could do. Then Bericus the Senior said simply, "We found this."

Lying sprawled uncouthly at the foot of the Red Dragon where the men had tumbled him down, there was a certain splendor about him still. An old man, an old giant, with bright hairs that shone like gold wires in the gray jut of his beard and the mane of wild hair outflung about his head. I recognized him first by the earl's bracelet twisted about his sword arm, for a spear had taken him between the eyes, but as I looked more closely into the smashed and blood-pooled face, I recognized the cunning iron-bound mouth, drawn back now in a frozen snarl. I recognized above all, I think, the greatness that seemed to cling about him still, an atmosphere of the thing that had made him a giant in more than body; this ancient enemy of Ambrosius's. Hengest, the Jutish adventurer who had grown to be a war lord of the Saxon hordes, lying flung down like tribute at the foot of the British standard that stirred faintly in the night air above him.

That left the son and grandson to deal with.

"So-o," Bedwyr said softly. "Earl Hengest goes at last to his own Storm Lords again. He should have died on a night of tempest, with the lightning leaping from hill to hill, not a still summer eve-ning with the scent of hawthorn in the air."

"He was a royal stag," I said. "Thank God he is dead."

Later, I had started out on a round of the watch fires, with a half-eaten bannock still in my hand, when Flavian appeared out of nowhere to join me. "Sir, all things are in order with the squad-ron. When do we strike camp in the morning?"

"At first light."

"Then if I am back an hour before that— Deva is only six miles away— If I gave over the squadron to Fercos—"

I stopped and turned to face him. I suppose I was tireder than I knew, and my patience went like a snapped bowstring. "Oh, for God's sake, Flavian! There are about five hours left to dawn; how much good do you suppose the captain of my third squadron is going to be tomorrow if he spends half the night riding about the countryside and the other half tearing his heart out in bed with a girl?"

Even in the dim light of the watch fire I saw how the blood surged up to his forehead, and I was as angry with myself as the instant before I had been with him. I said quickly, "I'm sorry, Flavian. That was unpardonable."

He shook his head. "No, I— It was foolish of me to think of it."

I set my hand on his shoulder. "It was; but not in the way you mean. Did you not say farewell to her before you came away?"

"Yes."

"And do you not suppose it hurt both of you enough that time? Send her word that you are safe; but if you go back now it will be all to suffer again."

"I suppose you are right. It is better for her, maybe—"

As I moved on, he turned back to the fire and took the knot of wilted hawthorn flowers from his shoulder buckle and dropped it into the flames. It was a gesture like a man making a votive offering.

Cei and his band came in during the night, having lost contact with the Sea Wolves in the dark; and at first light, our dead buried and our wounded safely back in Deva, we struck eastward along the Eburacum road on the scent of the fleeing Saxons, with the hunter of the Little Dark People who had first brought us word of their coming, riding with us for a guide. We had lost horses as well as men in the day's fighting, but thanks to the young half-bred stallions, we had still enough to remount any man left horseless, and keep a few spare mounts, even now.

I suppose that to any who have never tried, it must seem easy enough for cavalry to hunt down a fleeing enemy on foot. But the thing is less simple than it would seem, at the start of May in the mountains, when the grass is still sparse. Horses must be rested at times, too, if one would not have them burst their willing hearts, whereas men, if hard enough pressed, can carry on by some power of the spirit long after the spent body is beyond crawling another step. Then also, we were not merely hunting down fugitives but marching in our turn on an enemy stronghold. We had our baggage train and spearmen with us to slow us down, and the Saxons had left the road, as they had not done on their westward march, and scattered into the hills where it was often impossible for the horses to follow them. (We never knew whether they had found some renegade Briton to guide them, or whether, being desperate, they simply trusted to their gods to keep them clear of the mosses.) And among the immensities of those bluff-browed rolling mountains with the bracken and stone bramble springing among the rocky outcrops, where it seems that nothing moves save the wind in the sparse mountain grasses and the kestrel hovering overhead, but the glens are thick with birch scrub, it is not easy to find one man or a knot of men; nor wise to push on heedlessly, leaving the enemy in one's rear. We did find a few; they lay on their faces for the most part, each with a dark-feathered arrow scarcely larger than a birding bolt in the back. The Old Ones, the Little Dark People of the hills, had, it seemed, as little love for the Sea Wolves as we had.

Before long the reason for that became sickeningly plain, together with the way in which the hard-pressed Saxons had come by food to carry them on their flight. Twice in the first two days, we had seen smoke among the hills, smoke that was too dark and spreading to be that of a hunting fire; and on the third day, when we had left the road and were following our guide along a herding track where the grass was better than that along the scrubby valley through which the road ran, Owain sniffed the air like a hound, saying, "Smoke." And presently as we rounded a bracken-clad shoulder, we saw it rising from beyond a wind-shaped tangle of thorn and rowan and mountain juniper, pale like smoke that is almost spent. We checked the horses—I remember the sudden silence of the high hills, when the soft drum of hooves over the turf fell away; a buzzard circling the blue heights of the upper air, and faintly the sound of falling water; one is seldom far from the sound of falling water among those hills, any more than among my own hills of Arfon. I called to Bedwyr and to Gwalchmai who generally rode close to me, and with our little dark guide and a handful more, we turned the horses' heads toward the thorn tangle, leaving the rest of the war host under Cei to wait for us on the trail.

Beyond the belt of scrub, we came upon one of the settlements of the Little Dark People, half large farm, half small village; that is to say we came upon what the Saxons had left of it in their passing. A piteous huddle of huts half underground, the bracken thatch of their roofs still smoldering, blackened and fallen in, so that these that had been the homes of men were blackened and smoking pits gaping in the hillside; even the peat stacks had been wantonly fired, though among the densely packed turfs the fire had not taken hold. Spilled barley was scattered on the beaten earth (in the shelter of the mountain slope below the village showed the threadbare patchwork of small wretched fields). Dead cattle lay among the smoking wreckage; little hill cattle that had been famine lean even in their lives. Strips had been hacked from their flanks and shoulders; I suppose the Saxons had cut them to suck for the blood and warm juices, maybe even to eat raw. And among the sickening chaos of charred thatch and slaughtered cattle, lay the folk whose home this had been, hacked down in the uncouth attitudes of sudden death; old men, five or six dark narrow-boned warriors like our guide, women and bairns. There was a dead sheep dog lying at the feet of an old man whose brains were scattered among his bloody hair; a young woman with her body arched about that of the child she clutched against her, in a last effort to protect it. Both of them had their throats cut.

I turned to look at Bedwyr beside me, remembering what had passed between us a few nights ago. "No, Bedwyr, I do not love the Saxons."

Our little dark guide, who in the first moments had seemed more frozen than any of us, made the first move. He began to go from one to another of the bodies. He checked beside that of an oldish man with amber pins in his hair, who had been run through the belly, and stooping, drew the long slender knife from his belt.

I said quickly, "Irach, what are you going to do?"

And he looked up at me with the air of someone explaining a thing, simply, to a child, his knife point already at the still breast. "I do the thing that must be done. I eat my father's courage, that it may not be lost."

"Your father? Then this place—"

"This was my home, and my people," he said, and cut deeply and gently into the breast over the heart.

I looked away. My mouth was dry and my stomach crawled within me. I heard him say crooningly, "It is warm—it is still a little warm; that is good, my father," and was aware of a dark shadow that flitted away into the heather, with something in his hands.

No one moved for a long moment. Then someone said, "My God! The little savage!" and somebody else made the Sign of the Horns quickly, to avert evil, for it was not wise to speak so of the Dark People in their own place. I swung around on my armor-bearer and bade him go and bring up some of the others. He was greenish white, and in the act of hurrying to do my bidding, crouched suddenly and vomited, then went on again.

By the time he returned with the others, we had begun to topple the poor mutilated bodies into the smoke-hazed pits that had been their homes. I laid the sheep dog myself at his old master's feet, for the sake of Cabal, whom I would lief have had in like case to lie at mine. We piled over them everything that was loose or movable; charred beams, half-burned thatch, even the peats from the stack; anything that might serve to keep off the wolves and the scavenging mountain hare. Irach's father we left until the last, and he was still unburied when the little hunter came back and set to work quietly beside us. Some of the Companions drew away from him in a kind of horror, and here and there men echoed the Sign of the Horns. But he had only done as the custom of his people demanded, and the act had been performed in love. When the last body had been covered over, he drew the mourning lines on his cheeks and forehead with spittle and gray ash, and scratched his breast and arms with the point of his dagger until they bled, and then turned to us with a great and gentle pride, like a host on his threshold. "It is in my heart that the Saxon Wolves will have left little behind, but all and anything that remains here is yours, and you are most welcome."

But indeed the stouter-stomached among us had already begun hunting through the ruins in search of anything the Saxons had overlooked. There were few of us, I think, who would have cared to rout through a village of the Little Dark People in the ordinary way; but it was as though the Saxons had laid all open to the sky and the wind, and left behind nothing but the piteous wreck of human life; and maybe those of us who hunted through the ruins of Irach's village that day lost forever the sharpest edge of the fear that the people of the sunshine must always feel for the people of the dark.

The few beer pots were empty, and the grain pits had been emptied of the little barley that would have been left in them at this time of year, all save one that they must have overlooked in their desperate haste. The grain inside it was poor wizened stuff, but better than nothing. We scooped it into the grainskins across the backs of the pack ponies; the men and women who had grown and harvested it would not be hungry for its lack, and it would help us to avenge them. We cut more meat from the carcasses of the cattle on which the flies were already beginning to settle as the smoke grew thinner. Then there was no more to do. Myself, I cut the three branches of hawthorn and laid them across where the gateway had been, and sprinkled them with salt and a little of the wine that we carried with us for the cleansing of wounds.

Then we came away, some with a great silence upon us, some cursing, some harshly merry; and left the place under its haze of still faintly rising smoke. Our guide, with the death cuts on his arms and breast still bleeding, rode beside me on his shaggy pony; and as he rode, he made a little dark moaning mouth-music that sounded as though it had been wandering like a homeless wind before ever the hills first reared toward the stars, and made the hair creep on the back of my neck.

Next day, through the gap between two tawny breasts of the hills, we caught our first glimpse of the wide blue lands that ran to Eburacum. And so at last we struggled down out of the mountains that were the roof ridge of Britain, into lowland country again. Our pace was slowing by that time. We knew it, and pushed on without mercy for ourselves or the horses. If we could fling ourselves between Eburacum and the Saxon remnant, if we could even come at them before they had had time to complete their defense, it would mean one sharp and bloody battle, and an end; once they were secure behind walls, there must follow all the long-drawn heart-rotting business of a siege; and with the North already smoldering ready to flare into flame at any moment, we could not, God knew that we could not, spare the time for a siege.

But as we left the highlands and came down into the dale country that lay green with woods under the gray and russet of the fells, a thing began to happen that acted on us like a draught of rye spirit on a man far spent. Out of nowhere, as it seemed, out of the hidden villages and the dark dale forests, men began to gather to the Red Dragon. The Brigantes had always been a wild proud lot; they had never fallen fully into Roman ways, but the Saxon yoke, it seemed, was still more unendurable; and as news of our march swept through the heather, so they came, one or two well-to-do landowners whose farms so far had escaped the Sea Wolves, each carrying Roman weapons in good condition and with a small band of household and farm servants behind them; escaped thralls scarred with their shackles, warriors still free, with the woad-stained war shields that their tribe had carried against the Legions in the far-off days. They joined us on the march and fell in, loping among our foot, or on their fiery little ponies; during the brief night halts they came to our campfire, proud as stags and with the light of battle already in their eyes, saying simply and directly as men speak in the wild places, "My Lord Artos, I am Guern, or Talore, or Cunofarinus son of Rathmail. I come with you in this thing."

Toward evening of the last day's march but one, we came upon a small burned-out farm with the fire still glowing dully under the charred thatch and gray ash, and everywhere about the place, the traces of a great company having been there. Irach ran about sniffing houndwise into all things, then came back to me, rubbing his hands on his wolfskin kilt. "Not half a day since they passed this way. Here they gathered themselves into one host again. Let my Lord the Bear make haste."

I called up Bedwyr and Cei, and told them. "We shall push on with all speed while the daylight lasts; after dark we halt for an hour to eat and water the horses and let them roll. Then we shall push on again through the night, and we shall leave the foot to follow as swiftly as they may. The last lap of the race grows hot, my heroes!"

And so, save for that one break, we pushed forward through the darkness without halt, pressing the weary horses on across the softly rolling countryside, following again the metaled road; and next noon, almost within sight of Eburacum, we came up with the Saxon rear guard.

CHAPTER ELEVEN

The Witch's Son

I T was a ragged and running fight; a fight that split and re-
formed and scattered away across the green levels among
the sallows and the hazel thickets in a score of lesser fights, and
bunched together again, drawing always back toward the gray
walls of Eburacum that I began to see in the nearing distance.
Slowly, slowly the gate towers rose higher and more formidable
while the shadows lengthened from struggling men and white
curled hawthorn scrub. I had hoped almost until then to thrust
in between the Saxons and their stronghold and throw them back;
but far spent as my men and horses were, and lacking all knowledge of how many of the Sea Wolves had been left to garrison the
old legionary fortress, I dared not hazard them in such a position
now. Instead, I took the alternative risk, charging forward to
drive in amongst the enemy so close that there would be no space
in which to secure the gates against us. We drove them as dogs
drive sheep—not that there was much of the sheep about these
men; they were valiant fighters, and fell back before our rushes
steadily and with no sign of rout. Indeed they were steadier now
than at any moment since they broke on the Deva road; shields up
and swords biting, leaving their dead to lie in the track of the retreat without a glance.

There were only two or three hundred left when they gained the
gate, and we crashed after them so close that the triumphant forefront Companions were already mingled with Octa's house carls,
and the Red Dragon of Britain and the white horsetail standards
of the Saxons flying almost as one. I could hear already above the
yelling of my own lads, the bridge timbers ringing hollow under

Arian's hooves; I could see the folk within, women and old men
and boys beside the warriors of the garrison, poised to draw their
fellows in and hold the gate—and drive it to against us when the
last Saxon was inside. And if they succeeded in that, it meant death
to our own forefront, who would also be inside, cut off from all
help of their comrades.

I had chosen to take the hideous gamble, but now as I saw the
dark jaws of the gateway and the enemy swarms about it, I knew
for an instant the sick helplessness of the hunter who sees his
hounds running over a cliff. Too late to draw back now, too late
to do anything but set our teeth and drive forward, sweep the
Saxons away and keep the gates open by the thrust of our own
charge. . . .

I raised the war cry: "Yr Widdfa! Yr Widdfa!" and settled
lower into the saddle, and drove my heel again and again into
Arian's sweating flank, flinging him forward among the enemy
spears. "Keep close! For God's sake keep close! Keep the gates
back!" Beside me, Prosper was sounding the charge, and behind
me the Companions sprang forward. But already as the defenders
leapt to the aid of their reeling comrades, others had flung themselves yelling at the huge bronze-sheathed timbers of the gate. . . .

We were in the shadow of the gate arch. A flung spear took
Irach's pony in the breast, and the poor brute went down headlong, shrieking as it fell, while Irach himself leapt clear. The horse
behind it swung aside, snorting in terror, and for an instant our
whole forefront was checked and flung into confusion. The check
lasted only for the shortest breath, for a racing heartbeat of time,
but it would have been enough. . . . And then in that last black
moment of our charge when everything seemed lost, the marvel
happened—so swiftly that in the instant of its beginning it was in
full fierce flood. Sudden chaos roared up among the defenders,
wild figures were springing in from the rear, from the flanks, dropping out of nowhere as it seemed, into the midst of those who
sought to close the gates; men, and women too, gaunt and savage,
their tatters flying, thrall rings about their necks, with poles and
matchets and butchers' cleavers in their hands. They flung themselves against the valves of the gates to keep them open. All hell
had broken loose and was swirling about me in the dark cavern of
the gate arch; the shouting and screaming rose and gathered into a

[133]

solid whirlpool of sound and was sucked up and lost in great hoarse triumphant cheering that might have been the cheering of damned souls. Again I heard myself raise the war cry: "Yr Widdfa! *Yr Widdfa!*" It was caught up into a rolling roar behind me, and as it were upon a great wave of that cheering, we were crashing through upon that valiant rear guard, riding them down and sweeping them away as a sudden spate sweeps away all things in its path, while behind us the strong gate still strained and shuddered to and fro. Irach was running like a hound at my stirrup. We were crashing through the dark tunnel of the gate arch, deaf with the hollow thunder of our horses' hooves under the groined roof, through a reeling, howling, wild-eyed mob that was fighting itself now rather than us; and beyond the struggling Saxon rear guard, the straight main street of Eburacum opened, empty of life, before us.

On that moment, even above the dazing roar of battle, I heard the high, wolfish, blood-stirring howl of the Dark People's war cry, and Irach streaked forward, running with his dagger at the seething mass of warriors. He can have had no thought of breaking through, he was following again the custom of his own people who believe that victory must be bought with deliberate and willing sacrifice. And in that belief he flung himself upon the enemy spears. Truly the little man had eaten his father's courage—or maybe he had enough of his own.

"Come on, lads!" I shouted. "To me! Follow Irach! Follow me! Follow me home!" And the hunting horn took up the call; ahead of me, with his few remaining house carls about him, I saw the giant figure of Octa Hengestson, his golden hair matted with blood from a scalp wound, and the chain mail of his breast and shoulders stained brown with it, as though with rust. He had lost his shield, or cast it aside. I urged Arian toward him, and with a high defiant yell he leapt to meet me; and as he swung up his sword I saw for an instant his eyes that seemed to burn with a gray-green flame. I took him with the sword point in the strong curve of the throat above the golden collar. Blood spurted out, and I saw his eyes widen as though in surprise; and he crashed backward among his house carls without a sound.

After that, the heart went from them, and they began to give way more quickly.

Someone had fired the thatch of a Saxon hovel and before the

fresh evening wind the flames were spreading as wisps of blazing
straw drifted from one roof to another; smoke began to hang over
the broad street that was narrowed now by garbage piles spread
half across it; the high white basilica that stood like a cliff above
the huddled rook's-nest bothies of the Barbarians was dimmed in
drifting smoke, and the acrid smitch of it caught at our throats.
Men with unlikely weapons in their hands and thrall rings about
their necks were running beside me, all among the horses of the
Companions. . . . And then the Sea Wolves broke and streamed
back, and the thing was no longer a battle but a hunt.

Presently, with the fires already half quelled, I was sitting on the
rim of the ornate fountain in the midst of the Forum, my arm
through Arian's bridle while he drank, while cavalry, foot and
war-painted warriors ran questing through Eburacum in search of
fugitives, and Cei and a handful of the light horsemen swept on
after the others toward the coast, and the roaring flood of victory
surged all about me. A big man was standing at my elbow. I had
seen him in the forefront of the wild rabble at the gate; a man fair-
haired as any Saxon, but with the gray iron thrall ring on his neck,
and in his hands a naked sword which he was cleaning with care
on a tuft of grass pulled from the base of the fountain.

"Whoever you may be, friend, I have to thank you." My own
voice, thick and heavy in my ears, surprised me into wakefulness.

"As to who I am, I am Jason the Swordsmith—it is so that I
have *this* instead of a fence pole or a butcher's cleaver. And that"
—he pointed with the blade to another who passed staggering under
the weight of a big wine jar—"was a clerk in the tower corn store;
and that is Sylvianus who had land of his own and a whole roomful
of books to read—and *that* is Helen, our golden Helen." (Looking
where he pointed, I knew the woman again for one whom I had
seen in the thick of the fighting.) "The Sea Wolves treated her as a
common whore, and she liked it little, having been mistress of her
own house of girls for ten years and more. Thralls, most of us now,
as you can see." He touched the ring about his neck. "A fine following for the Count of Britain, are we not?"

"A fine following," I said. "As to the thrall rings, doubtless you
can deal with those, Jason the Swordsmith, with my armorers to
help you. But for you and your war host, the larger part of mine
would like enough be baying before the gates of Eburacum tonight,

[135]

while I and the foremost of us lay hacked to red rags in the city gutters." I looked up at him. Clearly he was the leader of the tatterdemalion band. "How did you contrive the thing?"

He shrugged thick shoulders. "We made our plans—two or three of them to be worked according as we found one better than another when the time came; a pleasure, that was. It was easier to come at each other with so many of the masters off on the war trail; easier to escape, too, when *that* time came. At first we meant just to break out, and then when word came of their defeat and Hengest's slaying, we guessed how the thing must go, and we thought we'd bide for a while, and then break out to join you or lend a friendly hand from inside, as seemed best."

"That was your plan, I think." The boldness of it accorded with the set of his mouth.

"Mine and Helen's." He jerked his chin toward the woman in her gaudy rags and glass bangles, who had turned in passing, to flash her painted eyes at the nearest of the Companions. "Helen's a jewel of a girl. She's worth ten of the rest of us any day, and she don't much care to be tossed around from one rutting boar to another without so much as a 'By your leave' or a 'Thank you dearling,' after being so long a madam in her own right." He chuckled, a warm rumble of amusement deep beneath the golden fleece of his chest. " 'Twas her idea to keep watch for you by sending up one after another of the girls with a bite of food and a beer pot for a kiss and cuddle with the men on the ramparts. And when the shout went up, and the girl that was up there then came flying down skirling that you rode upon the Sea Wolf's very tail, we knew that the time had come to set things rolling. We was most of us lying hid among the bushes of the old temple garden, by that time, and some of us crept up on the ramparts and dealt with the lookouts up there—" He made a small hideous jabbing motion with his thumbs. "Easy enough if you can get close enough to your man to come at the back of his neck before he hears you. There wasn't many of them, but their weapons added a bit to our store. The first of the Sea Wolves were falling back on to the bridge by that time, and the rest you know."

"The rest I know."

"Simple enough, when you come to think of it."

"When you come to think of it," I said, and we looked at each other with content.

All this while the hunt had been baying through the town, sometimes nearer, sometimes farther off, and the smitch of quenched burning came and went on the wind. A hurrying step sounded on the grass-grown pavement, and I looked around as Flavian came to a halt beside me. "Oisc is clear away, sir," he said. He was black with burning and none too steady on his feet, but he managed the old proud legionary salute with unusual precision. "We've turned the whole town out of doors, but there's neither hide nor hair of him to be found."

I shrugged wearily. "Aiee well, I should have liked to have made the kill complete and finished the whole brood, but I suppose that two generations out of three is not to be sniffed at. If he wins back to the Cantii then he'll be for Ambrosius to deal with—or for us another day. . . . It can't be helped, Minnow."

"No sir," said Flavian, and then quickly: "Sir—there's something else. We found a boy in one of the houses over toward the east gate. We think he's one of their great ones."

"Then why would they be leaving him behind? Is he wounded?"

"No, sir, he—"

"So then. Bring him along."

Flavian stood his ground in silence for a moment. Then he said, "I think perhaps—I think you should come, sir."

I looked at him, surprised and questioning, and then got up. "Very well, I'll come." I set my hand for an instant on the shoulder of the big swordsmith. "Later, I shall want to speak to all your band. Meanwhile, get whatever wounded you have to my surgeon Gwalchmai; any of my men will tell you where to find him."

I called to another of the Companions who was passing, and handed Arian over to him with a final pat on the horse's moist drooping neck; then turned toward the Forum arch, Flavian falling in behind me, and walked out into the main street. "The east gate, you say?"

"Down a narrow street just short of it."

We walked on in silence. The street, where smoking Saxon hovels huddled among the flaking walls of the Roman city, seemed strangely empty, for the hunt had swept to the farther end of the town and discovered the corn store; empty of the living, that is to say. There were enough bodies lying darkly sprawled in the glare of the angry sunset. Once a party of weeping women and children passed us, herded along by my men in the direction of the old fortress, where they could be more easily pent than in the town, but there were not many, even of them. A good number, I think, had escaped and would be heading for the coast; for the rest, there had been something of a massacre in Eburacum that fiery golden evening. Well, it might put the fear of God as well as Artos the Bear into the coastwise settlements. . . .

We reached the narrow street just short of the east gate, and turned into it; and instantly the fierce sunset light was cut off and the cool waters of the dusk flowed about us. Halfway down the street a gleam of saffron light shone from an open doorway, spilling already a faint yellow stain across the way. Several of the Companions stood beside the door, and they parted in the silence of men utterly weary, to let me through. Someone had brought a torch, kindled I suppose from a smoldering roof or someone's forsaken hearth; and by its light I saw that the floor beneath my feet was of fine tesserae, though white with the droppings of swallows from their nests in the ragged thatch, and there were traces of color as well as damp stains on the plastered evil-smelling walls. Another door at my shoulder was open, and one of the Bearers of the Blue War Shield stood aside from before it. I glanced at Flavian, and then turned in through it, the man with the torch following me.

The room was a smallish one, but even so the makeshift torch left the walls in shadow, the light, as the man raised his arm, falling full upon the two figures in its midst. A woman lay there on a low pallet bed; a woman in the long straight folds of a crimson gown, with the glint of royal goldwork about her head. And beside her crouched a boy of about fourteen, with one arm circled protectingly across her body. For one wing beat of time, stillness held the scene within it as a bee is held in the heart of a tear of amber. Then as I entered, the boy sprang up like a wild beast and whirled about to face me. But from the woman there came no movement, no quiver under the straight folds of the crimson gown that ran unbroken as the fluting on a column from the white neck to the rigid feet.

"Don't touch her!" he said between his teeth. I have seldom known anyone to do that in truth, but this boy did it. They were white strong teeth, and I felt that I was looking at some beautiful, shining wild animal that at any moment might spring at my throat. "Do not you dare to touch her!" And I scarcely noticed at the time that he spoke—after a fashion—in the British tongue.

I moved slowly forward, my hands open at my sides. "I'll not touch her."

I stood looking down at the woman, hearing the distant uproar of the city, the growl of voices in the outer chamber; hearing the short panting breaths of the boy beside me; and underneath, more potent than all else, the silence in the room. A great lady, dead and made ready for her pyre, in her finest gown with the goldwork of her rank wreathed about her head. A royal lady among her own folk, by the look of her; and a most beautiful woman. She was not young. It is hard to judge the summers of the dead, for sometimes youth comes upon the face, and sometimes age; but the hair that was spread over the pillow caught the torchlight with the ripe glow of a wheat field in low sunshine, despite the gray hairs in the brightness of it; and not all the gauntness of long fever, not the first faint stains of death beneath the eyes and at the corners of the winged nostrils, could dim the beauty of the face, nor soften its utter ruthlessness. Her eyes were decently closed, but as I looked down at her, the conviction grew on me that open, they would be the same greenish-gray as another pair of eyes that I had seen lately. I had never seen this woman before, I was as sure of that as I had been in Ygerna's case. But I was glad they were shut; I did not like the thought of them open—there might be too much power in them, and the power not for good. Suddenly, for no seeming reason, I remembered the words of old Aquila, describing to me the Lady Rowen, who in the days of his captivity he had seen once in her father's hall. "A witch, a golden witch in a crimson gown." The Lady Rowen, Earl Hengest's daughter, who had spell-drawn Vortigern the Red Fox into casting aside his own wife for love of her, and then used her power as a weapon against him in her father's cause. The Lady Rowen who had deserted him and returned to her own people when his shamed and outcast days came upon him—but not, it was said, before she had conceived his son.

I turned and looked at the boy who stood on wide planted feet, still as far as he could come between me and her, and found myself looking into a pair of gray-green eyes, the color of shallow water on a cloudy day—Hengest's eyes, though they had been smashed and full of blood the last time I saw them; Octa's eyes, blazing up at me under the white horsetail standard only that evening, in the moment before I struck. But the boy's hair was darker than theirs, darker than his mother's; it was the fierce russet of a fox's pelt.

So I knew the answer to my question even as I asked it. "Who are you?"

"I am Cerdic, son to Vortigern King of Britain. And the Lady Rowen who was my mother was daughter to Earl Hengest of the Jutish folk." His voice was level, with the levelness of a boy's who is desperately afraid that it may break.

"And what do you here, Cerdic, Son of Vortigern?"

"I bide with my mother."

"You must think of a better story. Oisc is safe away; and would you ask me to believe that your own people, your mother's people, would leave you here to the power of Artos the Bear?"

He was a valiant stripling; I could see that he was desperately afraid of me, but the strange gray-green eyes never wavered, and his head was thrown back, above the slim golden tore that circled his throat. "Not if they knew it. In a turmoil such as there has been here, it is easy enough to slip aside. They will be thinking me killed, no more."

"Your mother is dead," I said after a silence. "You know that, don't you?"

"She died yesterday. I saw her made ready for the pyre." The voice was steadier than ever.

"Then what purpose could you think to serve by staying here?"

This time the answer came at me like the clawed leap of the wild beast I had been thinking him. "I hope to guard her a little while. I hoped to kill at least one of you and maybe fire the thatch before you could come at her with your filthy ways, but you were too quick for me." His hand went to his belt, where the hilt of his dirk should have been, then fell away again. "Is it that you think I don't know the foul ways that you Christians have with the bodies of the dead? Is it that you think I don't know about the flesh and the chalice of blood when you feast with your God?"

And with the words scarce spoken, suddenly he was upon me as though he would have torn my throat out.

I caught and held him, pinioning his arms and crushing him against me, while a burst of voices and the thud of a swift footstep came behind me. "Let be, damn you!" I said to the voices and the footstep. I was crushing the boy's body to mine as hard as I dared. I was afraid to hit him. I was always afraid of hitting; the blow was prone to do too much damage. He struggled like a wildcat in my grasp. Once he managed to drive his head down and got his teeth in my arm, and held on; but his struggles were growing weaker because he could not breathe. I could feel his young breast fighting and thrusting for air under my own ribs, and tightened my hold still further. "Stop it, you young fool! Stop it or I shall have to hurt you." But my words never reached him.

And then suddenly he was drooping in my arms, half fainting; I loosed him slowly, letting the air come back into his lungs, and as he began to find his legs again, held him off at arm's length. He was quiet enough now, drawing his breath in great sobbing gasps, but I doubted whether if I relaxed my hold completely, he would not be at my throat again next instant. And all at once, looking into the sullen stone-set face, I knew that I could have loved this boy if he were my son. This boy and not the son whom I knew in my dark innermost places, was being reared for me by another witch among my own mountains. Indeed I think that in that one moment we were neither of us far from love of the other, so strange and wayward and terrible are the ways of the human heart.

The moment passed. "Who told you that?" I demanded. "About the flesh and the blood?"

He controlled his panting in one long shaken breath. "My mother. But all men know that it is true."

"Listen—listen to me, Cerdic, and believe me: it is *not* true, as you understand it. Your mother was—mistaken."

"I do not believe you."

"You must. In all faiths there are mysteries; you are old enough, maybe, to have been initiated into the mysteries of your own. When we who call ourselves Christians feast with our God, we eat bread and drink wine; the rest is the mystery. But before the mystery, the bread is but bread as other bread, and the wine is but wine as other wine."

"That is a thing easy to say."

"It is the true thing. No harm will come to your mother's body at our hands."

"That also is a thing easy to say." But I thought that there was beginning to be a flicker of uncertainty in his eyes. "How may I know that it is true?"

"I can give you no proof beyond my word. I will swear it, if you like."

He was silent a moment; then he said, "On what?"

"On the blade and the pommel of my sword."

"The sword which is to drive me and my folk into the sea?"

"It is none the less sacred to me."

He stood for a long silent moment looking me eye into eye. Then I released him and drew the sword from its sheath, and swore. The star of violet light woke under the torchlight in the heart of the great amethyst. "This is the seal of my great-grandsire, Magnus Maximus, Emperor of Britain," I said when I had sworn. And he watched the great jewel as I slammed the sword back into its sheath, then raised his eyes again to my face, with something of challenge in them, something else, too; a strange farsighted expression as though he were looking into a distance, not of place, but of time. But he spoke no word.

"Now it is time to be going," I said.

He swallowed, and suddenly the manhood left him and he was a boy again. "Going? Are you—not going to kill me, then?"

I had been aware for some time past that Bedwyr had come into the room and was standing close behind me. The familiar voice said very quietly in my ear, "Yes!"

"No," I said. "I do not kill boys. Come back when you are a man, and I will kill you if I can; and if you can, you shall kill me."

"It may be that I will do that—one day," he said.

But at the time I scarcely heard him. I turned on Flavian standing by. "Take a couple of the others and see him safely through the gate and three bowshots along the road to the coast." I looked again at the cub standing beside his dead mother. "After that, you will be on your own. If you run into any of the Blue War Shields, or find that the war boats have already sailed when you reach the coast, then that is the end. There is no more than I can do about you. Now get out."

He looked from me to the still body on the bed; one long look, and then back again. Then he turned without a word and walked to the door. Flavian turned in behind him, and I heard him call to two of those outside, "Vran, Conan, I want you—" and the knot of footsteps dying away down the narrow street.

In the torchlit room, Bedwyr and I faced each other beside the bed. "I would to God that it had been I who found him, and not that fool Flavian," Bedwyr said. "I could have arranged matters without troubling the Count of Britain." He never used that title save in the spirit of mockery.

"How?"

"By having him killed out of hand," he said simply.

"In Christ's name, why, Bedwyr?"

"Do you not understand that he is Vortigern's son? He understood it, if you did not. You blind, bloody fool, Artos, have you forgotten that there are still folk enough in Britain who count Vortigern's for the true Royal House, and yours for no more than a usurper's, fathered by a Roman general who was born in Hispania and took the flower of their young men with him to die at Aquileia? That may have little meaning now, while Ambrosius is the High King, but when the time comes for Ambrosius to die—"

Silence flashed down like a sword between us, and held us for a long harsh moment. Then I said, "I suppose I had forgotten something of that. I think I am glad, Bedwyr."

In the returned silence, the echo of receding footsteps still sounded, fainter with every breath that passed.

"It is still not too late," said Bedwyr.

I shook my head. "Fate does not allow it to men to unpick part of the pattern." As I said it, an odd foreboding brushed me by, a sense, not so much of future evil as of the fate that I had spoken of, a sense of the inescapable pattern of things. Whatever it was, it was gone as swiftly as a bird darts across a sunlit clearing, from the shadow into the shadow again. I glanced about me. "Na, the thing is done. Best see to this matter of the burning. Get in brushwood and loose straw and pile it around the bed. And clear back the nearer bushes in the garden. We don't want another fire spreading through Eburacum tonight."

"Fire? You want the whole house destroyed?" Bedwyr had said

what he had to say, and there was an end of it. So now he turned
to the next thing.

"Yes. Fire is the usual way, among her people; and the place
stinks anyway." But it was in my heart also that fire was a cleansing
thing, and I was still remembering Aquila's words, "A golden
witch in a crimson gown."

They were felling and uprooting the overgrown bushes in the
little town garden as I came out again into the street, and the
dusk had deepened to a soft blue darkness full of voices and hurrying shadows and the spitting flare of torches. They had lit great
fires in the Forum by the time I returned to it. Most of the foot had
come in by that time, and the whole war host was crowding close
about the flames. They had driven in a few cattle, and already the
smell of roasting meat was in the air. The whisper of another scent,
sweet and heavy with musk, curled across my nose, and the woman
Helen drifted out of the shadows and brushed across my path,
then checked, glancing up at me over her shoulder. Her bright
rags were allowed to slip just a little when she held them at her thin
breast; her eyes half laughing, at once bright and unutterably
weary under the lids whose green malachite had run in streaks, her
body touched against mine, lightly, with a mute invitation.

I looked down at her. "I am so deeply thankful to you, Helen;
tonight I cannot even find the words to tell you how thankful."

"There are other things than words, my Lord Artos; other ways
for a man and a woman to speak together." Her voice was soft
and throaty as a ringdove. "I have a little wine in my lodging."

"Not tonight, darling. I'm too tired."

Cei strutted into the light of the nearest fire as I spoke, and I
jerked a thumb in his direction. "You see that one with the russet
beard, and the bracelets? If you would be kind, go and offer him
your wine."

She looked at me without the least rancor, clearly with no sense
of rebuff—but indeed I had meant no rebuff—only with a little
mockery under the green-painted lids. "But perhaps he also is too
tired."

"He is never too tired," I said.

CHAPTER TWELVE

Trimontium

WE remained several days in Eburacum to rest both men and horses and get the weapons and war gear mended and renewed and see to the wounded. And almost at once the folk of the city who had escaped fire and seax when the Sea Wolves came, began to trickle back from the refuges to which they had fled farther inland. With their help we cleared the streets of the sprawling dead, and stripped the dead of their war gear, claiming for ourselves as usual the keenest weapons and most finely wrought mail shirts to replace the boiled leather and horn and age-eaten Roman hoop mail that still had to serve for some of us. As Lindum would have had us stay, so would Eburacum, and indeed with better cause, for the Coritani had been almost free of the Sea Wolves when we left, but here we had been able to clear only the city itself and the land toward the coast was still in enemy hands. But the North was smoldering into flame, and I could not bide in Eburacum any more than in Lindum City.

I gathered an oddly assorted council of war: one or two hungry magistrates, leaner than ever they had been in their lives before; a handful of tottering graybeards who had come forward to answer my call for men who had served with the Eagles in their youth; the leaders of Kinmarcus's tribesmen and of the Brigantian warriors who had joined us on the march; Jason the Swordsmith with the mark of the thrall ring red-raw on his neck, to speak for his own valiant rabble; my own lieutenants Bedwyr and Cei. I summoned them together into the Forum and told them I could not stay to finish the work that was begun, while the fire in the North swept down to engulf us all in the end. I would leave them a war band of trained spearmen to help them train themselves. I left them their own warriors, the Bearers of the Blue War Shields—and there were no fiercer fighting men under the sun, as the Eagles had good cause to know. I left them their old soldiers for wisdom and cunning in war craft, if their days for bearing a sword were past. (I saw how that made the men of the Blue Shield stand up straight like emperors, and the veterans begin to look down their noses at the Blue Shields; and began to harangue them on the need to forget all differences and stand together.) I forget now what I said, save that I did my best to strengthen their hearts and their sword hands, that I promised to come again and vowed that we would finish the work together. I know that I crooned over them like a bairn's nurse, and cursed them like a time-expired centurion with the gutter words of half an empire at his command, and appealed to them like a girl appealing to her lover. I think that many of us were near to tears by the end. I know I felt like a murderer. But I was sure in my heart that now I had cleared out the wolf's lair, they could hold their own—if only they could stand together! Dear God, let them be able to stand together! Let them learn that one lesson that seems impossible ever to be learned by the British kind!

Two days before we marched, a messenger came from the Prince Guidarius in Lindum, to tell me that the Coritani territory was still free of the Sea Wolves, but that even so, my old place still waited for me if I chose to return to it. I gave orders for the messenger to be fed and housed, and sent him back next day with word that I thanked the Prince Guidarius, but that I had not changed my plans. I had little time to weave courtesy into my reply, for I had both hands full with arrangements for food and war supplies to come up after us from Eburacum before the autumn's end. (I had already sent word back to Deva of the victory, together with a forewarning to Kinmarcus that we should need the same kind of supplies from him and from the Môn grainlands later.) With making plans for a supply depot at Corstopitum, the old depot town for the Wall fortress; with convincing the Bishop of Eburacum, who was among the returned survivors, that the income from certain Church orchard land, luckily undamaged by the Saxons, would be better spent on well-made arrows and salt and saddle leather, than laid by in gold to the Glory of God. He was not easy to convince, being less of a mouse than his brother of Lindum. But he saw my point in the end.

And the next day we marched out of Eburacum by the northern gate, and took the Legion's road to the Wall.

It must have been a fine sight in its day, the Wall, when the sentries came and went along the rampart walks and bronze-mailed cohorts held the fortress towers and the statues and the altars to the Legion's gods were thick along the crest; and between it and the road and the vallum ditch that followed it like its own shadow, one great string of towns, one long-drawn town under many names, straggling all the four days' march from Segedunum to Luguvallium. The towns were as dead as the Wall, now, for the menace of the North was too near, the raids too frequent for them to have outlived the protection of the Eagles; and we rode into a ghost town, the roofs long since fallen in and the walls crumbling away, the tall armies of nettles where the merchants had spread their wares and the Auxiliaries had taken their pleasure in off-duty hours, where the married quarters had been, and children and dogs had tumbled in the sunshine under the very feet of the marching cohorts, and the drink shops had spilled beery song into the night, and the smiths and sandalmakers, the horse dealers and the harlots had plied their trades; and all that moved was a blue hare among the fallen gravestones of forgotten men, and above us a hoodie crow perching on the rotting carcass of what had once been one of the great catapults of the Wall, that flew off croaking, with a slow flap of indignant wings as we drew near.

We camped that night around the crumbling gate tower where the road from Corstopitum, and Eburacum beyond, passed through into lowland Caledonia, into the old lost province of Valentia. I called the captains together after the evening meal, and took a bit of stick and began to draw maps in the ashes on the edge of the campfire. How often I had seen Ambrosius doing that, on the eve of a campaign. I was mapping, for my own information as well as theirs, a countryside that I had never seen; but it was not for nothing that I had spent those long winter evenings listening to Daglaef the Merchant. "See—here we sit now at the Hunnum Gate; from here the road runs—so, north and a little west, to Trimontium, three days' march." (It was odd how, never having known the Legions, one still thought of the old legionary march of twenty miles, when one wanted to work out a distance.) "Here it crosses the Tweed—so, and runs on through the lowland hills and into the fringes of the Caledon Forest, to come out in the levels below the Highland Line." Bedwyr and the others gathered closer in the firelight, peering over my shoulders. I went on scrawling lines and curves in the warm ash. "Now from Luguvallium, where I put this pebble, a second road runs north to Castra Cunetium, here, five marches by reason of the way the road sinks to avoid marsh country and high moors. And on, also, toward the Highland Line through the very heart of the Pict lands." I returned to Trimontium, trying to remember exactly how the merchant had described to me the run of the Tweed. "Here the Tweed Valley narrows into a gorge, running so. Easy to see the strategic importance of the place, isn't it, with the river valley and the road forming between them the main highways from Caledonia to the south; and the Inner Kingdom of the Picts thrusting down through the Forest in the northwest. . . . Then if Daglaef spake truth, there is a lateral road from Trimontium running thus, up toward the headwaters of the Tweed and across the high tongue of the Forest to those of the Cluta, and downvalley to Castra Cunetium. . . . Now have you all got that safely behind your foreheads? Then make sure that the rest of the lads have it, too, for it is in my mind that those three roads and those two forts are the pattern of our fate for a good while to come, for on our holding and our handling of them depends our hold of Caledonia."

Presently, when I had done, I threw the stick into the heart of the fire, and brushed my hand through the gray ash, blotting out the crude map as though it had never been, and got up to go and take a look at the horse lines, as I always did before lying down to sleep.

Next morning Owain with fifty light-riding tribesmen set off westward along the frontier road to Luguvallium; their task was to watch the back road, the flank road of my map, and send me instant word if the enemy chose to run the hazard (for we should be on their flank at rear), of trying a break through into Britain from that side.

And when they were gone, Bedwyr and I with our foreguard rode out through the gaping ruins of the Hunnum Gate, under the charging boar of the Legion that had built it. Beyond the Wall, the country seemed all at once darker and wilder, the distant hills more brooding, the very wind through the heather blowing with a more desolate song. But that was foolishness; nothing but the knowledge in our hearts that we were beyond the frontier, beyond the pale of familiar things.

It must have been almost two hours later before the last of the rear guard was through the gate, for we moved in the usual formation for a march through hostile country, the foreguard of cavalry scouting a few miles ahead of the foot and baggage train, the rear guard following a few miles behind, and the light horsemen scattered against the threat of flank attack on either side. I hated to ride in that formation; it lengthened the time of the day's march unbearably, or else cut the distance covered. But to take any other course would have been to go bleating for trouble like a lost lamb in wolf country.

We got the trouble soon enough, without bleating for it. From the Wall to Trimontium was a three-day march, and we did it in something over three weeks. There was no random turmoil throughout the country, the thing had passed beyond that stage. But clearly Huil Son of Caw had had word of our coming, and sent out his light war parties to hold us up while he finished the gathering of his own war host and the armoring of his stronghold against us. And the warriors of his skirmishing bands had the advantage of knowing the country they fought over, while we were strangers to it. We had to fight through almost daily skirmishes in which the enemy appeared from nowhere, and even when beaten off, simply melted into the hillside again, leaving very few dead behind them to mingle with ours. We were attacked at any brown stream or blind turn of the track, shot at from behind every furze bush; stretches of road were torn up ahead of us just where the ground was softest, so that we had to spend whole days in getting the horses across maybe a mile of ground where the white silken tassels of the bog grass gave us the only warning of the worst patches; and almost always we were attacked while doing it, so that all the while, though not heavily, we lost men and horses. Indeed if the road had been a valley one or led through forest country, I think that it would have gone hard with us; but it ran for the chief part through heather moors, and in most places where it was not a natural ridgeway, it had been raised slightly above the level of the surrounding countryside by the engineers who built it—for which I blessed those engineers, praying ease on their long-departed souls in the names of all the gods I knew. But apart from men, the very land itself seemed in league with the traitors and the Sea Wolves, and twice smoked up dense white mists against us, which, since there would have been a certain unwisdom in marching blind through unknown and hostile country in a mist that could have hidden a war host within a spear's length of us, held us captive for days at a time within the circle of the past night's defenses, with the horses under strong guard outside. (We ditched the camp every night, and each man set his spear upright behind the ditch; it was as near as light-moving troops such as we were could come to the old "thorn hedge" of the Legions.) The picket lines were attacked on both occasions, and several horses killed and a few hamstrung by men who paid for it with their own lives.

It was very early summer when we marched out through the Hunnum Gate, and we had numbered nearly seven hundred, counting the drivers, but the first heather was coming into flower over the moors, and we had lost something like a fifth part of our strength, when we came at last in sight of the great red sandstone fort crouched at the foot of three-peaked Eildon; Trimontium, the Place of Three Hills.

I had drawn the war host closer as we neared the place, and sent out a handful of light horse to scout ahead. And just as we were making the noon halt they rode in again with their ponies in a smother, and their leader came straight to me, breathless and stumbling in his run. "My Lord Artos, they are ahead of us in Trimontium. Saxons too, for there's one of their accursed horsetail standards peering over the wall. And Scots to judge by the glint of white shields on the ramparts."

I had been half expecting that. The Place of Three Hills must have been a good rallying point for them as it was a good base and headquarters for us. I called Bedwyr who was overseeing the noon issue of biscuit, and told him. "The wolf pack is ahead of us. We are going to have to fight for Trimontium if we want it. Pass the word to the rest."

But indeed the word was already running, as such tidings always do, like heath fire through the host. I sent a rider galloping back to summon up the foot and the rear guard, and when they came up with us we marched again, in changed formation ready for battle.

But before marching, the Companions, I also, picked sprigs of the big rose-purple bell heather and stuck them into our helmets and shoulder buckles, in the way that had become custom with us.

For a good while the fort was hidden from us by the slow moorland billows of the land between. But all the while three-peaked Eildon stood up before us, rising taller into the changing sky as the long miles passed. It was drawing toward evening when Bedwyr and I left the war host behind the last ridge, and riding forward alone, came out through the hazel and birch woods that had clothed the hills of the past day's march, and saw the lean red menace of the old fort, no more than five or six bowshots away. The scouts had spoken truth. Heads crowded the ramparts, and there was a dark swarm about the gateway where pack ponies were hurriedly being got inside and the barricades flung up behind them, and the smoke of many cooking fires billowed sideways in the wind that had begun to rise.

"I would to God I had some means of knowing their numbers," I said to Bedwyr, who had ridden out of the woodshore at my side. "The fort was built to hold a double cohort of a thousand for months on end; it would hold three or four times as many for a short space."

"So long as the water holds out," said Bedwyr.

I glanced aside at him. "You think they mean to stand siege here?"

"I think nothing—as yet—but I was ready to see them drawn up to make us welcome, on the clear ground yonder. They have had warning enough of our coming, and the Saxon at least has small love for fighting behind walls."

I was silent. I too should have thought to see them drawn up ready for us. It could be the siege, of course. If they were well provisioned they might be counting on the fact that we, in an alien and hostile country, would be likely to run out of supplies before they did. But there was the water; after the years that the place had been deserted, the wells had probably fallen in, and in any case, since there would be many more than the place had been built for, and the pack beasts also must be watered, it could not be long before the supply began to fail. They might of course merely be waiting for morning, believing that we should start nothing so late in the day as this. Or they might be planning a night attack of their own, when we had been lulled into a false security. I wished to God I knew. Meanwhile I remained silent for a while, taking in the lay of the land. From the shallow valley that ran down ahead of us, the land on the right rose gently in a kind of broad spur to the fortress walls, not cleared back, as it must have been in the old days, but overgrown with the wildest tangle of hazel and elder scrub. Beyond the fort and on either side, it seemed, as well as I could see, that the hillside fell away steeply as the swoop of a falcon, into the wooded river gorge below Eildon. The place, in fact, was a spur above the river, and if the three farther sides were what they seemed, only this, the southern side, could be attacked in any force.

A blast on Prosper's aurochs hunting horn brought no response save the ghost of an echo out of the river gorge.

The light was beginning to fade, and the rising wind sounded like a charge of cavalry when we turned back to the others beyond the ridge. I gathered a handful of our best scouts and trackers, and gave them their orders. "Get down the valley and lie close for a while. As soon as the day has dimmed to half-light, work your way in close to the fort. They may have pickets posted—I doubt it, but it is a thought to keep in mind. Work around the whole circuit, and bring me back word how steep the fall of the land is on the sides that one cannot judge from here, and what possibility there may be of sending in an attack from the river side. Notice also the condition of the walls, how the gates are held, any smallest detail that may aid us in the planning of the next move. Understood?"

When they had melted into the wind-swayed thickets, we made camp as best we could in the shelter of the ridge, leaving a few men to keep watch on Trimontium from the ridge itself; watered the horses at the stream which, rising somewhere in the high moors southward, flung its ferny loop around the far shoulder of the ridge and went purling down to join the Tweed; ate the evening meal of barley bannock and the inevitable hard yellow cheese, and settled down to wait as patiently as might be for the return of the scouting party. Sometime after dark—there was no moon that night, and the clouds were racing across the stars—they came slipping one after another out of the night and the wind-lashed woods to drop beside the campfire, and tell their story between ravenous mouthfuls of the food that had been set aside for them. There were no pickets, but also no possibility of mounting an attack of any strength from the farther side of the fort. "Scarce footing for the whin bushes," said the leader when I put it to him. But there was a deer track, and a postern gate on the north side, and in one place the wall was down to not much over the height of a man, with plenty of stone and rubble still outside to aid climbing, so that it might be possible to get a small band around that way to mount some kind of decoy attack to draw attention from the main gates. The gates themselves had rotted apart, but all of them were strongly closed with thornwork and stout timber barricades. Of the numbers of the motley war host gathered in Trimontium, save that they were very many, the scouting party had of course been able to gain no idea.

When it was all told, we looked at each other, Cei and Bedwyr and I, in the wind-torn firelight. Bedwyr had brought out his beloved harp as he did most evenings when the food was eaten; he plucked a little inquiring flight of notes from it that seemed to leap into the wind and be whirled away like the first yellow birch leaves. "Tonight?"

"Tonight," I said. "For one thing, we may not have a wind like this again, to cover the sound of Cei plunging through the undergrowth."

Indeed the wind stood friend to us that night in more ways than one. It covered the sound of our general advance as we made our way over the ridge and down through the birch and hazel woods into the shallow valley. (For though the main part of our horses were under guard on the far side of the ridge, even a few horses make more noise than many men in dense undergrowth.) It covered, with its soft turmoil among the bushes of the steep fortress hillside, the movements of Bedwyr and his dismounted squadron as they crept and clambered around beneath the red sandstone walls toward the unmended breach that the scouts had spoken of; though I think that they would have made little sound in any case, for they had laid aside their ring-mail shirts, which always chimed a little in action, however carefully one moved in them, and gone into their venture with nothing but buckler and drawn sword. . . . It covered the sound of brushwood and wagon straw being piled against the main barricades (five men it cost us, though, to keep it there) and when it caught light from the fire-brands that we flung into it, the wind caught and fanned the flames and roared them up and drove the licking tongues against the timbers of the barricade so swiftly that the first warning shouts had scarcely broken from the men within before the whole gateway was ablaze.

The archers, whom we had kept standing by, had light for shooting now, and crouching among the nearer bushes began to loose with a high trajectory that carried the arrows over the ramparts on either side of the gate towers, to fall on the heads of the defenders. Some of the arrows had flaming spirit-soaked rags tied to them, and their arc showed like shooting stars on a winter's night. A few enemy arrows answered, but not many; the defenders were too intent on the gate itself to have much time for shooting (surely we had their whole attention now, and Bedwyr had his chance if ever he was to have it!). The uproar inside the gate was so wild that at one moment, sitting old Arian with my own squadron, just beyond the reach of the flame light, I was troubled lest I should not hear Bedwyr's signal from the far side of the fort to tell me that he was ready, fearing even that he might not hear my horn sounding the charge. Where timing meant so much, we could ill afford to miss each other's signals.

The barricade went with a roar and a crash, and a sheet of flame leapt toward the stormy sky, its crest caught by the wind and bent over like the crest of a wave before it breaks; rags of flame were flying across the fortress; and faintly, in the moment's stunned hush that followed the fall of the barricades, I heard the war cry of Arfon sounding across the distance and the storm: "Yr Widdfa! Yr Widdfa!" and knew that the moment had come.

Arian was sweating; I felt him start and tremble under me, for like all horses, he was terrified of fire. All horses . . . How if they refused to face the flaming gateway? I should have ordered the whole assault on foot, but we needed the crash and sweep of a cavalry charge. No time for regrets or wavering now; no time to let the flames die down, though already our lads, close under the wall where the arrows and throw spears of the defenders could not reach them, were flinging on masses of fresh bracken to damp them down for the moment. The white steam hissed up, and the flame-wall sank and grew ragged as I called to my trumpeter, "Now, man—the Charge!"

The familiar notes of the hunting horn leapt into the wind, and I bent forward onto Arian's sweating neck. "Now! Now, brother!" He snorted and shook his head, beginning to swerve aside, and I flung a fold of my cloak across his eyes. Blind, I knew that he would go where I urged him, because he trusted me. "Git up! *On,* boy!" He hesitated an instant longer, and then with a defiant and despairing neigh broke forward into a canter, and I heard the hooves of the others drumming on his heels. The heat of the gateway struck at my face like a blow, the smitch of half-quenched flames choked and blinded me. My face was down against Arian's neck, partly to shield my own eyes, partly that my voice might reach him above the tumult. I was managing him with my knees alone, the reins loose on his neck, that I might have one hand for my spear and the fold of my cloak across his eyes. I sang to him, shouted in his laid-back ear. "On, brave heart! Sa sa sa—up, come up, bold and beautiful! Come up, my hero!"

And old Arian answered me like a hero indeed. He gathered himself together, greathearted as he was, and with the terror of the fire in his nostrils, galloped straight forward into the dark, through the steaming and crackling inferno of the gateway and the massed spears beyond. And after me crashed the rest, tramping the fire under round hooves and scattering the red embers like sparks from a swordsmith's anvil. I raised the war cry, and heard it echoed back to me from across the roaring chaos of the camp. "Yr Widdfa! *Yr Widdfa!*" The hunting horn was sounding again, and suddenly from the heart of the camp ahead of us came the hollow booming of the Saxon war horns, and the deep throbbing snarl of the eight-foot war horns of the Scots. We charged on toward them.

The fire arrows and torn-off flames from the burning barricades had fired the rough thatch on some of the buildings; and by the leaping wind-torn light, we charged and charged again through the solid masses of the enemy, carrying the Red Dragon of Britain on toward the heart of the camp where the war horns and the up-reared standards told us that we should come at Huil Son of Caw, his household warriors and his allied chieftains. Our foot swarmed in over the still-smoking embers that we had scattered for them, and hand-to-hand fighting had spread into every corner of the great fort. And from the northern quarter, where Bedwyr and his war band had leapt in over the crumbling wall, the war cry, taken up by a score of triumphant voices, was sweeping nearer.

I remember little of the last phase. When once all vestige of the pattern is gone, there is little to remember of any battle save the chaos and the smell of blood and sweat that are common to all battles; and one is very tired, and not very clear in the head. . . . In the end they broke and streamed away—those who could—over the broken parts of the wall, leaping from the rampart walks and down the bush-grown hill scarp, leaving their dead behind them.

The time came when the last fighting was done, and a sudden quietness fell over the great camp; and even the wind seemed to drop for the moment. Men were putting out the flames of the roofs that had caught, and I was standing beside the remains of a cooking fire, with an arm over Arian's neck, praising and consoling him for the red spear gash in his flank. Presently, I thought dimly, I must get it bathed; presently, if there was any water. Surely there had been something about a shortage of water, a long while ago? My head began to clear slowly, and I saw Bedwyr limping toward me, with the blood trickling from a gash just above his knee.

"A good hunting," I said, when he came up.

"A good hunting."

"Any sign of Huil?"

"None so far, but they have only just begun to go through the dead and wounded. There's a good few of them."

"What of our own losses?" (It might have been Eburacum over again, but after most battles there are much the same questions to be asked.)

"So far as we can tell as yet, not heavy. I lost several men getting in from the north rampart, but most of the wolf pack was faced to your blazing gate; yet it is in my mind that that charge of yours through the flames seemed more like a lightning flash than a thing that one could strike back at." And then he said, "We've lost nine horses; that I do know."

And the last of the fog lifted from my brain. (I think, looking back, that I must have taken a bang on the head without knowing it, for that kind of heaviness after battle was not usual with me.)

I looked at Bedwyr, scarcely noticing even when Arian muzzled at my shoulder. It was a worse loss than that of the same number of men; but there was no help for it, no help even in cursing. "Well, we have our winter quarters—though they stand somewhat in need of scrubbing out," I said. Amlodd came to take Arian from me, and I handed the old horse over, and then turned to the multitude of tasks and decisions, the general clearing up, that always wait for every commander after the fighting's over.

Gwalchmai as usual was serenely at work among our own wounded, gathered into a roofless barrack row; I heard a man cry out in pain, and his quiet voice in command and reassurance as I passed the tumble-down doorway.

Some of our men were throwing the Saxon dead and wounded alike over the ramparts at the spot where the escarpment fell almost sheer to the river; but not before they held a torch to each dead face to make sure that it was not Huil Son of Caw. Our own dead were being gathered and laid aside for burial in the long grave that their comrades were digging for them among the bushes where the ground was soft. I had made it a rule, years ago, that however hard and hot the day had been, however spent our bodies or sick our heads, however near the enemy and however little time remained to dawn, no dead body should be left unburied within the camp overnight. I do not know how it is; maybe evil spirits gather to bodies left lying so; but that way comes pestilence. I have seen it happen before, especially in summer weather. There would be no attack on Trimontium for a while and a while, and save for a few pickets, we could take the sleep we needed tomorrow.

The searchers found more than one Saxon chieftain, and a huge Pict with the blue spirals of his race tattooed from brow to ankle, and the gold collar of a noble, lying among the dead under the blood-dabbled horsetail standard where the last stand had been made. But when the last of the enemy slain had been dealt with, there was still no sign of any man who could be Huil Son of Caw.

"It is as well to have something saved for another day," said Cei, who had discovered a store of Saxon beer jars in one of the old store barns and was inclined to take a cheerful view. "Sir, will you give the order for an issue of beer all around? I'm thinking the lads could do with it."

For Cei was ever one to share good fortune.

"Well enough," I said. "Get in a couple of the captains and half a dozen of the Company to see to it."

But there was more than beer jars in that barn. A short while later, one of the Companions came to me in a hurry where I was standing with Bedwyr to see the baggage train brought in. "Sir, my Lord Artos, we have found a girl's body over there among the beer jars. Will you come and look?" He was a veteran of many fights, hardened in the fire, I should have said, as any one of my Companions, but from the color of his face, I thought for a moment that he was going to spew.

CHAPTER THIRTEEN

The People of the Hills

I CURSED inwardly as I turned to go with him. It was Eburacum all over again. I seemed fated always to find myself with the body of a woman to dispose of when the fighting was done. But this was no golden witch in a crimson gown.

The men had been working by the light of a pine-knot torch, and so there was light enough to see what lay at their feet, when they moved back with an odd hush on them to let me through.

More than light enough.

A young woman, hardly more than a girl, lay there among the beer jars, in the ugly, contorted attitude in which she had been flung down and kicked aside. She was no taller than a girl of fourteen or fifteen would be among our own folk, but she was of the Little Dark People, and among them a grown woman is no taller than that. I thought, looking at her upturned face among the tangled masses of black hair, that she had once been very good to look upon, in the narrow, fine-boned way of her people; but she was not good to look upon now, though her skin was still honey soft between the bruises and clawings of the brutal handling she had received, and her contorted limbs slim and fine. She was stark naked, and from the stains upon her she had been raped not once but again and again. The man who held the torch moved his arm, and as the light shifted I looked again into the girl's battered face. I had thought the look on it was one of torment and unutterable horror, but now I saw that beneath these things there was something else; a look of escape. She had possessed, this girl of the Old Race, the power which some birds and animals possess, when the outrage of living mounts beyond a certain point, of making the final withdrawal into the refuge of death where no tormentor can follow.

Cei was cursing in a sustained flow, his blue eyes blazing with a rage such as I had never seen in them before. "May their souls rot in Hell! By Christ! If I had the man here I'd unman him with my naked hands, and tear his living heart out afterward!"

"You'd need to unman a good few, I'm thinking—and maybe you'd need help," said Bedwyr's voice just behind me, still and cool as deep water by contrast with the hot rage of the other's.

One of the men looked to me. "What are we to do with her, sir?"

I hesitated. If she had been one of our own kind she could have gone into the same long grave as our battle dead. But she was of the Old Race, the Little Dark Ones. Many of our own scouts and camp followers had something of that blood in them (I have sometimes thought that there was a strain of it in the Royal House of Arfon itself, for Ambrosius, though taller, was narrow-boned and dark as the Fairy kind), and our own people worked alongside them contentedly enough, especially since Irach; though many a time I have seen one of my own Companions make the Sign of the Horns before sharing food from the same dish with one of them. But I knew that if I ordered the girl's body to be laid with our own dead, I should have trouble with my men, for fear that the nearness of the Fairy's dead might harm our own in some way.

"Scoop her out a grave to herself somewhere among the bushes," I said.

There was a sudden movement, a many-voiced murmur of dissent behind me, and swinging around I saw that a crowd had gathered, peering over each other's shoulders at the small outraged body in the torchlight. One of the mule drivers came thrusting his way through, or was thrust by those behind him; a small dark hairy man with prick ears like a faun's. "My Lord Artos, there is another word as to that."

"Speak it, then."

He stood with his feet apart, staring into my face, stubborn as one of his own mules. "My Lord Artos, I know something of these things, for my grandmother came from the Hollow Hills. They are not wont to lie alone, my people—my grandmother's people. If you lay her as you have ordered, she will grow lonely, and in her loneliness she may walk. Women who die as she died are given to walking, anyway; and she will be angry, not only with those who killed her, but with us, who cast her out. But if you bury her here in the midst of the camp, she will be quiet with life going on about her and the warmth of the cooking fires overhead. Her anger will be all for those who killed her, and she will bring us luck and help us to hold the Place of Three Hills."

Young Brys Son of Bradman protested furiously. "My Lord, do not listen to him, he will let her loose in our very midst!" And another added his word. "I've no wish to sleep at nights with *that* under my pillow!" And the refrain was taken up by others, while the mule driver stood his ground, still staring into my face, and behind him, the men who had thrust him forward muttered among themselves.

Cei demanded in his deep grumble, "Are you going to give ear to a bunch of mule drivers, rather than to your own Companions?"

"We shall still need mule drivers," I said. And then suddenly I had the answer: not perfect, but the best that I was likely to find.

Only a few paces from where we stood, there was a deep broad pit, probably once a supplementary grain store, for mildewed shreds of the hides with which it had been lined still clung to its sides and to the remains of the timbers that had once closed it in. It could never be used again, and I had given orders that the dead horses were to be tipped into it and covered over for tonight with whatever came to hand of clods and debris and old thatch. That would be a lighter task than to drag the carcasses outside and far enough from the camp. There had not been time yet for the order to be carried out, though the first of the carcasses had been dragged close in readiness; and horses were creatures of the Sun, sacred among the Sun people once, while nine has ever been a number of Power.

"Lay her in the old grain pit before the horses go in," I said. "Thrice three horses above her should make all safe, without keeping off the warmth of the cooking fires." And before anyone had time to raise further objections: "Go, someone, and bring a couple of baggage ropes," for I had no wish to tumble her into her grave as one flings a dead cat on a garbage pile; and while someone went to do my bidding and the rest stood by, few I think, even of her own kind, overeager to touch her, I flung off my old weather-stained cloak, and spread it on the ground, and lifted the poor broken body onto it. She weighed no more than a child, and some of the suppleness of life was still in her, so that I was able to lay her decently, and not in the crumpled attitude in which we had found her. Bedwyr knelt beside me, helping me to draw the dark folds close. "Cover her face," he said; and then, "I'll carry her."

But she seemed in some way to be my charge. I shook my head, and got up with the small close-wrapped body in my arms, and went outside with her to where the mouth of the old grain pit gaped darkly in the torchlight. Half the camp had come thronging around by that time, but there was no sound save a low muttering as here and there men looked at each other or at the burden I carried, and made the Sign of the Horns. In the end we did not need the baggage ropes after all, for Gault and Levin, making a jest of it, but a gentle jest, sprang down into the pit themselves, and one standing on the other's shoulders (they were much given to fooling together like a pair of acrobats) took the girl from me, and dropping clear as his friend crouched down, laid her kindly on the rough earth. We flung down fresh bracken to cover her, and the two warriors carefully wedged above her the beams that we passed down to them, so that they might keep the main weight of the horses off her. Then Levin climbed again onto his friend's shoulders, and caught the edge of the hole and scrambled out, ignoring the hands reached to his aid, and turned about to help Gault out after him. But the depth was too great. Straining, they could just touch fingertips, but could not get a grip on each other's hands. For the instant I saw them looking at each other, half laughing, one up from the pit that had become a grave, the other down into it, straining to reach each other. Then somebody tossed down the end of a knotted baggage rope and Gault swarmed up easily enough, and was standing among us again, panting a little.

The thing was over, and most of the weary fighting men were drifting away, while those that remained were stripping the dead horses of their gear before they went into the pit. I turned away to go and make sure that the whole baggage train had been got safely in, and find out the state of the wells. It was as I had expected; they had fallen in. There was water far down in one of them, enough for the wounded, anyway; the rest of us must do without water until the time came for taking the horses down to the river in the morning.

Morning was not so very far off, by that time, and a quiet was falling over the old red sandstone fort; dark shapes of sleeping men huddled in every corner, who stirred and cursed without moving if one fell over them; and the wind was lulling into soft fitful gusts with long exhausted stillnesses between, when I passed the old grain pit again. The last of the horses had been toppled into it, and the pit covered over with clods and half-charred thatch until tomorrow when it could be filled in properly. As I came toward it I saw that Bedwyr was ahead of me. I suppose he had checked in passing on some errand of his own. His little harp was in his hands, but I had not heard the notes of it until the moment before I saw him. He was playing very softly, faint plucked notes at long intervals, and the fitful wind was blowing the other way. He turned his head toward me (but I could not see his face for the nearest watch fire was sinking low), and went on playing, a note, and then a pause as though he listened for the next note before playing it, and then another note, spun so far apart that one could not carry the thing in one's head as any kind of tune, only as single moments of beauty that tore at one's heart, strung on those long dark silences of the dying wind.

"What is it?" I asked, when it seemed that the wind and the darkness had closed for good over the last note, and cursed myself for breaking the circle of perfection.

He struck another note with his thumbnail. "What does it sound like?"

"A lament—but I think not for the horses."

"Na. Another time I will make a lament for the horses; a fine lament, set with words to the harp song, swift and shining like the wind under the sun, for the Nine Steeds of Artos, and men shall sing it around their watch fires for a thousand years. This is only a small lament for a small matter, the merest spray of blackthorn blossom crushed under heel; and see"—he struck a final descending ripple of three notes and reached for the harp bag that hung over his shoulder—"it is finished."

Even as he spoke, I felt rather than saw his gaze go past me. He caught his breath in a snatch instantly stilled. "Look behind you, Artos my Brother. Were nine horses not enough after all?"

But I had already swung around. The fire, as a dying fire will, had leapt up as though in greeting; and on the fringe of the firelight something moved, then came forward into the full gold of the flames; a girl, a woman, though she was no taller than a fourteen-year-old child, with straight dark hair falling loose on either side of her narrow face, and huge eyes set long and slantwise in it. She was not naked as the other had been, but clad in a piece of some dark stuff—green and blue checker it was, when I saw it by the light of day, but in the firelight it looked almost black—flung across one shoulder and wrapped about her with a strap to hold it at the waist. Behind her came seven young men not much taller than herself and of the same dark, narrow make, naked save for kilts about their loins of the same dark plaid as hers or of otter or wild-cat skin, and each carrying a light spear and a small bow and quiver. In the first moment of their stepping forward into the fire-light, they made a strange and not easily forgotten picture, and a gasp ran through the men about me. Cei began to pray under his breath. But oddly enough it never even touched my mind that the girl was a ghost, though indeed she was white enough for one; and my first thought was to curse the men of the guard for sleeping on watch. But that was before I knew the pure-blooded People of the Hills as I came to know them later. When I did, I never again was hard on a sentry who let the Dark Ones slip through, for they move like shadows on the grass.

The men around the campfires had turned about to stare, and others loomed out of the shadows of the tumble-down barrack rows, drawn by some sudden sense of happening; and a great still-ness took us all so that for a long moment we stood and looked at each other, the girl with the seven lithe young warriors, and our-selves in the firelight.

"Who are you?" I said. "And what do you here?"

"I am Daughter among the People of the Hills, up yonder," she said, then, speaking the Celtic tongue with a hesitance and a strange cadence that betrayed it for a tongue that was not her own, "As to what I do here, I come—we come, my brothers and I, to say to you, 'Oh my lord, let you give back to us our sister.'"

There was a stirring and a harsh indrawn breath among the men around the campfire, and she looked about her quickly. "You know, then. You have seen her?"

"We have seen her. . . . How did she fall into the hands of those who were here before we came?"

"She was cutting sallows to make a basket, by the river; we both were by the river. And *they* came upon us—the Sea Wolves and the Painted People." She showed small teeth between drawn-back lips, teeth sharp and pointed as a field vole's, but there was no expression in her voice. "We ran, and they came behind us. Then I suppose she tripped and fell, and her hand was torn from mine, and when I looked around, they were upon her." She came a step closer, her eyes fixed on my face, her hands held out toward me. I smelled the faintly vixen smell of her, and the firelight splintered on the little bronze dagger, pointed as a bee's sting, that was thrust into her belt. "You are the one they call Artos the Bear, are you not? Let you give her back to us, my lord."

"Gladly, if I could," I said. "She is dead."

There was no change in the still, narrow face. "It has been in my heart all this night that she is dead. You found her dead when the strong place fell to you?"

"Yes."

"Then give us her body, that we may take it and lay it in the Long House, among her own people."

In the silence, we heard the wind harping softly across the crumbling ramparts, and the sudden spurt and crackle of the watch fire. Somewhere among the picket lines a horse fidgeted and was still. It was unthinkable to get those nine great carcasses out again; it would be a week's work with ropes and levers; and if it could have been done by the lifting of a finger, I knew that I would not let this girl see what came out from under them, for it seemed to me that they had been near each other, these sisters. "If I had known that her own people would come for her, surely I would have delayed. Now I cannot give you her body, for she is buried already."

"Where?"

I moved aside, so that she might see the mouth of the old grain pit with its rough covering of sods and thatch. Better that she should know it all, as swiftly as might be. "Here at the bottom of the pit, with the carcasses of nine war-horses laid above her. We wrapped her in a cloak and covered her thick with yellow bracken before we tumbled the horses in."

There was a sudden flicker of wild mocking laughter in her face, like summer lightning; the very air about her seemed to quiver with it, but she made no sound. "And all men know that horses are creatures of the Sun, with power over such as we are who belong to the dark warm womb of the Earth. You have taken pains that she should not walk in your sleep. Nine war-horses above her should surely hold her deep enough." And then the laughter died out of her face. "If indeed she lies there at all."

"If?"

"Listen. Listen, Great Man, Sun Man whom they call Artos the Bear. You have told us that our sister is dead. You have told us that you found her so when the strong place fell to you. You have told us that she lies here with nine horses to keep her down. But what proof have we of these things? It is in my heart that she is dead indeed, but fear and longing may trick the heart. If I may not see her body, how may I be sure that you do not hold her here alive for your pleasure? If she be dead, how may I be sure that it was the Sea Wolves and not yourself that brought her to it?"

"How could you be sure of that, though I showed her to you ten times over?"

She looked at me in silence for a while, her eyes wide and still like the dark bitter willow-bark water under trees. Then she said, "No, I am sure of that, though you will not show her to me at all."

"I cannot set my men to hauling nine horses out of a pit, when they are weary from battle, Daughter among the Dark People of the Hills."

She sighed. "Na, I see that you cannot. So be it then, she must lie where she lies. Only come back with me to the Old Woman in my hills, that you may tell her, and she may give you the Dark Drink to pour and the sacred herbs for her sleep-place."

There was a startled silence, and I was aware of the young warriors she had called her brothers, drawn close about her and watching me as intently as she herself, with dark inscrutable eyes.

Bedwyr, who had stood at my shoulder all the while, was the first to speak. "If there be need of this Dark Drink and the herbs, then send one of your brothers back here with them."

"It is for the Sun Lord to do," the girl answered, but her eyes never left my face.

"I am as the Sun Lord's sword hand. I will come, then, in his name."

"You will not, then," I muttered.

But it was as though neither of them heard me. "Thinking maybe that music is a powerful talisman against the spells of the dark." The low tone of mocking was back in her voice again. "But we also have our harpers in the Hollow Hills." Then abandoning him as though he had ceased to exist: "Will you not come, my Lord Artos? It is such a simple thing, but it must be done by the Leader, the Lordly One."

"Why should I come?" I asked at last.

And she moved closer still and set one hand on mine that was clenched on the hilt of my sword. "For a token of faith, maybe," she said.

So I knew that I must go, and I knew why. "When do we start?"

"So soon as you have laid aside your sword and dagger."

"That also?" I said.

"That also. Did I not say 'for a token of faith'?"

I pulled off my sword belt, with the dagger that was thrust into it, and handed both to Bedwyr, who took them without a word. It was Cei who cut in, his voice rough with urgency. "Artos, don't be a fool—armed or unarmed, for God's sake don't go with her!" His big hand was on my arm as though he would have held me back by force. "It's a trap!"

"I think not."

"*Don't* go!"

I shook off his hand. "I must."

"She has laid her spell on you! Don't you understand what she is? If you go with her you're risking your soul!"

I had thought of that, too. "I do not think so; but in any case, I must go."

"At least let me come with you," Bedwyr said, standing with my sword and dagger in his hands.

I shook my head, but I think I felt less steadfast than I seemed. "This is a thing for one man alone. . . . I am ready."

We went out through the narrow northern gate, leaving a hushed camp behind us; the girl moving ahead and I following. The young warriors, silent as they had come, insubstantial now as shadows, as though they had lost all reality when the firelight ceased to touch them, moved behind me and on either hand. From the foot of the fortress wall the hillside dropped almost sheer to the river, thinly covered with broom bushes, hazel and bramble scrub. "This way," said the girl. "Come," and dropped from sight almost as though over a cliff. I followed, and found my feet on a faint path, half lost, narrow and precipitous as a wild-sheep track, that swooped down through the scrub.

"Come," said the girl again; and the shadow-warriors fell back into single file behind me, as we started down. It seemed to me that we followed many paths that night, the thin faint trails made by the deer and the Dark People before ever the Legions drove their roads north. We crossed the road once, and running water at least twice—not the Tweed, but little swift hill streams coming down to join it. It seemed a very long way, but I realized afterward that the girl had led me by ways as twisting and mazy as the dance of a marsh light, and maybe my own weariness made it seem farther still, for I had ridden far and fought hard since last I snatched an hour's sleep. And dawn was spreading up the shining wind-tumbled heights of the sky, when at last we came up by some small patches of oats and barley, over a last shoulder and the open moor, into a shallow upland hollow where three small lost valleys came together.

A little below us, toward the far side of the hollow, where I suppose there was some shelter from the wind, I saw what looked in the first moment like a cluster of small bush-grown barrows—I had seen such a barrow torn open once in my boyhood, when a stream had burst its banks in sudden spate and changed course; and in the heart of it there was the skeleton of a man crouched on his side as a child lies in the womb, and a bronze dagger and an amber necklace. But almost in the same instant as I checked, looking down in the growing light, I saw the pale blur of peat reek rising from among the bushes.

"This is my home," said the girl, looking back over her shoulder. "I am sorry the way has seemed so long."

And we dropped into the hollow where the newly roused little dun cattle lifted their heads to stamp and stare at us as we passed, forded the stream under its stunted moss-grown elder trees, and followed the path that led to the village or steading. Heather washed to the very foot of the turf wall that fenced it around, and even when we passed within, and the small prick-eared hounds came out yawning their pleasure at their lords' return, the dwarfed bushes and briers that grew on the humped turf roofs still gave the place the air of a thicket. The girl made for the largest bothy, which stood, a mere turf hummock with a stunted whitethorn springing above its door hole, in the midst of the others. She ducked into the darkness under the roughly carved lintel beam, and I, following, had to crouch almost onto all fours to make my own way through the hole which was more like the mouth of an animal's lair than a houseplace doorway. The fetid smell that came out of the gloom was animal, too, the same foxy smell that clung about the girl herself, and the thick peat reek caught at my throat and for the moment blinded me, so that if the girl had not cried out a warning, I must have plunged headlong down the four uneven steps within. As it was, I groped and stumbled my way down them awkwardly enough, and found even when I had reached the foot, that I could not stand upright under the willow spears that upheld the roof.

The young warriors and their dogs entered behind me, and with their coming the place grew very full. My sight had begun to clear, and blinking, I saw the folk who were huddled there already; a couple of graybeards and three or four youngish women, and a tumble of dogs and children about the newly awakened central fire. The warriors who had returned last seemed to be all the young men that there were in the place, and I wondered if they were indeed brothers, or if the girl had used the term simply as we of the Company sometimes spoke of ourselves as a brotherhood. I never came completely to understand the relationships of the Dark People, maybe because they do not marry as we do, but seem to hold the women in common.

The girl had gone straight to a white-haired old woman who sat or rather squatted on a low stool beside the fire; a creature obscenely fat, thick-haunched and bag-throated and panting, like an immense toad; and flinging herself on the ground before her, burst into a quick torrent of words in her own tongue. I could understand nothing of it, but I knew that she was telling the old woman of all that had passed at the fort; and the huddled men and women in the big bothy listened to her and watched me. I was increasingly aware of their eyes watching me, seeing, as it were, without giving anything of themselves in return; while the girl and the old woman spoke together, question and answer, question and answer, in that quick dark tongue that reminded me of the patter of thunder rain on broad leaves. The young women against the walls had begun to rock themselves to and fro, wailing softly in the beginning of ritual grief. The place grew stifling so that there seemed no air to breathe, only the peat reek and the stench of fox.

At last the old woman looked up, shaking the cobweb hair back over her shoulders, and beckoned to me with a crooked earth-colored finger. I came and stood before her, with my head bent under the roof, and she craned back her head and beckoned again, downward this time. "Down, kneel down, Sun Man. How may I see you, let alone speak with you, while you stand above me with your shoulders thrusting off the roof?"

"Do as she says," murmured the girl. "She is the Old Woman."

I knelt down, squatting onto my heels so that my eyes were not so much above hers as she sat on her stool, and she leaned forward, peering into my face with bright toad's eyes. "You are he that they call Artos the Bear?"

"I am Artos the Bear, Old Woman."

"So, they said that you were tall as a fir tree, and mouse-fair, and they spoke truth. They said also that you come to drive the Painted People north again, and the Sea Wolves back into the sea."

"Who are *they,* Old Woman?"

"The wild geese when they fly north, maybe, or the wind through the hill grasses." She reached out suddenly and set her hands like twisted claws on either side of my face, drawing it close to her own. Her breath smelled of wild garlic and old sick flesh, and I wanted to look away from the dark eyes with their opaque bloom of light. Even now I am not sure whether I held her narrowed gaze because I would not look away, or because I could not if I had tried. "And so she is dead, the little one," she said at last.

"Yes."

"And you laid her in a pit with nine war-horses piled above her."

"If I had known that her own kind would come for her, I would have done otherwise."

"As to that, the earth will be as warm and dark for her there, as in the Long House of the Mother." Her eyes still held mine, and the wide toothless toad's mouth worked a little. "How did she come to the Great Sleep?"

"As to a way of escape, at the last." I heard my own voice saying: "She had been vilely used, and by many men, but though they would surely have killed her in the end, I think that she found her own freedom before that."

"So, you too have something of the Old Wisdom, the Earth Wisdom in you, Sun Man. . . . And indeed you speak the truth." Suddenly I felt my gaze released, as though she had seen all that she needed to see, but the touch of her hands was still on either side of my face. Then she released that hold also, and dropped them into the fine blue-stained marten skins on her lap. "She is not the first of our kind to take that way into death. . . . Men have always hated us; that is because they are fools, and always fools hate what they fear; but for the most part they have left us alone. But these men that swarm now in our hills, with them it is another thing, the Sea Wolves and the Pirates from the West and the Painted People. They think that because we are small they can crush us and so crush the fear too. They think also that there is gold in the place where we bury our dead. They burn us out as one burns out unwanted bees at the start of winter." (I thought of Irach, who had eaten his father's courage, and the small burned-out village above the road from Deva to Eburacum.) "They drive off our cattle and our women. This place is well hidden, and so far we have been safe from them, we small kindred. But now we too have our sorrow to avenge."

She was silent, and I grew more aware of the thin high keening of the women, and one of the warriors drawing in his breath with a sharp hiss.

"Are you afraid of us, Sun Man?"

"A little," I said. "But I have come in under your roof, Old Woman, when I need not have come at all, with neither a weapon nor a bunch of rowan in my hand."

"That is true," she agreed, "and because of that, and because you are who you are and your sword is a lightning against the Sea Wolves and their kind, it may be that if you call for the People of the Hills when you have need of their aid, the People of the Hills will come to your call. We are small and weak, and our numbers grow fewer with the years, but we are scattered very wide, wherever there are hills and high lonely places. We can send news and messages racing from one end of a land to the other between moonrise and moonset; we can creep and hide and spy and bring back

[171]

word; we are the hunters who can tell you when the game has passed, by a bent grass blade or one hair clinging to a bramble spray. We are the viper that stings in the dark—" She turned a little as she spoke, and summoned one of the young warriors with the same crooked finger with which she had summoned me. He came, and knelt beside me at her feet, not looking at her. Indeed I noticed that none of the men looked her in the eyes; she was sacred, taboo: "The Old Woman."

"Show the Sun Lord one of your arrows."

He reached to the quiver behind his shoulder, and drew out an arrow no larger than a birding bolt. It lay across his narrow palm, shafted with reed, flighted with widgeon's feathers, and barbed with the most wonderfully dressed blue flint. It was a beautiful little thing, a child's toy like the slender bow he carried; but as weapons of war, oddly pitiful.

"It is well made, is it not?" said the Old Woman. "And it flies like a bird. Be careful how you handle it, and do not touch the barb. It has only one fault, that it cannot be used for hunting—the poison remains in the kill."

"Poison?" I had taken up the small thing to examine it more closely, but laid it back with both care and speed in its owner's palm.

"One scratch from that barb—quite a small scratch—and you would be dead in a hundred heartbeats. Therefore it can only be used against man."

"With such weapons to your hand, I find it wonderful that you have not yet driven the Sea Wolves from your hunting runs."

"If we had enough of such weapons, well might you find it wonderful. But the plants that yield the poison are rare and hard to find, and there must be three to poison one arrowhead. Nonetheless, we have some store, and all that we add to it from now is in the hollow of your hand, Sun Lord. It is better and stronger when mixed with the black venom of hate; and we are good haters, we the People of the Hills."

The owner of the arrow slid it back into his quiver as casually as though no death hung in the barb, and getting up, moved back to rejoin his brothers in the shadows; and I heard him playing with a young hound, teasing it and rolling it on its back as I had done with Cabal when he was a puppy.

"Old Woman, I will remember the promise," I said, "for I think that I shall need good haters and skilled hunters in the time ahead." I did not speak of the poisoned arrows.

She settled back on her stool, planting her hands on her knees, clearly finished with one thing and turning to another. "Ah, but I grow old, and dim from walking with dreams, and forget the thing that should come first of all. You must have the Dark Drink, and the herbs to burn on the little one's grave about your nine great Sun Horses." She looked down at the girl who crouched, not rocking or wailing like the rest, beside the fire. "Fetch them, Itha, daughter's daughter; and fetch also the Cup, for the Sun Lord is weary, and must drink to the promise that has been made between us, before he goes again to his own people."

A sudden finger of chill touched me between my shoulders, as the girl Itha rose to obey. How often, in my earliest years, the woman who reared me had impressed on me the warning, "If ever you should be in the Hollow Hills, which the Lord of Life forbid, never let you touch anything to eat or drink. So long as you remember that, they cannot get you in their power, but one cup of milk or a crust of barley bread and you are theirs forever, and your own soul lost to you." It was the thing that all mothers and nurses told to all children; it was the thing one grew up knowing.

I went on kneeling before the Old Woman, trying not to let my hands tighten on my knees, a long time, a very long time; and then the girl was back, bearing in one hand a black pottery flask and a small leather bag, and in the other a cup of age-blackened leather, bound with bronze at the rim, and brimming with drink of some kind.

She laid the flask—which had no base to stand on—together with the bag on the filthy fern-covered floor beside my knee, and held out to me the cup. "Drink, my Lord the Bear, it will shorten the long way back."

I took the cup slowly, and sat looking down into the faintly amber depths of it, holding off the moment. . . . The Old Woman said, "Drink; there is no harm in it. Or do you fear to sleep and wake on a bare hillside and find when you return to it, the fort empty and your spear brothers dead a hundred years ago?"

And the chill that was on me seemed to deepen, with the memory of another woman who had spoken almost those same words.

I had drunk then—of all that she had to give; and wakened on my cold hillside, and though I joyed in the comradeship of my men, in the warmth of the sun and the balance of a sword and the willing power of my horse under me, something of myself had been on that cold hillside ever since.

But I knew that if I did not drink, I should have lost forever the friendship of the Little Dark People, I should have failed in the thing that brought me, and maybe gained enemies as deadly as the little poison arrow sheathed so lightly. I should quite possibly have lost Britain.

I made my stiff face smile. "No man fears to drink in the house of a friend—I drink to the Dark People and the Sun People."

I would have stood up, but under that roof I could not stand fully erect and put my head back. So I drank on my knees, draining the cup to the dregs, and gave it back into the girl's hands. The drink was cool and without the sweetness of heather beer, a forest drink with a flame at the heart of the coolness. I have never tasted its like again.

Then I picked up the flask and the little bag of herbs.

"Burn the herbs at sunset on the little one's sleeping place, and scatter the Dark Drink with the ashes over all, and it will be well with her," said the Old Woman; and then as I murmured some form of leave-taking and turned to the steep steps and the entrance hole: "Stay. My daughter's daughter will go with you to lead you back to your own world."

This time I think we traveled straight, for we left the valley at a different point from our entering it and without fording the stream, and the three peaks of Eildon were before us all the way; while the distance was not a quarter of that which we had covered in the darkness. We came to the foot of the fortress hill and began the upward climb. The wind had died away, and in the warm sunlight among the broom bushes the midges danced in shining clouds. How we escaped the sight of the watchers on the ramparts that time, I do not know, save that the girl Itha was with me and I suppose something of her own cloak of shadows covered us both. I know that at the time the silence from above added to my uneasiness, until vague sounds of movement and the whinny of a horse did something to ease the fear that was still chilly between my shoulder blades. We were almost under the red sandstone walls when Itha turned aside from the deer track, saying for the last time, "This way—come."

I had followed her so far that now I followed her unquestioningly this little way farther. She brought me to a small secret hollow among hazel bushes, not half a bowshot below the walls. Something in the formation of the hillside there must have blanketed sound, for it was not until I was on the very edge of it that I caught the least voice of falling water. It was only a small sound, even then, and oddly bell-like. The girl moved down into the tiny dell, and stooping, lifted aside a mass of bramble and hart's-tongue fern. "See," she said, and I saw a minute upwelling of water that sprang out between two rocks and dropped into a pool the size of a cavalry buckler, and then disappeared under the rocks and fern again. A man might pass within his own length of the water and never know that it was there.

"This is a wonderful thing," I said. "If you had not shown it to me it might have remained hidden until we came to clear the scrub."

"That was in my mind," she said. "At least it will save much water carrying uphill from the burn. The water is good and sweet. . . . When you have need of my people, hang a straw garland on the branch of the big alder tree that grows above the pool for watering the horses, and someone will come."

I was on my knee beside the water, splashing the cold sweetness of it into my eyes; and I asked, "Can I be sure of this tree? How do you know where we shall water the horses?"

"There is one place that is clearly better than all others, where the burn comes down to join the open river, close above the ford. We water our cattle there when we move them from pasture to pasture. You will know the place, and the tree."

She had been speaking quite close behind me, but when I turned, meaning to ask her some other question, she was not there. Only, a few moments later, something flickered below me on the hillside, that might have been some wild thing passing among the hazel bushes.

I got up, and turned to the postern gateway of the fort, which I could see above me, and began to climb.

An elder sapling had rooted itself in the cracked doorsill of a ruined guardroom. I had noticed it last night, as one notices small unmattering things; and as I came up toward the gate I knew one moment of icy foreboding that I should find nothing there but an age-eaten stump, and the familiar sounds of the camp made by men whose faces I did not know.

But the sapling was just as it had been last night, and suddenly the men of the watch were all about me, and there were shouts, and someone came running, running like a boy between the ruined barrack rows, and I saw that it was Bedwyr, with the Minnow and young Amlodd behind him. The last chill of the fear that had been like a thin wind between my shoulder blades fell away, so that the warmth of the sun broke through, and in the same instant weariness descended on me so that I could barely stumble forward to meet them.

"Is it well? Is it well with you?" they asked.

"All is well," I told them. "I think that all is very well. I have what I went for."

"Come and eat," they said.

But I shook my head, laughing muzzily. "All I want is a place to sleep—a corner to crawl into where no one will fall over my legs."

CHAPTER FOURTEEN

Cit Coit Caledon

THERE might have been two months more of possible campaigning weather, but after taking council with Cei and Bedwyr and the rest of the chiefs and captains, I determined against dissipating our forces at the summer's end in an attempt to round up the broken and scattered war host of Huil. Better to concentrate on making a strong winter quarters here in Trimontium and set about turning Castra Cunetium into a strong outpost while there was time for the garrison sent out there to dig themselves in before the winter closed down on them, and get the patrols going steadily to and fro along the road between.

The first thing must be to speak with the Little Dark People again, and make sure that Daglaef the Merchant had made no mistake as to the position of the old fort; make sure also whether it was open to our coming, or in enemy hands and to be fought for as we had fought for Trimontium.

So on the third morning after my return from the Hollow Hills, I bade Flavian hang a straw garland on the broken branch of the big alder tree when he took the squadron down to water the horses. The girl Itha had been right; there was one perfect watering place where the stream that we came afterward to call the Horse Burn paused in its headlong run, and broadened into an alder-fringed pool before it fanned over the piled-up wash of centuries that had formed the ford, and then plunged down its last steep stretch to join the great river. And above the pool one ancient alder tree stood out from its lesser and younger kind as a chieftain from among his sword brothers.

He came when he brought the horses back, to report the thing done, and that evening Druim Dhu, the warrior who had shown me his arrow, walked in through the narrow northern gate, saying to the men on guard there, "The Sun Lord sent for me, and I am come."

They brought him to me beside one of the evening fires on the old parade ground—we had not got as far as any fixed quarters yet, we were merely camping in the ruins of Trimontium as we had camped on open moor—and he squatted onto his heels in the firelight with the dignity of a wild animal, seemingly oblivious of the staring crowd about him; and with no word of greeting, fixed his eyes on my face and waited for me to tell him what I wanted.

When I had done so, he said, "As to this place you speak of, it is two days' trail along the Great Road toward the setting sun. I know, for I have followed the trail myself at the herding; and the walls are yet strong. Whether it is empty or man-held, I do not know, but give me a day, two days at most, to send the word and receive it back again, and I will come and tell you. Oh my lord, is there no more?"

"No more if the place be empty. If it be held, then bring me the number of the men who hold it, and their strength in weapons and stored food. Can that be done?"

"It can be done." He drew his legs under him to rise.

"Eat before you go," I said.

"I eat only by my own hearth."

But I knew that the trust must work both ways. "Eat! I drank by yours!"

He looked at me a long doubtful moment, then sank back beside the fire and held out his hand for the hot barley bannock that someone passed him; and ate, without taking his eyes from my face. When he had eaten, he got up, speaking no word of leavetaking as he had spoken none of greeting, but with a curious deep gesture of hand to forehead, melted out of the firelight into the dusk.

The next day there was no sign of him, but on the morning after that, when the horses were brought up from watering, Flavian came and sought me out. "Sir, Druim Dhu has come in again." He said, "I don't see how he does it, but it gives me the prickles! We started to get the squadron back from the water, and there he was in our midst!"

I glanced past Flavian, expecting to see the little dark figure behind him, but he shook his head. "He would not come up to the fort. He just said, 'Tell the Sun Lord that there is nought for him to drive out of the strong place we spoke of, save the hill foxes and maybe an owl or two'—and then he was gone. Maybe he turned into an alder tree." He laughed a little as he said it, but the laughter was not altogether easy.

"The ability to turn into an alder tree is no bad thing for a scout."

"I suppose not. It is unchancy all the same, the way he comes and goes." Flavian hitched impatiently at his shoulders, and looked at me with sudden gravity. "Artos, sir, are we to trust him?—*Them* —about Castra Cunetium, I mean? They have the name for being treacherous little beasts."

"Nevertheless, we are going to trust them. We shall send the usual scouting party ahead lest the state of things has changed since the message was sent. But that is all. It is in my heart that Druim Dhu and his kind will not prove treacherous to us unless we earn their treachery."

And so a few days later, with their share of the stores, weapons and raw materials of war loaded onto their share of the baggage beasts, Bedwyr with his own squadron of fifty cavalry, a war band of spearmen, and a few slingers and light horse for scouting, took the road westward up the river gorge, to garrison Castra Cunetium.

"We shall miss his harp in the winter evenings," said Cei, leaning beside me on the red sandstone of the west rampart to watch the little force grow smaller and smaller in the distance, until it was lost in the tawny dust cloud of the summer's end.

But that autumn we had little leisure in Trimontium for missing anybody or anything. We cleared the bushes and scrub for two bowshots around the walls, save for a clump of hazel shading the spring that had been as it were a gift to us from the Dark People. We set about clearing and restoring one of the two wells, which looked as though it might bear water again. We made the old latrines usable after a fashion, and patched up the rampart walls as best we could; we contrived, with bracken thatched onto hurdles, to reroof several barrack rows, some to serve their old purpose, some for outhouses, storerooms and stables. We got in peat and firewood, and bracken for fodder and bedding. Most of that work fell to the foot soldiers of our auxiliaries, who grumbled incessantly, as the warrior kind generally do when they are not fighting; for there was other work in plenty for the Companions and the light horsemen. Before September was out, we were regularly patrolling the lateral road, and from the first, I used small cavalry knots for foraging among the British villages and at the same time gaining some kind of control over the countryside. The clans of central and southwestern Valentia had not been drawn into the general flare-up; they were still, for the most part, friendly, and they had assuredly no longing for the Picts and the Sea Wolves trampling through their hunting runs leaving the inevitable wake of red ruin behind them. But on the other hand, many of the petty chieftains did not see why they should submit to a war host not of their own tribe in Trimontium, let alone help to feed them with the winter coming when they would have little enough for themselves. Sometimes it came to the direct threat. "Three bullocks or we fire the thatch," especially if Cei led the foraging party, for he could use threats with a kind of grim good humor that left few scars behind. But there was always the risk that if we pressed them too hard, the chieftains would bethink them that another way of saving their fields and cattle from the Barbarians was to make common cause with them; and so threats were not things to be used too often. And in the main we found that the coming of heavily armed cavalry, a thing that the tribes had never seen before, was at once threat and reassurance enough. For the same reason, I refused to allow any cattle raiding. Instead, we hunted. There was game enough for all in the scrubby woods around Eildon, tribesmen and war host and little dark hunters alike; especially as the wilder and younger of the war host chose to turn their hunting spears chiefly against boar or wolf, and so the better food game was left for the rest.

Late in the autumn our promised supplies came up from Corstopitum, and among the grainskins and tallow jars were the sheaves of arrows, the saddle leather and blocks of salt which I had bullied out of Eburacum's bishop. (May God be good to his tired old soul, he was a bonny fighter against paying his just dues, but he kept his word once it was given.) And after that most of what we killed was salted down and stored for the winter.

Winter came early that year, in a flurry of sleet that turned to snow and thawed and came again, and this time did not thaw, but lay week after week among the hills, adding to the stresses and hazards of both hunting and foraging; and for long spells at a time there was no grazing for the horses, so that they must be kept stabled and forage-fed; and in the long winter nights when the icy winds yowled through Trimontium and we heard the whistle of the wild geese overhead, we missed Bedwyr's harp, even as Cei said that we should.

In all those months we heard and saw nothing, either of the Barbarians or the Little Dark People.

But spring came suddenly and early as winter had done. There was a red flush among the alders when we went to water the horses, and the hills were loud with the crying and calling of lapwing, though the snow still lay thick on the northern slopes and the wind cut like a fleshing knife. And one evening when I brought my own squadron in from exercise—we were hard at it already getting the horses back into condition again—a shadow shook itself clear of the guardhouse door, and Druim Dhu with his little war bow in his hand was standing at my stirrup. He looked older, his eyes sunken back into his head. But then so did we all, it was the famine look, the wolf look that comes to most men at the winter's end when the food runs low.

"My Lord Artos." He touched my foot in the stirrup by way of greeting.

I reined aside, gesturing to the others to go on, and dismounted. "Greetings, Druim Dhu, do you bring me news?"

"The Cran Tara has gone forth," he said.

"So."

"To the settlements of the Sea Wolves along the land edge yonder." Druim jerked his head eastward. "Toward the Snow"— he meant the north—"and toward the sunset to summon the tribes and the Painted People. They were scattered back to their own places, to Manann, those who could get so far, last summer's end; and the White Shields from across the Sunset Sea wintered with them. Now the Cran Tara has gone forth, and they will be hosting again."

"Where to?"

"Into the Great Forest yonder between the two rivers, Cit Coit Caledon that we call Melanudragil in the dark tongue."

From that time forward, as the spring drew on, one or another of the Little Dark People appeared from time to time. Not always Druim nor even one of his brothers, but others whom I had never seen before. Once it was a little old man tough and twisted as a heather root, who materialized under the very hooves of the patrol as it came in. Once it was even a woman. It seemed that among the People of the Hills also, some kind of Cran Tara had gone out.

Each brought some word of the enemy's hosting, of the numbers growing in Caledon even before the snow was gone from the northern corries of Eildon; of Pictish and Scottish war bands seeping in by secret ways; of the long black war boats of the Sea Wolves prowling in up the Bodotria Estuary with reinforcements for their brothers of the settlements. And for the time being there was little we could do but hold all things in readiness, and wait until the red-hot moment came. I knew that to try to deal with the inflowing war bands piecemeal would be to fritter away our own strength almost certainly to no purpose. It was no formless skirmishing of war bands all across Valentia that we needed, but one smashing victory at the heart of things, Huil Son of Caw slain and his war host broken and scattered; after that the rest, however slow, would follow.

So I turned a deaf ear to the urging of the hotheads, and remained, as Cei told me to my face, "like an old eagle molting on his perch," in my half-ruined fort, while slowly the Barbarians gathered like thunder drawing in from the skyline.

Presently Bedwyr came in, leaving Owain in command at Castra Cunetium, and we held a council of war around the fire that burned in the entrance to the part-roofed Sacculum where I had made my own quarters. By that time it was clear from their movements, reported by the Little Dark People, that the enemy intended to cut the lateral road, and that once done, we should cease to be a system for quenching and holding down Lowland Caledonia, and become merely two isolated strongholds, each with its own perilously long and fragile communication line behind it, and no sure means of linking shields with each other.

"Added to which," said Bedwyr, thrumming softly at the harp on his knee, "that if Druim and his kind speak truth, we are like to be outnumbered by upward of three to one when Huil has the last of his war host gathered, and you have a most noble prospect."

"Cei has been urging me to deal with the inflow piecemeal," I said.

"And you are not of his mind?"

"I am of the mind to wait for the right time, and break the thing with one blow—or am I growing old, Bedwyr?"

"No," said Bedwyr. "That is Cei. It is always the old who are fiercest and most impatient." And he made music on his harp that was like a snapping of the fingers, and grinned across the fire at Cei, who grew purple behind his russet bush of beard.

"Why you—you lop-eared nightingale—" I caught his eye and he subsided into mutterings like an old hound when it is put out.

"Peace, children, and listen to me. I have let battle be forced upon me because I have very little choice in the matter, *but also because I believe that by doing so we may well gain our own choice of fighting ground.*"

"How then?" Cei put aside his anger for more important matters.

"By waiting until the last possible moment, to allow the enemy down into the most southerly tongue of Caledon; by not taking our own battle stand until they are within a few miles of the road itself. The forest is more open there, and on the watershed we shall have the river marshes below on either side to narrow the pass for us."

"For them also," Cei said.

"Aye, but at the least it will even the length of the battle lines and keep them from spreading out to engulf us, as they could well do with their greater numbers; and I think that we can take care of *their* flanks in advance. Therein lies one of the few advantages of a defensive action." I took a bit of charred stick from the fire and began to draw the pattern of fighting as I proposed it. I was not a stranger to Cit Coit Caledon, for I had hunted there, and ridden with the patrol more than once; it is no bad thing for a war leader to gain some knowledge of the lay of his campaign country.

And so on a March morning, drawn up in a somewhat unorthodox battle formation across the highest part of the watershed, we waited for the Barbarians.

The red-hot moment that we had waited for had come at last, signaled to us by the Dark People in smoke smother across the hills; and within an hour, all of us, save for a small and most

[183]

evilly tempered garrison left behind in Trimontium, had been on the march. It had been almost noon when the signal came through, and it was far into the night when we reached the agreed war camp and found Owain with his slim column from Castra Cunetium there just ahead of us. Found there also Druim Dhu, standing by one of the newly kindled campfires. But I had scarcely recognized him at first, through the war patterns of clay and red ochre daubed on his face and slight naked body. Only when he came and touched my foot in the stirrup in the moment before I dismounted, I had known him for sure by the familiar gesture. His hair was bound back with thongs, and the quiver of small deadly arrows hung well-stocked from his shoulder.

"The Wolves have made camp on the shoulder of Wildcat Ridge by the Mark Stones," he said. (To the People of the Hills, the Saxons were the Sea Wolves and the rest the Painted People; and the Tribes and the Scots raiders, when banded together, they often spoke of simply as "The Wolves.")

"How far is that?"

But distance meant little to Druim and his kind; they reckoned by the time that it took to make the journey. "If they start at first light, they will be well into the high ground whence the two rivers spring when the shadows lie so—" He stooped, and setting the foot of his bow to the ground, drew a line where its shadow would fall about three hours before noon.

"So. How many do they muster now?"

"Between two and three times the number that follow you, my Lord Artos. But there are brothers of mine—a few—not so far from here, who have scouted for you all this time and will serve none so ill as warriors."

And indeed a score or more of the Little Dark Warriors did come to our fire in the night, and disappeared again by morning. Whether they were the full tally, I did not ask. I had long since learned that where the Dark People were concerned, one did not ask; to try to use them as normal troops would have been like trying to forge a spear blade from the substance of a hill mist. One simply accepted what they gave.

We had snatched a few hours of sleep, and been astir at first light, with the fires fallen into ash, and after tending the horses, were gulping down our own hurried meal of hard barley bannock as we moved off into position, when the word came that the enemy were on the move—God knows how they got it through so quickly, for one could not send a beacon chain through the forest; but I thought that once just before first light I had felt rather than heard a distant rhythmic mutter of sound that might be a hollow log slapped by an open palm.

And so now, in the chosen place a few miles north of the road, our battle line was formed, and we waited for the first sign of the enemy. I was not happy, for I have always been a cavalry leader; my ways of battle are the ways of the horse, and yet save for our light riders far out of sight on the advanced flanks, the struggle ahead of us must be fought out on foot. Impossible to use heavy cavalry effectively in this scrub woodland, though it was far less dense than a few miles farther north. Waiting with my own squadron in the reserve, a little behind the center, I looked along the battle line, wondering, now that it was too late to make any change, whether I had made the best use of my strength. I had dismounted the whole of the Company, the heaviest and steadiest troops that I possessed, and set Cei and Bedwyr to captain them in the center of the battle line. On either flank the light spearmen, and beyond again, on the outer horns, the archers and slingers in isolated groups, curved forward so that the whole line formed, as well as it could in that rough country, a deep bow to bring the advancing Wolves under flank attack before ever their center could make contact with ours. Beyond again, hidden from sight, I knew where the knots of light riders waited; and I prayed to all the gods that ever gave ear to fighting men, that no pony would betray them by whinnying at the wrong moment.

We were strung across the neck of the watershed, making the best use of the natural slope of the country, with our left flank resting on a burn that ran down to join the young Cluta, and our right on the steep thorn-tangled scarp that dropped to the marshes of the Tweed. Behind me, if I looked southward, I should see the great hills of the frontier country, where half the rivers of Valentia were born, and through which, by way of Three Hills or its outpost fort, the roads ran to the Wall. Ahead of us opened a broad clearing where the young bracken was beginning to spring, and beyond, the forest rolled away and away like a dark sea washing about Manann the ancient heartland of the Pictish kingdoms; the Dark, the Forest, the ancient and savage and unknown; so that we stood as it were in the pass between two worlds, to hold it for one against the other.

It was a gray spring day, early in the year for the start of the campaigning season, and the starry white wood anemones turned their shivering backs to the wind and the scuds of rain that blew in our faces and darkened the crimson of the dragon on our standard to the color of half-dried blood. I thought how Arian's mane should be blowing back across my bridle hand, and I missed him sorely, missed his fidgeting and quickening, the thrusting urgency of him between my knees. My mail shirt dragged at my shoulders, weighing more heavily upon me with the long standing, the tramping up and down; and I wondered again if I had done a foolish thing in keeping the Companions in full war gear while dismounting them. But it was weight I wanted in the center, weight and steadiness; mobility was for the wings.

Ahead of us the forest seemed very dark—and indeed I do not think that was fancy, for I have noticed always the same thing about Cit Coit Caledon; partly of course it is the pines, the dark slow tide of pines such as we do not know in the South, but it is the same in the thinner places where the hills and the high moorlands thrust up through the scrub of oak and birch and hazel like gaunt shoulders through the rents in a shaggy cloak; always in my mind there is this quality of darkness, of wolfish menace in the land itself. It was as though maybe it were a very old forest and crouched brooding over secrets that it would not be well for men to know.

Something stirred behind me, and a dark shadow slid between my elbow and that of my standard-bearer. I caught the whiff of fox, and again Druim Dhu was there. "They are less than eight bowshots beyond the rim of the dark trees—a great host, a very great host. We shall have good hunting by and by," and he showed white teeth in a flash of silent laughter—his laughter was always silent, like his sister's. With the stripes of clay and ochre ringstraking his slight brown limbs like the early light striking through the bushes, it was hard to be sure, save for his voice, that he was there at all; and then suddenly—he was not.

But almost in the same instant, as though it were an echo or an answer to his words, we heard the roaring of the Scottish war horns, like some huge stag belling under the trees.

I saw a ripple run through the ranks ahead of me as a cat's-paw of wind through standing barley; and the whole center, who until now had been leaning on their spear shafts, crouched down, each man under his covering buckler, with his spear leveled in welcome to the nearing enemy.

The wind fell away, and somewhere a magpie scolded sharply; then a long gust came booming up through the woods driving a dark scud of rain into our faces, and with the wind suddenly there was a crashing among the undergrowth that rolled swiftly nearer, and a flicker of movement all along the shore of the clearing. It strengthened and gathered form and substance and became a swarming of men under the spring-flushed trees. The Wolves were here. They set up a great shout at sight of us, and came on, keeping what line they could among the bramble hummocks and the tangle of last year's bracken, sweeping toward us at a steady, menacing wolf lope that seemed slow and yet ate up the ground with a terrible speed. I had just time to make out the barbaric horsetail standards of the Saxons in the center, the white gull-wing gleam of the Scots' lime-washed shields on the left wing and the brave blue war paint of the yelling Picts on the right. It was a very great war host, as Druim Dhu had said, spreading out as it seemed forever, and as they swung nearer, I felt the tremor of the ground under their feet, as one feels it when a river breaks its banks after rain in the hills, and the very rocks are afraid.

Indeed I felt at that moment much as a man must feel who stands in the track of floodwater and sees the spate roaring toward him. I felt rooted in my heavy ring shirt, and knew that the same sense of nightmare was howling through every man of my heavily armed center.

The foremost of the Barbarians' rush was level with the tips of the curved horns now; and I prayed that the archers might not loose too soon. "Mithras, slayer of the Bull, hold back their arrow hands! Lugh of the Shining Spear—Christos, let them not loose too soon!"

The Barbarians were well within the trap when first from one side, and then a heartbeat later from the other, a ragged flight of arrows leapt from the undergrowth and thrummed into their midst. Men pitched and fell in their tracks, and for an instant under the barbed hail the charge wavered and lost impetus; then with a yell, gathered itself together and stormed on, men stumbling and falling on the flanks where the arrows wrought most havoc. Before me I saw the tense backs and braced shoulders of the men crouching over their leveled spears. . . .

A volley of light throwing axes came rattling against the bull-hide buckles of our front rank, and hard after it the enemy sprang forward yelling like berserkers upon the waiting spears. Shield rank and shield rank came together with a rolling thunder; the cries of men who had found the spears, the ring and clash of weapons and the grinding clangor of shield boss on shield boss; and the breath-held tension of the moments before had gone roaring up in bloody chaos. The Saxons were striving to take our spearpoints on their oxhide shields, jamming and bearing them down into uselessness, and in the first crash of the onslaught they were succeeding as, despite the weight, our center was forced back by the sheer ferocity of the rush. Then the Companions rallied and thrust forward again; swords were out now, and through the tumult and the weapon ring I heard Cei's bull voice roaring to his men, and all along the center the two battle lines were locked together like two wild animals struggling for a throathold. Behind me and on either side I felt the squadron taut as runners in the instant before the white scarf falls, but they were all the reserves I had, and I could not afford to fling them in too soon.

The Companions were superb. Unused to foot fighting as they were, they were holding stubbornly to the ground that they had taken, in face of the furious pressure that was being hurled against them. Once they even thrust forward again, before they were once more slowed into clogged immobility. For long moments that seemed to stretch into an aching eternity of time, the two centers strained together, so that even above the boil of battle it seemed that one could hear the gasping breath and the throb of bursting hearts. Men were falling on both sides behind the shield-walls, tangling the feet of the living, as the long death-locked battle mass heaved and swayed to and fro, with never more than a stride's length lost or won. God alone knew how long that hideous grapple might last, draining us of men, with nothing gained, and I knew that the moment to fling in the reserves had come. I put up my hand in signal to the trumpeter beside me, and he raised the aurochs horn on its baldric and sounded the charge, clear and high above the surf-roar of battle. It was the charge for the outlying cavalry knots as well as for us, and as we burst forward I was aware of a new sound swelling the tumult; the swift drub of horses' hooves sweeping in from the wings.

The struggling ranks ahead parted to let us through, as foot parts to let through a cavalry squadron. We had taken the blunt-ended wedge formation, and like a wedge we drove on into the battle mass of the enemy, yelling the old war cry, "Yr Widdfa! *Yr Widdfa!*" Chins driven down behind our shields, gray mailed wedge broadening behind the Red Dragon, we drove forward deeper and deeper into the Saxons, while at the same time—though I had no thought to spare for them now—the little bodies of horse had charged in on flank and rear, driving the Barbarians down upon our wedge. Archers and javelin men, tossing aside their now useless weapons, drew sword and closed in from either flank. The Wolves were driven in on each other, becoming so densely packed that each man's shield hampered his comrade's sword arm, and the dead clogged the feet of the living, and all their valiant efforts to force their way on only drove them the more deeply to our iron wedge.

Even now I am not sure how the day would have gone had the enemy been one war host, instead of four, each with their own ways of fighting, with little idea of how to combine, and nothing save courage and savagery in common between them. As it was, quite suddenly their battle mass began to waver in its forward thrust as its ranks thinned, and at last the moment came when with one supreme effort, with a slow long straining heave, we seemed to lift and upsurge and spill over them. Then, split well nigh in two by our wedge, overwhelmed and battered blind, they broke and gave back and began to stream away, trampling their own dead and wounded underfoot, trampled down in their turn by the small unshod hooves of the light cavalry.

We broke forward after them, cutting them down as they ran. Among the Saxons, only the great ones wore ring mail, while the lesser folk had no better body armor than a leather jerkin, and that only if they were lucky; the Scottish warriors, save again for their nobles, had little more, and the Picts, from the greatest to the least, had flung themselves into battle naked save for a leather loin guard. Yet some would not run but stood to face us, or retreated step by step, still fighting, and were cut down in their tracks, still proud beyond yielding. The hummocky ground among the bushes was clothed with trampled dead, and as we thrust on, I was aware of others running beside the war host; little shadows that slipped low from tree to tree. Something passed my ear with the high whine of a gnat, and the Saxon in front of me ran on a few steps with a small dark arrow no bigger than a birding bolt quivering between his shoulders, then dropped and lay writhing. The light riders were taking over the chase from us now, and I called off the Companions as one calls off hounds; most of them could not have heard me, and I dared not use the horn to sound the Retreat, for that would have called off the others also; but one by one, finding the chase taken up from them, they were dropping out, panting in their heavy war gear, wiping reddened sword blades on handfuls of long grass, turning back to me, gathering into their squadrons again. The sounds of the pursuit were dying away, and the wind and the soft chill rain still came scudding down from the north over our hunched shoulders as we turned back to our battle line and last night's camp beyond.

"Look there," said Bedwyr, suddenly walking at my shoulder. "And there—" He pointed. And there was a man lying among the dead with a little dark arrow in his back; and then another man, and another. . . .

"The Old Woman said they were the viper that stings in the dark," I said. "The pursuit is in sure hands, it seems."

It is in my mind that that was the cruelest fight I ever fought. It cost us dearly, too, for our own battle line was marked out now with its random line of bodies, piled in places two and three deep. More than fifty of the Companions died that day, apart from the auxiliaries, and jaunty little Fulvius lay among them, taking part of my boyhood with him; and Fercos who had followed me down from Arfon in the first spring of the Brotherhood. I looked up at the faint brightness beyond the drifting cloud wrack overhead, and saw that it was not yet much past noon.

The sun was still above the western moors and the weary work that follows battle not yet completed, and I was with Cei and Gwalchmai snatching a brief respite beside one of the watch fires while the tatterdemalion gaggle of women who had followed us as usual got some kind of meal together, when a crashing and rattling came through the undergrowth as though some great beast were heading our way, and as I turned quickly toward the sound, a man rolled, or rather was thrust, into the firelight. A tall man, naked and war-patterned with the Pictish woad, with a mane of tawny hair and frowning tawny eyes, who stumbled and almost fell, then caught himself proudly erect once more. I saw that he was dripping blood from a wound in the left knee; his hands were twisted behind his back and he was surrounded by a knot of little dark warriors. In the first moment of seeing him as he stood there in their midst, I thought suddenly of some proud wild thing brought to bay by a pack of little dark hounds, save that no hounds were as silent or as deadly as those that thronged about him.

"My Lord Artos," one of them said, and I saw that it was Druim Dhu, "we have brought you Huil, the spearhead of your enemies. Here is his sword," and he stooped and laid it at my feet.

The man in their grip was far spent, panting like a beast that has been run hard; sweat gleamed on his forehead when he raised his head to give me look for look, flinging back the tawny hair that he had no free hand to thrust out of his eyes.

"Is that true?" I demanded.

"I am Huil, Son of Caw." He gave me the answer in Latin little worse than my own. "And you, I know, are he that they call Artos the Bear, and I am in your power. That is all that we need to know, you and I. Now kill me and be done with it."

I did not answer at once. The man before me was not a Great One in the way of Hengest, but he was a man whom other men follow; I am such a one myself, and I recognized the kind. He was too dangerous to let go free, for if I did so, men would gather to him again. There were three courses open to me: I could have his sword hand struck off, and let him go. None of his own would follow a maimed leader, for by their way of thinking to do so would be to run upon disaster. I could send him south to Ambrosius, safely chained like a wild beast for the arena; or I could kill him now. . . .

"Why did you do it?" I asked, and the question sounded stupid in my own ears.

"Revolt against my rightful lords and masters?" He looked at me with something of laughter even in his despair and white exhaustion. "Maybe because, like you, I would be free, but for me, freedom is a different thing."

Others were gathering about us to look on, his name running from one to another, but he never spared them a glance; his fierce tawny gaze held unwavering to my face, as though he knew that it was the last thing he would see. "Kill me now," he repeated, and the tone was an order. "But strike from in front; I never yet took a wound in the back, and even in death a man has his vanities. Also let you first unbind my hands."

"There is nothing to bruise any man's vanities in dying with his hands bound," I said. I have wondered since whether I was wrong, but at the time I was taking no risk. I made a small gesture to Cei, who had stepped forward, his own sword drawn, to the captive's side. Huil Son of Caw smiled a little, confronting the blow with open eyes. Under the blue war patterns I saw how white his skin was, where the brown of the strong neck ended at the collar bone; white as a peeled hazel nut—until the red fountained out over it. The blow was swift, and he made it swifter by leaning to meet it.

That was the only time I ever had to do that particular thing.

We cut his bound hands free, then, and later, when our own dead had been laid away, we gave him honorable burial, deep against the wolves, and his sword with him. Only we raised no mound or cairn to mark the spot for a place of gathering. The wind was dying away and the rain turning soft and steady, what the folk of the Cornlands call a growing rain, as Cei and I turned away from the dark plot of newly turned leaf mold.

"It is in my heart that we shall not need to fight another pitched encounter among these hills," Cei said. "Your sword hand is something heavy."

"There are more wolves in Caledonia than died today."

"Truly. But I think that they will not again face the Bear as a war host in open battle. Better from now on, to look for the ambush behind the hill shoulder and the knife in the back, Artos my friend."

CHAPTER FIFTEEN

Midsummer Fires

CEI was right. There were no more enemy hostings, no more pitched battles among the lowland hills. Instead, from that time forth began a different kind of war, a war of raids and counter-raids, a patrol ambushed and cut to pieces in the hill mists, a village burned out in return, a stream poisoned by having dead bodies dumped into it. . . . It was more wearying than any campaign of open fighting could have been. For one thing it never quite ceased, even in winter, and so there was never a time when one could sit back and sigh and loosen the sword belt. That first summer and autumn I was striving by every means in my power to strengthen my hold over the great boss of lowland hills that was the chief barrier between the northern wilds and the rest of Britain; gaining the friendship, where I could, of the surrounding British chieftains, putting the fear of the gods into those that needed it. Presently I must follow up Cit Coit Caledon by turning on the last coast settlements to drive back the Sea Wolves, as I had done around Lindum. But first the lowland hills must be secured. And we carried fire and avenging sword and the terror of heavy cavalry that they had never known before, among the Duns and villages and the old turf-walled hill forts west and northward even into the heart of the Pict Country.

About a month after Cit Coit Caledon the supply train got through to us from Corstopitum, bringing, besides the grain and arrow sheaves, the spearheads and tallow and bandage linen in the great leather-covered pack panniers, the money (less than had been promised) to pay the men. And not many days later the supplies from Deva arrived at Castra Cunetium, together with

that year's draft of young horses, which Cei, who had taken over
the outpost by that time, sent on to me. With the supply trains came
our first news of the outside world in half a year. For me the
news came in a long dispatch from Ambrosius. Oisc and the boy
Cerdic who had escaped from Eburacum had both reappeared in
Cantii Territory. The Saxons under Aelle had captured Regnum
and sacked Anderida, slaying every man of the British garrison,
but Ambrosius had succeeded in hemming them into the narrow
coastal strip under the South Chalk though as yet he had failed to
drive them from their new hills. It did not make particularly good
hearing, but it all seemed oddly far away.

For Flavian also there was news, but his came up with the Deva
supplies. He took the letter off by himself to a quiet corner of the
camp before breaking the thread that held the two leaves of the
tablet together; and later he came to me where I was looking over
the new horses, the letter still in his hand. "Artos—sir—" He was
almost stammering in his eagerness, filled with a kind of grave delight.

"It is from Teleri. She has got a child!" But I had known as soon
as I saw the fool's face.

I said the due things and asked, because clearly he was waiting
for that: "Is it a boy—or a girl?"

"A boy," he said. "A son."

"Then we will wet his head in his absence, this evening when
the day's work is done." I set my hand on his shoulder in congratu-
lation. But God knows how I envied him.

Autumn came, and found us well strengthened in our position,
with a fruitful summer's work behind us. Winter passed and again
the alders by the horses' drinking pool flushed red with rising sap.
I had had few dealings with the Dark People since Cit Coit Caledon; they brought us news from time to time, and in return we
gave them all that we could spare from the winter grain stores.
That was all. But I knew always that I had only to hang a garland
on the Lord of the Alder Trees, and before night, Druim Dhu or
one of his brothers would come walking into the fort, and the
knowledge was good.

That spring also, I had another earnest of the Dark People, for a
small plant with silvery leaves and a fragile white flower sprang

up in the rough grass that now covered the place where the girl lay
with our nine war-horses above her. I suppose a seed must have
fallen from the dried herbs that Old Woman had given me, when
I burned them for the girl's spirit, and lain fallow for a year. I
never saw that flower growing anywhere else.

In the second spring, leaving Cei now in command at Trimontium, and Bedwyr harrying the East Coast Settlements, I took
Amlodd my armor-bearer, Flavian and Gault and a few others, no
more than would make up a hunting party, and rode far to the
southwest, into Dumnonia hunting runs. To me it felt almost painfully homelike to be in that land of heather moors and little shining
lochs within the sounding of the western sea; for the tribesmen
were the same breed as those of Cador's kingdom who were my
own kin. But I had not come into those western moors to savor
the sour-sweet of homing hunger, but in the course of my efforts
to bond together the loyal tribes and draw them to the Red
Dragon.

Maglaunus, one of the greatest of the clan chieftains, proved
also one of the most chancy to deal with. He was not in the least
hostile, merely determined, as it seemed at one time, that I should
have no opportunity of speaking at all of the matter that had
brought me to his Dun, and I knew, as one knows with a shying
horse, that it would be useless and worse than useless to force him
willy-nilly at the thing that startled him.

On the first and second of the three days that I had determined
to spend on him, we hunted by day, and by night listened to the
harper in his high painted timber hall, while around the lower fire
his three black-browed sons and the younger of the household warriors tussled together like hound whelps or diced or tried to fly
their hawks at sparrows among the house beams; and there was
no chance to speak apart with the chieftain at all.

And then on the third day—it was the eve of Midsummer—he
seemed to change his mind and be ready at any rate to talk; and
for most of the daylight hours we walked to and fro in the little
orchard below the Dun where the fisherfolk hung out their nets to
dry among the apple trees, arguing.

Maglaunus had a grievance, though he put the matter temper-
ately enough and without rancor. "Since you burst asunder Huil's
war host, the Scots raiders have returned to their usual ways; al-

ready by last summer's end they were slave-reeving along the
coast. It is no good turn that you have done us, my Lord Artos,
and if I give you this help that you press for in men and weapons,
I shall but have the less with which to defend my own coast."

"Would you rather, then, have had the whole Barbarian war
host sweeping through your lands?" I demanded. "You may have
that yet, Maglaunus the Chieftain, if I run short of fighting men
and the wherewithal to arm and feed them."

"That is as may be," he said, "but the Scots raiders are sure."

And from that, reason how I would, as we paced and turned
and paced again under the small wind-bent apple trees, it seemed
that I could not move him.

The day had seemed much like any other at first, save that
most of the men were out rounding up the cattle for the ceremonies
of the night; but when the light began to fade, a change came, the
change that comes over every Dun and camp and village when the
light fades on the eve of Midsummer. And when Maglaunus and I
turned back to the evening meal with our arguing still unfinished,
the Dun within its strong turf walls was throbbing like a softly
tapped drum. In the chieftain's hall as in every lesser houseplace,
men and women ate quickly and silently, as though their thoughts
were turned to another place. And when the eating was done, the
women quenched every hearth fire and torch flame, so that the
whole Dun held its breath in a waiting darkness; and in the darkness they went out, men and women, children and dogs, every
soul in the Dun whose legs would bear them, a thin trickle at first
but gathering more from every houseplace as they passed, through
the gateway in the strong turf wall and away toward the moors
that rose a mile or so inland.

Flavian and I and the rest of us, following Maglaunus and his
household warriors, joined ourselves to the dark silent ripple of
passing shadows, and went with them, no more than shadows ourselves in the deepening summer dusk.

It was an evening of warm whispering airs, when even the darkness that bloomed the earth seemed no more than a transparent
wash of shadow over the day, and the sky was a vast green crystal
bell still echoing with light in the north. But as we climbed higher,
the night grew less clear, and faint diaphanous wisps of mist
began to drift about us, the chill smell of the sea seemed stronger

than it had done lower down, and the earth became an older and a stranger place touched with the same dark potency as I had sensed in Melanudragil. We came to a place where the heather swept up into a little boss crowned by a circle of standing stones; nine tall stones I counted, that seemed, with their feet in the heather and the faint mist wreaths about their heads, to have checked into stillness from some mysterious movement of their own, only in the moment that our sight touched them.

On the level ground below the circle, where the heather fell back to make a dim dancing floor, a great stack of logs and brushwood waited in darkness, as the Dun was waiting, for the Need Fire, the Fire of Life, to be reborn.

So it had been among the Arfon hills in my own boyhood, and when the crowd spread into a great expectant circle, and from their midst nine young warriors stepped out to work the fire drill, I remembered like a physical thing the vibration of the bow cords under my hands, and my father's world meant nothing to me and my mother's world claimed me for its own.

They made the fire at last, after the usual long-drawn struggle, the curl of smoke and the sparks that fell on the waiting tinder, the sudden miracle of living flame. A great cry of joyful relief burst from the watching crowd—odd how one always has that fear: "This year the fire will not come and life will be over." To me it was this year—this year the dark will close over our heads, this is the black wilderness and the end of all things, and the white flower will not bloom again. . . . The small licking tongue of flame, so easily to be quenched, was a promise, not of victory maybe, but of something not lost, shining on in the darkness. And I shouted with the rest, out of the sudden hot exultancy leaping in my belly. They crowded forward to kindle torches at the wisp of crackling straw and thrust them into the dark waiting fire stack. And the inert mass of logs and brushwood woke from its sleep of darkness and roared up into the heat and smoke and leaping glory of the Midsummer Fire. The dark shadows leapt into reality as the red light touched them, and became rejoicing men and women, and as the licking flames spread farther and farther into the pile, long-drawn shout on shout of joy rose from them, breaking at last into a chant of praise that seemed to beat like great wings about the hilltop.

The chanting sank and the joy changed to merrymaking, and

for a while the wonder was gone from the night. The thing became a beer-drink, as it always does, as though men, having come too near to the mystery, sought now to shut it out behind a comfortable barrier of noisy and familiar things.

When the fire had sunk low, presently they brought in the cattle from the great hill corral where they had been penned in readiness, and began to drive them through the sinking flames that they might be fruitful in the year ahead. That too was from my boyhood; the wild-eyed, wide-horned heads uptossing in the firelight, the terrified mares with their foals at heel, the torrent of bobbing fleeces, embers scattered under a smother of sharp hooves, sparks caught like burrs in the horses' manes, the tumult of neighing and lowing, the shouts of the herdsmen and the barking of the driving dogs.

Men ran to dip branches into the scattered embers behind them, capturing the Need Fire before it was lost again, whirling them aloft until they became mares' tails of smoky flame. Some set off running back toward the Dun, the flames from their branches streaming bannerwise behind them. Others began to caper and dance, fantastic as marsh lights in the faint mist. Men and women began to be drawn into the dancing, and suddenly there was music for them to dance to—or perhaps the music came first; I have never known.

It was a thin music, a silver ripple of piping, but strong, for it drew the dancers after it as though strung on its shining strand. And as they pranced by, two by two in a chain that lengthened every moment, weaving in and out of themselves in the ancient intricate patterns of fertility, circling always sunwise about the scattered fire, I saw the woman.

She was standing somewhat aside, strangely remote from the wild scene around her; half lost in shadows save when the whirling torchlight touched her tawny unbound hair.

I knew well enough who she was; Guenhumara the chieftain's daughter. I had seen her again and again during the past three days as she waited on us, her father's guests, with the other women of the household. I had even received the guest cup from her hands, but beyond knowing with the surface of my mind that she was there, I had had no awareness of her. Now, it may have been the mood of the night, the piping and the mist and the tossing firebrands; it may have been only the heather beer—she entered in at my eyes as I looked at her, and I was aware of her in every fiber of my being. It was the first time in ten years that I had looked at a woman so, and even as I looked, she started and turned as though I had touched her, and saw me.

I started toward her, laughing like a conqueror: God help me, I was very drunk, but I think not with beer alone, and caught her by the wrist and swung her into the dance. Others joined on behind us, and far ahead, drawing us on and on, rose the white piping. We were flinging the circle wider now, to noose the nine stones within it, weaving in and out between them as garland makers weave the stems of flowers for a festival, casting our noose about the glowing embers of the fire, sometimes, at the will of the leader, crossing between fire and stone circle to form a vast figure of eight, twisting, looping, on and on until the mist circled with us above the heads of the stone dancers . . . and the loose hair of the woman flung the scent of vervain in my face. . . .

The spell was broken by a far-off cry, and the urgent blaring of a horn, small with distance, from below the Dun. The dancers checked and scattered apart, all eyes straining toward the coast, where, from the direction of the boat strand, fire that was certainly not the fire of Midsummer leapt up into the night.

"The Scots! The Scots are come again!"

I dropped the woman's wrist and shouted for my Companions. "Flavian! Amlodd! Gault—here to me!"

They gathered to my summons, shaking off the fumes of heather beer and ancient magic as they came, and freeing their swords in the wolfskin sheaths. Many of Maglaunus's warriors had come to the Midsummer Fire with no weapon save their dirks, according to the old and honorable custom; but we had learned the unwisdom of such custom, and paid away honor long ago, as part of the price for success against the Sea Wolves; and so the cry of Scots raiders found us better ready than it did many of our hosts.

Ahead even of the chieftain and his household warriors, we raced for the coast and the distant flames. We stumbled among the heather roots, hearts hammering within us, into the little sea wind that brought us the smell of burning ever more strongly as we plunged downward. There were two big skin-covered war currachs in the shallows below the boat strand, and dark figures leaping between us and the blazing bothies of the fisherfolk. Maybe they had counted on there being no watch kept when the Midsummer Fires were burning. They set up a shout, and closing together, swung around to meet us; and yelling with the little breath that was left in us we charged down upon them.

I remember little but confusion of what came after. Maybe that was the heather beer and the lingering spell of the past hour. To go into battle drunk is a glory worth experiencing, but it does not make for clear and detailed memory. Certain things I do remember, through a red mist of personal rage for the cutting short of wonder and beauty that I felt dimly might never come again. I remember how the heather ran out into soft sand, and the sand slipped and yielded beneath our feet; I remember the chill of surging water around our ankles when we had driven them from the keel strand to fight in the shallows; and the white lime dust of the Scottish shields turned golden by the flame of the burning currachs. I remember the uncouth tumble to and fro of a dead body at the water's edge, and somebody crying out with a great and savage laughter, that here were two less crows to come to supper uninvited in another year. And the surprised discovery that some time during the fighting I had taken a spear thrust in the shoulder and my left arm was dripping red.

I turned landward, sober now that the fighting was done, with my lovely red rage sunk to ashes, and holding my shoulder, began to make my way back toward the Dun. One of the women would bind the wound for me. The dead lay scattered like storm wrack along the tide line, rolling to and fro in the shallows as the little waves came in. Dawn was not far off, and between the flare of burning fisher huts and burning currachs there was enough light to see by; and close under the turf wall of the orchard where Maglaunus and I had walked up and down arguing yesterday, I saw the dark body of a man sprawled somewhat apart from his fellow dead. Something else I saw, too, and halted abruptly in my tracks, looking, not at the dead raider, but at the living dog who stood guard over him. I had heard—who has not?—of the great Hibernian wolfhounds; now I was seeing one. Standing there, head up and alertly turned to watch me, he was magnificent; tall at the shoulder as a three-month foal, his coat brindled in shadow bars of black and amber, save where his breast shone milky silver in

the flame light, just as Cabal's had used to do. He must have belonged to the chief of the raiders; such a dog would be worth his
place in any war party, and the gaping wound in his flank showed
that he had not shirked the fight. I took a step toward him. He
never moved, but he rumbled deep in his bull throat. I knew that
if I took another, he would crouch to spring, and at the third, he
would be at my throat. But I knew also, in a flash of certainty,
as swiftly irrevocable as the moment of lost virginity, that this was
what I had been waiting for ever since old Cabal died, the reason
why I had never called another dog by his name.

Flavian and Amlodd were with me, and the chieftain's three
sons. I gestured them back. "Sir—what—" Flavian began.

"The dog," I said. "I will have the dog."

"My lord, you should get that arm tended before you start troubling about any dog," young Amlodd urged.

"My arm can wait. If I lose the dog I shall not find his like
again." I knew how they were glancing at each other behind my
back, telling each other with their eyes that the Bear was still
battle-drunk or maybe dulled in his wits from loss of blood.

Then Pharic the second son said, "Come up to the Dun now,
Lord; he'll not leave his master, and my brothers and I will come
down again and rope him."

"You fool!" I said. "Let you drag him off his dead master on
the end of a rope, and he's ruined forever. Now go, if you don't
want to get your own throats as well as mine torn out."

We had been speaking at half breath, and all the while the great
hound made no movement, and his eyes like greenish lamps in
the flame light never left my face.

I squatted on my heels against the orchard wall, careful to make
no movement that might seem to him hostile, and settled into
stillness. After a while I heard the steps of the other men moving
reluctantly away through the long shore grass. I could feel the
blood still trickling, though more slowly now, through the fingers
of my right hand pressed over the wound, and wondered how long
I should be able to hold out; then put the thought away from me.
Still the dog did not stir. I was striving to master his gaze with my
own, and because no dog can bear for more than a few heartbeats to meet the direct gaze of a man, every little while he would
turn his head aside to lick at his wounded flank; but always after

a few moments he would turn it back to me again. I suppose to anyone looking on, it must have seemed ridiculous that I should spend the hours after battle in trying to outstare a hound; even to me, it seems a little ridiculous now, but it was not at the time. The thing was a battle of wills between us, that went on and on. . . . Dawn had come, the fires in the fisher village were quenched, the shadows of the small wind-shaped apple trees stretched far across the rough turf toward the sand, and little by little began to shorten. Once or twice the dog dropped his head to nuzzle at his lord's body, but always his gaze came up again to my face. His eyes that had been green lamps were amber-colored now, lucent, warm with the warmth of the sun, but lost in a great bewilderment, and I knew that behind them his love for his dead master was fighting me.

The sea wind ruffled the long grass and swung the shadows of the branches, and the gulls wheeled crying above the ripple-patterned sand that the tide had cleansed of battle. I heard a movement behind me, and someone said, quiet and urgent, "Artos, you must come—you must have that gash dressed. For God's sake, man, don't you see you're kneeling in blood?"

I said, "Listen, if any man comes near me or the dog before I give him leave, I swear I'll kill him."

The end came not long after that, suddenly, as such things generally come. It was a little like the moment in the making of horse or hawk, when the wild thing that has been fighting you with all its wild nature, fighting to the point of heartbreak for both of you, suddenly accepts, and gives of its own free will the thing that it has struggled so long to withhold. (For the thing is always in the end, in the essence, a free yielding by the beast, never a forced conquest by the man. With a dog, in the normal way, the thing is different, for a dog is born into man's world, and tries from the first to understand.) It passed between us, the acceptance, the recognition; a two-way thing as love or hate is almost always a two-way thing. For a long moment there was no outward sign. Then I made the first move, slowly holding out my hand. "Cabal—*Cabal.*"

He whined piteously, and licked at the dead man's neck, then looked at me again, making a small uncertain forward movement that checked almost as soon as it was begun.

"Cabal," I said again. "Cabal, *Cabal,* come." And crouching a little, inch by inch, he came. Midway between us he checked and swung back to his dead master, and I knew now his whole shadowy soul was being torn in two; but I could afford no mercy, now. Mercy was for afterward. "Cabal, here! Cabal!" He hesitated still, his great proud head turning from one of us to the other; then with a piercing whine, he came on again, crouching almost on his belly as though he had been flogged, but with no more looking back. He crept to my outstretched hand, and I began to fondle his ears and muzzle, letting him lick the blood crusted between my fingers, and all the while calling and crooning to him by his new name, repeating it over and over again. "Cabal—you are Cabal now, Cabal, *Cabal*."

Presently, talking to him still, I fumbled off my belt as best I could, and slipped it one-handed through his broad bronze-studded collar. "We are going now, you and I, we are going, Cabal." It did not matter what I said, it was the voice and the constant repetition of the name that was forming its bond between us. I pushed off from the orchard wall, and contrived to struggle to my feet, swaying with a queer drained weakness and stiff as though I were the man lying face down in the long grass, the man whose dog I had taken from him. I turned back toward the remains of the fisher huts, and the track up to the Dun, and saw Flavian and Amlodd waiting where they must have waited all night at the turn of the orchard wall, scrambling to their feet also.

The great hound paced beside me as I began to waver toward them; yet all the while I was aware that something of him belonged still to his dead master, and that to complete what we had begun would take many careful days. . . . Suddenly between one step and the next, sea and shore were spinning around me; I saw Flavian's face start forward, and then roaring blackness came up at me like a wave out of the ground.

When the light returned, it was not the cool light of the seashore morning, but the smoky yellow glimmer of a lamp. And as my head cleared a little, I found that I was lying on the piled sheepskins of the bed place in Maglaunus's guest lodging, with my left arm, as I discovered by an unwise attempt to move, bound close to my side. A shadow that had been squatting beside me leaned quickly forward, saying, "Lie still, sir, or you'll part the wound again," and the voice, and the face as I squinted at it, trying to focus, were young Amlodd's gruff voice and anxious freckled countenance.

"Where is the dog?" I demanded. My tongue felt as though it were made of boiled leather.

"Chained among the guard dogs in the forecourt," said my armor-bearer. And then as I made some movement of angry protest, "Sir, we had to chain him up. He's savage. We had to tangle him in a fishing net before we could get him at all, and even then most of us got mauled."

I cursed feebly. God knew what harm they had done, whether I should ever win the dog to me now. "Is he unloosed with the rest at cow stalling time?"

"No sir. I tell you he's savage; no one can get near him even at feeding time, save the Lady Guenhumara. Would one let a wolf run loose in the Dun? By and by, when you are stronger, if you still want to see the brute, a couple of us will strap his muzzle and get him along here somehow."

I shook my head. "I wish to God you hadn't chained him, but I can—see that you had—no choice, unless it was to kill the poor brute—outright. But since you *have* chained him—nobody must loose him again, excepting me."

"No sir," said Amlodd, with such evident relief that I laughed, and found that the laughter wracked my shoulder.

"Get Flavian for me. I must send word to Cei that I—I am laid by here with a spear gash in my shoulder, but that I'll be—back in Trimontium so soon as I can sit a horse."

"That has all been seen to, sir," said Amlodd.

And a woman moved forward out of the gloom beyond the lamp, and leaned over me with a bowl in her hands, and the strong tawny braid of her hair swung forward and brushed across my breast. "There has been enough of talking. Drink now, and sleep again. The more broth, and the more sleep, the sooner will you sit your horse again, my Lord Artos."

I saw that she was Guenhumara, the chieftain's daughter; but I was sober now, and I scarcely remembered at all how I swept her into the Long Dance with me up on the moors last night; the scent of vervain no longer clung to her hair, and the only thing that interested me was the hound, and what Amlodd had said concerning her and Cabal. "Why does he let you near him, when—he will not anyone else?" I mumbled, a little jealously, God forgive me, with the sleep that was in the broth already lapping its dark waves about me.

"How should I know? Maybe a woman spoke kindly to him and gave him warm scraps from the cooking, in his old life, and we are not terrible to him as men are, who chained him." She took the bowl away. "But even I, he will not have to touch him."

"There are other things than touching. Keep him alive for me if you can."

"I will do what I may. . . . Now sleep."

I lay in the guest place as the days went by, tended by the Lady Guenhumara, and the old woman like a hoodie crow who had been her nurse; while Flavian and the rest of the Brotherhood came and went, and Maglaunus himself would come and sit on the hide-covered stool, a hand on either widespread knee, and talk of all things under the sun, asking many questions. Some of these questions concerned my own way of life, whether or not I had a wife, or a woman to share my bed, and I told him "None," fool that I was, and never saw where his questions were leading.

On the third day my head grew hot and confused, and the wound was angry despite the women's herbs, and I remember little more with any clearness, for a while. The fever burned itself out after a time, and the wound began to heal. But the moon that had been young when the Scottish raiders came was young again when at last I was able to drag myself out, doddering as an hour-old calf, to sit in the sunshine before the guest place door, and watch the dunghill cock strutting among his drab hens by the midden. He was proud and possessive, that cock, the sun waking lights of beetle-green and bronze in the arched arrogance of his tail feathers. Presently, as I watched, he made a prancing spread-winged dash at a chosen hen; but she was just beyond his reach, and in the very act of leaping upon her, he was brought up short at the end of his tether, and tumbled, furious and undignified, in the dust. Three times it happened, before suddenly I had had enough of watching, and began to pull up brown flowered grass stems from around the doorpost, and twist them into a braid.

As soon as I was strong enough I made my crawling way to the forecourt. It was a hot noon of high summer, and the air danced in the forecourt that was empty of human life. The barn dogs lay asleep or snapping at the iridescent flies that buzzed about them. I looked around for the great wolfhound. It was a few moments before I saw him, for he had dragged the full length of his chain into the narrow band of shade along the foot of the peat stack, and the broken black and amber of his hide blended perfectly into his background. I stood still and called, not expecting any response. But he stirred and raised his great head from his paws, as though the name I had given him touched his memory. "Cabal," I called, "Cabal," and next instant he was up and straining toward me at the end of his chain, half choked, yet contriving to fling up his head and bay—a wild imploring note.

"Soft, softly now. I come!"

As soon as he saw me coming toward him he ceased his struggling and became quiet, standing with head up and grave golden eyes to watch me, his tail beginning uncertainly to swing behind him. The wound in his flank was healed, but for the rest, he was in a grievous state, his self-respect gone from him so that he was filthy with ordure, his coat staring and every rib starting through his once-beautiful hide, his neck rubbed into sores where he had dragged and dragged against his heavy collar. I learned later that he had refused to eat almost all the while. He must have come very near to breaking his heart.

I stooped and slipped free the heavy chain, and rubbed his muzzle and his ears—extraordinarily soft ears, for all the harshness of his coat—and he leaned against me with a tired sigh, so that weak on my legs as I still was, I staggered and almost went down.

When we left the forecourt he walked free beside me, with his muzzle touching my hand. I took him back to the guest place and shouted for whoever happened to be near. Flavian came running. "Go and get me some meat for this bag of bones," I demanded, while the dog stood by me, his mane stirring under my hand. "Hell and the Furies! How did you let him get into this state?"

"Amlodd told you, sir; we couldn't loose him. There'd have been murder done; and he would not eat, chained."

"The Lady Guenhumara—" I began.

"If it were not for the Lady Guenhumara he would have died.

But even her, he would not let touch him. She tried it once, to bathe the wound in his flank. That was when she got bitten."

"Bitten?"

"Not badly. Did you not see the tear in her arm when she came to tend you?"

"No, I—did not notice." I felt shamed then, but was still angry. "And could you not have told me?"

He confronted me with those grave level eyes of his. "No, sir. There was nothing that you could do; you would simply have fretted yourself into another fever."

And it was true. After a moment I admitted that, and nodded. "As you say. Go now and make love to the woman in the cook place for the meat. Then go away and keep the others away also; I have work to do."

And so presently with my hand still on his shoulder, and a huge bleeding mass of pig offal before him, Cabal ate his fill again at last.

A few days later, when I judged that the work was far enough advanced, and when more strength had returned to me, I slipped a strap through his collar in case of trouble with the other hounds, and took him with me into the chieftain's hall at the time of the evening meal. I was late, for I had been trimming my beard which had grown overlong while I was sick, and the task had taken longer than I had allowed for it; and most of Maglaunus's household warriors were already gathered. They sprang to their feet as I entered with Flavian and the rest of the Companions behind me, and gave us the salute for a chieftain, drumming with their dirk hilts on the tables before them, so that Cabal pricked his ears at the uproar and growled menacingly until I spoke to him in reassurance.

"It seems that you are a conqueror in all things," Maglaunus said, as I came up to the high seat, with the great hound stalking beside me.

Supper flared into a feast of triumph for our victory over the raiders, and I sat with Maglaunus at the upper end of the hall, on a seat spread with a magnificent red stag's hide, with Cabal crouched alert in the strewed fern at my feet, and ate broiled bear's hams and fine pale barley bread and ewe's-milk curds, while Flan

[207]

the chieftain's harper sang the song that he had made in my honor because it was I and my Companions who had played the foremost part in that matter of the Scots. It was not such a song as Bedwyr would have made, but it had a good strong lilt to it like the swing of a west coast swell and the dip of oars—it would have made a good war boat's song to keep the rowers together.

In Maglaunus's hall they still followed the old custom of the Tribes, and the women did not eat with the men, but apart by themselves in the women's place. But when the eating was over, they came in to pour the drink for their menfolk, while the little dark slaves who had served throughout the meal melted away or curled up among the hounds about the fire. So this evening, when the eating was done, Guenhumara came in as usual, walking up the hall with the other women behind her. She had tended me in my sickness as often as old Blanid her nurse, and far more gently, but save for those vivid moments of awareness beside the Mid-summer Fire, I had never seen her at all. Nor did I seem to see her now. And yet, looking back, I can remember very clearly what she looked like, and that is a strange thing. . . .

She wore a gown of blue and russet checkers, clasped some-where about the shoulder with red amber and gold, and the long tawny braids of her hair had small golden apples at their ends which swung a little as she walked, so that one expected them to ring like bells. She came up the hall slowly, carrying a great cup of dark green glass between her hands, and her face was so strongly painted that while she was still far down the hall I could see the green malachite on her eyelids; and the way her brows were drawn out long and dark with stibium, like the dark, dagger-sharp wings of a swift.

She came on slowly, slowly, while the hall fell quiet behind her, and mounted the step to the dais, and gave the brimming cup into her father's hands.

Maglaunus lurched to his feet and raised the cup, spilling a little as he did so. I saw the liquid dribble through his fingers, golden and almost as thick as run honey. He turned to look at me under his russet brows. "Shlanther to Artos the Bear. I drink to you, my Lord the Count of Britain. May the sun and the moon shine on the path of your feet, and may your sword arm never grow weaker." And he tipped back his head and drank; and when he had done so, stood holding the cup and looking at me over it with a kindling and speculative eye. I knew that something else was coming, and with a sudden warning beating in my head, I waited for what it might be.

"I have been thinking much of those things we spoke of before the raiders came—you see that I was right in that matter—but none the less, it grows in my mind that we must indeed come to stand shield to shield, even as you have said, against the Barbarians in the time that lies ahead. Therefore it grows in my mind also that there should be made a bond between us to bind our shields together; and to the bond between us, I drink again."

When he had more than half emptied the great cup, he held it out to me—I also had risen by that time—saying, "Drink you also."

The light of the flames on the central hearth shining through the thick glass filled the cup with a dimly golden fire as I took it into my hands. "To what bond shall I drink?" I asked, with the small clear sense of danger still beating in my head.

He said, "Why not to the bond of kinship? That is the surest bond of all. Let you take Guenhumara my daughter from my hearth to yours. So shall we be kinsmen, knit together by the blood tie of brother to brother and father to son."

For an instant I felt as though I had taken a blow in the root of my belly. I have never known what made Maglaunus broach the matter so publicly, risking his daughter's humiliation before every warrior in his hall; maybe he desired to put all his rejoicings together and make of the evening one grand and glorious blaze, and never thought of my refusing what he offered. Maybe he thought to force my hand. Maybe he was a gambler—or merely wiser in the ways of men and women than he seemed. Without will of my own, my startled sight jumped to Guenhumara's face, and I saw the tide of painful color flood up to the roots of her hair, and knew too that she had had no warning, but that unlike me, she had feared in advance; and that the heavy paint of her face had been put on as a young man takes up his armor. My mind was racing, seeking in all directions for a way out for both of us that would not make me enemies where I so sorely needed allies. Then I heard myself saying, "Maglaunus, my friend, you lay great honor upon me, but you must forgive me my answer for to-night. It is forbidden, taboo for me from my birth, even to so much as think of women, in each year between the dying of the Midsummer Fires and the kindling of the Lammas torches."

It sounded a wildly unlikely excuse, but after all, it was no more unlikely than the taboos laid upon Conary Môr, the Scottish hero, that he should never drive right-handwise around Tara nor sleep in a house from which firelight shone at night. . . . At all events, since no man could disprove it, it might at least gain me a breathing space. . . .

There was a murmuring all down the hall, a whispering among the women; the chieftain's brows drew together and they all but met across the bridge of his nose, and a dark flush burned beneath his eyes. Guenhumara, on the other hand, when I cast another quick glance at her, was so white that the paint stood out sharp-edged and ugly on her lids and cheekbones, though she met my look quietly and with the shadow of a smile.

Then the deep rumble of his laughter boomed into the moment's hush. "Aye well, what is five days? We can pass the time cheerfully enough, and at the end of it you shall give me your answer. Meanwhile, drink to the bond of friendship between us, my Lord Artos the Bear!"

Five days! I had forgotten how long I had lain sick; the late-ness of the summer. Well, five days' respite was better than none. "To the bond of friendship between us," I said, and drank off what was left of the sweet fiery stuff and gave the cup back into Guenhumara's hands as she stood to take it from me; and felt as I did so, that her hands were shaking. She smiled, and took it with a lovely dignity that made me the more aware of her armor, and turned to rejoin the other women.

The uneasy silence in the hall was engulfed suddenly in the snarling flurry of a dog fight as Cabal, who had lain quiet at my feet all evening, only raising his hackles and snarling a warning from time to time whenever one of the other hounds, stiff-legged and hostile, drew too near, rose with a full-throated roar of fury and flung himself against three of them at the same time. (I was to learn, when I knew him better, that he was not a fighter among his own kind, but that when he did fight, odds meant nothing to him.) Most of the other dogs flung themselves into the battle, and for a while we had hot work to separate them, even with a few firebrands and the contents of a pot of beer flung into their midst; and when finally I had succeeded in strangling Cabal off a howling adversary and most of the other dogs had been kicked outside to finish their fighting where they would, the scene that was just past seemed to be forgotten, and the beer went around faster than before.

I was as grateful to Cabal as though he had sprung into battle in defense of my life.

CHAPTER SIXTEEN

Lammas Torches

NEXT morning I whistled Cabal to heel, and took to the moors behind the Dun, heading for the high empty places as I had always done in time of stress since I was a boy. Also I was bent on testing my strength, for once Lammas was over, the sooner I was away from the Dun of Maglaunus the better. It was a day of hurrying storm clouds and swiftly changing lights that came and went across the great slow billows of the moor where the heather was coming into flower, so that at one moment a whole hillside would be bloomed dark as sloes, and the next, the color of thin spilled wine. And as the light came and went, changing and scurrying about the moors, so my thoughts changed and shifted, scudding about my mind as I walked. The only thing that remained constant amid the turmoil was my determination not to take Guenhumara from her father's hearth. It was not only that I flinched from the idea of taking any woman, but quite simply that I had no place for her in my way of life, no life to give any woman. Yet I knew that that would not satisfy Maglaunus; and there was the war alliance with him to be taken into the account, the hope of men and aid that we desperately needed, the necessity of bonding the tribes together that was our only hope of throwing back the Barbarians. Last night he had said, "Drink to the bond of friendship between us." But would that hold, after the slight that, however I tried to soften it, I must put on his daughter in four days' time? And the woman herself? Would it be better for her (supposing that I could get the word to her) to save her pride and maybe gain her father's anger, by herself refusing the marriage— or to be shamed by my refusal before the whole tribe and keep her father's favor? And would it make any difference whether she refused or not? Which was worse for a woman, the shame or the danger? The danger or the shame? As to my chances now of winning Maglaunus to the Red Dragon, whichever way things went, they were not worth a brown tufted rush in the wind. Oh gods! What a tangle! I cursed, and stumbled on, not taking much notice of anything about me, until a chill scurry of rain on the back of my neck woke me to my surroundings, and to the knowledge that I had walked too far and was spent.

I sat down in the lee of a hump of thorn trees, with Cabal lying nose on paws beside me, while the rain squall blotted out the moors, and then blew over and left the world refreshed and shining. I sat on for a while after, listening with one ear to the rich contented boom of bees in the young bell heather, and when I was somewhat rested, turned westward again and set off toward the coast, at an easier pace.

Presently I was walking into the eye of a wild sunset, with gray clouds racing across a western sky of saffron and silver gilt, and the sea running translucent gold to the skyline; and found that I was heading directly toward the hill shoulder with its ring of standing stones where we had danced on Midsummer's Eve. They stood up, shadow-bloomed, dark with rain against the tumbled brightness of the sky. The shining lances of the sunset were in my eyes, and it was not until Cabal pricked his ears at one of the standing stones, that I saw a figure standing in the shadow of it. I whistled the hound to my side as he started forward with an uncertain sound between a snarl and a whimper, and caught him by the collar. But the figure never moved, indeed in its utter silence it might have been one of the standing stones, and it was not until I was almost within reach that I knew it for Guenhumara in a tunic of unbleached gray sheep's wool that was one in color with the stone behind her.

"My Lady Guenhumara! What is it that you do here?"

"I was waiting for you," she said composedly.

"But how could you know that I should come this way?"

"Maybe I called you."

Fear touched me with a cold fingertip, and I was remembering another woman in a saffron gown, standing in a bothy doorway with that same air of stillness of having stood there since time began, saying, "I have waited for you a long time . . ."

Then Guenhumara laughed. "Na, I am no witch to comb my hair and call down the moon. I saw which way you walked, and came out after you, that is all. Here, from the Nine Sisters you can see far across the moors, and I hoped to be able to meet you on your way back. One cannot talk in the Dun without the very jackdaws crying the thing that one talked of from the rooftops next morning."

"I can well believe it. What is the thing that you would say to me?"

She had moved a little toward me, out from the shadow of her standing stone, and the light of the stormy sunset tangled in her hair and turned it to an autumn fire. She said, "When the Lammas torches are lit, what will you say to my father the chieftain?"

I was silent, not knowing what to reply; and after a pause, she said in a low faintly mocking voice—her voice was the lowest I have ever heard in a woman, yet very clear, vibrant as a bronze bell. "Na, my Lord Artos, you need not say it; I know. I knew while you were still searching under my father's eyes for your way out."

"Did I show it so clearly to all the hall, then?"

"To no more than half, maybe." Her eyes were fixed on my face, and suddenly I saw them dilate until the black swallowed all the color; and she laid the mockery aside as though it were a weapon. "I came to tell you something that it may be well for you to know, before the Lammas torches. If you take me as Maglaunus my father wishes, he will give you one hundred men with their mounts, for my dowry. That I know in truth. . . . Our horses are not so great as yours, but they are good horses, bred in the first place from some cavalry mounts of a Legion that was lost somewhere among the Lowland hills in the far-off days, and we have kept the strain pure."

I was more startled, I think, than I had been when Maglaunus first bade me take her; and when I spoke at last, it was more harshly than I had meant. "Did Maglaunus your father send you to tell me this?"

"If so, I would have died before I came!"

"Would you? I want horses and men, but not—like that."

I could scarcely have complained if she had spat in my face, but she only said with a small quickly suppressed sigh, "No, I suppose that you would not," and then, bracing herself to a yet more rigid stillness, "Artos, until now, I have counted myself a proud woman; and I am laying my pride at your feet for you to trample it into the dirt if you choose. I beg you to take me."

"Why?"

"Because I am shamed if you do not. It means little enough that you caught me with you into the Long Dance at Midsummer, though my father sets some store by it; men will say only that you were drunk. But my father offered me to you in the hall before all men, and if you refuse his offer, do you know what the whole Dun, the whole tribe, will say? They will say that you have had me, on Midsummer Eve or later—the Great Mother knows that I have been often enough alone with you in the guest place. They will say that you have had me, and found me not to your taste. It will be hard to live with open shame, in my father's hall."

"Is there less shame," I said ruthlessly, "in buying a husband for a hundred mounted men?"

"It is usual enough for a woman to be chosen for her dowry. And the shame would at least be only between you and me, not open before all men."

"Would that make it easier to bear?"

She made a small, infinitely weary gesture. "I don't know. For a man, maybe no; for a woman, maybe yes."

"Listen," I said urgently. "Listen, Guenhumara. You do not know what it is you ask for. We carry with us a few ragged whores in the baggage train; they help to care for the wounded and they keep the lads happy; but save for their kind, the life that we lead is no life for a woman. Therefore if we are fools enough to marry, we leave our wives at their father's hearths, hoping, one day, to see them again. Flavian will tell you as much; he married a girl at Deva, and he has a son more than a year old, but he has not seen him yet, nor the girl since she had scarce begun to carry him. It may be that next year I shall be able to spare him a few weeks to be with them, it may be not."

"You are the Count of Britain. There is no man to refuse you your woman with you, at least in winter quarters." And I saw by her ruthlessness how desperate she was in her purpose.

[215]

"I am the Count of Britain, and therefore my woman would have the hardest life of all, for I should have left for her only the few rags of myself that Britain does not claim." I was fighting as it were with my back to the last ditch, fighting not only her but something in myself.

"She might make do with those, in the winter nights," Guenhumara said gently. And then she laughed, suddenly and wildly. "But you have no need to fear that I shall prove too clinging a wife —I am more like to knife you one night in your sleep!"

"Why, when I have done your will?"

She did not answer at once, and now I could not see her face against the still brightening fires of the sunset. And when she spoke again, her voice had lost its vibrant quality. "Because you will know the truth. Because pity is not much easier to bear than shame."

I had not meant to touch her, but I caught her by the shoulders then, and turned her to the light so that I could see her face. The feel of her was good under my hands, light-boned and warm with life. She stood quite unresisting, looking up at me, waiting. And in the harsh westering light I saw her, for the first time, and not through firelight and the heady fumes of pipe music and heather beer. I saw that she was a tawny woman, tawny of skin as well as hair, and save for that hair with no especial beauty. I saw that her eyes were gray, under coppery brows that were level as the dark brows of her brothers, and the lashes tipped with gold like the hairs of a bay horse. I think it was in that moment also that I became aware of her atmosphere, the quiet that lay beneath her surface, even under the stress of the present moment. Young though she was, so much younger than Ygerna, it seemed to me that she had the essential quietness of autumn that contains both promise and fulfillment, while Ygerna had all the painful craving urgency of spring. "Listen, Guenhumara," I said again. "I don't love you. I don't think it is in me to love any woman, not—now. But if I am to take you, it will not be for any reason that should give you cause to knife me in my sleep, nor even for gratitude because you tended me while I was sick, and kept the dog alive for me. I shall take you because I can have a hundred mounted men with you—did you not say yourself it is usual enough for a woman to be chosen for her dowry? And because I like the feel of you, as though you were a well-balanced spear, and I like the sound of your voice." She made no sign, no sound, only went on looking at me; and I plowed clumsily ahead. "But you will have so much the worst of the bargain; go home now and think, and be very sure, and when you have thought enough, send me word."

"I lay awake all night, and have had my fill of thinking," Guenhumara said.

The first cold drops of the next rain squall were spattering about us, drawing a blurred gray veil across the last of the sunset, and I heard the gulls crying as they swept by. "You will get wet," I said, oblivious of the fact that she was wet already from the earlier rain, and pulled her against me and flung half my cloak about her; I knew by now that she was pleasant to the touch, but even so the nearness of her body was unexpectedly sweet in the warm dark under the folds, and the sweetness of it dizzied me a little. I put my arms around her and caught her hard against me, and bent my head and kissed her. She was a tall woman, and I had not far to go to stoop as I had done sometimes before. Her lips were cold and wet with rain under my mouth, and the rain hung chill on her hair and lashes, and for a moment there seemed nothing there, no more than if I had kissed the tall gray standing stone behind her. Then the fire of life sprang up within the stone, she seemed to melt, and leap up toward me within herself, and her mouth woke under mine into swift, eager response. And almost in the same instant she was remote again as one of the Nine Sisters. She slipped from my arms and from the shelter of my cloak, and turned and ran.

I was left looking after her, by the lichened standing stone in the rain, while Cabal, who had watched the whole scene sitting on his haunches at my side, glanced up at me, his tail thumping softly behind him. I was still feeling that instant of wild response, so quickly come and lost again that now I could scarcely believe that it had existed at all. But deep within me I knew that I had not imagined it.

In a little, when I had given her time to be well away, I whistled Cabal after me and set off once more for the Dun. The rain had died out again, and the wine color of the wet heather was turning smoky in the dusk.

That night before I slept, I sent for Flavian to the guest place, and told him what must be told. None of the Companions had spoken to me of the chieftain's offer and the taboo that I had invented on the spur of the moment, though I suppose they must have spoken of it among themselves; and Flavian did not speak now, only stood with one arm against the rooftree and stared into the flame of the little seal-oil lamp, until I had to break the pause myself.

"Well?" I said.

He brought his gaze back from the lamp. "And you are going to have her with you in winter quarters?"

"Yes."

"Then, of course, since we are to have wives among us at Trimontium, I may send for Teleri?"

My heart sickened and sank, and it was my turn now to stare into the flame of the seal-oil lamp. "No, Flavian."

"But how is the case different, sir?" His voice still had the levelness it had as a boy.

"Because I am the Count of Britain, the captain of you all," I said. "Sometimes the leader may have what he denies to his followers. Because I am the leader and there is only one leader, what I do does not make a precedent, but if I give you leave to do the same, how may I refuse it to any man in Trimontium—and within a year we shall be overwhelmed with pregnant women and squalling cubs, a danger to themselves and a danger to us, clogging our sword arms and dividing our hearts!" But the words tasted evil in my mouth, for never before had I used my leaderhood to take for myself anything that was not for my men also; not so much as a mouthful of sour soup or a wound dressed out of turn.

We were silent for a while, and then he said, "Don't do it, sir."

"I shall have a dowry of a hundred men and horses with her."

He looked up quickly. "And that is your whole reason?"

"It is reason enough."

"Then marry her and leave her at her father's hearth, as I have had to leave Teleri all this while."

"That—is not in the bargain."

He was silent again, a longer silence this time, filled with the soft boom of wind and the hush of storm rain across the thatch, for the night had fulfilled the promise of the sunset. The door apron flapped and bellied against its restraining pegs, and the lamp flame jumped and fluttered, sending fantastic shadows licking along the rafters. Then he said, "This is the first time you have ever done anything unjust, sir."

And I said, "That is not such a bad record. Bear with me in my injustice, Flavian, I am only a mortal man with my sins heavy on my shoulders, not an archangel."

"We are not the kind to know much about archangels, we of the Brotherhood; we have thought of you always as—maybe a little larger than life, that is all," he said, and moved very slowly toward the doorway.

I let him almost get there, but I could not let him go through it. I was fiddling with my sword belt, on the point of slipping it free, for I had sent Amlodd away early; then I abandoned it. I said, "Minnow, don't desert me."

He turned instantly, and I saw by the jumping light of the seal-oil lamp, the suspicious brightness of his eyes. "I think I could not." He came back quickly and dropped on one knee to free the sword belt himself. "Where does Amlodd keep the silver sand? This clasp needs burnishing. He's not such a good armor-bearer as I was."

But I lay awake most of the night with a bad taste in my mouth.

In the days that followed, the life of the Dun went on seemingly much as usual, but down in the dark beneath the surface of familiar things, a wild tide was rising. No outward sign told of its rising, and had I been of my father's world, I doubt that I should have sensed anything at all; but my mother in me knew the look in men's eyes, and heard the dark familiar singing in the blood.

Three days before Lammas, Maglaunus the chieftain was not in his accustomed place at supper in his high hall; but no man glanced at the empty seat with its great black bearskin spread over it, nor spoke of his absence, for we knew the reason for it. No man can take the godhead upon himself without time apart to make himself ready. . . . Always there must be one to wear the Horns; one to give life and fruitfulness out of his own substance, the King and the Sacrifice in one, to die for the life of the people if need be, as the Christos died. Sometimes it is a priest that becomes the Incarnate God, sometimes even a Christian priest, for in the wilds and the mountain places men do not set such rigid frontiers to their faiths as they do in cities; sometimes it is the king, the chieftain, and that is the old way, and holds within it the true meaning. Lammas fell on a Sabbath that year, and for the first part, the day was as other Sabbaths.

Early in the morning we went down from the Dun to hear mass in the small bracken-thatched church that served both the Dun and the fisher village below it. For once, Cabal was not with me, being too much taken up with the hut where Maglaunus's favorite hunting bitch was in season; but I remember that Pharic had his hawk with him—indeed he seldom moved far without her—and carried her still, when we reached the church door and went in under the stone lintel. There was room in the church for Maglaunus's household, and for the small band of Companions who followed me, but for few more, and so for the most part the lesser folk of both Dun and village remained outside in the forecourt like a low-walled sheepcote. It made little difference, for they could hear all that went on through the open doorway, and at the appointed time the three monks of the Holy House at Are Cluta, who lived in the humpbacked bothy beside the church, would bring out to them the Bread and Wine.

I heard little of the service, for with my eyes schooled straight in front of me, I seemed all the while, with every sense I possessed, to be watching Guenhumara with her maidens about her, in the women's part of the church. When the time came for the Sacred Meal, I knew how she looked around for her brothers, for Pharic most of all, that they might go up together, and I knew that they had always gone up together. I went up next, and knelt at Pharic's other side—his left side on which he carried his hawk; and it is so that I remember the small unvoiced battle of wills between priest and princeling, the one denying and the other maintaining the right to bring his hawk to the Lord's Table. Clearly it was a long-standing struggle, and when after a few moments the priest lowered his eyes in defeat, it was a defeat that he had known many times before.

The three dark-frocked brethren must have realized the chieftain's absence, and understood its reason. They must have known, when they carried out the Host to the kneeling warriors and fisherfolk in the forecourt, that in a few hours they would be up on the moors with the Nine Sisters, stretching eager hands to an older and deeper-rooted Lord than the Christos. But they made no sign; they were withdrawn, showed nothing in their quiet faces; and I knew that they would ask no questions.

When we came out again through the forecourt gate, with the mass of worshippers already thinning, Pharic, still carrying his hawk, was gentling the back of her neck with one finger, so that she bobbed her unhooded head, hunching her shoulders in pleasure. "It is a good hawking day," he said suddenly, and glanced about him, at his brothers and the rest of us. "The Lord knows we may not have many more chances before the autumn molt, and I am away up to the moors. Laethrig, my Lord Artos—Sulian —Gault—who comes with me?" And swinging on his heel without pause for any answer, to shout for horses and others of his hawks to be brought down.

But indeed the plan fell in with our mood well enough, for I think all of us wanted some outlet for the unrest that was growing in us, something to fill the hours until dark. And when the horses were brought and a couple more hawks, each with its familiar glove, we mounted, and gathered up a few dogs to flush game for us, and headed for the marshy glens northward, in search of heron.

We had a good day's hawking, but the thing that remains clearest of it in my mind came when Pharic had seemingly wearied of the sport; and lagging behind with him, while the rest moved on to try some pool farther up the glen, we came walking the horses up a long slope where the midges rose in clouds from the bracken as we brushed by, and over the crest of the ridge reined in and sat looking down into a widely shallow valley running to the marshes and the sea. Directly below us a small leaf-shaped tarn lay as in the hollow of a big quiet hand; and listening, I thought that I could catch the whistling call of sandpipers that always haunt such places. And between us and the pebbly shore lay all that time had left of an ancient steading, the ground dimpled with hollows and bush-grown mounds that must once have been bothies and byres and store pits, and showing here and there curved outbreaks of stones that had faced a turf wall, so that I was reminded of a village of the Little Dark People. But in the midst of the place, on ground a little higher than the rest, the stone drum of the old strong point, the chieftain's tower still stood to almost twice the height of a man, and had a roof of ragged thatch.

"What happened to it?" I asked, after we had sat looking down in silence for a few moments.

"No fire nor sword; not the Scots this time. The place was too prone to flooding in the winter, and some forefather of mine with a misliking for wet feet abandoned the place to build the present Dun on higher ground."

I had something of the story from this one and that. "It seems not quite abandoned, even now. So far as one may see from here, that thatch is sound enough, and someone has been cutting bracken fodder over yonder on the far side of the valley, not more than a week or ten days since, to judge by the clean yellow gleam of it."

"The herdsmen use it at the spring and autumn herding, and sometimes in the summer, on passage from one grazing ground to another. They keep a roof on the tower for shelter, and fodder for the beasts and maybe a creel or two of rye meal for themselves stowed above the house beam. It's a humble end, isn't it, for a stronghold that's known the clash of weapons and the music of the chieftain's harper—but there's times, even now, when the place comes into its own again for a while and a while."

"And what times would those be?"

"When there is a marrying in the chieftain's line. Always it has been our custom that when the sons of the chieftain's house bring home their brides, they must pass the first night in the old Dun. That is for courtesy to the chieftains of the older time—to bring the incoming women to their hearth."

I glanced around at him. "The daughters, too?"

"The daughters, maybe, though for them it is not greeting but farewell. When a woman marries she goes to her husband's hearth." He turned his head deliberately, and looked at me under black brows as level as his hawk's wings when she rested on the upper air. "It is not forbidden to the daughters, too."

We looked at each other, the horses shifting under us eager to be moving on, and the little breeze that could not reach down into the midge-infested glen behind us stirred the hair on our heads and brushed through the tawny late summer grass. "Guenhumara has told you, then," I said at last.

"Something—it is a matter that concerns me, after all, since if she brings you a war band for her dowry, it must be I who lead it."

"You especially?"

"It is for one of the chieftain's sons to lead such a band. Laethrig is my father's first son, and Sulian is already knotted in a girl's long hair, while I—I am free, and have an itch to the soles of my feet that I shall not find easement for, here in my father's hall."

I looked at him in the clear upland light, the set of his head that matched that of the hawk on his fist, the hot red-brown eyes under the black brows; and I thought that he might be well right in that, and thought also that it would be good to have this frowning youngster among my captains.

"I can maybe find the means for easing the soles to your feet," I said. "And if there is a like itching in the palm of your sword hand, I can find you a fine way to appease that also."

"Then while my sister is your woman, I am your man. But I forget—" He flung up his head and laughed. He had a hard short laugh that when he grew older would be a bark like a dog-fox's. "You may not speak of such matters until the Lammas torches are lit!"

"It is none so simple a thing, to be faced with the offer of a wife, all unwarned, in a hall full of strangers," I said, "and with more matters than a bride-wreath hanging on the Yea or Nay."

"Sa sa, I can well believe it, and a man might snatch at any means to gain him breathing space. Only when the breathing space is past, and he has made his choice, and struck his bargain, let him abide by it, remembering that hall full of strangers, who are not strangers to the woman, but her own people, and remember that among them she has three brothers, and among those three brothers, one in particular."

I had liked the boy before, and I liked him the better for that clumsy threat. "I will remember," I said. And I suppose I must have shown my liking in some way, for suddenly his dark bony face lit up as though in answer, and the moment of stress was gone like a plume of thistle seed on the small soft wind.

"And speaking of the Lammas torches," I said, "the shadows are growing long—time, maybe, that we were away back to the Dun."

He shook his head, looking back the way that we had come. "Ach, no need for a while yet. It is good out here; a good time of the evening, and we are none so far, across country. We can meet up with the others at the glen head, and send two or three of the young ones back with the hawks and the dogs; no need for the rest of us to be making for the Dun at all. We can ride straight over to the gathering place, and leave the horses in the little wood close by."

So it was that dusk had deepened into the dark, and a blurred moon was rising over the high moors, when we dismounted and tethered the horses in the hazel thicket below the gathering place, and set our faces to the steep heathery slope beyond. The little soft wind of the day had quite died away, and the sky was overspread with the faintest rippled sheet of thunder haze, and even as we climbed, there was a flicker of summer lightning along the hills. The circle of the Nine Sisters stood above us on its shoulder of the moors, darkly outlined against the snail-shine of the moon, and about its feet the dark multitude was already gathering. We could hear the awed hushed murmur of tongues, the faint brush of feet in the grass. . . . As we stepped out from the heather onto the smooth turf of the dancing floor I saw that every face was turned inward to the circle of standing stones, and looking the same way, I saw—or thought I saw—that despite the luminous clearness of the night, a faint mist clung there still; no, not so much a mist as an obscurity that one could neither see nor see through. So must the magic mists have been, that the priests of the older world could raise for the cloaking of an army.

Pharic had disappeared, with his own lads about him, and young Amlodd, still panting with the speed that he had made from the Dun after his errand with the hawks, came dodging through the multitude to join the little knot of Companions. But he, too, kept his face turned all the while to the Nine Sisters. The tension of thunder was on us all, but another tension also, that rose and rose as the moments passed, until it reached almost to the limit of physical endurance; as certain prolonged notes of a horn will do. I heard Flavian gasp beside me. I was sweating in the palms of my hands, and it began to seem to me that at any moment now the whole night must crack wide open under pressure of this intensity of waiting.

The faint whisper of scuffing feet and low-pitched voices had fallen away into complete stillness, and out of the stillness came the Beginning. Not any note of horns, but the sudden overwhelming stench of animal potency, as though some great rutting beast were nearby.

A low thrilling murmur, a kind of moan, rose from the crowd, and as one man they surged inward almost to the outer surface of the standing stones, as though drawn by the thing within them, the thing that drew me with the rest, as it had drawn me when I was a boy among my own hills, but so long ago that I had forgotten. . . . The mist seemed to have gathered more thickly within the stone circle, and out of the midst of it, tangible as the musky stink of rut, was flowing a vast Power. Somewhere a pipe called silverly, small and remote as a bird over the moon-washed moors, more compelling than the war horns of an army. And as though at the command of the pipe, the mist began to lift. Somewhere at the heart of it came a blurred blink of bluish light, that strengthened into a small clear jet of flame springing from between a huge sweep of shadowy antlers.

On a throne of piled turf in the exact center of the Nine Dancers, his arms folded on his breast, sat a tall man, naked and shining, with the head of a royal stag.

At sight of him the people set up a great throbbing cry that rose and rose and seemed to beat vast wings about the hill shoulder; and then in one great surge of movement like a breaking wave, they flung themselves to the ground.

And I, I was on my knees with the rest, the old men and women, the warriors and the children, the maidens with the magic vervain and the white convolvulus braided in their hair; my face hidden in my hands, and the feel of young Amlodd's shoulder shaking against mine.

When I looked up, the Horned One had risen and was standing with arms upstretched, showing himself to his people. The flame between the glorious crowning sweep of antlers bathed his breast and shoulders in a radiance that was like the cold blue fire that drips from the oar blades in northern seas; his flanks and thighs seemed insubstantial as woodsmoke, and the shadows engulfed his feet. And slowly, as though drawn upward by his raised arms, the crowd rose to their feet, and again the wild greeting cry was beating about the hill shoulder; and this time it did not die

away, but changed by little and little into a rhythmic chanting, into
the ancient intercession for the harvest and the mating time that
one hears with the loins and belly rather than the head.

It was not quite as we sang it among my own hills, but though
word and cadence may vary a little, the core of the mystery remains the same. The ritual slaying of the God, the dark gleam of
the sacrificial knife, and the wailing of the women, and the rebirth
coming after. . . . I remembered Bedwyr with his harp beside the
horse-dung fire at Narbo Martius when the world was young, and
the merchant in his blanket robes swaying to and fro. "So the
women used to sing when I was a boy—singing the lament for
Adonis, when the crimson anemones are springing from the
rocks. . . ." And I remembered the bracken-thatched church in
the cool light of that morning and Guenhumara kneeling at the
Lord's Table; and I saw the oneness of all things.

And then the ritual was over, and the reborn Lord had seated
himself once more on his throne of turfs; and I thought that there
had been other beast-headed figures among the standing stones,
but could not be sure for the mist that seemed to hang there still.
And people were catching up unlit torches from the fringe of the
dancing floor, and crowding forward to kindle them from the blue
flame burning on the very forehead of the God.

The light flared brighter moment by moment, a wheel of ragged
fire-tongues circling the Nine Sisters. The fierce coppery light beat
farther and farther up the weathered flanks of the standing stones,
driving back the moonlight; and among the tawny smoke, now
glimpsed, now lost, were surely uptossed heads, horned and
winged, hound-snouted and prick-eared. . . . And in the very
heart and center of the flaming circle, the stag-headed figure sat
immovable, the red patterns of ritual death and ritual birth still on
his breast and thighs, and the old dry scars of war and hunting
such as men carry who are not gods. I had lost my sense of oneness, and I could have wept for it like a child who falls asleep at
the warm hearth and wakes to find itself in the alien dark beyond
a closed door; only I knew that it had been there. . . .

Something of the godhead was fading from him, as the blue
light dimmed before the red flare of the torches, so that one became aware once more of the man's head within the mask. And
yet he lost nothing by returning humanity. The god was incarnate.

None the less the Life of the People because we knew that he was also Maglaunus the chieftain, none the less terrible and apart.

All at once the crowd fell back a little, and there was empty torchlit space between me and the still figure on the high turf throne. The antlered head was turned toward me, and I felt the eyes behind the mask reaching out to mine across the emptiness; felt at the same time, as though it were in myself, the appalling weariness of the man, the first lonely and terrible awareness of returning self.

"My Lord Artos, Count of Britain."

Maglaunus's voice was scarcely recognizable, hollow under the mask. He made a small summoning gesture with one hand and was still again. And I knew that the moment had come. I walked forward across the trampled turf and stood before him. He tipped his head far back to look at me, and for an instant I caught the flicker of reflected torchlight behind the eye slits under the stag's muzzle. "I am here," I said.

"The Lammas torches are lit," he said. And that was all.

CHAPTER SEVENTEEN

Guenhumara

AN old warrior with a headdress made from the feathers of a golden eagle—it is in my mind that he was one of the chieftain's many uncles—came forward to stand beside the turf throne and speak with me as to my taking Guenhumara, as to the bonds of friendship, and the dowry that she would bring me. For it was not for the Horned One to speak of these things, though it would have been well enough for Maglaunus the chieftain at other times. I heard the old man talking, and the mention of a hundred armed and mounted men with the chieftain's second son to head them; I heard my own voice making the replies that courtesy demanded. I saw the little blue veins that writhed about the old man's forehead, and the torchlight shining through the silvery down at the base of the eagle's feathers. But all the while my awareness was going out beyond the old man, beyond even the Stag-Headed One on the throne, to the place where the torches had moved apart, leaving a gap of smoky darkness; and in the darkness something stirred and was still, giving no more to the torchlight than a blink of gold.

I turned once more full to the still figure on the throne. "The dowry is good, for horses and armed men are of greater worth than much gold to me, and gladly I accept it with the maiden." I made my voice ring against the standing stones, so that all the shadows lost in the farthest dark might hear it. "The Lammas torches are lit, and now that it is no longer taboo, I ask that I may take the Maiden Guenhumara from her father's hearth to mine. So shall the bond of kinship be made complete between Maglaunus, Clan Chieftain of the Damnonii, and Artos, the Count of Britain."

There was a long pause, and then very slowly the antlered head inclined; and the hollow voice spoke behind the mask, using the old form of words that belong to every asking: "What can you give the maiden in place of what she leaves for you?"

"My hearth for her warmth, my kill for her food," I returned. "My shield for her shelter, my corn for her quickening, my love for her contentment, my spear for the throat of the man who offers her harm. There is no more that I have to give."

"It is enough," said the hollow voice.

And Guenhumara with the golden apples swaying at the ends of her hair came through the gap of darkness that they had left for her between the torches.

The thing was done, and not to be undone again. The Horned One himself had taken the flint knife and nicked first my wrist, and then Guenhumara's where the vein showed blue under the brown skin, and let them bleed a few drops into the cup of wine. We had drunk from the cup, both at the same time, our hands linked on the rim as custom demanded, and all the while we were strangers looking at each other with stranger's eyes, when we looked at all; as though there had never been that other moment up here beside the Nine Sisters, when I had held her under my cloak and felt the life in her leap toward mine.

But stranger or no, she was my woman now, and together we were swept into the wild merrymaking that had begun to boil up through the wonder and the awe. The central part of the mystery was accomplished, and the god had stepped down from his throne to lead the dance that whirled and spun, as the torchlight and the shadows flew, its flaming circle about the smaller circle of standing stones that seemed to join in some secret dance of their own that had nothing to do with movement. We were dancing to the rhythmic stamping of our own heels, to the music of the pipes that whirled us this way and that as a wind whirls through dry leaves and sends them skyward and spins them along the ground—until at last the ring dance burst apart of its own spinning, into groups and couples and single leaping dancers.

Guenhumara danced with me. She had moved through the

rituals of her marriage as one moving perfectly, but in her sleep, through the complicated patterns of quite another kind of dance, but now she was awake and under the same spell as the rest of us. The same laughter came from her as from the others around us, the same soft cries from deep in the throat. And we danced our own dance to our own patterns, among all the swirling multitude (but indeed many were doing that, by now), the man-and-woman dance that is one with the buck tearing with his antlers at a bush and the goldfinch showing off the yellow under his wings.

The beer pots had begun to go around and men and women crowded to light more and more torches from one another, and dance with them whirled aloft in ragged mares' tails of smoky flame, that shone on laughing or sweating faces and clinging hands and flying hair. In one place, a man in a wildcat-skin kilt had withdrawn into a world of his own, and with drawn dirk was spinning and stamping in the complicated rhythms of the war dance. Close beside me, a half-naked girl slipped from the arms of a young warrior and went down, skirling with laughter, and I saw the love-bites on her throat and shoulder before the youngster flung himself joyfully upon her.

With the drum-pulse of stamping heels throbbing in my blood and the pipe music breaking in little sharp waves against me, I do not know how long it was before the knowledge came to me, nor quite how it came at last, that unless I found a way out quickly, I was going to have to take Guenhumara then and there. It seemed only after my brain had begun to clear that the long glances cast in my direction warned me what was expected of me.

And I knew that the thing expected of me was not possible. If it had been any girl plucked at random from the women's side, I could maybe have played the stallion without much more thought of the rest of the herd than the stallion has when he covers his mare. If I had loved her, then the rest might not have mattered to either of us. As it was . . .

In the same instant I caught the frowning red-brown gaze of Pharic, across a dozen heads between. He was half laughing, but the message was serious; and receiving it, I knew why he had shown me the ancient stronghold, why he had so arranged matters that my horse was within reach.

Scarcely knowing that I did so, I had caught Guenhumara by

the wrists and swung her out of the dance. Gault and Flavian were close at hand and still looked to be in their right minds; and I called them up with a jerk of the chin. "Go and get Arian up here, as close as may be," I muttered to the Minnow, making believe to play with the golden apples on the end of Guenhumara's braids, while she stood panting a little, with her face in the shadows.

"The other horses, too?"

"No, just Arian. Bring him up to the edge of the torchlight, and whistle for me when you are there. Gault, go and get Amlodd and the rest. It is time to be carrying off the bride, and we shall need you to cover our retreat."

The thing had passed over so swiftly that I think no one of the swaying, prancing throng about us knew that we had fallen out of the dancing for anything much but to fetch our breath, or maybe because we too were ready for the next thing. And as Gault and Flavian slipped away on their separate errands, I reached out and caught a beer jar from a passer-by, and held it for Guenhumara to drink. There was little enough left in it; a mouthful for each of us, but it served to cover a few moments of time, and she looked up at me over the rim, with a swift and willing understanding of what I was about, her eyes in the ragged torchlight no longer those of a stranger. I flung the empty jar aside, not caring under whose feet it fell, and it was caught by Pharic, who I had not known was still so near. I flung my thanks after it and he put up his hand in a swift odd gesture as though to catch and toss them back. "Am I not one of your captains now?" he said, and was gone again into the swirling crowd as I caught Guenhumara's hands and swung her in the opposite direction. Then I heard beneath the tumult and the sweet fierce piping, the dull trample of a horse's hooves on turf, and a moment later caught the moth-pale gleam of Arian's flank on the farmost fringes of the torchlight, and the high white whistle that a boy makes with his fingers in his mouth.

I laughed, and a sudden warm drunkenness took me, and I was every man who had ever carried off his chosen woman from among her kin. "That is for us! Come, Guenhumara!" and I caught her up and ran. She began to laugh too, and flung her arm around my neck to ease her weight for me, as I headed for that white gleam on the edge of the torchlight. Only the dancers nearest to us could know what was happening, and for an instant, surprise held them from breaking the dance or making any offer to prevent us. And in that instant I reached my horse and flung Guenhumara up across the saddlebow. But as I mounted behind her, Pharic raised the shout, "See! He carries off our sister!" and instantly the tumult of half battle that ends most bride feasts broke out.

I caught the reins from Flavian as he leapt back, and driving my heel into Arian's flank, swung him half around; my own few lads were springing in behind me for a rear guard, the young warriors, headed by Guenhumara's three brothers, striving to break through to her rescue. Glancing over my shoulder as the startled horse plunged and snorted under me, I saw Flavian and Pharic straining together in a wrestling grip that was only half laughing. "Ride!" Flavian shouted. "We'll hold them while we may!"

I jabbed my heel into the white flank and we were away at a full flying gallop, leaving the laughter and the shouting of battle behind us. And Guenhumara was clinging to me, laughing still, with her hair bursting loose of its braids flying like cool spray across my face and throat.

So soon as I was sure of no hunt on our heels, I slackened to an easy canter, for it is not good to ride full tilt among unknown hills by the light of a fading moon, especially with a woman to hamper your bridle arm. And as though with the wind of our going, that other wild warm wind that had swept us together for a while fell away. Guenhumara had drawn herself together, and sat light and undemanding in the crook of my arm now, so that I scarcely felt her there at all. "Where are we away to?" she asked in a little, as though nothing of the past hours was left in her at all. I spat out hair.

"To the Old Dun. Where else?"

"Do you know the way?"

"I hope so. Pharic showed me the place of it—I think in case of need."

"You do not mind, that I told Pharic?"

"You could scarcely do otherwise," I said, "seeing that his life also is caught into the thing."

"Into the tangle," she amended.

"I did not say that."

"No, you did not say it." She put up her hand and very gently gathered the long strands of hair that had snarled into my beard and the Medusa-head brooch at my shoulder, and took them back into her own keeping.

And we rode on, not speaking any more, for there seemed nothing more to say.

The blurred moon was still up when we came over the last wave crest of the moors, and looked down into the valley where the small upland tarn caught the glimmer of the sky. And in the soft white light, the ruins of the forsaken Dun looked more than ever like a village of the Little Dark People.

"They use the tower sometimes for a herding hut, nowadays," Guenhumara said then, much as her brother had done, a few hours earlier. "But when there is a mating in the chieftain's line it remembers again that once it was the chieftain's hall."

We rode down through the heather that had long ago engulfed the track, and in through the gap in the soft wavelike ridge of turf that showed where the gateway had once been. The heather had flowed in, washing to the very walls of the tower; and in the blurred moonlight the late harebells which drifted against the rough-piled walls of the cattle yard were shadow-white. And all the while the faint summer lightning flickered along the hills.

On a patch of open turf I dropped from the saddle and lifted Guenhumara down after me. I gave her my strike-a-light, and leaving her to gather sticks and heather snarls and get the fire going, set to unsaddling Arian and rubbing him down with a handful of grass. I took the old horse down to the tarn shore to drink, and afterward knee-haltered him and turned him free to graze where the runnels of open turf wound among the heather and bush-grown mounds, and went back to the tower.

A light as dimly and threadbare gold as fallen sycamore leaves shone out to greet me. Guenhumara had made the fire, and now she sat beside it, shaping little cakes of rye meal and honey, ready for the hearthstone when it grew hot. The round stone walls ran up out of the firelight and disappeared into the shadows overhead, so for all one could see, the ancient strong point might have been standing again to its full height; and behind her against the far wall, her shadow fell across the high-piled bracken and tumbled skins of the herdsmen's broad bed place.

She looked up when I entered, with a faint shadow of a smile, and pointed to the black pottery jar she had set just within the doorway. "I have found their store, you see; I dare say they'll not grudge us a wedding feast. Do you take that down to the lochan for water, and then be gathering some fresh fern for bedding."

I took up the jar and brought the water, and then armfuls of fern to scatter over the stale stuff on the bed place, kicking aside the stinking skins. And by the time I had done, the fire was burning with a clear red heart and the honey cakes were browning on the hearthstone. I sat down on the man's side of the hearth, my hands hanging across my knees, and sometimes looked at Guenhumara and sometimes away. And Guenhumara on the woman's side turned her hot rye cakes and fed the fire with heather sprigs, one at a time, and never looked at me at all. And from time to time there came the faint low mutter of thunder among the hills.

It was hard and harder to believe that I had not imagined that moment of wild response in her; but I knew that I had not; it was there somewhere, waiting to be wakened again. . . . Presently the cakes were done, and we ate them, hot and sweet and crusty, washing them down with cold lochan water from the black pottery jar; and still neither of us could think of anything to say.

The uncomfortable wedding meal finished, I got up and went out to see that all was well with Arian. The night was stiller than ever, the stillness of it seeming only intensified by that faint half-heard muttering below the skyline, and the occasional summer lightning was all but lost in the milky whiteness of the moonlight. I could hear lochan water sucking at its pebbly shore, and a hunting owl cried among the bushes; that was all. And suddenly I wished that the storm would break, longing for the relief of crashing thunder and storm wind, and rain lashing down the valley.

When I ducked under the lintel stone back into the tower again, Guenhumara was already lying on the bed place where I knew that I should have carried her. She had stripped off her gown and shift, and laid them with her copper and enamel arm rings and her shoes at the foot of the bed place, and in the close warmth of the tower she lay naked on my old weather-worn cloak, with her hair unbraided and flung about her. And a little white moon-moth, drawn indoors by the fire, danced and flickered about her head. And looking at her, I saw even in the uncertain mingled light of the fire on the hearth and the low moon through the doorway, that the skin of her body was not white where the clothes had covered it, but the pale brown of clover honey. She was a tawny woman from head to heel. She turned a little, her head on her arm, to watch me as I crossed to the hearth and set down the saddle which I had brought in in case it rained later. Oddly, the strain between us had relaxed, as though we had both been holding off something, and now we had let go and opened ourselves to the inevitable.

"I left you the fire to undress by," she said, "but I think the moon would have been light enough." And then, as I kicked off my shoes, and freeing my sword belt began to strip, "How many scars you carry! You are fang-gashed like an old mastiff that has spent its life fighting wolves."

And I think that she must have been seeing me for the first time in the way that I had first seen her four days ago, for she must have seen most of the scars often enough when she tended me in my sickness, and never spoken of them before.

Standing by the hearth, I looked down at the new crimson scar on my shoulder, and the white seams of old ones on my thighs and sword forearm. "I suppose that is what I am."

"Why do they come again and again so close about the same places?"

"You can always tell a heavy cavalry man by the position of his scars. They come on the thighs below the edge of one's war shirt—I have heard of thigh guards, but they hamper one in mounting—on the thighs and on the sword arm."

"Why not a long sleeve?" she asked, practically. It was an odd conversation for a wedding night.

"Because it would hamper the sword swing; also because the Saxon armorers do not make their sarks that way."

I stood by the fire, stretching, then stooped to set on the turfs that I had laid by for smooring it. As I did so, she said in the same tone of quietly detached interest, "You're beautiful. How many women have told you so?"

I thrust the fire together and set on the sods, and the firelight died, leaving only the fading moonlight to bar the darkness. "A few," I said, "but very long ago."

"How long? How old are you, my Lord Artos?"

"Thirty-five. That is another reason why you should not have married me."

"And I am twenty—almost one and twenty. We are old, you and
I."

I had not thought of her as being of any special age, but I had
realized, without much thought, that she was long past the age at
which most women go to a husband's hearth; and I wondered for
the first time why it was that she had not done so. As though she
caught the question in my mind, as though, also, she had lowered
her own defenses a little further, with the quenching of the too-
probing firelight, she said, "When I was fifteen, I was betrothed to
a chieftain's son from farther south. It was arranged in the usual
way, but I loved him, none the less—I *thought* I loved him. I am
not sure now; I was only fifteen. He was killed hunting, before the
time came for him to take me, and I thought that the sun and
moon had fallen from the skies. His memory came between me and
all things, between me and all men, and when my father would
have betrothed me again, I begged and prayed—I swore that I
would kill myself; and in the end—I was beside myself, and I think
he feared that I had it in me to carry out my threat—he yielded
partway, and promised that at least I should have five summers'
respite."

"And this is the sixth summer," I said.

"This is the sixth summer. But—" I heard a small bitter laugh of
self-mockery. "Scarcely two summers were gone by before I knew
that I had been a fool. I tried to hold his memory, but it turned
thin like woodsmoke and melted through my fingers, and I had
nothing left."

"Why did you not tell your father?"

"I was too proud. If you were a girl of seventeen who had
shrieked down the roof of her father's hall, vowing to die for her
dead love if she were forced into another man's bed, could you
have gone to your father and said, 'Oh my father, I made a mistake, a simple mistake; anyone might make it. It was not love; I
have forgotten what his face looked like, and the sound of his
voice, and now I am ready for a living husband, after all.'"

I took up my sword and carried it across to the bed place and
laid it to hand. Then I lay down beside Guenhumara. The moon-
moth fluttered across my face, but there was no other movement in
the dark beside me.

Her body was good to the touch, to explore; the skin smooth

and silky despite its brownness, and I could feel the strong light bones under it; the light cage of her ribs, the long slim flanks. She was too thin for most men's taste, but suddenly I loved the feel of her bones. I had seen, while she lay there in the firelight, that there was a rose mole on her left breast, and I searched for it by touch and pressed my finger onto it. It was soft and curiously alive, like the bud of a flower, like another smaller nipple, infinitely small and soft, and the feel of it sent a shimmer of delight through my body and into my loins. I flung my arms around her and strained her against me. She lay completely passive, neither giving nor withholding, as the furrow lies passive for the seed at sowing time. . . . And in that instant came like a black frost the memory, the very flavor, of the last time that I had lain with a woman, a mating half battle, half ecstasy, like mating with a wildcat. The cold miasma of hate seemed all about me, suffocating, chilling me to the soul, sapping all my powers. I clutched Guenhumara closer—no, rather I clung to her as one drowning—struggling to drive out the horror of my spirit, struggling to drive out the chill with her warmth, the death with her life. Her body was no longer passive under mine, and I must have hurt her, for she cried out, and I knew in that moment that she was a virgin; but even so, I hurt her more than is the nature of things, and I had no mercy. I was fighting desperately against some barrier, some denial that was not of her making. . . . It was, save for one other, the bitterest fight that ever I have known.

In the end I managed the man's part none so ill, but it was empty and joyless, the mere husk of what had once been a living thing; and I knew that for Guenhumara also, there had been no joy to transmute the pain. I remembered my first girl, taken laughing in the warm lee of a bean stack, clumsily but with delight. That had been whole and sweet, but this was a maimed thing. And I knew to the full then what Ygerna had done to me; that in some way she had robbed me of the spearpoint of my manhood.

I released Guenhumara, and rolled away from her. I think I groaned. I know that I was sweating and shaking from head to foot like a man after a mortal struggle; and I buried my head in my arms, waiting for her to turn away from me in disgust or bitter mockery.

Instead, she said calmly, but as though something in her throat was tight, "It should not be like that, should it?"

"No," I said. "It should not be like that." I drove my face harder onto my arms and little clouds of colored light whirled through the darkness before my eyes. I heard my own voice, muffled in my arms. "A few days since, I was watching one of your dunghill cocks. He was tethered with his hens about him, but the one he wanted was beyond his reach, and every time he leapt on her his tether brought him up short at the last moment, and tumbled him in the dung, until his feathers were all mired and draggled. God have mercy on me, I thought at first that it was funny."

There was a long silence; and then Guenhumara said, "Has it always been so?"

"If it had, do you think that I'd have taken you with a whole war host for your dowry? I haven't been with a woman for ten years. I did not know."

Another silence; the flutter of the flames had died away and outside I heard the soft whisper of falling rain; the scent of it on the warm earth breathed in at the open doorway. And beyond again, I heard the silence of the forsaken Dun.

Then Guenhumara said, "What happened? Let you tell me the once, and be done with the telling."

And lying there with my head still buried in my arms, I told her the whole foul story that I had not told in ten years, even to Bedwyr who was nearer to me than my own heart. It was her right to know.

When the thing was told to the last word, I waited for her horror and her drawing away. She did not speak for so long, in the end I lifted my head from my arms and turned again to look at her in the dark. And as I did so, a strange thing happened, for she turned a little toward me, and felt for my face and took it between her hands, and kissed me like the mother I never had. "God help us both, my dear," she said.

CHAPTER EIGHTEEN

The Lovers

WORD of what had happened was in Castra Cunetium and the Place of Three Hills ahead of me. Maybe the word had run through the tribes, maybe it had been carried by the Little Dark People, who know everything. I saw it in men's eyes that met mine a little too long or not quite long enough, as I rode in, but only two of my Companions spoke of the thing without waiting for me to speak first.

Gwalchmai came limping into my quarters while I was still washing off the dust and sweat of the summer tracks. He had ridden in only a few hours ahead of me, on some business of supplies, and began by giving me a report of how things were going with Bedwyr among the Saxon settlements, so that at first I thought that was all he had come for. Indeed he had actually got up to go, when he turned back to me, clearly hesitating over something more that he wished to say. He was a man who seldom found it easy to speak of the things that mattered to him. "The whole fort is throbbing with the word that you have taken a wife from the Damnonii," he managed at last, "and that she comes here to join you when we settle into winter quarters. Artos, is it true?"

"It is true that I have taken a wife, yes," I said.

"And that she comes here?"

"Yes, also a hundred of her father's best horsemen, captained by her brother."

"The hundred will be welcome, at all events."

"But not the *one?*"

He hesitated. "We are not used to the thought of the *one* and the thought is strange to us. You must give us a little time." He

[239]

changed the subject. "Artos, they did not send up any bandage linen or salves with the last supplies. We have had a good few wounded, as I told you, and we cannot go on tearing up our cloaks forever. I cannot go myself, I must get back to Bedwyr tomorrow, but give me leave to send Conon down to raise hell at Carbridge and get some more sent up."

But Cei was less forbearing, later that night, before we started out to make the late rounds together. "In God's name, if you wanted the girl why didn't you take her—and leave her with a pretty necklace, and no harm done?"

"Maglaunus her father would perhaps not have given me a hundred well-mounted men for tumbling his daughter under a broom bush."

"Aye, there's no denying that it is a dowry worth the having," Cei admitted; and then in a deep grumble between disgust and speculation: "But a woman prinking in her mirror. I suppose she'll bring a swarm of giggling girls to serve her?"

"One woman. I told Guenhumara she might bring one hench-woman: she chose her old nurse—no teeth, Cei, one foot already in the grave and the other on a lump of tallow."

"An asset indeed!" Cei's speculation was swallowed up in disgust.

"Agreed, my old ram, and a foul nuisance here in the fort, but by the God's grace, the other foot will slip one day," I said savagely. I was angry and sickened with all the things under the sun, myself most of all.

"Love does not seem to have sweetened your temper, Artos mine."

I was pulling on my rawhide boots, and I did not look up. "Who spoke any word of love?"

"Na, it was a hundred horsemen, wasn't it? But great God! Man, you can't have her here, just her and the hag in a fort full of men."

"There are the gay girls of the baggage train," I said, and stood up and reached for my sword which lay on the cot beside me.

"If she's a good woman, she'd sooner die than touch little fingers with one of the sisterhood."

"Cei, do you know much about good women?"

He laughed unwillingly, and shrugged, but looked up from the lamp flame with trouble in his fierce blue eyes. "You must have the thing your own stubborn way. But Christos! I foresee storm water ahead!" Then he shook himself as though shaking off the trouble like an old cloak, and laughed again, and flung his heavy arm around my shoulders as we went out from the lamplit room into the darkness of the hills. "Like enough I shall try seducing her myself, in the pursuit of further knowledge."

"Thanks for the warning," I said, tranquilly enough, and tried to ignore the black pain of jealousy that stabbed through me. In that moment I first understood that I loved Guenhumara.

In the next I fell headlong over a pig—we kept a good deal of livestock by that time—who rose in squealing affront and lumbered off into the night, leaving me to rub a bruised elbow and curse the Fates who must need strip a man even of his dignity, making a clown of him even while they turn the knife in the wound that they have made.

Everything in Trimontium was in good shape, for despite his hot temper and his wenching, Cei was as reliable as a rock, and so next morning when Gwalchmai headed eastward again, with the reliefs who were going up to free some of the other men for rest, I rode with them. And a few evenings later, I stood with Bedwyr in the lee of a clump of wind-shaped elder scrub that marked the lower end of our picket lines. There was a smell of smoke about him, not the fresh tang of campfires, but the acrid and faintly greasy reek that comes of burning out the places where men live. Bedwyr had been busy since I saw him last.

He was saying, "It is in my mind that the world would be a simpler place if the God that Gwalchmai believes in had never taken a rib from Adam's side and made a woman for him."

"You would miss her sorely, when you came to tune your harp."

"There are other matters for a harp song, besides women. Hunting and war, and heather beer—and the brotherhood of men."

"It is not many days since I found that I must ask the Minnow not to desert me," I said. "I did not think that I should have to ask it of you, Bedwyr."

He stood looking out over the camp, where the smoke of the cooking fires trailed sideways into the dusk, and a faint mist was creeping in over the moors from the sea. "If I were to desert you, I think that it would be for something more than a woman."

"But this goes beyond the woman, doesn't it?"

"Yes," he said. "This is more than any woman." And then he swung around on me, his nostrils flaring, his eyes brighter and more fierce than I had ever seen them in his twisted, mocking face. "You fool, Artos! Don't you know that if you were deservedly frying in your Christian's Hell for every sin from broken faith to sodomy, you could count on my buckler to shield your face from the flames?"

"I believe I could," I said. "You are almost as great a fool as I."

And we went up past the horse lines together, through the salt-tasting mist that was thickening across the high moors.

Two days later, Gault's squadron was ambushed and cut to pieces by a Saxon war band. They rode back into camp—what was left of them—battered and bloody, their dead left behind them, the more sorely wounded roped to their horses.

I saw them ride in, and the rest of the camp turn out with grim acceptance of the situation, and few questions asked, to rally around them, help down the wounded and take charge of the horses. I bade Gault see to his men and get a meal, and come to me with a full report afterward—he looked very white and staggered for an instant in dismounting, as though the ground had tilted under his feet; but to see one's squadron cut to bits is enough to account for that in any man. Then I went back to finish looking through Bedwyr's muster lists, in the half-ruined shepherd's bothy that I had taken for my own. It is good for a commander to have some such place when he can, he is easier to find at night, and matters which are not for the camp's ears can be spoken of in private.

I was sick at heart for the dazed and tattered remnant of my fourth squadron now gathering to the fire and the hastily brought-out food, sick for the loss of so many of my Companions, but it would serve no useful purpose to neglect the muster lists. So I crouched on the packsaddle which generally served me for a seat in camp, and returned to the work in hand. I had just reached the end when a figure loomed into the opening where the door had been, shutting out the blue dark and the flare of the campfire beyond; and looking up, I saw that it was Gault.

He moved in from the doorway, and there was no doubt that he staggered now. "I've come to report, sir," he said in a strained voice that was not like Gault's at all, and stretched out his hand to the crumbling turf wall and leaned there. I could see the sweat on his ashen face in the lantern light. "But I think I've—left it too late."

I sprang up. "Gault, what is it? Are you wounded?"

"I've—got a Saxon arrow in me," he said. "I broke off the shaft so that the rest shouldn't see it, but I—" He made as though to push aside his cloak, and in the act of doing so, pitched head foremost into my arms. I laid him down and hurriedly thrust back the concealing folds of his cloak and found the short bloody stump of an arrow shaft projecting from just below the cage of his ribs. The horn scales of his war shirt had been split there by a glancing axe blow some while since, and for days he had been intending to get the weak place mended. Now it was too late. He was quite unconscious, not much blood on him, but he must have been bleeding inwardly for hours. I sat for a few moments on my heels beside him, then got up and strode to the door and shouted to the man who stood outside leaning on his spear against the light of the nearest watch fire. "Justin, go and fetch Gwalchmai; no matter what he's doing—he must have finished with the worst wounded by now. Get him here at once!"

"Sir," he said, and I turned back to the lantern-lit bothy and the still figure crumpled on the floor. I thrust away Cabal's inquiring muzzle, and ordered the great hound to lie down in the far corner. I felt Gault's heart and found it still beating faintly, and straightened him into an easier position, thinking as I did so, that it was so that one straightened the crumpled dead.

Gwalchmai came very soon. I heard his uneven step outside, hurrying, and next instant he was in the doorway. "What is so urgent, Artos?"

"Gault," I said, and moved aside to give him more space. "He's taken an arrow under the ribs."

Gwalchmai limped forward and knelt at Gault's other side. "Reach down the lantern and hold it for me. I can't see in this gloom."

I did as he bade me, and we leaned together over the wound in the pool of yellow light. "Who broke off the shaft?" Gwalchmai demanded. He had already drawn his knife and was cutting the lacing of Gault's war shirt.

"He did it himself, so that his men should not know."

"So—well, I daresay it will make little difference in the long run. It would have given me a better purchase. . . ." He cut the last thong that held the battle shirt together on the right side, and lifted it back, with the blood-sodden linen tunic beneath; and was silent, looking down at the wound that was laid bare. At last he raised his eyes to mine. "Artos—what am I to do?"

"Light of the Sun, man, that's for you to say. Get the barb out, I suppose. Why else should I have called you?"

"Not quite so simple. If I leave the barb where it is, he'll be dead in three days—an ugly death. If I try to get it out, the chances are around a hundred to one that I shall kill him here and now."

"But there is the hundredth chance?"

"There is the hundredth chance."

We looked at each other across Gault's body. "Do it now," I said, "while he is unconscious. At the worst, death will be quicker and kinder that way."

Gwalchmai nodded, and got to his feet, and I heard him shouting from the doorway for hot water and barley spirit and more rags. He remained there until the things were brought, then returned and knelt down, setting out the tools of his trade beside him. "Get something to put under his back—we must have him arched backward to draw the belly taut."

I grabbed the old cloak and an armful of bracken from my bed, and made them into a firm roll, then lifted Gault while Gwalchmai arranged it under him, so that when I laid him down again his body was bent backward like a half-drawn bow, the skin drawn tight over breast and belly.

"So, that will serve. Now the lantern again."

I knelt there for what seemed as long as a whole midwinter night, intent on holding the horn-paned lantern perfectly steady, that no tremor of light might confuse eye or hand at the crucial moment, while Gwalchmai, working with the complete absorption that shut him off from all men at such times, bathed away the blood so that he might see exactly the edges of the wound, and again took up his knife. I watched the sure, intent work of his hands as he began with infinite care to enlarge the wound. Later, he laid down the knife and took up a fierce little probe, then another, and later still, returned to the knife again. It seemed to grow unbearably hot in the bothy, I could feel the sweat prickling in my armpits, and beads of it shone on Gwalchmai's forehead, and yet the night was a cool one, and I had no fire under the turf roof. From time to time, whenever Gwalchmai bade me, I felt Gault's heart. His upturned face was frowning, the teeth bared as though in intolerable pain, but I think that in truth he did not feel anything. I hope to God that he did not. At one time I thought his heart was stronger and his breathing more steady, but maybe it was only my own desire that deceived me; or maybe it was a last flicker of life. . . . Quite suddenly, both began to grow fainter.

By that time we must have been working on him for the best part of an hour, and the thing was almost done. "Gwalchmai—can you give him a respite? His heart is fading."

Gwalchmai gave an infinitesimal shake of the head. "Respite will not serve him now. Moisten his lips with the barley spirit."

And only a few moments later he sat back to draw his own breath, then leaned forward once more and took hold of the short end of arrow shaft which now lay in a little oozing blood-filled hole. I shut my teeth and for an instant my eyes. When I looked again, he was laying a reeking arrowhead on the ground beside him. Blood gushed out in a red wave, and Gault drew a great choking breath that seemed to tear itself free of breast and rattling throat, while a convulsive shudder ran through his whole body —and we, kneeling alive in the lantern light, knew that the hundredth chance had been denied to us.

Gwalchmai sat back on his heels, and said with a great weariness in his voice, "Hang up the lantern again. We shall not be needing it any more." He rubbed his hands across his face, and when he took them away, his forehead was smeared with Gault's blood. "We know so little—so hideously little."

"Better he should go now than in three days' time," I muttered, trying, I think, to comfort myself as much as him. I got up, suddenly as tired as though I had just come out of battle, with no glow of victory to sustain me, and turned to hang the lantern again where it had hung before. And even as I did so, the pad of hurrying footsteps sounded outside, and Levin was in the doorway. "Gault bade me take over and see to the men while he made his report," he began in a rush, "and so I could not come before. I—" His gaze fell on the body on the ground, and the rush broke off short, into silence. Then he said, slowly and carefully, as though he were a little drunk, "He is dead, isn't he?"

"Yes," I said.

"I knew something was amiss, but he would not tell me. He said only to see to the men while he came up here to make his report. So I could not come before."

He came a step nearer, and saw the bloody arrowhead and the few surgeon's tools that Gwalchmai had begun to gather up for cleaning, and looked at Gwalchmai, his mouth flinching. "You killed him, you bloody butcher!"

"We both killed him," I said. "Gwalchmai will tell you that if the barb was left in, he must die within three days; if it was cut out, there was one chance in a hundred of saving him. That's long odds, Levin."

"Yes, I—" He pressed the back of his hand across his forehead. "I am sorry, I—n-not sure what I'm saying. . . . Did he—say anything?"

"He was already out of his body," Gwalchmai said, getting to his feet.

But the other had knelt down beside his dead, bending forward to look into the set frowning face, and I do not think he was aware of us any more. He cried out sharply and shudderingly, "Why didn't you wait for me?—Gault, why didn't you wait for me? I would have waited for you!" and slipped down full length with his arms around the body as a woman might have done.

Gwalchmai and I looked at each other, and went out of the bothy.

Outside the door hole, he said, "I'll send a couple of men to carry the body away." And then, "Best have a care, or we'll be needing a grave dug broad enough for two."

"Not if I can help it," I said. I heard his footsteps die away into the darkness between the watch fires, gauging his tiredness by the slur of sound as he dragged his crippled foot after him. I stayed where I was, under the Red Dragon on its lance shaft beside the door hole, listening for any sound from within the bothy, until I heard the feet of the men Gwalchmai had sent; and then turned back into the lantern light. Levin was kneeling beside the dead man, staring down at him, and seeing them there with the lantern spilling its pool of dim yellow radiance on the two wild-barley-colored heads, I realized as I had never quite done before, how alike they were. It was as though the link between them was so potent that even in their outward seeming they could have nothing apart from each other. "The men are coming up from the camp to carry him away," I said.

Levin raised his haggard gaze to my face. "I must help bear him."

"Very well, but return to me here, as soon as all is done."

He did not answer, but in the last moment before the men were at the door, he ripped his sword from its wolfskin sheath.

I sprang forward. "Levin! No!"

And he looked up again, choking with an ugly laughter. "Ah no, not yet. Time for that later," and with a movement as swift as the other had been, he drew the blade that lay by Gault's side, where I had put it down when we cut away his harness, and slammed it home into his own empty sheath. "You'll be returning one sword to store, but I'll have the one *he* carried," and got to his feet as the newcomers ducked in through the doorway.

When the heavy tread of men carrying a burden had stumbled away into the night sounds of the camp, I sat down again on the packsaddle to wait, and Cabal shook himself clear of the shadows and came, a little uncertainly, as though questioning whether the reason for his banishment was yet over, and collapsed with a gusty sigh in his usual lying place at my feet. After a moment he raised his head and looked up at me, whining and uneasy, and as I reached my hand down to stroke his head I felt the harsh hairs raised a little on his neck. He was a war dog, and killing in battle he understood, but not this. The lists that I had been working on lay scattered beside me. There was blood on them now, the stains turning brown around the edges as they dried. There was blood soaked into the beaten-earth floor, and the smell of it was everywhere, and the smell of death. It is one thing to have the friend killed beside you in battle (though that strikes sore enough), but quite another to feel him die under your hands in the cold blood that comes afterward. I wondered whether Levin would come back, or whether I should have to send for him, for I was not sure that he had even heard my order.

I had waited a long time, and was on the point of sending, when he appeared once more in the doorway.

"You have been a long time, Levin."

"The ground is hard and stony in these parts," he said dully. "What is it that you wish with me, Artos?"

"Gault should have furnished me with a full report of what happened, but he had no time. Therefore, as his second, the duty falls to you."

He got through it quite creditably; there was not, after all, so very much to tell, and then, when it was finished, he broke down, with his arm along the rotting roof beam and his head on his arm. I gave him a little time, and then said, "A sorry business, and has cost us dear in men and horses. But it seems that no blame clings to Gault."

He swung around on me, his eyes wide and blazing. "No *blame?*"

"None whatever," I said, pretending to misunderstand him. "And you have given your report well and clearly."

"Thank you, sir," he said bitterly. "Is there anything more?"

"First, have you anything to say to me?"

"Yes. I wish to ask for leave to go away from here."

"And fall on your sword?"

"What is it to my Lord Artos what I do, when once I am no more of the Brotherhood?"

"Only this—that we are short of men as it is, and I cannot spare another for no good cause."

"No good cause?"

"None," I said. I got up and walked across to him. "Listen to me, Levin. For more than ten years I have counted you and Gault among the best and bravest of my Companions. That is because each of you has striven always to outdo the other in valor and endurance, not from any rivalry, but that each of you might be worthy of his friend. So it has been since you were boys; and are you going to be a shame to Gault, to break the old covenant between you, now in the first hour that he is dead?"

He stared back at me with dilated eyes. "Maybe I'm not as strong as Gault. I can't go on—I can't."

I took him by the shoulders and shook him a little. "That is a weakling's cry. There's water in that jar in the corner; wash your face, and go down and take over command of the squadron. Choose whichever of your lads you judge most suitable for your second; that is your affair, so don't come troubling me with it."

"You—you're giving me command of the squadron?"

"Assuredly. You have been Gault's second for five years, and you have it in you to make a good leader."

"I cannot do it," he said pitifully. "Artos, have some mercy on me—I can't. It is all true as you say, but I *can't go on!*"

But already, though he was not yet aware of it himself, I could feel him strengthening under my hands, bracing himself to take up the intolerable burden.

"Oh yes you can. One can always go on. And as to mercy, I keep that for when and where it is needed. If Gault could break off the arrow shaft so that his men should not know and lose heart, and get the rags of you out of ambush and back to camp, with a mortal wound in him, then you can wash your face so that the rest won't mistake you for a woman, and go and take over his squadron and keep it what he made it, one of the best squadrons of the Company." I gripped and gripped at his shoulders, driving in my fingers until I felt the bone. "If you cannot—then you were never as he thought you were, after all."

He stood unmoving for a long moment, though I had dropped my hands. Then his head went up very slowly, and I saw him swallow thick in his throat; and he turned and crossed to the jar of water in the corner.

Through the rest of that summer I watched him anxiously. But there was little need. He proved, as I had believed he would, to be as fine a leader as Gault had been; and under his handling, the battered remnant gathered itself up and began to be a squadron again. He was careful of his men, but utterly careless of himself—so reckless that, though there was no more talk of falling on his sword, it was clear he hoped for death. And as so often happens when a man is in that state, death passed him by as if he had a charmed life.

We campaigned late into October that year. At most times in the North, one cannot hold to the war trail much beyond the end of September, but it was a soft autumn, and the last yellow leaves were still clinging to the birches when at last we rode into Trimontium to make our winter quarters again.

There were only a few days left, and many things to be seen to in them, before I must ride for Castra Cunetium to meet Guenhumara. But in the time that I had, I did what I could to make ready for her. I furbished up the much larger chamber next to the nar-

row one in the half-ruined officers' block where I had slept since
we first came to Trimontium. The commandant's dining room, I
think it must have been, to judge by the crudely painted trophies
and goats' masks that still showed here and there like shadows on
the shreds of plaster that still clung to one wall. I bought a thick
striped native blanket and a rug of soft beaver skins from Druim
Dhu and his brothers, who bought and sold all things in common,
to cover the piled fern of the bed place. I pegged up a fine embroidered hanging of some saint or other, all glimmering blues and
russets, kingfisher colors, to cover the crumbling red sandstone of
the most ruinous wall and give some richness to the chamber. It
was part of the loot that we had taken from the Sea Wolves that
summer, and they, I suppose, had reaved it from some rich religious
house in the gentler Lowlands. Well, the Church could count it as
part of the debt they owed me, there was a certain satisfaction in
the thought.

All the while I was aware of my men watching me, with a kind
of suspended judgment that might turn into anything. . . . The
awareness did nothing to ease the waiting days. I half longed for
her coming, as those days went by, half dreaded it, sometimes wondered whether she would come at all.

She came, and we swept her into Castra Cunetium by torchlight. It was a wild night, the feast of Samhain, and I remember
how the torches flared in the wind, sending their tawny smoke
billowing all across the forecourt, their light beating like bright
wings in the darkness upon the faces of the men who thronged
around us, and clatter and jink and hoof drum of the cavalry
swept in after us through the gates. Guenhumara rode between
her brother Pharic and myself, with her cloak flying loose from its
shoulder clasp. I had not known her in the first moments of our
meeting, almost a day's march farther westward, for with her tall
slight body clad in plaid breeks for the long ride, and her hair gathered up under a soft woolen cap, she looked for all the world like
a fine-boned stripling. And indeed I think that few among the
crowding garrison realized who she was, for I saw them craning
behind her for the commander's woman. That was until we clattered to a halt, and I dismounted and turned to help her down; for
I remember, then the roar went up.

I had not touched her until then, for we had not dismounted

at our meeting. There were still grumblings of trouble in the hills, and we had ridden hard to reach Cunetium before full dark, and in the instant before she kicked free from the stirrup and slid into my arms, I knew a wild expectancy; but as it had been before, among the Nine Sisters, I felt as I caught and set her down that there was nothing there, that I might have been holding one of the cool gray standing stones; and this time there was no time for the fire and the life to kindle, for she turned from me at once, swaying with exhaustion as she was, to face the new life about her, with all her defenses like a drawn sword in her hand.

Pharic and the rest were swinging down from their horses, and Bedwyr, who was once again in command of the outpost garrison, had come out from among his squadron to bid her welcome.

I said, "Guenhumara, here is Bedwyr, my sword brother and lieutenant."

I had wondered how it would be between Bedwyr and Guenhumara when they came together, and I was left still wondering.

I remember him making the bent knee to her that a man makes to a queen; I remember his ugly, crooked face smiling down at her, faintly mocking, his reckless eyebrow flaring like the wind-blown flames of the torches, saying with the drawling tenderness in his voice that I had never heard him use on a woman before, "I never thought to see a flower springing in the hard ground of this old fort—and it not even summer."

"A hand for the harp as well as the sword." Guenhumara's gaze touched on the embroidered lip of the harp bag that cocked above his shoulder. "Was that grace note plucked from the last song you made?"

"Na na—but I may find it fit in well enough when I come to make the next. There is something tells me that you set little store by the minstrel kind."

"I have known only the one harper in my father's hall," she said gently. "He can outplay any of his kind along the west coast, when it comes to Oran Môr, the Great Music; but I have heard over-many light lilts to the Lady Guenhumara's shining hair—especially when he would have another arm ring or a new bull calf for his herd."

"Be assured, at least, that I have no use for an arm ring, nor for a bull calf," Bedwyr said, with the smile flickering around his lips. "And alas! I have not yet seen the Lady Guenhumara's shining hair!"

Standing by, it seemed to me that I was watching two swordsmen playing for the feel of each other's blades, but whether the foils were blunted or sharp, I could not yet be sure. I have thought since, that they were not sure themselves. I made the late rounds with Bedwyr that night, neither of us speaking any word of Guenhumara, and after he had gone back to the mess hall and the evening firelight, I lingered behind, leaning my elbows on the crumbling stone breastwork that still faced the old turf ramparts, and staring out into the blustery darkness of the hills. I meant to follow him at any moment, but I was still there when something moved below and behind me, and as I swung around, Guenhumara herself came up the rampart stair. She was close-muffled in the heavy folds of her riding cloak, but the light of a distant pine-knot torch behind her made a bright copper-dust nimbus through her unbound hair, and I knew by that, and by her way of moving, I suppose, that she had changed back into women's gear.

"Guenhumara! You should be in your bed."

She reached out her hand to Cabal, who had risen from his place beside my feet to welcome her better than I had done. "I am too restless for my bed. Everything is so strange; I felt caged in that little room with its face turned nowhere save into a courtyard, and all the wind and the darkness outside." She came beside me, and set both hands on the cold age-eaten coping. "So this is a Roman fort—a Dun of the Red Crests?"

"Is it not at all as you expected?"

"I do not know. Yes, I suppose so. They say that the Romans like to have their lives boxed into squares and fenced with straight lines. . . . One was telling me, a while since, that in Roman cities the houseplaces have high square rooms to them, and that they are built all along ways so straight that they might have been ruled with a spear shaft. Would that be true?"

Memory twinged at me, and out of the dark and under the wind it seemed for a moment that another woman's voice was in my ears, a low voice, and mocking. "They say that in Venta there are streets of houses all in straight rows, and in the houses are tall rooms with painted walls; and Ambrosius the High King wears a cloak of the imperial purple." And I wanted to catch Guenhumara into my arms and hold her fast against all threat to take her from me, defying Ygerna, defying God Himself if need be. But I knew with a sick helplessness that I could not so much as touch her until she gave me leave.

"It is true. The better houses, and the main streets, anyway," I said, and hoped that my voice was steady. "There are small crooked ways behind the straight ones, and they creep out farther in these days, as the grass creeps farther between the wheel ruts in the streets."

"The grass is not Roman," Guenhumara said with a small tired whimper of laughter. "It flows in curves when the wind blows over."

"You will grow used to it all in time."

"I will grow used to it in time," she agreed, "but tonight it is all so strange—so many strange faces in the torchlight. Do you know, save for your trout-freckled armor-bearer, I have not seen in this Red Crest's eyrie, one of those who were with you in my father's hall."

"They will be most of them at Trimontium," I said. "Flavian rode this far with me, and then on south, to winter with his wife and bairn."

She looked around quickly. "Was that his price?"

"His price?" I did not fully grasp her meaning for a moment, and could only repeat the words, stupidly. "His price?"

And I think she must have seen how it was, for suddenly she was trying to catch her words back. "Na na, that was a wicked thing to say—stupid, which is worse; I shall be less stupid when I am not so tired. You told me before, that it might be you could let him go this winter, and it might be not, and I am glad that you could let him go." She moved a little nearer to me as she spoke, as though to make up for some hurt or failure, and I knew that I had the beginning of the leave that I had waited for, and put my arm around her as we propped side by side against the rampart wall.

"What of the one with the barley-colored hair—Gault, his name was," she asked in a little.

"Why Gault in particular?"

"I don't know. I thought of him at that moment—just a thought that passed by."

"Maybe it was himself that passed, coming in to the fire," I said, thinking of the empty places kept beside the mess hall hearth, and the food and drink set ready for men who came no more in the body to the evening meal among their comrades. But it would be at Trimontium that Gault's place was kept for him, beside Levin, this Samhain night.

I felt Guenhumara startle and stir in the curve of my arm. "Dead?"

"Almost two months ago."

"Was there a woman left lonely for him—or a bairn?"

"No, Guenhumara." I put both arms around her then, and pulled her close, as though trying to shield her from something, I am not sure what. She was too weary to quicken, spent as a bird that one finds sometimes fallen on the shore after a long storm-driven journey over the sea. But she leaned against me as though there was some kind of shelter in that. And standing there in the wind and the sharp spitting darkness, I had a sudden sense of light and strength and quietness, and it seemed to me that Ygerna's power could not last forever; that it might even be fought off and broken, and in the end I might be free, and Guenhumara with me.

"May the fire be warm for him," Guenhumara said softly, against the breast folds of my cloak, "or may the birds of Rhiannon sing for him, if it hurts less, to forget." ("Forget . . . Forget . . . Are you afraid to hear the singing of Rhiannon's birds, that makes men forget?")

And the light went out, and I knew that the Samhain wind was dreary cold, and the rain spitting down my neck, and no man may escape his doom. I kissed Guenhumara, and it was like kissing her good-bye. "Anwyl, you must go in to your bed."

She kissed me again, with a great and lovely kindness, as she had kissed me on our wedding night. "Come soon, then, Artos the Bear, for it is lonely in this place."

"I will come soon," I promised.

And she drew back out of my arms, and went away down the rampart stair.

CHAPTER NINETEEN

The House of Holy Ladies

FLAVIAN returned to us early in the spring, before even the first supply carts of the year got through. I was out on old Arian, beginning the long business of getting him back into condition after the winter, and we came together with a suddenness that set the horses trampling, at the bend where the Cunetium road ran out from the shadows of the river gorge. "Artos!" he shouted, and I, "Minnow!" and laughing and exclaiming and cursing the horses, we leaned together from the saddle to strike hands, while Cabal sprang around us with his tail lashing.

"How is it with Teleri and the bairn?" I asked, when we had quieted the beasts and turned them back toward the gates of Trimontium.

"It is very well with both of them; he is a fine cub and uses his fists like a warrior already." He spoke with the lingering tone and inward-turning smile of a man looking back on past contentment so strong that the flavor of it lingers with him still. And then in a changed note, "She came then?"

"Guenhumara? She came. But what tells you so?"

"You have a new cloak."

I glanced down at the dark thick plaid I had flung about me against the March wind that cut like a fleshing knife. Guenhumara had not been two days in Trimontium before she asked for a loom, and when two of our craftsmen made it for her, the first thing that she wove on it had been a cloak for me. "I have a new cloak," I agreed, "but must it be of Guenhumara's weaving?"

"They always weave a cloak for their lord, to keep him warm," said Flavian, with the air of one grown suddenly wise in the ways

of women. "Mine wove this for me," and he shook out and re-
settled the folds of a fine dark blue cloak bordered with black and
flame red.

"It is a bonny cloak," I said, "and a bonny target for Saxon
arrows you'll make wearing it. Now I have but to squat still enough
in this dim plaid of mine, and the Dark People themselves will
take me for a hole in the hillside."

"Ah, you are jealous, my Lord the Bear!" And so I was, but
not of his cloak with the black and scarlet border.

We rode on, exchanging the news of the camp for news of the
world outside, until we came down to the ford, and splashed
through; and as we set the horses to the steep rough-paved slope
on the far side, Flavian said suddenly, "Fool that I am. I should
have told you at first. Hunno bade me remind you that he will be
sending your Signus up with the horse drafts, this spring."

I had almost forgotten that the white foal would be three years
old now. In war and in the wilderness one easily loses count of
time. I twisted in the saddle to look at my companion. "You have
seen him? He has fulfilled his promise?"

"I believe you will think so. He's a good hand taller than Arian,
and more powerful, and his heart is as high as his crest. Hunno
says he is the crown and the flowering of all the colts that ever
came under his hands, and that the Horned One has granted it
to him to make a perfect horse at the end of his days. . . . I think
he forgets that the dam had anything to do with it."

"The end of his days?" I said quickly. "Is anything amiss with
Hunno?"

"Nothing but that he grows old," Flavian said, and suddenly he
sighed. "It happens—it happens to all of us."

"You have noticed that? Sa! You are growing up, my Minnow."

"Even Teleri was a little older than when I saw her last. Her
breasts are not pointed any more, but round. Maybe by the time
I see her again she will have found a white hair and pulled it out
and grown seven more."

It was the best part of a month later that Hunno sent up the
yearly draft of horses. They were a good lot. Trained on for battle (that was the task that fell to the summer garrison every year),

they would serve to remount some of Pharic's contingent before the end of the campaigning season.

And among them, as promised, was Signus. The big white war-colt was certainly, I thought, walking all around him in the first moments of our reunion, everything that Hunno had claimed for him. He stood rising sixteen hands at the shoulder, strength and endurance promised though not yet fulfilled in his deep shoulders and long, finely sloping haunches, pride and fire in every line of him from high crest to sweeping, restless tail, and as he stamped and tossed his head and wheeled about to keep me in view, my soul went out to him as it had done at our last meeting, when his muzzle was still flecked with his mother's milk. I went closer, and felt the quivering bowstring fineness of the tendons at wrist and hock, the life and the instant response shiver through him as I ran my hands over his body. He swung his head toward me in interest, his wariness forgotten, his ears pricked forward, nuzzling with delicate outthrust lip for the lick of salt that he was all at once sure I had brought him. I shook some into my palm from the small raw-hide bag I usually carried with me, and gave it to him, drawing my free hand again and again down his nose from forelock to quiver-ing nostril, while he sucked and slobbered at the gray salt. His head was broad and intelligent, his eyes like a falcon's, dark and lumi-nous, under the veil of white lashes. "Did I not say that we should go into battle together, you and I? Did I not tell thee?" I said, in the British tongue that he would be used to. And he ruckled softly in his nose, butting against me for more salt.

I had him saddled up, and called to Amlodd standing by to bring a spear and follow me, and took him down then and there to the practice field to try him out. We had cleared the old practice field during our first long months in winter quarters, hauling out the elder bushes and the furze that had overrun it, and setting up the brushwood jumps and spear targets. And there I spent the better part of that evening, one of the happiest evenings, I think, that I have ever known. I tested his paces, and tried him for ease in maneuvering, bending him this way and that, reining him up short and wheeling him almost on his haunches; and found his mouth sensitive and his heart high and willing even when clearly he did not understand what I wanted of him. I took him over the jumps and ditches—it is very seldom that one needs a war-horse to jump, but when one does, one needs it as never anything in life before. In his eagerness he was prone to stretch out his neck and jump off too soon, but confidence and scorn of the obstacle ahead was in the very gathering of his lean haunches under him, and his landings were sure as a cat's. He must be schooled against overconfidence; ah, but too much fire, too fierce a scorn of obstacles, are better than too little, in horse or man. I took him at full gallop down the curved line of practice posts, swerving him in and out with the torn sods flying back from his hooves, and fell more and more in love with him at every drumming hoofbeat. He shook his head, when I brought him to a halt at last, scattering foam on his breast, and I could sense in him as though one life flowed through both of us, the joy in his own speed and power and the hand beginning to grow familiar on his reins. This would make a war-horse indeed! Only when I took the spear from Amlodd and set him at the target, he was somewhat lacking, for he did not yet understand what was wanted of him, and the target itself, which looked like a man and yet was not a man, was a thing to be shied and snorted and trembled at, lest there be some hidden menace in it. But time and training would amend that. And in the ultimate task of a war-horse I knew that he would need scarce any training at all, for the use of his own teeth and front hooves as weapons is born into every stallion.

By the time that I had done, the sun was low and the three-peaked shadow of Eildon had engulfed the whole river valley and the old red fort on its headland and the marshes eastward. I turned Signus toward the gateway, and saw what looked like half the war host crowded there to watch the show. From deep within the gloom of the gate arch one figure moved forward and started down the length of the practice field toward me, and I saw with a small sharp stab of pleasure that it was Guenhumara. Cabal, who had gone through every trial and test with us, bounded to meet her, and mouthed the hand she held to him in his great jaws. That gentle pretense at savaging, which had in it all the loving laughter of intimacy, was a thing that he bestowed sometimes on me, very occasionally on Guenhumara, on Bedwyr and Druim Dhu, never on anyone else. I noticed that in the curve of her other arm, she carried a small deep rush basket, tenderly as though it contained something fragile and precious.

I had dropped from the saddle, with my tunic sticking to my back, for the evening was warm for April and Signus had been no armchair ride; and when she reached me with Cabal stalking beside her, she stood watching while I rewarded the big colt with another lick of salt. "Flavian told me that you were trying out the white colt, and so I came to watch. Is he all that he should be?"

"He is all that I hoped and believed he would be," I said, fondling the muzzle that thrust against my breast.

"Believed? You have seen him before, then?"

"Three years ago—a foal still running at his mother's heel. I marked him for mine, then, and gave him his name for a covenant between us."

"And the name?"

"Signus. He was an autumn foal, and a white one, and I called him for the star of the Great Swan that rises at the time of the first autumn gales."

"So—and he is swift and fierce and beautiful like the wild swans that used to fly over my home. It is a good name for him."

Amlodd had come panting up from the far side of the practice field, and I handed the white colt over to him, and once more turned toward the fortress gates with Guenhumara.

"What will you do now, with Arian?"

"For the next year or two, God willing, I shall ride him equally with Signus. In two years the young one will have gained experience, and I shall send Arian back to Ambrosius who first gave him to me. He will be past his best by then, poor old lad."

"He will hate that."

"He will remember Ambrosius. It would break his heart to hear the trumpets and know that I had gone into battle without him."

"Poor Arian. It is sad to grow old."

"It happens," I said, "to men and horses, and I suppose to the stars themselves, until the time comes that they fall from the sky on a winter's night. . . . You sound like Flavian; he says that Teleri's breasts are not pointed any more, but round."

"That is not age," said Guenhumara, softly. "That is because she has borne a child and given suck."

And a sudden silence took us as we walked, a small silence, but painful.

All through the autumn, even while I dreaded her coming, I

had hoped, hoped for some kind of miracle, I don't know what. But when she came, nothing had been changed between us. And Guenhumara, though she never spoke of it, I think had hoped for a miracle, too. If we could have spoken of the trouble, we might have drawn closer together, but we could not. And the silence made a sword-blade barrier between us more impassable than the thing itself. The fact that I could not be fully a man to her made me shy of her in other ways, and as I held back and drew away, so, by no will of her own, it seemed, must she draw away also. And yet I believe she loved me then. I know that I loved her.

"What have you in that basket that you carry as though it were eggs?" I asked at last; anything to break the silence.

And she laughed a little breathlessly and hurried to help me. "But it *is* eggs! Look!" And coming to a standstill, she turned to me and put back a wad of grass and moss with which the basket seemed to be filled, and showed me, lying as it were in a nest of moss, seven greenish waxen-surfaced mallard's eggs. "Gwalchmai found them in the marshes and brought them to me to hatch."

As she carefully re-covered them to keep their warmth in, I thought that that was like Gwalchmai, thought also that the gift showed the place that she had found for herself among us and taken with quiet certainty as her own. "I'll have no married women to raise trouble among the men," I had said, long ago, to Flavian. But if trouble of that kind were to come with Guenhumara, it still lay hidden in the future days. Maybe that was in part because she was mine, and I was Artos the Bear, with a bear's blow to defend my own; maybe, a little, because they too were mine; but chiefly, I think, it was something in Guenhumara herself.

"And how is it you think you are going to hatch them? Will you make a nest and sit on them turn and turn about with Blanid?" I asked, making a foolish jest of it.

We had moved on again, and the onlookers about the gate, now that the show was over, were beginning to drift away.

"One of Caradawg's hens has gone broody," she said. "That was why Gwalchmai brought them to me, because he thought that there was a good chance of hatching them."

It was more than I did. Caradawg the armorer whiled away the time when work was slack by breeding fighting cocks and trading them through the fort and with the merchants who came occasionally in the summer, and I could not see one of his fierce little red game hens sitting placidly on a clutch of mallard's eggs. "I was going to find Caradawg when Flavian told me about the colt, and I saw the crowd gathering and came down to watch with the rest." Guenhumara checked, and added after a moment, "Only of course I shall not be here to see them hatch out; Caradawg must see to that for me. That was the one thing that Gwalchmai forgot."

"Yes," I said, "that is the one thing that Gwalchmai forgot."

"Let me stay a while longer," she said suddenly, "until the ducklings are safely hatched."

I shook my head. "Mid-April is late enough for you to be making the journey. It is not even as though I could spare the time to ride all the way with you and leave you safe in your father's hall."

"Is not Pharic's arm strong enough to get me there, even with an escort behind him?"

"In mid-April, yes. By mid-May, for all that we can know, it might take the whole war host."

There was a small pause. We were out on the roadway now, and had slackened to a snail's pace; as though without actually admitting it by stopping, neither of us wished to reach the gates. Then Guenhumara said, "Very well, if you fear an ambush for me on the journey, let me stay here all summer. I shall be safe enough within these great red walls."

"Will you? We hold Trimontium with a garrison cut to the very bone in summer, to free every possible man for the war trail. You have a certain value as a hostage, and if word that the Bear's wife was here with so small a force to guard her came to the ears of our enemies, broken and divided as they are, you might bring deadly peril both on yourself and Trimontium. I can't afford to lose either of you."

"But principally Trimontium," said Guenhumara, and drew away from me a little as we walked. "Ah well, I promised, did I not, that you should not find me a too clinging wife."

I made a clumsy, protesting gesture of some sort toward her, and then checked it because of the men who still lounged in the gateway. Even alone with Guenhumara I was shy of any intimate gesture, being a hamstrung lover in all things; and before other eyes I could not touch her at all. The gate was very near now, and she spoke quickly and very quietly, with a breath of unhappy laughter. "Na na, you need not pretend, my lord; part of you will breathe a great breath of relief when I am gone."

"And part of me will miss you as a newly blinded man misses the first light of morning," I said in the same suppressed tone.

She looked around at me, then, and in the last few steps, drew nearer again. "God help us both!" she said, as she had said it on the first night of all. The long evening shadow of the gate towers fell across us.

By the end of that year's war trail, I knew that I could safely leave Valentia to itself, at least for a while, and turn south at last, to redeem my four-year-old promise to Eburacum. And that following summer I did not send Guenhumara back to her father, but for the first and only time in our years together, carried her with me. It seems an odd decision now, and looking back, I am not sure how I came to make it. I suppose at the roots of the thing, because I wanted to so sorely. I knew that the small Sisterhood who had fled with the rest of Eburacum when the Sea Wolves came, had returned to what was left of their house in the city; and I could leave Guenhumara with them, and perhaps, if the chances of war fell so, see her from time to time through the summer.

So we rode south, leaving behind us the usual small garrisons in Three Hills and Castra Cunetium. Old Blanid rode with the baggage train, like a battered old rook clinging to the tail of a wagon, but Guenhumara put on again the breeks and short tunic that, with her hair hidden, still made her look like a boy, and rode ahead with the Companions.

The men of Eburacum welcomed us back as though we had been their long-lost kindred, crowding the streets to cheer us in. I looked for Helen among the throng, and did not see her until a knot of poppy-red ribbons flung from above hit Cei on the mouth as he rode beside me, and glancing up, I saw her raddled face laughing down from an upper window. She waved to both of us, and I waved back. Cei thrust the ribbons into his bosom and blew her smacking kisses through his fiery beard as though he had not loved every girl of the baggage train and a score of others besides, and wearied of them all since the last time that he lay in her arms.

They had given a good account of themselves in the past four years, the men of Eburacum and the Brigantian territory; they had held their city free of the Sea Wolves, and here and there even thrust back the Saxon settlement from along the coast and river mouths, and they carried themselves like hounds with two tails. But there still waited work enough for us to do. We made camp in the old fortress as we had done before, while the war host made itself battle-ready; and for days the bargaining that rose from the corn merchants' stores and the sellers of dried meat and sour wine, the fletchers and the leatherworkers bade fair to drown the rasp of file and the ring of hammer on anvil from Jason the Sword-smith, and the armorers' shops throughout all the city.

It was not until the last day before we marched out that I took Guenhumara, with Blanid still grumbling and flapping in attend-ance, to the House of the Holy Ladies. It was a long low building turning a blank eyeless face upon the Street of the Clothmakers that ran toward the fortress gates. The patched walls with scars of burning still upon them, the clumsy new thatch that showed the ends of charred beams here and there under the eaves, told clearly enough of the state in which the Saxons had left it. We spoke with the Mother Abbess in her little private chamber, and after Guen-humara had been made gently welcome, and led away from me by a small scurrying Sister like a sad little bird, I lingered for a last word with the woman who ruled this narrow enclosed world.

She was a tall woman, and I think had been beautiful. Her hands folded in her dark robed lap were beautiful still, and strong, though knotted with rheumatism and yellow-white as the ivory of the crucifix hanging on the lime-washed wall behind her, a big hand that I could imagine holding a sword. She would make a foe worthy of any man's blade, I felt that instinctively, and liked her the more for it, as one good fighting man recognizes his brother-hood with another. "There was something more you wished to say to me, my Lord Count of Britain?"

"Only this." It was a thing that must be set clear and straight between us. "That I would not have you shelter the Lady Guenhu-mara under any false hope of a gift for your nunnery. What money I have, whatever treasure I can gather, goes to feeding my men, in the purchase of war-horses and the retempering of sword blades. And furthermore, it has been in my mind these many years that since I fight, among other matters, to keep the roof over the Church's head and the light unquenched on the altar and its holy ones with their throats uncut, it is the Church that owes to me, not I that owe to the Church."

"So I have heard, these many years also," the Abbess said gravely.

And I had another thought, and came a step nearer to the tall chair in which she sat. "One thing more, Holy Mother; I mean no disrespect in this, but I ride away tomorrow, and Guenhumara will be in your hands. I am not greatly loved by the Church of Christ, as both you and I know, and to speak truth that has not held me long from my sleep at nights; and if, when I come back, I find that my wife has not been well and kindly used in every way, then women as you are—"

"You will see whether this house of God will not burn as brightly a second time as it did the first," said the Mother Abbess. "Do not spend your threat on me, Artos the Bear, for there is no need, I assure you." Suddenly and most unexpectedly she smiled, a smile that was somewhat grim about the mouth, but danced behind her eyes. "As Abbess of this house of Holy Sisters, it is my duty to tell you that you are a most sinful man, a despoiler of Christ's Garden second only to the Saxon kind, and that on the day when Almighty God in His Glory parts the sheep from the goats, you are assuredly damned. But as a mere woman, and one perhaps not overblest with meekness, it is in my heart to spoil all by telling you that if I were a man and fighting to hold back the Barbarian flood and the darkness from the land, I believe that I should feel and act much as you have done, and deserve damnation also, in the Day of Judgment."

"Holy Mother," I said, and did not realize until the words were spoken, how unseemly they were, "I wish I had you among my Companions."

"Maybe I should make a better fighting man than I do a nun," she said, and I do not think she felt the words an outrage. "Though God knows that I strive to live by His rule and be worthy of my trust. But as to the Lady Guenhumara—we are a small sisterhood, and poor; we live for the most part on the charity of the good people of this city, and on the outcome of three fields beyond the walls. We have no store of gold, no jeweled image or worked altar cloth to give you for the purchase of horses or sword blades, but we will share most willingly what we have with your wife, and strive to make her happy among us until you come for her again. Let that be our gift, some payment of our debt to you."

"There could be none greater," I said. I pulled off a bracelet of enameled bronze that I had worn since I was a boy, and set it on the table beside her. "That is not to destroy the gift, but that Guenhumara need not live on the charity of the good citizens of Eburacum. I thank you, Holy Mother. I am ashamed."

I knelt for her blessing, the first time I had received a blessing from the Church since the day that I took Gwalchmai from his fenland monastery. And the small scurrying Sister, summoned by a little bronze bell that stood on the table to the Abbess's hand, led me away and thrust me out into the fine spring rain that was scudding down the Street of Clothworkers, and I heard the heavy door rattle shut on the women's world that I had left behind me.

That summer we rode the war trail all up the coast, northward and northward and northward, burning and harrying as we went, and gathering an ever-growing war host from the hills and moors, until we rounded the end of the Wall at Segedunum and came up with the traces of our last summer's southernmost harryings, and knew that at least for an hour, until the next tide rose and the next wind blew from across the sea, our coasts from the Bodotria to the estuary of the Metaris were free of the Saxon scourge. But it was a long trail and a hard one, and there was no return to Eburacum in all that time, so that it was full autumn before I saw Guenhumara again.

We rode into the city on a still October evening full of woodsmoke and the smell of coming frost, with great rustling flights of starlings sweeping homeward overhead. And I do not think that there was one living soul in Eburacum who could walk or crawl or be carried, from the age-palsied beggar on two sticks to the wide-eyed baby held up against its mother's shoulder, from the chief magistrate with his formal speech of welcome, to the very dunghill curs, who did not come swarming into the streets to see us clatter past and give us a welcome fit for heroes, as though we were newly in from some battle of gods and Titans, instead of a summer spent in burning out Saxon hornets' nests and getting well stung for our pains. Their voices broke about us in great waves of sound, they cast branches of golden leaves and autumn berries before our horses' feet, they crashed forward and surged about us so that at times we could barely force a way onward at all. I was riding old Arian, for it was his last campaign that we returned from, and I felt that the triumph was his due—he had always loved a triumph; he was playing to the trumpets now, tossing his head and all but dancing—and indeed it was as well that I did so, for Signus, although magnificent in a charge, was still inclined to fret and turn difficult in a crowd.

I had meant to go straight up to the fortress, get out of my filthy war gear and if possible shake off the crowd, and then go quietly down to the House of the Holy Ladies and ask Guenhumara if she would come with me now or bide where she was for the few days until we marched for Trimontium again.

But as we turned into the Street of the Clothworkers that led up from the main street to the fortress, and I saw the blind wall of the house close before me, it was as though I heard Guenhumara call, not with the ears of my body, but in some quiet place in the very midst of myself, beyond the reach of the joyous uproar all around me. She was calling me, needing me, not later when I had gone up to the fortress and shed my harness and was at leisure for other things, but *now* in this present moment. I told myself that I was a fool and imagining things, but I knew that I was not—I was not—and in a few moments more I should be swept past the house, with the Companions torrenting up the street behind me, and the light troops and the rattling baggage train, on and up toward the fortress gate, and Guenhumara left crying after me. . . .

"Sound me the Halt!" I cried to Prosper. He shouted back, something that had the note of a question or a protest, but I did not hear the words. "Sound me the Halt, damn you, and keep on sounding it!"

I was already swinging Arian out of the main stream, forcing him through the onlookers, who bunched and scattered squealing, to give me passage, as I heard the horn sounding its brief imperative message. "Halt! Halt! Halt!" I heard the shouts of the watchers and the turmoil break out behind me, the trampling and cursing as the cavalry obeyed the unexpected order. Bedwyr had thrust through to my side, and leaned half out of the saddle to catch Arian's bridle from me as I dropped to the ground. I turned to the small strong door, thrusting back Cabal, who would have followed me, and beat on it with the hilt of my dirk.

The same small scurrying Sister came in answer to the summons, glancing past me into the street with a white startled face, even as she saw who I was. "My Lord Artos?"

"I have come for my wife," I said.

In a short while I was standing again in the small lime-washed chamber with the ivory crucifix on the wall. The room was dim with the autumn evening, and empty. But almost at once a slight sound made me swing around to the door; and the Mother Abbess stood there. "This is a house of prayer and contemplation. Are you responsible for this uproar before our door?"

"I have a war host with me, and the people of Eburacum are glad to see them come again. . . . I am come for my wife, Holy Mother."

"Would it not have been better to have gone up to the fortress first, and come for her in a gentler manner, when the welcome had died down?"

"Much. That was what I meant to do, but when we turned into the Street of the Clothworkers and I saw the nunnery wall before me I—changed my mind."

She moved aside from the small deep-set door. "So. Go then and fetch her as swiftly as may be; I think that you will find her in our little herb garden, waiting for you. And—" The shimmer of a smile crept once more into her dry low voice. "I believe that she will give you a good enough account of us to save the nunnery roof from a second taste of fire." She had moved to the table and picked up the little bronze bell that stood there. "Sister Honoria will show you the way."

A nun, a stranger this time, with the soft anxious eyes and surging flanks of a cow ripe for the bull, answered the summons, and to her the Mother Abbess said, "Take my Lord Artorius into the herber, and send someone to bid Blanid bring out her mistress's bundles. The Lady Guenhumara is leaving us."

She turned to me for the last time. "You have been hunting Saxons into the sea all summer, they tell me. Our gratitude and our prayers together with those of all Britain must be yours for that—and I think you may need our prayers more than you do our gratitude. Do not bring Guenhumara to take her leave; Sister Ancheret

[267]

our Infirmarer is sick herself, and I am very busy in her place, with the poor sick folk who come to us morning and evening. She has my blessing already."

I thanked her, and followed the broad black back as it surged deliberately down a stone-flagged passage, through a bare hall set with trestle tables and benches, and out into a narrow courtyard with a well in the midst of it. A young nun was drawing water at the well, but never looked up as we passed. I suppose it would have been a sin. On the far side of the courtyard was an archway in a high curved crumbling wall that looked as though it might have been part of the outer wall of the theatre in the old days. And the fat nun took one hand from the loose sleeves of her habit and pointed to it, never lifting her eyes to my face. "If you go through there, you will find her. But pray be careful for our little cat. She will suckle her kittens always in the midst of the path; and striped tabby as they are, it is not easy to see them if they chance to be in the shade of the cherry tree. . . . I will go and tell Blanid about the Lady Guenhumara's clothes. She has such pretty kirtles, blue and violet, and a checkered cloak; but she has only worn a gray one here. . . ."

I heard the flap of her clumsy sandals recrossing the court behind me, as I went on through the doorway in the wall.

Beyond was a long irregular strip of garden, high-walled on all sides, and seemingly with no way out save the one by which I had come. A place filled with the soft dusty grays and greens and silky mouse-browns of herbs and medicinal plants now run to seed, where the sinking turmoil of the street outside came only as the roar of surf on a distant shore. And at the far end, her face turned to the archway, stood Guenhumara, dim-colored as the garden, save for the brightness of her hair.

She took a hurried step forward when she saw me, then checked, and stood quite still to wait my coming. I came near to treading on the tabby cat after all, for my eyes were filled with Guenhumara, but I was aware of it just in time, where the striped shade of the cherry tree lay in the last dregs of sunlight across the path, and stepped safely over it and the guzzling kittens. Then I was with Guenhumara, taking the hands she held out to me. I wanted to fling my arms around her and bruise her body, and her mouth against mine, but she seemed so remote in the old gray gown she wore, remote and far away from me, like a nun herself, and I could not.

"Guenhumara! Guenhumara, is it well with you?"

"Well enough," she said; and then echoing my tone in that low vibrant voice of hers: "Artos! Artos, are you really here so soon?"

"I did not mean to come until I had got rid of my war gear and the good folk of Eburacum. But I had a sudden feeling that you wanted me—it was as though you called to me, Guenhumara."

"And so you came."

"And so I came." I had her by the hand and was drawing her back toward the archway. I did not know why I had the feeling that there was no time to be lost in getting her away from the place. It was certainly nothing to do with the tumult outside; it was more like a sudden sense of danger. And yet it was hard to see what could menace her in that quiet nunnery garden.

"I left the good folk of Eburacum and the whole war host giving tongue like the Wild Hunt before the door. *Did* you call me, Guenhumara?"

She looked up into my face with grave smoke-colored eyes under the feathered tawny brows. "Yes," she said. "Old Marcipor who chops wood for the Sisters and helps with the heaviest part of the gardening, he brought us word this morning that the Count of Britain would ride in before dusk; and all day the city has been humming to itself, and all day I have waited. And then I heard the shouting and the trumpets and the horses' hooves, and I knew that you were back in Eburacum and that you must pass up this street to the fortress, and I thought, Presently, when he has seen his mess safe into camp, and stripped off his sweaty harness and perhaps eaten, and found time to breathe, then he will come for me. Tonight, or maybe tomorrow morning he will come for me. And then quite suddenly I knew that I could not wait. I have waited, not too impatiently, all summer, but when I heard the horses, and the people shouting 'Artos!' I knew that I could not wait any longer—it was as though I were suffocating within these walls. I believe if you had passed, I should have made them open the door, and run after you to catch your stirrup." She broke off. "No, I should not—of course I should not. I should have waited somehow, till you came."

We had passed under the narrow arched doorway into the courtyard again. The strange sense of danger was less pressing now, and I had begun to tell myself that I was a fool. I checked beside the wellhead and turned to look at her. She seemed not so remote now, as though from her, too, the shadow was passing, as though the life were waking in her again; and I noticed for the first time that she had left off her braids and knotted up the heavy masses of her hair at the back of her head after the manner of Roman women; that was partly what had made her seem strange to me. I would have caught her into my arms and kissed her then, heedless of the eyes looking on, but she held me off with both hands on my breast, begging with a strange urgency, "No, Artos! Not here! Please, *please* not here!" and the moment passed, and there were the dark figures of nuns about us, and she was turning from one to another, taking her leave of them, with old Blanid clutching her bundle on the outskirts of the cluster. "God be with you, Sister Honoria, Sister Rufia—pray for me—Sister Praxedes." But it was not a time to be lingering over farewells. I caught her up and bore her out through the fluttering black-robed throng, across the eating hall and down the passageway and the shallow steps beyond. A Sister scurried ahead to draw the bolts and bars of the door. Blanid flapped along with toothless cluckings of delight in our rear. And so, much as though I were bearing off a bride by force, I carried Guenhumara out into the crowded street.

We were greeted by a roar from those near enough to see what was happening, a high, delighted squealing from the women, a crash of laughter and shouted welcome from my own Companions. Bedwyr had dismounted, and stood holding Arian's bridle besides his own horse's, while Cabal, sitting alert and quivering where I had left him, sprang up with wildly lashing tail. I tossed Guenhumara up onto Arian's back and taking the reins from Bedwyr, mounted behind her and settled her into the crook of my bridle arm. Bedwyr was laughing up at me, his crooked face alight and on fire with his laughter. "Sa sa! Bravely done, old Hero! Here is matter for a harp song!"

"Make it for us after supper!" I cried, and struck my heel into the horse's flank.

Arian broke forward, Bedwyr swung into his saddle, Pharic pressed up on my other side calling greetings to his sister, and the rest of the Company came jingling and clattering after me. Guenhumara looked back over my shoulder at the small deep-set door in the eyeless nunnery wall, and I felt her shiver. The kind of swift convulsive shudder that is supposed to mean a gray goose flying over one's grave; and instinctively I tightened my arm about her. "What is it? Were you unhappy there? Were they not kind to you after all?" Under the roar of voices, the clatter of hooves and jinkety-jink of harness, we could speak together as privately as though we were alone on Eildon slopes with only the curlew to overhear. "Because if that is the way of it, I'll—"

She shook her head. "They were very kind to me, the Sisters, and even the Mother Abbess whom they all fear. But it was like being in a cage. I could not breathe or stretch my wings—and no fresh wind ever blew through the bars. . . ."

"You have always hated cages, haven't you—cages and chains."

"Always. I think in a way I have always been afraid of them." She gave a small shaken laugh. "When I was fourteen, the man I was to marry gave me a pair of linnets in a wicker cage. You were supposed to hang it in a tree, and the linnet would sing to you all day long. I kept them for three days because they were his gift and I loved him, and then I could not bear it any more, and I opened the little door and let them go."

The corner of the street hid the House of the Holy Ladies from view, and she fetched a quick sigh that sounded like relief, and turned face forward again.

CHAPTER TWENTY

The Beast and the Flower

I HAVE never known such an autumn for berries as we had
that year. Every dog-rose tangle was flame-flecked with hips,
every whitethorn looked from a little distance to be the color of
dried blood, bryony and honeysuckle ramped along the wood-
shores scattering their red fire-jewels among the gray seed-smoke
of the clematis, and old Blanid shook her head and mumbled
darkly of a cruel winter on the way. But it has often seemed to me
that the threat of an especially hard winter after a big berry crop
is no more than a tale that the old wives tell each other; and I
paid little heed. We always made ready as best we could for a
hard winter, at Trimontium, and most years we got it.

On the third day after we returned to our winter quarters, word
was brought to me that Druim Dhu had come into camp, seeking
to speak with me. By this time the Dark People of our nearest
hills had lost much of their strangeness in our eyes. Many of our
lads even forgot to cross their fingers if they stepped in a Dark
One's shadow, and the Dark People on their side had lost much
of their fear of us. It was no unusual thing nowadays for Druim
Dhu or one of his brothers to come and set themselves down by
our cooking fires, even eat if they were hungry, borrow a hammer
or a cooking pot—they were great borrowers, but more scrupulous
in their returning than many churched Christians are—and perhaps
leave a gift of a freshly taken wild honeycomb or a couple of salmon trout behind, when they disappeared as silently as they had
come.

So I found Druim now, squatting beside the master armorer in
his dark cavern of a workshop, and watching with attentive in-

terest, head a little on one side as a dog sits beside a mousehole, while he renewed some broken links in a war shirt. He got up when he saw me coming, and came to meet me with his usual palm-to-forehead salutation. "May the sun shine on my lord's face by day and the moon guide his feet in the darkness."

I returned the greeting, and waited for whatever it was that he had come to say to me. It was never any good trying to hurry matters with Druim Dhu, or any of his kind. One waited for them to be ready, and when they were ready, they spoke. He watched a peregrine hovering above the fort until I could have shaken him, and then said without any preamble, "Let my lord send the horses south this winter."

I looked at him keenly. That was a course that I had always striven to avoid. "Why?" I demanded. "We have always kept them with us in winter quarters before."

"Not through such a winter as this one will be."

"You believe that it is going to be a hard one?" If he talked to me of berries, I should send him to old Blanid, and they could tell each other their old wives' tales until suppertime.

"There will be such a winter as there has not been since I was a cub scarce done with sucking my mother. A winter like a white beast that strives to tear your heart out."

"How do you know?"

"Earth Mother has told the Old Woman in my house."

There was something in the way he spoke, something in the dark wild eyes, that chilled me suddenly. This was a different thing from Blanid's talk of berries. "What do you mean? How does Earth Mother speak to the Old Woman in your house?"

He shrugged, but his gaze never left my face. "I do not know. I am not a woman, and not old. Earth Mother does not speak to me, though I too should look for a hard winter, taking my fore-tidings from the changed ways of the deer and the wolf kind. I know only that when Earth Mother speaks to the Old Woman, what she tells is true."

"And so in my place, you would send the horses south."

"If I wished still to be a horse lord in the spring. There will be no grazing-out in mild spells, this year; and the Hairy Ones, the Wolf-People, will hunt to the very gates of the fortress."

[273]

"So. I will think upon it. Go now and get something to eat. My thanks for bringing me the warning of Earth Mother."

I did think upon it, deeply, all the rest of that day; and when the evening meal was over, I called Cei and Bedwyr and Pharic and the rest of my chiefs and captains to my own quarters. We had a little fire of peat and birch bark and wild cherry logs in a battered brazier, for already the evenings were turning cold, and when all of us were gathered about it, I told them. "Brothers, I have been thinking; and out of my thinking, I am decided this year to make a change in our usual custom, and send the horses south for the winter."

A dozen startled faces looked back at me in the red upward glow of the brazier. Cei was the first to speak, playing in the way he had with the blue glass bracelets on his wrist. "I thought you would as lief part with your sword arm as with the horses."

"Almost as lief," I said.

Bedwyr, squatting on the pile of wolfskins that sometimes served me as a bed, his harp as usual on his knee, leaned forward into the light that turned his face into a copper mask. "Then why this sudden desire for amputation?"

"Because Earth Mother has told the Old Woman in Druim's house that this will be a winter like a white beast that strives to tear men's hearts out. There will be no grazing-out in the mild spells, and the Wolf-People will hunt to the fortress gates. So says Earth Mother."

Pharic's black brows drew together. "And think you that Druim's word and the word of the Old Woman and Earth Mother are to be trusted so much?" He broke into a somewhat scornful grin. "Oh, I doubt not that they are speaking the truth as they believe it. So is old Blanid when she babbles of autumn berries. They believe so much, the Little Dark People, but need we believe also?"

"I—think so, yes. I propose to act on it as though I did, at all events; and if I am wrong, I give you leave to point the finger of laughter at me for all time."

Within a week the horses had all gone south, save for three or four of the hardy hill ponies that we kept against possible need of a messenger. Most of our light riders were of course needed to take them, one half directly south to the Corstopitum depot and on to Eburacum, and the other by Castra Cunetium and down to

Deva. And with each, I sent half a squadron of the Companions
—Flavian, as it chanced, in command. I gave orders, since there
seemed little help for it, that the men were to winter with the horses,
and bring them up again in the spring.

We had brought up the last of the winter supplies with us from
Corstopitum, and with good stocks of meal and salted carcasses
in the long store barn, we settled down to make all secure and
galley-shape for the winter that Druim Dhu had promised us. We
mended again the cracks in the barrack-row walls, where the autumn rains had washed out the mud of our previous repairs (we
were almost as great workers with mud, by that time, as the swallows who built every spring under the eaves of the Praetorium), we
got in extra peat and firewood, melted down every scrap of fat for
candles, and piled up great ricks of russet bracken for bedding and
the ponies' fodder. This being our fifth winter in the Three Hills,
we must push farther afield in our foraging and woodcutting, and
without the aid of the wiry little pack beasts that in past winters we
had relied on to carry the loads. But with no horses to tend and
exercise, we had more time than usual on our hands even so; and
we hunted hard, that autumn, eating fresh meat while we could.

I had thought, naturally, to see no more of the horses or the
men who had gone with them, until spring, but in half a month the
Eburacum part of the squadron under Corfil, who had stepped
into Fercos's place as Flavian's second, plodded in on foot, having
done the march, so they reported without undue humility, in the
exact nine days laid down for the Legions in the days of good
roads. And two days after Samhain, as though his arrival was the
signal for the white beast to begin his prowling, Flavian himself,
with his half squadron behind him, staggered in through the Praetorium Gate in a blinding snowstorm.

"I didn't think we were going to make it," he said, when he came
to me in my quarters.

I cursed him where he stood. "You bleeding fool! Didn't I give
the whole lot of you orders to stay south until the spring—and you
with a wife and son in Deva!"

He blinked at me in the light of the lantern, the snow on his
shoulders melting into dark wetness at the edges, and grinned, weary
but unashamed. "It is a different matter for the auxiliaries. *We*
are the Brotherhood, and we have always been an unruly lot. We

didn't like the order, so we took a vote on it and decided to mutiny."

Earth Mother had spoken truth. By mid-November we were sunk so deep in winter that we might have been in a world that had never known spring. At first the snow was not deep, save in the hollows and the northward-facing glens, for the first fall had melted, and the stuff that followed it was wet, sleet and half-frozen rain that drove and drenched across the fort before bitter gales from the northeast. Eildon must have sheltered us a little, but I think not much, and the wind howled day after day down through the hazel woods to fling itself like a living enemy upon the old red sandstone fort above the river. The woods boomed and roared like a great sea beating upon a wild coast; and indeed for days at a time, for all that we could see of Eildon and the hills beyond, we might have been perched on some headland high above a raging sea. And then after a month, the wild gales fell still, and out of the stillness came snow, and an ever-increasing cold that made the sword hilt sear the hand, and narrowed the spring under the hazel bushes that had been the gift of the Little Dark People to the merest dribbling thread of water, under a curtain of black ice. And in the long nights the strange, colored fires that Pharic's people called the "Crown of the North" and Druim's "The Dancers" played more brightly than ever I had seen them, across the northern sky.

But under the covering of snow, our log and brushwood piles were broad and long, and the peat stacks rose beside the living place doors, the stores were gathered in, and we had even a cartload of sour wine to help out the local heather beer at the times when men need to make merry. And with no need to trouble for the horses' fodder (but God of gods, how we missed the stamping in the picket lines, and how the loneliness, the sense of being utterly cut off from the world, increased upon us with the horses gone!) we felt that we could outlast the winter well enough.

That was until Midwinter's night.

For all of us that night had some meaning. For those of us who were Christians, it had become the custom in our fathers' fathers' time to celebrate the birth of the Christos on that night, when the old year goes down into the dark, and out of the dark all things are born anew. To those who followed the Old Faith, it was the night of the Midwinter Fires, when one made all the light and heat one could, to help the sun grow strong again and drive out the darkness and the cold. For the few among us who bore the small telltale brand of Mithras between the brows, it was, just as to the Christians, the Saviour's birth night. To most of us it was, I suppose, in some sort a mingling of all these things, and to all of us, when the worship was over, it was a night for as much merrymaking as could be crammed into it, and as much heather beer. In an open winter when the hunting was good, we were able to get fresh meat for the Midwinter feast; but this year there had been no hunting for upward of a month, and we should have no release from the tyranny of boiled salt beef and mutton. But there was always the beer. Each year I released three days' supply of beer to make up for the shortage in other directions. That meant the portion of the garrison who had weaker heads than the rest, or who got more than their fair share, were drunk by midnight, and greeted the next day with aching head and bloodshot eyes and tempers. What would have happened if the fort had ever been attacked at that time, I sweat to think; but I knew the limits of my power with the wild auxiliaries; they were not the Company, and it did not extend to keeping them sober on Midwinter night. Besides, men do not remain at their best, especially cut off in the wilds, if they may not make merry to the full, now and then.

But I, I dreaded Midwinter, and was always devoutly thankful when it was over for another year and the fort not burned down about our ears.

This particular Christ's Mass night was no worse than its forerunners had been, until one of the mule drivers having (so his mates said afterward) drunk himself into a state of deep suspicion of the world, got the idea that he was somehow being cheated of his fair share, and stealing a half-full beerskin, departed to make merry by himself in a corner of the derelict mill shed which backed onto the main store barn. What happened after that, no one can ever know. In all likelihood he kicked over the lantern he had brought with him and it opened as it fell, the guttering flame caught the dry-bracken fodder stored there, and the wind blowing through the holes in the roof did the rest.

The first that anyone knew of the danger was when one of the guard (we always kept a small and comparatively sober guard, even on Midwinter's night) saw smoke curling up through the rents in the mill shed roof.

I was with the main uproar in the mess hall when the man came running with his news, and the Companions and most of the auxiliaries gathered there with me; but the baggage train folk had quarters of their own beyond the old parade ground, and there would be small knots making merry all over the camp, many of them half drunk by this time. I got hold of Prosper, who was still smiling somewhat owlishly into the fire while the other men stumbled cursing to their feet all about him, and shook him into awareness. "Get out of here and sound me the alarm, and keep on sounding it!" I told him, and casting a hurried glance around me, saw that most of the Companions, at least, still looked reasonably serviceable.

"They'll think it's an attack," someone objected.

"What in Hell's name does that matter, if it gets their heads out of the beer jar?" I was already running for the door, Cabal leaping ahead of me in wild excitement. I ran as though for my life across the empty parade ground and down toward the lower camp, most of the Brotherhood pelting at my heels, and behind us, clear and true and rock-steady—it is wonderful what habit will do—I heard the notes of the great aurochs horn sounding the alarm.

By the time we reached the clear space before the mill shed and workshop, there was a crowd that thickened every moment, as men tumbled out from their merrymaking in answer to the urgent summons of the horn and, as word leapt from man to man like heath fire itself, headed down toward the disaster. There could be no doubt now as to where the fire was; flame had followed the smoke; it was already bursting through the rough thatch in a score of places, leaping up into the night, and the flickering glare of it brightened over the gaping faces of the crowd. The wind that had been rising all day was blowing hard from the northeast by that time, driving dark rags of cloud across the frost-fierce stars; driving also the licking flames along the thatch toward the store barn.

They got the door open just as I arrived, and the red furnace burst of flame that leapt up behind it on the instant drove them back as though from a charge of horsemen. I forced my way through them, yelling, "Leave that, you fools! The flames are spreading to the barn roof. Get the stores out!" Pharic and I and a couple more of us, heads down behind our arms, managed to get the door shut again, while Bedwyr was already busy organizing a bucket chain from the well, with any and everything capable of holding water—we had enough men to fight a score of fires, scarce enough water to quench a candle. But there was the snow; it did not serve so well as water, but it was better than nothing. We blanketed the flames with it as best we could, while men swarming onto the roof strove to tear away the thatch and rafters in the path of the fire. The ponies in their nearby shed were shrieking in terror as the smoke reached them, but they were in no danger as yet. Others of us, the women among them, were working desperately to get out the stores. They might have saved the whole, but the door, which we had made ourselves to close the gap where the old one had rotted away, was of green wood because we had no seasoned timber, and prone to jam. It jammed now; perhaps the heat had something to do with it; and by the time it had been broken in, while several of the lads getting onto the roof and tearing up the smoldering thatch, dropped through into what might like enough have been their deathtrap, the fire was there ahead of them.

Our store of mutton tallow added to the blaze, making the whole store shed a torch. Rags of blazing thatch had begun to tear off and whirl away downwind like birds of fire, and I sent men running to watch against other outbreaks. The flames leapt higher, bending over at the crest, and the flickering light beat upon our scorching eyeballs, the thick smoke cloud choked us, and the fire seemed to be in our very lungs. In the end we got less than half the stores out, before the roof came down with a rending crash and a roar of flame, engulfing two men.

The fire was beginning to sink, the darkness creeping back over the fort, and we had kept the flames from spreading to any other building. But that was the best that could be said. I remember, as one remembers a dark dream, men bringing lanterns, now that the fire was low, to light the work of salvage, and myself standing in the trampled slush that was already freezing over again, surrounded by scorched men and half-charred carcasses of meat, and grain baskets with the coarse meal seeping out through the blackened slits in their sides. I was rank with sweat, and the sweat was turning icy on me in the bitter wind, and the palms of my hands seemed flayed and full of pulsing fire. Guenhumara was there too, with a great smear of black across her forehead. I suppose I must have asked her what she did there—I always made her go with Blanid to her own quarters, and bolt the door, when the drinking started—for she said breathlessly, "Carrying water. Was I to stay in my rooms, with the horn sounding the alarm, and men crying fire through the camp?" And then, "Artos, your eyebrows are singed off," and then in quick concern as Cabal crouched panting against my legs, and I made to fondle his poor scorched head, "Oh my dear, your hands! Your poor hands! Come up with me and let me salve them."

But I had other things to do just then. There would be time presently for Guenhumara's salves, there was none now.

We had lost three men, and half the rest of us had burns and scorches to show for that night's work. Three men not counting the mule driver. We found the charred stump of his body next day, lying in its snug corner behind the millstone with the shriveled remains of a burst beerskin beside it. He seemed never to have moved at all, so deep in drink that like enough he never even realized what was happening until the smoke suffocated him. We did not trouble to give him decent burial, but simply flung what was left of him over the ramparts at the place where the hill dropped almost sheer to the river, and left him to the wolves if they did not mind their meat somewhat overcooked.

That day after taking exact stock of the stores that were left to us, we held a hurried council to decide our course of action. But, in truth, there was little choice left to us. To try to break out and get south to Corstopitum through the drifts and the blinding blizzards would have been nothing but a deliberate marching on death, and it would be equally impossible—as well as useless—to attempt getting a message through to them. The same applied to any attempt to get word through to Castra Cunetium; the deep mountain roads were utterly impassable to anything heavier-footed than a hare, and even supposing that the word could be got to them, and the stores got back again, the garrison was so small that if they parted with enough to make any appreciable difference to us, it would result merely in their starving in our stead. There was nothing to be done but stay where we were and make the remaining food last out as long as possible. After working the matter out carefully, it appeared that if we went on half rations from that day, we could hold out until about midway through February.

"An early spring might save us," said Gwalchmai, who, though no captain, always had his place at our councils.

And Bedwyr laughed. "The sun cannot complain that we did not make him a fine enough Midwinter blaze!"

But the weeks went by and the weeks went by, and winter seemed to have claimed the world for good. There was never a day that offered a chance of hunting, only snow and gales, and bitter black frost that bound up the land even under its white furs. The snow lay drifted in slow curves to the eaves on the northern side of every building, and every day fresh paths must be cleared to stable and well and store sheds, not that that was altogether a bad thing, for digging keeps a man warm—though it also makes him hungry. Now and then, by putting out the bones of a finished carcass in a good spot of a moonlit night, and then putting a couple of archers on the walls, we managed to get a wolf or two, but they were so famine-thin themselves, poor brutes, that there was little that the women could do with them save make broth; and already the men grew gaunt and hollow-eyed, with heads that seemed too big for their sharp shoulders.

One day Cei came to me and said, "Maybe the Dark People have food. Why do we not go foraging? *You* know where one village is, at all events."

"They will have little enough for themselves; they will have none to spare for those that come asking."

"*Asking* was not in my mind," Cei said grimly.

I caught him by the shoulders to drive home what I had to say. "Listen, Cei; the Dark People are our friends. Na na, I am not being womanish, I do but use my head as it seems that you have forgotten to do. They are our friends, but they are not the kind that hold to friendship in the face of an injury. I have no wish to find the water supply fouled and our men on the walls picked off with those hellish little poisoned arrows of theirs."

So we did not go foraging, and whatever the Dark People had, they kept. We saw nothing of them in all that winter, but then we never did, during the dark of the year. It has often been my thought that the People of the Hills burrow deep into their holes and sleep through the cold months almost as the field voles and the badgers do.

After a while we gave up sleeping in separate quarters and barrack rows, and huddled all together in the big mess hall, for though our fuel stocks had not suffered, we needed more warmth than in other winters, because our hunger let in the cold; and by the same token, a man needs less food when he is warm. So we put all the peat and firewood to one blazing fire that served both for cooking and for warming the hall, and which we could keep up even at night when need be. And there we crowded at nights, and in off-duty hours in the daytime also, from the captains to the mule drivers, the women of the baggage train, the dogs curled among us, and even the three ponies in the foreporch stamping and fidgeting through the bitter nights; drawing, all of us, I think, comfort and encouragement, even in a strange way life itself, from each other's nearness.

The behavior of the men in all that time is a thing I scarcely understand even now, looking back on it across the gulf of more than thirty years, but at the time it seemed nothing strange. At first the usual stresses and strains of winter quarters seemed stretched unbearably by hunger and hardship and the little hope that any of us had of seeing the spring again. Old quarrels flared up, the troublemakers stirred up whatever mischief came to hand, again and again men were rightly or wrongly accused of trying for more than their share of the day's allowance. But as time went by and our state became more desperate, all that changed, and men drew further away from the wolf pack. It was as though we all felt death too near to waste our substance in such barren ways; as though under the shadow of the Dark Wings, there was a growing quietness, a growing gentleness among us.

Not that this quietness had any outward seeming; indeed our evenings were louder-voiced that winter than ever they had been in Trimontium before; and besides the old heroic sagas that he could declaim as well as any king's bard, I do not think that ever harper made so many songs as Bedwyr made in that one; songs of hunting and drinking, lewd love snatches that made the women of the camp squeal and giggle; songs that called down mockery on all things under the sun, from my height, which was supposed to tempt the eagles to rest on top of my head with disastrous effect upon the shoulders of my war shirt, to the master armorer's habit of scratching his behind when thinking out any problem of his craft, and Cei's supposed adventures with a great many girls, each of which was more outrageous than the last. And never a lament in all those long dark months.

February came at last, and the evenings were growing lighter. But the White Beast still had his fangs locked in our throats. Sometimes there was a little thaw at noon; always it froze again an hour later, and indeed as the days lengthened, so the cold increased. We were down far below half rations now, to one small rye cake a day for each man, and every two days a lump of meat about the size of three fingers, black as coal and hard as boiled leather. When the dried meat was all gone, we began to eat the dogs, drawing lots for the next to go; they had lived so long only by killing the weaker among themselves and if we kept them longer, they would be nothing but staring hide over dry bones. Even as it was, they had no more on them than the wolves. I began to regret bitterly that we had not kept back more of the ponies, for then we could have eaten them too. As it was, we ate one, but the other two must at all costs be kept until the very last.

By mid-February not only starvation but sickness was among us. There was always scurvy in the camp by winter's end, owing to the salt meat, but this year it was more widespread than usual. Guenhumara and old Blanid worked with the other women, tending the sick, and their days were full. Old wounds opened and refused to heal—I was having trouble myself with the old gash in my shoulder, and with my burned hands which refused to skin over properly. Men began to die, and we scraped shallow graves for them in the iron-hard ground outside the fort, and piled the frozen snow high over them and hoped that the wolves would not find their bodies.

Young Amlodd died holding to my hand, with his eyes on my face like those of a sick dog that expects you to help it when there is no help to be given. And it was after his burial that Levin said, "Who will bury the last of us? I wonder."

"The wolves, Brother," said Bedwyr, and glanced up at a golden eagle quartering the sky. There were always one or more of the great birds over Trimontium. "And maybe an eagle or so. Sa sa, it is an ill winter that blows nobody any good."

The Minnow said, "And yet I could have sworn that there was a softer feel in the air this morning," and there was a raw longing for life in his voice. None of us answered him. I too thought that the icicles were at last beginning to lengthen under the eaves; but we knew, all of us, how small our chances were, even if the thaw came tonight. In the state that we had sunk to, with scarcely the strength left to dig a comrade's grave, we could never reach Corstopitum, even if we abandoned our sick, and as for help coming from the depot, they had no reason to suppose that we needed any. The winter had been the worst for a score of years, but so far as they knew, we were well stocked with corn and meat; the first supply wagons would come up as usual toward the end of April, and that, I reckoned, would be too late for most of us by something over a month.

"All that we need is a talking eagle such as that Tuan who told his tale to Saint Finnen. The flight south would be nothing to him," said Pharic, and his straight mouth quirked into laughter that did not touch his eyes. "A sad thing it is that the high days of heroes and marvels are over!"

The next day Levin was missing, and so was the day's food for his whole squadron. I remember, when the news was brought to me, feeling a little sick (but it did not take much to make one feel sick, just then). What had happened? Had he run mad, as happens sometimes when strain becomes too much for the spirit of man? Had he crept out into the white emptiness to meet death because he could not wait for it any longer? The disappearance of the food did not look like that, and I remember, also, sending in my own squadron of walking corpses to beat up a few swords, when Levin's squadron gathered themselves to do murder on the spearmen who maintained that Levin had stolen the food and then fled away to join the Little Dark People because he dare not face his own kind. *I* had another thought, but I did not voice it. If there was the least chance of a man getting through before the thaw came, and the snow waters had had time to abate, I should have sent one long ago.

That night the air turned suddenly soft, and we thought, all of us, that the thaw that was too late to save us was coming at last. For two days the snow sank before our eyes, and everywhere there was the sound of running water. In three days more it might

be possible to try to send a messenger out; a faint flicker of the
hope that had been dead in us so long, revived. But on the third
night the frost came back, with a black bitter wind swooping over
the white skirts of Eildon, and then a soft air and snow that whirled
in mealy clouds across the ramparts, blotting out the world, and
then frost again. The White Beast had not yet loosened his grip.
I forget how many days it froze, that time, but I know that they
seemed as long as the whole winter over again, before the wind
went booming around to the southwest with a new smell on its
wings, and the slow steady thaw set in.

That must have been the best part of three weeks after Levin's
disappearance; and with the steady drip and trickle of melting
snow once more in our ears, we knew that the time had come to
draw lots, not for the dogs this time (we had eaten most of them
by now, anyway), but for two of us to make the desperate attempt to get through to Corstopitum for help. Castra Cunetium
we did not take into the account at all; apart from anything else,
the mountain road would remain impassable long after the road
south was open. That night I could not sleep. I knew, as we all did,
that whoever drew the two longest straws tomorrow would be going
out to almost certain death; and yet there was the one chance in
a thousand, and it must be taken. . . . Anyway, what was the
death of two men, now, when we were all for the Dark Road
close after them? And yet I knew that whoever they were, those
two, their deaths would lie heavy on my heart when my own time
came—unless—I prayed to Mithras and the Horned One and the
White Christos that I might draw one of those two straws. I even
began to wonder if there was any means by which I could tamper
with the draw. But the choice belonged to Fate, not to me. And
still I could not sleep. We no longer kept any watch at night;
nothing could come at us, and in our cold and weakened state,
the two hours' guard duty would have been too likely to kill the
man who stood it on the walls. But I had grown into the way of
getting up some time in the midst of the night, and taking a look
around the fort to make sure that all was well. What I thought to
find, I do not know; the thing had become a habit. That night,
too restless to lie still any longer, I got up rather earlier than usual,
quietly, so as not to wake Guenhumara. We had done our best
to keep her a little privacy, by giving her the place at the farthest

and darkest end of the mess hall, with only one sleeping space beyond her; that, the cold place against the wall, was taken in turn by myself and Bedwyr and her brother Pharic, the other two sleeping between her and the rest of the war host. Looking down at her now, as I stood stretching, I thought how, on the first night, Bedwyr had drawn his sword and laid it between them, laughing, and said, "No man shall say that I was not as nicely nurtured as Pwyl, Prince of Dyfed." But it is not good to lay sword between one and another when the need is to huddle close for warmth, and his sword remained in its sheath now.

There was nothing save for a glint of distant firelight on her tumbled hair to show that a woman lay there, for the slim leg from which the muffling folds of her cloak had fallen back showed cross-gartered breeks. She had taken to her boy's riding dress long ago, for the great warmth. Her cheek was cuddled against Pharic's shoulder, and there was a certain likeness between them that was not there when both were awake.

I stretched until the muscles cracked behind my shoulders, trying to draw a little strength into myself. My belly felt weak, and my head swam so that it was as though the whole mess hall lifted and fell gently under my feet like a galley in a quiet sea. I doddered down the hall, picking my way among the sleepers, but in the light of the fire that threw enormous shadows under their sunken cheekbones and pinched noses and brows, they had the gaunt set jaws and sunken eye sockets of those already dead. The famished shadow that had been Cabal stalked at my heels. So far he had escaped the death draw, but his turn must come soon. . . . I opened the door, and thrusting it gently to behind me, went out past the two wretched ponies into the night.

After the crowded mess hall (not so crowded as it had been, though) that stank like a fox's earth, the smell of the thaw struck at me keen and chill as the blade of a knife; there were no stars, and despite the snow it was very dark, with the kind of breathy darkness that makes one aware of the world as a living thing.

In places, where our feet passed most often, the snow had become black slush, but it still lay unblemished over the shallow mound where the woman of the Dark People lay beneath the bones of nine war-horses. She had protected us well from the Saxon kind, I thought, but even she was powerless against the

White Beast. I made my usual round longer than usual, but when it was finished I knew that I still could not go back and lie down again beside Guenhumara.

On an impulse, I turned in through the entrance to the Praetorium, and crossed the narrow courtyard to the quarters that I had shared with her, and went into the small chamber that had been my sleeping cell before she came and was now my armory and office. I felt for the lantern on the roof beam, took it down, and opening it, felt inside. There was about half the candle left, and when that was burned out, there would be no more. We had eaten the small amount of tallow that was saved from the fire. Well, soon enough now, we should have no more need of candles. I struck flint and iron and got a light, and then, with the lantern, wandered through into the bigger chamber that was Guenhumara's, and set it on the wicker chest against the wall; then stood looking about me, wondering why I had come, and what I should do now that I was here.

The chamber had a lived-in look that spoke vividly of Guenhumara, who still came here sometimes during the day. The soft beaver-skin rug on the piled rushes and bracken of the bed place still softly hollowed where her body had pressed it, a gold eardrop hanging half out of a painted wooden casket; even the faint scent of her seemed to hang on the cold air as though she had only that moment passed out through the door and left something of herself behind. I stooped and pulled a handful of rushes from the bed place. Somebody must cut the lengths for tomorrow's draw; it made a good enough reason to myself for being there. I rummaged in the box of painted wood—there was a running deer on the lid —and found Guenhumara's silver scissors among a tangle of small gear and woman's things, huddled my cloak about me and settled down on the inevitable packsaddle to cut lengths of brown rush stem into my iron cap fetched from next door. Cabal crouched down beside me, his great gaunt head on my knee, and broke into the deep snoring throat-song that in him meant contentment in my company; and I broke off to pull his ears in the way that he loved, wondering what I should do with him if I drew the long straw tomorrow; then returned idly to my clipping.

The light of the lantern was beginning to sink, and the shadows gathered in the corners of the room; the dim blue and gold and russet saint in the embroidered hanging seemed to waver on the edge of living movement. I did not hear footsteps coming nearer through the thawing snow, but suddenly the door latch lifted, and as I looked up quickly, the door opened, and Guenhumara stood on the threshold.

I sprang up. "Guenhumara! What are you doing abroad in the dark of the night?"

"I came to look for you; you were gone so long, and I was afraid." She came in and snibbed the door behind her, and stood with her back to it. All her bones stood out in the sinking lantern light, and the tendons in her neck stood out like cords, and her lips were chapped and flaked and bleeding, and my heart flew out to her like a bird out of the cage of my breast.

"I did not think you knew when I went out. I hoped you were asleep," I said.

"I always know when you go out. What is it that *you* do here in the dark of the night?"

I looked at the work of my hands. "Ruin your scissors by cutting up lengths of rush with them."

She came forward from the door, and looked into my battered helmet and then at me, and held her hand to Cabal. "More dogs tomorrow?"

I shook my head. "Na, tomorrow we draw lots of another kind."

"What kind, then?" She sat down rigidly on the chest top.

And when I told her, she said, still looking into my helmet, "A straw for a life. . . . Every life in the garrison?"

"Not so many. A straw for each of the Companions, and only for such of the Companions as are within reason free of scurvy."

"Has the gash in your shoulder healed up again since yesterday?" she asked after a moment, and I knew what she meant.

I said, "Within reason free. If we keep to those who have no taint at all, it is in my mind that there will be none to draw the straws, at all."

"And so you also will draw?"

"I do not lay this kind of hazard before Bedwyr and Pharic and the rest, and then step aside from it myself. It is stupid, isn't it, to give so much weight to that when, long straw or no, we are all going to die so soon?"

She was silent for a while, and then for the first time she looked up. "You have no hope, then, of their getting through?"

"None," I said, and we were silent again. Then I laid aside helmet and scissors, and knelt down beside her and put my arms around her under the rough thickness of her cloak. "Try not to be afraid, Guenhumara."

"I don't think I am," she said, wonderingly. "I don't want to die, but I don't think I am afraid—not very afraid." And then a swift change of mood came on her; her eyes in her famished face were suddenly shining and enormous in the last guttering light of the lantern, and her voice had a low vibrant quality like the musical throb of a swan's wings in flight. "I am so glad that the thaw has come. I should have hated to die while the world was still dead; it would have seemed so—so hopeless. But tonight the world is stirring into life again, it is breathing in the darkness. There's something in the wind—can't you smell it? Almost like the scent of wet moss."

"I know," I said. "Yes, I can smell it, too."

"It is so sad that it is too late for us. One day there will be moss soft and damp under the trees again, and wood anemones, and they will light the Beltane Fires—and somewhere a vixen will mate and have cubs . . ."

"Don't, Guenhumara. Don't, Heart-of-my-heart." I tightened my arms around her and felt how she was shivering from more than the cold. And scarce knowing it until the thing was done, I caught her up and, lurching to my feet, carried her across to the bed place and—for my strength was so far gone from me—collapsed headlong beside her. I dragged the beaver-skin robe over us both, and under its soft darkness, held her close. I could feel the light bones that had so delighted me, sharp and brittle through the thick stuff of her tunic, and the icy shuddering that wracked her, and dragged her against me as though I would have drawn her inside my own body and warmed her there. I kissed her face, the sunken eyes and poor cracked mouth and the corded column of her throat, trying to comfort her for the spring and the summer and the harvesttime that she would not see; until at last her shuddering ceased, and she lay quiet with her arms around my neck as mine were around her body. And lying so, gradually, I knew that

Ygerna had no more power over me, because in a few days, a week or two at most, I should be dead.

I do not know, I have never been able to remember, whether it was she or I who unclasped the strap about her waist; I only know that it was accomplished as something inevitable. There was a great sense of peace in me, peace so strong that it formed a refuge, and the old foul fly-cloud of hate could not break in to smother and drive me back as it had always done before. I was aware of the present moment as something with the light shining through it, a gift, a revelation, a flower growing on the edge of an abyss, with nothing beyond it; but it was the flower that mattered and not the abyss. And I loved Guenhumara then as I had so longed to love her. I came free and untrammeled into her deepest sanctuaries, and she sprang to meet me and make me welcome, and give me what I had never known that she or any other woman had to give. For a little while we were healed of the loneliness, the amputation of being separate people, and fused into one, so that the circle became perfect.

Next morning when the lots were drawn, the longest straws fell to Alun Dryfed, and to Prosper, my trumpeter. Food from the little that still remained to us had been made ready in advance for whoever were Fate's chosen, and the two thickest cloaks in the fort, and whatever else might be of use to them. The two remaining ponies stood ready loaded, and there was nothing to wait for. We thronged the old red ramparts to cheer them and watch them plowing away down the road to the south, or rather, down the line of the hidden road that still lay deep under the thawing snow. Presently, when the loads were lightened and by God's grace the snow grew thinner, the men would ride—if they lived so long— but now, at the outset, they led the ponies, and it was four figures that we watched, four shapes of darkness dwindling into the distance, floundering up the steepening slopes into the hazel woods. They looked very small in the white immensity of the hills, and I seemed to see beyond them all the long hopeless road to Corstopitum stretching into eternity. When the shoulder of the valley had taken the last dark laboring speck from our sight, we dragged ourselves off about whatever there was to do with the rest of the day. Gwalchmai had of course taken no part in the draw, but held the helmet for us; if he had not been lame, we still could not have spared him with so many sick in the camp; but I shall not forget his face.

It was not long past noon of that same day when a hoarse incredulous shouting from the southern walls brought half the fort crawling and stumbling (few of us could run) toward the Praetorium Gate. The man on watch there came staggering to meet us, his eyes wild in his head, crying and jibbering out something about four men, four riders on the road. We thought that his wits were gone, but in a few moments more, others had swarmed up onto the crumbling rampart walk and out through the gateway, and then they too were shouting and pointing. I scrambled up the rampart steps, thrusting through the men who were there ahead of me, and stared south, shielding my eyes with one hand against the dazzle of snow in the sun that had that instant burst through the drifting rain clouds.

Far off on the edge of the hazel woods, four horsemen were struggling toward Trimontium, and as they drew nearer, I saw that two of the riders were Prosper and Alun Dryfed. The third was a stranger, or at least no one whom I knew well enough to recognize at that distance. The fourth, I could have sworn, was Druim Dhu or one of his brothers! Nearer they drew, and nearer yet. We lined the walk and thronged the gateway, more and more of us every moment, waiting for them, straining our aching eyes in their direction. But I do not think that we made any sound now. We did not dare to hope. . . .

Level with the far end of the practice field, the horsemen urged their ponies into a floundering canter, throwing up the snow behind them like spray. They were waving to us, then we heard them shouting, but we could not catch the words. They came up the slope, the grossly overladen ponies stumbling and rocking, and were in through the gate. Men surged forward to surround them as the ponies staggered to a floundering halt; and suddenly word was spreading back from those nearest, to the outermost fringes of the throng. "It's the supply train! The supply train's coming! God's mercy. They are almost through to us!"

Garrison of walking corpses that we were, we set up a hoarse aching roar that might surely have been heard in Corstopitum itself. I thrust through to the core of the crowd, just as the four men dropped wearily from their mounts, and demanded dazedly of the stranger, "Man, is it true?"

He was dirty gray with exhaustion, leaning on his foundering pony for support. "Surely, my Lord Artos. They'll be here by tomorrow night. We were sent ahead to bring you word." He indicated with a jerk of the head the small dark man beside him, and I saw that it was indeed Druim Dhu.

"But how in God's name did you know our need?"

"The first man you sent got through to us," he said.

The supply train arrived at dusk next day, a ragged stumbling file of mules and pack ponies led and driven by panting and straining men, almost as spent as we were, though less gaunt. And among them were some of our own auxiliaries, and also of the Little Dark People.

The train was not a large one, and the leather-covered pack panniers were only lightly loaded, for with the normal loads the beasts would never have got through at all. But the food that they brought would tide us over until the next lot could get through. We helped as best we could, to get the pack teams unloaded, and later—much later it seemed—we sat down all together in the mess hall to our first full meal in three moons.

"I'll not deny," the small red-bearded train master was saying, "that it has been a desperate business, even with the help of the Dark Folk over the last lap; and I'll not deny that if this Levin you sent us had lived to argue, like enough we'd have argued too, and hung back a bit for the thaw. But when a man dies to bring you a call for help, why then that's a better argument than any that you're like to be able to put up against him."

I looked around quickly. "Dies?" Somehow, I don't know why, I had assumed that Levin had remained at the depot to recover strength before coming up with the next supply train.

"Aye. I'd not be knowing myself, how he kept on his feet to get through to us at all. They were pretty well rotted off him with frostbite. . . . He died the same night."

I was silent for a while, and then I said, "But how in God's name did he even find the way? The thaw had not come by then."

Druim looked up from the strip of salt meat in his hands. "That was simple enough; we showed it to him."

"You showed it to him?"

"Yes; even we, the Little Dark People, we have our uses. A party of hunters out after wolf found him already strayed from the road. They gave him meat when they had made their own kill, and set him on his road again, and then went home and made a smoke on the crest of Baen Baal to tell those to the south that he was coming and must be passed on to the next watcher, and then they made the snake pattern for him about the ashes of the houseplace hearth; for they knew that he went to his death."

"And knowing that, they let him go?"

"What else could any of us do?"

"If you could send him on so, from one to another" (I was using "you" for the whole People of the Hills) "could you not have sent his message on in the same way? Could you not have raised one finger to save his life?"

Druim Dhu looked at me as though puzzled at my lack of understanding, and answered also for the whole of his people. "It was in his face. Also, Sun Lord, you heard what the train master said: had it been one of us who brought the cry for help, who would have hearkened to us? Besides, he would go on; he said his friend was waiting for him."

There was a long pause, in which we heard very loudly the green trickling of the thaw. Cei broke it. "That must have been close on three weeks ago. Why was no word sent up to the fort?"

"The smoke was sited to carry its message south," Druim said, "so we in my village did not know of the thing ourselves until a few days since. When we did, I would have come, but the Old Woman looked into sand and water, and said that the pack beasts would be here in five days at the most, and that my coming would serve no end save the lightening of your hearts."

"Even that might have been worth doing," grumbled Cei.

"True; and still I would have come, but the Old Woman said that there were taller crops than mouse grass and laid it upon me, upon the whole village, by the wrath of the Corn King, that we should not come."

"And why would she be doing that?" someone asked, through cracked lips.

Druim shook his head. "I am not the Old Woman. I do not know."

Later, I wondered a good deal as to his meaning, but at the time I was no longer listening closely. Across the fire I met Bedwyr's bright gaze reaching out for mine. And that night he made a harp lament, the most winged and wildly haunting, I think, that he ever made.

That night, as before, I could not sleep. Life and the urgency of life had taken hold of me again; we were saved, and death that had been at our elbows drew away into the darkness. And for me, the freedom was gone: Ygerna's power was over me again, and all was as it had been before.

No, not quite all. Two months later, when the horses had come north to us once more, when the curlews were at their mating and the furze was a yellow fire above the river marshes, Guenhumara told me that she was with child.

CHAPTER TWENTY-ONE

Earth Mother

THAT summer, the last as it proved that we spent in the lost province of Valentia, was a time of final scouring, sharp and without ruth while it lasted, but not lasting long, a time for a last strengthening of the ties that I had labored so long to make among the chiefs and princes; and the first frosts had scarcely set the burns running yellow with fallen leaves, when I rode back to Maglaunus's Dun. All summer I had been wondering as to the thing that Guenhumara had told me, scarcely daring to believe that she had not made some mistake; and the native tracks and ridgeways after Castra Cunetium seemed endless to my wild impatience. But when I rode into the Dun and dismounted with Pharic and the rest of my small knot of Companions before the hall threshold, and she came out to bring me the guest cup, her thickened body was enough to tell me that she was about her woman's work.

"So it is true," I said.

She looked at me, half smiling, over the tilting rim of the guest cup—and it was as though touching her would be like touching something that drew its warmth and living kindness direct from the earth, like an apple tree.

"Did you doubt it?"

"All summer I have been doubting. I think I did not dare to believe."

"Foolish," she said. "Blanid knows about these things."

Later, lying with my arms around her on the broad guest bed, I tried to make her see the wisdom of remaining at her father's hearth that winter. But she would have none of it; the bairn would not be born for two months yet, and she was perfectly well able to make the journey back to Trimontium, protesting that it must be born, when the time came, under the shelter of its father's sword, and that if I left her she would follow me on foot. She held me about the neck, even while I felt the child stirring and impatient in her body, and her hair fell all across my face in the darkness. And in the end, I yielded.

God help me, I yielded; and next morning, with Guenhumara and old Blanid in a light mule cart, we started back for Trimontium.

We traveled slowly and reached Castra Cunetium without harm done. I breathed a sigh of relief, knowing that the journey was more than half over, and now at least Guenhumara could rest a few days. But at Castra Cunetium an ill wind blew up, for on the last day of our sojourn Blanid fell down the granary steps and hurt her back. There did not seem to be much amiss, but assuredly she could not go forward for the time being.

"It seems that your journey ends here, at least for a while," I said.

But again Guenhumara put out her will against mine. "And yours?"

"I ride on with the patrol tomorrow. I have been apart from the war host long enough."

"Then so do I also ride on with the patrol."

"That is foolishness," I said, "and you know it. What will you do without Blanid to care for you, if the bairn comes to be born, before she can follow after you?"

"There are other women in the fort," she said tranquilly.

"Yes, a score or more—the gay drabs of the baggage train."

"Firewater Chloe, who counts herself Queen among them, knows how to deliver a child, all the same."

"How can you know that?" I was fighting a losing battle, and I knew it, but I fought on. "There has never been a child born at Trimontium in these years."

"You fool!" she said, softly mocking. "Do you think that because you have not heard a child cry, none can have been born? Do you think that none of these women has ever miscounted her days? There have been three bairns born in Trimontium in the winters since I first came there. They smothered them at birth like unwanted kittens, and put them out on the hillside for the wolves.

But it was Firewater Chloe who held their mothers in her knees when the birth time came upon them."

"Guenhumara, if you knew, could you not have done something?"

"What?" she said. "What do you think they would have had me do? A bairn clinging to the breast is a heavy burden to carry in the wake of a war host. Also it is bad for trade. . . . Even I, who am the wife of the Bear and have no trade to think for, I shall not find it a light thing to carry a bairn in the wake of the Bear's war host. I have lived in the women's quarters of my father's hall. But if there were no other woman in Trimontium, I should not be the first of my kind to bring her own young to birth. I have seen too many of my father's hunting bitches whelp, not to know how to bring out a child and sever its life from mine."

And again I yielded. If only I had been stronger then, and weaker the next time she set her will against mine. . . .

It had been a long dry summer, as though to counterbalance what had gone before, and though the birch leaves were yellowing, there had been little rain, so that from the first the dust of the dry tracks rose in a dun cloud from under the horses' hooves and almost blotted out the tail of our little band; and the burns ran low, and whenever we could we took to the long soft moorland grass, tawny now as a hound's coat, until heather drove us back again to the track. The grass made gentler traveling for Guenhumara. On the second day (the usual two days' march must be made into three by slowness of the mule cart) the little wind failed us so that the land was bathed in a still golden warmth that comes sometimes in early autumn, and the last of the ling blossom was loud with bees and smelled of honey, and the sky had paled from its autumn blue to the color of curdled milk. We flung off our cloaks and strapped them to the saddlebows along with the iron caps that clanged there already. Riada, the latest in my long line of armorbearers, who besides being native to these hills like the rest of Pharic's hundred, had a nose for weather that would have rivaled a stag's, sniffed the air and foretold thunder and more than thunder.

The horses were restless that night, when we camped beside the high water of the Tweed, and I remember that when Guenhumara let down her hair and began to comb it, sitting by the low campfire, the sparks flew out of it as they do out of a cat's fur when thunder is brewing. Once, in the darkest hour of the night, a little cold moaning wind blew up out of the heart of Cit Coit Caledon, and died down again, and left the world still and heavy as before.

When we yoked the cart mules and saddled up again next morning, it seemed to me that Guenhumara was quieter than usual, or rather that her normal quiet had densified into stillness, and that her stillness was like that of the world about us; a kind of long-drawn breath before the storm breaks. And she moved with a new heaviness when I helped her into the cart. I asked her if all was well with her, and she said yes, that all was very well. But I was thankful in my bones that it was the last day's journey.

It must have been close on noon when thunder began to grumble among the hills southward; scarcely more at first than a quivering in the air that one felt in the back of the neck rather than the head; then drawing closer, a low, almost continuous muttering, then dying again to that deep distant quivering of the air. The storm was circling over the hills, but for a long time it never came near to us; even the sky swept clear to the southern rim of the Tweed Valley. And slowly, far ahead of us, Eildon, which had been no more than a shadow on the sky haze when we broke camp, was rising higher, gaining depth and substance, so that I could make out the three peaks marching one behind the other, and see where the hazel woods of the lower slopes gave place to the bare grasslands and scree above.

And then the thunder spoke again, deep and menacing, a snarl this time, nearer—much nearer—than it had been before; and from behind the hills south of Eildon, the clouds came banking up, higher and higher while we watched; a blue-black mass of cloud, teased into forward-creeping rags and ribbands at its upper edge, by a wind that we could not yet feel in the Tweed Valley. Pale wisps of vapor drifted against the darkness of it, and the heart of the mass seemed to churn and swirl as though someone, something, were stirring it over a fire; and out of the churning storm-heart leapt flashes of blue light, and the thunder came booming hollow toward us along the hills.

I was riding alongside the mule cart, and I looked anxiously at Guenhumara huddled behind the driver in the mouth of the tilt. She was sitting oddly braced, as though to resist every jolt of the wheels under her, instead of giving to the movement in the ordinary way, and her face was very white, but that might be only the strange and menacing light. "Best get back under the tilt," I said.

She shook her head. "It makes me sick if I cannot see where I am going. See—I will pull my cloak well over my head."

And the anxiety in me quickened sharply, but there was nothing to be done save press forward while we could.

We were heading straight into the storm, but it seemed to me that the hideous swirling vortex at its heart was swinging to our right, and I began to hope that the worst of it might pass over the hills south of the Tweed. The fringes of the black cloud were above us now, swallowing up the sky, and we rode in an unnatural brown twilight, while southward of us the storm trailed its path across the hills, dragging with it out of the belly of the clouds, a black blurred curtain of rain that blotted out everything in its passing. "Christos! There'll be homes washed out and drowned cattle and women weeping among the hills tonight," someone said.

Presently the storm had circled away behind us, but there was no returning light ahead; and suddenly, spinning in its path as such storms do among the hills, it was coming up on our tail—coming swiftly as a charge of cavalry! Already in the heat, the dank breath of it was parting the hair on our necks, and the long grass bowed and shivered away from the gust as though in fear. . . . "Up the side glen yonder," I called to the men behind me. "There'll be better shelter among the scrub."

It was a thin shelter enough, among the half-bare birch and rowan, but better than none, and we gained it, dismounting and manhandling the cart the last part of the way, just as a second, stronger puff of wind came over the shoulder of the glen; and a few heartbeats later the storm was upon us. Stab on jagged stab of blue-white light split the gloom, and the thunder crashed and boomed and beat about our heads like a great hammer. We got the mules unharnessed lest they bolt, and then turned to the horses. They, poor brutes, danced and snorted in terror, and it was all we could do to get them edged back into some kind of shelter and keep them together there. Guenhumara was crouching back under the tilt, and I bade Cabal stay with her and left them to do as best they could for the moment, while I gave all my attention to Signus who was flinging this way and that, squealing with mingled rage and panic. And save for a confused awareness of blinding white forked light that leapt crackling from black sky to black hillside, and the ceaseless crash and tumbling boom of the thunder that seemed as though it would pound the very hills asunder, that storm, for me, was one long struggle-royal with the whirling white stallion.

At last the lightning became less incessant, and the thunder trod less swift upon its heels, the whiplash crack of it that had all but split the eardrums dulled to the rolling of great drums that throbbed and reverberated among the dark glens. And I knew that for the time, at least, the crown of the storm was past—so far, that is, as the thunder was concerned; for after the thunder came the wind and rain. We got the horses quieted at last; wind and rain they understood, whereas thunder is a thing that no horse ever understands—nor any man either, which I suppose is why we have always given it to our highest and most angry gods.

Presently the tilt went, ripped away like a torn sail. I got Guenhumara under the cart, and in a while, with Signus's bridle pitched over an alder branch nearby, I was crouching beside her, my arm around Cabal's strong rain-cold neck, trying to shelter her with our bodies from the in-driving lances of rain; while the wind roared up the valley and the wet drove by in solid sheets, in gray trailing curtains that blotted even the far side of the narrow glen into nothingness, and beat and drenched through the thin moaning woods.

And as we crouched there, in the space of a hundred heartbeats, every summer-dry runnel in the heather became a rushing ale-colored water course that leapt over the stones and sprang out among the heather roots and went swirling down to join the little burn that was already swelling into spate; and under the chill of the storm, the smell of wet refreshed earth rose all about us, aromatic as the rising incense of bog myrtle in the sun, and was drowned by the gray deluge and washed back into the ground. It was well on toward evening when the rain began to slacken and the light to return, but we still had six or seven miles to go, and with the warning of the swollen burn in my ears I dared not wait any longer.

Guenhumara was whiter and more pinched than ever, her eyes enormous and nearly black, so that they seemed to shadow all her

[300]

face. And when the driver had yoked up the mules, I had to all but lift her to her feet. "Guenhumara, *is* there anything amiss?"

She shook her head. "I hate thunder, I've always hated thunder. It is no more than that."

Pharic, who was standing near with his arm across his horse's neck, turned quickly to look at her, the straight black brows almost meeting above the bridge of his nose. "That is the first I've ever heard of it, then. You must have changed since the days when you used to stand on the bull shed roof to be nearer to the storm, while Blanid shrilled at you like a black hen from underneath."

"Yes, I've changed," Guenhumara said. "It is because I am growing old." She turned to me, gathering her drenched garments into bunched folds as though suddenly aware of how they clung to her swollen belly. "Artos, take me up before you on Signus. Not— not the cart any more."

So I took her up before me, with a drenched sheepskin saddle rug flung across Signus's withies to give her softer riding, and felt how tensely rigid she was in the hollow of my bridle arm. I gave the mule driver orders to follow after us, left two of the patrol with him, and again we rode on.

Below our left, the Tweed was roaring like a herd of bulls. The sky was clearing as the storm rolled away into the dark heart of Manann, and the evening blue was beginning to show through the rags of the fraying storm clouds, when we came around the flank of the high ground and dropped through hazel woods toward the burn that came down there from the high moors to join the river. But the roaring of the burn warned us what we should find, even before we came in sight of it. Farther south, the storm must have broken with a wilder fury even than we had suffered, and the burn was coming down in a roaring spate of white water. It was far out over the banks on either side, clutching at the roots of the hazels and swirling in yeasty turmoil about the red earth of the lower hillside, tearing away great lumps of turf and boulders. The ford was completely lost; it might even be carried away; bushes, tree roots and clods of earth were sweeping past, and even as we checked in consternation at the water's edge, the body of a half-grown roe deer went by, rolled and tossed like a wineskin in the surf.

Pharic was the first to make a move, and as usual with him, it was a reckless one. "Well, it's a cheerless prospect, biding here all night," he said, and urged his horse straight forward into the rush of water above the submerged bank.

I yelled him back. "Don't be a fool, man. It's death!"

And the horse neighed in sudden terror as the spate caught at its legs and all but swept it down into the full flood. There were a few hideous moments of struggle and then with a heavy crash of hoof-flailed water, and a slipping scramble, he was on solid ground again. I had opened my mouth to tell my marriage-brother a thing, but in that instant Guenhumara gave a tiny gasp, almost a moan, but checked before it broke surface, and I felt her make a convulsive movement as though she would have drawn up her knees against her belly as one does in cramp. And looking down, I saw her whole face clenched and twisted together, small in the shadow of her sodden cloak hood. Fear shot through me. "What is it?—Guenhumara. Is it the baby?"

Slowly and with care she unclenched her face as one unclenches a fist, and opened her eyes with a long sigh. "Yes, the baby. It is better now, until the next time. I am sorry, Artos."

"Oh God," I said, "what do we do now?" And I know that I could have howled like a dog against the sense of utter helplessness that overwhelmed me. It might be many hours before the spate ran down; if we tried making any kind of footbridge by uprooting the hazel saplings and laying them across, that too would take time; and even when it was accomplished, our own Horse Burn would be in a like state, between us and Trimontium. And meanwhile, Guenhumara's child was on the way.

"How long do you think it will be?" I asked her. The others, dismounted for the most part, were probing about the banks.

"I do not know, I have never borne a child before—I think it may not be for a long while—oh, but it hurts me sore already, Artos—I didn't know it hurt as much as this." She broke off in a little gasp, and again I felt that bracing of her body, the cramped convulsive drawing up of her knees, and held her close while the pang lasted. When it was over she began to speak again, hurriedly. "Artos, find me a sheltered spot—a hollow of some kind among the bushes, and spread me the driest saddle rug you can find, that the child does not lie like a lamb dropped into the wet—"

"No," I began stupidly.

"No, listen, for we have no choice. I have told you that I know what to do. Give me your knife to sever the child's life from mine, and I shall do well enough, if you keep guard that nothing comes out of the woods upon me while I am—busy."

But suddenly I also knew what to do, and while she was still speaking, I wheeled Signus toward the half-lost herding path that led up from the ford into the hills. "I've a better way than that. Hold out for a small while, Angharad, and you shall have surer shelter than a wet hollow in the ground, and another woman to help you."

"Artos, I can't—I can't bear the horse much longer."

"Only a short while," I said. "Bear it for a short while, Guenhumara." And I called to Pharic and the captain of the patrol. "Pharic, come, I am taking Guenhumara up to Druim Dhu's village. Two of you come with me, and the rest of you bide here and pick up the cart when it arrives, and get across when the spate goes down. Keep Cabal with you."

"But you've never been there." Pharic urged his horse up beside mine on the verge of the drowned droveway.

"I have once—six or seven years ago. I've been close to it since, on the hunting trail."

"And you can find it again?"

"Please God, I can find it again," I said.

In the last wild light of the fading day, with the cloud flitters flying low above the hills and the low shining of a sodden yellow sunset in my eyes, and Guenhumara hanging a dead weight on my bridle arm, I came over the last heather ridge, and checked for an instant, with an almost sick relief, looking down into the shallow upland valley that I had seen once before.

But the valley of Druim Dhu's homestead was not the peaceful place that it had seemed that other time. Here also, the little burn that had come down shallow over its bed of trout-freckled stones had run mad and become a roaring torrent, bursting out of its old course to cut a new one for itself that deepened and broadened even as I urged Signus into the downhill track, rending away great chunks of the bank and spreading itself all abroad in a swirl and tumult of white water that swept perilously near to the little huddle of turf bothies within their hawthorn hedge. All across the shallow cup of the valley, men were struggling to get the lowing, terrified cattle up to higher ground, while others, women too, were struggling waist-deep in the water to shift the dam of torn-down bushes and debris that had built up across the true course of the burn. Above the roar of water their shouts and the barking of the cattle dogs came up to us, small and sharp and desperate, even reaching Guenhumara, so that she turned her head to look down into the valley ahead of us. "What—is this place?" she demanded, and then with a sudden thrill of fear in her voice, "Artos, what *is* this place? Those little green howes? Artos, you'll not be taking me into the Fairy Hills?"

"The Fairy Hills, or Druim's village. It is all the same."

"It is a bad place!" she cried. "They are all bad places, the Fairy Hills!"

"Not to me and mine," I said. "Listen, Guenhumara, I have been inside this place. It is only a living place, as your father's hall. I have drunk heather beer in there, and no harm came to me. Druim Dhu and his kin are our friends."

She made no more protest, but I do not think the fear left her; it was only swallowed up in the urgent needs of her body.

Thank God, the village was on the near side of the water; I rode down toward it, Pharic and Conn just behind me. A small dark man dragging a sheep hurdle staggered past us, with dazed eyes that seemed not to see us until he was almost past. Then he turned about, not knowing me even then, and demanded fiercely, "What do you here, big man on a big horse? This is our place; go home to yours!"

"Great God, man, I had better welcome last time I came here," I said, and as though his eyes cleared, I saw the recognition come into them.

"Artos—my Lord Artos!"

"As to what I do here—the way into the Place of Three Hills is cut off by the burns in spate, and my woman is far gone in labor, therefore I have brought her to Itha. Is she in the houseplace?"

He shook his head, then jerked it in the direction of the straining figures about the dam.

"The water 'll be in the houseplace soon, if we can't turn it."

"Meanwhile I take my woman there. Send Itha to me—I'll come back and take her place as soon as may be." I had dismounted by that time, Guenhumara scarcely conscious in my arms, and called to the other two, as the little man staggered on toward the desperate struggle that was being fought out around the dividing of the burn. "Tie up the horses and then go down and help with that dam. I'll be with you in a while."

I found the houseplace by the feather of smoke rising from the crest of its bush-grown roof, and the smell which came from it, and ducking low under the lintel, carried Guenhumara down the four turf steps into the smoky darkness. In the first moment I thought no one was there but the Old Woman on her stool, looking as though she had never risen from it, and a handful of children huddled about her, staring at me under their brows like little wild things. And then from behind her came a small fretful wailing, and I saw another woman crouched against the far wall and bending over a child in her lap.

At sight of me, Old Woman cackled with laughter that set her enormous belly heaving. "Artos the Bear! So you come back, Sun Lord. Maybe those that drink in the Fairy Hills must always come back." And she nodded at Guenhumara in my arms. "No need to ask what ails that one."

"No," I said. "Her time is on her two moons early, and the burns in spate, even as yours, between us and the gate of the Place of Three Hills. Where may I lay her down?"

"Over there." She jerked her head toward a pile of skins against the wall, and I carried Guenhumara over and laid her on it. I had scarcely done so when, with no sound of her coming, the girl Itha was at the foot of the steps, standing there like something drowned, to wring the water from her long black hair. Not that she was a girl now, but worn and weather-lined. They are beautiful young, but they age quickly, the women of the Ancient People. Some of the children ran to her, clinging to her drenched skirts, but she paid no heed to them. "Istoreth told me that you were here, and your woman needing my help."

"As you see," I said. "I am going now, Itha. Your menfolk need help too, with the burn."

"You trust me?" she said, looking up from where she already knelt by Guenhumara. "I that am a woman of the Hollow Hills?"

"The water of the little well was good and sweet, and the faces in the fort were still the faces I knew, when I got back to them. I trust you."

And I went out into the wild evening, down to join the men by the parting of the burn. The sun was set by now and some of the women had brought out torches, and in their flaring light the rush of water was fired with gold over swirling depths of immeasurable darkness, and the alder trees stood up gaunt and black against the last bright rags of the stormy afterglow. Pharic and Conn had joined those who were fighting to clear the dam of uptorn bushes, and I joined another band, who, waist-deep in the racing water, were striving with hurdles and sods and uprooted furze bushes to guide the threatening flood away from the village and turn it back into its true course. Again and again we saw our work torn away and the water pouring through the breach; again and again we restarted the desperate struggle to make good the damage. Most of that night, by the windy torch flare, I worked thigh-deep in the racing flood, one with the Little Dark Men about me, as I had not been even at Cit Coit Caledon. I lost all count of time, all my world was the white fury of water that must be fought like a killer horse, and the strength of my own body pitted against it; and Guenhumara in the turf house, fighting as I was fighting.

At last I became aware of a slackening in the rush of water, and shouted to the others that the spate was passing. And later still, I was standing only knee-deep in the flood, steadying myself by an alder branch and drawing in great gulps of air that I seemed to have no time for before, and looking about me. It was not yet dawn, but through the rents in the still tattered sky I could see the morning star that we call the Cock's Lantern; and the world was spent and quiet all about me, and the level of the flood was going down, down; our dams and brushwood walls had held at last, and the water, its fury spent, was turned back into its old course.

There would be a heartbreaking deal of damage to make good, but the village was safe. I left the rest to finish the work, and crawled back, blind weary, to the turf house within the hawthorn hedge.

Itha met me in the entrance that looked, in the first light, to be no more than a dark burrow mouth in the side of the bush-grown mound. "It was in my mind that the voice of the burn was sinking, and soon you would come."

"Itha, is the babe born? How is it with them?"

A bleating cry like that of a newborn lamb came out of the gloom behind her, to answer my question before she spoke.

"The babe is born," she said, "and it is well with them both." She drew wider the heavy skin apron behind her, and the dim flicker of burning peat came to meet me, and the usual smell of such places, mingled with another, sharper smell that I had met with in stables when one of my mares had foaled.

I ducked under the lintel and stumbled down the steps. The place was more crowded than it had been last night, for some of the women were back, and through the throat-catching peat reek I could just make out Guenhumara lying on the pile of skins where I had laid her down last night. I would have gone to her at once, but Old Woman sat on her stool across my path and looked up at me through the fronding smoke of the hearth, and I stopped as though she had caught me by the hair, and waited for whatever it was she had to say to me, suddenly afraid.

I remembered the woman I had seen before, still crouched against the far wall, nursing the child in her lap. And I heard the child cry, not the young bleating that had reached me on the threshold, but the dim tired wailing of something sick.

"It is a girl child," Old Woman said, and the little bright-filmed eyes went searching in through mine, to read my inmost answer.

And I could have laughed aloud in relief. I believe I had never thought of it being anything but a son; but Old Woman's news was not bad, to me, only surprising. And she saw that, and scorned me for it, with the slantwise scorn of her people; and spat into the fire. "Aiee, aiee, and so you will keep it. Now we, the Dark People, are wiser. When we have a girl child too many we put it out on the hill for the Wolf-People. It is not good to have a daughter before a son, it is a sign that the Great Ones are angry, and it should be put out for the Wolf-People. But *she* would not have it so."

"*She* was right," I said, "for this is not a girl child too many, but a daughter greatly longed for."

I would have gone on, then, but her eyes still held me from the last few steps, and suddenly I saw that there was trouble in them. The words came so softly, so mumblingly out of the toothless toad's mouth, that I could scarcely catch them. "There was a time —the Sun Lord knows it, when I made the patterns in sand and water and learned certain things concerning the Sun Lord, and forbade Druim Dhu the Young Man of my house to bring a certain word up to the Place of Three Hills, accordingly."

I nodded, bending toward the small bright eyes. "You told him that there are taller crops than mouse grass, I think. Something of more matter than the easing of our minds?"

"So, the Sun Lord remembers and understands. . . . But there was a grayness about the Sun Lord, a mist between me and him, and I could see into it a little way, but not enough. I could not see whether the child would be of the holly or the ivy; only that there would be a child, if Druim Dhu took no message to the Place of Three Hills. But now it is on my heart that the child had best be given to the Wolf-People."

"That is not our way, among the Sun Folk, Old Mother, and I believe that in this thing at least, the Great Ones are not angry." And I felt myself released and I took the last few steps to Guenhumara.

For the moment I thought she was asleep, but when I knelt down beside her she opened her eyes—enormous eyes whose grayness seemed to shadow her whole drained face. The hair on her forehead was darkened with sweat, but the work was now over. Her body lay so flat that it scarcely raised the otter-skin robe that covered her, and something moved and bleated again, infinitely small, in the curve of her arm. She put the soft covering back without a word, and showed me the babe. It was very crumpled, but the crumpling was no more than the damp crumpling of a newly opened poppy bud that will unfurl to silken softness in the sun. It was almost as red as a poppy bud, too, with a little fine dark down on its head, and dark eyes, when it opened them, that wandered as the newly opened eyes of a kitten do. It yawned, the triangular smile of a kitten, and went to sleep again, one small hand outside the otter skins, and when I touched it in the palm the thing curled around my finger seemingly of its own accord, and bonelessly as a sea anemone. A foolish whimpering delight woke in me, because my daughter was clinging to my finger in her sleep.

"How is it with you, Guenhumara?"

"I am tired, but it is well with me now," she said, and then, "You see that it is a girl child?"

"I see; and Old Woman told me."

"It is strange, I never thought of it being a daughter—I suppose that is because I wanted so sorely to give you a son to train up to handle a horse and a sword and be a great warrior by your side."

"I would as lief have a daughter," I said. I was a little drunk. "A small soft daughter to hold in my heart. She shall have a Saxon bracelet to cut her teeth on—the Saxons weave very pretty jewels out of gold wire for their women—and a white wolfhound puppy to grow up with; and a great warrior one day to sweep her into the Chain Dance at Midsummer. . . ."

Guenhumara laughed the soft shadow of a laugh. "Foolish, you are—my Lord Artos the Bear of Britain is no more than a foolish cub himself, when he is pleased!"

Neither of us said, "Next time it will be a son: next time . . ." But the contentment of the moment was enough for us, without looking forward or back to stress or strain or joy or heartbreak.

Guenhumara reached out and touched my sleeve. "You are as wet as though you had been drawn up out of the sea."

"I have been in the burn all night with the men of the village, working to turn it back into its own course."

"And now that is done?"

"Now that is done, and the water is sinking. There has been much damage to the grazing land, but the village is safe, and I think none of the cattle have been lost."

"You must be weary, too. This has been a hard night's work for both of us, my dear."

Presently I heard the voices of the men outside, and Itha's voice, and a grumbling as they turned away to make themselves a fire and dry off elsewhere, and the living hut began to empty as the women went out to tend their menfolk. I had forgotten that no man save myself who owned other gods than theirs might enter here again until the place had been purified, lest the nearness of a woman who had newly given birth should rob the warriors of their fighting powers. Truly, I had laid a burden on these people. Well, maybe my help and Pharic's and Conn's in the matter of the burn might repay a little. Later I would bring them a gift—the fort's biggest copper pot, perhaps; and meanwhile the least that I could do was to take myself out of the women's way as quickly as might be.

I took my finger from the small clinging grasp, and said to the enormous figure on the stool beside the hearth, "Old Woman, when may I come for her?"

"In three days," she said. "In three days she and the child— since you are set on keeping it—will have gained strength enough for the way, and you may take them safely. Also in three days her purification will be accomplished."

"In three days, then," I said.

But in the same instant Guenhumara's free hand was on my arm, clutching at me as though I were the only thing between her and drowning; and I saw that her peace had broken all asunder and she was afraid. "Artos, you are not—Artos, don't leave me here! You must not—you must take me with you—"

"In three days," I said. "In only three days."

"No, now! I shall do well enough on your saddlebow, and Pharic can carry the babe."

I looked down at her questioningly. "What is it, Angharad, Heart-of-my-heart?"

"I—we must not be left here, the bairn and I—Artos, I am afraid!"

"Of what?" I bent close over her, and her words came muffled against my shoulder, so that I hoped Old Woman would not hear. I did not clearly hear myself, but I caught something about the babe, about three days in the Hollow Hills. And I tried to soothe and reassure her, putting back the damp hair from her forehead. "Listen, listen to me, love. These people are my friends; there is nothing here for you to be afraid of."

"For me, maybe no—but for the babe. You heard what *She* said: you can hear the other one wailing now—over there against the wall. Artos, they hate this one because it is a girl child and strong, and comes of the Sun People, and theirs is a son and sickly—"

I dared not listen to any more. I kissed her and got up, refusing to see the look in her eyes. I had told her not to be afraid, but I knew that she was still afraid, though she made no more pleading; and there was nothing that I could do about it. I could not pass on to her my own certainty of friendship in this place, nor could I carry her off with me now, unless I wished to likely kill both her and the babe. A gray wave of helplessness broke over me, so that all my peace, like hers, was broken, as I turned to the entrance.

CHAPTER TWENTY-TWO

The Last of the North

AT the appointed time, I took my gifts of gratitude to Druim Dhu's village, and brought Guenhumara back to Trimontium.

Itha had tended her well, and she was already able to stand on her feet again and even walk a little, with my arm around her. Only she had a strange unchancy look about her eyes. She said nothing as to the three days and nights that I had left her there against her pleading; indeed for the rest of that day she scarcely spoke at all, but often seemed to be listening, and once I saw her bend her head to the babe as she was suckling it, and snuff the little warm body as a bitch snuffs the puppy against her flank to be sure that it is her own.

That night, when the lamp was out and the moon patterning the beaver skins across the bed, I remember asking her how it had gone with the sick child—for she had been waiting for me in the curve of the windbreak before the entrance hole, and I had not gone into the houseplace at all.

"Better," she said. "It began to gather strength in the night, and Old Woman says that it will live now. Children mend so quickly. At sunrise they are in the doorway of death, and the next they are sitting up and crying for honey cake." Her voice was hurried and breathless, the words tumbling a little over each other, running on: "So quickly—they mend so quickly—often I have seen it happen among the bairns in the women's quarters . . ." And I knew that she was telling it to herself rather than to me, and that she was still afraid.

But when I asked her what was amiss, she only laughed and

said Nothing—Nothing—Nothing, and shivered, though the night was not cold. I could feel the faint tense quivering under my outstretched hand on her flank, and wanted to draw her close and warm it away against my own body, but the bairn in the curve of her arm was between her and me.

Whatever the thing was, it passed—or Guenhumara locked it away in some inner place and buried the key; and by the ninth day, the bairn's naming day, she seemed almost as she had been before it was born.

We called the little thing Hylin; there is almost always a Hylin among the women of the Royal House. And old Blanid, who had by then rejoined us, wept a good deal and talked of the day that Guenhumara had been named; and the whole of Trimontium demanded extra beer in which to wet the baby's head, on promise of not burning down the fortress a second time. And I wondered if any of the women of the baggage train remembered a babe of her own, put out for the wolves. If they did, at least it did not prevent them from taking their full pleasure of the heather beer.

Indeed the last sore heads were scarcely sound again when the supply train came up from Corstopitum, bringing the winter stores.

Bringing also, letters and news of the outside world. It was strange how, between the supply wagons, one first hungered after the world beyond the southern hills, and then almost forgot that it was there at all, until the next train got through. This one brought me letters from Ambrosius as usual, and one (he generally wrote about once a year) from Aquila; and both told the same story of increasing Saxon pressure, a new tide rising, a new wind setting from the Barbarian quarter, upon the Icenian coasts; a new restlessness among the southern settlements.

I think it had been in my mind all that end-of-summer that my work in the North was done, and now I knew it without doubt. My plans of campaign had been turned toward the level horselands of the Iceni that the Saxons were already calling for their own Northfolk and Southfolk, before ever the sudden flare of revolt in Valentia had called me across the Wall. Now when the time for winter quarters was past, it would be time for turning south again, taking up the old campaigning plans where they had been laid down. . . . Time, perhaps, to be standing shield to shield with Ambrosius once more. . . .

On our last evening in Trimontium there was a soft growing
rain that later turned to mist, and the green plover calling unseen
from the skirts of Eildon. There was a certain sadness over most
of us, that evening, a sense of leave-taking; and as the mist thickened, it was as though the familiar moors, knowing that we no
more belonged here, had withdrawn themselves from us and turned
their faces away; even the roughhewn walls and the ragged thatch
that dripped mist-beads from the reed ends had lost something
of substance and reality, and the fortress was already returning
to the ghost camp that it had been before we came.

"It might have waited until we were gone," Bedwyr said, looking
about him as we made our way up from the baggage lines where
everything stood in readiness, toward the mess hall at suppertime.

"The mist?" I said. "It will clear by dawn, it's not the sort that
lasts." Because I did not want to understand what he meant.

We passed the mound where the girl of the Hollow Hills lay,
and the horses above her. I had never known her name. The Dark
People do not speak the names of the dead. It was grassed over
now, and brambles arched about it, and it looked as time-rooted
as the rest of old red Trimontium; the small white flower that was
nameless also was in bud already, the bud of a white star among
gray soft hound's-ear leaves. And I had the sudden foolish thought
that I hoped she would not be lonely when the cooking fires were
quenched and there were no more voices in the Place of Three
Hills.

When we got back to the mess hall, there beside the fire, having
appeared out of nowhere in his usual manner, sat Druim Dhu in
his best green-dyed catskin kilt, white clay patterns on his arms
and forehead, and about his neck his finest necklace of dried
berries and blue glass beads and woodpecker feathers.

He sprang to his feet when I came close, and stood in the firelight holding up the bow that had been resting across his knees,
and conscious of his decorated beauty as a flower or a woman
might be.

"Is it a festival?" I asked.

"Na, I do honor to my friends that are going away." But the
dark eyes were inscrutable as ever; and even now, though I would
have trusted him with my life, I did not know whether the strange
forehead patterns and the glowing necklaces had been put on in

sorrow, for a kind of parting gift, or in triumph that the Dark People were left masters of their own hills once more.

When the food was ready he ate with us. Silent as usual—but indeed it was a somewhat silent meal for most of us, though from time to time the silence flared up into sudden noisy horseplay and somewhat unreal merriment—and after the meal was over and he had eaten his fill, and most of the men had scattered again to the various tasks and preparations that were still to be accomplished before tomorrow's march, we walked together toward the postern gate above the river, and I went out with him a short way onto the track.

A little above the spring that had been, as it were, Itha's gift to the war host on our first coming, we stopped, and stood silent.

"We have had good hunting together, Sun Lord," Druim Dhu said at last, "in Cit Coit Caledon above all. That was a great hunting, a most great hunting."

"A most great hunting," I said, "Dark Man."

"And now it is over."

"Maybe I shall come back, one day."

"Maybe, Sun Lord," he agreed with courtesy; but we both knew that I should not come back, one day or any day. And I knew suddenly why he had painted his forehead and put on the necklaces—and that I was going to miss the little dark hunter, south of the Wall, more than anything or anyone that I left north of it.

"It will seem strange to hear the foxes barking again in the Place of the Three Hills," he said. "And whiles and whiles, when we are moving the cattle over, I will be looking to see if there is a garland on the branch of the big alder tree up Horse Burn."

I said, "And whiles and whiles, I will be looking across the fire between sleeping and waking, and thinking to see the white clay marks and the green glint of woodpecker feathers."

It was a light enough leave-taking, yet as I watched the small lithe figure dissolve into the hill mist, I knew that I was bidding farewell not only to Druim Dhu, but to a whole part of my life. As in Ambrosius's study on the night that he gave me my wooden foil of freedom, so now on this steep hill path with the river sounding through the mist below me, I was standing on a threshold. . . .

I turned, and went back up the track to the postern gate, and stepped across the foot-hollowed stone sill, and the guard thrust the dead thornbush into place behind me.

It was the familiar room in which Ambrosius had given me my wooden foil. The familiar frescoes of bulls' heads and garlands on the walls a little more faded than they had used to be, in the fading daylight; the bronze brazier in the center, casting its dim rose of light up to the rafters, for the spring evening had turned cold with an east wind; the dim black and gold lozenge pattern of scroll ends on the shelves of the far wall; Ambrosius's sword lying where his sword always lay when he was not wearing it, ready to his hand on the big olivewood chest. Only the man standing with his back to me and his head bent to catch the last light of the west as it fell through a high window, on the scroll in his hands, seemed a stranger. A slight, faintly stooping man, with hair the dim silken gray of seeding willow herb, bound about the temples with the narrow gold fillet that so many of the Cymric nobles wear.

I even wondered for a moment, who was making free with Ambrosius's private quarters. And then as I checked in the doorway, the man turned—and it was Ambrosius.

I suppose we said something, cried out each other's name. And the instant after, we had come together with arms about each other's shoulders. In a little, we held off at arm's length, and stood looking each at the other. "Well may men call you the Bear!" Ambrosius said, laughing, "especially those who have suffered your love grip! Ah, but it is good to see you again, Bear Cub! The hours since your messenger came have seemed long indeed!"

"And to see you, Ambrosius! It is Sun and Moon on my heart to see you again! I waited for nothing save to leave Guenhumara and the bairn in my old quarters—not even to wash off the dust of the road, before I came seeking you."

His hands were on my shoulders, and he looked up, searchingly, into my face. His own dark narrow features looked strange under the paleness of gray hair, but his eyes were the same as they had always been. "Ah yes, this Guenhumara," he said at last. "Do you know, I used to think that you would be all your life as I am, who have never taken a woman from her father's hearth."

"I used to think so, too."

[315]

"Is she very fair, this woman of yours?"

"No," I said. "She is thin and tawny, but she has beautiful hair."

"And she brought you a hundred horsemen for a dowry, which I think might make any woman beautiful in your eyes."

"It was the horsemen that were beautiful. Guenhumara does not need to be. She is like—" I hesitated, trying to think what Guenhumara *was* like, for I had never sought to describe her before, even to myself.

And the laughter twitched for an instant at Ambrosius's lips. "A flower? Or a falcon? I have heard it all before, Bear Cub. Na na, never trouble, I shall see her for myself before long."

But I was still trying to think what Guenhumara was like. "Not a flower—maybe one of those dry aromatic herbs that only give out their full scent to the touch."

Presently he was sitting in the cross-legged camp chair with the wolf heads carved on the arms, that had been his seat as long as I could remember. I had pulled up the same old stool to the brazier, and Cabal, who had stood until now, watching us, with slowly swinging tail, collapsed at my feet with a contented grunt, seemingly as much at home here as that other Cabal had been. And we looked at each other with the strangeness of the long separation making a sudden silence between us. Ambrosius broke it at last. "You will have brought your whole Company south with you?"

"A full muster of three hundred, with spare mounts and the usual baggage train."

"So, that makes good hearing. What became of the auxiliaries you wrote of?"

"They went back to their own places—they were always a shifting population. They gathered to the Red Dragon to fight for their own hunting runs, and each time I moved on a few would follow me, and the rest drift back to their own hearths, while others gathered in their stead. It meant training raw troops all the time; but they were good lads." I fell silent, staring into the red heart of the brazier, realizing suddenly a thing that I had never thought of before; that the Companions, also, were a shifting population. I was remembering men who had marched with me from Venta thirteen years ago, men from the Wolds and the wide-skied Lindum marshes; men out of Deva and Eburacum, little bands of hotheads from my own hills, from the Lake Lands and all across the dark North of Britain, all my Companions in their time, lying dead among the heather through the length and breadth of Lowland Caledonia, their places filled by the young warriors of the land that had killed them. Yet I had not thought of the Brotherhood as a thing that shifted and changed. When we rode south once more and the last of the auxiliaries fell away, I had been glad that we were just the Company again, the old tight-knit Brotherhood that we had been at first. And sitting beside the brazier on that chill spring evening in Ambrosius's chamber, with a thrush singing in the old pear tree under the courtyard wall, I knew that that was because the Company had a living entity of its own, stronger than the individuals who made it up.

"If you have work for us, I think you will find us equal to somewhat more than the same number of spears drawn at random," I said, thinking that he might be regretting those fallen-off auxiliaries.

He too had been staring into the heart of the brazier, but he looked up, smiling behind his eyes. "I am very sure of it. As to the work that I may have for you—I sent you the word last autumn of a new tide flowing."

"It came to me."

"That tide flows more strongly now. The Sea Wolves are on the move again, swarming into the Trinovantes territory, spilling inland over the old Icenian lands from the Abus River to the Metaris. We are holding them, but none the less, you are come in a fortunate hour, you and your three hundred."

"What of the Cantish settlements?"

"As yet, nothing; but it is in my mind that they also prepare to move. Have you heard in your northern fastness that Oisc, Hengest's grandson, has proclaimed the Kentish Kingdom and that our kinsman Cerdic grows to be a mighty war leader in his own right?"

"No," I said, "I have not heard that. Oisc slipped through my fingers at Eburacum, but I had Cerdic in my hand, and I let him go. I was a fool not to have him killed. But it is hard to be wise, with a fifteen-year-old boy standing at bay over his mother's body."

He nodded, and then a few moments later, raised those pale

[317]

bright eyes of his abruptly from the red heart of the brazier. "How soon can you take the war trail?"

"Give me ten days," I said. "We've had a long hard march after a long hard winter, and we're still out of condition, horses and men alike. Some of us—you remember Flavian, Aquila's son —have to send for waiting wives, and I have arrangements of my own to make, for getting down part of the Deva horse herd. We're new out of the wilderness, Ambrosius; give us ten days to see to our own affairs and taste the fleshpots—get drunk for a night or two and play Jupiter among the women of the town, and straighten our sword belts again thereafter, and we are all yours."

The smile flickered again behind his eyes. "That seems a modest enough request. The last time it was a whole campaigning summer."

"I promised you the North, in exchange for that summer," I said, and picked a withered ivy leaf from among the stacked logs by the brazier, and handed it to him, "and here it is."

He took it and began to play with it between his fingers; but it was so dry that it crumbled away.

We sat talking on in the fading light, discussing possible plans of campaign, discussing the broader issues that I had all but forgotten, fighting my own war away in the North, exchanging the story of the years that lay divided between us. Presently, speaking of the fortifying of the Royal Territory, the Old Kingdom that was one of the chief things he had to show for those years, of his plans for defense in depth, using again the hill forts of our forefathers, Ambrosius pulled a bit of charred stick from the brazier and fell to drawing maps on the tesserae, as I had seen him do so many times before; until there was no more light to see by save the dim rose-red glow of the brazier itself, and he shouted for his armor-bearer to bring lights.

The boy brought candles in a tall three-branched bronze pricket, and set them on the chest top beside Ambrosius's sword, and went away again. Sitting there with Ambrosius in the gathering dusk, I had forgotten the change in him, but now as the light strengthened and steadied, I saw him again clearly as I had done in that first moment of entering the room, the deeply bitten lines of his dark narrow face under the gray hair, the way his eyes had sunk back into his head, and the faint discoloring of the skin about them. I thought that he looked not only old, but ill.

He caught me looking at him and smiled. "Yes, I have changed."

"I did not say so."

"Not in words, no. Have I not always told you that you showed too clearly in your eyes everything that is going on behind them?"

"Ambrosius," I said, "are you sick?"

"Sick? Na, na, I grow old, that is all. An old gray-muzzled sheepdog. . . . Ah well, I shall sleep in the sun now, and scratch for fleas, while a younger dog guards the flock from wolves. . . ." He bent forward and set another log with meticulous care over the red cavern of the brazier. "It is thirteen years, Artos."

Thirteen years. Wonderful what one could forget in thirteen years. . . . Almost, I had forgotten that my own war with the Saxons was not all the war there was. Almost, seeing the Sea Wolves flung back at this point and that along the coast, I had forgotten that, like the harsh gods of the Saxon kind themselves, we were carrying on a struggle which must end in darkness at the last. It was another kind of coming back from the Hollow Hills . . . Remembering again . . . Finding all things and all people a little changed, a little strange, and myself the strangest of all . . .

"On my way here a while since, I could have thought it was a hundred," I said. "With the campaigning season started, there was scarcely a face I knew, and two boys that I passed exercising hounds stared and whispered as I went by as though I were something out of another world."

"I can tell you what they whispered: 'Look at his scars! He is head and shoulders taller than anyone else hereabouts—and that great hound with him—it must be Artos the Bear!' And then as soon as you were safely by, they ran to tell their comrades that they had seen you. You are something of a legend, Artos. Didn't you know that?"

I got up and stretched until the small muscles cracked between my shoulders, laughing. "I am a very weary legend—and I must away and see how all things are with Guenhumara and the babe."

"Tomorrow," Ambrosius said, "I will have the stores cleared out of the Queen's Courtyard chambers, that Guenhumara may have them."

"Your mother's chambers? You will give her *those?*" I knew that he had used them as storerooms ever since his own return to Venta, that he might avoid having to let anyone else live there after her.

"You are all the son I have," he said, "and she is your wife, this Guenhumara. Therefore it is fitting that she should use them, and bring them back to life again."

CHAPTER TWENTY-THREE

Threnody

WHEN I got back to my old quarters, Riada my armor-bearer was squatting before the door with his sword across his knees. "I have looked to them as you bade me," he said, getting up, "and I got them fire and a lantern."

"Sa, that is good. Off with you now, and see if you can still find something to eat."

The door behind him stood just ajar, spilling soft yellow light across the colonnade, and I pushed it open and went in. Guenhumara was sitting beside the small brazier, combing her hair, which I saw was damp and clung about her temples in darkened wisps, though the ends were already feathery dry. She looked at me through the strands as she swept them this way and that. "I have washed my hair; it was full of all the wayside dust from here to Trimontium."

"It was still bonny," I said, "but it's bonnier without the dust." I glanced about me. "Where is Hylin?"

"Asleep in the little room through there, with Blanid."

I went quietly and looked into the room that had been my sleeping cell since I was a boy. A rushlight burned like a star on its bracket high on the wall, and by its light I saw Hylin curled asleep in a soft dark nest made from the old beaver-skin rug at the head of the cot, just as she had done at Trimontium. Guenhumara always took her up at sleeping time, and lay with her in the curve of her arm. Blanid slept also, against the wall at the foot of the cot, snoring gently; and I stepped over her and bent to look at Hylin. She was as white as she had been red on the day that she was born, and the blue showed through at her tight-shut eyelids;

and I thought, as I had thought often before, she was too small for a half yearling and thin like the small one of a hound litter that gets pushed out from the milk. But that was like enough, for Guenhumara had never had enough milk for her and maybe the milk of the little baggage mare had not agreed with her as well as Guenhumara's milk would have done. Maybe we could do something about that now; there must be a woman in Venta with milk to spare.

"Well?" Guenhumara said without looking up, when I went back to the outer room.

"She was asleep with her thumb in her mouth."

She flung back all her hair and looked up at me then, with a pinched spent face. "If you say maybe it is because she is hungry, I shall hit you!"

"I was not going to," I said quickly, for I knew how she hated that she had not enough milk.

But she flared out at me like the veriest spitcat, none the less. "And do not you use that quieting voice to me! I am not a child nor yet a mare to be gentled past a white rag in a thornbush!" And then before I could answer, though indeed there was no answer in my mind, she got up and tossed the comb aside and came and laid her head against my breast. "Artos, I'm sorry. It is that I am tired. We are both so very tired, the bairn and I, that is why she looks so gray."

I put my arms around her and kissed the top of her damp head —I always loved the smell of Guenhumara's hair when it was clean and wet. "Go to bed, love. I must find Bedwyr and make sure that all is well with the lads, and wash off a layer or two of dust. But I'll not be long behind you."

"I can't go to bed yet, I'm too restless. Maybe I'm homesick." She looked up at me. "When do you take the war trail and leave me alone in this great strange place?"

"Not for ten days. Ambrosius will give you his mother's chambers that he has let no one use since her day, and I shall be able to see you settled in there before I go. Venta will not seem so great and strange to you, then." I kissed her again. "Try to be happy here in the South; it is not my country either, but it is a good land, none the less."

"At least we can be homesick together in the winter evenings," she said with a shaken breath of laughter.

A familiar step came along the colonnade and she moved back quietly out of my arms as Bedwyr's voice sounded beyond the part-closed door.

I bade him enter, and he pushed the door open and stepped into the lamplight, with my iron cap in his hand and a shapeless load of glimmering mail flung across one shoulder. "I've seen your baggage ponies unloaded," he said, and flung down cap and war shirt with a chiming crash onto the end of the big olivewood chest. "Riada will bring up the rest of your gear later."

"That should all have been Riada's work, but thanks, Bedwyr."

He shrugged. "The boy had not eaten, and I had. The rest of the lads are fed and in some kind of shelter for the night. Cei is seeing to the horses, still—some difficulty about finding a good place for them in the picket lines—you know what horse masters are when there is any question of disturbing their own arrangements."

"I also know what Cei is. I will go down to the horse lines and see what goes forward, before I head for the bathhouse." I turned again to Guenhumara. "I may be some while seemingly—longer than I had thought. If you will not go to bed, wake Blanid to keep you company."

"I shall do well enough with the fire for company."

But I hated to think of her sitting there alone, combing and combing her hair, it might be far into the night. And then I had a happier idea. "Bedwyr—can you bide for a little? Maybe she will give you a cup of wine for a song. Can you weave a harp spell that is good for the homing hunger?"

He put a hand to the strap of his harp bag, and checked, looking at her with that wild left brow of his flying in inquiry. "If my Lady Guenhumara would have it so?"

Guenhumara hesitated also, and then stooped for her comb. "Anything, so that you play softly and do not wake the baby."

And he lounged down onto the chest beside my war gear, unslinging his harp as he spoke. "As soft as the wild swan's down. . . . Bide while I tune the darling, and you shall have the very birds of Rhiannon sung from their tree into your hollow hands, if that will help to pass the evening."

[323]

I whistled Cabal to heel, and went out; Guenhumara's voice in my ear, calling after me, "Come back soon," as though I were going, not merely to the horse lines, but on a long journey.

I wished that Bedwyr had not said that, about the birds of Rhiannon.

Within half a moon the old struggle with the Sea Wolves had claimed me again, and with the Brotherhood I was far up into the old Icenian hunting runs. We saw fierce fighting all that summer; but what remains of it to me now? No man remembers the battles of his later years with the clearness, the joy and fire and anguish of the warfare of his youth. I had fought out half a score of pitched battles by then; how many skirmishes and forays and lesser fights, the war gods only know; and the details of one encounter become confused with the details of another, so that now, of all those battles of the later years, the only one to stand out clearly in my mind is the one we fought below Badon Hill. And that was the red flowering and the crown of all that had gone before. But in that first summer of our coming south, Badon was still five years away; and better than the whistle of arrows and the smoke of burning camps, I remember the smell of the saltings, and the wide wind-rippled marsh skies that reminded me of those first campaigns about Lindum when all things were younger and we were still a Brotherhood in the making.

I returned to winter quarters on a day when, after a month of bitter wind and rain, with the evenings already drawing in to early lamplight, the year turns back for a last regretful look at summer. And when I came to the Queen's Courtyard, I found Guenhumara and another woman sitting on the colonnade step in the late sunshine, while Hylin and two more babies tumbled about the old beaver-skin rug at their feet, and a dark grave boy of eight or nine, with a wooden sword, went gravely through the practice position of sword fighting. One look was enough to tell me whose son he was, and therefore who the other woman must be—and indeed she was little and brown, even as Flavian had described her. Guenhumara had risen and stood waiting. I think that in all our years, she never ran to meet me, but stood waiting for me to come to her, quite still, not from any lack of welcome but as though she were making something last, not wasting it in flurry

[324]

and soft outcries; and with the same wish to make the moment last, I seldom hurried toward her. I checked for an instant beside the boy, and asked, "Do they call you Minnow?"

He lowered his guard and looked up. "How did you know, sir?"

"I just thought they might. Keep your point two inches lower when you make that lunge, Minnow. You're laying yourself open to a belly thrust else."

He made the movement again, stamping his small feet and recovering as neatly as many a grown man. "Sir—is my father come back?"

"He is with the horses now."

I went on, Cabal stalking behind me, to where Guenhumara waited at the entrance to the colonnade, while Teleri gathered her brood and flurried softly away into the shadows behind her.

The winter that followed has a sheen to it, a silken texture in my memory, like a flower with the light through its petals, and not much longer-lived. Hylin seemed much stronger, the summer sun had burned her soft skin brown and bleached the ends of her soft wispy hair; she had filled out, and though she could not talk yet—I had half thought she might, but Guenhumara said no, that a year was too young—she had learned to laugh, a small crooning bubbling laugh that was the prettiest sound I had ever heard. I bought her a white boarhound that winter, choosing her a bitch since they are more gentle than dogs and less likely to stray—out of a litter of squirming and whimpering whelps in a huge willow basket which one of Ambrosius's hunters brought to the courtyard with their anxious mother sniffing behind. I got Bhan the leather-worker to make a puppy collar with tiny five-petaled silver flowers on it, where a grown hound would have had studs of bronze. It was the first time in my life that I had bought a pretty thing for my daughter, and I enjoyed it more than I should have enjoyed laying captured treasure at the feet of a queen. It was a mild winter, so mild that at midwinter there was still one tattered blossom on the little thorny white rose that grew in an old clay wine jar at the angle of the colonnade; and Guenhumara picked it and brought it in to lie on the table at suppertime on the Eve of Lights, and the scent of it in the warmth of the brazier was fit to tear the heart out of the breast.

[325]

With spring came the time to ride the old weary war trail again. And by the next autumn Hylin was growing thin once more, and had begun to get strange little sweats that came at night and were gone again in the morning; and Guenhumara, tending her, seemed to have gone away from me to a great distance. I got Gwalchmai to look at the child, and he came with me for kindness' sake, but when he looked, he said only, "Na na, I have become something of a surgeon in these years; but I know nothing of the sicknesses of bairns. Get Ambrosius's leech to see her." So I asked Ambrosius for the loan of Ben Simeon his physician, and the little burly Jew came and looked at her, and shook his head, snapped his fingers and clicked his tongue to make her laugh, and went away using strange words that we did not understand and I think were not meant to understand, and saying that he would send something to help the cough, and soon he would come again.

All that winter the only thing that seemed to soothe Hylin when the fever was on her was the sound of Bedwyr's harp. And God alone knows how many evenings he came up weary from the colt-breaking yards, the sweat of his day's work still rank on him, to squat beside the Small One's cot and make little tunes for her—tunes simple enough to teach to a whistling starling, which must have seemed to him as it would have seemed to the man who carved the marble Demeter in the Forum, had he set himself to fashioning dolls from grass stalks and poppy heads turned inside out.

I was glad that I had already given him a farm from my own estates in Arfon, Coed Gwyn, where the snowdrops whitened the woods in spring, for if I had done it afterward, I should have been afraid that it might seem like payment, and unforgivable.

I carried a heavy heart with me down the war trail that spring, and yet there was relief in the familiar feel of my battle harness. I have always been a fighting man, and for me there was the release, the small sweet death of forgetting, in the clash of weapons and the dust cloud of battle that other men find in women or heather beer.

We were encamped a short way east of Combretovium with the Saxons across the valley within their laager of wagons, and I had gone out to a small isolated knoll to get a good view of the enemy and make some guess at their movements, when a messenger came seeking me out, with word from Guenhumara that Hylin was dying.

It was a very still evening, I remember the shadows lying long from our camp toward the Saxons, and in the stillness I could hear the faint small sound of shouting voices and the ring of the armorer's hammer across the valley between.

I do not know what I said to the man; something about getting a meal, I think. Then I went on studying the enemy camp. Cabal looked up into my face, whimpering, sensing something amiss. Presently Bedwyr brushed out from the furze bushes and came to a silent halt beside me. I looked around at him, carefully, and saw it in his eyes, that he knew. I suppose the messenger had spread it all over the camp by that time. Neither of us spoke, but he laid his hand briefly on my shoulder, and for an instant I set mine over it. We very seldom made any outward showing of the long-familiar bond. "I have told Riada to saddle Signus," he said at last.

"Then you must be telling him to unsaddle again. I'll not be needing Signus until the morning."

I suppose he thought that I was stunned by what had happened, for he said, "Artos, don't you understand? The message has been a day and a night on its way to you, already—"

"And if I do not leave now, I may not see the bairn alive. Yes, I understand."

"Then why—"

"If I go now, I leave my men to face tomorrow's Saxons without their leader."

"Don't be a fool, Artos. Have Cei and I never led troops against the Saxons, yet?"

"Never troops that the Bear had deserted on the eve of battle, to ride off about his own affairs. . . . With three squadrons away, the chances hang unevenly balanced between us and this particular pack of the Sea Wolves. Listen, Bedwyr, I know you and love you, every man, and I know that I can depend on your loyalty to the last ditch; I know there is not one man among the Company will blame me, if I ride away now. But there are the others—I know also what a chancy thing is the mood of a war host. I do not think that I can be well spared until tomorrow's fighting is over."

"How if you were killed or laid out in the first charge? We should have to spare you then."

"That would be another thing. I believe that you would all fight like fiends out of Tartarus to avenge me." I patted his shoulder clumsily. "Go and tell Riada I shall not be wanting Signus until mounting time at first light tomorrow."

"And Guenhumara?"

"Guenhumara knows that I will come when I can. She will remember that I was Comes Britanniorum before ever I took her from her father's hearth; and the old bargain between us." But in that, I suppose I was expecting Guenhumara to think like a man.

Of the next day's fighting I remember nothing at all. They told me afterward that at one time we were as near to defeat as ever we had been without being actually driven from the field. And I heard men talking among themselves outside the bothy as I was stripping off my harness while Riada brought around my spare horse, and one said to the other, "Trust the Bear to know the perfect moment to fling in his charge," and spat appreciatively. So I suppose that I played my part none so ill. A wonderful thing is habit.

I left the clearing up of the day's end to Cei and Bedwyr, the wounded to Gwalchmai as usual; and when I had snatched a bite of bannock and a hurried draught of beer, and went out to the horse which Riada had brought around, I was surprised to find that the shadows had scarcely begun to lengthen. The smoke of a great burning rose from the Saxon camp, and all across the valley the women were moving among the dead and wounded; and already the ravens were gathering overhead.

I mounted, and rode out of the camp that was silent and full of faces, and set my horse's head toward the low ridge of hills that carried the old Icenian Way. Riada had provided for me the swiftest and most enduring of my remounts, since Signus, having been in battle, was in no state for a long hard ride that day; but I would have give much to have had him between my knees now, for I never knew his like for speed and endurance. I came near to breaking the willing heart of my mount, for I rode as though the Wild Hunt were on my heels. I rode the sun out of the sky and the moon clear of the hills, drumming mile after long mile down the old ridgeway without let or pause or mercy. Toward midnight I came to the hill fort at Durocobrivae, the first outpost of Ambrosius's stronghold, and there changed my foundered horse for a fresh one, and rode on again.

Dawn was not far off when, my horse rocking in his stride, I came up the last straight stretch to the north gate of Venta, and the guards opened the great valves, the ironshod newels shrieking in their stone sockets, and passed me through. I was clattering up the still-sleeping streets. The guards at the palace gates passed me through in turn, and I dropped from the saddle in the outer courtyard, staggering as the solid pavement heaved up to meet me like the deck of a galley in a swell. I tossed the reins to someone who came with a stable lantern as though he had been waiting for me, and headed at a drunken stumbling run for the inner court and the Queen's Court beyond.

The moonlight broke in a silver wave against the far side of the courtyard, whitening the leaves of the rose in its great jar and casting its tracery of shadow in perfect echo on the wall behind it. The door of the atrium stood open and the lantern light spilled its yellow pool across the colonnade, together with the sound of a woman keening. Guenhumara came into the doorway, and stood outlined against the light waiting for me; but it was not she who was keening.

I had checked my headlong pace, and came across the courtyard at a walk—it seemed very wide, a vast space like an arena—and up the step of the colonnade into the lantern light. I remember trying not to hear the keening, trying not to hear its meaning in my heart and loins and belly.

"The bairn?" I croaked; and put out a hand to steady myself against the doorpost, for I was almost as near to foundering as the horse that I had ridden half to death that night. "How is it with the bairn?"

Guenhumara never moved. She said, "The bairn died an hour ago."

CHAPTER TWENTY-FOUR

The Fetch

GUENHUMARA was still standing in the doorway. I said something, or tried to, I do not know what, and she replied in a hoarse flat tone that had nothing of her voice's usual beauty. "Why did you not come before?"

"I came as soon as I could, Guenhumara."

"I suppose you had some fighting to finish first." Still the same hoarse level tone.

"Yes," I said. And then as she never moved from the doorway, "Let me in, Guenhumara."

She moved back quickly, before I could touch her with the hands I held out, and I lurched through into the atrium. The room seemed strange, the lantern set low so that the shadows leapt gigantic up the walls; making the blue and russet saint in the tapestry stir as though on the edge of life, and I was vaguely aware of the black huddle that was Blanid in the corner, rocking to and fro and keening as the Northern women keen for their dead, and another woman on the edge of the lantern light, who I suppose must have been Teleri.

"Where is she?" I said.

"In her usual sleeping place."

I turned to the open doorway of the sleeping chamber, and went in, all but stumbling over Margarita, the boarhound bitch, who lay across the threshold. There was a quietness in the room that seemed to shut out the keening from the atrium, as though it had passed beyond such things. There was a scent of burning herbs, and the rushlight on its pricket glimmered like a small high star, its yellow light quenched and washed away by the silver tide

of moonlight that flooded in through the window and lay across
the bed. Small Hylin lay as she had always done, in her soft nest
of beaver skin at the head of the bed, but straight and stiffly neat,
not curled like a kitten. Why could they not have left her thumb in
her mouth, I wondered dazedly, and buried her as one buries a
favorite hound, in the familiar position of his lifetime sleeping?
Cabal, who had followed me in, thrust forward his muzzle inquir-
ingly, then looked up into my face and whimpered, crouching away
into the shadows. Margarita had crawled to my feet, whimpering
also, and pawing at the bed rugs, frightened by what she could not
understand. Guenhumara stood at the foot of the bed and never
moved.

The stillness seeped with an icy chill into my heart, numbing it,
and I could have turned away I think without much show of my
grief. . . . Then a nightingale began to sing somewhere in the
tangled wilderness of the old palace gardens, and the white throbbing ecstasy of the notes pierced through the merciful numbness
with a sharp sword of beauty that was more than I could bear.
And I knelt down by the bed and drove my face into the soft darkness of the fur beside the little still face that no longer looked like
Hylin's, and cried.

The moonlight was graying into the cobweb darkness of day-
spring when I stumbled up from my knees, and the song of robin
and willow wren was waking in the wild garden. Guenhumara still
stood at the bed foot, unmoving as the Nine Sisters on the moors
above her father's Dun and as remote. I would have put my arms
around her, but she stepped back, saying quickly, "Na, don't touch
me, not yet."

And I let my arms fall to my sides. "I could not come before,
Guenhumara."

"Oh, I know," she said drearily. "All that I accepted for part of
the bargain on the day that you took me from my father's hearth.
. . . It was of no great matter that you were not here, it was not
you she cried for—she cried for Bedwyr and his harp, before she
fell asleep."

The blow was struck quite deliberately, and she was not a woman
given to striking with such weapons. Suddenly I had a panic sense
of Guenhumara's going away from me, and I caught hold of her

whether she would or no. "Guenhumara, what is it? For God's sake tell me what you are holding against me!"

For a moment, standing there beside the Small One's body, she put out all her strength to fling me off; then the resistance went out of her, and she said in a low wail, "Why did you leave us those three days and nights in the Fairy Howe?"

"Because you were both too weak to be carried off within an hour of bearing and being born. If I had carried you off then, I might so easily have lost you both."

"If you had, then at least I should have died very happy, and the bairn would have escaped all that she has suffered these past months," she said. "As it is, I think that you have lost us both, now," and the chill of her words struck me through as the nightingale's song had done.

"Guenhumara, cannot you understand? I left you safe among friends for three days, because I was afraid for you if I did otherwise. In God's name tell me, is that so great a sin?"

"Safe among friends," she flashed. "Because you were afraid? What do you know of being afraid? Oh yes, you know the tightening of the belly that comes before battle. You have never known in all your big trampling sword-smiting life, what it is to be afraid as I was afraid, those three long days and nights! I begged you— I knew how it would be, and I begged you to take us away, but you would not listen, you would not even hear—and now the bairn is dead."

"Because she spent her first three days of life in a house of the Dark People? Heart-of-my-heart, how can you believe such a thing?"

"Everyone knows what the Dark People do to the children of men—it was in the very air of that place. And on the last night, the third night, I dreamed dark dreams and woke with a start, and they had taken the babe from my arms! That terrible old woman was sitting by the fire, holding her up and crooning over her—a little dark song that made my heart beat cold. And there was a man there, with a badger's pelt over his head and shoulders and his face painted in badger stripes, and he was making signs on her forehead with his thumb as a potter marks clay; and Itha and all the other women were there, and they threw herbs on the fire so that it leapt up with a strange bitter smell and curled all about the bairn. I cried out, and Itha brought her and gave her back to me and said that I had dreamed ill dreams and must sleep again, and despite all that I could do, I slept as she bade me."

"Anwylin, Anwylin, there was no waking; it was all the same ill dream."

"The smell of the bitter smoke was still about her in the morning."

"Then it was some ceremony of purifying. All faiths have their hidden ceremonies."

"They were drawing her life out," Guenhumara said. "I know. They were drawing her life out, to give it to their own sick child—it began to mend next day—and they left her not enough for three years."

The thing was hopeless. I would have trusted the household of Druim Dhu with my own soul or hers, but I knew that nothing I could do or say would change her own belief in the matter. Nevertheless, I tried once more, desperately. "Guenhumara, there was good faith between me and the people of Druim Dhu, and whatever of evil the Dark People may work from time to time, they do not break faith unless one first breaks faith with them. If I had let slip Cei to forage among their corn pits that winter—"

But she was not even listening. She was not conscious of my hands on her, and I dropped them to my sides with a feeling of leaden hopelessness. When she spoke again, it was more gently, but the gentleness brought her no nearer to me than she had been before. "I know that you loved her too, and I know that you could not understand what you were doing. But I shall remember always that it was because of you that the bairn died. . . . No, don't touch me; I don't want to touch you or be touched by you—not for a long while, maybe never any more."

I was defeated, and I knew it with a helpless despair.

I took one last look at the Small One's body, and went past Guenhumara, Cabal faithful at my heels. It was her right to be left alone with the child. I went out through the dim-lit atrium and across the courtyard to the storeroom, where a cot was always kept furnished with rugs and a pillow in case I sent back a messenger or came myself too late at night to rouse the household, and flung myself down there. And the strange thing is that I slept until close on noon.

We buried Hylin the next night, and so I was able to help carry the little bier, before I rode back to join the Brotherhood next day. Aquila, who was at home nursing a breast wound, came with me; and Ambrosius and a few others. I had not many friends in Venta at that time of year. We carried her from the house after dark, with torches, in the Roman manner. The men of the Roman heritage who were old when I was a boy used to say that a woman's whole life was "lived between the torches," for she left her home at night and by torchlight only twice, the first time in her bridal litter and the second on her bier. But for small Hylin there was only once, and she would never know a bridal litter.

It was a windy night, and the torches streamed raggedly in the wind that made a soft turmoil in the leaves of the poplar trees; and the shadows leapt and ran all about the small grave.

Afterward there was no funeral feast. It was such a little death, too little for such things. We walked back in a silent knot, the torches quenched, and parted at the gate of the old Governor's Palace. Aquila would have walked with me all the way and so I think would Ambrosius, but I wanted no man with me, and they knew and loved me well enough to let me go alone.

The moon was several nights past the full, but when I came into the Queen's Court there was enough light to show me the figure of a man sitting on the broad rim of the old cracked fountain basin.

Cabal growled softly in his throat, until I stilled him with a hand on his collar. And the man got up and turned toward me. I could see little in that light, save that he was of nearly my own height, fair-haired, and very young, but something in his voice, when he spoke in the British tongue, stirred and crept in my memory. "You are Artos the Bear, him that they call the Count of Britain?"

"I am Artos the Bear. You have some business with me? A message?" But I knew he was no man of the war host that I had ever seen.

"No message," he said. "A matter of my own, but hearing of the sorrow upon your house, it seemed better that I wait for you here, rather than walk in unheralded at such a time."

"Surely it must be a matter of great urgency, that it will not keep until the morning, even over such a night as this one."

He said, "Forgive me. I am a stranger here, new come from the

[334]

mountains and unused to cities of any kind. What place should I
turn to on my first night in Venta Belgarum, save to my father's
house?"

Utter silence came upon me; a dark and icy stillness. And in it
the words seemed to spread and spread like the ringwise ripples
when a pebble is dropped into still water. And when the last ripple
died into the dark edge of the stillness, I could only repeat his last
words, and set them spreading again.

"Your father's house?"

So Ygerna had kept her word. I knew the timbre of his voice
now. Across the years I heard it again: "May you have much joy
in your son, my lord—much joy in your son—much joy . . ."

"I am called Medraut," he said. "My mother said that she told
you I should be called Medraut, after the pet white rat that she
had, with ruby eyes."

"She did; and that she would send you to me when you came
to manhood. It will have cost her something to redeem that promise, for she must miss you sorely—or are there others born after
you?" I tried to catch the insult back, remembering that she was
his mother. "Forgive me, Medraut, I should not have said that."

He gave a small bitter laugh. "Na na, I make no mistake as to
the cause you had to love my mother, or she to love you. But she
will not miss me. She is dead. It was when she lay dying that she
bade me come to you."

We were silent again, and then I said, "For your sake, I should
be sorry."

"Sorry?"

"Doubtless you loved her."

"Loved her?" he said musingly. "I do not know. I have learned
more of hate than of love. I only know that I was part of her and
she of me, as though there was still some cord between us. . . ."
He was fingering the carved acanthus leaves of the old fountain
curb, watching his own hand in the moonlight. Then he looked
up, and said a horrible thing—horrible in its piteousness and self-
betrayal. "It is cold outside my mother. I know now why the newly
born draw their first breath in weeping."

And in reply I had a thought that was equally horrible. I wondered if he was in truth born into life even now, or whether his
mother had devoured him as a wildcat in captivity will devour her

young. But I only said, "It is cold in this wind. Come into the house, Medraut."

"As my father bids me," he said.

There was no one in the atrium, but a low fire still burned in the brazier, and the candles were lit as usual in their tall prickets, and from Guenhumara's private chamber came the click of a shuttle to and fro. I left him standing by the brazier and crossed to the farther door and went in, letting the heavy curtains fall again behind me.

Guenhumara stood weaving at her loom—a piece of saffron cloth with a border of some intricate many-colored design. She never turned around when I entered, though she must have heard me, and Margarita, crouched against an upright of the loom, lifted her head from her paws and thumped her feathered tail as Cabal padded into the room. "Guenhumara," I said.

She tossed the shuttle across and let it fall into its resting place; then turned slowly to face me, and I saw by the dry brilliance of her eyes that she had not shed one tear. "Artos—it is over, then."

"It is over." I glanced about me into the shadows. "How long have you been here alone? Where is Teleri and old Blanid?"

"I do not know. I sent them away, sometime. They did not want to go."

"It is not good that you should have been alone!"

The gray shadow of a smile touched her mouth but never the hot bright eyes. "You mistake. It is good for me to have been alone. Better than to be stifled by the soft sympathy of other women. Who is the man that I heard come in with you? I thought it was agreed there was to be no death feast for the child."

"A man I found waiting for me outside. Bring wine into the atrium, Guenhumara."

"Wine?" she said. We had a very small stock of wine, three amphorae at that time, I think, but we saved it for the greatest of occasions.

"Wine, Guenhumara."

She turned without another word and went out by the far door into the colonnade, and I heard her footsteps going quickly along it to the storeroom. Then I went back to the atrium.

Medraut stood where I had left him, beside the brazier, and for the first time I was able to see him clearly. His head was up, a half smile on his lips. He waited for me to take stock of him at my

[336]

leisure, at the same time taking his own stock of me. He was as tall as I had thought, his shoulders not yet broadened into a man's, under the shapeless garment of sheepskin with the wool inside, which was belted by a wide bronze-studded strap about his waist. His legs were very slightly bowed, as are the legs of most of us who are bred in the saddle; "suckled on mare's milk," as we say in the mountains. His hands too, like my own, were horseman's hands, and when I looked into his face under the mane of mouse-pale hair, it was as though I looked across five and twenty years or so, at my own fetch, in the days when my beard was a golden chicken down along my jaw, as his was now. And I knew the chill stirring at the back of his neck, that a man may well feel, seeing his own fetch in the firelight. Only his eyes were his mother's, deeply and hotly blue, veined like the petals of the blue cranesbill, and with the same discolored shadows under them, and they gave to his face a startling beauty that I had never possessed. He was so nearly a son to be deeply proud of; and yet something, somewhere, was horribly amiss with him. He had been too long within his mother, and some part of him was marred and twisted—I could feel the deformity as I could feel Ygerna in him. Lame flesh may be carried off like a tattered cloak, without harm to the spirit—I thought of Gwalchmai; but Medraut was crippled somewhere in his inmost self, and that is another matter.

I told myself that I was merely remembering Ygerna and grafting what I remembered onto her son, and almost made myself believe it.

Then he turned a little, quite deliberately, shaking back the heavy fold of sheepskin from his upper arm, and I saw above the elbow the coiled and entwined dragon of red gold that his mother had shown me on the morning after his begetting. "No need to show me that," I said. "No man, seeing you, could doubt the truth of your claim."

He smiled a little, and turned back to the fire, but left the fold of dappled sheepskin flung back from his shoulder.

The outer door opened, and Guenhumara came in, bearing the great silver guest cup with the ram's-head handles. "Drink, and be welcome," she said, bringing it to Medraut.

He took it from her with bowed head, saying, in place of the usual formula, "God comfort you, my lady, and ease the sorrow of the house." I came to know in after time, that he might always be counted on to say the right thing when he wished to. Guenhumara looked up at him, a long clear look that turned from him to me and back again. Then she took the guest cup from his hands, and set it down on the table within easy reach, and without another word, went back through the curtained doorway into her own chamber.

After she was gone, I pulled a stool to the brazier, bidding Medraut to do the same, and we both drank from the guest cup, but the thin cool wine of Burdigala brought no fellowship; only after we had drunk it, it seemed easier to speak.

"It is in my mind that your mother will have taught you to hate me well," I said, scarcely knowing that I was going to, until the words were spoken.

The dark blue eyes met mine, but I could not see into them, as I had not been able to see into Ygerna's. "Did I not say? I have learned more of hate than of love. Is it my fault?"

"No," I said. "What is it that you wish of me?"

"A horse and a sword. I am your son. It is my place and my right to ride among your squadron and sleep at your hearth."

"Do you care a jot for our struggle against the Saxon flood?"

He shrugged very faintly. "It will not submerge the mountains."

And I leaned forward, studying him through the faint smoke of the brazier. "Then how if I say to you that there is no place among my squadrons for a man who neither knows nor cares what he fights for?"

"I should say to you that surely it matters little if a man cares what he kills for, so that he is skilled enough as a killer. Give me a horse and a sword, and I will prove to you that I can use both." He smiled, an odd, unexpected, tremulous smile. "One day I may even learn from you to care for the cause behind the fighting."

I was silent, still studying him across the brazier. I did not believe in this sudden hint of a hunger after better things, and yet I think that at the moment, he believed in it himself. He was one of those who can always believe as they wish to believe. At last I said, "Tomorrow I ride to rejoin the Company. You shall have your sword and your horse."

"I thank you, my father."

"But first, you shall take off that arm ring."

"It is mine," he said quickly, and made as though to cover it with the protection of his other hand.

"You fool. I have no wish to take it from you. You can carry it in your breast for all I care. Only I say that you shall not wear it above your elbow, in the sight of all men."

"My mother gave it to me, and she had it from her mother—"

"Who had it from Utha, my father and your grandfather, on the morning after he mated with her. All that I know as well as you do, and it is for that very reason that you shall take it off."

"Why?" he demanded, still covering it with his hand.

"Because it is mate to the one which Ambrosius the High King wears above his elbow. It is a royal arm ring of the Princes of Britain."

He took away the shielding hand and looked down at the heavy gleaming thing.

"The royal arm ring of Britain," he said musingly. "Yes, it might perhaps be—tactless to wear it about Ambrosius's court." Very slowly he pulled off the great arm ring, and thrust it into the breast of his rough sheepskin tunic. "See what a dutiful and obedient son you have, my father."

I got up, and he rose instantly, with exactly the right show of deference. "It is past midnight, and we must make an early outset in the morning. Come, and I will show you where you can sleep."

I did not rouse out any of the servants; truth to tell, I shrank too much from anyone else seeing him. I had had all that I could take for one night. The thing would be all over Venta soon enough without any help. I took a spare lantern and lit it at the brazier, and led him out across the courtyard to the small turf-floored storeroom where I had slept for the past two nights.

In the doorway, when I would have left him, he stayed me, standing against the lantern light. "Father—"

"Yes?"

"Are you going to acknowledge me? Or do I ride with you to-morrow simply as a new spear out of nowhere, to join your war bands?"

"Since no man who looks at you can doubt for one moment that you are my son," I said, "it is in my mind that neither of us has much choice in the matter."

"Father—" he said again, and checked, and then, "Can you not speak one gentle word to me, on this first night of my coming to you?" and his voice shook.

"I am sorry," I said. "This is not a night when I have many gentle words to spare," but I touched his shoulder, and realized with a sense of shock that, like his voice, he was shaking.

He drew a long breath and suddenly thrust out his hands to me as a woman might do. "Artos my father, it is an ill night that I have chosen for my coming; yet how was I to know. . . . And in the child's death, do not quite forget that I am your living son! May not a son's coming redeem the night a little for the other loss?"

It might have been a child's appeal for warmth, it might have been only an incredibly clumsy attempt at consolation, but I knew already that Medraut was never clumsy, that when he wounded, he did it of deliberate intent; and I could have struck him across the mouth. But he was my son. My God! My only begotten son! I thought blasphemously. And I could not trust myself to speak again, but turned and went back to the atrium.

I had nowhere to sleep now, but I did not want to sleep; I felt as though I should never sleep again. I sat down on the stool by the brazier with my elbows on my knees and my head in my hands, and shut my eyes at the light that seemed to claw at my aching eyeballs. The sense of doom was heavy on me, and the room seemed full of Ygerna's hate reaching out to me still from beyond death. And Medraut was alive, and the child that I had loved was in her grave; and everything that was in me seemed broken and bleeding, and I was lost in a great wilderness.

Guenhumara came and found me there. I heard her step come across the tesserae and caught the faint indefinable scent of her, and knew that she was standing just behind me. But I did not look up.

"So that was your son," she said, after a waiting pause.

"There'd be little use denying it, would there?"

"He is very like you. As like as a son can be to his father; only one cannot see into his eyes as one can into yours. And that makes him the more dangerous."

"Only if he is dangerous already," I said dully.

"A son of yours, as like to you as that one, coming out of nowhere with the Royal Dragon of Britain on his arm, and if I mistake not, something of your own power to draw men after him."

"All that is nothing by itself," I said, defending him, I think, to myself more than to her.

"By *itself*, no," she said, and then, "Send him away, Artos."

"I cannot—I must not."

"Why? Are you afraid of the mischief he may work against you elsewhere, if you do?"

"Maybe," I said. "Na. The thing is not so simple as that. If I send him away, I am no more than a horse swerving away from the jump that it *must* take at last. He is my fate, my doom if you like, Guenhumara. When I first saw him it was as though I looked at my own fetch. No man can escape his doom; better to face it than be taken between the shoulders as one tries to run."

"Artos, you make me afraid when you talk like that. It is as though you were already half defeated."

"Not unless I try to run."

"Then if you will not send him away, I pray to God that he may get his death in battle—and soon."

I had not been aware that my eyes were shut until I opened them and found myself staring into the red hell-mouth of the brazier. "No! Guenhumara, for Christ's sake no—I am too near to praying that already."

"And knowing the things you know, why should you not?"

"Because whatever he is, it is my fault, mine and my father's who unleashed the evil."

"Your father's, maybe, though he did nothing that many another man has not done before him," she said quickly. "Not yours! No more yours than the bear's when he falls into the trap that has been dug for him."

Suddenly her hand was on the back of my neck, hesitantly, moving to brush my cheek. But when I put up my own to touch it, it remained only a moment, as though to avoid seeming to repulse me, and then was gently but finally withdrawn. "Come to bed, Artos. You need sleep sorely, and as you said, you must ride early in the morning."

And so I lay beside Guenhumara again in the wide bed, and there was a certain peace in being near her. But the child was between us, as surely as she had been on the night that I brought them both home from the Hollow Hills; as surely as the naked sword that Bedwyr had laid between Guenhumara and himself in the bitter winter before the child was born.

CHAPTER TWENTY-FIVE

Shadows

NEXT morning I gave Medraut his sword, and a big roan from among the reserve herd, and we rode out of Venta in the soft summer rain that had come up with the dawn. Cabal loped ahead as always, and beside him ran the smaller, lighter form of Margarita, both of them looking back at me from time to time. "Take the bitch with you," Guenhumara had said. "She will be happier with you." But I knew that the white boarhound's constant whimpering and searching the same places over and over again were more than she could bear.

At Durocobrivae we made a halt for the night, and I picked up my own horse again; and toward sunset on the second day, we rode into camp.

I took Medraut to my own bothy, and sent him off with my waiting armor-bearer to draw his war gear from the baggage train and get something to eat—turning away to fling down my cloak and saddlebag even as I gave the orders, so that I need not see the look on young Riada's face. I had seen too many looks on too many faces already; the startled glance and lengthened stare, the suddenly widened or narrowed eyes, as I rode in with Medraut beside me.

Left to myself when they were gone, I stood staring at nothing, fiddling with my dusty harness but getting no further with stripping it off. I should have gone out at once; God knows there were matters enough for me to see to; but still I lingered, giving the news time to run through the camp.

Presently a step came over the trampled turf, and Bedwyr loomed into the ragged doorway, his figure shutting out the rippled flame of sunset as he ducked through. "Artos—they said that you were back. What news? What news of the Small One?"

"Dead," I said. "She died an hour before I reached home," and heard the leaden words as though somebody else had spoken them.

The silence closed over them. I could not see Bedwyr's face, but I heard him swallow harshly in his throat. Then he said, "There are not any words, are there?"

"No," I said, "there are not any words."

"How is it with Guenhumara?"

"Much as it would be with any woman. If she could weep it might be the better for her."

Not even to Bedwyr could I tell that story to the full. I had taken up my iron cap and was burnishing it with the rag which Riada kept for that purpose. The sunset light through the doorway was reflected red in the smooth curved surface. "She said the child cried for you and your harp, before she fell asleep the last time."

He gave a smothered exclamation, then nothing more, and after a while I said, "So here's another lament for you to make."

He folded up abruptly onto a packsaddle, his hands hanging across his knees. "No more laments. I have made overmany laments in the past fifteen years."

"So long?" I said. "We are growing old, my friend. One day it will be time for the young ones to take our swords in hand, and make one last lament for us—if they remember—and step into our places. And for us the aching will be over."

"The young ones—such as the son who rode in with you this evening?"

My hand checked on the war cap of its own accord. "You have heard, then?"

"I have seen him. You never told me you had a son, Artos."

"Until two nights since, I hoped very greatly that I had not."

"So? Was he, too, fathered under a whitethorn bush?"

"It amounted to that. . . . Bedwyr, will you take him into your squadron?"

"Mine?" I knew from his voice the upward quirk that would set his left eyebrow flying. "I should have thought that you would wish to keep him in your own."

"Should you? Na, it is better that he should not ride too much in my saddlebag. He must go to you or Cei, and Cei will not know how to handle him."

"Will he take so much handling?"

"Listen, Bedwyr; he was begotten in hate. It is a foul story, and save for Guenhumara, it is between myself and God—and in hate he was bred up by his mother, and held by her all these years. It is the only thing he truly understands; he is a stranger in the world, and at odds with it, because his mother never truly gave him birth until her own death tore him from her." I was struggling for the words I needed. "He wants to get back to the warm darkness of his mother's womb; and failing to escape from it, he will be revenged on the world if he can. How much of all that will Cei understand? Cei, whose idea of hating is a blow and a flare of sparks?"

"Whereas I . . . ?"

"I think that at least you know how to hate."

"A strange recommendation."

"Not so strange, since a man understands better in another the thing that he knows in himself. And may even have a surer mercy for it."

"That sounds oddly like a counsel of love."

"Love?" I said. "No, not love. But I remember also that Cei could never have ridden the Black One as you rode him."

There was a silence full of the small sharp sounds of the camp about us, and then Bedwyr spoke again, with a curious cold stillness in his voice. And I realized that after all the years that we had been closer than most brothers, I still knew scarcely one thing about him that belonged to the time before Narbo Martius. "At least it is true that I know how to hate. I hated my mother. She drowned my bitch's puppies before my eyes, and the bitch took the milk fever and died. I used to lie awake at night thinking of the different ways to kill my mother, and the only reason, I think, that I did not do it was that once it was done, I should not have it to look forward to. And then I grew to manhood, and I knew that I had left it too long and I should never kill my mother now. So I left home by the road to Constantinople, and you know the rest. . . . Yes, I'll take the boy into my squadron."

He never suggested that I should send Medraut away, as Guenhumara had done; but few men, I think, have the ruthless logic of a woman.

[344]

For a while Medraut's coming was a subject for talk and jest around the watch fires, but the war camp had more pressing matters to occupy them than the Bear's youthful wenching and its resulting bastard, and soon the thing was to all outward seeming as though it had never been otherwise. It seems strange now, that the ripples should have died so soon. . . . But indeed my son had an eye for country and an uncanny knack of blending into it which, on one level, enabled him to find and fortify a place for himself among us almost unnoticed (even Bedwyr, I think, was at times, and at first, scarcely aware of the new rider in his squadron) and on another, combined with a kind of cold panache, aided him to swift success in the type of warfare which is carried on by ambush and foray. He began to get a name for being lucky to follow in battle, and that goes far with men who live with their swords in their hands; and so presently some of the young ones began to follow him.

He had plenty of opportunity to enhance his name among them in the next three years.

Three years of ebbing and flowing warfare, while the Barbarians clung onto Cantii Territory and the land strip between the South Chalk and the sea, unable to gain further ground in the face of Ambrosius's troops; while more and more of the Sea Wolves swarmed into the old Trinovantian and Icenian lands; always, it seemed, a new skein of the tattered black war boats before each easterly wind, a new war camp or settlement springing up overnight in place of the one we had burned out in the morning. For the sea crossing is shorter in the South, and the Sea Wolves, it seemed, better combined and of more steadfast purpose, so that it was like trying to sweep back a river spate with a besom broom. And always, if we turned our backs for an instant in dealing with the flanking thrusts to the north or south, the settlers in the Tamesis Valley would put out another probing tentacle toward the heart of Britain.

For the most part, now that Ambrosius and I had again joined forces, the wolds and marshlands of the East Seax and Northfolk and Southfolk were my hunting grounds even up into Lindum Territory, where the Saxon inroads had begun again; while Ambrosius turned his forces against the Barbarian swarms south of the Tamesis. But as the years went by, Ambrosius himself took the field less and less often. He was High King as well as military commander; for him, not only to lead his troops in war, but to rule the broad central territory that was the heart and the ultimate fortress of Britain; and often affairs of kingship held him in Venta while other men led his war hosts on the outer frontiers. And so little by little the pattern between us changed and codified; and we were no longer sword brothers of a like kind, in our fighting, but he the Monarch and I, who had been the Count of Britain, the Rex Belliorum, the chosen war leader.

But all too often it was not the duties of kingship alone that kept Ambrosius prisoned in Venta. Increasingly, through those years, he was a sick man. One could see it in the gradual wasting of his flesh—he had never much to spare—in the yellowish color of his skin and the growing brilliance of his eyes, and the drawn look of his mouth which bespoke endurance. Those of us nearest to him could see it also, in the way he drove himself—not as one who rides a well-trained horse and rides him hard, but as one with the wolves behind him, lashing a spent beast. But at any suggestion that something was amiss, he simply laughed and went away into his own remoteness where other men could not reach him; and lashed himself the harder, afterward.

It was when we returned to winter quarters in the fourth autumn since we came south, and I saw the change that there was in him since I saw him last, that I asked Ben Simeon, his Hebrew physician, what ailed the High King. He looked at me under his brows, the dark luminous gaze brooding on my face, as he hitched his greasy old kaftan about his shoulders in the way that he had, and inquired, "How many of those nearest to the King have asked me that, do you suppose?"

"More than one, I imagine," I said. "It so chances that we love him."

He nodded. "So so, and all of them I have put off with answers that sound well and mean nothing. But you are in a son's place to Ambrosius, and therefore it is right that you should know the truth. In Alexandria where I learned my trade, and where the priest kind have not yet made it a sin to explore the bodies of the dead for knowledge of the living, they call it the Crab Sickness."

I did not know what he meant, and I said so.

"It is a thing, a very evil thing, that grows like a crab in the body; and sometimes it spawns into many of its own kind, and sometimes it remains but one; but either way it devours the body."

I found it hard to speak through something that seemed to close my throat. "And is there no checking this thing?"

"None," he said. "Neither by herbs nor by the knife. The secret of it is as deep beyond us as is the secret of life itself—or the secret of death."

"Death," I said. "Is that the end?"

"Whether the thing runs its course mercifully swift, or crawls through years of time, it is death in the end."

I remember that I was silent for a while, drawing patterns on the beaten earth with the chape of my sword. Then I asked, "Does Ambrosius know?"

"One does not keep such news from the like of Ambrosius, with the work that he has in his sword hand, still to do, or to be passed on in good order to someone else."

So I was right; he had been working against time all that year and more, striving to leave Britain strong for another hand to take from his, building toward a victory that, if it ever came, he would not live to see. I could have gone home through the streets of Venta howling like a dog for Ambrosius who had been to me father and friend and captain, not for his death, but for the manner of it, and for its shadow reaching out before.

The early weeks of that winter went by, much as the same weeks in other years. By day we slaved in the training grounds and the colt-breaking yards; or when chance offered, took a day's hunting in the forests about Venta. Our evenings were passed, for the most part, about the fires in the gymnasium of the old Governor's Palace, which the Companions had taken for their mess hall; sometimes, the chiefs and captains among us, in Ambrosius's High Hall which had been the great banqueting chamber, or in my case, and all too seldom, in my own quarters with Guenhumara, like a mere tired soldier or farmer or merchant returning to his woman at the day's end. And these evenings were at once a deep joy and an abiding sorrow to me.

It was always a joy to me to be with Guenhumara, to look at her, and breathe her quietness; yet beneath the joy, and in some way part of it, as though one were the shadow of the other, lay always the sorrow, the sense of distance between us that I could not cross; the loneliness. She had said that she did not want me to touch her, and I could not come near enough to touch her, nowadays—oh, not physically: physically, when once those first few days after Hylin's death were past, she never withdrew herself from me, nor did she ever withdraw her kindness, but kindness is not of necessity the same thing as love; and I knew that something within her, her deepest and inmost self, her soul perhaps, had gone away from me and was going further. I think that she did not wish it; I think that at that time she would have come back if she could; but she could not find the way, and I could not find it for her.

Sometimes on those rare evenings, we would be alone together; sometimes a little knot of friends, Cei and Gwalchmai, Pharic and the Minnow . . . very occasionally Bedwyr alone; and those were the best evenings of all.

On those evenings we abandoned the atrium, and sat in Guenhumara's private chamber, or at least Bedwyr and I sat, while Guenhumara returned to her weaving. I can see her now, as though I were still sitting on the stool beside the brazier with Cabal sprawled on the warm tesserae at my feet, lordlily indifferent to the white boarhound bitch Margarita suckling his squabbling puppies close by. She would be working at her standing loom, and Bedwyr sitting on a pillow beside her, idly fingering his harp, and glancing up at her; she turning perhaps to glance down at his ugly laughing face, and their two shadows flung by the lamp onto the web of her weaving, so that it was almost as though she were weaving them into the pattern of the cloth. And behind the wandering harp notes, the whisper of sleet against the high window shutter.

I liked to watch them so, for it seemed to me good that the two people I loved best in the world should be friends, that we should be a trinity; the clover leaf or the yellow iris, not merely three in row, with myself in the center. On those evenings, too, it was as though Guenhumara came back a little out of her distance, so that I felt that a little more—a little more—and we should find each other again.

Medraut never made one in those quiet evenings. He had begun to gather a following of his own, among the younger of the Companions, and they had their own ways of passing the free hours.

And I was only too thankful that it should be so. Perhaps if I had been otherwise, if I had tried harder to fight his mother in him, instead of leaving him in her power, it might have saved much sorrow later. And yet—I don't know—I do not know. I think he was destroyed, and not merely held captive; and only God can remake what has been destroyed.

The dark of the winter was past, and the days lengthening, and the hunter in me had begun to sniff the distant unrest of the spring, when Ambrosius sent for me one evening.

I found him in his private chamber, sitting in the great chair beside the brazier. Gaheris his armor-bearer squatted with hunched shoulders on the floor beside him, cleaning a piece of harness, and in the farther shadows I could just make out the dark shape of the Jew physician. We talked for a short while of things that mattered little to either of us; and then in the midst of some quite different subject, he said: "Artos, I am like a beast in a cage, here in Venta. I must get outside the bars for a while."

"So?" I said.

"So I am going up to the villa for a few days. They tell me that the hunting in Spinae is good after the soft winter." He smiled at my silence, the old swift smile that kindled his whole face as though a lamp had sprung up inside it—there was little flesh now to shield the light. "Good hunting for the friends who come with me, even though maybe my own hunting days are gone by." And I saw in his eyes that he knew that Ben Simeon had told me.

"Can you ride so far?"

"Surely. It is but a forenoon's ride, and my old fat Pollux grows less like a horse and more like a goose-feather bed with every day that passes."

It would be useless to argue against the plan, I saw that; and indeed I had no wish to. "Who goes with you, Ambrosius?"

"Not many: yourself and Gaheris here and Aquila—my war leader and my armor-bearer, and the captain of my bodyguard. I shall not lack for care and guarding."

"And Ben Simeon?"

He shook his head. "I have no more need of physicians, Bear Cub."

And the figure in the shadows made a movement that was the beginning of urgent protest, and then was still again.

CHAPTER TWENTY-SIX

The Sword in the Sky

TWO days later we were up at the small villa house—scarcely more than a farmsteading—in the wooded hills north of Venta, which Ambrosius and his father before him had used for a hunting lodge. The old smoke-darkened atrium was full of stored grain baskets and so were the wings, save for a few rooms where the steward and farm servants were housed, as was the case with almost every villa out of the Saxons' path, for in these days when there was no longer any export trade, the people had given up wool and turned back to corn. But Ambrosius had always kept the two long rooms of the upper story for his own quarters, and the servants sent on ahead had made all ready for us.

On that first day we none of us hunted, but left the dogs in idleness, though Kian the chief hunter told of a twelve-point stag well worth the hunting, and remained together about the farm, lingering over the day as friends linger over a parting meal before each goes his separate way. We supped—the three of us, for young Gaheris had been dispatched to join the hunters in the steward's quarters—in the long upper chamber, a good country meal of hard-boiled duck eggs, dark rye bread and ewe's-milk cheese, and the last of the withered long-biding apples that the steward's woman brought proudly from the storeroom for our pleasure; and washed it down with thin wine made from the little pinkish grapes that grew on the south wall.

The meal over, and the winter dusk already drawing in from the ends of the room, we gathered about the brazier; gathered close, for the clouds had rolled away and the evening was turning cold under an ice-green sky; and huddled our cloaks about us,

scuffling our feet into the rushes where the dogs lay sprawled. The
fire was a sweet-scented one, of apple and knotted hawthorn wood
laid over the glowing charcoal; the smoke of it fronded upward
into the blackened bell-mouth of the smoke louver, touched to
gold by the flickering of its own small flames—hawthorn burns
neatly, in licking flames like fringed flower petals—and the burning
wood gave back the warmth of the sun that it had gathered through
a score of summers.

We had not lit the fat-lamp, and the light of the brazier beat
up into our faces, throwing curious upward shadows from cheek-
bone and jaw and brow. Ambrosius sat forward, with his hands
hanging relaxed about his knees, as he had always done when he
was very tired, and his face in the upward light was the face of a
skull wearing the gold circle of kingship about its hollow brows.
Aquila's face with its great hooked nose was that of an old out-
worn falcon. He had been sick a long time with the breast wound,
and though it had healed at last, he would never be fit for hard
service again; it was for that reason that Ambrosius had made
him captain of his guard. But a worse wound to him had been
the loss of his wife the previous summer—a little brown fierce
thing with a taste in plumage that was bright as a woodpecker's;
but I think to Aquila she had not seemed like that. . . .

Presently Ambrosius roused from his thoughts, and glanced from
one of us to the other with contentment, a great peace and quietness on his face. The wooden bowl of apples stood on a stool
close by, and among them a couple of handfuls of sweet chestnuts
from the tree in the courtyard. He reached out and took one of
them, and sat turning the glossy brownness of it in his fingers with
the lingering touch that means memory. "Constantine my father
brought me up here on my first hunting trip, in the winter before
he—died," he said after a while. "Utha he had brought up for
three years, but that was the first winter that I was judged old
enough. I was nine, and a man among men. . . . Utha and I
used to roast chestnuts in the evenings; but in those days we still
used the atrium and there was the hot edge of the hearthstone to
roast them on." He smiled ruefully, as though at his own foolishness. "I suppose one couldn't roast chestnuts on a brazier."

"I don't see why not," I said. "You have been High King so
long that you have forgotten how to make one thing do the work

of another. You have forgotten cooking ribs of stolen beef over a watch fire in a snowstorm," and I got up.

He made to stay me, laughing. "Na na, it was but a trick of the mind—a whim of the moment."

But suddenly, and out of all proportion to the size of the matter, I was determined that Ambrosius should have his chestnut roasting. "The whim is a pleasant one, though. I also have roasted chestnuts here before I was old enough to carry my shield." And I went down to the steward's quarters where the cook place was, and called to the steward's woman, "Mother, give me a shovel or an old fry pan. The High King has a mind to roast chestnuts."

When I came back to the upper room, bearing a battered shovel, I had the impression that Ambrosius and Aquila had been in earnest speech together, and that they had stopped abruptly when they heard my returning foot on the stair. I was vaguely surprised, but they had been sword brothers when I still ran barefoot among the hunting dogs, and must have many things to speak of in which I had no part. I showed them the shovel in triumph, and set to building the glowing hawthorn logs into the best shape for my purpose, feeling suddenly my own morning time come back upon me as I did so; and setting half a dozen chestnuts on the shovel, slid it into the hot heart of the fire. "See? I have not wasted my years in the wild places."

So we roasted chestnuts, like three urchins, while Cabal propped himself against my knee and looked on, singing his deep throat-song of contentment in the warmth; and scorched our fingers raking them out, cursing and laughing, but never very loud, for a mood of quiet seemed to hold us all, that evening. . . . After a while Ambrosius looked up from the hot chestnut he was peeling, and I found the gaze of his sunken eyes drawing mine across the firelight. Then he leaned forward, the hot nut forgotten in his fingers.

He said, "Artos, when I determined on this hunting trip, and spoke of feeling caged in Venta, did you think 'sick men have odd fancies'?"

"I know too well the feeling of the cage bars that comes upon a man toward the end of winter quarters, when the life of the world is stirring but spring and the time to march out again is still far away."

He nodded. "Yet that was not the whole reason, nor the chief reason that I wished to come up here into the hunting hills."

"So? And the chief reason?"

"There were two," he said. "Two, conjoined like the two halves of a damson stone. And one of them was this, that I knew the time had come to speak to you of certain matters concerning the man who takes the Sword of Britain after me."

Aquila made a harsh sound of protest in his throat; and Ambrosius answered it as though it had been spoken. "Ah, but it has. . . . Na na, my friends, never wear such grim faces for me. I am not an old man—not old in years—but assuredly I am not going out in my flower. I have had a long enough life, and a good one that has brought me faithful friends and a few to love me; and there is little more that any man can ask—save perhaps that there shall be one to carry the tools of his trade after him and work more greatly with them than he has ever done."

He was silent for a long moment, looking down at the half-peeled chestnut in his hand, and we also were silent, waiting for what came next. I had an odd feeling, though I do not think he had actually moved at all, that Aquila had drawn back from us a little, as from a thing that was chiefly between Ambrosius and myself. "The time has come when I must choose out a man to carry the tools of my trade after me." Ambrosius raised his head again and looked full at me. "Artos, save for the small accident of birth, you are my son; all the son I ever had. I have told you that before. Furthermore, you are of the Royal House in blood, as surely as I am myself."

I cut in, thinking to make the matter easier for him. "Utha's son in blood, but not in name, and so I cannot be the one to carry the tools of your trade after you. Never fret, Ambrosius, I have known that always. I am the war leader. I have no hunger to be the High King." I reached out, I remember, and set my hand over his. "Long ago, you promised me Arfon, and that is enough for me."

"Na, you do not understand," he said. "Listen now: If I set you on one side, the choice must fall upon Cador of Dumnonia, or upon young Constantine, his son. They are the last that have the royal blood of Britain in them, and I am not sure of Cador; he has the inner fires of a leader, but his flame flares and sinks, and his purposes shift like wind-driven sand dunes. I cannot feel in my heart that he is the man to hold together a mixed kingdom and a pack of native princelings straining at the leash. The boy's mettle I have had no chance to judge at all, but whatever he may be later, he can be little but a half-broken colt yet."

(I thought of the dark young man I had hunted with, that spring before Gaul, and the babe into whose nest Maximus's great seal had fallen.)

I said, "Ambrosius, should not all this go before the Council?"

A smile twitched at his lips. "I scarcely think so. Listen again: If I call the Council together and tell them that I have chosen Cador of Dumnonia to follow after me, I am putting Britain—all that was our heritage, all that we of the war host have spent our lives for, all that we still mean when we speak of Rome—into the hands of a man who I am not at all sure is strong enough to hold them; and if, when I am dead, it appears that my doubts were well founded, it will not be I who suffer, but Britain. Britain and the whole western world that will see the last lights go out."

"Who, then?" I said.

He looked at me very straightly, speaking no word; and after a moment, I said: "Oh no, I am not the stuff that usurpers are made of."

"But can you be sure that you would be left the choice? If I were to name Cador of Dumnonia as my successor, I think that for the most part the British princes would accept him, with a certain amount of muttering among themselves. 'He is no greater man than we are,' but also, 'He is the last of the blood-royal.' But the whole of this Kingdom of the South, and besides your own war band, the whole of the war host would rise for you, to a man."

"Not if I did not lead the rising," I said.

"Artos, my simple Bear Cub, you overestimate—or perhaps underestimate—the power of your hold. When men rise for a leader it is not always at the leader's instigation. . . . You are the man with the strength to hold Britain after me, and because you are baseborn, I cannot name you formally as my successor before the Council. But I can at least leave you free to win the High Kingship for yourself."

"I think that still I do not understand," I said slowly.

"Do you not? If I die without naming my successor, most men

will turn to you as a matter of course, and the rest will be for you to handle. Therefore I shall be at pains to die suddenly, without time to name an heir. It will inconvenience the Council somewhat, I imagine, but—"

I sprang up. "My God! Ambrosius! You are sick in your mind! To leave us with no named heir—that will be to leave Britain rent with inward war, at a time when our only hope is to stand together —you cannot have thought—you—"

He sat in the heavy carved chair and looked up at me, his head tipped back, the eyes clear and resolute in his dying face. "Oh yes, I have thought . . . I am not a gambler by nature, Artos, but I can throw the dice when need be. I know perfectly well that in this I am throwing for the highest stakes of my life, and that if I lose, Britain will fall apart like a rotten apple, and lie open for the Barbarians to swarm in; but if I win, we shall have gained a few years more to carry on the battle. And I believe that I shall win—at least with more likelihood than if I were to name Cador of Dumnonia to come after me." A shadow of wry laughter crept into his tone. "It is a pity that, in the nature of things, I shall not be here to know whether I win or lose; whether I have thrown Venus or the Dog."

"I still think that it is madness!"

"Madness, maybe; but there is no other way. Sit down again, Artos, and listen to me for a while longer, for we have not all the time in the world."

I sat down, feeling as though I had taken a blow between the eyes, and aware all the time of old Aquila's frowning gaze bent in judgment upon me. "I am listening, Ambrosius."

"So. Then, you know as surely as I do, that the campaigning of this coming summer is not likely to follow the pattern of the past few years."

I nodded. "So says every wind as it blows over. Yet it is hard to see why the thing should come now, this year and no other, if it did not come five years ago. We have shown the Barbarians clearly enough that in pitched battle in anything even faintly approaching even numbers, we can cut them to pieces with our cavalry; and they must know, for their scouts are not fools, that we are steadily building up the strength of our cavalry forces."

"It is maybe for that reason that they determine to throw their whole strength against us before it is too late." Delicately, he shelled off another strip of brown husk from the creamy kernel of the long-cold chestnut. "It is in my mind that the Saxons are learning to combine at last. Certainly the coming and going that there has been all this winter between the Cantish Kingdom and the East Seax would seem to point that way."

The captain of the bodyguard smiled down his great hooked nose into the fire, and raked out a smoking chestnut with his dagger. "We also have our scouts. It is a good thing, seemingly, to have friends among the Little Dark Men of the hills and forests."

"Ambrosius, if there is indeed a great push coming in the spring, then at least wait until, by God's mercy, it has been flung back, before you make your decision past unmaking it again."

"I shall not last until the spring," Ambrosius said, simply, and tossed the half-peeled chestnut that he had been playing with so long, back into the fire with a gesture of "Finish." And then he said—it was the first and only time that I ever heard him speak of his sickness—"I have stood up in my place as long as I could. God knows it; but I am worn through with carrying a wildcat in my vitals—I am rotted and eaten away. Soon there must be an end." I saw the sweat on his forehead in the firelight.

After we had sat in silence for a while, he spoke again. "Artos, I have a sense of fate on me. It is not merely that our scouts report certain movements of the Saxons. I believe in my bones, in my very soul, that a Saxon thrust such as we have not seen before is coming this spring—by midsummer at latest: and when it comes, there will be a struggle compared with which the battles we have known will be but candles held to a beacon blaze. And believing that, I must believe that this, above all others, is not the time to be leaving Britain in the hands of an untried king, but rather in the hands of a strong and well-proved war leader. As to what comes after, so far as the question of my successor is concerned, the victory in such a struggle would be a mighty weapon in your hand, Bear Cub, and if you fail, then Britain will not need a High King again."

His voice had died almost to a whisper, hoarse in his throat, and his brilliant eyes were haggard, clinging to my face. Yet still I was half resisting; and not from humility but from lack of courage. I had always been one who dreaded loneliness, the loneliness of the spirit. I needed the touch of other men's shoulders against mine, the warmth of comradeship. I was a fine war leader, and I knew it, but I shrank from the very thought of what Ambrosius was asking of me. I did not want the loneliness of the mountaintop.

Aquila had risen some time before, and tramped over to the window at the end of the room; he was something of a lone wolf, old Aquila, and his own deep reserve made him flinch from the least probing into the reserves of other men; and I suppose he did not want to see our faces while the last stages of the thing were fought out. Suddenly he spoke, without turning from the window. "Talk of beacon blazes, there's something big burning over yonder beyond Ink-Pen, by the look of it!"

I got up quickly and went over to him. "Saxons! Open the window, Aquila." He lifted the pin and swung wide the glazed leaf, and the cold and the smell of frost flowed in against my face. The window looked north, and as the dazzle of the firelight faded from my eyes, and the stars began to prick out in the clear sky, I could make out a dull red glow in the sky, like red reflection of a great fire.

Even as I watched, the glow was spreading, rising higher into the stars. "It would take a whole city burning to yield that glare," Aquila said, and I could hear the frown in his voice. And then the formless glow began to gather to itself a shape, a great blurred bow, and out of its brightness suddenly a streamer of light flickered up into the dark sky, and then another, and another; and I wondered why I had been such a fool as not to know the thing at once— I suppose because in my mind it belonged to the North, and so I was blind to it here in the South Country. I laughed, and something in me lifted as though at the touch of a familiar magic. "No Saxons tonight, old wolf. It is the Northern Lights, the Crown of the North. Dear God, how many times I have watched those flying ribbons of fire from the ramparts of Trimontium!" I glanced aside at Aquila, whose exclamation told me that he had recognized the thing he looked at, at the same moment as myself. "Sa sa! You too! You must have seen them often enough in your thrall winters in Juteland."

"Often enough," he said. "They used to grow and grow until they were like great banners of light flying all across the sky; and the old men would say that they could hear a rushing of great wings overhead. . . . But one scarcely ever sees them here in the South, and then no more than the red glow that might be a farm burning in the next valley."

There was a movement behind us, the scrape of a chair being thrust back, and a slow slurred step on the tesserae, and we moved apart to make room for Ambrosius between us. "What is this marvel? This Crown of the North?" He set a hand on my shoulder and the other on Aquila's, breathing quickly and painfully, as though even the effort to rise and cross the floor had been a day's labor to him. "So-o," he said, lingeringly, when he had got his breath back. "A marvel indeed, my brothers." For in that short while that we had been standing there, the light had strengthened and spread, until one got the impression of a vast arc spanning the whole night, if one could but have seen over the northernmost hills that hid it from our view; and from that unseen arc, as though it were indeed the headband of a crown, a myriad rays sprang out, darting and wheeling to and fro, flickering out half across the sky, like ribbons of colored fire that licked and trembled and died and darted forth again, changing color moment by moment from the red of blood to the green of ice, to the blue of the wildfire that drips along the oar blades of the northern seas in summer nights.

"I too have seen the glow like a burning in the next valley, and a flicker or so in the northern sky, from the high shoulder of Yr Widdfa," Ambrosius said, in the tone in which a man speaks in the place where he worships his God. "But never the like of this. . . . Never—the like of this."

Voices, scared and hushed and excited, were sounding in the courtyard, a babble of tongues and a running of feet. Down there they would be pointing and gesticulating, their faces awed and gaping in the strange flickering light. "The others have seen it now," Aquila said. "They could scarcely make more starling chatter if it were a golden dragon in the sky."

"There will be many pointing to the north and bidding each other to look, tonight," Ambrosius said musingly. "And later, all Britain will tell each other that there were strange lights in the sky on the night before Ambrosius Aurelianus died; and later still, it will become Aquila's dragon, or a sword of light with the seven stars of Orion set for jewels in the hilt."

I remember feeling as though a cold hand had clenched itself in my belly, making it hard to breathe, and knowing in that instant the second of the reasons that had brought Ambrosius up from his capital to this half-derelict hunting lodge that he had known as a boy; turning back in the end to the place that had been dear at the beginning, just as I, with my own hour upon me, would have turned back if that might be, to some lost glen in the lap of Yr Widdfa of the Snows.

I flung my arm around his shoulders, as though I would have held him to me, and felt the sick skin and bones that he was, and I wanted to cry out to him, "Ambrosius, no! For God's sake not yet!" But I wanted to cry out for my own sake, not for God's, not for his. "I have lost too many of the people I love; there is time yet, stay a while longer—" But the pleas and protests died in my heart. Besides, any that could be made, Aquila would have made before me.

So we none of us spoke of the thing in words. And after a while, when the glory of the Northern Lights had begun to fade, and the stars to show again, Ambrosius said conversationally, "I think that the frost will not be hard enough to spoil the scent tomorrow."

"The scent?" I said. "Oh no, Ambrosius, no hunting; we bide together, we three."

"Of course. We shall bide together, and together we shall hunt old Kian's twelve-point stag. The hounds will grow stale else, and the huntsmen also. A day on the game trail will do the three of us more good than all Ben Simeon's black potions."

I turned on him, and in doing so, caught sight of Aquila's face in the strange bluish light, and knew that he was as unprepared for this as I was.

"Ambrosius, don't be playing the madman! You could never last an hour's hunting!" I blurted out.

And in the same bluish light, I saw him smile. "Not as I am now; but sometimes it is given to a man, by the Lords of Life, to gather all the strength that is yet in him, enough for a few days, maybe, or a month, and spend it all in an hour or a day as a single moment; that is, if the need be great enough. I believe that it will be so given to me."

The great lights were dying from the sky, and his face was sinking into the shadows as through dark water, as the winter night returned to its usual seeming. "I have roasted chestnuts with the two dearest friends I have, and I have seen the glory of the God beyond gods in a winter sky. That is a good way to spend a parting evening," he said, and turned from the window and walked steadily back to the fire, as though something of the strength he spoke of had already come to him.

Aquila slammed the window shut, and tramping after him, defiantly took up the fat-lamp and lit it.

I followed last of all.

The few remaining chestnuts, left forgotten, were charred and glowing on the glowing shovel, each sending up curled tendrils of smoke. As the lamp flame sprang up and steadied, and the soft light flowed out to quench the fierce red dragon's-eye of the brazier, Ambrosius stooped and took up a half-full wine cup from the table where we had supped; and turned to us, smiling, the cup held high. "Brothers, I drink to tomorrow's hunting. Good hunting and a clean kill."

But seeing him standing there, the lamp turning his mane of hair to tarnished silver and filling his eyes, always so pale in the darkness of his face, with a rain-gray light, and burnishing the gold fillet about his skeleton temples; seeing the faint half-triumphant smile on his mouth that was unlike any smile that I had ever seen there, and the great cup burning in his hand, and the shine upon him that was not the lamplight alone, it seemed to me that I was not looking at the Ambrosius I knew, but at the King decked for sacrifice, and my heart shook within me.

Then we heard young Gaheris pounding up the stair to demand whether we had seen the marvel, and he was only Ambrosius again, standing in the candlelight with an empty wine cup in his hand.

CHAPTER TWENTY-SEVEN

The King's Hunting

NEXT morning when the horses were brought around, Ambrosius mounted Pollux almost as lightly as the rest of us (he had had to be almost lifted into the saddle when we set out from Venta, two days before) and sat there in his greasy weather-stained old hunting leathers, discussing the day's prospects with Kian his chief huntsman. An extraordinary return of strength had come to him from somewhere, and even his face seemed less skull-like than it had done for a month past, so that all last night might have been no more than a dream.

Yet his renewed strength seemed not quite to belong to the world of men, and something of last night's shining was still upon him, after all, and the huntsmen and farm folk looked somewhat askance at their lord, and seemed more shy of going near him than ever they had been before—for he was never one to wear the Purple among his own folk, and I have heard him arguing with an armorer about the placing of a rivet, or with some old falconer as to the handling of an eyas, and getting the worst of it in the way of any man who argues with an expert on his own ground.

The world was gray with hoarfrost, under a skim-milk sky still barred with the last silver and saffron of the dawn, but the frost had not been a hard one and would not spoil scent; and the horses danced after their day's rest, even old Pollux, and the hounds strained forward in eagerness against their leashes as we rode out from the farm courtyard and skirted the brown of the winter wheat field beyond, scaring up the little crested lapwings as we went, and headed for the dark shoreline of the woods beyond.

The sun came up, and the frost melted around us as we rode,

giving place to a thin white mist lying close to the ground in the hollows. The horses waded through it as through shallow seas of gossamer as we dropped into the valley, and small bright drops trembled in the light, hanging from every dried hemlock head and half-silken, half-sodden feather of last year's willow herb. And I remember that over the open fallow the larks were singing. In a sheltered hollow of the woodshore, the first hazel catkins were hanging out, and as we brushed through, shaking the whippy sprays, the air was suddenly stained with a sun-mist of yellow pollen for yards around. And I wondered how it all seemed to Ambrosius: whether he had yet freed himself utterly from the dearness and strangeness and piercing beauty of the world, from the lark song and the smell of melting frost on the cold moss under the trees, and the thrust of a horse's flanks beneath him, and the faces of his friends. His own face betrayed nothing, but I thought that he looked about him from time to time, as though he wished to see very clearly the winter woods dappled like a curlew's breast, the prick of a hound's ears, the crimson thread tips of a woman-bud on a hazel spray, the flying shadow of a bird across the turf, to draw them in and make them part of himself, part of his own soul, so that he might carry them with him where he was going.

The hounds picked up the scent of the stag beside the pool where he had come down to drink at dawn, and the instant they were slipped from the leash they were off and away, filling the winter morning with their music under the high thin sounding of the hunting horn. So, following the hounds, and with the hunters running hound-swift alongside, we swung westward and up onto high ground. Ambrosius rode that day like a sound man. I have wondered since, if Ben Simeon had given him some such draught as they say the Jutes give to their berserkers, but I do not think so, I think it was something that, at God knows what cost, he himself had summoned up, the last valiant flare of a dying torch before it gutters out. He had drawn a little ahead of Aquila and me, and we glanced at each other and marveled; and young Gaheris had a look of puzzled hope as though he half believed his lord's sickness was passing.

We hunted long and hard, and it must have been close on noon when, toiling up a slope of bare winter-tawny turf, we sighted our quarry on the skyline. A magnificent twelve-point stag, a royal hart, in the instant before he bounded forward over the ridge. Old Aquila sounded the View, and the hounds who, for some time past, had been running almost in silence, businesslike, muzzles to ground, broke out into fierce music and sprang forward with a burst of eagerness.

When we crested the ridge, the stag was nowhere in sight, but a few moments later he came into view again, flying like the wind above his own shadow along the opposite hillside. The hounds were hunting by sight now, and swung right-handed, streaming out on a line that would carry them straight across the valley to cut him off; but he saw us in time, and doubling in his tracks was away down-valley toward the refuge of the woods that crept up from the low river country, and for a while we lost him among the hazel scrub and thickets of thorn and wayfaring trees that were the outer fringes of the forest; and the music of the hounds turned thin and querulous. "He has taken to the water," said the chief hunter, and we swung away down the riverside, splashing our way across by a shallow stickle, the hounds swimming for it, and pushed on down again, along the farther bank. Sure enough, a mile or maybe more downstream, at a place where the bank had been pulled away, exposing torn earth and a tangle of willow roots, the hounds picked up the scent again. Hunters and hunted swung back toward open country, for the quarry could not strike into the denseness of the damp-oak forest with its low growth of branches to entangle his antlers, any more than we could force a way through on horseback. And when next we had him in full view the great stag, though running swiftly as ever, was clearly laboring. "I think we have him!" I cried, and the big brindled hounds swept on, baying and belling. Our horses were tiring, but we urged them on to one last burst of speed. Ahead of us, the stag was slowing visibly, struggling on with his proud diadem of antlers lowered now; once he all but stumbled to his knees, then regathered himself and fled on in one last desperate flare of swiftness, with the hounds almost upon him.

Over a last hill shoulder and down into the valley beyond, stumbling and struggling through the sodden wreck of the past year's bracken, with the brindled hounds running low and baying on his heels, and behind, crouched on our horses' necks, we four, and Ambrosius's hunters racing and leaping at our stirrups. In a

narrow side combe, scarcely more than a stream channel down
the slope of the hill, among flint boulders and the tangled roots
and spiny maze of ancient thorn trees, the stag turned at bay; his
head up, the great antlers like tree branches themselves; a king
again, and no mere hunted fugitive, though his eyes were wild and
his flanks sobbed in and out, and his nostrils seemed full of blood.
And as we reined in below the great beast, there was a majesty
about him that gave us all pause; not a hunted beast but a king
brought to his death. Ambrosius flung up his hand, I remember,
and it was as though brother greeted brother.

The brindled hounds checked an instant, then sprang in, yelling;
the hunters making a wide bow on either side and siccing them on
with jibes and encouragement in the dark tongue in which hunters
talk to the hound pack. The rest of us dismounted, for it was impossible to take horses up into that steep tangle. But Ambrosius,
who yesterday had been a dying man, had flung himself from the
saddle, with the familiar hunting shout "I claim kill!" and was
away ahead of us, scrambling among the tree roots and under the
low thorn branches, and I caught the wintry light flash on the
blade of the hunting knife in his hand.

He was among the hounds now, and I saw that he meant to make
the kill himself. I had seen him do that before, in the Western hills
when I was yet the height of another hound. It is accounted the
crowning feat of a hunter, also the most hideously dangerous, work
for a young man in the flower of his strength and speed; but to put
oneself forward to aid in the kill after another man has cried his
claim is one of the unforgivable things, and I knew also, as surely
as ever I had known anything in this world, that Ambrosius had
cried it for a warning to us to hold back from more than his kill.
Only Gaheris, not knowing the truth, ran at lung-bursting speed
to reach him against all the law of the hunting trail. But the boy
caught his foot in a thorn root and fell headlong, driving the wind
from his body, and by the time he had struggled still crowing to his
feet again, and Aquila and I, with our own knives drawn, had
come pounding more slowly up behind, the thing was finished.

Ambrosius had run in among the hounds that were yelling all
about the stag as it confronted them with lowered head. Even as
he did so, one of the dogs, impaled on a deadly tine, was flung
aside with its belly split open like a rotten fig. I heard the dying

howl of the dog, and in the same instant a strange cry of triumph from the High King. I saw him spring to meet the great animal, scarcely attempting to avoid the deadly antlers, seeming rather to court them as naturally as a man goes to his woman's arms after a long parting. The upward thrust of the strong branched and weaponed head and the flash of the hunting knife came in the same bright splinter of time, and as though in a dream or at a great distance, I saw the crumpled body of a man who did not seem in that moment to be Ambrosius flung up as the dog had been, and slither writhing across the stag's shoulders, and crash down untidily, all arms and legs, among the thorn roots and the boulders. Then the Red Lord of the Forest swayed and staggered a step forward and plunged down upon him.

The hunters were shouting, running from all directions. And we —we were running too, now that it was too late, bounding upward with bursting hearts. He can have been only two or three spears' lengths ahead of us, but it seemed a mile before we reached him. Then I was kneeling beside the tangle of beast and man, hauling the still faintly kicking stag off Ambrosius's body, while Aquila and the boy drew him clear, and the hunters whipped off the hounds. Ambrosius's knife was still in the great brute's throat, and when I drew it out the blood burst out after it in a red wave. There was blood everywhere, soaking into the thorn roots, curling in rusty tendrils downstream with the flow of the little hill torrent. I dispatched the deer, and turned back to Ambrosius. And all the while the words of the old saw were chanting themselves maddeningly over and over in my head. "After the boar, the leech; after the hart, the bier."

Ambrosius was quite dead, horribly dead, the whole lower forepart of his body smashed to red rags, one great gash where the tine had entered at the groin and burst out again below the breastbone, gaping raggedly over blood and torn gut and wet soft things that I could not look at. I was not Ben Simeon who had been to Alexandria. But his face was not touched. It wore a look of faint surprise (so many dead faces that I have seen have looked surprised; it must be that death is not like anything that we have imagined it to be), and under the surprise, a look harder to define, something of triumph, but not personal triumph, the look, perhaps,

of a man who has fulfilled his fate, and gone gladly to the fulfillment.

Above the battered and mutilated body, Aquila and I looked
at each other, and then bowed our heads. I don't think any of us
spoke—any of the three of us, that is; the hunters were murmuring
among themselves, white-faced, as they got the dogs leashed, and
turned again and again to stare in our direction. I looked at the
ashen face and quivering mouth of Ambrosius's young armor-
bearer, and knew that the boy must instantly be got away and
given something to do. Besides, he was the obvious choice, for he
was the lightest rider of us all. "Take the least tired of the horses,
and ride back to the farm. Tell them the High King is dead, and
bring back a hurdle—no, stay—three of the hunters had best take
the other horses and go with you. You'll be quicker so than by
rounding up three of the farm people."

When they were gone Aquila and I straightened the King's body
somewhat, that it might not lie tumbled and unseemly when it
began to stiffen. Then I stripped off hunting leathers and undertunic, and tore the tunic into strips and bound them about his
loins and waist, that none of the red wet ruin of things might fall
out when we came to move him. Aquila held him for me the while;
and when it was done, I picked him up and carried him down to
the foot of the narrow combe, clear of the thorn scrub where they
would be able to get the hurdle, clear of the blood and mess. The
remaining hunters with their hounds had gathered at a little distance, and we forgot that they were there. I do not think that in all
that time either of us spoke one word. Only I remember Aquila's
harsh painful breathing, for with the running and the struggle he
must have all but torn the breast wound asunder.

In a while the party from the farm came back with the hurdle,
and stood gazing down at the dead King, almost as silent as ourselves. Then we lifted his wasted body—he was nothing but yellow
skin over the light bones—and laid him on the hurdle, and set off
back to the farm. Somebody had gralloched the deer, and they
flung its carcass across the back of a pony and brought it after us.

It was not so very far, traveling straight across the country, for
the stag had looped and doubled many times in his flight, and the
dusk had scarcely deepened into the dark when we stumbled into
the courtyard, where the flare of torches beat harshly on our eyes

and the farm folk came crowding around, and the sound of women's wailing was in the air.

We carried him upstairs and laid him in the long upper chamber, at just about the time that he had stood last night with the half-empty wine cup in his hand and that strange brightness upon him, crying to us, "I drink to tomorrow's hunting. A good hunting and a clean kill!" But he himself was the kill, as he had known that he would be.

We left him to the women, and when they had done their work, and he lay stiff and seemly on thinly piled bracken from the fodder stack, his sword beside him, Aquila's cloak for a royal coverlet, and the household's best honey-wax candles burning about the long chamber, Aquila and I took up our stand at his head and feet to keep the death vigil. We had brought the hounds into the room —my old Cabal and a leash of his own hunting dogs—that they might draw any evil spirits from his body, according to the rites of Mithras, though presently he would be buried according to the rites of Christ. That was the one thing that we could still do for him.

I had sent Gaheris off on the steward's horse to carry the word back to Venta, to Bishop Dubricius the father of the Council, to Justus Valens the second-in-command of the guard. "Tell them that we shall start to bring him back at dawn, and bid them come to meet us. Hurry, and you should be there well before first light." He had not wanted to go, he had begged to share our watch, and I remember that he was crying. And I had promised him that he should share the watch that must be kept in Venta, and that for the moment he was of more service to his lord on the road south.

It was very quiet in the long upper chamber, for the farm folk and the hunters had betaken themselves to their own quarters in their own huddle of shocked stillness; only we heard each other's breathing, and the soughing of the thin north wind in the bare chestnut tree outside, and the creaking of the old house at night, and once a dog howled and a voice stilled him, and later he began to howl again. I could understand why Ambrosius had wished to come back to this place to die. Tomorrow there must come all the solemn panoply of a High King's death, the slow chanting of the Christian priests, the flaring torches illuminating the bull masks of

[367]

Mithra, the bier hung with gold and imperial purple, the curling smoke of the death incense making the senses swim. But tonight there was only bracken to lie on and familiar rafters overhead, the smell of the winter night and burning hawthorn logs, the harping of the icy drafts along the floor; and Aquila who was not a brother to stand at his feet, and I who was not a son to stand at his head.

Ambrosius's face had lost the look of surprise and the other, more strange look that had been upon it earlier. It had no expression now save a sternness infinitely remote. It was no longer a face but a mask, with the brand of Mithras showing between the brows more clearly than it had done between those of the living man; a head nobly carved in gray marble for his own tomb, that had caught the austere strength but missed the gentler things. It was not even very like Ambrosius any more. But looking down at it as I stood leaning on my sword, I saw it for the face of the King Sacrifice; older than either Christos or Mithras, reaching back and forward into all time until the two met and the circle was complete. Always the god, the king, the hero, who must die for the people when the call comes.

I suppose there must have been something in his ending, of the man who goes out to meet a quick death rather than wait for the slow and hideous one that he knows is coming to him. But more than that, he had chosen his way for the deliberate purpose he had spoken of so reasonably last night, peeling chestnuts beside the fire, and for another that had nothing to do with reason. . . . I remembered suddenly across the years, Irach flinging himself forward upon the Saxon spears at Eburacum. And for the second time in my life I glimpsed the oneness of all things. . . .

The hilt of my sword shifted a little in my hands which were crossed upon the grip and shoulders, and the light of the candles caught the royal purple of Maximus's great seal, and set a star of brilliant violet light blazing in its depths. I had never told Ambrosius that I would take up the task that he laid upon me, but I knew now that if by any means, by the grace of all the gods that ever men prayed to, I could gain the High Kingship of Britain, I would do it.

I think that Ambrosius had known it all along.

[368]

CHAPTER TWENTY-EIGHT

Rex Belliorum

ON the third day after Ambrosius's burial the Council of the Kingdom met, as I had known that they must before many days went by. My place in the government of the land had always been a carefully unformulated one; I had sat at the Council table whenever I was in Venta at the time when a meeting was called, but always, as it were, as a guest. And that morning, as on so many other mornings, I received my formal invitation. And I knew, with a tightening of the stomach, that the time had come for the opening phase of the trial of skill and judgment that lay before me.

An hour after noon, when she brought me my best cloak of violet cloth with the black and crimson border, Guenhumara set her hands on my shoulders and said, "Will they talk of who is to be the new High King?"

"Assuredly," I said, "but it is in my mind that now, with the Saxons stirring beyond the borders, is not the time to be king-making."

She gave me a long clear look. "You know that the apple is yours, to stretch out your hand for."

"I believe that it may be, but I cannot afford to break Britain apart in plucking it."

"You are always afraid of breaking something, aren't you?" Guenhumara said, and she drew my head down and kissed me, with nothing but duty and gentleness behind her lips.

The Basilica at Venta must have been a place of beauty and splendor in the days when the world was still firm underfoot. Ever since I could remember, it had been half derelict, the frescoed plaster falling from the walls, the fine Purbeck marble cracked and damp-stained, the gilding blackened. The huge wrought-bronze screens that had shut off the Council Chamber from the main hall had been taken down in my grandsire's time, and melted down for harness of war. But the place had a certain dignity and beauty still, though a beauty of decay and fallen leaves compared with the pride of high summer.

I made a good businesslike swinging entrance through the west door, with Cei and Bedwyr and Pharic behind me for a ceremonial guard, tramped across the tesselated floor, and mounted the three steps to the Council Chamber, and stood before the Council of Britain.

There was a stir and a ripple and a thrust of movement as those already there rose for me in all courtesy—save for Dubricius who, being a Father of the Church, rose for no man save the High King himself. A cold diffused light shone down impersonally from the three high windows, and searched out rather than lit the faces of the men about the table. Dubricius himself, with eyes alight and alert and cold as a seagull's in a plump many-folded subtle face that seemed to be made of the finest quality candle wax, would be my chief opponent, I knew, and the two other churchmen would follow his lead. The rest, I thought, would be more open to reason; some of them had been fighting men in their time, and two were soldiers still: Perdius, who commanded the main cavalry wing of the war host, gave me the brief nod that was the nearest approach to a greeting that he had for anyone, and I caught Aquila's dark frowning gaze as it came out to me like a handclasp.

The King's Chair, on the right of which Dubricius sat, was empty in the cold uncaring light, and opposite to it, a chair of state had been set for me. And when the grave courtesies of the occasion had been exchanged, and the Bishop had prayed for the soul of Ambrosius the High King, we turned first to the lesser matters that must be dealt with; the mere camp routine of state, while the recording clerks on their stools scratched away at their tablets in the background. When the camp routine had been disposed of, I remember that there came a pause, as though every man drew breath for the true business of that day's meeting of the Council.

Dubricius leaned forward, his big pale hands folded on the table before him, the great ruby on his thumb making one point of pride and fire in the clear emotionless light of the February day, and looked about him at each of us in turn. "My dear friends, my brothers of the Council—" He had a pleasant voice, unexpectedly dry to come from so unctuous a body, unexpectedly moderate to come from a man with those eyes. "A short while since, in the opening moments of this sitting, we prayed for the soul of our late most beloved lord, Ambrosius the High King. Now, since it appears that our Lord Ambrosius took his leave of this life without having at any time named his heir—" The lively seagull's eye turned first to Aquila and then to me: "That is so, my Lord Artos?"

Aquila sat very still and gave no sign, but I felt his gaze on me. "That is so," I said.

And Dubricius bent his head in acknowledgment until the broad chins flattened on the breast folds of his mantle. "Since it appears that our Brother Ambrosius has at no time named his heir, there falls to us assembled here, the heavy and grievous task of considering the man best fitted in all ways to succeed him, and for that purpose above all, we are met here today."

"If the High King had but left a son!" murmured a dejected-seeming Councilor renowned for his fruitless "if onlys."

A carefully controlled impatience twitched at the Bishop's brows. "The whole necessity for this meeting of the Council, Ulpius Critas, arises from the fact that the High King left no son."

Aquila, who had been staring at his own hard brown sword hand on the table, looked up quickly. "None in blood."

"We all know, I think," Dubricius said with dry courtesy, "where Ambrosius's choice must have fallen, were it not that—" He seemed for the moment at a loss how to go on, and I helped him out.

"That Artos the Bear, his brother's son, was chance-begotten on a farm girl under a hawthorn bush."

The Bishop again bent his head in acknowledgment and acceptance, though I thought with a trace of pain, such as a well-bred man might fail to conceal, were a guest to spit at his supper table. "There remains, then, unless my memory plays me false, but one other on whom the choice may rightly fall: Cador of Dumnonia also is of the Emperor Maximus's line."

"Only on the dam's side," another man put in, and a third added reflectively into the gray bird's-nest of his beard, "But no hawthorn bush."

Perdius, the cavalry commander, said impatiently, "Shall we lay aside this question of hawthorn bushes, which has to my mind very little bearing on the case, and choose whoever seems like to be the man best fitted for the High Kingship? We have no experience of this Cador's powers, but we know well the Bear's. May I state now, once and for all, that I believe Artos, the Rex Belliorum these many years, to be that man."

"Speaking as a soldier?"

"Speaking as a soldier, in a day when we need above all things, a soldier to lead us."

But Dubricius was a churchman, bound by the laws and the formulas of the Church. "So; but then again, Perdius, there may be others among us who may believe that the High Kingship, which is of God, calls for other qualities, other qualifications, besides a strong sword arm. And in the judgment of these others, Cador of Dumnonia, the true-born son of his father, and a ruler already in his own right, may seem to have the stronger claim."

The soldier snorted. His broad reddish nose had been badly broken in his youth, and he possessed, as legacy of the damage, a peculiarly offensive one-nostriled snort which had caused many a man larger than himself to curl up like a wood louse, but I do not think that he had ever used it on the Bishop of Venta before.

"A ruler? A petty princeling with no better claim to the High Kingship than a whole fistful of others, save for this one small matter of a few drops of blood, which he shares with Artos the Bear."

"And with one other," a lesser churchman said; and the implied warning and reminder that Artos had a son to follow him was clear in the small sharp silence that followed. One or two of those about the table glanced at each other and away again. Medraut's following was among the younger of the war host; the older men, the Church and the war-scarred veterans did not, I think, even then quite trust him.

I was suddenly weary of sitting in my seat of honor and being argued over as though I were not there at all. I slammed back the heavy chair and stood up. To be the tallest man in any company is a thing that has its uses. "Holy Father Dubricius, my Lords of the Council—here is a great arguing that it seems to me may well drag on until this day year and still be no nearer to its settlement; and I

[372]

would suggest that this, with the Saxons slinking to and fro like a wolf pack on our borders, waiting only for spring to be at our throats as they have not been for a score of years, is not the time for a king-choosing at all. We have enough on our hands without that."

Dubricius looked at me with a wakening gleam in his eye and there was a sudden stillness of close attention all around the table. "Surely, my Son, if the Barbarians are indeed moving—though of that, we have little sign that differs from the signs in other years —then this, of all others, is the time to be swift in choosing a king, lest when the time of testing comes, we must face it without a leader."

"If the thing might be done peacefully, yes," I said, "but do you not see that whichever way you throw the apple, there will be trouble, *bad* trouble, afterward? See now, the choice lies between Cador and myself—" I quelled a sudden movement from the Bishop. "Oh yes it does; I am not standing aside from this in humble apology for my left-hand birth; bastardy makes me no less fitted to carry the Sword of Britain—and if the choice falls upon me, I know well enough that I shall have almost the whole body of the Christian Church ranged against me—"

The churchman cut in, querulously. "Have you shown yourself so much a friend to the Church that she should open loving arms to you now?"

"Meaning that I have pastured my horses on monastery land, and demanded a share in the monastery plate when the war kist was empty? Yet I have kept your roofs over your heads for twenty years, your lights burning in your sanctuaries and your monks inside their own whole skins. And I am thinking with a certain saying of your Christos that the laborer is worthy of his hire. If the choice falls on me, the Church will set its face against me, as I say, and with her certain of the Celtic princes who love not the ways of Rome even now, and like enough Cador of Dumnonia will join you. Sa! But let you choose Cador of Dumnonia to carry the Sword of Britain, and you will find that not only my own Company, but the whole war host will rise against him and you. Oh, I will not stir the thing up, I swear you that, but none the less they will rise, without my stirring. Holy Father Dubricius, my Lords of the Council, for God's sake believe me. It is not the moment to be risking such a split in the kingdoms—a split through which the Saxons may come in on us, as an army through an undefended pass!"

Bishop Dubricius said wearily, "How may we be sure that all this talk of a Saxon thrust is more than an attempt to gain time?"

"For what, in God's name?"

"For perfecting plans of your own, for making more sure of the war host."

Aquila spoke, slowly and deliberately. "I cannot speak for the Companions, but for every man of the war host, I can speak. They will not accept a Western princeling thrust upon them without having yet earned their trust. The Rex Belliorum has no need of time to make more sure of them."

And behind me, the leveled voice of Bedwyr said: "*I* can speak for the Companions."

Dubricius's gaze flicked past me. "I did not know that we had a new Councilor among us."

"No? Nevertheless, as lieutenant to Artos the Bear, I claim the right to speak for his personal cavalry." (A thunderous growl from Cei supported his words.) "We are the Bear's men to the death, and whether he leads us or no, we will not see another man sitting in the place that should be his."

Someone was trying to silence him, but the Bishop made a quick gesture with the hand on which the great ruby was brilliant as a gout of fresh-spilled blood. "No, let him speak—it appears, then, that you care more for a personal leader than for the good fate of Christian Britain?"

"We care for the good fate of Britain, oh yes, for the last-leavings of Rome, for the last lights that must be shielded as long as we may shield them from flickering out. Quite a few of us have died for these things from time to time. You have maybe heard? But we do not think that an untried princeling on the High Seat, instead of a war leader who has spent half a lifetime in arms against the Sea Wolves, would be for the good fate of any save the Sea Wolves themselves, at this time. You speak of Britain as though it were one, my Lord Dubricius; but we are from many tribes and many peoples. Some of us were bred up in the last lingering ways of Rome, some in the free wilderness where Rome's shadow scarcely fell. We are from the broad hills of Valentia, from the marshes of the East and the mountains of the Cymri. Myself,

I am not of this land at all, save by ancestry, but was born and bred in Armorica beyond the Narrow Seas. We have only one thing to bind us together, we are the Bear's Companions, and our swords belong first to the Bear and *then* to Britain. That is a thing for you to remember, my Lords of the Council."

He of the bird's-nest beard leaned forward abruptly. "You speak with a loud voice, Bedwyr, Lieutenant of the Bear; yet one remembers that there are but three hundred, or maybe a few more, of you."

"How many rode with Alexander of Macedon when he set out to conquer the world?" inquired the deep singer's voice behind me with great sweetness. "He called them his Companions, too."

There was a long, long pause in the Council Chamber, and the scratching of the clerks' quills was silent. Very slowly the Bishop bowed his head and sat thinking, the thick blue-white rolls of his jowl resting on the fine embroidered stuff of his mantle, his eyes half closed. In a while they flashed open again, making their usual disconcerting change in his face, and he straightened himself in his chair. "Let me be clear as to this before we carry the matter further. What, precisely, are your demands? Not of necessity the High Kingship for yourself?"

"Not of necessity the High Kingship for myself, but that it shall not be set upon any man, at this present time."

"And why does it seem to you that the thing will come better at another time?"

"When this spring's fighting is over, if the victory is ours, we may have leisure to fight among ourselves, with the wolves driven off to a safe distance. If we taste defeat, then we shall be dead, and all need to choose a new High King gone from us with our last breath." I stared around the Council table into face after face that looked back at me, in support, in rejection, in complete blankness. One of the more ancient Councilors had fallen asleep. "Father Dubricius, you speak of our need to choose a ruler before the Saxons come, but for the civil matters of state, surely this Council, this Senate, is competent, while for all that has to do with the leading of a fighting people, does not the Rex Belliorum suffice, as he did in the old days, when a confederacy of the Tribes, with no High King over all, would choose out one chief from among themselves to lead them on the war trail?"

[375]

Dubricius seemed to have withdrawn deep inside himself, his eyes half closed once more. Then again he opened them, not swiftly this time, but with a slow deliberation, and fixed them on my face as a man might look into the pages of a book that interested him.

"Yes," he said, when he had read enough. "I retract certain words of mine that I spoke just now. I believe, at all events, that you believe in this great Saxon thrust. Now tell me why?"

I remained standing, as though to sit down again would be to lose some advantage. I leaned forward with my hands on the table, and told again all that I had learned from our scouts, of the stirring beyond the Sea Wolves' borders, of the coming and going between the Cantii territory and the East Seax. Most of that, of course, was known to them already, but they had not before had the small pieces fitted together to form the whole picture. I told them of Ambrosius's views (which were indeed my own also) as to why the thrust should come now, when it had not come last year nor the year before; I told them of the likelihood that the Barbarians were at last learning to combine, and the men about the table listened and nodded wisely and listened again; and when I was done, a small buzzing murmur rose from them until Dubricius silenced it with a movement of the hand.

"So," he said. "You make out a good case, and clearly it is one that you believe in. . . . That, I have allowed already. You might still be mistaken."

"I might, though thirty years of the war trail give one something of an instinct in these matters. But Ambrosius had it also, and I never knew him to be mistaken."

There was another long and dragging silence, and in desperation I was just about to plunge in again, though indeed I did not know what more there was to say, when the Bishop turned his hand over and laid it flat on the table in a gesture of "Finish," and said most surprisingly, "No, nor did I."

He swept his gaze around the whole circle of the Council—and yet one knew that he had taken in every face as he came to it. "Brothers, shall we cast our votes on this matter? Will those of you who are in favor of leaving this choice to wait for a while, signify your judgment by putting your right hands on the table before you."

Aquila's hand and that of Perdius slammed on the table almost before he had finished speaking, and three other Councilors followed almost as swiftly; the lesser churchmen sat rigid with their hands in their laps; Ulpius Critas half raised his arm, then changed his mind and pretended to rub his nose, then changed again and laid three fingers on the edge of the table after all. Vericus of the bird's-nest beard took his time to think, then set his hand before him with a small decisive slap. One more Councilor refrained, and the Bishop, smiling a little sleepily, left his own hand lying where it was, big and plump and pale on the polished wood. The ancient was still asleep, and nobody troubled to wake him; the verdict was clear enough without his vote.

I parted from my grimly triumphant escort within the gates of the Governor's Palace, and went on home, to find that one of the scouts had come in and was sitting on his haunches half asleep in the corner of the courtyard where the evening sun yet lingered with a little warmth. He roused at the sound of my footsteps and was up with the swiftness of an otter, and came to meet me, touching joined palms to forehead in the gesture that the Dark People make before their chiefs.

Noni Heron's Feather was well known to me, a man half bred between the Dark People and our own, with the skill as a hunter and tracker that only the Dark People possess. I had followed the game trail with him more than once, and there are few better ways of coming to know a man than by hunting with him; and it was so that he had become one of the chief among my scouts.

"What word do you bring, Noni my friend?" I said, stooping to fondle Cabal's great gray-muzzled head as he came to greet me.

He thrust the long black hair out of his eyes, and stood up straight in his wildcat-skin mantle, as he had seen the Companions do when they spoke with me on parade occasions. "The Sea Wolf who walks by the name of Cerdic has gathered his war bands and moved up from the hunting runs of the Cantii, driving much beef cattle with him on the hoof, and has made his camp two days eastward of the frontier on the old track under the North Chalk. In other places also, the Wolves are driving off the herds. Indeed, that I tell as a thing from my own heart, for they have driven off the red cattle from my father's village, and if my father's folk had not contrived to hide the cows in calf among the forest, next winter they would have starved." He paused for breath, for he had told the thing at a racing speed. "Another thing I tell, but this thing not of my own knowing: Erp the Otter bade me bring you the word and say that he will come in a while and a while when he has seen what follows, and tell it again himself, but that meantime you should know as soon as might be." He paused again, a little anxiously, for in general I did not like secondhand information. But from those two, I knew it might be relied on.

"So?"

"Erp came from the edge of the Great Water, that way—" He pointed south and eastward. "And met me at a certain spot, and bade me tell you that he had seen three boats come in to the place that you call Dubris."

"War boats?" I asked quickly.

He shook his head. "Na, not the long war boats, but broad-bellied like a woman in whelp, and out of them, men carried ashore new weapons rust-spotted with salt, and ironbound caps, and barrels, and one of the barrels broke open and out came much sawdust, and packed in the sawdust—" He broke off yet again, searching this time for the right word, his fingers making flickering filigree patterns over his own body. "War skins, like this—like salmon skins."

"Mail shirts," I said. "So they still have to bring in their best sarks from the Rhenus armorers, do they?"

"Mail shirts? That is the word? Aiee! I will remember." He came a light half step nearer. "My Lord the Bear, one thing more I tell. I heard it spoken of around a Sea Wolves' campfire, while I lay hid in the shadows beyond the firelight—and since, in other places also: they say that they have chosen out Aelle of the South Seax to be Battle Lord of them all, of all the tribes of the Sea Wolves, and lead them on the war trail!"

Like all his kind, Noni betrayed nothing through his eyes, but I think, from the almost prick-eared look on the rest of his face, that he wondered why I laughed.

CHAPTER TWENTY-NINE

Badon Hill

SUNSET was past, but the web of light still lingered behind the hills northward, and the nights are never very dark in midsummer. And from the hawthorn-crested barrow that was the highest point of the camp, I could look out over the clustered wattle huts of the regular garrison (we always kept a small garrison there, even in times of so-called peace, for Badon Hill was one of the main strong points in Ambrosius's system of defense in depth) and make out still the shape of the surrounding country. A familiar shape, for I served along the northern frontiers when I was a boy.

I could see how the huge hill shoulder thrust out from the main mass of the Downs, commanding the Ridgeway and the sweep of the White Horse Vale, and the pass where the road dives southward through the bare rounded turf hills. Once through that pass and into the rich lowlands beyond, the land would lie open to the invaders, to swing westward through the lead-mining hills into the reed and withy country south of Aquae Sulis—we might be able to do something there, but it would mean holding a perilously long and slender line, and the marshes would hamper our cavalry—and so on to the coast, and the main strength of Britain neatly sliced in two behind them. It was the old game, the same game as they had tried at Guoloph, twenty years ago. But between the Sea Wolves and all these things, like a giant on guard, stood Badon Hill with its triple crown of dikes and ramparts that had been a stronghold to our British forebears before even our Roman forebears came.

If the White Horse Vale is the gateway into the heart of southern Britain, then Badon Hill is the key to the gate. It remained to be seen whether the Saxons could turn it. . . .

Ambrosius had been right. In the face of our growing cavalry strength, they had dared delay no longer in mounting their great attack. And for the first time in their lives, it seemed that the Saxons were indeed learning to combine. With Aelle of the South Seax for their chosen War King, and Oisc for his lieutenant, they had drawn together, the Jutes of Cantii Territory and the Tamesis Valley settlements, the East Angles and the Northfolk and Southfolk of the old Icenian horse country. Up from the south and swarming down the Ridgeway from north of the Tamesis, they had come, to converge at last on the White Horse Vale; and all the way, we had harried them, by flank attacks from Durocobrivae and Calleva, by night raids and ambushes, and the dog-pack tactics of slingers and mounted archers on their lines of march by day, striving by every means in our power to slow them up and thin their ranks. It had had some effect, but not enough, we could not spare sufficient light troops for the task; and the last messengers to come in had reported that the enemy had joined forces and were camped for the night astride the Ridgeway some six miles off, and that despite the valiant efforts of the light troops who were now keeping watch on them, they still numbered some seven or eight thousand men.

Against them we could muster not much over five. But we had the cavalry.

Below me in the camp where the light of the fires was biting more sharply as the last of the daylight died, arrows and fresh bowstrings were being given out, while men with torches moved along the picket lines, checking foot shackles, and from the field forges came the ring of hammer on anvil where the smiths and armorers were at work on last-minute repairs. And from the cooking fires the smell of the evening stew began to mingle on the air with the tang of woodsmoke and horse droppings.

I had called the Council of War to sup with me, for when there is not much time to spare, it serves ill to waste it by eating and conferring separately when both may be done together, and so in a little, Aquila the firstcomer tramped into the light of the council fire that burned almost at the foot of the bush-grown barrow, flinging back the heavy blood-red folds of his cloak, and half turning to speak to Bedwyr, who stepped out of the shadows be-

hind him, into the fire flicker that touched as though with explor-
ing fingers the pale feather of hair at his temple. And I went down
to them, with old Cabal stalking at my heels.

Perdius was the next to join us, and little grim Marius who commanded the foot of the main war host. The Lords of Strathclyde
and the North, and the princes of the Cymri, for I too had sent
out my own Cran Tara that spring; and Cador of Dumnonia,
grayer than when we hunted together in the spring before I sailed
for Gaul, thicker in the shoulder and inclined to a paunch; and
when the stewpot and baskets of barley cakes had already been
set beside the fire, Cei arrived, clashing with cheap glass jewelry,
from our sister fort across the road valley, where he held command
of tomorrow's left cavalry wing.

So we ate, and while we ate, worked out with bits of stick and
ale cups and daggers, the pattern—so far as one can ever make
such a pattern in advance—of tomorrow's fighting.

When the food was eaten and the War Council ended, and the
captains and leaders gone their own ways, I went to put on my war
shirt. The day had been hot, and in summer no man wears link
mail more than need be; and there would be little leisure for arm-
ing in the morning. Old Aquila walked with me, for the bodyguard
was camped beyond the garrison huts, and so his way was mine.
Before the mud bothy where my personal standard drooped on its
spear shaft by the doorway, we checked, and lingered looking out
over the great curve of the Downs silvered now by the moon, and
by very contrast with the quiet of the summer night beyond the
ramparts, the awareness of tomorrow's battle was strong on us.

"We have waited a long time for this," Aquila said.

"Ever since we drew breath after Guoloph, I suppose. Twenty
years. And yet it seemed at the time, just for that one time, that we
had fought the greatest fight that ever there would be between us
and the Saxon kind. And afterward—"

I hesitated, and he said quietly, "A new Heaven and a new
Earth?"

Cabal nosed at my hand, then began the old familiar pretense
at savaging my wrist in his great jaws, until I took it away and began to gentle his ears as he wished.

"Something of the kind. Most of us were young, then, and drunk with victory. Now there comes a greater fight, and we grow old and sober."

"So—and afterward?"

"If God gives us again the victory—the old Heaven and the old Earth patched up to seem a little more secure. A few gained years in which men may sow their fields in reasonable hope of reaping the harvest."

Aquila's harsh hawk face was remote in the moonlight, as he looked far off between the dark bothies toward the rim of the Downs, every line of it deep cut as a sword gash; and under the frowning black brows, I had a feeling that it was not the shape of the rounded slopes against the sky that he was seeing, but something further and beyond. "Even that might be worth whatever price was asked for it."

Abruptly he turned to me. "Bear Cub, will you do something for me?"

"I expect so," I said. "What is it?"

He pulled the flawed emerald from his signet finger.

"Take this in charge, and if I die tomorrow and Flavian lives, give it to him to wear after me."

"And if you do *not* die tomorrow?" I said quickly, as though by that I could turn the thing aside.

"Then give it back to me at sunset."

"And how if I am no more weapon-proof than you?"

"The mark is not on your forehead yet," Aquila said, and put the ring into my hand.

I stowed it in the little pouch of leather hanging around my neck inside my tunic, in which I kept sundry other matters of my own. "Until sunset, then. Maybe we shall meet in the thick of things, tomorrow."

"Maybe," he said, and touched my shoulder, and went on his way toward the guards' part of the camp.

When he was gone, I turned into the bothy behind me, where a lantern hung from the center pole and my war shirt from its wooden cross against the wall. I did not call Riada, for the mail was laced at the side, and could be put on easily enough, not like the kind one pulls on over the head, and which is all but impossible to get into without help. I took it down and heaved into it, and was busy with the lacing when a step sounded outside, and Bedwyr ducked in through the low door hole.

He sat himself down on the packsaddle which as usual served the purpose of a chair, and watched me as I drew the broad thongs through the eyelet holes. "Artos, what do we take for our badge tomorrow?"

We still kept up our old custom of riding into action with a sprig of some flowering thing tucked into helmet comb or shoulder buckle—brown feathered rushes in the East Coast years, or sometimes yellow loosestrife or the little white many-thorned roses of the sand dunes; heather in the Caledonian years ("Taking Heather" had come to be the term men used in those years for joining the Companions). It was a privilege jealously guarded from the rest of the war host, a flourish, a grace note that was ours alone. But there was neither feathered rush nor royal heather on Badon Hill. Wild cranesbill along the foot of the chalk ramparts, but the blue flowers would be limp and dead before the first charge.

The grass for my bed had been cut from the northwest face of the hill, where it grew long and thick in tawny waves, for the fall of the land was too steep for the horses that had trampled it flat elsewhere. A few stalks of it were spilling out from under the old half-bald otter skin that Riada had spread for me to lie on, wisps and feathery shreds of seeding grasses and among them the withered head of a moon daisy. I stooped and picked it up, thinking suddenly how the steep drop of the hillside there was freckled white with the swaying flower heads.

Nowadays we number the moon daisy among the flowers of God's Mother; the gold for her love and compassion, the white for her purity, and the raying petals for the glory that shines about her. But underneath in the warm dark places we have not forgotten that the flower of the moon belonged to the Lady, the White Goddess, before ever men gave it to the Maiden Mary. The Church, claiming as she does that the Old Ones have no place left in the people's hearts, must forget that, or pretend to forget, and I knew that if I and my Companions were to ride into the coming battle with the flower of God's Mother for our badge, it must help to strike the weapon against me from the Church's hand, while still, for those of us who still held to the Old Faith, the old meaning would be there. Also it would show up well in the dust and turmoil

[383]

of the fight. I looked down at Bedwyr as a man sharing an unspoken jest with his brother, and tossed him the limp wisp of flower head. "This would make a fine panache, and there's plenty on the west side of the hill; easily picked out in battle and surely most suited of all flowers to a Christian war lord and his Companions."

And I saw by the quirk of that most devilish eyebrow, that he took my point. "Give it fifty years, and the harpers who sing tomorrow's battle after us will tell how Artos the Bear rode into Badon Fight with a picture of the Virgin on his shoulder."

I was finished with the lacing of my war shirt and began to fasten the shoulder buckle. "If there are any harpers of our own people still singing in fifty years' time."

Bedwyr was playing with the withered moon daisy, twisting the limp stem between his fingers. He tipped back his head to look at me through half-shut eyes, still fiddling.

"Not so did you speak to the war host a while since."

"I have the oddest fancy to win this battle," I said, testing the buckle, "and choose my words to the war host accordingly."

"Sa! That was a magnificent harangue you gave us."

"Was it?" I had no clear idea now of what I had said. The usual kind of thing, I suppose. It had not seemed so usual at the time.

It had been just at sunset, and my shadow had streamed away from me forward over the hilltop with a vast fiery arrowhead of sunlight between the straddled legs, and I remembered the coppery glare of the sunset on the faces of the war host turned up to mine, answering to me so that I could play on them as Bedwyr played on his harp. And that and the length of my shadow had filled me with a drunken sense of being a giant.

"You should always speak to your war host before battle, at sunset with the fires behind you," Bedwyr said. "That is for any leader. It would make even a small man look like a tall one, and a man of your height becomes a hero-giant out of our oldest songs; a fit rider, half a hillside high, for the Sun Horse of the White Horse Vale, with the seven stars of Orion for the jewels in his sword hilt."

("A sword of light with the seven stars of Orion for the jewels in its hilt.") I seemed to catch again the echo of Ambrosius's voice on the night before he died. But Bedwyr had not been there, only Aquila and I.

"I will remember another time," I said, and reached for my sword.

We made the late night round of the pickets and guard posts together, as we had made them on so many nights before. There is always something strange, something not quite canny, in making the rounds of a camp at night; the increasing stillness that comes at last to be broken only by the fretful stamp of a horse from the picket lines, or a standard stirring in the night wind, the spear gleaming out of nowhere across one's path in the moonlight, to vanish as one speaks the password. It is a little like moving through a world of ghosts or, alternatively, like being a ghost oneself. One's own footsteps seem unnaturally loud, and any incident, the face of another waking man glimpsed in the red glow of a dying campfire, seems fraught with meaning and significance that it would not bear in the daytime.

So it was with Medraut's face, that night, suddenly seen in the flare of a picket-line torch. By day, to pass Medraut coming up from the horse lines was the merest commonplace of life, save for the vague sense of a shadow passing between me and the sun which any sight of him always woke in me; but at night, that night, in the dark solitude of waking men in a camp full of others "sleeping on their spears," the brief unmattering moment stands in my mind even now as vivid as a duel.

Yet he only moved aside to give me right of way among the harness piles, spoke something of having thought at exercise that the big gray might be going lame, and melted on into the dimness of the moon.

Bedwyr glanced after him, and said, "The odd thing is that in some ways he is very much your son."

"Meaning that in the same circumstances, I also should be down at the picket lines playing leech to a horse that I thought might be going lame? It is not really the horse that he cares about, you know."

"No," Bedwyr said, "he cares no more for his horses than he does for his men. But tomorrow will be his first action in command of a squadron and he cannot bear that anything should go amiss under his leadership, be less than perfect as he sees perfect. . . . I was thinking rather of a certain capacity for taking pains, together with a conviction that if a thing must be done, it is needful to do it oneself." We walked on for a few paces between the horse rows, and then he added thoughtfully, "Yet if he has that conviction, assuredly it is the only one he has. In all these fighting years, he has never learned to care for anything beyond the fighting; for him it is enough to strike, without heed as to the thing he strikes for. He likes to kill—the actual skillful process of letting out life—that is a thing that I have met only a few times among fighting men."

"He is one of the destroyers," I said. "Most of us have something of destruction in us, I suppose, but mercifully not many are destroyers through and through. Dear God! That I should speak so! It was I who made him what he is!"

"How?"

"His mother ate him as a she-spider eats her mate, but it was I who gave him to her destroying love."

Neither of us spoke again until we were clear of the horse lines and into the moon-whitened space that lay between them and the wagon park; and there Bedwyr checked as though to tighten a slipping sword buckle. He said at half breath, and with an extraordinary gentleness, "Say the word, Artos, and he shall find an honorable death in tomorrow's fighting."

The long silence that followed was ripped asunder at last by the sudden murderous scream of Pharic's hawk, which he had with him in his bothy.

I stared at Bedwyr in the moonlight, sickened, and then angry, and then neither. "You would take that stain on your hands for my sake?"

"Yes," he said, and then, "But you must speak the word."

I shook my head. "I can't cut this particular knot with a sword; not even yours. You made no such offer the first time, the last time that we spoke so of Medraut."

"I had not had him in my squadron, then . . ." Bedwyr said.

I did not ask his meaning. Probably he could not have told me, if I had. Medraut committed none of the evils that can be put into words; it was not in what he did, but in what he was; no man may hold the hill mist between his thumb and forefinger nor catch the hovering marsh light in a grain jar.

The clouds blew up from the south that morning, their shadows sweeping like charges of cavalry over Badon Hill and down the long bay of the Downs; like the ghosts of armies that had fought there when the world was young. Turn southward, and you could see the wind coming, laying over the ripening grasses in silvery-brown swathes like the waves of the sea. Turn north again, and from where I stood on the crest of the bush-grown barrow, I could see the whole bay of the White Horse Vale with its flying cloud shadows, rising to the gentler hills again at its farther side. Badon Hill thrust out from the main mass of the Downs a great summer-tanned shoulder, high over the Vale, so that one looked down upon it as a buzzard circling on wind-tilted wings must do. I could see the green Ridgeway with its ragged line of hawthorn trees passing scarce the throw of a slingstone below the strong green wave-lift of our ramparts, dipping to cross the paved road from Corinium where it climbed more gently out of the Vale, to strike southward through the pass; and beyond, where the steep swell of the Downs upheaved itself once more into the sunlight from the morning shadows of the pass, the triple turf ramparts of our sister fort, that the garrison in Badon had always called the Cader Berywen from the sour hill-juniper scrub that speckled the ditches between its earthworks. And everywhere, lining the mouth of the pass, among the thorn scrub of the downland flanks, and thronging the turf ramparts of the forts, was the gray blink of sun on spear blade and shield boss and helmet comb, and the flecks and flashes of color where Marius's standard flew with Cei's flickering cavalry pennants above the triple-staged entrance of Cader Berywen, or where Cador and young Constantine gathered their war bands beneath the saffron-stained banner of Dumnonia, and the tattered Red Dragon of Britain lifted and half flew from its spear shaft in the midst of the Companions where they stood or sat at ease on the grass about me, each man with his arm through his horse's bridle. There was plenty of time, now, and it is not good to keep men or horses longer than need be in the last stage of waiting.

Signus, who smelled what was coming, snorted down that proud imperial nose of his, tossing his head so that my buckler clanged against the saddlebow; old Cabal lifted his gray muzzle and snuffed the wind, and Bedwyr, who had just ridden up on his raking sorrel, turned beside me and laughed in the old fierce gaiety that had always come upon him in the time before fighting. He no longer carried his harp into battle as he had used to do, but with the knot of moon daisies white in his shoulder buckle, he looked as though he were riding to a festival.

There was a sense of pause, a sense of rising tension, as when the wine in a slowly tilted cup comes to the rim and rises above it and hangs there an instant before it spills over. And in the waiting moments one had time for little things, for the dark crescent-winged swifts darting along the flanks of the Downs, as unaware of us, it seemed, as they were of the cloud shadows drifting by; the fading milky scent of the last pinkish blossom on the hawthorn trees, the way the renewed leather lining of my war shirt chafed my neck where the armorer had made a clumsy job of it. I thrust a finger inside the neckband, seeking to ease it, and tried not to watch Medraut walking his black horse up and down at the foot of the barrow, pausing in passing to break down with his foot the blue cranesbill that grew almost on the edge of last night's fire scar, and grind it with absorbed precision to pulp under his heel.

The scouts had come in soon after dawn while we were snatching a hasty morning meal, to report the Saxons stirring, but it must have been within two hours of noon when, maybe two miles off along the ridge of the Downs, there came a shadow, not much darker at first than the cloud shadows, but not traveling with the wind. The Saxon war host was in sight.

I waited a short while longer, the chiefs and captains murmuring about me; then spoke to Prosper, my trumpeter. He was growing gray-muzzled like the rest of us, but his wind was as good as ever, and he put the silver mouthpiece of the aurochs horn to his lips and sounded the View. There was a moment's silence, and then like an echo the call was tossed back to us from the ramparts of Cader Berywen.

Other horns and trumpets were sounding now, the voices answering each other to and fro across the valley; and the great camp of Badon, which a few moments before had been a place of waiting, sprang into eager life, as the fighting companies made for their appointed places, some to guard the entrances against enemy surprise, or man the northern ramparts where great piles of throw stones waited for hurling down on the heads of the Saxon host, while the rest went swinging out through the wide gateway and downhill into the pass.

I was mounted by that time, and sitting my great old Signus on the crest of my lookout place. I was like Janus, half of me turned upon the British line that was forming like a great threefold chain slung across the pass to the south between Badon and Cader Berywen, half of me turned with straining eyes upon the shadow that was not a cloud shadow creeping slowly nearer along the high roof ridge of the hills, deepening to a stain like that of old spilled wine, to a spreading swarm of ants. And then, far off still, and soft with distance, came the booming of a Saxon war horn; and Prosper beside me again raised the horn to his lips and sent the bright notes crowing their defiance across the warm summer wind. Save for those who would remain on guard, the great camp was emptying about me like a cup. Only my own Companions were left now, and they also were swinging into the saddle, squadron after squadron with the spear pennants fluttering, heading at a trot out through the gateway.

Bedwyr was beside me again, his horse dancing. He shouted to me that all was in order. I nodded, still watching the nearing swarm. I could see now how even as they rolled toward us their flanks were torn and harassed by the flying knots of light horsemen that skirmished about them, and my heart went out to Maelgwn and Cynglass, to the men and the little fiery ponies of my own hills. But it was a vast host, still, a spreading murk of men that engulfed half the countryside like the shadow of an advancing storm.

"Sa, here comes the Darkness," Bedwyr said.

"If ever you prayed to any God, pray now for the strengthening of the Light."

He leaned a little from the saddle, and set his hand on my shoulder. "I have never known how to pray, unless maybe through Oran Môr, the Great Music—I will make you a song of light driving out darkness, a song of the lightnings of the war host of Artos, when the day's work is over." And he wheeled his horse and clattered off to his post with the Companions. And I was alone with Riada sitting his horse just behind me, and the scouts and messengers who came and went.

The advancing darkness had been without sound at first, but

now there began to be a soft quiver in the earth rather than the air, the tramp of thousand upon thousand feet, the faint surf of shouts and weapon ring; the merest ripple of sound that came and went at the will of the summer wind that tossed the moon daisies to and fro, but gathering strength, solidifying into the distant earth-shaking many-voiced thunder of an advancing war host. A fold in the Downs had swallowed the vanguard from sight, and then along the nearer ridge, maybe half a mile away, ran a dark quiver of movement, and over it lifted the rain pattern of upraised spears and the white gleam of the horsetail standards; more and more, and then the brown of the war host, with our light horsemen wheeling and re-forming about them and sending in their flights of arrows and slingstones—growing sparse now—as chance offered. The sun splintered into shards of light on shield boss or spear blade, among the onward-rolling mass, and the deep crash of tramping feet and the formless surf of shouting seemed to spring forward ahead of them.

Then I wheeled Signus, and with young Riada his half length behind me, rode down from my vantage point and out by the wide three-angled gate gap to take my place at the head of the Companions. For a few moments, as I came out onto the open hillside, I checked Signus and sat looking down to the road far beneath me, and up the slope beyond to the green triple crown of Cader Berywen, seeing the whole battle line slung between.

Marius with the pick of the veteran foot fighting troops; and forming the center among them, clearly recognizable by their blood-red cloaks, the old royal bodyguard; on either side, the javelin men and light horse of the irregulars, forming the wings. Seeing also, as the advancing Saxons would not see it, the glint of weapons and the small movement of men and horses among the thorn scrub that swept about the lower slopes of the Downs and closed in upon the ancient track where it dropped toward the broad paved road into the heart of Britain.

Then I touched heel to Signus's flank and rode on around the flank of the hill. Well back beyond the crest, the Companions were waiting, squadron by squadron, each with their captains out in front; Bedwyr and Flavian, my son Medraut and black-browed Pharic and the rest; they tossed up their spears in salute, and my place was waiting for me as the familiar glove waits for the hand.

Beyond, farther down the hillside and screened from the road by a dense bank of elder and thorn scrub, the main light wing of the cavalry waited, the horses fidgeting and swishing their tails against the midges.

The sounds of the nearing Saxon host, which from here had been blanketed by the bulk of Badon Hill, began to swell and sharpen again, but much of the ragged shouting had fallen away, so that I knew that the skirmish troops had broken off action and dropped back to their appointed stations. Yet a long time we waited, while the sounds drew a little nearer, until at last the van of the war host came sweeping down into the mouth of the pass, and the roar of their coming burst upon us like the roar of a charging sea when a sand bar goes. We could not see them as yet, we could see only the farther part, even of our own battle line—but the boom of war horns, the ominous roar of joining battle, told us that their van had met with our own advance troops, and the high note of rage and furious anguish cried aloud the crossfire of arrows from the thorn scrub on their flanks, and one could sense how they checked an instant, then drove forward at an increased speed. I rode forward alone, save for my trumpeter and young Riada, to a little spur of the hillside from which I could see what went forward.

The roar of conflict beat up to me now, with the vast impersonal roar of storm water on a rocky coast, and the whole bell-mouth of the pass was a solid mass of Saxons. At first sight it seemed that this whole bay of the White Horse Vale had turned to armed men, a dark Barbarian tide surging up against the slim barrier of our battle line. Here and there among them men were falling under the flights of arrows, but with such a war host as this, the hidden archers could do little save fret and thin the ranks a little, while the main rush of the Saxon vanguard swept on, their deadly loping battle trot quickening almost to a run. Again Saxon horns and old legionary trumpets flung defiance back and forth between the hosts, and again I heard, as I had heard it so often before, that long-drawn terrible German battle shout that began as the merest cold whisper and rose and rose until it beat in waves of sound upon brain and breast and belly, and then answering it, the shorter, sharper yell of the British.

The Sea Wolves were within casting distance of our main first defense line now, and as the long-drawn battle howl shattered on its final beast note, a volley of throwing axes came rattling against the British shields. Looking down from my high place as God might look down upon the battlefields of men, I saw a gap crumble here and there in our own ranks, but for the most part our men were used to the little deadly missiles, and knew how to cover themselves, and wherever a gap opened in the front rank, the man immediately behind stepped forward to fill it, so that even as the Sea Wolves sprang in across the last few yards, the British ranks were whole again. Next instant the forefront of both war hosts crashed together with a yell and a terrible thunder of meeting shields that no man who has heard it can ever forget.

For an incredibly long time our first line held the full weight of the Saxon charge, but at last, slowly, they began to yield ground. Slowly, slowly, the bright stubborn lightnings of leaping spear and sword blade never for an instant ceasing, they were giving back and back until they merged into the second line behind them, and again the Saxon thrust was held. The boil of battle that had been concentrated at first across the road and the valley bottom was spreading now up the flanks of the Downs among the thorn scrub on either side, where no battle line could be kept; and scarce a spear's throw below the waiting cavalry the woods were full of struggling knots of warriors, the clash of arms and the high-panted war cry, the thrum of parting bowstring and the squeal of a wounded pony and the death cry of men. And beyond, where the main conflict set the whole valley roaring as a narrow gorge when a river bursts together in spate, our first and second lines, fighting desperately for every foot they yielded, were being forced back, slowly and dreadfully upon the third, the last line, the only line of reserve we had. I had given orders that the task of the center was less to hold ground than to kill men (and truly, if I had not, I think that they would have died where they stood, and Britain gone down into the dark, that day), and most assuredly they were killing men. . . . The ground that the Saxons pressed over was thick with bodies, and Saxon bodies more than British, though there were enough of British bodies, too; God knows that there were enough and more than enough. . . . And always, in the midst of the ragged line, I caught the blood-red color proudly marking out the dwindling ranks of Ambrosius's old bodyguard.

We no longer had three lines of defense, but one, one seething line that bowed and wavered like a ribband in a high wind, yet somehow never parted, one last supple barrier of gray iron through which it seemed that the Saxon war host could not break.

For a time—short or long—the close-grappled line reeled and strained to and fro, as the ebb and flow of battle set now this way and now that, and then the British broke their hold and drew back, but as a wild animal draws back to spring, and with a bound and a roar, sprang forward with uplifted spears. Again came that rolling thunder of shield meeting shield, for a long desperate moment the two war hosts strained together, locked and immovable; so I have seen wrestlers strain together, or a pair of antler-locked stags in the rutting season, neither for the moment able to gain the least shadow of advantage over the other. And then, with a slow long heave, the British seemed not so much to thrust the Saxons back as to lift up and pass over and engulf them.

By that time the white dust cloud was hanging half the height of the valley, but through it I could still make out dimly how the Saxons gave ground, slowly at first and then more swiftly, falling back in something like disorder upon their own reserves, who had not so far been engaged. Open ground littered with dead and wounded had appeared between Briton and Barbarian, and it was as though both sides paused to draw breath. I remember now, the quietness that rushed in to fill the place of the tumult as it died away, an acute and shining quietness, wind-haunted and filigreed with the churring of grasshoppers among the seeding grasses and the blue cranesbill flowers.

The dust cloud had begun to sink, and through it I saw Aelle of the South Seax, the War King, with his house carls about him and his white horsetail standards, come forward with his reserves. The pause was over and with a roar and a bellowing of war horns, the two hosts sprang again for each other's throats.

And again, after a sharp and bitter struggle, I saw the British battle line begin to give ground; slowly as ever, and contesting every yard of the way, back over ground that had been fought over before, back beyond it; they were level with the concealed cavalry wings now; and I knew that it was time to fling in the horse. And in that same instant, I saw what remained of the bodyguard—a score of men, maybe—led by old Aquila, heave forward from the rest of the battle line, cleaving like a wedge of red-hot metal into the battle mass of the enemy.

They too knew it was time for the horse, and were drawing the attention of the whole war host upon themselves to give the best possible chance to the cavalry charge; they were throwing away their lives for the price of taking the greatest possible number of the Barbarians with them. It was a superb and glorious piece of waste, one of those things that men do when for the moment they cease to be quite men, and walk with the high gods.

My hand was already lifting in the signal; Prosper raised the horn to his lips and the swift notes of the cavalry charge took wing across the valley, to be caught up before the last note had died, by the trumpeter on the ramparts of Cader Berywen. Among the thorn scrub a sword flashed up, and the next instant, with Perdius at their head, the cavalry broke forward and were away at a canter, at full flying gallop, their spears swinging down as they went.

I watched them away, as one watches one's hounds slipped on a boar, but there was no time to see how the charge took effect. I caught up my buckler, and sent Signus plunging back to rejoin the waiting squadrons of the Company. "Our turn now! Come on, lads!"

For us it must be the longer way around, for with the steep slope of the hill northwest, and the spread of the fighting up the flanks of it, it was impossible to bring a rear charge around that way without arriving in disorder that would rob us of half our striking power. We flung our curve right-hand-wise around Badon Camp, riding like the Wild Hunt, for we must have had the best part of a mile to cover. I heard the drum of the squadrons' hooves behind me and on either side; the wind of our going filled the standard so that the Red Dragon of Britain seemed to spread its wings in flight above us. We struck the Ridgeway and thundered down it toward its meeting point with the road south. Signus's flying mane whipped back over my buckler, and the round sods flew beneath his shod forehooves; and as we swung into the mouth of the pass, at full pitch of my lungs I raised the war cry of Arfon: "Yr Widdfa! Yr Widdfa!" and heard it caught up behind me into a challenge, into a paean.

From both sides the cavalry wings had driven home their charge, crumpling and driving inward the Barbarian flanks to jam their own center, breaking the force of the deadly thrust against the British battle line; and now it was for us to give the crowning blow.

We took the Saxon war host in the rear, crushing in the hastily formed shield-wall as though it had been a thornwork hedge. And

I saw before me a swaying and struggling mass of yelling, battle-crazed faces under horned and flanged helmets, a crimson deadly leaping of spears and short seax blades over the rims of the linden bucklers; and then it broke and crumbled back, and with a roar, we hurled through upon the reeling battle mass of the enemy beyond.

The battle of which I had decreed the pattern, and which, so short a while before, I had looked down on, magisterially aloof, seeing it spread below me in its entirety, became for me as for the youngest boy with a javelin, the few yards of howling turmoil closest at hand, the feel of my weapon striking home, the snarling face of the man next before me, the reek of blood and horse's sweat and choking chalk dust.

My spear broke in my hand at last, as I wrenched it from the body of a gigantic Saxon, and I flung the shaft away and drew my sword as we thrust on. I was making for the place where, dimly through the rolling dust cloud, I could glimpse the white horse standard with its crimson tassels and gilded skull that staggered to and fro above the mob, marking where Aelle of the South Seax fought among his house carls; and suddenly it seemed that the solid battle mass before me was thinning, breaking up as the mailed wedges of cavalry drove into it. The muzzle of a black horse swept up on my right, and snatching a glance that way, I saw Medraut flinging his squadron forward as though the battle were his alone; his face, with a small east-wind smile on it, was white as the moon daisies that he wore like a plume in the comb of his war cap, and his sword blade was blooded to the hilt and over the hand that held it.

An alley of clear space opened for an instant, and as I thrust Signus into it, a naked figure sprang across almost beneath his breast. The Saxons had learned long since that their berserkers were the most terrible weapon they possessed for use against cavalry. For a splintered and sickening instant of time, I saw the drugged, dilated eyes, the lean body reddened from head to heel, the wicked disemboweling blade; then, as the creature dived for Signus's belly, I took the only chance there was, wrenched the great horse away, and sent him up in a rearing half turn, screaming with rage, his hooves lashing for the man's head. It was a hideous expedient, for the least misjudgment of time or position would give the berserker a perfect opening for his belly thrust; as it was, hampered by the reeling throng about me, I doubt if I should have made it, but in the same instant, with a deep singsong snarl, Cabal crouched, and launched himself at the man's throat. Between the lashing forehooves I saw them go down together, and could wait to see no more . . . no more . . . but thrust on toward the white gleam of the horsetail standard that still showed above the sea of conflict. I was within half a spear toss of the royal shield-burg, when a young man—a chieftain to judge by his dragon-scale war shirt and the red gold about his neck—sprang in before me at the head of a yowling knot of his own kind, and caught at Signus's bridle, and clung on, and even as the horse reared and plunged squealing with fury, his sword rang against mine; and the westering sunlight, slipping over the downland shoulder into the shadows of the pass, fell full upon his face. And for a moment as his fellows swept forward to meet the squadron the fighting that boiled around us fell away. His war cap had been struck off and the wild mane of hair that sprang to his shoulders was red as a fox's pelt, and the eyes that blazed into mine were filled with a gray-green fire, a kind of furious laughter. And across the years that had made him a man and a leader of men, I knew him again, and he knew me. He shouted to me, "Did you not say that I should come again, and kill you if I was able?"

And I shouted back, "Or I you, Cerdic, son of Vortigern!" and caught his stroke with a shock of blade on blade that ran up my arm in numbing flight of pain sparks, and sent it spinning from his hand, then struck again, at the neck. I saw his face contort into a choking snarl, and the bright spurt of blood, and without a sound, he was gone among the trampling hooves and feet of the battle.

But the horsetail standard had also disappeared from sight.

Presently the host of the Saxons had become a mass of swirling separated war bands that swayed and surged to and fro, each battling desperately for itself; with the cavalry busy among them. They were breaking away in flying groups, and later still, at twilight, when people in houses would be lighting candles for the women to weave by, after the evening stew, we were hunting the defeated rabble of a proud and mighty war host down the White Horse Vale.

Not today, not today, would Britain go down into the dark.

CHAPTER THIRTY

Hail Caesar!

WE hunted hard and slew often, and I remember that we were singing as we rode, one of the old triumph songs out of the Western hills. The singing made me think of Bedwyr who had so often sung us home from battle, but in the deepening twilight I could see no sign of him, and there was no time for asking of this man or that. No time for feeling much, at all, neither for triumph—despite the singing of the squadrons about me—nor for grief; I was spent and empty as I rode, the empty husk of a thing created for the purpose of killing Saxons.

The dusk was almost deepened into the dark when we came to the place below where the Ridgeway crossed the Calleva road. There was a sickly smell to the place, and the ground, even down into the Vale, was cluttered with bodies, British and Saxon; and ahead of us the red gleeds of watch fires showed where the Barbarian host had left their wagon laager. We set up a shout, and settled down into the saddle for more fighting, but the men who had been left with the baggage train had joined the rout of their comrades and nothing and no one was left to draw seax against us. With one accord, the irregulars and a good part of the cavalry dropped out in search of plunder. I could have whipped them off, I suppose, as a hunter whips the hounds off a carcass, but it scarcely seemed to matter now what they did. I left them to their scavenging, and rode on with whoever cared to follow me. But I remember that there was no more singing, we were all too weary.

Indeed we carried the hunt little farther ourselves, but a few miles down the Vale, drew rein by a little chalk stream to breathe and water the horses; and knew as by common consent that for this night, the hunting was over.

The stream ran under the lee of a hazel coppice, and the snail-shine of the rising moon was silvering the world about us, and, unbelievably, in the hazy depths of the thicket a nightingale was singing. A big shadow loomed up beside me, and I saw that it was Cei, drooping in the saddle, with his buckler hanging almost in two halves at his shoulder.

"God! What a day! What a thundering victory! Is this all, or do we hunt them further?"

"Let them go," I said. "Tomorrow will be time enough to scour out the countryside—when we have learned our own losses and bound up our wounds." I was looking at the figures on the wood-shore, some still sitting their horses, some sliding like cramped old men from their saddles. Those who, for the most part, still wore somewhere about them the withered rags of a moon daisy had thrust up closest to me. There were maybe two squadrons of them, or rather less. "Is this all that is left of us?"

Someone laughed thickly in his throat, and I knew it for Owain. "Na, Pharic and his wild men dropped off to help rifle the baggage wagons."

"*I* did not, then!" Young Riada pushed up beside me. "I am my lord's armor-bearer."

"And there are likely a good few of us back among the wounded!" someone else put in.

"What of Bedwyr?" I asked after a moment. "Does anyone know?"

Flavian answered me, that time. "I saw him go down. No more than that."

And the nightingale was singing as it had sung in the old palace garden on the night small Hylin died.

In a while, when we had breathed and watered the horses, and ourselves drunk and bathed our hurts at the stream, I gave the order to remount, and got them going again.

The moon was well clear of the Downs by now, and as we turned the horses' heads back the way we had come, there shone out at us, from the turf of the Downs glimmering and gigantic, distorted by the slopeway of the hillside, the chalk-cut sacred Sun Horse of the White Horse Vale.

At the same time we saw, far up the curve of the Vale and sweeping closer, the flare of torches; and a few moments later caught the first faint throb of hooves. "Sa, they have rifled even the watch fires!" someone said. "They have finished with the wagons and remembered the hunt again."

A flying cloud of dark shapes was taking substance under the torches, heavy cavalry and men on little fiery mountain ponies; some of the light cavalry from the battle had come up, the riders leaning sideways in their saddles, with men on foot leaping along beside them clinging to their stirrups, and man after man carrying makeshift torches kindled from the Saxon watch fires, that streamed in mare's tails of flame above their heads. Signus stamped and snorted at the nearing fire, and the foremost of the wild riders saw the Red Dragon on the edge of the stream, and set up a great hoarse shout and swung toward us. In a few moments the first of them were dropping from their horses all around, then more and more until the whole loop of the stream was full of men and horses and the swirling, dancing flare of torches that drove out the white light of the rising moon. Some were dumb and dazed with utter weariness, others beginning to be drunk, as much with the aftermath of battle as with the honey beer that they had found in the wagons. One—a long lean man with a brilliant eye—capered wildly in an open spot, wearing a woman's flame-colored gown hitched to his knees; and another, dismounting from his weary horse while it drank, sat on the stream bank with his head on his knees, and wept bubblingly for a dead friend. It might as well have been myself. Many had twists of blood-soaked rag somewhere about them, and the horses too showed gashes on breast and flanks, so that some of them it was pitiful to see. Men and beasts alike made for the water—even those men who were already awash with Saxon ale, so that for a little, with the bathing of many hurts, as well as drinking, the stream below the torchlight must have run fouled and reddened.

They were all around me, also, a sea of torchlit faces turned up to mine as I sat the great battle-weary horse above them. Men were thrusting in for a closer look, to touch my knee or my sword sheath or my foot in the stirrup, and all I wanted was to get them into some kind of order and back as far as the wagon laager for the night. And then—even now I do not know how it started—one of the veterans, with enough years behind him to remember the old way of things and the last imperial troops still in Britain, set up a shout of "Hail Caesar!" And those nearest about him caught it up, and the thing spread like the ripples in a pool, until the whole of the war host—or such of them as were mustered there—were shouting, bellowing it out and beating it home upon their shields and the shoulders of their comrades. "Hail Caesar! Caesar! Caesar!"

Wounds and weariness were forgotten, and the whole night took fire about us and roared up in triumphal chaos. They plucked me from Signus's back and flung me up again onto a royal throne made of the shoulders of men; a tossing and swaying throng that lurched to and fro, the whole night lurching with it as the mob surged about us. Cei and Pharic with his tall Caledonians and the rest of the Companions fought their way in to make a bodyguard about me, baying as loud as any. I looked down on battered and filthy faces exultant in the torch glare, spears shaken aloft, a vast, blasphemously uproarious mob, and flung out my arms, shouting too—I do not know what, save that it was no order to be still. Few of them could have heard the words, anyway; but at sound of my bellow they ceased for a moment the roar of "Caesar! Caesar!" and began to cheer, a fierce hot thunder of cheering that rolled the breadth of the war host and curled back and burst upward in waves of sound that set the horses plunging. And then as the cheering sank, somebody cried out, pointing with a spear toward the great beast that pranced half-hillside-high, cut from the turf of the White Horse Down. And that cry too was taken up, and still carrying me shoulder high in their midst, they set off toward it at a stumbling run, the torch flames streaming out behind, until their speed slackened with the steepening slope of the ground.

The White Horse lost all shape as we drew nearer, becoming only a series of vast white scars across the turf, but never shall I forget the sight of swarming dark figures running low under the moon and the torches, panting up the steepening hillside toward it, myself in the midst of them, in the midst also of a kind of running fight among those who would take next turn when my bearers changed beneath me.

The crowd swelled moment by moment, as the men who had remained behind to tether the horses came panting after us, and others fresh from looting the wagons, some of them still on horseback, joined the comet tail of torches.

We were across the shallow outline ditch and out on the bare chalk now, and the featureless whiteness of it under the moon dizzied and made the head swim, so that any clump of couch grass or sprawl of rest harrow that had escaped the yearly scouring was good to let the eyes cling to, and I could feel the panting of my stumbling steeds under me, as they faced the last steep slope up which, like a royal road, the arched neck of the sacred horse ran to a head that had looked bird-small from the valley. In the midst of the lake of whiteness that was the head, a spear-blade-shaped island of grass, maybe four or five times as long as a man is tall, formed the eye, proud and open, staring back at the sun and the moon and the circling stars and the winds of the sky. In the very midst of this eye, the spark that is the Sun's answer and touch place, the divine point of power, where Earth Life and Sun Life meet and quicken, stood a rough boulder, a block of limestone, green on the north side with moss almost as the grass about it, but as the torches beat upon it, the probing glare picked out strange circles within circles of eternity, that the weather had all but worn away.

And on this great roughhewn boulder, where I think the forgotten kings of a forgotten people had been enthroned, they set me down for my own throning—not as High King, after all, but as Emperor, even as his own troops had crowned Magnus Maximus my great-grandsire Emperor. Assuredly no emperor of the Roman line ever had a stranger crowning, nor a stranger congregation to see it done. For by this time the uproar had called back the men from the villages who had rounded up their cattle and taken to the hills when they got word of the Sea Wolves coming, and sometimes I thought, though I was never sure, that I glimpsed little dark men in skins on the edge of the torchlight.

And I was made Emperor, I think, with something of the rites of every faith that could still claim a follower among the war host. Pharic and his Caledonians set a circle of seven swords point down in the grass about me, and in all that followed, no man entered the circle save between the two swords at my face, and I was chrismed with armor grease brought from the captured wagons, but the priest who anointed me was a wild-eyed creature who came out of the dark with the villagers, a Christian priest by his

frock of undyed sheep's wool and his shaven forehead, but he wore
the Sun cross carved from red amber around his neck, and he
made the King marks on my forehead and breast, feet and hands,
not in the Christian form but in older symbols. And my own men
brought a hastily made circlet of oak leaves from the hill spinney
close by, where the young leaves still retained a flush of their
springtime gold, and thrust it down on my head for an imperial
diadem; and someone—who, I never saw—hoisted an old cloak on
a spear point above the heads of the crowd and tossed it to those
nearest me, who caught and flung it about my shoulders. It was
ragged, and spattered at the hem with dried blood, but it was of
wine-red so deep and rich that in the torchlight it had the proud
glow of the Purple. I got up and stood before my war host while
they roared their acclamation, aware of the Purple and the Diadem
as though I were clothed in flame. My sword—I did not remember
having drawn it—was naked in my hand. I felt the great carved
stone at the back of my heel, and something in me, in the touch of
my heel against the stone, in my very loins that linked me with the
earth and the gods and the stones of the Earth, and the Sun and
the Power of the Sun, and in the thing in the dark at the back of
my head that came from my mother's world and knew the secret
of the strange concentric circle that my father's world had forgotten, told me that this was not a throne but a coronation stone like
the Lia Fail of the High Kings of Erin, a stone for the King to
stand on at his kingmaking, and I sprang onto it and flashed up
my sword to the shouting war host, and all around me a thousand
weapons were tossed up in reply, and for a while and a while I
knew my feet one with other feet that had been planted on that
flaking stone, and other men's hearts beating in my breast, and a
wild weeping exultancy swept through me and on through the human sea around me. And then behind the exultancy, my father's
world pressed in again and I knew soberly that I was a man wearing a crown of oak leaves and a tattered cloak that was almost, but
not quite, of the imperial purple, but that none the less, I was
chosen by these men, my men, to carry the ragged heritage; and
I had as much right to it as many another sword-made emperor
of Rome's latter years.

So I stood above them, alone in my circle of seven swords, and
looked down on the roaring sea of torchlit faces, chilled suddenly

by a foreshadow of the loneliness above the snow line. And when
at last the tumult sank enough for me to make myself heard, I cried
out to them in the greatest voice that I could muster, that it might
reach to the farthest fringe of them. "Soldiers! Warriors! Ye have
called me by the name of Caesar, ye have called me to be your
Emperor as your great-grandsires called mine, whose seal I carry
in the pommel of my sword. So be it then, my brothers in arms.
After forty years there is an Emperor of the West, again. . . . It
is in my heart that few beyond our shores will ever hear of this
night's crowning, assuredly the Emperor of the East in his golden
city of Constantine will never know that he has a fellow; but what
matters that? The Island of Britain is all that still stands of Rome-
in-the-West and therefore it is enough that we in Britain know that
the light still burns. We have fought today such a battle as the
harpers shall sing of for a thousand years! Such a battle as the
women shall tell of to the bairns at bedtime to make them bold,
and the young men whose fathers' fathers our great-grandsons
shall beget, shall speak of when they boast among themselves at
the harvest feast. We have scattered the Sea Wolves so that it will
be long and long before they can gather the pack again. Together,
we have saved Britain for this time, and together we will hold
Britain, that the things worth saving shall not go down into the
dark!" I must speak also to my mother's world. "But because I
am not Emperor alone, but Prince of Arfon and a lord in Britain,
because I am native-born and native-bred, and learned my first
words in my mother's tongue, I can claim to be yours as no other
emperor has ever been, and therefore I swear my faith to you now,
by the oath that we of the Tribes have counted most sacred since
first we came out of the West. And after, you shall swear your
faiths to me."

I sheathed my sword. Some oaths are sworn weapon in hand,
but that one must be taken with the hands empty, since it concerns
things that no man may hold. "If I break faith with you, may the
green earth gape and swallow me, may the gray seas roll in and
overwhelm me, may the heaven of stars fall upon me and crush
me out of life forever."

There was a moment's silence after I had sworn, and then a
tempest-roar of acclamation and a drumming of spear butts on
shield, such as even that night I had not heard before. But I was

[403]

so tired that it boomed and roared hollow in my ears as the sea in a cavern, and when I would have stumbled down from my high place, they had pulled up the circle of swords, and from all sides the chiefs and princes and the captains were thrusting in to kneel and set their hands over my battle-fouled feet. Connory the son of old Kinmarcus, Vortiporus of Dyfed, big wild Maelgwn my kinsman who held the reins of Arfon for me and had brought my own war bands down from the hills; young Constantine, dark and blazing as his father had used to be, but burning, I thought, with a steadier flame. In cold blood he might have been my enemy in this, but caught up with the rest, he swore his faith to me with the rest, and I knew that he would keep it. And among the others came Medraut my son. He cast himself down before me with the grace of a woman or a wildcat, and made the solid, ritual gesture of faith-taking into a thing as airy and delicate as though he played with a feather. Yet there was a filthy rag bound around his sword wrist, and the blood that clotted it was as red as any other man's, and the face he turned up to mine gray-weary, the face of a man who had spent all his fires. His eyes were without expression, not blank, but veiled over their secrets more closely than I had ever seen them before, so that one could see nothing but the blue color and the surface light reflected from the dying torches. "I fought well for you today, did I not, my father?"

"You fought well today, Medraut my son," I said, stooping to take his hands and raise him up, and so felt him shaking again. Dear God! Why must he always shake like a nervous horse? And once again the old sense of doom was upon me, a floating down of dark wings, because of the thing I could not see behind my son's eyes.

In the first gray light of a morning that had turned wild and squally, we returned to Badon, and heard the trumpets sounding from the green ramparts for watch setting. And those who were in the forts cheered us in through the soft rain, but we were far too spent to make a gallant entry.

The Saxon wounded had been dispatched in the usual way, and our own carried up to the hill fort and housed in the wattle huts that normally served the garrison; and cooking fires were bright in the rain under their ragged shelters of wet skins. Men came thronging around me, spoke to me, looked at me with alerted and

oddly lengthened gaze, and dazed and drugged as I was with the
aftermath of the day and night, I scarce thought to wonder
why. . . .

Presently there would be many things to see to. Perdius came
with a report of sorts, Marius hard behind him, almost before I
was dismounted. I listened, a little drunkenly, while they told of
Aelle of the South Seax dead among his house carls, and no sign
of Oisc among the bodies, nor of Cerdic. ("Maybe his own men
carried him away," I said. I could have sworn that my blade had
found the life.) While they reported on the numbers of dead and
wounded both in men and horses; while around us the camp clamored with demands for news, and the news itself shouted from man
to man.

I listened, and asked further details of this thing and that, the
present placing of troops, the supply situation. . . . And then at
last, as Signus was led away, I was free to ask, not Caesar's questions, but one question of my own. "Bedwyr—what of my old
Bedwyr?"

Someone pointed up toward the wattle barrack huts. "Up there,
my lord. They have taken the wounded up there."

For a moment I felt stupid with relief. "Not dead, then?"

"It would take more than a smashed elbow to kill that one,"
somebody said. But their tone toward me was subtly changed, and
they stood a little farther off, and when I turned to make my way
up to the barrack huts, I heard the burst of low eager voices behind me, and felt eyes following me as I went.

The scout Noni, who came running to me before I had gone a
dozen paces, was the first person to look at me with unchanged
eyes since I entered the fortress; but the eyes of the Dark People
seldom betray much, and his mind was full of other things. "My
lord, it is the great hound—him you call Cabal."

I stopped in my tracks. I had accepted in my heart that the old
hound was dead. "What of Cabal?"

"I have him under one of the wagons. It was in my belly to
hope that I might save him for you, but the hurt is too sore." He
laid a narrow brown hand on my wrist; it is very seldom that the
men of the Dark People or their near kin will touch a Sun man
(it is different, with a woman); but I think he must have hoped

[405]

very greatly to be able to come to me with the word that he had saved me my dog. "Come now, and do what must be done."

I turned aside toward the wagon park, Noni moving like a shadow beside me.

The disemboweling knife had done its work too well, but Cabal knew me and tried to thump his tail, though clearly the whole hinder part of him was as good as dead, and as I knelt down beside him and touched his great savage head, he even began a whisper of the old deep throat-song that had always been his way of showing his contentment in my company. I did what had to be done with my dagger and got up quickly to go, but checked a moment to look back at the small dark brooding figure of Noni Heron's Feather. "Who brought him up here?"

"He crawled some of the way himself—Aiee! He was a hero! The throat of the man he slew was torn clean out—and the rest of the way we carried him, one of the drivers and I."

I thanked him, and again checked on the edge of going my way, because he still seemed to be waiting for something. "What is it, Noni Heron's Feather?"

"Are you not going to take his heart?" He spoke with a hint of reproach. "He fought well for you; it was a great heart—worthy even of an emperor."

I shook my head. "That is not the way of the Sun People. We believe that to each man and each hound his own courage."

But I remembered Irach, as I went on toward the barrack huts.

The camp women were moving to and fro among them, and there was an all-pervading smell of pungent salves and torn humanity mingled with the acrid smoke of the horse-dung fires where the great water crocks were boiling, and once or twice, passing a doorway, I heard a man curse or cry out in pain. In the doorway of one bothy, I found Gwalchmai with a couple of the men he had trained to help him, laving his hands in a pail of reddened water. His face was blotchy and leaden with weariness, but he too looked at me with a suddenly arrested eye. "We laid him in your own quarters when the barrack huts grew overfull," he said in answer to my question, beginning to dry his hands on a piece of rag.

"Is he—" I began, and changed the end of the sentence. "How bad is the wound?"

"Much as an arrow through the elbow joint usually is," Gwalchmai said. "I have cut out the barb, and the wound itself will not kill him, unless he takes the wound fever. But—"

He hesitated an instant, and I heard myself speaking the last word after him. "But?"

"He has bled almost white—the arrow severed an artery."

I remember noticing the little red streaks in Gwalchmai's eyes, the eyes of a man who needs sleep and knows that he will not get it for a long while yet. I said, "Has he any chance at all?"

Gwalchmai made a small expressive gesture with his hands. "If he still has the life in him three days from now, I believe that he will live."

I found Bedwyr lying flat under the old otter-skin rug on my bed place, surprisingly flat, not like a grown man at all, but like a young boy, or a woman who has given birth. His left arm, swathed in bloody rags and laid across his body, seemed a thing that did not belong to him at all, and his fantastic face, when I squatted down beside him, had the whiteness of something long since drained of life, fine-lined and skeletal, empty shell and sea-scoured bone, so that for a long moment not so much of grief as of a curious stillness, I thought that he was already dead.

Then as one of the camp women, who had been pounding something in a bowl in the far corner of the bothy, got to her feet to take herself elsewhere, he opened his eyes and lay looking up at me, frowning a little as though not quite sure that either he or I were there. "Artos," he said after a while, half questioningly, and I do not think he knew that he had fumbled out his sound hand to find mine; and then, "Was it—a good night's hunting?"

"A good night's hunting," I said. "It will be a while and a while before the wolf pack can be done with licking its wounds and gather against us once more."

"You will—know about Aquila—all the bodyguard."

"I have Aquila's signet ring around my neck," I said. "He gave it into my keeping for Flavian, the night before."

He was quiet for so long after that, that I thought he was drifting off to sleep, but in a while he opened his eyes again and fixed them on my face, and I think that by a conscious effort he saw me for the first time. Until then he had only seen someone bending over him, and known that it was me. "Hail Caesar!" he said, and then—his voice was no more than a spent whisper, but that wild

mocking left brow of his flickered up and flew like a banner—
"Greatly am I honored! It is not given to every man to die in an
emperor's bed!"

I had forgotten that I was still wearing the diadem of withering
yellow oak leaves. I put up my free hand and pulled it off and let
it drop onto the old skin rug beside Bedwyr. "That was a jest in
vile taste! Listen to me, Bedwyr, if I am Caesar, you are Caesar's
captain. I cannot and will not do without my captain—listen to
me, Bedwyr, listen!" I was bending over him, trying to hold him
by the eyes, but already they were closing again. He was not listening any more—I doubted if he could even hear me, and I had to
reach him for my own sake I think as much as his, before maybe
he went altogether away from me. I bent lower quickly and kissed
him on the forehead. The taste of the black pain-sweat was sour
and salt on my mouth.

Then I got up and went out to find Flavian and give him his
father's ring, to take up the reins of the many tasks that waited for
Caesar's handling.

CHAPTER THIRTY-ONE

The Bargain

T HE mighty war host of the Saxon Confederacy had been broken asunder, and we drove the scattered war bands out of the White Horse Vale, out of the Tamesis Valley basin where they had had their settlements for twenty years and more; everywhere, from Portus Ardurni around to the Metaris, we flung them back to their coastal runs, and indeed I believe—I still believe— that we could have flung them into the sea.

But be that as it may, a day came, an autumn day with the gale booming up through the forest from Anderida Marshes, when Artorius Augustus Caesar (few men called him Artos any more) and three Wolf Kings, each with a picked handful of chiefs and captains behind them, met together in the main chamber of the long-derelict posting station on the Londinium road.

Outside, the horses stamped and fidgeted in the old cavalry corral, made restless by the wind, and the wind swooped all ways at once through the holes in the fire-scarred thatch, filling the place with smoke from the burning ashe logs on the hearth that had been cold for years. Always an ashe fire for a peace council—maybe because it is the only wood that will burn green? The green branch of all envoys and those who come in peace . . . ? We had brought our green branch in another form also, Flavian's young son. I had asked Flavian to bring the boy with him (to his mother it would be excuse enough that he was rising thirteen and it was time that he began to see the ways of men) for an added sign that we had no ill intent and the council was indeed one of peace, for no man takes his twelve-year-old son on the war trail. The Saxons had had the same thought, it seemed, and one of the East Anglian chieftains had come to the meeting place trailing a son like a half-trained puppy at heel. Anlaf and the Minnow; they had eyed each other under their brows at first, stiff-legged and wary; finally they had departed together, walking at arm's length. "They will come back when their bellies bid them," someone had said.

We sat, British and Saxon, facing each other across the hearth. I had Perdius with me, and Cei, and Cador of Dumnonia and young Constantine, and Flavian, sitting with the hand on which his father's ring blinked green as a wolf's eye in the firelight, clenched on his knee. I longed for the help and support of old Aquila's wisdom now, almost as deeply as I longed to have Bedwyr beside me.

But at least Bedwyr was alive. It had been five days before we could be sure that he would live, and then after all the wounded had been got back to Venta, the wound had turned sick, and he had been like to die all over again. That had been when I took him out of his bare little cell in the old officers' quarters and brought him across to my own, for Guenhumara to tend as once she had tended me. If I had not done so, I think he would indeed have died, for we had many sore wounded and there was fever among the troops that summer besides, so that Gwalchmai and his henchmen and even Ben Simeon had more work than any man could do with; and the wound kept shedding bone splinters, and reopened again and again, so that even now it seemed not sure that it was truly healing.

I looked across at the big fair men on the far side of the hearth. They were the lords of a broken kingdom, for the most part very young or very old. Cissa of the South Seax and Ingil of the East Angles were the young untried sons of newly slain fathers, one gray-bearded warrior with the long white scar of an ancient spear wound on his forearm spoke for the Northfolk and the Southfolk who had no king left to them at all. They were defeated, but they did not bow their heads, and despite myself, I felt the stirring of respect for them. They were Barbarians—they are still Barbarians, the Saxon kind, and they will be for centuries yet, for they are a younger people than we, and have never known in any way the Rule of Law. But they had courage, not merely the hot valor that flares in battle, but the courage that continues after the fires are out. These men were of the breed that had burned out Irach's village and slaughtered his kin; creatures who in some ways were less like men than beasts—the Sea Wolves that we had named them. But now they faced me as though we were equally met, and prepared to fight still for their continuance. And courage I have always loved in any man, no matter what else I have hated in him. Even in Medraut—even in my son.

So we spoke together, to and fro across the blazing ashe logs and through the smoke, with the boom of the wind through Anderida Forest sounding behind our words.

The graybeard had been chosen—for the garnered wisdom of his years I suppose—to act as spokesman for the rest, a gaunt old man with eyes under a gray shag of brows, that were as yellow as a wolf's, and teeth like an old wolf's, too, yellow and long in his beard. "We are the conquered, and you are the conquerors," he said. "Therefore it is for us to ask your mercy and for you to give it." But he did not ask so much as demand.

I leaned forward with my arms on my knees, and stared into his proud old face. "I am thinking of burning farmsteads and nuns slaughtered like cattle at their altar steps," I said. "I am thinking of living men mutilated on spent battlefields. I am thinking of a girl I saw once, whose spirit had been driven from her body not by one man's rape but by many. What mercy did you ever show, when yours was the conqueror's hand?"

There was a dim growl of voices from both sides of the fire. The old man gave the ghost of a shrug. "War is war. Nay then, we do not ask for mercy, we propose a bargain."

"A bargain?" I said. *"You* would talk of bargains with *me?"*

"A bargain which would be of advantage to us both. It is this, my Lord Artos the Bear. You shall grant to those of us who are left in Britain (the high gods know we are something fewer than we were) leave to abide in the coastal strips where our first settlements were made; cornland and timber and common land sufficient for our needs; and in return, we will undertake to hold those same southward and eastward facing coasts secure from the incoming of others of our kind."

"I seem to have heard such a tale before," I said. "Ah, but tell me now, in your country, beyond the North and Narrow Seas, is it a common custom for the hunter to bid the wolf in over his threshold?"

A brief, appreciative twinkle lit the wolf-yellow eyes of the old warrior. "Yet a wolf brought in over the threshold, warmed by the hunter's fire and fed the occasional bone from the hunter's hand, may become as a guard dog, in time, and bold to drive the wild wolf pack from the door."

"So Fox Vortigern thought, forty years ago."

There was a small, quickly controlled movement among the Saxons behind the spokesman, and looking up to meet the eyes of the man who had made it—the tall red-haired man leaning against the wall a little withdrawn from the rest, as though proclaiming, even with something of a flourish, his awareness that this talk of bargains was a thing that he had no part in—I saw again the newly healed scar on his throat, between the copper of the young beard and the gold of the collar he wore. It had been something of a shock to see Cerdic at the council fire, even though I knew by then that my blade had somehow missed the life spot. I suppose the first sight of a face one last saw in the moment of striking what one believes to be the deathblow, must always be a little as though one saw a ghost. The flickering gray-green eyes were hot with anger at any reference to his father, and yet I could see that he accepted the inference, because he knew as well as I did that it was just.

"Vortigern was one man, and Artos the Bear is another," said the ancient.

"Honey drips from thy tongue, Old Father," I said mockingly.

And he shook his head, coughing sharply as a puff of smoke curled across his face, suddenly pettish. "Na na, I speak the thing that all men know. Vortigern was one man and Hengest knew it, Artos is another, and we, the kings and chiefs who follow after Hengest, know that also. *We* are not fools!"

And looking into the fierce red-rimmed eyes of the old man as the smoke cleared, I knew that at least he was no flatterer of kings. "Yet though I were Tyr himself, and Woden, and the first Caesar joined in one, why should I accept this most dangerous expedient of keeping the brood of Hengest within my borders, when I have the strength to thrust them off the last headland into the sea?"

"Because maybe a thousand miles of coastline facing the Saxon and the Anglish and the Jute lands and needing always to be defended, needing always vigilance and a shield-front maintained, while the Scots folk creep in from the back with their long knives,

[412]

has its dangers also. I know the land that we come from, from Manopia and the Rhenus mouth around to the northern coast of Juteland; I remember the lean harvests and sea shifting among the sodden islands, and the folk driven too close for the poor land to feed them, and I tell you that so long as ever a wind blows from the east or from the north, my people and the Saxons and the Jutes will come down upon these richer shores." His face spasmed for an instant into a mass of sword-gash wrinkles, which was his nearest approach to a smile. "It was not we alone who lost good fighting men this summer."

I was silent, my chin sunk between my fists, hearing the wind roaring up from Anderida marshes; and I knew that what he said was true. I had known it for a long while past, or I would not have been sitting here today, not have bidden Flavian to bring the boy with him. If I had been still the man to whom Ambrosius gave his freedom and his wooden foil, I think that I should not have been there at all, that nothing would have seemed possible to me save to hurl the last Barbarian into the sea. But I had the first white hairs in my muzzle now. . . .

"Tell me why I should trust you the length of my thumbnail?" I said at last, lifting my head from my hands.

"Sa, I will tell you: over that way"—he jerked his head southeastward toward Dubris—"over that way, I saw once a winged horse carved over a gateway, and one told me it was a Totem of the Second Legion, because they had held that place and so marked it for their own. Now from where did the Second Legion draw its men?"

I was silent for a long moment, looking at him. "From the tribes along the Rhenus," I said slowly.

"From the tribes along the Rhenus. Aiee! I have heard also that the great Magnus Maximus, my lord's great-grandsire, served a while with the Second Legion and loved them well, and that long, long before that, the Emperor in Romeburg himself made them an Augustan Legion, and none, I think, accused the Second Legion of broken trust!"

And that also was true.

And I had learned some things and lost others in the process of growing old—for I felt old that evening, with the weight of five and forty winters lying heavy on me as though there had been added to them another score. And so I made my decision, though I did not yet let it appear that I had done so, to the men about me. It was a decision that proved sound, insane though I know that many of my own folk thought it; and when the black sorrow came, it was not from the Saxon shore, not from the men with whom I struck that day's bargain, after all.

"It is in my mind that you speak both truth and something of wisdom," I said at last. "So be it then, let us go further into this matter of a bargain between your people and mine."

There was much talk after that, much argument, while the clerks waited to make copies of a treaty, and beyond the door the tawny sunset flamed and faded between the trees, and the light of the burning ashe wood began to bite into the deepening shadows. And then at last the arguing was done, and I stood up to state the final terms, while the clerks scratched on their parchments, a small, hurried, insect sound. I spoke of boundaries and tribal territory, of landholding in yard-lands per man, and rights of wood and water, pasturage and the hunting spear, and of the military service to be rendered in exchange. ("The coasts from Portus Adurni around to the Metaris we will keep for you from all inroads," the aged spokesman had said, after conferring with the others of his kind, "but you shall not call upon us to carry our spears into any other war of yours, in any other part of Britain." And I had agreed, for the thing seemed fair enough.) And all the while, as I spoke, something yammered within my head, in stupid astonishment at myself and the words that I was measuring out, as a man issues out arrowheads from a basket. Northfolk and Southfolk, East Angles and South Seax and the Cantii Kingdom, I dealt with them each in turn, so far as they could be dealt with before the agreed frontiers were drawn out in detail.

Last of all, I turned again to the red-haired man with the scarred throat. And when, meeting my gaze, he straightened and stepped forward between two others to the hearthstone, it was as though he had been waiting for me all the while, and I for him. "Cerdic, son of Vortigern, between you and me there can be no bargain struck."

He stood looking at me, half smiling so that the white dogtooth just lifted his lip at one side. And more even than at our first meeting, he seemed like some fierce and beautiful and dangerous animal. "Is it death, then, my Lord Artos?"

"*I* do not kill in the council circle," I said and there was a small thunderous stirring among the Saxons, an eye cocked here and there among my own men, for every man there knew the old ugly tale of how Hengest had called a council feast for Fox Vortigern, and bidden his warriors of the feasting circle to slay each the Briton at his left hand, and how Vortigern had bought his own life with half a British princedom that was not his to pay with.

Cerdic knew it, too. His nostrils dilated, quivering like a stallion's, and his hand went to the place where his sword hilt should have been—but the weapons were stacked outside, for no man comes armed to the council, unless, like Hengest's Saxons, he carries his knife hidden in his sleeve. His hand remembered and fell away again. "What does my Lord the Bear propose for me, then?" he said, breathing quickly.

"Nine days to be gone from Britain."

I saw the surprise flicker in his eyes, and the red brows twitched together. I think he had been prepared for death, but he had not thought of the other thing. "Do I go alone? And in what like? Am I to thank Most Noble Caesar for leave to take my sword with me? If not, I will find means to gain another before I come again."

"Take your sword. Take your long war boats and any of your own war band who choose to follow you," I said. "You are free of all the sea that your keel can sail over, and any landfall that opens to you. Only you shall be gone from these shores in nine days."

"Sa! You offer a prospect strangely pleasant," said the adventurer in him, in a tone of lingering and half-mocking surprise, and then with a sudden snarl of fury as though the beast crouched to spring: "Tell me in what I have differed from these others, that my fate should differ from theirs? That I should bear a wolf's head and go landless and driven out, while they hold the lands that Hengest my grandsire took by the strength of his arm?"

Oisc of the Cantish lands looked up from the fire and thrust his word angrily between us. "Hengest was my grandsire also, let you remember!" but neither of us paid him heed.

"I will tell you: for the unjust, yet sufficient reason that you are

[415]

your father's son, the blood of your father's line running in your veins."

"The royal blood of Britain!" he said.

"I would call it, rather, the blood of a Prince of Powys, who married and abandoned a High King's daughter, and claimed through her the kingship in his turn. The sorry thing for you is that there are still men in Britain who support your father's claim, and so you are a danger to Britain, Cerdic, son of Vortigern, for your heart goes with your Saxon kin. Therefore run your war boats down the beach and gather your sword companions, and carve yourself a kingdom if you can, elsewhere."

He stared at me in silence for a long moment, with his eyes half closed over their cool flickering affrontery. "The first time we met you bid me go. You bid me go free and said that I should come again when I was a man, and you would kill me if you could, and if *I* could, I should kill *you*." The flash of a smile that had no mirth in it showed for an instant those strong white dogteeth, and his hand went to the scar on his neck. "The thing is not yet ended between us, my Lord Artos the Bear of Britain."

He would have swirled about, then and there, and stridden out through the doorway, but I called him to heel. "It may be that the thing is not yet ended between us, as you say. But the end must wait for another day. The women are busy about the cooking fires and soon we shall be at the evening meal. Bide then, and eat and drink and be warm at the fire with the rest of us."

"If I am to be away from my father's shores within nine days, I have more pressing calls upon my time."

"Yet all men must eat. I give you half a day's grace, that you may find the time to sup with the rest of us tonight."

The smile still lingering at one side of his mouth grew sardonic. "Do you fear that I shall fire this somewhat battered thatch over your heads if you let me from your sight?"

"No more, I think, than you fear my ambush on your road to the coast."

And suddenly, his gaze still locked with mine, the smile that had been shut and ugly flashed open in his face, fierce and oddly joyful, and he said swiftly in the British tongue, "So be it, oh my brother and my enemy; we two, both of King's blood, will drink the stars out of tonight's sky, among this pirate royalty!"

So presently, when the deer and badger meat was brought in smoking from the spits, and the mead began to go round, Cerdic and I drank from the same cup and dipped our fingers in the stirabout bowl together, among the rest of the Companions and house carls who had played no part in the council that went before. The two boys had, as foretold, "come back when their bellies bade them" and took their supper squatting among the hounds. What they had done with their day no one asked, nor did they tell without the asking, but from the state of their faces, it seemed likely that they had spent part of it fighting, and another part in eating blackberries. Now they sat bunched shoulder to shoulder, the dark head and the fair one together in the firelight, while they picked companionably at each other's brier scratches.

That seemed to me a thing that had in it the seeds of hope for the future. But every time I glanced that way, I saw beyond them the face of Medraut my son, among the other squadron captains, and every time the shuttered and yet strangely devouring gaze, lit to the color of sapphires by the firelight, was on me or on Cerdic beside me, so that at last, even when I did not look, there seemed no escaping it.

The night seemed so full of him that I was not surprised when later, as I went to the sleeping place that had been made for me of turf and branches against the wall of the ruined fodder store, I found him waiting for me. He unfurled his height from the sleeping bench as I entered, and asked in a suppressed voice if he might speak with me alone.

I said to Riada, who had followed me according to custom, "I'll not be needing you for a while. Go and keep a lookout that we are not disturbed. I'll call you later." And when he had gone, I moved forward, letting the heavy wolfskin apron fall again behind me. "Medraut? What is it then, that brings you here?"

"Is it so strange that a son should come to his father's bothy?"

"It is scarcely a habit, with you."

"Is that all of my choice?" he said. "If my company gives you pleasure, you have hidden it well." And then suddenly, "Father, what is it that is amiss between you and me?"

I went and sat on the piled sheepskins of the bed place, and stared into the sea-blue heart of the tallow candle flame. "Is that what you came to ask me? I don't know. Before God, I don't know, Medraut; but whatever it is, I admit the fault of it, I and my house—I who kindled the spark of your life in your mother's womb, my father who first taught *her* mother how to hate."

"Hate, yes," he said broodingly. "I am your guilt made flesh, am I not, Father? You will always smell the dark birth-smell of my mother's hate on me, and hate me in turn."

"God forbid that I should hate any man who has done nothing to earn it," I said. "It is not so simple as that. There is a shadow cast between you and me, Medraut, a web of shadow that there is no escape from, for either of us."

He came toward me, and before I knew what he was about, knelt beside me and bowed his head onto my knee. It was a horrible womanish gesture. "No escape. . . . It is in what you are and in what I am." His voice came muffled against my knee. "No, don't draw away from me. Whatever else I am, I am your son— your most wretched son. If you do not hate me, try to love me a little, Father; it is lonely never to have been loved, only devoured."

I did not answer. I have never been a man to whom words came easily in the time of most need. The wrongs that had been done to him sickened me, I was torn with furious pity as for some hideous bodily hurt. And for the first time, in that desperate cry against loneliness, I knew something of myself in the son I had begotten, and through my own dread of loneliness, that had made me flinch from the Purple, like called to like. In a moment more, I think that I should have put my arm around his bowed shoulders. . . .

But before I could do so, he wrenched himself away and sprang to his feet, and the chill, jibing note was back in his voice when at last he broke the silence between us. "Ah, na, that is too much to ask for, isn't it?"

And the moment was gone beyond catching back. "That would be to ask for a gift, and I must not ask for a gift, I am only your son. If I were a chieftain of the Sea Wolves, then the thing would be different, and we might laugh together, even with the dagger naked between us. Sa, then I demand only my rights."

I got up from the bed place, and we stood facing each other. "Your rights, Medraut?"

"A son's rights in place of a son's gift." He was speaking half wildly now. "Today you sat in council with the lords of the Sea Wolves, Flavian with you, and Cei—the son of a Roman house who cannot even speak our tongue without the gutturals of the Rhenus half drowning whoever stands nearest him—and Connory and that young whelp Constantine and the rest; and where was I? Outside sitting on my rump with mere squadron captains around the cooking fire!"

"Are you not, then, one of my squadron captains?"

"I am also Prince of Britain; it was my right to sit at the council table—all men know that by blood I am Prince of Britain."

"By blood, yes," I said.

"Oh, my father the Emperor, there is small need to remind me that we are both bastards; have you found it to stand in *your* path?"

In the long silence that came after, the wind lifted the wolfskin over the doorway and teased the candle flame, and high in the darkness overhead, over toward the marshes, I heard the whistle of the wild duck passing. I was thinking suddenly that even on that last night in the upper room, Ambrosius had never spoken of Medraut; it was as though we both knew and tacitly agreed that his entrance into any plans for Britain's future was unthinkable. Now I was thinking of Medraut coming after us, his hand on the Sword of Britain, and the fear was black on me, for all that I believed in and held sacred.

"If I were to bid you sit in council with me, it would be as though I stood up and cried before all men, "This is my heir, to come after me! But that is the thing you have in mind, isn't it?"

"I am your son," he said again.

"Among the wearers of the Purple, the diadem has never passed of necessity from father to son. Your son's rights, Medraut, do not include the Sword of Britain after me, unless I speak the word."

The usual veil over his eyes seemed to thicken until the blueness of them was completely blank; and he said after a moment, in a voice that was suddenly silken: "How if *I* speak a word, then? How if I shouted the whole foul truth of my begetting to the camp?"

"Shout, and be damned to you," I said. "The chief shame will not fall on my head, who had no knowledge of that truth, but on your mother's, who knew it well!" There was another pause, filled with the sea-surge of the wind in the trees. Then I said, "You see, it is not so easy after all."

"Na," he agreed, in the same silken voice. "It is not so simple after all. Yet maybe we shall find a way one day, my father. It is in my heart that we shall find a way." The threat was clear.

"Maybe," I said, "but meanwhile it is time for sleep, for the rising time for both of us must come early in the morning; and truth to tell, I wish to be alone."

And when he had made me his low bow that was a mockery of respect, and ducked out through the skin-hung door hole, I sat thinking for a long while before I called Riada to me. I thought, among other things, that it was as well that there should be no public talk of Constantine coming after me. Cador and I understood each other well enough, that in the nature of things, the boy must be my heir; but it would be better—safer for Constantine and for the kingdom—that the thing should not be put into words and cried aloud in the Forum.

CHAPTER THIRTY-TWO

The Queen's Captain

BEFORE the end of the month I was back in Venta. We rode in between roaring crowds who surged forward to fling golden branches and jewel-colored autumn berries under our horses' hooves, and it seemed that the rejoicing of the whole city clamored like a clash of bells.

It was conqueror's weather, not the half-regretful glancing back to summer that occurs sometimes in early autumn, but the sudden valiant flare of warmth and color on the very edge of winter that often comes toward the time of Saint Martin's Mass. The sun shone like a bold yellow dandelion flower tossed into a cloudless sky, and a wind last night had dried the mud of the autumn rains so that the dust curled up beneath the horses' hooves, the poplar trees stood along the streets as yellow torches, with their shadows under them reflecting the blue of the sky. And next day, when I was able at last to draw breath and turn my back for an hour on matters that concerned the war trail and the kingdom, the sun was still warm to the skin in the Queen's Courtyard, where Bedwyr and I lounged side by side on the colonnade steps. The light was westering, and the sand-rose in its great stone jar laid an intricate tracery of shadow at our feet, and denser shadow stole out from the far side where the pigeons crooned and strutted on the roof of the store wing. But on the colonnade steps out of the wind, there was warmth to let one's cloak hang open, a still warmth, lingering like the savor of old wine in an amber cup. The smell of the evening meal stole out from the cook place, and the movements and voices of women, and the fat bubbling laugh of the woman who had taken Blanid's place when the old creature died last year.

[421]

I had been telling Bedwyr of all that had happened at the council table, and the course that I had taken as to the Saxon settlement, while he sat forward with his maimed arm supported across his knees, his narrowed gaze following the pigeons, listening to me without a word. I wished that he would speak, it was hard to tell the thing against this wall of silence. But when I had finished he still maintained it, until I asked him directly, "When I was young, I'd have torn out their living hearts, and my own also, before a Saxon should be left on British ground. Am I learning other things than the use of the sword, Bedwyr? Or am I merely growing old and losing my grasp?"

He stirred then, still watching the pigeons strut and coo. "Na, I do not think that you are losing your grasp; it is that you must learn to play the statesman now. For Artorius Augustus Caesar it is no longer enough to be a soldier, as it was for Artos the Count of Britain."

I rubbed my forehead which felt as though sheep's wool were packed behind it. "I have not slept much, these past nights, wondering if I have chosen the wrong course and maybe the ruin of Britain. And yet it is still in my mind that it is the lesser of two dangers."

"In mine also," Bedwyr said. "We cannot stretch our shield-wall to cover the Forth to Vectis Water—it may be that this way will at any rate gain us more time."

Time. . . .

We were silent again. And then I heard my own voice, as it were thinking aloud. "I remember once, long ago, Ambrosius said to me that if we fought well enough we might hold back the dark for maybe another hundred years. I asked him, seeing that the end was sure, why we did not merely lie down and let it come, for the end would be easier that way. He said: 'For a dream.'"

"And you? What did you say?"

"Something about a dream being often the best thing to die for . . . I was young, and something of a fool."

"Yet when there is no dream left worth dying for, that is when the people die," Bedwyr murmured, "and there is the advantage to it, that the dream can live on, even when hope dies. Yet hope has its value too. . . ."

"Sa sa." I turned abruptly on the colonnade step, to face him.

[422]

"Bedwyr, all our lives we have fought a long fight without hope"—
I hesitated, seeking the words I needed—"without—*ultimate* hope.
And now, for the first time, it is in my heart that there is a kind
of hope for us, after all."

He turned from the pigeons. "What hope would that be?"

"You remember that I asked Flavian to bring the Minnow with
him to the council camp?"

"I remember."

"There was another boy there, a little younger than the Minnow,
the son of one of the Saxon nobles. Like enough, he was brought
for the same purpose. They walked around each other on stiff legs
at first, like young hounds, and then they went away, and no man
saw them again until evening. They came back at suppertime, being
hungry, and told no one what they had done with their day, and
no one asked, but they looked as though they had spent part of it
fighting, and the rest in eating blackberries. They shared the same
broth bowl and spent the evening among the hounds by the fire,
picking bramble thorns out of each other's feet. And suddenly I
knew, watching them—Ambrosius never knew it—that the longer
we can hold off the Saxons, the more we can slow their advance,
even at the cost of our heart's blood, the more time there will be
for other boys to pick thorns out of each other's feet and learn
the words for hearth and hound and honey cake in each other's
tongue. . . . Every year that we can hold the Saxons back may
well mean that the darkness will engulf us the less completely in
the end, that more of what we fight for will survive until the light
comes again."

"It is a good thought," Bedwyr said softly. "It would be a better
one if you could live three or four lives."

"Surely. And there's where the harness chafes. Having only
one, and that more than half spent— If God had but given me a
son to take my sword after me."

He turned sharply to look at me, but did not speak, for the
thought of Medraut leapt naked between us. "In the end it must
fall to Constantine," I said at last. "Cador knows that."

"And Constantine is—a fine cavalry leader in his own wild way,
and will doubtless make a fine prince for Dumnonia."

"He burns with a steadier flame than his father. But the young
ones are of a lesser stature, a lesser breed—both Saxon and British,

they are a lesser breed. The giants and heroes are dead, and all save one, the men grow smaller than they used to be when we were young."

"And that one?"

"If I could have had Cerdic for my son," I said slowly, "I should have been well content."

Neither of us spoke again for a long while. Bedwyr returned to his watching of the pigeons, I to staring down at that arabesque of shadows that the sand-rose cast across the pavement at my feet, neither of us thinking much of what we saw. And the slow long silence fell like the soft dust of years over the things that we had been speaking of.

A dry-edged poplar leaf, caught by an eddy of wind, came spinning across the sunlit courtyard to flatten itself for an instant against the bottom step, and in the way that one does such small pointless things, Bedwyr flung out a hand—his left—to catch it, and snatched at his breath swearing softly, and let his arm settle gingerly onto his knees again, while the leaf whirled away.

I looked around at him, seeing afresh the discolored hollows around his eyes and the way the bones stood out under the skin that had bleached from its usual brown to a dingy yellow, and the parching of long-recurrent fever that had left his mouth dry and chapped. "It still catches you, then?" I said. I had asked for that arm of his before, but he had swept my questions aside, caring for nothing but to hear what had happened at the council table.

"It is well enough."

" 'Well enough' is an answer for the birdcatcher's grandmother."

He seemed to be drawing back his mind from a long way away, to give me his full attention. "It still catches me," he said with mocking exactitude. "The ache runs down here like a red thread— a little red worm in the bone—and catches me up short when I would be catching poplar leaves in flight." He flung back the loose fold of his cloak and held it out to me, and I saw that from the elbow down, the arm was somewhat wasted and brittle-looking, and the elbow itself, below the heavy bronze arm ring that I had given him years ago, was wickedly seamed with livid scars, not only of the wound itself, but of the many lancings and probings after the splinters of shattered bone, some of them scarcely healed even now. "It also does not bend." I saw the painful drag and thrust of the muscles, but the joint remained immovable, bent at about the angle at which a man carries his shield and bridle.

"What does Gwalchmai say? And Ben Simeon? Has Ben Simeon seen it?"

He quirked up that wild eyebrow, the other grave and level, so that his face wore two expressions at once. "That I am fortunate to be alive. . . . I shall even be able to use it by and by, seeing that it is not my sword arm. When I knew that it must stiffen I bade Gwalchmai to set and strap the thing in the position that I bade him, and before spring I shall be handling horse and buckler again; I shall be fit for service as Caesar's captain."

"And the Emperor's harper?" I glanced at the embroidered doeskin bag that lay as usual beside him.

"Surely, and that already, since a one-handed skill will serve." He took up the harp and drew it from the bag, using his left arm with a kind of clumsy acquired skill, and settled the slim well-worn instrument between his knee and the hollow of his shoulder. "It is easier with a sound arm, admittedly," he said, frowning as he fumbled for the familiar supporting hold.

He struck a swelling ripple of tuning notes that sounded like a question, made his adjustments, and began to play. It was a tune from my own hills, that he had picked up from Ambrosius's harper, small and jaunty as a water wagtail. And listening to him, I lost the Queen's Courtyard in the westering autumn sunlight, and was back again in the dark of the mountains that walled Nant Ffrancon, with the thunder of horses' hooves in my ears, and a herdboy playing that tune on his pipes; and for an instant the taste of my youth came back to me, and the green freshness of the morning before Ygerna's shadow fell across the day.

A quiet step sounded behind us, and I looked up as Guenhumara came across the colonnade with her spindle and distaff. I moved aside to make space for her on the step, but she smiled and shook her head, and leaned herself against the cracked plaster column, looking down at us.

Bedwyr had dropped his hand from the harp strings, and as the small prancing melody fell silent, she said quickly, "Na na, let you go on playing; it was the harp song that called me out." And he made her a little bow, and caught up the tunelet again where he had tossed it down. And while he played, I had time to look at

Guenhumara as I had scarcely had time to look at her since I came home. She was wearing a gown of some soft red-brown stuff, faded a little as the earth fades with sun and rain, and it seemed to me suddenly that there was a new softness about her, a look of harvest. I searched for the woman I had kissed into that one moment of passionate response beside the gray standing stone in the rain, and could not find her, but knew that she had her part in this other woman and was not lost, as the green shoot is not lost in the red corn. There was a warmer quietness in her, fulfillment and content as a cornfield at harvest time. The Corn Queen, I thought. She is like the Corn Queen, and pushed the thought away, for the over-tones of sacrifice that clung to it. I wondered whether she was—not forgetting the Small One, but perhaps remembering with less pain.

The small rippling tune that was now the wagtail and now the water, burst into a last running phrase, and was silent. And in the silence, all at once, Guenhumara laughed, with strangely darkened eyes, and the bright color flooded up from her throat to the roots of her hair. "Artos, why do you look at me so?—As though you had never seen me before?"

"Do I? I am sorry. It is that I am looking for the first time at the Queen."

"The Queen," she said slowly and carefully, as though testing a strange word on her tongue.

And Bedwyr, laughing also, as he looked up at her with eyes narrowed against the westering light, struck a small triumphal flourish of notes from the leaping harp strings. "Sa! They will sound the trumpets for you, now that Caesar is home, and open the treasure chests and bring out the blue and purple and golden silks that tear like withered leaves, and the queen's jewels laced with cobwebs, but meanwhile, here is a queen's fanfare for you that at least has never been worn for a garland by any queen before."

"Do not listen to him," and it was as though the same spirit of small quiet laughter had entered into me also. "All that, the Red Fox and his kind carried off long ago. There will be no dusty silks and weight of dead woman's jewels for you, Cariad. . . . If I were Lord of the Eastern Empire" (the memory of some picture gleaming behind the altar of a church must have put it into my head) "you should have a crown of golden stems and leaves curling in and out together like the sand-dune rose but without the thorns

[426]

—and in every arch of it a bell of crystal to ring when you walked."

"Bedwyr told me that a circlet of oak leaves was all the diadem my lord had to crown him Emperor. Then a crown of golden corn-stalks—so that my lord give it to me—will serve well enough for my royalty. With that, and your fanfare, Bedwyr, I shall not feel the lack of any dead queen's jewels."

A sudden rush of warmth rose in me, and I reached out and put my arm around her knees, these being the nearest part of her. "Oh Guenhumara, it is good to be at home with you again." Oddly, I was much less shy of touching this new Guenhumara than I had been of touching the old one.

I had half hoped that she would say, "It is good to have you at home with me again," but she only said, "Is it, my dear?" And I felt her startle for an instant under the heavy folds of her gown. Then she stooped and brushed her hand across my cheek, and I let myself believe that what she had not said in words, she had said in that brief touch.

Bedwyr was returning his beloved harp to its bag, and slinging the strap across his shoulder, and something in the way he did it made me think of a traveler picking up his dusty bundle before he turns again to the track. And without thinking, I said, "You look like a man setting off on a journey."

He laughed. "Do I? If so, it is but a short one. It is in my mind that tomorrow I will be away back to my own quarters."

I sat up abruptly, releasing Guenhumara. "You're not meaning it?"

"I am so."

"Bedwyr, you're not fit yet to go back to that kennel of yours."

"You underestimate the Lady Guenhumara's care of me. I am almost a sound man again."

"Almost! And what wrong have I done you, or you me, that you should run like a hen with the wind in your hind feathers, the moment that I am home off the war trail? Guenhumara, Heart-of-my-heart, tell him that he cannot go."

I thought that a shadow had fallen on Guenhumara, but it was only that the westering sun had slid behind a broken column. She said quietly, "Bedwyr knows that there is his place and his welcome here for as long as he cares to stay, and that they are waiting whenever he chooses to come back. And that he is free to come and go as he chooses."

Bedwyr was making some adjustment to the harp strap. His fingers checked on the buckle at his shoulder, and he looked up, faintly jibing over his own dark depths. "I have just thought, that we are forgetting the Purple in all this. Men might say that it was an unwise thing, even a dangerous thing, to go when the Emperor says 'Stay.' "

"If the Emperor ordered you to stay, would you do it?" I said.

"I must needs obey the imperial command."

We looked at each other a long moment, eye into eye, no longer laughing. Then I said, "Your sword brother bids you go where you will and when you will, and come back when you will."

We were aware, all of us, that we had lost the fragile contentment of a few moments past, and made, I think, a conscious effort to catch it back. Bedwyr saying that a little later he should maybe go up for another look at the farm I had given him, and Guenhumara asking what it was like. "Hill pasture and upland horse run," he said, "three cornfields and a cluster of turf bothies. I have not seen it in summer, but there will be snowdrops in the woods above the house in February. That is why they call it Coed Gwyn." Only for some reason this time I could not enter into the thing that was tossing to and fro like a colored ball between the other two. And suddenly it seemed that Guenhumara gave up the game. She shivered a little. "It grows cold now that the sun is gone. Let us be away to the fire."

So the small quiet hour that had in it something of sanctuary was over, and a few moments later I stood with Guenhumara in the colonnade and glanced back over the half wall to watch Bedwyr weaving his still slightly uncertain way across the courtyard to make ready for supper. "Guenhumara, do you think that he should go yet?"

She had been watching the retreating figure too, and turned with a little start toward me. It was already dusk indoors though the light still lingered in the courtyard, and Nissa had brought the atrium candles, and in the light from the open doorway her face was softly golden, with its shadows blotted in from the gray twilight. "Yes, I think he should," she said, and took my hand to lead me into the atrium.

I had another and more formal coronation to undergo in the Basilica, a few days later, but to me it was no more than a husk of the true crowning that I had gone to on the night after Badon; and I remember little of it now, save a vague blur of gold and colors and the gray of naked mail, and the bright cold seagull's eye of Bishop Dubricius as he set the gold circlet on my head. And the moment when I sprung the great dragon arm ring of Ambrosius onto my arm, and knew that I stood where he would have had me stand.

Life changed, tipping over to a new angle, and I who had been the war leader and was now the High King (crowned Caesar but High King in all things other than the name) had become something of a stranger in a strange land, striving as best I might after the ways of kingship, in the state halls and Council Chamber where Ambrosius had worked himself to death the winter before. But I had the help of Guenhumara, sitting beside me in the Queen's great chair that had been empty and stored away so many years. . . . Indeed she was nearer to me in that winter than she had been since the time before Hylin died. Bedwyr, on the other hand, seemed farther away.

In the days that followed my second crowning, Venta grew quiet, and quieter yet, as the war host broke up and men drifted off to their own homes to plow for the next year's harvest and beget the next year's children. But for the Companions, of course, as well as for a few standing cavalry squadrons and spear bands, there was no breakup; and the usual winter's work began, as the newly broken two- and three-year-olds came up from the horse yards to be "trained on" for war, while all the while the made warhorses must be kept in fighting practice. Old Hunno had died some years before, and since Amgerit his son was too valuable where he was, to be spared from the breeding runs, my new horse master was a yellow-haired small savage from the Old Iceni country. I had been somewhat anxious as to him at first, not quite believing that any man save Hunno could turn me out the younglings trained as I needed them; but in all justice, I do not think that our cavalry suffered by the change.

Midway between Christ's Mass and Candle Mass, we held, as we had held them every year, our Winter Cavalry Maneuvers. It helped to keep men and horses on their mettle, and brightened a little, even for the watching townsfolk, the dark of the year when the Midwinter Fires were burned out and spring (which in any case, for these many years, had meant also the Saxons) was still very far away.

I can see now the level meadows below the town walls, winter-pale in the thin sunshine, the shadows blue and opaque like wood-smoke among the bare dappled woods of the surrounding hillsides, the rustling flights of starlings overhead, and the curved sweep of the squadrons that seemed to echo the starlings' flight; I can hear the drub of hooves and the trumpet sounding thin across the water meadows, which is the music to which my life has been set.

Ever since noon, it had been going on, watched by the crowd huddled thick before the city gates and along the fringes of the practice ground. We had maneuvered all together, the squadron streamers flying in the silver-gilt light, in the mimic warfare that trains hand and eye toward the real thing. We had divided up, squadron by squadron, champion by champion, and with the horses seeming almost to dance to the sound of the trumpets, had thrown off, for the watchers' benefit, changing and complicated patterns of wheeling lines and arrowheads and spinning circles (but these too, make for skill and control in the day of battle). I had had my squadron out there already, putting them through their paces, and the roar of the crowd and the soft thunder of hooves on the winter turf behind me was still in my blood, as I sat watching Bedwyr take his turn.

He was sweeping his squadron after him down the long line of practice posts that had been set up, weaving them in and out as the shuttle through the weft, his second behind him with the squadron streamer flying from his spear shaft like a flame of saffron and peacock blue; and I watched anxiously, wondering how it was with him, wondering if, despite the strap across his shoulder, the weight of the heavy black bullhide buckler was dragging too cruelly at his maimed arm, watching for any sign that he was finding it hard to control the big red roan. But he had always had the harper's trick of controlling his horse with his knees so as to have both hands free for his harp, and it stood him in good stead now. In my anxiety to see how it went with him, I urged Signus forward a few paces, past a clump of bare willows that slightly blocked my view, and as I reined in once more, became aware of a knot of young men still partly screened from me by the branches who, their own part in the day's work over for the time being, stood talking together while they watched the horsemen. Nearest to me of all, stood Medraut, his hair—he had pulled off his war cap—shone mouse-fair in the wintry light, and he played and finicked with his war mittens as a nervous horse plays with the snaffle bars. They lounged together, watching the horsemen, talking in quick light snatches with laughter between; and I sat my old Signus a little to their rear and watched them, wondering if it was only in my mind that they seemed not of the same metal as the men who had been young when I was young, only that to the old dog the young one seems never to be what his own pack fellows were. These lads were hardy and strong-shouldered as we had been, they had ring-mail shirts gray-bright as salmon skins, where *we* had ridden to war in old boiled leather, and yet in some intangible way, they seemed diminished, lacking in something that we had possessed. Indeed these—all members of Medraut's squadron—seemed scarcely to be of the Companions at all. . . . "It has to be so," I told myself. "This is a different life to the one we knew twenty years ago, and the Company must change with the rest." It was true, and yet I was aware suddenly, looking at the broad young backs of these lads I felt I scarcely knew, that the old strength of oneness had begun to go out of the Company and it was growing blurred at the edges. And under my own war sark, something ached a little in my breast for the old close-knit brotherhood.

Busy with my own thinking, I heard their voices only as sound, until someone among them spoke Bedwyr's name, and as though at the opening of a door, I heard the sense of what they said. "He is a tough one, the old Satyr. Christ! He leads like a young man still." And another returned with half-angry admiration, "If when I am as old as that and one-armed, I can lead as well, I'll not be complaining. . . . He's none so ill-looking, either, on a horse and at this distance when you can't see his face."

Medraut laughed—a brittle, whinnying laugh, an unhappy sound —and flicked the war gloves he was fiddling with toward the place at a little distance where Guenhumara, with the hood of her marten-skin mantle fallen back from her head, stood with little plump

Teleri and a knot of the other women about her. "You're not the only one of that mind, I'm thinking, though I doubt if she will be finding much amiss with his face at close quarters, either—or with the rest of him, for that matter. Look how our Royal Lady watches him now."

A third member of the group said, I thought with something of discomfort, "After all, she is not the only one to be watching Caesar's captain."

Medraut said softly, almost musically, "Caesar's captain? The Queen's captain would be nearer the mark, my child." And they all laughed.

And despite the stab of anger that had shot through me, I could have laughed too, listening to them; these callow lads who knew nothing of the bonds that ten or twenty years of life could forge. Of course she was watching him, as I was watching him; it was the first time that he had tried out his arm in full war gear.

Still laughing, one of Medraut's fellows looked around and saw me. The laughter trickled out of his face, and he muttered something to the rest, and flicked out a foot to kick Medraut on the ankle. Medraut gave a small start for appearance's sake, but it is in my mind that he knew I was there all the while. He looked over his shoulder, and met my eyes with a stare of cool antagonism that assuredly was not the look of one whose words have been overheard by the wrong man, indeed there was a strange kind of satisfaction in it. Then he put up his hand in sketch of salute, and moved away, the others, somewhat unsurely, following him. We had long ago given up all pretense at anything between us that should be between father and son.

I thought that I put the whole thing out of my mind as no more than a casual thorn prick administered by my son in a moment's idle malice (as though Medraut ever did anything casually!) and yet a little later, when we formed the whole Company in two halves, Bedwyr leading the blue squadron and I the red, and came thundering together from the far end of the practice ground, a strange thing happened, for as the two ranks closed upon each other, and I saw the leader on the tall roan rushing toward me, my sight darkened, and for a strange damned moment I saw the face of my enemy. I even made the first move to swerve Signus in his tracks, that instead of passing between the roan and the next horse,

I should bring him crashing into Bedwyr's mount. I don't know why, it was certainly no part of cavalry fighting; I suppose with some blind black instinct to kill, not at the remove of a weapon, but with my own hands. . . . The thing was over almost in the instant that it came upon me, the merest flash of darkness, and I saw Bedwyr's face, crooked and ugly and familiar as my own heartbeat, laughing at me, and yet with something of surprise behind the widened eyes, and wrenched Signus back onto his true line again, so that we drummed past almost brushing knee against knee and crashed on to our two ends of the field.

CHAPTER THIRTY-THREE

"It Was Warm Between Thy Breasts, Lalage"

A FEW days later, Bedwyr asked for leave to go up to Coed Gwyn for a while, and for the first time in my life, part of me was glad to see him go. Na, not glad, but conscious of an odd relief in his going, that had in some way to do with that strange evil moment during the final charge, though what, I did not know, for I took care not to look too closely.

Winter wore away while, still deeply meshed in the unfamiliar tasks of kingship, I scarcely noticed that the evenings were growing long and light, and the still-bare woods full of the clear surprised twitterings and flutings of thrush and wren and robin, trying over again the song that they had forgotten since last year. And then suddenly the pale promise of spring was fulfilled and running like the green Solas Sidh, the Fairy Fire, through the woods and heaths; and in the tangle of the old palace gardens, the fragile white stars of the anemones turned their backs to the wind. And when I took three squadrons of the Companions and rode up to see to the defenses around Sabrina head, where the Scots' attacks had still to be reckoned with, Bedwyr had not yet returned, and Owain took command of his squadron.

It was about the half of a month before we turned the horses' heads home again.

On the last day of the return ride we reached the derelict villa on the Sorviodunum Road a little before dusk, and in the usual way of things I would have ordered camp there, and covered the last seven or eight miles in the morning, but all at once, even as I drew rein before the nettle-choked gateway of the cattle yard where we often corralled the horses, I was filled with a wild impatience to be home that was in part the mere wish of a tired man to see the lamplight shining from his own door, and his own woman with her hair tumbled on the pillow, in part a sense of desperate urgency, of something wrong, that came to me clear and unmistakable like a bird's call out of the evening sky. It was a glorious evening, the kind on which the last luminous twilight lingers on far beyond its usual time; there would be the last half of a moon later, and the big sorrel colt I was riding seemed fresh enough, as did the other horses.

I called to the rest, "How say you, brothers? There's a moon coming. If we bait the horses and ride on again when we've eaten, we can be in Venta by midnight. Shall we push forward and give our wives a start?"

We off-saddled the horses, watered them and turned them loose to graze and roll while we ate hard oaten bread and dried curds, and stretched saddle-cramped legs for a while. And all the time I was possessed of that wild impatience to be pushing on, mingled more and more strongly with a sense of dread without cause; a shadow without substance to cast it. It seemed an unbearably long time until I could decently give the order to saddle and remount.

The moon was high when we came up the last straight stretch between the graves and the poplar trees to the west gate of Venta. The gate towers stood up against the glimmering sky, black, like a cliff. But the clatter of our horses' hooves had given warning of our coming, and the yellow glim of a lantern blinked in the lookout above the gateway, voices sounded, giving orders, and the heavy valves began to grind open before I had need to shout for admittance. And we clattered through into the wide main street of Venta, streets whitened by the moon, between the dark walls of the houses, which might have been the streets of a deserted city for all the sign of life in them, save for a half-wild cat who turned with eyes that were twin green sparks of hate to spit at us before streaking off into the shadows, and here and there a woman flitting like a tawdry night moth along the dark side of the way; and once a strayed reveler late out of some wineshop, and wavering his unsure way home, who shouted something about folks that must come clamoring up the street like the Wild Hunt, waking other folks in their beds, and then continued on his way, singing mournfully but with surprising sweetness:

> *"The wind blows cold tonight,*
> *And the black rain falls chill,*
> *And the hillside's cheerless sleeping*
> *Wi' a broken sword to hand . . .*
> *It was warm between thy breasts, Lalage."*

I have hated that song ever since.

We dismounted in the wide forecourt of the palace. The horses were led away by the grooms and stable servants who came running with lanterns, and the sleep still in their eyes like a century or so of dust, to take charge of them, and the Companions clattered off to their own quarters. I had an idea that Cei wished to come with me, as though he thought that I might have some need of him; if so, I must have got rid of him some way, for when I went on toward the Queen's Courtyard, I was alone, save for my armorbearer. But all the happenings of that night are confused and darkened in my mind.

I passed one of my own lads on guard duty at the courtyard entrance, and a few moments later (the door was never barred) was in the atrium. The place was dark save for the few red gleeds still glowing in the brazier, and Margarita, when she sprang up from her place and came with her usual grave delight to greet me, was an enchanted creature, flushed to the color of a pink pearl shell. Nothing could be very wrong, I thought, with the house quiet in sleep and Margarita in her usual place, and I began to call myself all kinds of a fool. I bade Riada light a couple of candles and bring some wine, for there seemed no point in rousing the household, and while he groped for the candles in their prickets and kindled them with a twig from the charcoal embers, I flung off my cloak and stood holding my hands over the dim warmth of the brazier, for there was a chill in me, though the night was not cold.

The light sprang up, quickening from candle to candle, and the familiar room grew warmly out of obscurity, and Margarita was more enchanted than any white hound by candlelight. I glanced about me as Riada departed to carry out the second part of his orders, as I had done at so many homecomings, seeing the kingfisher-colored saint on the wall above the big olivewood rug chest, the signs of Guenhumara's occupation that had made the big smoky room, so long deserted, into my home. Indeed it was as though she had only just left the room, for a small red Samian bowl on the table, half full of water, still contained a few chill white anemones and beside it lay her scissors and thread and a length of plaited green rushes, as though she had been making a garland or a festival wreath.

And suddenly, looking at these traces of Guenhumara, it seemed to me strange that she had not awakened and come down to me. We had not made much tumult, in our coming in, but she was a light sleeper—light as a leaf—and I had never come home before, even at this hour of night, that she had not roused. Suddenly the sense of disaster, which the sight of all things in their usual places had quieted in me for a short while, flared up again, and I turned from the brazier and ran up the narrow stairway.

The room was white with the moon as it had been on the night that the child died, but it was too early in the year for the nightingale. It had the blank anonymity of emptiness so that I knew Guenhumara was not there, even before I saw the rugs smooth and unrumpled on the bed place, only a faint hollow on the side, as though she had sat there for a while.

I stood for a long moment, thinking too, while the cold emptiness of the room seeped into me. *It was warm between thy breasts, Lalage;* the old song scurried senselessly round and round in my head, as though in search of escape. I wanted some way of escape, too, but I did not know from what. I went out and down the stairs again.

Riada had returned with wine in my own big silver cup with the ram's-head handles, and a couple of servants had appeared, blinking and in hurriedly dragged-on clothes. I turned on Sasticca, she who had taken old Blanid's place, and demanded, "Where is my Lady, the Queen?"

She gaped at me, scarce fully awake. "Eh, my lord, we did not expect you this night, or there should have been a better welcome—"

"The Queen," I said, "where is the Queen?"

"My mistress could not sleep, she said the moon was too bright.

She went out to walk in the garden, and bade us not to bide waiting for her."

Relief of a sort swept over me. In the garden that stretched beyond the widespread warren of the palace, she would like enough have heard nothing of our return. For a moment it was in my mind to go out after her, and meet her in the crown of windflowers that she had made herself for some whim; but if she had gone to walk in the garden at night, it was maybe because she wanted to walk alone. I could wait a while at least.

So I dismissed the servants back to their sleeping places, and, when they were gone, took the wine cup from Riada, and drank. As I did so, I saw his gaze go past me to the colonnade door at my back, which he had left open when he brought the wine; saw him stiffen a little, and the thick russet brows draw together.

I swung around, and there in the doorway, with the cold sheen of the moonlight behind him, stood Medraut. I had not heard him come, for his footsteps were almost silent, the same light prowling tread that I have noticed in a hunchback before now. But there he was, and there it seemed that, like his mother, he might have stood waiting for a lifetime or so. His eyes pricked with spangles of cold blue fire that seemed not to come from the candles, in a face that would have been a mere white mask save for the working of the muscles about the mouth. I could not see what lay behind the mask. But whatever it was, I knew that it threatened my whole world.

He said—and in some strange way his voice, like his face, gave the impression of being masked—"Artos, my father, thank God that you are back. There is sore need of you here!"

"What need?" I demanded.

"Is there so much trust between you and me that you will believe my word? Come quickly and know the thing for yourself!"

"If you do not tell me, I do not come," I said.

He stood as still as ever, looking at me; and I could have sworn that whatever else, there was a kind of struggling grief behind the white mask. I daresay he really believed in his own grief just then, for save for hate, he was so empty that he could feel whatever it suited him to feel. "Not even for my stepmother's sake?" he said.

There was a moment's complete silence in the atrium, and one fear that was already in me began to thicken like a cold mist. "Very well," I said at last, and put down the half-empty wine cup.

[438]

Young Riada cried out to me sharply, "Sir—my Lord Artos, don't go," and his voice cracked with anxiety.

I felt for his shoulder and gave it a little shake, my gaze still holding and held by Medraut's. "I'll be back."

In a kind of cold nightmare, the more terrible because the fear was for no known thing but fear existing in its own right, I walked out into the courtyard. Medraut drew back for me to pass, and then turned in with his light prowling step beside me. "Across the garden, that is the quickest way," he said. I did not ask where to; I knew that I might as well ask the question of the winter rain as of the man beside me. In some ways he was stronger than I was. We went out through the furry blackness of the low arched alleyway under the store wing, and cut across the corner of the tangled garden, to the sprawl of courts and tumble-down buildings on the far side. This was the oldest part of the palace, dating from the first days of Rome-in-Britain, and had fallen into disuse save as storerooms and the like. A veritable honeycomb of courts and chambers linked one to another, black and white under the moon, empty of life as the city outside had seemed. In one place only, the remoteness of the moon was challenged by a smudge of smoky gold, where a torch high on the angle of two walls shed a little light into the alleyway that made a shortcut to the mews. Medraut reached up and took it from its iron sconce as we passed, and the shadows spun and darted flying before us and crowding in behind as we went on again.

At a gateway in the wall, I felt Medraut's hand on my arm, urging me through without a word, and then we were in a narrow courtyard in the heart of the old palace. I knew the place well, though I had seen it seldom in the past thirty years, for I had kept my mongrel dog pack there when I was a boy. A well, whose water was still sweet—or had been then—was sunk in the midst of the place, and a wild pear tree overhung the wellhead. It had been a bird-sown sapling when I first came there; it was dead now, black and stark in the moonlight, its beauty turned skeletal, save for one living branch on which a few white flowers still unfurled their fragile petals in a last reaching out to the springtime.

The shadow of the flowering branch fled across the face of the storehouse opposite as Medraut, with the torch held high, moved forward, and the probing torchlight picked out the figure of a man standing with his drawn sword before the arched entrance, and other figures in darker corners, striking out in each case that glint of a drawn weapon.

I remember that for the split instant of time before the scene sprang to life, I wondered whether I had walked into a trap, and was to die as Constantine my grandfather had died, and whipped my hand to my sword hilt. Then as they stepped forward into the full torchlight, I saw that they were four or five of my own Companions, four or five boys of the new generation that I felt I scarcely knew. Now, clearly, they were acting under Medraut's orders as they moved in toward the storehouse doorway, and Medraut himself stood back formally, that I might go first. I checked in the arched opening, and looked around at him, trying once more to see behind his mask. "What has Guenhumara to do with this place, Medraut? Why all the ugly mystery?"

"Let my father forgive me," he said. "There was no other way," and made a little gesture to me to go in and climb the steep curved stairway whose bottom steps showed waveringly in the torchlight.

I went in and began to climb, my giant-wise shadow climbing remorselessly ahead of me in the light of the torch which Medraut carried close behind. At the midway turn of the stair where the tawny light ran up into the darkness, my son slipped past me, and checked before a small deep-set door, and tried the latch with a small decisive rattle. Then, as the door did not open, he whipped out his dagger and beat upon the dusty timbers with its hilt. In the enclosed space of the stairway the sound seemed to beat upon one's ears, and the echoes woke and flung to and fro like startled bats, but nothing else answered to the summons, and after a moment Medraut began to beat again, crying out in a strange high voice like that of a woman on the edge of hysteria. "Open up! Open in Caesar's name, or we'll smash the door in!" And I felt the other men pressing up behind me, eager as hounds that wait for the quarry to break cover. And suddenly I knew that the thing that mattered to me most in the world was that I should not see what lay behind that door.

I caught Medraut's dagger wrist and dragged it down. "No! Either tell me the meaning of this foolery or else have done with it!"

But in the same instant the man on the step behind me reached forward and caught up something that lay like a snowflake on the

threshold of the doorway, and when he held it up to the torchlight
with a small puzzled laugh, I saw that it was a wood anemone, one
fragile white windflower already beginning to wilt. And I knew
that there could be no shelter for me, from what lay beyond that
small deep-set door.

There was the light grating sound of a key turning in the lock,
the door was flung open from within and the softer light of a fat-
lamp flowed out into the stairway to mingle with the flare of the
torches, and Bedwyr stood in the doorway, naked under a hastily
flung-on cloak, and with his drawn sword in his hand.

There was an instant's silence so intense that it pressed upon the
ears, and in the heart of it—the stillness at the heart of the storm—
Bedwyr and I stood face to face. I think that he was scarcely aware
of the other men, only of me, and of Guenhumara standing against
the wall behind him. "I did not know that you had returned to
Venta," I heard my own voice saying in the stillness, "but it seems
you have your reasons that I should not."

I rounded on the young men crowding the stair. None of them
were against me especially; they were against the Queen and
Caesar's captain, because Medraut had taught them to be. Only
Medraut had known that the blow was aimed at me, and the ruin
of the other two only incidental. "You have done your night's
work, now get out!" I shouted at them, and their faces stared up at
me, surprised, angry, resentful, out of the gloom of the stairway.
"Get out," I said again, more quietly, "back to your kennels—and
for you, Medraut—you too have done your night's work, and
most nobly! I would say that surely there can be no more cunning
spy among all the Little Dark People than you have proved yourself, but the Little Dark Ones I have always counted as my friends,
and I would not seem to insult them now."

The white mask was haggard, and I will swear that there was
sweat on his forehead. He had lowered the torch somewhat and
the copper glare of it beat like a gong in both our faces, and for one
instant it was as though his eyes flashed open upon me and I saw
in them twin blue sparks lit by the flames of hell. Then the veil, the
inner lid, descended again, and he said humbly, "If I have done ill,
let my father forgive me. I could not bear that men should laugh
behind your back—your own men; and even the Sea Wolves who

must come to hear of it, and think the less of Artorius Augustus who let himself be cuckolded by his dear familiar friend!"

"And doubtless all that you told to your dupes who were here just now," I said. "You have taken great care for my honor, somewhat less for your own. Now get out of my sight, and for God's sake keep out of it, for if you come near me again for a while, I think that I shall kill you."

He stood staring at me while the torch spluttered in his hand, and for a moment the muscles worked about his jaw and throat as though there was something more that he would say. Then he turned, with one long look at Bedwyr in passing that could not quite conceal his triumph, and ran down the curling stair as though the hounds of hell were after him.

Bedwyr still stood unmoving, as though on guard before the small deep-set doorway. "Get back inside," I said.

I saw him swallow, but he did not move, and deliberately I drew my sword and brought up the point to his throat. "Get back."

His hand tightened convulsively on his own sword hilt, and it hung by a hair, whether or not the next instant we should be fighting for the doorway.

Then Guenhumara cried out harshly, "Bedwyr! Do as he says!"

He hesitated an instant longer, then with his eyes still leveled on my face, took a step backward, and another. I followed, with the point of my sword still kissing his throat, until both of us were within the room; then crashed the door to behind me, and stood leaning against it, looking from him to Guenhumara and back again. The place was a store chamber, half full of cloth bales and raw fleece; several of the fleeces had been pulled out from the stack and piled to make a couch, and on the black ramskin spread uppermost of all, lay a broken garland of wood anemones. I saw all that by the soft light of the fat-oil lamp, yet I never looked at anything but Bedwyr's face and Guenhumara's.

"Did you ever go to Coed Gwyn at all?" I drove my sword back into its wolfskin sheath and my own voice seemed to rasp at my throat as the blade rasped against its casing. "Have you had good hunting in the Arfon hills, this half winter past, or was there richer hunting here? Did you merely lie up within a day's ride of Venta, until I was safely away and the Queen could send for you?"

Bedwyr spoke for the first time, tossing down his own sword, since the sheath was not on him. "The hunting was good in Arfon, and I returned from it yesterday, not even knowing that you were away."

"A fortunate chance!" I said. "And it seems that you wasted little time in making good use of it!"

Silence took us by the throat. Guenhumara still stood pressed against the wall as though impaled there, so that I might almost have thought to see the spear shaft between her breasts. Her unbound hair fell in a strong tawny smoke about her, and her eyes, straining to mine, seemed mere blind black holes in her deathly face.

"Artos," Bedwyr said at last, "I plead no excuses for either of us; to do so would be a waste of breath. Guenhumara and I have loved each other, tonight. But I swear to you before whatever gods there be, that this was the first and only time."

I laughed, and the sound of the laughter was foul and brutal in my own ears. "Did love come on you so suddenly, then? Did you sup with her to keep her from another lonely evening, and find too late that Sasticca had mingled mandrake in the wine cup? How is it then, that all men know what has been going forward? Even my armor-bearer cried out to me not to go with Medraut tonight, knowing well enough what I should find!"

Bedwyr showed neither shame nor anger, only grief in the haggard lines of his face, and of all strange and unexpected things, a certain grave kindliness. He could afford to be kind. "No need for mandrake," he said. "The care that is between Guenhumara and me grew slowly and in the dark."

"In the dark!" I echoed bitterly.

"But not as you mean it. Listen to me, Artos, whatever comes after, listen to me now. For more than ten years, you and I and Guenhumara have been closer to each other than to any other living soul, and Guenhumara is a woman. We did not know, any more than you knew, the thing that was happening, until you brought me to her, sick with my wound after Badon."

"And you had all the summer together, while I was sweating on the war trail."

"And we had all the summer together, while you were sweating on the war trail. Was that our fault?"

I thought of the autumn evening and the light nonsense that we had tossed like a golden ball, to and fro. "So that was why you went back to your own quarters?"

"Yes, when you came back I knew that I must go because she was yours."

"You forgot that easily enough tonight. Your memory, it seems, is not of the best."

"I had been up in the mountains alone, all the end of winter, all the bitter waking spring, sleeping alone and eating my heart out. And when I came back, and saw her again, I forgot that she belonged to you, and remembered only that my love clung to her, and hers to me."

I remember that it was then, in the pause that followed, that Guenhumara came away from the wall to stand beside him. "It is true, Artos, it is true, every word of it," she said.

And I, God help me, I knew now where her new kindness, her air of harvest, had come from; and it was as though the dark lifeblood were draining away from some wound in me. I had always sworn to myself that if Guenhumara took a lover, I would not be jealous, remembering that I had failed her; but I had never thought, never in my darkest and coldest dreams, that the lover would be Bedwyr. Strange are the ways of the heart. I think that truly I could have allowed Guenhumara her lover: I know that if Bedwyr had taken any other woman it would have troubled me no more than did Cei's wenchings. But they had turned to each other, the two people I loved best in the world, and doing so, each had taken the other from me, and I was left outcast and alone, and betrayed. The black bitterness rose and rose within me, and there was a little drum pounding, pounding, behind my temples.

Guenhumara came half a step toward me, with her hands held out, and her voice had the throb of a swan's wings in flight, that had always shaken the heart in my breast. "Artos, for your own sake as well as for ours, try to forgive us!"

And I said, "What is there to forgive? There is only once in your life and mine, that ever I was more than half a man to you. It is but the way of things that the mare needs the stallion at the right season!"

She cried out at that as though I had struck her. "Artos, no!" and gave back the half step again.

And I saw something in her face and in Bedwyr's that made the hammer stop beating in my head. "My God! You never told him that, did you!"

[444]

It was Bedwyr who answered. "No, she never told me that."

"That was—merciful of her."

"No," Guenhumara said. "The things that are between you and me are not for sharing with Bedwyr."

"Nor the things which are between you and Bedwyr for sharing with me. Did ever you love me at all, Guenhumara?"

She did not come back the half step, but I think that something of her longing was toward me, even then. "Yes," she said, "only we could never cross each other's thresholds. I tried as well as you, but we could never cross."

I stepped sideways from before the door, for it seemed to me that this thing was ended. "That is all there is to say, isn't it?"

Neither of them moved, and I turned on Bedwyr, who seemed to have drawn aside in spirit from what concerned only Guenhumara and me. "Well then, what now? You have tasted her, and it seems that the taste pleases. Are you not going to claim her from me?"

The old mocking smile twisted his lips an instant. "Does a wise man claim Caesar's wife from Caesar?"

Guenhumara said quickly, "That is what you will do? You will send us away?"

"What else did you think I should do?"

"I don't know. If you were a different man, I think that you might have us killed. As it is—I don't know." She drew a long shaken breath, and began to bargain, or I thought at the time that she was trying to bargain, though I could not grasp her purpose, for I knew well enough that the queenship mattered little to her. I understand now that she was striving desperately to save something out of the ruin, to salve some rags of good for all three of us, for me most of all. "If you will forgive this one night—" Her voice broke and she steadied it, too proud to use a woman's weapon of tears. "If it seems to you that the years that I have been your faithful wife, and Bedwyr your loyal lieutenant, have any weight to set against this one night, I will promise you—on my knees if you like— that we will never again be alone together, nor speak one word to each other when you are not by."

Fool! To think *that* was the thing that mattered, the mere fact of lovemaking. Fool not to understand that I would have had her lie with Bedwyr a score of times, not loving him, rather than know her

[445]

heart crying out to him while she lay faithful one night in my arms. Bedwyr understood, but in some ways Bedwyr and I were nearer to each other than Guenhumara and I had ever been.

"Bedwyr would need to make the half of that promise," I said harshly, "and I think that he would not make it. Na na, Guenhumara, you offer a thing too hard for mere mortals, for me as well as you. You are no more my wife—nor you, Bedwyr, my lieutenant and my sword brother; all that is finished. . . . It should be pleasant at Coed Gwyn now, though I fear that the snowdrops will be over. You have until noon to make what arrangements you need, and be out of Venta."

Guenhumara began to plead again, desperately. "Artos, listen— oh listen! Not both of us! Surely it is enough if you banish one? Send *me* away—send me home in shame to my father's hearth, for a bad woman who dishonored your bed; or if you are more merciful, let me go back to the House of Holy Ladies at Eburacum, as of my own free will. Only let you not send Bedwyr from you; the time comes when you will need him as you never needed him before!"

Bedwyr still stood unmoving, an image of silent grief, his chin sunk into his cloak and his sword fallen at his feet. He raised his head and looked at me, and I know we were both thinking of the House of Holy Ladies in the Street of the Clothworkers, and Guenhumara clinging to me, looking back as I carried her away, with that shudder as of a wild goose flying over her grave. . . . "Will you abide by that?" I cried to him. "Great God, man, will you let her take the whole payment on her shoulders?"

"In the part assigned to me, there would perhaps be something of payment also." His words blurred a little, as though his lips were stiff. "But I think that the question does not arise."

All the flame of my anger had sunk to gray ash, and I was cold to my inmost soul, and suddenly very weary. I said, "Na, it does not arise, there is no more place for you here than there is for her. Take her and go, for I want neither of you near me ever again."

I dragged open the door, and with Guenhumara's voice in my ears, calling my name for the last time, stumbled my way down the stairs in the dark, blundering against the walls like one very drunk.

In the courtyard a breath of wind tossed the last living branch of the wild pear tree, and scattered a few fragile petals into the dark well water. . . .

CHAPTER THIRTY-FOUR

Thinning Ranks

THE next day was the third Sunday in the month, a day when, by long custom, Ambrosius, whenever he was in Venta, had sat in audience for any man who had a wrong to be righted, a grievance to air, a plan to put forward, to come to him in the Great Hall. I had continued that practice after him and so that Sunday I sat in the High Seat on the dais with certain of the Com- in this man's need for release from military service, and that wom- an's complaint against the corn merchant. The old cloak of im- perial purple that had also been Ambrosius's hung on me as heavily as did the custom of the day, but it was good that I had something that must be done. I think if I could have rested that day, I should have gone mad. . . . The first humblebee of the year had strayed in from outside and was bruising its head against one of the windows that still had glass in it, in futile attempt at escape, and the sound teased and tangled at the edges of my atten- tion. "No escape, no escape—" I frowned, striving to concentrate on the rights and wrongs of the case being poured out before me.

There were more people than usual that day, but of course all Venta must know by now; they stared and whispered, or I thought they did, and I did not care, if only they would go, if only I need not sit there seeing their faces—faces after faces after faces—through a haze made by the throbbing in my head.

It was over and the last of the waiting throng in the forecourt chair empty at my side, and strove to make my bruised brain take panions ranged for a ceremonial guard behind me, and the Queen's had melted away, and the gray light of day was fading in soft spring rain beyond the windows. And I was about to rise and go back to Ambrosius's quarters—I had given orders for my gear to be fetched from the Queen's Courtyard, which was home to me no longer—when a confused tramp of many footsteps sounded outside, and Pharic's voice answered by another, and as I glanced questioningly at Cei who stood big and grim and gray-golden beside my chair, Guenhumara's brother came in by the lower door, carrying his favorite falcon hooded on his fist, and followed by all that were left of the mounted band who had come to me as her dowry.

He strode up the hall to stand before me, his tall Caledonians tramping behind him. He made the customary salute before the High Seat, and stood there with his head tipped far back and the level black brows joined into one bar, frowning, and stared at me out of hot red-brown eyes.

"You have something to say to me?" I demanded, at last.

"Aye," he said. "It is this, Artorius Augustus. It has been told to us that last night you sent Guenhumara my sister and your Queen from the court in shame."

"It was not I who set the shame on her forehead," I said coldly.

"Na, and for that reason, because she herself wove the shame, we seek no feud between you and us, no vengeance for your putting her away. Yet still, to me, she is my sister, and to all of us she is the daughter of our chieftain's hall, and therefore we, who have been your men loyally for ten years and more, count ourselves no more among the ranks of the Companions, because you put her away in shame."

"I understand," I said. "You have my leave to go north again to your own place."

The hot hawk's stare never changed or wavered from my face. "We seek no leave. We go north, back to our own hills, taking with us the women we have married and the bairns we have bred here in the South. We come to tell you this, no more."

I remember sitting there in the High Seat, with the carved wolf's heads on the foreposts biting into my hands, staring and staring into the midst of that proud unswerving gaze. "So be it," I said at last. "When do you ride?"

"The horses are already saddled, and there will be something of a moon, later."

"Then it seems that there is nothing more to be said."

"One thing more." Pharic's gaze, leaving my face for the first time, moved deliberately to that of my armor-bearer, who sat in attendance on the dais steps with my spear and buckler across his knees. "Come, Riada."

He got up slowly but without hesitation; clearly he had expected the summons and knew that it must be obeyed. But he turned to look at me with a troubled and wretched face. "Sir, I do not wish to go. But they are my tribe."

"They are your tribe," I said.

He knelt for an instant and touched my foot in the old gesture, then rose and went to join Pharic. And with a last grave salute—there was no hot blood in this parting; it was, as it were, a matter of honor, almost of ritual—the whole band turned about and strode down the hall.

When they were gone, the great chamber seemed very empty, and I was aware suddenly of the rattle of spring rain against the windows, and the bee still bruising its foolish head against the thick greenish panes. I got up slowly, and turned to the door behind the dais. Cei followed me in silence like a big faithful hound, and I turned to him in the doorway, resting a hand on his shoulder for the comfort that I might have found in resting it on Cabal's head. "Do you remember my saying to you once that I'd have no married women to make trouble among the Companions? That when two men desired one woman, that was when the Brotherhood began to break?"

"Something of the sort," Cei said heavily.

"I was right, wasn't I?"

The faithful core of the Brotherhood never broke, save by death, which is another matter. But neither Flavian nor Gwalchmai, not even Cei, were as near to me as Bedwyr had been, and I knew to the full the solitude above the snow line that I had dreaded all my life. And since, in the years that came after, even fighting had for the most part given place to statecraft, there was little to do save work. So I worked, while the springs and autumns passed and in the courtyard where I had kept my dogs as a boy, the last branch of the wild pear tree died. I worked at the task of making Britain strong, of hammering out a stable government; I labored over the treaty with the coastwise Saxons, that the thing might not fall to pieces when I could no longer hold it secure in the hollow of my hand. It is all without life in my mind as a badly tempered blade. All my life I have been a fighting man by nature, an administrator only by difficult adoption. Also, so far as might be, I stopped feeling, in those years, and the things that enter only by the head, no man remembers as he does the things that enter by the heart.

Cerdic had taken the three war boats that were his, with a full crew of sword companions to each of them, and before his days of grace were all run out, had left the shores of Britain. We heard of him from time to time, briefly and uncertainly as the flicker of summer lightning at twilight, now here, now there, chiefly as a raider, occasionally as a sailor of strange seas. We began to hear of him at Portus Namnetus on the Gaulish coast; the place was the perfect stamping ground for the son of Fox Vortigern and the Lady Rowan, for in the country about the Liger mouth, Celt and Saxon for no reason had come together and made a mingled race. And as time went by, it seemed that he had made his home quarters there. Until the ninth or tenth summer after Badon, that was all.

By then, in my efforts to keep the four tribal runs of the Old Kingdom knit together, I had come to spend almost as much time in Sorviodunum, Aquae Sulis and Calleva as I did in Venta, and that year about midsummer, I took the court up to Sorviodunum. It was a dim and sultry summer, the kind of weather in which fever breeds, and the Yellow Hag had come earlier than usual to the towns; but I had never taken the fever—indeed I have seldom in all my life been sick without a wound on me—and so when an aching head and a shiver between the shoulders came upon me on the day after our arrival, I thought only that I had got chilled in the thunder rain that had drenched us on the long ride up from Venta. But within two days I was raving.

At first there were clear intervals, when I returned from the whirling flame-touched world of the fever-madness to the misery of my own body; to darkness that suffocated me or light that clashed like a hammer even when my eyes were closed. And swimming out of a fiery fog into one such interval, I was aware of sounds of gathering and preparation in the world outside, feet, and voices, and the yelp of a trumpet call that was answered from the far side of the city, aware also of Cei and Gwalchmai in urgent low-voiced conclave in the doorway of the long room among the rafters of the King's Chamber where I lay.

They looked toward me, and with the preternaturally sharpened hearing that comes sometimes with fever, I heard Gwalchmai say: "Yes, now. Be as swift about it as you can; there's no means of knowing how long before the Yellow Hag claims him again."

Then Cei was standing over me, with his thumbs thrust into his sword belt in the way that he had, bending forward to peer into my face. "My Lord Artos," he said, faintly questioning.

"What—is it, Cei? What—all that trampling and trumpeting— outside." My tongue felt as though it was made of boiled leather, and the worried weather-burned face and burly big-paunched figure slipped to and fro on my sight the more I tried to hold it still.

"It is Cerdic—Artos. Can you hear what I say?"

"What of Cerdic?"

"He's landed on the west side of Vectis Water, and a young war host with him. They got in in the rain and murk two days since and were ashore before the coast wardens knew a thing of their coming. We got the news last night."

I remember struggling to my elbow and cursing him that I had not been told before—as though any word could have reached me; I remember striving to be out of my bed, and shouting to Gwalchmai for a draught of some kind that would give me the strength to ride for a few days even if it killed me after, and the two of them holding me back and striving to quieten me as though I were a fire-maddened horse. . . . Later, when I was quiet again, I have a dim half memory of setting some kind of scrawl that might serve for a signature to the marching orders and to an authority for Cei to take command of the war host, and pressing Maximus's seal onto the hot wax, while Cei steadied the blade of the great sword above my wavering hand. No memory of Cei leaving the room, for I was off and away on my travels once more.

It seemed a very long while later, and indeed I think it was many days, when I began to know myself within the dark shell of my body again, and later still, grew slowly sure that there was a dagger in my back, below the left shoulder blade. Presently I found there was no dagger there, only the blade-shaped pain of the dagger. But the pain pierced deeper and deeper all the while, until I was snatching at my breath like a winded runner, and the world that had just begun to return dissolved about me again into fiery chaos in which the only sure thing was Medraut's face like a white death mask hanging in the air wherever I looked, until at last that too was burned up in the fires, and the fire itself engulfed in a last great darkness.

How long I lay slung between life and death, I have never been able to judge with any certainty, but it cannot have been far short of a month between the time I first fell sick and the time I awoke in fading lamplight and felt the air of very early morning on my face, and knew that I could breathe again and that I was lying cool and sodden in a pool of sweat.

I tried to drag myself out of it, and could not. And then the Minnow, who was now my armor-bearer, was bending over me, feeling my body with eager hands. He said, "Oh sir, we thought that you would die!" and most surprisingly I felt what seemed to be a drop of warm rain on my face.

I mumbled something about being wet enough already, and the boy began to crow and whimper with laughter, and then Gwalchmai was beside me also, and they were lifting me out of the sodden rugs and spreading over me dry warm ones that smelled of the storage herbs. And sleep gathered me into a gentle darkness.

Day after day I lay flat on the rug-piled bed place under the musty-smelling thatch that twittered with swallows' nests (it was the King's Chamber, but conditions were harsher at Sorviodunum than at Venta), tended by Gwalchmai and the Minnow, and the small tubby Jew who had stepped into old Ben Simeon's shoes. There was a sense of gulf behind me, and everything about me seemed small and bright and far off, like its own reflection in a silver cup. I had no more strength at first than a half-drowned puppy, but at least my mind was my own again, and I was able to demand and attend to news of the fighting—though indeed there was little news that had any form or coherence to it, only a long confused talking of skirmishes and small-scale indecisive actions; of Cerdic's brilliant use of salt marsh and sea inlet and steaming damp-oak forest, which were home conditions to him now to hold off our own war host from coming to grips with the Saxon kind. At any other time I should have been wild and fuming to take the command myself, but I was so weak, so newly back from the edge of all things, so possessed still with the sense of everything being small and far away, that I was content to lie still and leave the campaign, such as it was, in Cei's hands.

Gwalchmai was the impatient one, wanting to be with his wounded. He took pains to hide it, but I had not known my Hawk of May for the better part of a lifetime without being able to read his mood and his longings. . . . One evening, when he came to see me after supper as he always did, I remember grumbling to him at the snail pace of my returning strength, and he raised his brows at me. "It is not usual that a man who has passed straight from the Yellow Hag to the Lung Fever finds himself ready to outwrestle the wild aurochs within the week. You are mending, my friend. You'll do well enough now."

"And so I suppose you want to leave me and be away to the war host," I said.

He sat down in the big carved cross-legged chair beside the hearth, with a small grunting sigh, and rubbed his knee. "I'll bide as long as you need me."

I turned toward him, seeing with a sudden warm rush of affection, the tired old man that he had become, dried and withered like the wild pear branch in the well courtyard, and I knew that he was not fit for the camp and the war trail, and knew also that he must go. "As to that, I've Ben Eleaza to brew my poisons for me. There's others needing you more than I do now."

"I'll not deny that I'll be glad to get back to the war host and the wounded," he said simply. "My chief business has been with them a good few years."

"A mere thirty or so. There's a good few of us would be dead at least once before this, if it wasn't for your sharp little knife and stinking fever potions."

"There's a good few of us dead, even so," Gwalchmai said soberly, and we were both thinking back, as men growing old do think back, remembering comrades living and comrades dead, who had been young with us when the Brotherhood itself was young. So the thing was settled and we bided talking for a while, until it was time for Gwalchmai to make his preparations for the journey.

When he got up to go, he swayed suddenly and caught at the back of the chair to steady himself, and for the moment, as he stood brushing his hand across his forehead, it seemed to me that a

[453]

gray shadow stole over his face, and fear brushed me by. "What's amiss? Oh good God, Gwalchmai, not you, now!"

"Eh?" He looked up, shaking his head as though to clear it. "Na na, maybe a little tired, that's all. Sometimes I think I'm getting old."

"You're ten years younger than I am."

"I daresay I'll last a few years more," Gwalchmai said, and limped serenely to the door—his limp had worsened in the last few years.

I never saw him again.

I had regained just enough strength to crawl from the bed place to my chair beside the hearth, and sit there muffled in rugs, generally with a couple of hounds at my feet (but no hound of mine was ever called Cabal again) when there came to me a certain dispatch from Cei. My lieutenant's writing was never overeasy to decipher, oddly small and cramped for such a big tempestuous writer, and I pored over it, holding it to the flickering light of the fire, for though it must be still daylight outside, the shutters were closed over the small ragged windows in the thatch, to keep out wind and rain. Moreover, the letter deserved careful reading, for at last there was something to report; the Saxons brought to action at last, and a full-scale battle on the Cloven Way, almost half distance between Venta and Cerdic's landing beach. Cei had written me the plain account of it, move by countermove and phase by phase, together with certain facts or seeming facts concerning the left cavalry wing which made ugly reading. I could imagine how he would have bitten at his quill and glared in trouble at the lines as he set them down. And in the end, though the Sea Wolves had indeed been halted and even turned back, at cost of bitter manloss to ourselves, no decisive victory to report; little gained from the whole summer's campaigning, save that Cerdic was still penned to the south side of the Forest. And the first of the equinoctial gales was beating its wings against the rattling shutters as I read, and I knew that the campaigning season was over for that year.

When I had reached the cramped signature, I sat for a long time holding the unrolled parchment in my hand. Then I called up the Minnow, who was squatting between the hounds burnishing a shield, and sent him for one of the clerks to take down a letter in my turn. But mine was to Medraut. I don't know quite what

purpose I hoped to serve by summoning him; I suppose I had
some idea that if I confronted him with the thing face to face, I
might know whether my almost formless suspicions of him were
just or not.

A few days later, sleeping before the fire—I slept a great deal at
that time—I dreamed of Coed Gwyn, the White Wood, dreamed
of the struck notes of a harp, and Guenhumara combing her hair
beside a peat fire and Bedwyr sitting with his head against her
knees; and great wings that beat me back when I cried out and
would have gone to them. . . . And woke with the wet feel of
tears on my face, to the wings of another storm drubbing at the
shutters and driving the smoke down from the fire hole, and
Medraut standing by the hearth.

The rain was still dark on the shoulders of his flung-back cloak,
and he stood with one foot on the warm hearthstone, staring into
the red eye of the fire, and stripping and stripping his riding gloves
between his fingers; the look on him, as always when one saw him
suddenly and alone, of having stood there, quite patiently waiting,
for a very long time. His cloak was clasped at the shoulder by a
new brooch, a black opal set in braided gold wires, that had the
look of a gift from some woman. Generally he had something of
the sort about him, for I have seen that often an aging woman
with a young lover will make him such gifts, and Medraut picked
and handled his loves with care, always older women, and those
that would dance the man-and-woman dance charmingly with him
and raise little trouble when the dance was over. And yet, lightly
and cynically as he turned from one woman to another, I think
that some part of him was seeking always his mother. It was that
that made his womanizing both foul and oddly piteous.

For an instant, I saw him without his being aware of any eye
upon him save those of the hounds at my feet, yet his face betrayed no more than it would have done had he known himself
under scrutiny. He had grown a shell of cool assurance that he
had not possessed ten years ago, and looking at him it was easy to
believe that he was a magnificent cavalry commander—but it would
have been as easy to believe that he was anything else, in the
empty chamber behind his eyes. As he could blend into the surroundings of his life, so it seemed that he could take on the color

of one's own thoughts, so that I could never be quite sure whether I saw Medraut, or only what I imagined Medraut to be. Only in the opal on his shoulder, the flame and peacock colors woke and shimmered and died again, and I had the strange fancy that in the dark fires of the jewel one might read what never showed behind his eyes.

Then one of the hounds stirred, growling very softly—most dogs disliked Medraut—and he looked my way and saw that I was awake and watching him and stopped playing with his wet riding gloves. "God's greeting to you, Artos my father. You are better, they tell me."

"God's greeting to you, Medraut my son; I grow stronger each day." It was the first time in ten years that he had stood before me in my own quarters.

"You sent for me," he said at last.

"I sent for you—in the first place that you may explain to me why this summer's campaigning against Cerdic and his followers has had no better success."

He stiffened for a moment and then said quickly, "At least we halted their northward advance, and thrust them back into the lower forest and the marshes."

"But not back to the coast—and that by the loss, it seems, of many men to our war host and few to theirs."

"My father knows that the fever has thinned our own ranks; and also what like of country that is to fight over."

"A land blurred between land and water, swamp and forest. A country, more than any other part of our coastline, well nigh impossible to clear of an enemy, once they have made good their landing."

"Well?" he said softly and on the faintest note of challenge.

"I have been thinking it something strange that Cerdic should know so well where the soft belly lies most open to the knife. I have been thinking it fortunate for him that he should choose a summer when the Yellow Hag is rife among the war host ranged against him."

I wondered if it was possible, remembering the night we made the East Coast treaty, that this son of mine, who had come to me eaten with jealousy of Cerdic my enemy, should have common cause with him now. I had a sick feeling that it was perfectly possible. Christos! If only I could look just once behind his eyes. . . .

"Doubtless Cerdic has his scouting parties—and alas! there are traitors in every camp."

"Not in every camp," I said, "but undoubtedly in some." I pulled myself up in the great chair, thrusting back the dark warm wolf furs, for suddenly I seemed suffocating, and reached for the narrow parchment roll that lay on the table beside me, but I did not open it, I knew the contents by heart. "Your arguments are unanswerable. See if you can do as well with the final engagement on the Cloven Way."

He dropped his gaze for an instant to the letter I held, then raised it again blandly to my face. "Cei will have given you a better and fuller account of that than I can do."

"Better, doubtless, but not so detailed at certain points. There is, for instance, a curious lack of detail in his account of the breakup of the left wing that robbed us of a fully decisive victory."

"The left wing being my command," Medraut said, and began again to play with his gloves. "The detail is very easily supplied. Cei failed to second me at the crucial moment."

"Cei states that you were in no need of seconding, and he had sharper call for the reserves elsewhere, until the whole center of the wing crumpled without warning."

"But then, Cei has always hated me," he said.

"Cei doesn't know how to hate—not as we understand the word," I said. "He's too like a Saxon. It takes the Celtic blood to know truly how to hate."

And we looked at each other, eye to eye, in a small and powerful stillness in the heart of the storm that battered the shutters and drove the white rain hushing across the thatch. But the opal at his shoulder caught fire from an infinitesimal movement and for an instant was an eye opened on some strange and beautiful half-hell.

Then Medraut retreated a little. "In battle it is not always easy to choose—even to know—where lies the sharpest need. *I* know that my need of seconding was as the need of lifeblood, but it seemed that Cei did not. Let my father believe I fought the best action that I could without."

"Cei states here that you wheeled your charge-back on too close a curve, so that the formation became clogged and ragged, and consequently the impact lost its force."

"It seems that the account was *not* so lacking in detail!"

"There is no more to it than that," I said. "But Name of Names! That is the mistake of a raw squadron captain on his first maneuvers; you are among the most able of cavalry commanders, Medraut; that kind of mistake is not for you!"

He gave me a small bow; his face had drained of color so that in the light of the fat-lamp, the faint discoloration of the lids made his eyes seem painted like a woman's. "My father is overlavish with his praise. . . . There is always, of course, the question of land shape to be considered; this has been a wet summer, and the valley turned oversoft for horses a short distance below our fighting ground. Unfortunately even the most able of your cavalry commanders cannot command a countryside to give him sufficient elbow room."

I had the sense of trying to hold a marsh light between finger and thumb that one always felt when dealing with Medraut, and knew that whatever purpose I had hoped to serve by this interview, I had served none; none in the world. "So." I laid Cei's letter back on the table beside me. "You have accounted for all things most nobly," and my voice sounded old and hopeless in my own ears.

"That was all my father wished to say to me?"

"Yes. No, one thing more." I struggled to clear my mind from the gray cloud of weariness that still descended upon me so easily. "I have said that you are among the most able of my cavalry commanders, and that is no more than the truth; you also have the trick of drawing good fortune to you in battle, and so you have a large following. But men do not follow you for love, any more than you lead them for love. If you make more mistakes of that kind you will begin to lose your reputation not only for skill, but for luck, and if you lose that, you will lose your following."

He smiled, a smile that was light and sweet as honey smeared on aloes leaves. "My father has no need to warn me, I know to the thumbnail's breadth what I can afford, and I shall not afford more. I never gamble beyond my means."

"See that you don't," I said, "only see that you don't, Medraut."

The smile became yet sweeter, but he still played with his gloves and maybe that was to hide that his hands were shaking. "I have my father's leave to go? I made great haste to answer his summons, and I am something wet."

In the doorway, his hand on the golden Ophir rug that hung

[458]

across the ill-fitting door, he checked and turned once more. "Has any news come to my father lately out of Arfon?"

"What news should there be out of Arfon?"

"Only women's news, to be sure. They say that Maelgwn has taken a second bride."

I was surprised, not at the news (for Maelgwn's first wife had died the previous year, and he was not one to sleep long alone), but that Medraut should trouble with it.

"And begun to build another oratory," added Medraut.

"So? Is there some connection?"

"The bride was his nephew's wife—not his half sister, I grant you, but still, his nephew's wife—Gwen Alarch, they call her." He was as malicious as a gossiping old woman with a young one's name in her hands. "The boy was killed hunting, and some say not by accident, but I doubt if Maelgwn loses as much sleep over *that* as for another cause. . . . Maybe he'll get him a son yet, and I'd not count too much on his faith-keeping hereafter, if that happens."

"Na?" I said.

He shook his head. "Na. After all, the Saxon flood will not rise far into the mountains; and with a son to follow him, it must seem the more desirable to make sure of the Lordship of Arfon after you."

And noticing that he set himself aside from all claim to Arfon, I knew well enough the reason—that he flew at higher game. And again it crossed my mind that it was as well that I had never allowed Constantine to be openly named as my heir. Medraut must know clearly enough where the choice must fall, but as long as nothing was said, he would be in no hurry. There was a deadly patience about him, as there had been about his mother.

The golden rug swung back into place and his light step was swallowed instantly by the wind and the rain—unless he was still standing outside, smiling that light swift sweet smile that made one's blood feel thin.

Gwalchmai died about that same time, as quietly and suddenly as a tired man falling asleep by the fire after a hard day's work, Cei told me, weeping for him, when a few days later the first of the Company returned to winter quarters.

The ranks were thinning fast.

CHAPTER THIRTY-FIVE

The Traitor

NEXT spring I was prepared for another thrust of the Sea Wolves, but though we heard of more of the long war boats following in the wake of last year's, and others with women and even children, the thrust never came; and when we moved against them in our turn, they simply melted among the forest and marshlands like a mist.

And so as the years passed, the thing settled into a fitful border warfare which has served to keep the Sea Wolves penned within some kind of frontier, but no more. It seems strange, when one comes to think of it, that we have not been able to drive them back into the sea. And yet—I don't know—there is Pictish blood in the folk of those parts, left over from the great Pict Wars of Maximus's day; the Picts are second only to the Little Dark People for knowing the secret possibilities of their own countryside, and they do not love the smell of Rome.

Also, we have never, in all these years, been free to turn the whole war host their way; there has been Eburacum and the Lindum coastline in need of our aid, and the Scots from the West every summer, and not even a whole heart within ourselves, for among the princes of the Cymri, who have always fought like dogs whenever the High King's hand was off them, the word was running to and fro like a little furtive wind through the grass, that Artos the Bear was one who had forgotten his own people to carry a Roman sword. Maybe someone set that word running; I do not know. I know that three years since, I had to deal with the princedoms of Vortiporus and Cynglass as one deals with enemy territory. . . .

This summer the Scots made a sudden attack on Môn and the

coast of all the northern Cymri (last summer the harvest failed
and last winter was a lean one; that always sets the young men
wandering) and I went up with two hundred of the Companions,
leaving Cei in command at Venta, to the aid of Maelgwn and the
coastwise princes who were for the most part still loyal. The Scots
are brave men though their fires flare too windily over too little of
red heart; and it was the beginning of harvesttime before the flurry
of small buffeting wide-spaced attacks were dealt with to the last
one.

We made our base camp, our central stronghold all summer, in
the old Roman fort of Segontium that clung to the foot of the
mountains commanding the Straits of Môn, until with the shores
quiet again, it was time to be turning the horses' heads south once
more. It was a soft evening, that last one I spent—the last that I
shall ever spend—among my own hills, the sun westering into a
smoky haze beyond the low hills of Môn, and every comber of the
western sea shot through with translucent gold as it came in to
crash and cream below the fortress walls. Arfon tore at my heart
that evening, all the shadowed glens of Arfon and swift white falls
of mountain water, and the high tops that were tawny now in late
summer as a hound's coat, and the moss-fragrant woods below
Dynas Pharaon where I shall not walk again. I would have put
off the parting for a few days longer, lingering, finding some excuse, but I knew we should have slow traveling on the way south,
for I intended to swing wide of the direct road, in order to pass
through as many of the Cymric and border princedoms as might
be, and sup in hall with as many of their lords. I thought it might
serve some good purpose, that they should see the High King at
their own hearths. God help me, I was still fool enough to cling
to that old hopeless dream of a Britain strongly enough bonded
to stand with shields still linked, when I was no longer there.

Fool! Fool! Fool!

With a short while to waste before supper, I had gone up with
Maelgwn into the old watchtower at the southeast angle of the
fort, to look at the falcons we had housed there—Maelgwn was a
falconer to his fingertips, like Pharic, and where he went his hawks
went too. I can see the small round chamber now—lit partly by the
coppery sunset light through the archer's window, partly by the
flare of the newly kindled torch in its sconce by the winding stair-

head. The hawks and falcons hooded and unhooded on their perches, with the startling black and white slashes of their mutes patterning the wall behind them. I can smell the smoke curling up the stair from the driftwood and sea-wrack fire that the falconers had lit in the chamber below, and hear the harsh cries and wing clappings of feeding time. Maelgwn had pulled on an ancient hawking glove, and was feeding the birds himself, taking from his falconer the gobbets of meat, and holding each in turn to the bird that snatched it from him. The last, and clearly his favorite, was a young golden eagle, whom he took up to feed on the fist. "This one I took myself from the eyrie in May; a small thing of down and quills, but a demon even then—eh, my Lucifer?" He held a bloody partridge to the bird, who took it with a lightning strike of the talons, and began to break it up with the delicacy of its kind; and then, the food being gone, rattled his feathers and sat with distended crop, brooding on his lord's fist, like a chained Caesar and outglaring the world in general with a mad topaz eye. They were two of a kind, I thought, watching the man standing where he had moved into the window with the great bird on his fist; both predators, both knowing no law but their own, both magnificent in their way, and I wondered again if they were true, those tales of his first wife's death being no natural one. It was certainly true that he had killed the boy for the sake of Gwen Alarch's pretty hair and little soft breasts. Well, he would hold Arfon with a strong hand after me, he might ride the princedom with a wolf bit himself, but assuredly no other would encroach on its borders. I wished that I could be as sure of Constantine's strength.

Suddenly Maelgwn's likeness to the eagle sharpened, as his eyes widened, focusing on something a long way off, and his finger checked in the light repeated movement of drawing again and again down the burnished neck feathers.

He said nothing, but I got up from the box on which I had been sitting and crossed to the window.

Far up the track that had once been the military road from Moridunum and the South a small puff of dust caught the last of the sunlight and turned to a golden smudge with a seed of darkness at its heart. It was scarcely larger than a plume of thistle silk, and yet I knew—or maybe it only seemed afterward as though I knew—that it was the doom I had waited for almost forty years, that the rider hammering down the old road through the mountains, with his dust cloud rolling behind him, was the Dark Rider, for me.

"Someone has an urgent tale to tell, that he carries it at that speed," Maelgwn said.

I nodded, but I do not think I spoke; watching that small ominous plume of dust spin nearer at breakneck speed, dropping out of the sunlight that still clung to the skirts of the hills, into the shadows that were already creeping in across the coast. And a few moments later I heard, faintly, faintly as the blood in my own ears, above the soft voice of the sea, the beat of horse's hooves. In a little, I could see the horseman, bent low over his horse's neck, and the drum of hooves rose pounding and urgent; it was almost dusk now, below the fortress walls, and men and torches were gathering to the gate. I pushed off with my hands from the high cold window ledge; time to go down. . . . "It will be for me," I said, and turned and clattered down the winding stair, my own shadow wheeling darkly ahead of me on the torchlit wall. Maelgwn followed me, still carrying the golden eagle, and at the foot of the stairway Flavian joined us, hurrying from the stables.

The gates were open when we reached the clear space before them, and in the midst of a small startled crowd a man was dropping from the back of a foundered horse. The poor brute was black with sweat and crusted with the summer dust, his flanks heaved distressfully, and the foam dripping from his muzzle as he stood with drooping head was rank and bloody; and the rider, staggering where he stood, was in little better case, white from head to foot with the dust that had made raw red rims around his bleared eyes, save where the trickling sweat had cut channels in it down his haggard forehead and cheeks. Indeed it was small wonder that in the first moment of seeing him neither Flavian nor I recognized his son.

Then Flavian uttered a startled exclamation, and it was as though a film dropped from my eyes. "Minnow! What word do you bring me?"

He looked up at sound of my voice, and came and stumbled onto his knees at my feet, his head and shoulders hanging. "An ill word." The dust was in his throat too, and his voice a mere croak. "An ill word, my Lord Artos. Do not make me speak it; it is all here in this letter—"

I took the roll which he pulled from the breast of his tunic and handed up to me, broke Cei's familiar seal and snapped the crimson thread, and opened it out. Someone was holding a torch for me, and the flames of it, teased by the light sea wind that was rising with sunset, fluttered over the crabbed writing. Yet I had none of my usual difficulty in reading anything from Cei's hand; it was as though it read itself, every word striking up at me from the ill-cured parchment with a small cold separate shock. I read on, neither slow nor quick, and when the last word was reached, looked up, with a head that felt cold and clear and oddly separate from my body. I saw the faces of my own Companions and those who followed Maelgwn turned toward me in the torchlight, stilled in waiting and unspoken question.

"This is from Cei," I said. "He sends me word that Cerdic of the West Seax has been strengthened by a great war fleet from the Ligis Estuary—a lean summer and a hard winter we had last year, you'll remember—and that Medraut my son has raised the standard of revolt against me. He has left the war host, taking a goodly following of our young warriors with him, and joined himself to Cerdic at Vindocladia. They have sent out the Cran Tara for the Scots and the Painted People in Gaul to join them."

The silence closed in over my voice, and went on and on, the sound of the sea echoed hollow in it, and a crying of gulls like lost souls.

Nobody spoke; they were waiting for me to speak again; only somebody swallowed thickly, and I saw Flavian's hand clench on his sword belt until the knuckles shone waxy white as mutton bone. In the end it was not I, but Maelgwn's great golden eagle that broke the silence when it had begun to seem unbreakable so that it must endure forever. Disturbed by what he felt around him, and swift as all his kind to catch the mood of men, he began to bate wildly from the fist, leaping against his jesses while his jarring screams tore the silence across and across and his vast beating wingspread seeming to shut out the sky. Maelgwn fought to quieten and control him, cursing softly, while the great wings thrashed about his head, and now that the silence was broken, men's voices splurged up, and incredulous and impotently raging.

When at last the great bird was quieted, and the men, answering to my upflung fist, had grown silent again, I heard my own voice against the wash of the tide. "It will be moonrise in about three hours. In three hours we ride south, my brothers." And the words seemed to be an echo of something said before.

("For God's sake come!" Cei had written. "Gathering all men possible by the way. We need every man, but above all, for God's sake come yourself with all speed, for if ever we needed you to lead us, we need you now!")

Within the half of an hour, Companions and tribesmen were snatching a meal in the crumbling mess hall. Around the upper fire a little apart from the rest, I had gathered to me Maelgwn himself with a couple of chieftains who had not yet dispersed to their own places after the summer's fighting, Owain and Flavian and the Minnow still in all his dust; and while we ate we held a hurried council of war. From outside came the sounds of the aroused camp, men's voices, and the trampling and neighing of horses as they were brought in, the clang of weapons fetched out from the armory and flung down in heaps.

"If Medraut has but now sent out the Cran Tara, it must be some while before the Scots or the Picts can gather to him in strength," I said. "If the Fates are not against us we may well be able to take him and Cerdic before their friends can reach them."

The Minnow, who had been staring with red-rimmed eyes into the fire, looked up and shook his head, which with the dust of his wild ride was grayer than his father's. "If Noni Heron's Feather and his sons speak truth, the Cran Tara must have gone out in the spring, for a war hosting at harvesttime. With a northwest wind to speed the currachs, the Scots and the Painted People will not be late to the feast."

And it seemed to me that my heart settled, cold and heavy as flint, under my breastbone. For the wind which had risen at sunset and was siffling through the sand-dune grasses and across the ramparts of the fort blew from the northwest. . . .

Flavian beat his open hand on his knee. "Harvesttime! And three quarters of the war host at home in their own villages, getting in the barley!"

"So the call must have gone out at least two months before he left Venta," I said, but I was speaking more to myself than to the other men about the fire. "While he still supped in hall with the rest of us. It is true that one cannot see into his eyes. . . ."

"He has the forethought and the gift for seeing and acting

[465]

swiftly on the chances of a situation that becomes a High King, if nothing else," Maelgwn said, in his throat, not without admiration.

A High King. Yes, the High Kingship was the quarry that Medraut hunted. The Purple would mean nothing to him, it belonged to another world than his. There would not be another Emperor of the West; all that would be over with my going. If he was victorious there would be a High King, and half a length behind him, as it were, a Saxon holding the greatest power in Britain; just as once it had been with Vortigern and the Sea Wolf Hengest. And then when the time came, as it must, for a trial of strength between them, there would be only the Saxon, and Britain would be torn between the tree and the stallion, and the end would be darkness, after all.

I must have groaned aloud, for there was a small swift movement among the men around the fire, and suddenly they were all looking at me as though I had drawn their attention by some sound. I laughed, to cover the thing, whatever it had been, and tossed the last of my barley crust to the nearest hound, and looked around at them, gathering them in. "It is in my mind that with Cerdic and Medraut striking up from Vindocladia, the obvious place for a landing of the Scots, and presumably the Painted People with them, is well up the Sabrina Sea—somewhere in the marsh and reed country northwest of Lindinis—away beyond the Apple Island, maybe—low shores and small wandering waterways to run the war boats inland and ground them, and having landed, they will cut through to join hands with the Saxons as soon as may be."

"The old game of cutting the kingdom in two," Owain said.

"Partly, partly also, of course, to combine into their full strength before we can come to grips with them. It seems that they are all too likely to succeed in that, yet even now, if we ride like the hammers of hell, there is still a chance that we may meet one half of the enemy host in time to deal with it before it is joined by the other."

"And so?" Flavian said.

"We ride like the hammers of hell. But before we ride, I have a Cran Tara of my own to send out. Maelgwn, can you furnish me with ink and parchment or tablets?"

"Na," said Maelgwn, lordlywise. "I am no clerk."

"But good God, man, have you no clerk here with the means of writing a letter?"

In the end he brought, with his own hands, a breviary rich with monk's work in gold leaf and glimmering colors, that I think he loved next after his hawks and his women, though for its beauty rather than its content, and tossed it to me like a thing of no account. And I tore out the pages I needed, and tossed it back to him. One page, I remember, was half taken up with the initial S, fashioned into the likeness of a dragon with long arched neck and fantastic foliated tail, that was like the royal dragon arm ring that I had worn for twenty years. Another was gemmed with tiny trefoil flowers and leaves among the prayers, another bordered with delicate interlaced strapwork ending in birds' heads. I turned them over and wrote on their blank sides on my knee, reading the hurried words aloud as I did so, that the others might know what orders I sent, and where.

I wrote to Connory at Deva, to rouse the Northern war bands and bring them down as swiftly as might be; they could not reach us until many days after battle joined, but whichever way it went, they might serve some purpose later. I scrawled my orders to Aurelius the Dog, the Lord of Glevum, to rush every man he could gather, down the Sabrina coast to prevent a landing if it were not already too late. But it would be too late, I knew that in the dark of my bones. To Cador of Dumnonia to get his war bands out before the fangs of the trap closed, and join Cei at— I hesitated, looking at the country in my inner eye—at Sorviodunum. Lastly I wrote to Cei himself, honoring him with the dragon page, bidding him call back the war host from their harvesting (but he would be doing that already); bidding him take the gathered host westward as far as Sorviodunum, and make his rallying place there while he waited for my coming. That would put them about midway between Venta and the southern Mendips. If they pushed farther west they might become engaged with the enemy before I could reach them, and I dared not risk the outcome of that.

I had already sent out a summons to any of the tribesmen of my own hills who could join me before moonrise, and Maelgwn had his orders to gather what troops he could within the next day, and bring them after me.

When the letters were written, someone brought me balls of beeswax, and I sealed them with Maximus's great amethyst seal in the pommel of my sword, with the spread-winged eagle and the proud surrounding legend IMPERATOR. I called up three of the young warriors about the lower fires, all well known to me as swift horsemen and for their knowledge of the hills and hill tracks, and gave Cador's letter to the first, bidding him take the shortest way south to the Silures coast, and for God's sake keep out of Vortiporus's hands, and cross by fisher boat into Dumnonia. The letters for Aurelius the Dog, and for Cei, I gave to the other two, bidding them ride together as far as Glevum, and the one to drop off there while the other pressed straight on to Sorviodunum. And when they had snatched up the last of their supper, flung on their cloaks and gone from the hall, that left only Connory and the North.

I remember looking across the fire to where the Minnow sat half asleep and propped against his father's knee, and saw how Flavian's hand with the great flawed emerald rested on the young man's dusty shoulder. The last man to wear that ring had died in my service twenty years ago; in all likelihood Flavian would be dying with me in a few days from now. Three were too many to take in direct succession from one man's line.

"Minnow," I said, and as he roused and shook himself upright in his place, "eat first and sleep after. I can give you four hours for sleeping, after that take a fresh horse—see to that, Maelgwn my brother, since I shall be on the road south before then—and carry my summons up to Connory at Deva. If you can get two changes of horse on the way you should be there in less than three days."

"Sir—let someone else carry the message," he said after a moment. "I am one of your Companions, I have been your armor-bearer. It is my place to ride with you."

"It is your place to obey my orders," I said, and he got up and came and took the packet, hesitated a perceptible moment longer, then touched it to his forehead before stowing it in the sweat-stained breast of his tunic.

When he flung on his cloak and went out into the night as the others had done, his father got up and strolled after him. And I knew that somewhere in the dark outside—probably Flavian would have taken him to his own sleeping place—they would be taking their leave of each other, almost certainly for the last time.

They wasted no time over it; the Minnow needed his few hours' sleep, and Flavian had work to do like the rest of us. He came back into the mess hall alone, just as we were making ready to leave it, looking much as usual, save that the old scar on his temple showed up more clearly than was its wont, an odd thing to betray a man. He gave me a long steady look of gratitude, and I noticed that the battered signet ring was no longer on his hand, only the skin was very white where it had been.

We were tightening sword belts and kicking the last bones to the hounds, when he paused beside me and asked in an undertone the question that no other man had asked me yet. "Sir—of the men who followed Medraut, did Cei say were there any of the Company?"

"Sixty-seven," I said, picking up the cloak that I had laid aside in the heat of the hall.

"Oh God!" he said, and choked on the words, and as he turned to pick up with needless care a fallen ale cup, I thought I heard him sob.

"It will be mostly the young ones—the cubs grow weary of following an old leader." I gripped his shoulder for an instant in passing. "Not *your* cub."

And he was beside me, master of himself again, when I came with the rest of the fighting men behind me, to the entrance. Men and shadows were hurrying to and fro, and the soft blustery darkness of the hills was teased with torches. Maelgwn's summons had begun to take effect already, for among our own big horses standing ready saddled or being walked up and down on the grass-grown parade ground, the fitful light touched on the shaggy flanks of more than a score of the wiry hill ponies and the bright hair and enameled dagger hilts of the tribesmen who rode them. And for a moment my heart lifted at the sight.

The moon was just shaking clear of the mountains inland when we rode out from Segontium, each man with a rolled-up cloak and a bag of cheese and bannocks strapped behind his saddle, for on this road we must cover the ground too swiftly for even the lightest of pack beasts. At the last, Maelgwn with his household warriors behind him had come to my stirrup, and promised again to be after me with a full war host before the dust had settled behind our horses' heels. I had leaned down to him from the saddle, and we spat and struck palms on it like men sealing a bargain. He meant his promise, but I knew that he would fail me, even then, as surely as I knew that old Cynglass and Vortiporus of Dyfed were already my enemies. There was a small son up at Dynas Pharaon, with Gwen Alarch, his mother.

[469]

CHAPTER THIRTY-SIX

The Last Camp

WE struck away inland by the mountain road to the head of the Lake of Bala—from there one may look up the long tangle of glens southwestward toward Coed Gwyn, not much over an hour's ride away—and then turned farther southward by a half-lost herding track, and began the grueling business of getting the horses across country by ridge crests and up and down slopes of rock and scree where even the sure-footed mountain ponies could scarcely pass. Much of the way we walked and scrambled, leading and dragging the poor beasts behind us. The second night we slept chilled and dripping above the cloud line, slept for no more than a few hours and then pushed on again. Once we came near to losing three of the horses in a peat moss. But we got through at last, and in better time than if we had followed the long road around by Mediomanum. The sun was well up, and the mists of the summer morning rising, when we came down from the high moors, past the worked-out copper mines at the head of the stream that fed the first beginnings of the great Sabrina. The cotton grass was in flower and the first harebells in the shelter of the old mine workings, and the little amber bees were busy among the bell heather. And looking back I could still see Yr Widdfa upreared like a cloud shadow in the sky. I made my salute to it, as one does to a chieftain, in farewell, and we pushed on the flagging horses down the broadening streamside toward the Sabrina head, and Viroconium in the lush lowlands.

At Viroconium we managed to get remounts for the worse spent of the horses, and pushed on again, south by Glevum and Corinium and on down the Cunetio road that carried us within a few miles of Badon Hill, and out along the last long rolling stride of the downs to Sorviodunum.

And all the length of our wild ride, as the news spread like forest fire, men came in to join us in ones and twos and little reckless bands of horsemen, so that when we came in sight of the small fortress city crouched on its hilltop, I had more than four hundred flying cavalry behind me, in place of the two hundred that had followed me north. We had been just under six days on the road, but five of the horses died in their picket lines that night.

The war camp was spread across the low ground about the gray walled mount which rose for a citadel in its midst, and the smoke of evening cooking fires lying over it in a haze that softened the outline of fodder stacks and branch-woven bothies; and out of the haze the familiar many-mingled sounds of a great camp came to meet us, the cracked bell note of hammer on armorer's anvil over all. At any rate Cei had received my message. Our coming must have been seen by the scouts while we were still at a distance, for already men were hurrying down from the higher fringes of the camp to press about the stockade gateway and cheer us in—cheer us as though we had come to lead them to another Badon. And Cei was at my stirrup before I had well reined in—or rather, a gaunt, gray, red-eyed, avenging ghost in the likeness of Cei, with his buckler already clanging behind his shoulder.

"What news?" I demanded.

"The Saxons and the Scots have joined shields, something over a day's march to the west."

So we were too late. Well, I had had little hope of catching the two halves of the enemy host before they could combine. I swung a leg over my tired horse's back, and dropped heavily to the ground. "How many do they muster?"

"All told, some eight thousand, if the scouts make no mistake. Noni Heron's Feather is in the camp now, if you would speak with him."

I nodded. "How many of ours?"

"Not much above half that as yet. I dared wait no more than four days before marching. Marius and Tyrnon are gathering more to bring on after us, but the gathering is none so easy, in these times—may his soul rot for it!"

"That he chooses harvesttime? In his place I should do the

same," I said. Neither of us spoke Medraut's name in that first moment.

He looked at me with a furious grief in his hot blue eyes. "I was not thinking of the harvesttime, not so much of the harvesttime. I was thinking that one toad's poison may spread a long way. It isn't only the men who have marched out with him to join the Saxon camp; even over those that bide still in their own places, even over some of those who answered the muster call, he has smeared his own foul slime. Three days since a man said to my very face, 'Why should we not have peace with Cerdic and his kind as we have with the men of the Saxon shore? With Artos it is all fighting, even with his own people among the hills, and we must leave the harvest to ruin. Medraut knows a better way.'"

We stood grimly silent for a few moments; there seemed nothing to be said.

Then I asked, "Have the Glevum troops come in?" for the city had been empty of its fighting men when we rode through (one messenger rides faster than a whole war band) but they might still be scouring the Sabrina marshes for the landing that they had been too late to stop.

"This morning. As soon as they found themselves too late to prevent the Scots landing, they pressed on to the hosting place—indeed, they were here and making themselves free of the city wine-shops when our foreguard came up."

I was glancing about the camp, seeing the great dragon standard upreared among the cooking fires, and farther off, the black deer-hound of Glevum, but nowhere the saffron flash of the Dumnonian banner. "What of Cador and Constantine?"

"No sign as yet."

"No word at all?"

He shook his head, like that of a gray and ragged old sheep dog beset by flies.

"If they are not here by dawn tomorrow, it will surely mean that they could not get out in time," I said, "and we must count them lost to us and do as best we may without them. With the traitor princes of my own people already flighting south to join the Saxons, we cannot afford a longer delay, even for Marius and Tyrnon to come up. Call me a council, Cei; we can make plans as we eat as we did at Badon."

But of all that hurriedly called council I can remember little, save that I ordered a general advance westward at dawn, save also—and this I remember clearly indeed—that seeing how sorely we were outnumbered, I proposed a battle formation that had never been used before, but which seemed to offer some hope of holding off the threat of the longer enemy wings, and that somehow I hammered the rest of the council into agreeing to it. All the rest is lost in a gray shifting murk like the smoke of the cooking fires. Also it seems very long ago—longer ago than our council before Badon fight, and yet it cannot be many days—God knows how many or how few; it grows hard to keep count of time. . . .

In the lag end of the night the long-awaited messenger got through to us from Constantine. "From Constantine?" I said when he was brought to me. "What of Cador, the King?"

"My Lord the King grows old before his time. He is sick and cannot ride," the man said, standing before me in the cold flare of torches in the windy dawn. "Therefore he sends his son to lead the war bands."

"How soon can they join us?"

"Here?" he said, doubtfully.

"No, we march westward in an hour; we shall be within a few miles of the enemy when we camp again."

"So, then maybe not long past noon tomorrow. They make forced marching."

"By noon tomorrow the work may be for the wolves and ravens rather than for the men of Dumnonia," I said. "They must force the march still farther. How large is the force?"

"The household warriors, and such of the war host as we could gather quickly. It is harvesttime."

Harvesttime, harvesttime!

I said, "Go now and get something in your belly, then get back to Constantine and tell him the need that we have of his coming swiftly."

Within the hour, we marched; pushing westward over the great summer-pale combers of the Downs, following the Legion's road at first, then by the alder green ridgeway into the low-lying country below the Mendips. And that night we camped on a patch of rising ground in a soft country of deep woods and ferny hillsides, with the downs of our day's march rising cloud-dappled, chalk-scarred, behind us, and far ahead, the gleam of water and the curious lightening of the sky that told of marsh country. Far ahead also, unglimpsed, unhinted at in the summer quiet land sweep, were the enemy war host; the enemy war host led against me by my son and the man whom I would have had most joyfully for my son if Fate had woven the pattern that way. They were encamped some five miles off, reported the little dark scouts who brought in word of them, and I would have pushed on then and forced the battle, for there were still some hours of daylight left, and in that way we would have had the advantage of surprise with us; but half my men were blind weary, and to go into battle next day with men strengthened by a few hours' sleep, would, I judged, be a thing to outweigh the loss of surprise. So we made camp, and mounted a strong watch, with a screen of outpost pickets beyond. And while the main camp was being pitched, I rode the rounds of the outposts with Cei, from one to another of the knots of men lying up wherever there was cover and command of the country westward, in small ferny hillside hollows, or the fringes of an alder thicket, among the last pink smoke of the summer willow herb, while the horses grazed nearby. In one such outpost as we rode nearer, they were singing softly, with their mouths full of bannock; an unlikely war song, but I have noticed that men only sing of fighting in time of peace.

> *"Six bold warriors riding home from war,*
> *Five fair maidens, spinning at the door,*
> *Four swans flying, at the break of day,*
> *Three-leaved clover makes the sweetest hay . . ."*

Singing very softly with a swing that was at once grim and merry, their eyes on the track where it passed below them. They rolled over and scrambled to their feet at my coming, and the youngling in charge of them came and stood at my stirrup, looking up, eager for my approval because this was his first command of men. "All well?" I said, in the usual form.

"All well, Caesar," he returned, and then, forgetting his dignity, grinned, and flashed me the "Thumbs Up" that men used to use in the arena, but only boys use now. I stuck my own thumb skyward, laughing, as I turned my horse away.

I saw his head on a Saxon spear before the same time next evening. It was still recognizable by the big crescent-shaped mole on one cheek.

It was sunset when, the round completed, we turned back toward the camp. But I remember that as though by common consent, with no word spoken between us, we wheeled the horses on a low billow of rising land, and looked westward once more, and having looked, could neither of us look away. I have seen wild sunsets in my time, but seldom, surely never, a sky quite like that one. It was as though beyond the dark, gold-fringed cloud bars of the west, the world itself were burning, and the torn-off rags of the burning, spreading into great wings as they went, were drifting all across the sky so that even when one looked upward to the zenith, still the sky was full of the rush of vast wings of flame. Far off toward the Island of Apples, the winding waters of the reed country caught fire from the burning west, and earth and sky alike blazed into an oriflamme. It was a sunset full of the sound of trumpets and the flying of banners, a sunset that made one feel naked under the eye of God. . . .

"If tomorrow we go down into the Dark," Cei said at last, with awe in his deep grumble of a voice as the radiance began to fade, "at least we have seen the sunset."

But for the moment I was looking at something else, at red petals of fire brightening far out in the dusking marshes. The campfires of the Saxon war host.

In a while we turned the horses and rode on into camp, to find Marius and Tyrnon there with their hastily gathered reinforcements who had marched in just ahead of us. God's face was not turned from us in all things, it seemed.

When all things were in train, we ate well that night, knowing that there would be little time for food in the morning, and as soon as the meal was done with, men began to roll themselves in their cloaks and lie down with their feet to the fires.

I withdrew to my own quarters, to the hut of hurdle roofed with the striped awning of a captured war boat, gay as a horse-fair wine booth save that in place of the vine garland my battered personal standard hung before it for a sign. I pulled off iron cap and sword belt and flung down, still in my war shirt, on a pile of bracken with my saddle for a pillow. A saddle makes a good enough pillow, but a hound's flank makes a better. . . .

[475]

At most times I have been able to sleep on the eve of battle, if I had an hour or so to lie down, but that night I could not, for the thoughts and pictures that whirled through my head almost as though I had the fever.

I lay for a long time staring at the small bright flame-bud of the tallow glim in its lantern, and the flame had no more heart nor comfort to it than the Solas Sidh, and the long upward shadows that it threw all up the wattle walls were the shadows of the future pressing in upon me, crowding me with mouthless questions to which, God knows, I had no answer; shadows that came trailing the past behind them also, so that I caught again the acrid smell of the dung fires at Narbo Martius, and the thunder of my horse's hooves in Nant Ffrancon and heard again, across the years, my own voice and Ambrosius's: "Then why don't we yield now, and make an end . . . ? They say it is easier to drown if you don't struggle." "For an idea, for an ideal, for a dream." "A dream may be the best thing to die for." But I had no dream left. . . . "When the dream fails, that is when the people die." But Ambrosius had not said that—Bedwyr had said it—something of the kind—in the sunlight of the Queen's Courtyard, with the pigeons crooning on the store-wing roof.

So that I longed with a small whimpering longing to set my finger one time more on the rose mole on Guenhumara's breast, but could not remember whether it was on her left breast or her right. . . .

Gradually past and future began to mingle; tomorrow's battle and Ambrosius's last hunting becoming one, as the light of the candle spread and blurred into the shadows, and the sounds of the nighttime camp that had been sharp-edged and assertive grew blurred also, by little and little, until they were no more than the wash of the tide behind the sand dunes that faced toward Môn. . . .

I heard a voice outside, a challenge and a sharp exclamation beyond the nearest watch fire, and shook myself clear of the little dark lapping waves of sleep, thinking that maybe another scout had come in. Then somebody put aside the loose fold of the awning at the bothy entrance, and I turned on my elbow, and saw a man standing there caught between the lights of the watch fire and the tallow glim. A lean old man in a war shirt of glimmering mail. His proud mane of iron-colored hair, bound about the hollow temples with a strip of crimson leather, showed one lock as white as the grinning mask stripe of a badger. And he stood looking at me strangely under one level brow and one that flew wild.

"Bedwyr," I said. "Bedwyr?" and sat up slowly, and drew my legs under me and got slowly to my feet, and we stood confronting each other for a long time.

"Is it yourself, then, or your ghost?" I said at last, for caught between the two lights, he might have been a ghost indeed, called up to me by my need, by my own nearness to the crossing over.

He moved then, one step forward, and let the striped fold of the awning fall behind him, and I saw that he was living flesh and blood. "No ghost," he said. "I have disobeyed your orders, and come back, Artos."

I could have cried out to him, as Jonathan to David, by the forbidden love names that are not used between men; I could have flung my arms about his shoulders. Instead, I stood where I had risen, and said, "Why did you not join me on the road south?"

"The news did not reach me until you were many miles on your way, and from Coed Gwyn the swiftest way is by the coast road so that one does not fall into traitor hands on the way, and so that one can get a fisher boat across the Sabrina. Can you spare me a mount? A river currach is no horse transport."

"A mount maybe, though we are somewhat short of horses," I said. "Your old command is Flavian's now." Almost I might have been speaking to a stranger.

"I did not come seeking my old command. A fighting place among the Companions, no more."

The aching silence fell between us again. The loose end of the awning flapped in the light wind like a bird with a broken wing, and the candle flame leapt and fluttered, casting strange shadows on the rough hurdles that formed the walls.

"You will have no illusions as to the likely outcome of tomorrow's fight?" I said (but already it was today's).

"Not many." There was a twist of the old reckless laughter on his lips.

"And so you came back."

"I have always been one to choose with some care the company that I die in."

Age had made him uglier than ever; the lines of his face that had been fantastic in his young manhood tipped over into the grotesque. It was a face made for a bitter jest by some God with a crooked sense of humor, and Christos! My heart whimpered for joy at the sight of it.

"Take me back into your service, Artos."

"What of Guenhumara?"

He said steadily, "I left her at the gate of the little nunnery in Caredegion, out on the headland. You know it? They keep the holy fire burning always for Saint Bride. She will be happier there, I think, than at Eburacum, even if I could have spared the time to take her there."

And I remembered the House of Holy Ladies in the Street of the Clothworkers, and Guenhumara shuddering in the curve of my bridle arm as she looked back toward it, as though a wild goose had flown over her grave. "She hated cages. She was afraid of them," was all I could find to say.

"She went in through the door of the wall, of her own free wish," he said dully.

"Were you not happy together, all those years?"

"Not very."

"But—Bedwyr, you loved her, and she you?"

He said simply, "Oh yes, we loved each other, but you were always between us."

It was a small bothy, one step brought us to meet in the midst of it; my arms were around him, and his around me, the strong right arm and the maimed left that felt sapless and brittle as a bit of dead stick, and we held fast together, and wept somewhat, each into the hollow of the other's shoulder. Maybe it is easier to weep when one grows old, than it was in the flower of life. The strength ebbs, or the wisdom grows. . . . It no longer tears at the soul; there is even something of catharsis, of healing, in it. . . .

In the dark hour before dawn, I was roused to the news, brought in by one of the scouts, that the enemy were showing the first sign of stirring, and with him another rider from Constantine. The men of Dumnonia were pressing on to the limit of their endurance, but the marsh country had forced them around by the long way and they could not be with us much more than an hour before noon. I got up and swallowed a few mouthfuls of bannock and beer, while I armed and made ready. Bedwyr, having no duties of command to hold him now, came and served me as armor-bearer—he was skillful enough with that arm, though he lacked much strength in it—and afterward I did the same for him, so that in the end we armed each other like brothers.

I took especial pains that morning, combing out my hair and beard, and settling the folds of my old weather-worn cloak with care, arranging and rearranging the plume of yellow corn marigold in its shoulder brooch—those of the Brotherhood who yet remained still rode into battle with some such grace note about them. I knew, I had accepted, that Fate had finished the pattern, that the doom was accomplished, and I was to come by my death that day (but I thought that it would be swift and seemly, as the thing should be, as it had been for Ambrosius; not this untidy lingering by the way!). And I could only hope that my death might serve also as ransom for the people. I knew, too, as surely as I knew the other thing, that the pattern demanded that I should take Medraut with me, and prayed that, so, the old sin might be wiped out and the final defeat of Britain not demanded. At the least, with Medraut gone, Britain might be saved the fatal split within herself that must let the darkness in. And hurriedly, for already I could hear through the wattle walls the sound of the squadrons mustering, I made ready as though I rode to take a bride or a triumph, for it was as though something in me, older than my own life, the thing that I had felt at my crowning, knew that there was a certain fitness of things, an outward and visible sign of willingness, to be made in the sight of the gods. . . . I remembered all at once how carefully Ambrosius had made his young armor-bearer trim his hair for him on the morning of his last hunting.

CHAPTER THIRTY-SEVEN

The Corn King

THE stormy promise of last night's sunset had been fulfilled in a day of soft blustering wind and squalls of rain, and the standards and the squadron pennons flew as though already carried at the charge. Beyond the huts and the cooking fires the whole war host was already mustered, horse and foot, archers and spearmen. The wild riders of my own mountains, sitting their small shaggy steeds as though they and the horses were one; the men of Glevum under the black hound banner of their prince; the men of the high chalk downs, with something of the formidable steadiness of the Legions about them still. If only, among them, I could have caught the saffron gleam of Cador's standard, but the men of the West must be still many miles away. I wondered how near were Cynglass and Vortiporus. . . . My own Companions were drawn up before the rest, yellow-touched with the corn marigolds that each man wore in his helmet comb or shoulder buckle, waiting with Flavian at their head, for me to join them. My grand old Signus had died three years ago, and the big silver stallion Gray Falcon, who had taken his place as chief among my war steeds, was being walked up and down close by. He whinnied at sight of me, and the men shouted my name in greeting, so that it sounded like the sudden crash of waves on a sandy shore.

I flung up an arm to them in reply, and mounting, wheeled Gray Falcon in among them, with Bedwyr at my side on a tall raking sorrel drawn from the reserves, and suddenly knew the Brotherhood complete again. Pharic and his Caledonians, whose tribe had first loyalty with them, the traitors who had followed Medraut over to the Saxon camp, they were cut away; the familiar faces that were lacking and long since rotted into skulls were another matter, for it was not death could break the Brotherhood; what was left was the hard core, the men who, new-joined last year or with forty years of service behind them, chose to tuck the corn marigold in their war caps and ride into this last battle with me. These were the Companions of the Bear. And I have never loved them quite as I loved them at that moment.

I should speak to them now; almost always before battle I had made them some kind of fighting speech, but there had been so many battles, so many fighting speeches, that there seemed nothing left to say, and looking at their grim faces, I knew it was no time for false heartening. So I cried out to them only, "Brothers, you know the odds against us today; therefore let us fight so that whether we win or whether we die, the harpers shall sing of us for a thousand years!"

I flashed up my hand to Cei in command of the main cavalry, and old Marius who led the foot, and the great aurochs horn sang harshly merry and was echoed across the camp, the notes that ordered the march tossed to and fro on the squally wind that ruffled up and silvered the hazel leaves. And the first band of horse moved off, raising their spears to me in salute as they passed.

Hail Caesar! Those about to die. . . .

We rode in the usual formation for hostile country, for we could not be sure how near the enemy scouts and advance parties might be: foreguards flung out ahead, and knots of light horse screening the flanks of the main body, and I remember that Bedwyr, riding beside me, had his harp slung on his shoulder, as he had used to ride into battles, and presently, though he did not unsling it, he began to sing, so softly that it scarcely broke through the beat of his horse's hooves, but I caught the breath of it and it was the first song that ever I had heard from him, the lament for the Corn King that helps the crops to grow, the promise of his return—*out of the mists, back from the land of youth, strong with the sound of trumpets under the apple boughs* . . . and I remembered the big stars and the smell of dung fires and the mule drivers listening on the outfringe of the firelight. . . . He must have heard himself at the same instant as I did, for we glanced aside at each other, and he laughed and flung up his head and broke baying into a cattle-reeving song of the Berwyn Hills.

Presently three of our scouts came riding back over the skyline of the low ridge as though the red-eared hounds of Anwn were after them. The foremost reined up in a smother of dust almost under Gray Falcon's nose so that the big horse snorted and danced in his tracks. "Caesar, the advance guard is tangled with the Saxon outposts! They're falling back—"

I sent the three of them out again, and rising in my stirrups shouted to the Companions to come on. The trumpeter beside me raised the great aurochs horn to his lips and sent the echoes flying out over the marshes, and we broke forward at an increased speed, the whole war host changing pattern and deploying for action at full march, so that we became, as it were, two advancing battle lines one behind the other, each with its own spear center and cavalry wings, and the small free bodies of light horse that flanked and partly joined the two together.

Just below the crest of the shallow ridge I checked them, and with Bedwyr and two of my captains rode forward through the furze to get a view of the Saxon position. It was a spur of the same ridge from which, farther back into the hills, I had seen the Saxon watch fires brightening under last night's sunset.

On the very fringe of the marshes, where soft ground and winding waterways must limit the use of cavalry, the enemy battle line was drawn up not much more than a mile distant. Medraut, with the war training that I had given him—and the inborn skill that I had given him too—had chosen his ground well. In the clear between the soft showers of blowing mizzle, the Barbarian battle line was sharp-edged and pricked with detail; I could make out in their center the horsetail standard of Cerdic, where the Saxon leader held his heavy shield warriors, his hearth companions, white as a gleam of bog grass against the blurred greens and grays of marsh and reedbed; more white, that was the lime-washed Scottish bucklers; the dull glint of shield boss and spear blade and war cap splintering into sudden light where a gleam of wet sunshine fled across the marshes and the northward swell of the hills. No sign as yet of the pied and checkered standards of the traitors Cynglass and Vortiporus. God be thanked for that at least. Above all I saw the blood-red gleam on the right flank where the main part of the enemy cavalry was posted. (Cavalry wings on a Saxon war line!)

Medraut was flying the Red Dragon of Britain for his battle standard, and my gorge rose at the sight.

Between the Saxon host and the ridge from which we looked toward it, our advance cavalry was falling back, scattered and pursued by a flying mob of light horsemen and running spears, and even as I looked, another band of riders appeared from behind some thick hawthorn scrub, and came curving across like a skein of wild geese in flight, to cut off our men from all hope of retreat.

I had hoped to draw the enemy up from their chosen position onto ground that would allow us better use of our advantage in cavalry, but to delay for that now would mean the sacrifice of the whole of our advance force. Again I spoke to the trumpeter, and again the notes of the war horn sang thin over the western countryside. The tramp of feet and the smother of hooves came sweeping up behind me, and I swung Gray Falcon into place at the head of the Companions as we spilled like a wave over the comb of the ridge, and on down to join with the advance guard. The enemy broke off as they saw us nearing, and scattered back to their own battle line, and we swept on and down, the advance troops wheeling about once more to join with us. It is seldom good to take foot any distance at the full charge, lest they lose formation and breath together; but there were bowmen among the ranks of the great Saxon battle line, and I must get them across the open ground as swiftly as might be. The first flight of arrows thrummed out at us as we came within range, and men pitched in their stride and went down; then our own horse archers opened up in reply, and in the enemy ranks, also, gaps darkened for an instant, until each was closed up by the springing in of the man behind. Forward and away at the canter and the long loping run, the standards lifting and flying on the air of our going, the war horns yelping, and under the horns I raised the war cry: "Yr Widdfa! *Yr Widdfa!*"

The enemy also had broken forward, to the booming of their own bulls' horns and the long-drawn shuddering German war howl, having learned the unwisdom, I suppose, of receiving a cavalry charge while at the halt. And so we swept together, yelling at the speed of both armies.

Far on either side of us spread the Barbarian wings, and I glanced back once as we rode, to make sure that the second line on which our hope depended was keeping station, and saw the

[483]

solid wave of men and horses sweeping after us, under the standards of Powys and Glevum. So far, so good; but in this country
where there could be little free maneuvering for cavalry, to engage
solidly all along the line would be to ask to be engulfed, and I began to swing the whole war host slantwise so as to bring the Companions and the flower of the spear ranks against, as I judged, the
weakest span of the enemy battle line, that held by the Scottish warriors. The spears were flung, a dark whistling shower, and we
charged home with drawn swords. War front and war front rolled
together with crash of meeting shields that filled the marsh skies
with wheeling and calling clouds of birds, and instantly there rose
the clash and grind of weapons, the full-throated roar of war cry
against war cry, the screams of horses, all blended into the great
formless smother of sound that is the voice of all battles.

The line of white shields wavered, and clouds of lime dust rode
into the air, choking and blinding friend and foe alike, and in the
midst of the sharp white haze we were hacking and trampling our
way forward. Almost it seemed, in one short triumphant burst of
time, that we should break through to take them in the rear before
our own weaker left wing, which I had held back somewhat by
the slantwise charge, became fully engaged. That was when
Medraut's cavalry took us on the flank. The charge was brilliantly
timed and handled and, save for the unmounted spearmen I had
set amongst us, we must have been crushed in by it. As it was, our
outer ranks were forced back, and the thing that I had dreaded and
prepared for began to happen: the enemy's longer flank was curling
around our own to engulf us. Behind me I heard the trumpets
sounding, and knew that our second-line warriors were wheeling
about to make their stand back to back with us, while the farthest
right of my own wing, withdrawing under the crash of Medraut's
charge, were linking shields with them.

Now we were a long narrow island, thrust and driven at from all
sides, but an island that stood like rock, while again and again the
dark waves of destruction came roaring in on us, and again and
again we flung them back. I had pulled back the Companions into
the slim space between the two fighting lines, to re-form them, and
that I might have freedom of movement to come at any part of the
war host. And I remember Flavian grinning at me from under the
standard. He had lost his helmet and his forehead was streaked

with blood, and he shouted to me above the furnace roar of battle: "A hot day, and somewhat dusty!" I saw Cei with every cheap glass ornament he possessed bright upon him, standing like a giant in his stirrups in the midst of a battle all his own. I saw men going down, and others stepping forward to fill their places, and knew that soon the lines would grow perilously thin; soon the island, the British shield-burg, must begin to shrink. Constantine and his war bands could not be far off now—and nor could the traitor Cymri. . . .

In the spot where the Barbarian host had come together, encircling us, it seemed to me suddenly, more by a kind of hunter's instinct than by anything I could see, that the joining place was weak. I sent the order to Tyrnon and saw him unleash the flower of the war host's cavalry. They rolled forward, not fast, but remorseless as a wave, the spearmen parting to let them through. . . . And suddenly the pressure against us on that side began to slacken. I heard the triumphant yell as it was torn apart and flung off, and the whole battle mass that had been knotted fast seemed to shake free of the bonds that had held it and grow fluid again. With the incredible swiftness with which the entire nature of a battle can change, the whole field had opened up and was now on the move. The fighting lines were swaying to and fro over ground that had been fought over all morning and was cumbered with dead men and dead horses, slippery with blood, stinking. Our hands and war gear were stained red, and here and there a man with his shield torn away would lift a battered corpse in front of him to receive the enemy spears. In the midst of the swifter swirl of cavalry and light troops, Marius with the heavy spearmen had made for the white horse standard, and was locked with Cerdic's troops like a pair of tusk-locked boars, while again Medraut's flying squadrons were sweeping down upon us.

The Saxons had unleashed their berserkers some time before, and when a shadow slid up from the undergrowth of battle almost under Gray Falcon's breast and turned about with knife in hand, my heart jumped cold and I had already flung myself sideways in the saddle in desperate essay to cut the creature down when I saw that it was no drug-maddened Barbarian, but one of the Little Dark People, and turned the sword point just in time. He cried out something to me, but in the tumult I could not hear and shouted to him in return, "Up! Come up here, then!"

And he set one foot over mine in the stirrup, and next instant was clinging to my saddlebow for support, his narrow face streaked with the clay and ochre war patterns on a level with my own, the three buzzards' feathers thrust into his knotted-up hair bowed and shivering sideways in the squally wind. "My Lord the Bear, the men from the North are near, those that come to join with the Wolves."

"How near?"

He held up a spread hand. "As many bowshots as there are fingers on my hands and toes on my feet, maybe less—they come swiftly, swiftly, like a wolf pack on the trail."

And as swiftly as he had come, he sprang down and was gone into the thickest storm of the fighting, where our ranks were desperately striving to rally under the hammer blow of Medraut's last charge. One more such charge as that . . . and we should scarce be rallied from this one before the newcomers were upon us also. . . .

I wrenched Gray Falcon half around on his haunches, and thrust in beside Cei who was standing in his stirrups to steady his men, his eyes blue fires in a face smeared with blood and filth, and shouted to him, "Constantine can't be far off now, but it seems that Cynglass and Vortiporus will be here first."

"How near?" he roared back, as I had done. ("Ya-ai ya ya ya! Stand firm, you rabble!")

"Something well under a score of bowshots. Take over, Cei. I'm going to try and draw Medraut off for a while."

"Don't be a fool, Artos, you can't!"

"If I can't, then there'll be nothing but the bits for Constantine to pick up when he *does* get through. It's your battle now."

He looked around at me, grinning like a dog in the gray jut of his beard, then flung the half shield away from him, and sent his horse plunging forward, and the fight closed over between him and me.

I drove back somehow through the turmoil to my own squadron, flinging off my cloak of the betraying purple and bundling it under my shield, shouted to them to throw away the yellow corn marigolds and follow me, and a few moments later, with my trumpeter beside me and young Drusus, with my personal standard dragged from its lance pole and bundled under one arm, was leading them out of the boil of battle.

"Is it some game that we play?" Flavian cried, leaning from his saddle toward me.

"A game of marsh lights and played with Medraut. The curs of the Cymri are overnear, and Cei and Marius can do without his attentions as well."

"This is a game that my father would have enjoyed," he said, and choked on the last word and pitched from the saddle with a flung spear between his shoulders.

We swung wide, with a small ragged pursuit on our heels, and into cover of the alder woods that fringed the rising ground, then turned and charged them. They scattered back, and we did not wait to ride down the survivors, but turned about once more and headed at full gallop into the soft rolling country that lifted above the marsh to the north. Bedwyr had taken Flavian's place, and rode stirrup to stirrup with me as we had ridden in the early days, as we struggled upward in desperate haste toward the hill track from Aquae Sulis. Just before we lost the full cover of the woods I called a few moments' halt. "Now, Drusus, get the standard back on its spear shaft, and you Alun Dryfed, and you Gallgoid, your cloak is a good bright one. Tear it in half and it shall serve us for two—" I flung on my own cloak of the unmistakable purple at the same time, and when we rode on again, widely spaced now to allow for the phantom cavalry among us, we carried on long hazel branch or spearpoint what seemed to be the pennons of a dozen squadrons. We came out on to the bush-scattered ferny hillside, and turning Gray Falcon aside a short distance down the woodshore, I could see the whole battle spread before me, and the pied flicker of the traitor standards already on the fringe of it. The Little Dark Warrior had spoken truth. I could see also, but still a long way off, the faint dust cloud of marching men on the great causeway road from Lindinis.

"They've a long way to go! My God; they've a long way to go!"

I turned back to the rest again. "All's well, raise the standard again. Now your turn, Aidan. Sound me a fanfare." And touching heel to Gray Falcon's flank, I rode forward with Drusus close behind me, choosing my line so as to give an uninterrupted view to

the enemy, and pausing to let the gleam of the horse's coat and the
red and gold flame of the standard show up against the deep summer colors of the hillside. Beyond me, the bushes and tall form of
the trackside would break and blur the numbers and movement of
the rest of the squadron, leaving only the pennons clear—those
pennons of a dozen squadrons: Artos and his heavy cavalry reserves sweeping around through the higher ground to take them on
the flank! Even from that distance I could hear the roar as we
were sighted, and looking back before I rejoined the head of the
squadron and swung them northward again following the track
into a shallow fold of the hills, saw a mass of cavalry already
shaking free from the main mass of the Saxon war host, and swinging toward the higher ground.

A short while later we let ourselves be glimpsed again on the
crest of another soft billow of moor, then rode like the hammers
of hell for the place where the track forded a stream coming down
from the higher hills, and beyond it became a stony scramble half
lost among the heather of a narrow combe. We gained it ahead of
Medraut and his horsemen, splashed through, and wheeled about
on the farther side.

"We are not like to find a better place to hold them," I said.

And Bedwyr nodded, cleaning his sword blade on his horse's
mane that was almost as red, that it might be bright for further
use. "I never saw a place more to my mind," he said, "nor a Company," and met my eye, and I thought how he had said last night,
"I have always been one to choose with care the company I die in."

Far off and dulled by the swell of the land, I could hear the
rumor of battle like the rumor of a storm rushing through distant
forest country, and already the nearing beat of hooves drumming
up toward us. I looked around me once, I remember, seeing the
pocket of level in the quiet lap of the moors, the stream silvering
over the ford, the furze coming into its second flowering, bean-
scented in the sun and wet. There were linnets in the furze, I heard
their song; and the great cloud shadows sailed up from the south
as they had done on the morning of Badon fight. A good place for
a last stand, with the combe narrowing behind us, and the river
ford before.

I remembered, across more than half a lifetime, Irach leaping
upon the enemy spears, and for an instant felt again the oneness

of all things, that is man's comfort under his knowledge of being alone. Yes, a good place for a final stand. By the time the last of us fell, Constantine should surely have come up. . . .

I glanced behind me and on either side at the score of men ranged there with me, and saw it in their faces, that they knew their purpose here as well as I did. I wanted to say something to them now, something to toughen the fiber and kindle the heart, but that is for an army, and this was a knot of friends, and instead I said: "My most dear, we have fought many fights together, and this is the last of them and it must be the best. If it is given to men to remember in the life we go to, remember that I loved you, and do not forget that you loved me."

They looked back at me kindly, as friend looks at friend. Only one of them spoke and that was Drusus my standard-bearer, the youngest of them all. He said: "We have good memories, Artos the Bear."

And then in a new burst of cloud shadows sweeping up from the marshes, Medraut's cavalry burst out of the valley before us. They reined in on the farther bank, and for a long trampling pause, each looked to the other across the running water. There were faces that I knew among the horsemen on the farther bank; in the midst and forefront of them, Medraut sitting his tall roan with his naked sword across its neck and on his arm the great dragon arm ring of a Prince of Britain, that was brother to the one I wore on my own. The stream was little more than a couple of spear lengths wide, and we could have spoken to each other as one speaks to the man across the hearth. We looked eye into eye and I saw his nostrils widen and tremble. Then he cried out and heeled his horse into the water, and instantly the foremost of his riders plunged after him.

And we, on the near bank, braced ourselves and spurred forward to meet the coming shock.

We fought hock-deep across the ford, up to the girths on either side, and the water sheeted up, boiling to a yeasty turmoil, white and then stained with rusty streaks that spread down the run of the stream. Men were in the water, and a horse screamed and went down, rolling belly up into shallows like a great wineskin. Again and again they hurled against us, yelling, and again and again we flung them back. More horses were down now, and men fought on foot, knee-deep, thigh-deep, in the boiling shallows, and so far, not one of the traitors had reached the western bank. Small difference if they had; but men fighting as we were must have something to hold, some rampart which is of the spirit as much as of pass or narrows or running water; and for us it was the ford and the line of that lowland stream. . . . Bedwyr was beside me, the rest of the surviving Companions close-knit on either hand, and if we never fought in all our lives before, God of gods! we fought then! And in the midst of all, Medraut and I came together, naturally and inevitably, as to a meeting long appointed.

Spears had no part in this kind of fighting, it was work for swords, whether on horseback or on foot, and we strove together almost knee to knee, while the water boiled and the spray flew like the spume of breaking waves. The horses slipped and scrambled among the stones of the ford, neighing in fury, and both of us had flung aside the bullhide bucklers which hampered the bridle arm in maneuvering. Medraut was fighting on the defensive, waiting to pounce. His face was set in a small, bright, curiously rigid smile, and I watched his eyes as one watches the eyes of a wild animal, waiting for it to spring.

But in the end it was I who broke through his guard first with a blow that should have landed between neck and shoulder, but in the same instant his roan stumbled, and the stroke caught him on the comb of his war cap and swept him from the saddle.

He went down with a shuddering splash in his heavy mail sark that sent the water sheeting upward, and was on his feet again, still gripping his sword, while the roan plunged snorting away. He leapt in under my guard with shortened blade, and stabbed upward. The point went under the skirts of my war shirt and entered at the groin, and I felt the white shrieking anguish pierce through me, up and up until it seemed to reach my heart; I felt death enter with it, and was aware of the dark blood gouting over Gray Falcon's shoulder, and Medraut's face with the small bright smile still frozen upon it. The sky was darkening, but I knew quite clearly that I had time and strength for one more blow, and I wrenched the horse trampling around upon him, and thrust at the throat, bare above his war sark, as he flung back his head to hold me still in sight. The same blow that I had struck at Cerdic, all those years ago. But this time it did not go amiss. The blood burst out with the blade, it spurted in little bright jets through his fingers when he dropped his sword to clutch with both hands at his throat, and in the moment before he fell, I saw his eyes widen in a kind of wonder. That was the moment when he understood that the doom between us demanded for its fulfillment, not that he should kill me or I him, but that each should be the death of the other.

He opened his mouth gasping for air and blood came out of that too, and with it his last breath in a kind of thin bubbling retch.

As he fell, the whole world swam in one vast darkening circle, and I pitched from the saddle on top of him. I remember hitting the water, and the circle turned black.

I tried to cling to the darkness, but the pain was too bright, too fiery, and tore it from my grasp. And I was lying in this place, in this small cell where I lie now, and the cell was full of tall shadows on the lamplit walls. The hooded shadows of monks, the barbed shadows of gray men in war harness, like the ghosts of some long-forgotten battle. But at first the shadows seemed more real than the men, for I had not thought to wake into the world of living men again. I heard a low mutter that might have been prayer or only the beating of a moth's wings about the light. I heard someone groaning, too, and felt the slow-drawn rasp of it in my own throat, but did not think at first to connect the two. A shadow, darker than the rest against the lamp, was kneeling beside me; it stirred and bent forward, and I saw that it was not a shadow at all, but Bedwyr. But whether all that was of the first time, or whether other times came into it, I do not know; indeed all time has seemed confused these last few days, so that there is no saying, "This thing happened after that," for all things seem present together, and most things far away, farther, farther away than the night that Ambrosius gave me my wooden foil. . . . I said, "Where is this place?"

Or at least the question came to my mind, and I must have spoken it, for an old ancient Brother, whose tonsured head had a silver nimbus like a rain cloud with the sun behind it, said, "Most often men call it 'The Island of Apples.'"

"I have been here before?" For the name chimed in my head, but I could not remember.

And he said, "You have been here before, my Lord Artos. I took your horse, and led you up to the hall, to Ambrosius at supper," and I thought that he wept, and wondered why.

I fumbled out a hand to the dark shadow between me and the lamp, which was Bedwyr, and he caught it in his own, the sound one, and drew it to his knee and held it there, and something of life seemed to flow from his hand into mine, so that the leaden chill lifted from my heart and brain, and I was able to think and remember again. I said, "Did we gain time enough? Did Constantine get through in time?"

And Bedwyr said, bending closer, "Constantine got through. The victory is yours, Artos, a narrow victory, but it is yours."

A great wave of relief rose in me, with the next wave of pain, but the pain outstripped the relief so that for a while I could neither see nor think nor even feel save with the feeling of the flesh. Thank God it no longer comes like that—and when at last it ebbed again, the relief that I had known ebbed with it and grew small and thin. *"How* narrow?"

"As when two hounds fight until their flanks are laid open and their throats in ribbons, and one breaks off and runs howling; and yet for both hounds alike, there is no more that they can do for a while and a while save crawl into a dark place and lick their wounds." He began to tell me how Connory of Deva had come in together with the Lords of Strathclyde, and were hounding the surviving Saxons and their allies through the reed country and back toward their southern settlements, while Marius was mustering the remains of the war host to regarrison Venta. I did not ask as to Cei and Flavian; I knew. But I asked after a while, "How many of the Company lived?"

"Of those that remained with the main action, something under half," he said. "Of your own squadron, Alun Dryfed and little Hilarian"—he told off two or three more names—"and myself."

"It is more than I expected," I said, "but then I did not expect to live myself long enough to hear the tally."

"Medraut's men lost heart after he was dead. They ran. After that it was easy."

"And so we have won another lease of time," I said by and by. "A few more years, maybe."

"Do you remember saying, once, that every year we gained

would mean that just so much more of Britain would survive when the flood overwhelms us at the last?" Bedwyr put his face very near my own as though he were trying to reach me across a great distance, as once I had tried to reach him.

"Did I say that? Pray God the truth is in it. I have labored hard to build a Britain strong and united, but it is in my heart that unless Constantine can hold them, the Tribes will have sprung apart once more before three harvests are gathered, and so presently the Saxons will walk in. . . . Yet maybe we have held the pass long enough for something to survive behind us. I don't know —I don't know—"

And then another time, I think it was another time, I asked Bedwyr when we were alone together, "Bedwyr, does the war host know how it is with me?"

"We have told them that you are wounded."

"Who knows that it is the death wound?"

"Myself and Alun Dryfed, and maybe the reed cutter whom we borrowed with his boat, to bring you here by the swiftest way. The Council must know by now, and Constantine, of course. For the rest, we have let them believe that you are sore wounded and we have taken you up to the monastery for tending. A few may guess, but none will know anything more."

"That is good. Now listen, my dear; presently there will be more fighting; therefore, lest the Barbarians make a triumph out of my death, and our own soldiers lose heart in the knowledge of it, leave the matter there. Nobody save yourself and the brown Brothers here must see my body once the breath is out of it, and no one must know the place of my grave. So they will maybe fight on with a better heart. You understand?"

"I understand," Bedwyr said. He was trying to feed me with warm salted milk all the while, like a woman with a sick child, but my belly would not hold it.

"I think you do. It was for that reason that you brought me here instead of carrying me back to camp with the rest of the wounded, was it not?"

"Try to sleep," he said.

But there was still one thing that I must do. "Constantine, send for Constantine."

He came, and stood in the doorway until I called him closer; a dark square-set man with his father's windy fires sunk to a steadier glow in him.

"Constantine, son of Cador, you know that I have no son to hold Britain after me?"

"That I know," he said, "and I am sorry."

"Are you? Did the women often tell you how Maximus's great seal sprang from my sword hilt into your nest of skins beside you, when you were a babe lying at your mother's feet?"

"The women always tell such things."

But he knew as well as I did, why I had sent for him.

"Sometimes they may be worth listening to. Now listen to me. Long since, I set my sealed word in the Council's keeping, naming you, who are the last of the royal blood, as my heir to come after me. But that will scarcely serve now."

He shook his head.

So I sent for the Father Abbot and his Senior Brethren; Bedwyr I needed not to send for, for he was already there; and with a clerk to make a written record, I called them to witness that Constantine, son of Cador of Dumnonia, is to be High King of Britain after me, and added: "Until I come again."

And held Constantine's gaze with my own, until he bowed his head, saying, "I am not Artos the Bear, but I will hold Britain as best I may, or may God turn His face away from me."

I bade Bedwyr take the great dragon arm ring from above my elbow, and spring it onto Constantine's arm, and he stood looking down at it, as though he waited. I think he half expected me to add my sword to the gift, until he remembered that it would be taken as certain proof of my death by all who saw him wear it. And yet I knew that in some way I must give it to him; it was his, the Sword of Britain, and carried the High Kingship with it.

After a long pause, he said, "How shall I know when I am in truth the High King?"

"You will not have long to wait," I said, thinking only that he was impatient. "The death smell has been in the wound for days, now. Does it signify?"

"Because the people will not know? It signifies to me, to know whether I am but Regent or have in truth the right to my sacring."

And by his use of the word, I knew that he understood and accepted all that the kingship carried with it.

And so I knew what I must do with my sword.

"There is a wildfowl mere only a few miles north of this place, and eastward of it the land rises somewhat. Set a watcher there among the alder woods—one that you can trust—and when I am dead, Bedwyr shall bring my sword and throw it into the mere. That shall be your sign. Will it serve?"

"It will serve," he said.

In the red sunset light I can see Bedwyr's face that is darkened when the lamps are lit, and the angry crusted wound that has laid it open from jaw to temple and drawn out that devil's eyebrow into a yet wilder flare. And when I fumble up my hand to touch it, it is wet with tears like a woman's—but I do not think I ever knew Guenhumara weep.

But there is something changed about him; something lacking. . . .

"What has happened to your harp, Bedwyr? I have scarcely ever seen you without your harp in all these years."

"It was torn apart in the fighting. No matter; there will be no more songs." His head is low so that I cannot see his face any more; his sound arm under my head, a better pillow than a saddle —as good as a hound's flank when you sleep beside the watch fire with the apple tree branches overhead.

But he is wrong. Suddenly I know he is wrong. We have held the Pass long enough—something will remain.

"There will be more songs—more songs tomorrow, though it is not we who shall sing them."